本书为——

宁波市社会学学会2020—2021年度学术项目资助成果

浙江省高校一流专业网络与新媒体专业建设成果

2019年本科高校省级一流课程“网络新闻实务”建设成果

2021年浙江省高校课程思政教学项目成果

浙大宁波理工学院思政工作质量提升工程成果及校园文化建设成果

"行走的新闻—用声音叙事"
纪念中国共产党诞辰100周年特别田野调查

浙里是我家

100个中国青年的100个中国故事

HERE I AM, ZHEJIANG

100 FAMILY STORIES
FROM 100 CHINESE YOUNG MEN

刘建民　王军伟　李　炜　等◇著　林晶晶　周　维　蔡　亮　等◇译
Terence Noel（爱尔兰）◇审校

ZHEJIANG UNIVERSITY PRESS
浙江大学出版社

图书在版编目（CIP）数据

浙里是我家：100 个中国青年的 100 个中国故事 / 刘建民等著；林晶晶等译. —杭州：浙江大学出版社，2021.6
ISBN 978-7-308-21470-4

Ⅰ. ①浙… Ⅱ. ①刘… ②林… Ⅲ. ①新闻—作品集—中国—当代 Ⅳ. ①I253

中国版本图书馆 CIP 数据核字（2021）第 109314 号

浙里是我家
——100 个中国青年的 100 个中国故事

刘建民　王军伟　李　炜　等著
林晶晶　周　维　蔡　亮　等译
Terence Noel（爱尔兰）　审校

责任编辑　李海燕
责任校对　孙秀丽
封面设计　雷建军
出版发行　浙江大学出版社
（杭州市天目山路 148 号　邮政编码 310007）
（网址：http://www.zjupress.com）
排　　版　杭州好友排版工作室
印　　刷　杭州高腾印务有限公司
开　　本　710mm×1000mm　1/16
印　　张　48.75
字　　数　1100 千
版 印 次　2021 年 6 月第 1 版　2021 年 6 月第 1 次印刷
书　　号　ISBN 978-7-308-21470-4
定　　价　160.00 元

打开"浙"扇读懂中国的窗

胡征宇　杨德仁

三分匠意，七分文心。中国人自古以来对"窗"情有独钟，"窗"与"门""户"相映照，成为"家"的代指；同时又与"里""外"相贯通，在窗内、窗外间观照内心以达天下。透过"窗"，可以含蓄地表达寄托与勤勉；透过"窗"，也诠释着中国的开放观念与中国人心中的天下观。正如"学向勤中得，萤窗万卷书""望远不上楼，窗中见天外"等诗句，不仅描绘了"窗"建筑学上的直观之像，而且更多地蕴含着以"窗"之名，借"窗"言志、以"窗"咏怀的深刻意涵。

窗间过马、驹窗电逝。又是一年新墨香，在迎来中国共产党建党百年华诞之际，在习近平总书记考察浙江、赋予浙江"努力成为新时代全面展示中国特色社会主义制度优越性的重要窗口"一周年之际，也在浙大宁波理工学院建校二十周年之际，案头这部由学校宣传部、传媒与法学院、外国语学院、马克思主义学院共同推出的青年学子"行、访、察、叙、写、译"合集《浙里是我家》即将付梓。全书是在中国共产党成立 100 周年的时代大背景中，透过 100 个浙江家庭故事，向世界展示中国发展速度的一扇窗口，向世界传递中国奋进力量的一扇窗口，向世界讲述多彩中国的一扇窗口。

浙江，是中国的一扇窗。一百年前，中国革命的红船从浙江嘉兴南湖启航；一百年来，浙江儿女在中国共产党的坚强领导下，筚路蓝缕、实干担当、砥砺奋进。特别是 2003 年实施"八八战略"以来，浙江大地发生了精彩蝶变，实现了从经济大省到经济强省，从对内对外开放到深度融入全球，从基本小康到高水平全面小康的跃升，成为"中国之治"的"浙江之窗"。青年，是中国的一扇窗。一百年前，在国家和民族生死存亡的危机之时，一批又一批爱国青年挺身而出；一百年来，一代又一代中国青年满怀对祖国和人民的赤子之心，积极投身党领导的革命、建设、改革伟大事业，为人民战斗、为祖国献身、为幸福生活奋斗，把最美好的青春献给祖国和人民，谱写了一曲又一曲壮丽的青春之歌，用青春之我创造青春之中国、青春之民族；处在"两个一百年"交汇点上的新时代中国青年，正以前赴后继、接续奋斗的姿态，努力成为实现中华民族伟大复兴中国梦的"青春之窗"。高校，是中国的一扇窗。一百年前，中国的高等教育在风雨飘摇中矢志办学，艰辛求索教育救国的道路；百年大计，教育为本，一百年后的今天，中国高校正在展开一幅“中国特色、世界一流”的炫彩图景，成为连接世界、展示中国的科学与文化之窗。

在浙大宁波理工学院，就有一群用行动践行中国精神、展示蓬勃力量的新时代青年。自党的十九大以来，他们连续四年步履不停、笔耕不辍，围绕改革开放四十周年、新中国成立七十周年、全面建成小康社会、建党一百周年等重大主题，聚焦“家”这一社会单元，行走在祖国大地，扎根实践大课堂开展田野调查，先后完成了《我家四十年》《国是千万家》《我的小康之家》《浙里是我家》四部思考与观察的成果，持续讲好中国的“家庭故事”，厚植家国情怀，为属于中国的新时代构图画像，用稍显稚嫩的笔触书写一个饱满、丰富、真实的中国，打开了一扇读懂中国的窗口。

值得一提的是，“家”的四部曲，曲曲动人悠扬，曲曲有传承与创新。《我家四十年》《国是千万家》是学校“行走的新闻”课程思政十四年实践的延续。《我的小康之家》在这一延续的基础上，独具创新地设计了观察者、叙述者双重视角，以对观察者的再观察方式，达到了观察者与叙述者时空碰面、情感碰触、思想碰撞的多层效果。即将付梓的《浙里是我家》，在继承中又有了进一步的创新探索，一方面，观察者的角色更多元、参与更广，并在观察方式上作了优化调整，呈现出对“浙江家庭故事”在学术、精神等层面的提炼与升华，更具融合度和张力；另一方面，实现了学校两项育人品牌——“行走的新闻”和“用声音叙事”——的联合创作，既保留了“行走的新闻”田野调查鲜活力，又发挥了“用声音叙事”注重跨文化、国际化传播优势，让浙江的家庭故事在中文、英文双语呈现中更加立体，更具传播力。

为世界了解浙江、读懂中国打开一扇窗。透过《浙里是我家》这扇窗，我们读到了同学们铭记历史、讴歌时代的青春之信，读到了同学们懂得感恩、珍惜生活的青春之悟，读到了同学们立志奉献、策马扬鞭的青春之志，读到了同学们积极向上、勇毅拼搏的青春之行，读到了同学们放眼世界、笃学笃行的青春之美。透过《浙里是我家》这扇窗，我们更读到了一幅千万个家庭共筑中国梦、共逐中国梦、共圆中国梦的历史画卷、青春画卷与未来画卷。正如同学们在感言中所写：“习近平主席在新年贺词中说到，幸福都是奋斗出来的，我们作为新时代的新青年，要将上一代的奋斗精神传承下去，将我们的‘小家’和‘大家’建设得更好。”

为同学们点赞！向每一位潜心育人的师者致敬！

胡征宇　中共浙大宁波理工学院党委书记

杨德仁　浙大宁波理工学院院长、中国科学院院士

目　录

讲好中国故事浙江篇

刘建民　王军伟　李　炜

习近平总书记指出，讲故事是国际传播的最佳方式。“行走的新闻”从2007年至今，正式出版新闻调查作品集19部。近4年来结合重大时代背景推出4部“中国故事—我家故事”系列作品：2018年，《我家四十年——纪念改革开放40年特别田野调查》记录历史；2019年，《国是千万家——庆祝新中国成立70周年特别田野调查》献礼庆典；2020年，《我的小康之家——00后眼中的中国小康之家样本观察》呼应时代，为小康之家画像，为全面小康构图；2021年，《浙里是我家——100名中国青年的100个家庭故事》从红船出发，到“两山”之下，共迎百年华诞。

百年百家浙江故事，百年百世青年中国。《浙里是我家》这本书是浙大宁波理工学院党委宣传部、传媒与法学院、外国语学院共同推出的青年学子“行、访、叙、写、察、译”中国故事的最新集合。全书收录100个中国浙江家庭故事的中英文对照文本，并组织教师、专家、学者、媒体界人士和部分学生对每一个故事展开社会学、新闻学、文化学、人类学、生态学、传播学等角度的学术观察。传媒与法学院网络与新媒体专业2018级、2019级，新闻学专业2018级、2019级、2020级专升本班部分同学，以课程实践的方法参与调查写作；外国语学院英语2018级的同学以课程实践的形式参与本书部分文稿翻译。

■ 高校新闻传播教育的中国故事实践范式

范式的概念在新闻学的语境下更多地体现为新闻理论研究的方法与共识，以及新闻实践中主要采用的报道理念、结构方式等。而新闻实践范式中又存在譬如以党性为核心的宣传范式等多种新闻实践范式。新闻业作为社会知识生产的行业，新闻范式可被看作一种以客观性为核心的信息收集的模式，并被嵌入新闻实践中，主要是为了确定事件的新闻价值和报道给受众的方式。记者像科学家一样依赖于一个范型来提供实践指导，并分享它的基本假设来“理解这个世界”。新闻范式是新闻从业者运用一个社会或时代对什么是新闻以及如何制作新闻的共享理解。

在全球化大背景下，如何讲好中国故事、让世界读懂中国，成为各级各类媒体加强国际传播能力建设所面临的重要课题。中国高等教育在新闻传播人才的培养过程中如何确立自身的新闻实践范式；如何做到在马克思主义新闻观的理论引领下，实现知识传输和思政教育融通；如何通过课程实践加入中国故事内容生产的队伍，汇入新时代的新闻实践洪流；如何探寻新闻实践教育规律，创新新闻实践策略，探寻专业教学和课程思政突破路径，"行走的新闻"做出了有益的尝试。

中国故事的新闻实践范式的第一要义是讲述者。以访谈方式发掘、采集、整理与保存口述者（当事人、亲历者、见证者、受访者、整理者等）的历史记忆，呈现口述者亲历的史事——"行走的新闻"让青年学生当好中国故事的主讲人。近现代中国每个家族百年史中的沉浮，都是中国大历史发展前进的微坐标。因而以家史来证百年史，可以将每个个体家庭融入到大历史的洪流中去，以历史亲历者和参与者的身份，去更好地体会历史的变迁、国家的进步、社会的发展。习近平总书记曾寄语青年："要坚持学以致用，深入基层、深入群众，在改革开放和社会主义现代化建设的大熔炉中，在社会的大学校里，掌握真才实学，增益其所不能，努力成为可堪大用、能担重任的栋梁之材。"[①]新闻实践范式是新闻从业者共享的一套关于何为新闻、如何报道以及怎样区分好新闻坏新闻的世界观。高校新闻传播教育培养新时代的准记者、未来的新闻接班人，其新闻实践范式自然要求创新中国故事的青年认知、创设中国故事的青年叙事。

中国故事的新闻实践范式更要强调的是素材范畴。自 20 世纪 70 年代以来，家庭史研究成了西方历史学和社会学等学科共同关注的领域。把家庭史与社会变迁结合起来考察，尤其是研究家庭演变与近现代社会形成的关系，从家庭变革的内部探讨社会发展的动力；形成了一些理论模式和研究流派，如"生命进程"论、"家庭策略"、"原始工业化"等。家庭史是人类共同生活的基本单位，形成演变的历史，家庭的发展史是社会发展史不可分割的组成部分。

家史承载着国史的变迁。对成长于新世纪、生活在新时代的青年一代来说，通过对家史的搜集整理，能够更好地从血缘传承中理解自己从哪里来到哪里去的人生基本问题，更可以在社会历史的大潮下，去探析家庭及家族在大历史变迁下的命运，从个体及家族变迁中更深刻地理解历史的发展，理解我们个人在家族乃至国家发展中的位置和作用。同时，将历史与现实结合起来，从历史感悟现实，促进对国史的理解，增强家国情怀，培养责任担当意识。历史长河悠悠，每一

① 2013 年 5 月 4 日，习近平总书记来到中国航天科技集团公司中国空间技术研究院，同各界优秀青年代表座谈并发表重要讲话。

个参与讲述家庭故事的青年人，都可以在家史家训的传承中感悟历史变迁，并成为不断延续的历史的一部分。

“行走的新闻”实现了高校学子中国故事内容生产和话语建构，形成中国故事的青年“话语共同体”。“中国故事—我家故事”系列作品聚焦重大主题与历史叙事的新闻聚合、探寻知行底蕴与行学本色的实践整合、创新课程思政与时政观察的学术融合。激活中国故事的家庭细胞，创新新闻叙事的载体和方法——通过行、访、叙、写、察，记录家国奋斗历程，感受家庭、社会和国家日新月异的变化，体悟中国精神。

■ 新闻叙事视角下的“我家故事”口述实录样本

“行走的新闻”是用口述实录故事写出的新闻通讯。学界对新闻通讯的定义中都出现了“形象、生动、具体”等词汇。无论是人物通讯，还是事件通讯，都是运用“叙事+情节”的故事模式，以“场景再现”的方式，给人以感同身受。通讯则更侧重于叙述新闻过程。故事技巧是指通过结构布局、视角选取、场景建构的方式，增加故事的趣味性和可读性。一篇用故事技巧写出的新闻通讯，不仅是客观的和真实的，还能引起受众的共鸣。口述实录是一种新闻体裁。口述实录诞生于20世纪40年代的美国，“萌生于美国史学界，渐次浸染到全球的史学、新闻和文学领域”。口述实录可被归入新闻报道中人物专访这一类别，是记者通过对人物的采访，由口述者讲述个人亲身经历的新闻事实、表达个人观点，并最终以第一人称的形式见诸媒体的新闻体裁。口述实录最初出现时，是作为一种搜集史料的手段。从历史记录的广度而言，口述实录提供了相当广阔的空间，既有井然有序的宏大叙事，也不乏细节化的个体叙事，能够展现更为多元的社会场景。“行走的新闻”我家故事系列具备史料价值，能够增强人们对社会的认知。

“行走的新闻”生产了带体温的中国样本：“我家故事”系列已建立基于600个中国故事、浙江故事的家庭样本数据库。这些样本书写饱满、丰富、真实的中国，打开一扇读懂中国的窗口，成为研究这一时代社会发展历史的微观样本。“行走的新闻”构建了带情感的新闻叙事：叙述者的视角、故事素材有助于发现中国普通家庭喜怒哀乐，厚植家国情怀，为属于中国的新时代构图画像，成系统、见规模。“行走的新闻”发出了带热度的学术观察：泥土味、现实性和第一人称视角为触及社会学研究末端提供参考范式。观察者与叙述者为师生关系，青年学者从学术初心出发，在新闻调查中找到丰沃的学术土壤。

受社会历史变迁的影响，特别是多元现代性的影响，记忆、情感和认同越来越成为当代国家、群体和个人寻找意义感的途径和表现。对记忆、情感和认同的研究也为我们认识社会历史变迁提供了极佳的视角和窗口。在诸多有关记忆、情感和认同的研究之中，口述史作为一种方法和认识论，因其对“活的历史”和“多元历史”的强调而显得尤为重要；通过对个人历史与公共议题的结合，口述史不仅连接了记忆、情感与认同，也十分鲜明地展现了米尔斯所说的“社会学想象力”的核心要义。

“行走的新闻”数据库中的“我家故事”均为自述家史，既是个人史、家族史，也是社会发展史，是社会变迁史。最大的特点是个性化、情感化。既是局限，也是特色和优势。事实上，作为认识论的记忆、情感和认同不仅在社会学理论上有其重要价值，也为我们理解转型之中的中国社会提供了不可多得的分析视角和框架。“行走的新闻”通过青年学生引导和帮助那些身体和记忆力尚好的老人将回忆的时间跨度拉长，将个人的家庭传承、人生经历、见闻和思索统统讲出来，写出来。每一位口述者都是站在自己在历史上所处的“那一个”独特的“点”上，来接受社会的风雨洗礼和冲击，经历、感受和体味着生活的艰辛与快乐，也用自己的方式书写着人生和历史。而经过几次变换的社会主流观念改造和重塑，沉淀在心里的历史记忆，有的被遗忘和淡化了，有的又扭曲和变形了，有的却坚定和鲜明了。但无论命运把他推向何处，漂流到什么地方，都是历史的轨迹，也都是人的灵魂史。这看似隐藏在个人心灵深处的记忆，却是社会发展的核心和精神。所以，每一个样本不仅是个人和家庭的私产，也应当成为社会的宝贵财富和共享思想。

新闻是社会变迁的纪录。无论从新闻的角度还是历史的角度观察，“行走的新闻”这些鲜活的故事文本中的每一个都是安放个人和家庭灵魂的神圣殿堂。个性化和感性化也是其社会价值和生命力之所在。以新闻为表征的历史已经从精英历史转向大众历史；新闻历史叙事已经从宏大叙事、间接描述、意义阐释转到“人”的“自我言说”和意义再生。

■ 中国故事的浙江窗口，百家故事的青年中国说

浙里出发、浙里创造、浙里奋斗、浙里见证——在浙江这一片改革开放的热土上，每一个人，每一个家庭，都演绎着经典的中国家庭故事。一己之家百年风云，一曲之江百年辉煌。家庭进步变迁是社会的发展记录。百年回眸，从南湖红船，到“两山”之下，《浙里是我家》100 个家庭故事映照着普通浙江百姓在民族复兴路上的寻梦之旅。

“你们响应习总书记的号召，讲好中国故事、浙江故事、宁波故事，用身边故事、生动实例，弘扬正能量，歌颂党、祖国人民。”浙江省省长郑栅洁连续三年给“行走的新闻”批示或回信：“用一个个鲜活生动的案例，记录了党带领人民群众全面建成小康社会的光辉历程，以‘小家’见‘大家’，从小切口反映大时代，为世

界了解浙江、读懂中国打开了一扇窗。”

100 个青年笔下的 100 篇家庭故事构成的家庭史、个人史，真诚、真实、真挚、真切。这些新闻叙事作品有真实的素材，有情感寄托的访谈场域，和多维感知的家庭视角，从不同个人、不同家庭的角度，展现浙江小康之路的坚韧、光辉的发展历程。

乐居的“浙里”话语——从贫居到安居，安居到乐居，《爸爸与房子》（金华胡安）、《房屋的变迁》（湖州沈静）、《房屋进步史》（桐乡徐淳迪）、《老房翻新》（金华姚冯胜）、《漏雨的日子不再来》（台州阮箭芬）、《买房记》（温州黄雨欣）、《平凡岁月中的四套房子》（温州肖研萱）、《我曾生活过的四个房子》（金华楼康婷）、《我住过的五个家》（衢州张淼）、《小家变迁史》（义乌金煜盛）无不述说着房子是最大的民生，房子是用来住的这个真理。

创业的浙江叙事——“大众创业，万众创新”已成为中国经济社会发展的新引擎，读着《爸爸的柜台》（温州黄冰茹）、《从船夫到店主》（温州洪莹莹）、《从打工到创业》（湖州温纯）、《从修鞋匠到房东》（温州郑佳慧）、《大不了重头再来》（绍兴薛佳颖）、《轰鸣声中成长》（嘉兴沈晓琳）、《舅舅与他的厂子》（义乌马旭灿）、《摸爬滚打生意经》（温州林温铋）、《失败，再出发》（杭州邵怡娜）、《叔叔的店》（衢州陈梦洁）、《四海为家》（温州项婷）、《踏平坎坷成大道》（台州尹飞宇），感受着浙江民众创业的浪涌。

迁徙的浙江形态——《从贵州到湖州》（湖州吴诗雨）、《从山里走出来》（温州潘俊）、《开往义乌的绿皮火车》（义乌邹姗姗）、《来浙江，没有返程车票》（湖州殷吉梅）、《落地生根》（嘉兴谭静怡）、《妈妈的杭漂史》（杭州徐莹）、《你在义乌，我在鹰潭》（金华季燕婷）、《吾心安处是家乡》（杭州刘玫）、《一路打拼到浙江》（海宁严文洁）……植根故土，掘金他乡，一个因为经济和生存而迁徙的时代，掠过浙江大地的不是“候鸟”，他们都定居了下来。

代际的浙江传承——《爸爸向前冲》（台州卢婷）、《百年家史》（温州郑博）、《不同的“二十年”》（宁波张诗雅）、《花屋下的三代人》（湖州金颐宁）、《开过火车的父亲》（嘉兴顾笑笑）、《三代人的三种生活》（湖州许费凡）、《四世同堂》（杭州沈层娇）、《细流成河老一辈》（丽水刘施婷）、《爷爷的奋斗》（绍兴徐涵）、《一位老教师的大学梦》（温州郑玺）等故事告诉我们，代际传承，不仅是物质的，更是精神的。

小康的浙江画图——浙江“八八战略”总统领下的小康家庭之窗，在《奔波在东栅塘汇之间》（嘉兴陆宇婷）、《闯出个名堂》（宁波蔡盈盈）、《从海中岛到城中村》（舟山王楚琪）、《从无到有的日子》（绍兴胡淡燕）、《旧物屋》（杭州江薇）、《离岛，归岛》（舟山王永明）、《踏上幸福的路》（绍兴谢子弘）、《一山更比一山高》（绍兴蒋依诺)等故事里得以微观显现。

永远的浙江精神——求真务实、诚信和谐、开放图强的浙江精神,在《扎根前溪村工业区》(温岭郑婧怡)、《浮沉二十年》(温州蒋明瑜)、《虹桥镇上那点事》(温州胡露敏)、《老钱家的“支柱”》(衢州程书棋)、《摸爬滚打半辈子》(金华余沁怡)、《守寒窗,跃农门》(杭州何流)、《“万能师傅”》(湖州朱智凤)、《硖石镇上的普通人家》(嘉兴高恺悦)、《在溪口打拼》(宁波樊佳瑜)等故事里,显示出浙江人民强大的生命力和创造力。

百姓的浙江传奇——《漫漫岁月起高楼》(杭州韦红)、《没有迈不过去的坎》(杭州吴梦婧)、《每个第一次都是非凡》(杭州钟齐淇)、《我与 TA 的关系》(嘉兴张晓宇)、《向上的“楼梯”》(温州高婷婷)、《向未来砥砺前行》(绍兴李东腾)、《雁荡镇上卖海鲜》(温州王亚琦)、《一船五车》(绍兴汪雅琴)、《这三亩五分茶地》(杭州张恬)、《只要肯登攀》(宁波张微)……每一家每一户,都为浙江成为“新时代全面展示中国特色社会主义制度优越性的重要窗口”书写了百姓传奇。

■“行走的新闻”:行基层、访现实、叙中国、写未来

习近平曾寄语青年:“中国比较大,国情比较复杂,各个地方的情况可能都有差异,但是,如果我们要真正地想为国家做一些事情、有报国理想的话,应该更多地深入到基层,真正了解实际的国情是怎么样的。同学们的忧国忧民,只有到基层中去、到实践中去、到人民中去,才能真正知道所学的知识如何去发挥、如何去为社会作贡献。”①

“行走的新闻”思政元素发掘和内容供给集中体现在对“中国故事”的挖掘与讲述之中。青年学生们从新闻传播人才培养“故纸堆”里走出来,探索一条增强社会观察力和学术洞察力的创新探索之路,在实践中感受中国体温、看见中国社会、讲述中国生活、发现中国精神、体会中国智慧、读懂中国未来。

“行走的新闻”价值塑造、知识传授和能力培养以“行访叙写”为落地实践的核心抓手,实现“四向四做”卓越新闻人才培养落地发芽。“行”是走向社会,“访”是关注现实,“叙”是中国叙事,“写”是专业突破。坚持马克思主义新闻观知识传授与讲好中国故事价值引领相统一,将价值塑造、知识传授和能力培养紧密融合,引导学生“课堂上学习、课堂外思考,走出校园提问、走进社会实践”。

行之有效的知识教育、实践教育和课程思政三位一体的育人实践——“行走的新闻”,破解当下新闻观教育与新闻实践环节落地“两张皮”、学院式新闻教学

① 1990 年 7 月下旬,北京大学黄誌、李树峰等 60 名学生赴福州开展为期 12 天的社会实践活动。时任福州市委书记习近平获悉后非常重视,利用晚上休息时间到实践团驻地看望大家并座谈。

与新时代背景下新闻内容生产“两条道”、新闻传播专业教育与课程思政教育“两股劲”的困局，为课程思政提供了一个特色的样板。

坚持不懈的新闻传播教育教学的创新实践——理论教学，教师在顶层领跑；实践教学，学生在田野奔跑。课程理论教学以马克思主义新闻观为指导，实践教学以“为家国画像，为青春构图”为行动指南，以学生时政视野的开阔和国情认知教育为教学主题，致力于通过课堂上学习讨论和课堂外全真实践的全面结合开启并提升学生内在潜力、学习动力和专业能力。

与时俱进的课程思政教育与专业教育的融合实践——专业教育，教师铸就“知行”底蕴；思政教育，学子尽显“行学”本色。课程设计观察者、叙述者双重视角，以学术随笔等方式关照和回应叙述，增强专业知识的学术表达，达到师生时空碰面、情感碰触、思想碰撞的多层效果，是师生合作、教学相长、心灵相契的教学新方式。

“年轻人不能认为进了大学就进了保险箱，就等着将来直接分配到机关。一定要多接触社会，补上社会实践这一课。你们虽然读了很多书，但书里有很多‘水分’，只有和群众实践结合，才能把‘水分’挤掉。要给书本上的知识‘挤挤水’，才能得到知识‘干货’。”[①]牢记习近平总书记的教诲，“行走的新闻”会一直在路上。

刘建民　浙大宁波理工学院传媒与法学院高级编辑
王军伟　浙大宁波理工学院传媒与法学院副教授
李　炜　浙大宁波理工学院党委宣传部常务副部长

① 1985年冬天，正在厦门大学读书的张宏樑同学因一封信结识了时任厦门市委常委、副市长习近平，并经常得到习近平的指导和帮助。

“温州精神”的前世今生

邱子桐

如今提起温州，很多人都会想到改革开放以来作为经济制度创新的“温州模式”以及温州人务实求利、敢于创新创业、敢为人先的温州精神。郑一博同学的《百年家史》一文，呈现了一个与家庭经验紧密相关且更为宽阔的时间维度：展开了跨越了四代人的家庭系谱。我们现在在媒体中认知的温州人精神在郑一博的百年家庭叙事中被清晰地勾勒出来。

郑一博同学首先追溯了在辛亥革命那一年出生的太爷爷和民国时期出生的太外公的人生。16岁的太外公带着14岁的二妹翻山越岭去山区任教，从而开启了家族与教师职业之间的联结。新中国成立前两年出生的爷爷在上世纪70年代务农，同时还做了兼职的船夫，起早贪黑为改变家庭生计而努力；1978年改革开放后，外婆开展副业努力赚钱；尽管“70后”父亲在读大学之前遇到了被人冒名顶替的糟心事，但是他仍然凭借自己的奔波与努力成为家中的第一位大学生；母亲也在读完大学后顺利成为高中老师。“00后”的郑一博和姐姐出生于中国全面全球化的时代，他们的求学与未来工作的轨迹似乎与温州的土地渐渐远离。

如今在媒体中所被呈现出的温洲精神，几乎在郑一博同学的每一位家庭成员中都有所体现：敢于改变，坚毅地为家庭而努力，柔韧而灵活的思想。同时，一代比一代富裕的轨迹也紧紧地依附于国家的百年历程：从辛亥革命到新中国成立、从革命到市场、从改革开放到全面全球化。

（浙大宁波理工学院传媒与法学院副教授，博士）

故事

温州

郑一博（网络与新媒体专业193班）

百年家史

1911年，我的太爷爷在浙南乡下一个赤贫的农民家庭中出生，老家就是现在的温州市龙港市云岩片区；4年后，我的太外公在几公里外镇上的一个小手工业者家庭中呱呱坠地。两个男人从此开启了完全不同的人生。现实中的他们从未有过交集，作为他们的后人，我追本溯源，借助长辈们只言片语的回忆，循着一些零星的线索，才得以透过尘蒙的时光一窥他们当年的风貌。我想，就以两位太祖的出场作为这篇百年家史的开端，并让他们以这种特殊的方式完成一次跨越时空的会面吧。

我的太爷爷在家排行老三。贫穷的家境使他不能像同龄人一样早早娶妻，到了25岁那年，他入赘邻村一户人家，太奶奶姓鲍。十多年后，太爷爷因故返回老家，带回了三个年幼的孩子，我爷爷是其中的老二。太爷爷以划船、挑矾为生，干的是体力活，劳累异常，但收入很微薄。太爷爷在上世纪60年代便因病逝世，只活了54岁，他去世时，几个儿子都还没有成家。

太外公家住温州市苍南县宜山镇。太外公上过小学，由于家境不是很宽裕，毕业后难以继续学业。他心有不甘，跑到市区中学的教室门外偷听老师上课，隔着窗子大声回答老师的提问，从而引起了老师的注意。抗战时，日军的敌机曾经在太外公家房屋的上方呼啸而过，太外公的三妹妹体弱有病，竟惊吓而死，给家人留下了难以磨灭的伤痛记忆。

当太外公还是个十六七岁的少年时，便带着自己14岁的二妹翻山越岭去山区任教。这段经历也成为这个家族与教师职业结缘的伊始。太外公18岁时便已结婚，太外婆是典型的江南女子，身材娇小，面貌姣好，她一辈子生育了5子5女，是当时名副其实的“光荣母亲”。太外公非常重视对孩子的培养，10个子女中有4人成为教师，在家乡传为佳话，甚至还上过报纸。他还颇通文墨，写一笔好字，擅长替人写打官司的讼状，是当地有名的“状师”。

我的爷爷生于1943年，本有一兄一弟，但是由于家境窘迫，他的弟弟在16岁时便被送往一位老人家中作为养子，从此面临颠沛流离的一生，不过好在最后也是落叶归根。1968 年,我爷爷 25 岁时,娶了我 17 岁的奶奶。两家都是家徒四壁,以致当他们结婚时,不仅摆设的家具,连衣服和鞋子都是向他人借来的。爷爷奶奶都没有上过学,只能以体力谋生,仅有的依靠就是家乡那块瘠薄的土地。除了务农,爷爷还伐木、划船。在最困难的日子里,爷爷奶奶甚至吃不上饭。在漫长的岁月里,如何解决温饱问题一直是他们生命中沉重的话题。

爷爷奶奶以务农为主,70 年代初期,村里有人去江西吉安做松香,他们也设法取得了公社人员的联名签字同意书,离开家乡远赴江西讨生活。后来,他们还带上了幼小的孩子。我父亲便曾在江西的小学念过书。1975 年左右,爷爷奶奶重返家乡继续务农。农事之余,爷爷做起了船夫。他划着手摇船,运载去海边运输海鲜回乡贩卖的客人。他天不亮就起床,站在船头划动双桨。小小的木船在浙南平原宽阔的河面上慢慢地、吃力地前进着,船舱中是一批昏昏欲睡的客人。

与爷爷奶奶不同的是,我的外婆从小到大都没饿过肚子,而且她顺利地完成了小学、初中的学业,并考取师范学校,毕业后成为小学教师。我外公也是一名教师。1964 年元旦,外公外婆和另外两对教师夫妇一起,共同举行了一场集体婚礼。外公有机会上学,并且成绩优异,考上了市里一流的师范学校。后来,外公在小学和初中都教过书,担任过校长。

外公外婆新婚时,仅有的家具是一张长辈留下的老旧婚床。他们和父母一起挤在老家低矮的屋檐下,生活负担加重的外婆在教书之外,还要插田,割稻,晒谷,养鸡养鸭,种植菜蔬瓜果。在辛苦而拮据的生活中,她带大了三个孩子。

在我母亲的记忆中,我的外婆与外公都曾做过她的老师。我妈妈日后也成为一名教师,其中受她父母的影响颇深。

70 年代初,我的父母都已出生。1978 年后,我的外婆也效仿他人开展家庭副业,比如帮人剥蒜头,组装开关,利用边角料缝制内衣裤售卖到周边地区等,并尝到了赚钱的甜头。这些劳动,当时尚在念小学的我母亲和两个舅舅都参与过。1982 年我母亲升入镇上的初中,外婆的教书地点也从村小转向镇小,一家人开始了小镇生活。

爷爷还继续做着船工,但船的动力由人力转向了柴油,行驶起来就省力多了。再后来,村里通了公路,船运渐渐被陆运取代,这时爷爷也年事渐高,才结束了前后长达廿余年的船运工作。

值得一提的是,我的爷爷奶奶虽然没有文化,却坚持供孩子们上学。而我的父亲也没有辜负他们的一片苦心,从小发愤苦读,初中毕业时不仅考上了高中,打破了老家那所乡村学校高中升学率为零的纪录,而且上了县中的分数线。但造化弄人,在不知情的状况下,他的县中名额竟然被人悄悄地冒名顶替,使他几乎不能继续完成学业。经过一番奔走,他得以升学,上了镇上的普通高中。1987

年,他终于凭借自己的努力考上了杭州师范学院(今杭州师范大学),成为家中的第一位大学生。1991年,他大学毕业后返乡执教,当了一名高中老师。我父亲的经历,正是知识改变命运的经典案例。

我母亲自小在我外婆外公的庇荫下长大,正常完成了学业。1988年她县中毕业后考取了温州师范学院(今温州大学),毕业后也做了一名高中老师。1994年,我的父母结婚。他们在镇上安了家,不久买了自己的房子,过上了跟他们的父辈完全不同的安稳日子。

我与姐姐一同出生于2001年,是一名"零零后"。和父辈祖辈不同的是,我一出生便住在镇上的商品房中,从小疏离了泥土。年幼时,当我在水泥路上奔跑,偶尔抓获几只路边杂草丛中腾跃的蚂蚱时,还会激动地将其装入瓶中。后来经历了一次搬家,住进了更好的小区后,我与土地的距离更远了……

百年沧桑家史,几千字的短文难以尽述,只能通过零星的碎片管窥尚未消散殆尽的回忆,录之以作纪念。

Wenzhou
Zheng Yibo (Class 193, Majoring in Network and New Media)

A Family Story of One Hundred Years

In 1911, my paternal great-grandfather was born in a poverty-stricken peasant family in the countryside in southern Zhejiang province, which is now located in Yunyanpian District, Longgang City in Wenzhou. Four years later, my maternal great-grandfather was born in a small handicraftsman's family in a town several miles away. Since then, these two men had started completely different lives. They had never known each other in life. As their descendant, I looked back on their past. With the fragments of the elders' memories as scattered tracks to follow, I finally got a glimpse of their life in the old days. I would like to start with these two ancestors, and let them meet each other across time and space in this special way.

My paternal great-grandfather was the third child in the family. His poor family made him unable to marry as early as his peers. At the age of 25, he married into a family of the village nearby and lived with them. My paternal great-grandmother was surnamed Bao. More than ten years later, my grandfather returned to his hometown and brought back three young children. My paternal grandfather was the second child. My paternal great-grandfather made a living by rowing and carrying alum. What he did was physical work. It was extremely exhausting, but he earned very little. In the 1960s, he died of illness at the age of 54. When he died, none of his sons were married.

My maternal great-grandfather lived in Yishan Town, Cangnan County, Wenzhou City. He was able to study in the primary school, but his family was not well-off, so it was difficult to continue his study after graduation. He felt frustrated, so he went to the downtown high school to audit classes unofficially by standing outside the classroom. He would answer teachers' questions loudly outside the window, which drew their attention to him. During the War of Resistance against Japanese Aggression, the Japanese planes once roared over the house of the maternal great-grandfather. His third sister, who was weak and sick, died of fright, leaving an indelible pain for his family.

When my maternal great-grandfather was just a boy of 16 or 17, he, taking his 14-year-old sister with him, climbed over the mountains to teach in the mountainous area. This experience also became the beginning of the family's connection with the teaching profession. My maternal great-grandfather got married when he was 18 years old. My maternal great-grandmother was a typical female in the south of the Yangtze River. She was petite and pretty, and she gave birth to five sons and five daughters in her life, which made her a truly "glorious mother" at that time.

My maternal great-grandfather attached great importance to the cultivation of his children. Four of his ten children became teachers, which became a much-told tale in his hometown and was reported by the newspaper. He was also well versed in writing and calligraphy, especially writing indictments for others, which made him well known locally as a "plaint writer".

My paternal grandfather was born in 1943. He originally had an elder brother and a younger brother. However, due to the poverty of his family, his younger brother was sent to an old man's family as an adopted son when he was 16 years old. From then on, he suffered a total dislocation of his life, but fortunately, he finally returned to his hometown. In 1968 when my paternal grandfather was 25, he married my paternal grandmother, who was 17. Both families were so impecunious that when they got married, they borrowed not only the furniture, but also the clothes and shoes. My paternal grandparents did not go to school, so they could only make a living through labor. What they could rely on was the barren land in their hometown. Apart from farming, my grandpa also cut wood and rowed a boat. During the most difficult days, my paternal grandparents even had no food to eat. For a long time, how to deal with the problem of food and clothing had been a heavy task in their lives.

My grandparents mainly took up farming. In the early 1970s, some villagers went to Ji'an of Jiangxi province to make rosin. My paternal grandparents also managed to get a consent form signed by members of the commune and left their hometown for Jiangxi to make a living. They took their young children with them later. My grandparents returned to their hometown to continue farming around 1975. My grandpa worked as a boatman besides farming. He paddled his boat to the beach to carry passengers back home to sell seafood. He got up before dawn and rowed in the front of the boat. The small wooden boat advanced slowly through the wide river in the plain of southern Zhejiang. Inside the boat were drowsy passengers in the cabins.

Unlike my paternal grandparents, my maternal grandmother had never been hungry since childhood. Moreover, she successfully completed her studies in primary school and middle school. After that, she was admitted to a normal school and became a primary school teacher after graduation. My maternal grandfather was a teacher, too. On Chinese New Year of 1964, my maternal grandparents, together with another two teacher couples, held a group wedding. My grandpa had the chance to go to school. With excellent grades, he was admitted to the top normal school in the city. Then my grandfather taught in primary school and middle school and held office as a headmaster.

When my maternal grandparents got married, the only furniture was an old wedding bed left by the elders. They lived with their parents in the small house in their hometown. Besides teaching, my grandmother, who had a heavy living burden, had to transplant rice seedlings, harvest rice, dry grain, raise chickens and ducks and plant vegetables and fruits. She brought up three children when having a life of hardship and privation.

In my mother's memory, both my grandparents once taught her. My mother later became a teacher, which was greatly influenced by her parents.

In the early 1970s, both my parents were born into this world. After 1978, my maternal grandmother followed the example of others to start a family sideline, such as helping people peel garlic, assembling switches, using leftover materials to sew underwear and sell them to the surrounding areas. This made her taste the benefit of making money. My mother and two uncles, who were still in primary school at that time, were all involved in this work. In 1982, my mother entered the middle school in the town, and my grandmother's teaching place was changed from the primary school in the village to the primary school in the town. From then on, the family began to live in the town.

My paternal grandfather continued to work as a boatman, but the power of the boat changed from manpower to diesel fuel, so it was much more labor-saving. Afterwards, roads had been built in the village and shipping was gradually replaced by land transportation. My grandfather didn't end his 20 years of shipping work until he got older.

It is worth mentioning that my paternal grandparents insisted on sending their children to school even though they were illiterate. My father also lived up to their expectation. He studied hard since childhood. When he graduated from middle school, he not only got into high school, ending the history that the high school enrollment rate of the village school in his hometown was zero, but also reached the passing score of high school in the county. However, the fates conspired against him. Without knowing it, he was secretly replaced by an impostor, making it almost impossible for him to continue his studies. After a lot of efforts, he was able to go to school, but it was just a regular high school in town. In 1987, he was finally admitted to Hangzhou Normal College (now Hangzhou Normal University) by his own effort, and became the first undergraduate in his family. In 1991, after graduating from the college, he returned home and became a high school teacher. My father's experience is a typical example of how knowledge changes people's lives.

My mother grew up under the care of my grandparents, and she pursued her studies successfully. In 1988, she graduated from high school and was admitted to Wenzhou Normal University (now Wenzhou University). After graduation, she also became a high school teacher. In 1944, my parents got married. They settled in town, and soon bought their own house. They lived a stable life, which was very different from that of their parents.

My sister and I were born in 2001, and I am Generation Z. Unlike my parents and my grandparents, since my birth I lived in a commercial house in the town and grew up without dirt. When I was a young boy, I ran down the concrete road and occasionally caught several grasshoppers leaping in the roadside weeds. I would be excited and put them into a bottle. Later, after moving into a better community, I was further away from the land.

A short article with only thousands of words is difficult to describe a family story of one hundred years. I could only learn about those memories that are buried in mind through fragments, so I wrote down this article as a commemoration.

生活充满意外，生命之树长青

刘炳辉

卢婷是一个文静内敛、个子高挑的女大学生，大学期间也时常来参加我们转型中国读书会的活动，2019年夏天还跟随读书会一起在宁波市象山县茅洋乡开展暑期社会调查。但卢婷的成长历程，我也还是通过这篇文字才有了更深入的了解，说起来有些惭愧，平日里对卢婷的关心还是少了些。

人都有来时路，卢婷的来时路也有些不易。父辈的创业之路看似寻常，却也艰辛，偌大的一辆车，居然就这么丢了。一个中学生本来如常的日子，却突然迎来了一场手术。这些都是生活的意外，都是难以预料的。

面对这些突如其来的生活意外，我们该如何面对？这才是人生的大问题和真问题。没有谁会永远一帆风顺，人生不如意事十之八九。战胜艰难险阻的关键，就是生命的顽强不屈，永远乐观，永不放弃。这是我从卢婷的家庭故事中读到和学习到的。

我的恩师曹锦清老先生时常教育我们，要乐观，要永远乐观，因为悲观没有出路。

（浙大宁波理工学院马克思主义学院副教授，博士）

故事

台州

卢婷（网络与新媒体专业183班）

爸爸向前冲

我的老家位于浙江省台州市仙居县大战乡的一个小村庄——格垟村。我们家世世代代都扎根在这片土地上,过着日出而作、日落而息的生活。村子四面环山,是大山的宠儿,主要的农作物有水稻和油菜,每到春季,村里的油菜花便盛开了,放眼望去是一望无际金灿灿的油菜花海。

爸爸出生于1974年,新中国成立以前爷爷只是个放牛的,土地改革后,爷爷当上了民兵,负责剿匪、站哨……听爷爷说,刚解放的时候土匪仍然很多,那时候枪弹不长眼,剿匪很危险。爷爷和奶奶的文化水平都不高。爷爷有5个兄弟姐妹,个个都读了书,数爷爷最惨,因为实在穷并且年龄大而被搁在家中放牛、做农活。奶奶在她外婆去世之后也就不再读书了,所以他们从小干的都是一些苦力活,也因此爸爸小时候的生活很艰苦。

渐渐地,爸爸到了上学的年龄,因为他在家中排行最小,有4个姐姐,经济实在是周转不过来,所以只读到初中就不再读书了,那年他17岁。"改革开放前的学校很多都是一座座破旧的土木结构房屋,土墙都脱落了,窗户上一块玻璃都没有,一到冬天,呼呼的寒风就刺骨,遇到下雨,雨点从破瓦片上的窟窿里落下来。那时候哪有什么柏油马路、水泥路,只有厚厚的泥土上踩出的窄窄的一条小道,要是放学遇到下雨,就泥泞不堪,路上到处是水潭,如果不小心踩到水潭,整只脚就会陷进去,好不容易把脚拔出来,可鞋子却留在了泥潭里……"

1998年12月25日,我的爸爸迎来了他人生中的一个重要时刻,他结婚了。妈妈是经人介绍的,且爸爸家的老房子就在外公家旁边,因此熟识。彼此有了好感之后,两个人还经常一起骑车去城里的烈士陵园爬山,车程大概1小时。他们就这样吹着风慢悠悠地骑着,迎着日出或晚霞,想起来也够浪漫,爸爸说的时候脸上也不自觉溢出了笑容。2000年2月29日,他们迎来了我。

爸爸17岁初中毕业以后,去城里跟修卡车师傅学了两年多的修车技术,那时当学徒是没有工资的,后来和仙居的几个老乡一起去了广东省中山市那边工厂打工,打工时长约两三年。

在我出生没多久时,爸爸买了一辆二手的工程车,那时家里都没有什么钱,但为了生计,不得已向亲戚们借钱买车。可是天公不作美,可怕的一天来临了,爸爸的车被偷了。那年我只有四五岁,并没有什么印象,听爸爸说车是停在干爸家门口被偷的,可是这么大的车被偷走真的令人很震惊,让原本不富裕的家庭再一次雪上加霜。在准备再买一辆回来的时候,我外婆突发脑出血,在医院抢救了一段时间,最后不幸成了植物人。那时爸爸和妈妈一起专心照料外婆,大概4个月之后,外婆去世了。

之后爸爸又借钱买了第二辆工程车,在我的记忆中,小时候经常会坐着爸爸的工程车陪他一起去工地。那时候,爸爸的副驾驶座永远都是我的,儿时的天真仿佛让我不懂得害怕。十几年过去,我依然记得那车的样子,蓝色的车身由于岁月的冲刷已经没了那般崭新、锃亮，颜色逐渐泛黄，磕磕碰碰有了印痕，引擎盖上的不起眼处也长出了蚕豆大的锈斑，玻璃不再像镜子般明亮，车轮子也换新了很多次。似乎唯一不变的是它的高大，就像爸爸在我心目中一样，撑起了我们的家。

后来爸爸把车卖了，2008 年开始在仙居县兴宇有限公司工作，工作也和汽车零部件有关，工资不高，全家 6 口基本上靠着爸爸的微薄工资糊口。2015 年，在爸爸辛辛苦苦工作，买车梦快要实现的时候，又一个噩耗降临——我脊柱侧弯要进行大手术，得花约 10 万元。向亲戚们借钱送我去杭州做了手术，全程陪着我的，就是这个话不多但深爱我的爸爸。

2016 年爸爸买了辆小型汽车，也类似小面包车，这车可以坐下七八个人，一直开到现在。车子虽然不贵，但是爸爸对它也精心照料。亲戚们出去玩时，爸爸就开着这辆车载他们去；我要上大学时，爸爸就送我去；去城里时，爸爸都会带一些爷爷亲自种的农家菜、水果等给大姑妈……有了车子，就不用再担心骑电瓶车或摩托车时装不下三个人，不用经历下暴雨时雨衣“衣不蔽体”的浑身湿漉漉的难受感，也不用担心乡下到城里的往返路上东西太多装不下……这车子虽然普普通通，但是给我们家实实在在帮了很多忙。

家中建房有三个阶段。第一个阶段就是上面所说的古老屋，在爸爸 17 岁那年，不幸被火烧掉了。

第二个阶段是改革开放后，1993 年爷爷奶奶盖房，那时农村人基本上仍都是自己盖房，因为没钱请人。说起盖房的经历，奶奶仿佛回到了当年：“那个时候啊，真的，一切都是我和你爷爷自己弄的，你爷爷亲自上山砍树、做地基……当时路又窄，车子也开不进来，石头运不进来，我们两个人就自己一块一块地搬进来，和水泥的沙子也是我们俩一箩筐接着一箩筐扛进来的，那时候真的不容易……才盖成了两层楼外加前面一个厨房。”后来一直到我出生，家也还是两层楼。

第三个阶段是大约 2008 年，家里经济状况稍微好了些，爸爸妈妈一起努力再加上花钱请人来造。将原本的两层楼改造成了四层楼，一层的厨房也往上再盖了一层，并且贴上了瓷砖和瓦片，内部也进行了略微装修。那时候在左邻右舍之中，我家还算是最早一个装上瓷砖的。到现在我们都还生活在这里。

爸爸妈妈在我初中那年就在城里租了个房子，后来因为我考上了当地的重点高中，家又搬到了离学校很近的地方，如今仍在，他们工作结束就会回来看看；而我，只要一放假就会往乡下跑，因为住着舒服，也因为有爷爷奶奶。

父亲这辈子承受了太多，如今爷爷奶奶儿孙满堂，生活虽也不算十分富裕，但是一家人整整齐齐就是最大的幸福！相信在我们全家的共同努力下，一定能过上更好的生活！

Taizhou
Lu Ting (Class 183, Majoring in Network and New Media)

Dad, Move Forward

My hometown is located in Geyang Village, a small village in Dazhan Township of Xianju County, Taizhou City, southeastern China's Zhejiang Province. Our family has been rooted in this land for generations, a place where our ancestors have lived and toiled from sunrise to sunset for years. The village is surrounded and favored by mountains, and crops like rice and rape are grown here. When spring comes, a sea of golden rape flowers which are all in bloom stretches out as far as we can see.

My father was born in 1974. My paternal grandpa, once a cowherd before the founding of the new China, became a militiaman responsible for bandit suppression and standing sentry after the nationwide land reform (1950—1953). My grandpa told me that there were still many bandits shortly after liberation. It could be life-threatening with bullets flying in every direction on the battlefield. Both grandpa and grandma were not very well educated, and they worked and toiled all day long from a young age. My grandpa's five siblings all received education, but being the eldest child in a poor family, grandpa had to look after cattle and do farm work instead. My grandma dropped out of elementary school after my great-grandmother passed away. Therefore, life was tough in my father's childhood.

My father is the youngest in the family, and he has four sisters. When he was old enough to go to school, the family could not afford to pay for his tuition fees, so he discontinued his education after graduating from junior high school at the age of 17. He said, "Before the reform and opening up, many school buildings were made of earth and wood, with plaster falling off the walls and no glass installed in the windows. In winters, these shabby buildings failed to keep the chilly winds out, and in rainy days, the rain fell from the holes in the broken tiles. There was no asphalt road or cement road leading to the school, only a narrow path covered with thick mud that was trampled out by passers-by. The path became muddy once it rained. Puddles were here and there, and passers-by might tread into one if they were not careful. In that case, the whole foot was trapped inside and the shoe might be left in the mud when they finally pulled out the foot."

On December 25, 1998, my father got married, an important moment in his life. My father got to know my mother on a blind date, and his old home happened to be next to my maternal grandfather's house. After my parents developed a crush on each other, they often rode for about one hour to the city to climb mountains in the Martyres's Cemetery. The bike tour, during which both of them faced the morning sun or against the sunset, was so relaxing and romantic. My father couldn't help smiling at the thought of these sweet memories. On February 29, 2000, I was born.

After my father finished junior high school at 17, he found an unpaid apprenticeship in the city and learned from a truck repairman for more than two years. And then, together with several fellow townsmen, he went to Zhongshan City, southern China's Guangdong Province, where he worked in a factory for about two or three years.

Shortly after I was born, my father bought a second-hand truck to earn a living. He didn't have enough money for it and had to borrow some from relatives. But then bad luck followed—the truck was stolen! It was such terrible news. I can't recall the details now for I was only four or five years old then. As my father said, the big truck was parked in front of my godfather's house and then it was gone! This shocking incident left the impoverished family even worse off. Yet misfortunes never come alone. When my father decided to buy another truck, my paternal grandmother suffered a brain hemorrhage and was resuscitated in the hospital for some time. Unfortunately, she was left in a vegetative state. Afterwards, my parents took care of my grandmother in her final four months.

Shortly thereafter, my father got himself a second truck with some borrowed money. In my memory, I often took the truck and accompanied him to the construction site when I was a child. I was always on the passenger side, with no fear of what might happen at all. It has been more than ten years since then, but I still remember what the vehicle looked like. Its blue body was no longer new and shiny, but became yellowed with age. I could see traces of the bygone years from the scratches, the bean-sized rusty spots hidden on the engine hood and the lackluster glass. Its wheels also had been replaced many times. What remains vivid and unchanged in my memory is its giant size, which coincides with the image of my father in my heart, tall and strong enough to support the whole family.

But then my father sold the truck and began to work in a local company, Xingyu Co., Ltd., in 2008. The job was also related to auto parts, but it was not well paid. A family of six had to struggle to make ends meet with father's subsistence wage. My father worked really hard in an attempt to get a new truck. But more bad news came upon him in 2015 which smashed his dream. I had to receive scoliosis surgery, which would cost about 100,000 yuan. My father borrowed money from relatives and sent me to Hangzhou, the capital city of Zhejiang Province, for the surgery. He was always right beside me at that time, sparing in speech yet deep in love.

In 2016, my father bought a small car, something similar to a minivan. It can seat 7—8 people and remains in use today. The car is not expensive, but my father takes good care of it. This car, though commonly seen, is a great help to my family. It has come in handy for my father when some relatives want to hang out, when I go to college, or when my father wants to bring some home-grown vegetables and fruits to my aunt in the city. With the car, my father can take three of us for an outing, which is impossible if riding an electromobile or a motorcycle; when there's a rainstorm, he can find a shelter instead of getting himself wet even in a raincoat; and he can load the car up with as much as it can take when traveling to and fro between the village and the city.

As for our house, it has been renovated three times. At first, my father lived in the old house described above, which was destroyed by fire when he was 17 years old.

Then in 1993, after the reform and opening up, my grandparents built a house on their own, which was then quite common in rural areas, for nobody could afford to hire workers. My grandmother later recalled, "At that time, we got all things done by ourselves. Your grandfather cut down trees in the mountain and made a base. The road was too narrow for a truck to drive in, so we had to carry the stones piece by piece. The sand used to mix with cement was also put into large bamboo baskets and carried to the construction site by us. It was really hard at that time. Finally, we built a two-story house, with a kitchen in front." The building still had two stories until I was born.

In around 2008, as life was better-off then, my parents worked together on the third renovation project with the help from workers they hired. The former building was transformed into a four-story house, and above the kitchen, another floor was built. My parents even got the kitchen tiled and made small changes to the interior decoration. My family was even one of the first to have ceramic tiles in the neighborhood. To this day, we still live in this house.

My parents rented a house in the city during my junior high school years. As I was admitted to a local key senior high school, they moved to a place close to the school. The rented house is still there and they would go back once finishing their work. However, I prefer to live in the house in the countryside on vacations. It is more comfortable, and more importantly, I can live with my grandparents.

My father has suffered a lot all his life. Now my grandparents can enjoy the company of children and grandchildren. We are not very rich, but luckily, we can spend time with each other. I believe that with the joint efforts of our family, we will live a better life!

感情深藏于故事里

毛信意

爸爸，房子，金华。当这些字眼跳入我眼帘的时候，一种久违的亲切感油然而生。作者的家乡金华市婺城区罗埠镇胡家村，与我30多年前就读的浙江师范大学相距约30公里。贫瘠的黄土地，零落的泥墙屋，香味诱人的酥饼，勤劳和善的村民，那是融入我青春的记忆。作者讲述的“爸爸与房子”，对于从小生长在农村的我来说，恰似讲述我家的故事，备感亲切而温暖。

“橘子味和汗味是我在孩童时期记忆最深刻的味道。”文章一开头，作者就以生动形象的一句话，抓住爸爸的特点，切入儿时对爸爸的记忆，“装下我和爸爸在饭前的快乐。”把父子之爱深藏在简洁的文字里。

作者娓娓道来，在不同的时间节点，用具体生动的故事，刻画出吃苦耐劳、奋发向上的有血有肉的爸爸形象。“人穷手艺不穷。”爸爸除了会种洋葱、卷心菜，会赶集市销售农产品外，还是能工巧匠，会做木工和厨师。爸爸积极进取，进城务工，寻找“致富经”，回乡从事建筑业，最终成了小包工头，期间，自家也建起了崭新的砖瓦房。

文中对妈妈的描述虽少，但“缝纫工”妈妈的形象还是比较丰满的，勤劳善良又可爱。爸妈之间的相互欣赏和夸奖，更像一股暖流，烘托着父母之爱和家的温馨幸福。

总之，全文有三个特点：真，写真事；清，脉络清；简，表态简洁，以时间为线。第一人称纪实性表达，把感情深藏于故事里。岁月宛如一首歌。读后有余韵，有回味。

（宁波日报报业集团主任记者）

故事
金华
胡安妤(新闻学专业201专升本班)

爸爸与房子

橘子味和汗味是我在孩童时期记忆最深刻的味道。

在夏天,每天下午四五点的时候,我会去打上一桶井水,用最传统的方式冰镇上一瓶橘子味的汽水和两瓶啤酒,有时还会放进一个西瓜,用一只红色的桶,装下我和爸爸在饭前的快乐。至于汗味,这与爸爸的工作有关。爸爸是一名建筑工人,顶着夏日的骄阳工作一天后早已汗流浃背。妈妈总是习惯性地念叨着爸爸身上的汗味,而我却格外地期待这独特的味道,因为爸爸下班回家总是会带上很多好吃的。

爸爸于1965年在金华市婺城区罗埠镇胡家村出生,为人憨厚。

爸爸在成为一个正式的建筑工人之前可是干过很多活的。在爸爸年纪还不大的时候,就跟着大伯父一起做米升子、砧板之类的小物件,做完之后,就和同村的人一起拿到集市上去卖。碰上洋葱、卷心菜等收获的季节就起个大早,用车子将它们拉到兰江的码头上去卖给批发商。除此之外,爸爸也是我们村子上的一把厨艺好手,碰上有人家婚丧嫁娶,爸爸就会帮他们炒炒菜,能收获不少好评。

居住环境的艰辛是促使爸爸改变的主要动力,在那时,爸爸便萌生了重新造房子的念头。于是他就开始跟着师傅学做更难一点的木工活,从做凳子、桌子到开始造木头房子一共花了两年多时间,此时的爸爸23岁。学成之后,就四处寻找需要木工的人家,给他们做一些木工活或者对房子进行一些修修补补。这样一天下来有固定的工资,虽然工资不高,但为生计四处奔波的时候爸爸积攒下不少人脉。

日子趋于平淡,生活并没有因为爸爸换了工作而变得更好,但好在也没有变差。过了几年,爸爸妈妈以最传统的方式,经人介绍相识、相知之后结了婚。后来我问起妈妈,爸爸在当时两手空空,可以说的上是一个穷小伙,而妈妈的原生家庭条件可以说比爸爸的好很多,那为什么要选择爸爸。妈妈说:“在那个时候你爸爸的条件是不好,但是人穷手艺不穷,而且他为人忠厚老实,这样的人总是不错的。”

爸爸和妈妈结婚两年之后生下了姐姐，又过了五年我也出生了，可惜的是，在我出生的那一年爷爷去世了，所以我脑海中的爷爷都是从别人口中得知的。因为姐姐的到来，让爸爸工作变得更加卖力，一辆崭新的二八自行车骑到锈迹斑斑。

1993年，从出生便一直呆在农村的爸爸和他的几个朋友决定到城市去找一份工作。爸爸和他的朋友们租下了一间房，吃喝拉撒都在这几十平方米的空间里。爸爸在城市中奋斗了三年。

在村子里，从前的土房子大都推了重建，也开始用更坚硬的预制板来造高层数房子，但会造的人还是少数。爸爸意识到了这一点，也想着能离家里近些，就决定回到农村，开始着手建造这类房子。毕竟从事这一工作有些年头了，而且认识的朋友也多，想找着活干并不是什么难事。

时间到了2001年，距离爸爸想造房子到现在已经有十几年的时间了。在这期间也完成了两件人生大事，娶了媳妇，生了孩子。妈妈的辛勤和踏实让我有一种莫名的安全感。从妈妈开始工作到现在，一直坐在一张四四方方的缝纫机前，虽然期间也换过工作，但终归没有离开这台机器。

能造完家里房子也离不开妈妈的心血。

在2001年年初，家里的新房子开始动工，从打地基到盖完最后一片瓦，爸爸都亲自参与，当然，也还请了一些爸爸在工作时认识的朋友。虽然我对当时的记忆已经模糊了，却也还记得家中的房子拖了好久才完工。现在我的记忆大多是已经住进了新房子之后，我问妈妈："你和爸爸在造这个房子的时候是不是很辛苦？一边忙着外面的工作，一边还要操心着家里的事情。"妈妈说："辛苦啊，在外要上班，还要顾家，你爸爸也不能因为自己家造房子就耽误了别人家的，不过好在你爸人缘好，大家都愿意过来搭把手，虽然当时生活困难，但还好现在都熬过来了。"

到2002年家里的房子才算完工。爸爸站在顶楼，双脚实实地踏在地板上，细细地看着眼前的所有，想着终于达成了十几年前的心愿，在心中的不仅有高兴，还有感动。爸爸说："自从你妈妈嫁过来之后啊，我们家的日子就越过越好，别人都说我们家，五年前还欠着债呢，现在就造起了新房子。"

爸爸不甘心每天拿着那份死工资，就改变了以往的模式，开始承包下一幢幢的房子，与屋主谈下承包的总价。经过多年的打拼，爸爸认识了不少朋友，而且大都愿意跟着爸爸一起干。就这样建立起了一支小队，爸爸就当起了他们的"小老板"，尽管这只队伍到现在都还没有壮大起来。

家里的小日子就这样越过越好。

晴天和雨天是交替存在的。

转眼间就到了2016年，爸爸出事了。爸爸往楼下丢建筑材料的时候有铁丝钩住了他的衣角，爸爸就被这些东西瞬间带到了地面上。因为伤得严重，术后的恢复期很长。有时候，爸爸会静静地看着那成堆的木料发呆，好像在想着什么时候才能像从前一样，或者还能不能恢复到像从前一样。好在爸爸原本开朗的性格还在，没有让阴郁的情绪围绕在身边太久，在家待了一年多的时间之后就又可以从一些较轻的活开始工作了。

后来，政府颁布了"三改一拆"的法令，家中的老房子已属于危房，也被列入了拆除、整改的行列。这幢老房子在巨大的挖掘机面前是那么不堪一击，轻轻地推了几下就变成了一堆残渣散在了地上，好像一位生命垂危的老人走到了生命的尽头。这幢老房子曾经见证了三代人的喜怒哀乐，难免让我有些不舍。就在去年，村子里对土地进行了重新规划，老房子这儿建了篮球场，我就没有特意去过那，只是几次偶尔经过时心中泛着莫名的酸楚。

现在，2020年，还是一家五口，还是住在同一屋檐下。

其实爸妈在前几年也有过几次想重建新房子的念头，但因为一些土地上的问题就一直搁置着。到了现在，爸妈已经放弃了再造的念头，爸爸说："女孩子么，总要出嫁的，你们也都长大了，不能像我们这样一辈子留在这个村子里，房子也就没有造的必要，我和你妈住在现在的房子里也就够了。"

Jinhua
Hu Anyu (Class 201, Majoring in Journalism)

Father and His House

To me, the smell of tangerines and sweat left the deepest impression on me when I was still a child.

Every summer at 4 or 5pm, I would put a bottle of tangerine-flavored soda, two bottles of beer, and sometimes a watermelon in a bucket of well water and cool them off—a most traditional method in the old days. The red bucket contained all the pleasure for my father and me before dinner. As for the smell of sweat, it was closely related to my father's job as a construction worker. He was bathed in sweat after one day's hard work under the summertime sun. While my mother tended to complain about my father's smell, I, on the contrary, expected this unique odor because this also meant my father had come back with a lot of delicious snacks.

My father, born and raised up in Hujia Village, Luobu County, Yucheng District, Jinhua City in southeastern China's Zhejiang Province, is an honest and good-natured man.

He tried different jobs before finally becoming a full-time construction worker. For example, he used to make small utensils like chopping blocks and rice containers with his elder brother and sell them in markets with fellow villagers. He had to get up very early during harvest seasons for vegetables like onions and cabbages, and then sold them to wholesalers at wharfs by Lanjiang River. Besides, my father, a skilled chef, also frequently helped with cooking whenever there was a wedding ceremony or funeral.

The harsh living environment was the driving force behind my father's changes. It was during that hard period of time that my father decided to build a new house. Having made up his mind, he started honing his carpentry skills following his master. Over two years passed, and my father was able to make stools and desks and build wooden houses independently. He was then 23 years old, and started doing woodwork or repairing houses for clients. He thus had low yet stable incomes, as well as a wide circle of friends and acquaintances.

Life didn't change for the better or for the worse after my father became a carpenter. Several years later, my father and mother were introduced to each other and finally got married. I later asked my mother why she chose my poor father whose family was much worse-off than hers. I remember she replied like this, "Though very poor, he had skills and was honest. Such people must be good chaps."

Two years after they got married, my sister was born, and five years later, I came to this world. Unfortunately, my paternal grandpa passed away the same year, so everything I know about him was told by others. Ever since my sister was born, my father had worked even harder; his brand-new bicycle turned rusty and worn-out after years of use.

My father, who had spent almost his entire life in the village, decided to try his luck in the city together with his friends in 1993. They shared a rented house which covered only tens of square meters, and my father toiled and struggled for three years in the bustling city.

Most of the adobe houses in the village had already been demolished and rebuilt and some of them were even turned into high-rise prefabricated residential houses. However, there were still very few people who could actually build houses. Realizing this and hoping to be closer to home, my father planned to build houses of this kind in the village. It shouldn't be something difficult since my father was experienced after years of work and had lots of friends from different walks of life.

Time flew and it was 2001, over ten years since my father first thought of building a house by himself. He got married and had children while he was working hard for his dream to come true. My mom, industrious and always down-to-earth, gave me a sense of security. She changed jobs several times, but has never left the sewing machine she has been using ever since she started working.

The house couldn't have been built without my mom's hard work.

My father began the construction of our new house in early 2001, and was personally involved in the whole process from laying house foundations to laying tiles. Of course, he also asked some of his friends for help. I had a vague memory of the days before the house finally took shape, but I still remember it was a very long time before we moved into the new house. I later asked my mom, "Back then, you and Dad needed to take care of jobs and the family at the same time, so days must have been extremely harsh for you, right?" My mom replied, "Of course. It was such a hard period of time, working outside and taking care of the family. But your father couldn't disturb others' lives just because he was building our own house. But luckily, your father was well-liked and everyone was willing to come over and give a hand. Life was tough at that time, but thankfully, it's all in the past now."

The house was completed one year later. Standing firm on the top floor and seeing everything before his eyes, my father was elated and deeply touched since his dream finally came true. He said, "Life has been better ever since I married your mom. See, we were in debt five years ago, but now we have a new house!"

Not content with just earning stable yet fixed salaries, my father broke the old business mode and started contracting housing projects. He had made a lot of friends, most of whom were willing to work with him. Gathering those friends together, he later formed a construction team and became the "leader", though it remains the same size today.

Life was getting better.

Yet sunny days and rainy days alternate.

My father had an accident in 2016: he was taken down to the ground by the iron wire which snagged his clothes when he was dropping construction materials. It took a long time for him to recover from severe injuries. My father would stare blankly at stacks of woods, and it seemed he was wondering when he would completely recover or whether he could recover. Luckily, my father, whose optimistic life attitude didn't surrender himself to gloomy moods, was able to start from some light work after more than one year's rest at home.

The old house was later listed as a dangerous building and was supposed to be demolished when the government issued relevant decrees. Faced with giant excavators, the vulnerable and fragile house collapsed and fell apart, becoming debris on the ground, exactly like an elderly man on his death bed. I couldn't help feeling wistful about the demolished house for it witnessed joy and sorrow of three generations of my family. The village administration replanned land last year and built up a basketball court there. I didn't go back there purposefully but still felt grieved when I passed by.

Now it's 2020, and the same five family members are still living under the same roof.

Actually, my parents thought about building a new house a few years ago, but the plan was dropped because of some issues concerning land ownership. Now, they have completely given up the plan. My father said, "You and your sister will eventually get married and live in your husband's house. And you shouldn't stay in this village for the rest of your lives like your mother and I. The current house is big enough for your mother and me to live. Therefore, there is no need to build a new one."

“温州一家人”的现实案例

邱子桐

黄冰茹同学的《爸爸的柜台》中用了特别多的词来描绘温州父母创业的艰辛：出身农民家庭的爸爸考上了大学却为了缓解家庭经济压力而选择放弃，之后先去了江苏昆山舅舅的电器店打工，住仓库，每天吃便宜的盒饭，但在一年后靠攒下的钱开始自己当老板，用仓库里的两个柜台开始做电器批发生意。接着便每天起早贪黑为拥有自己的门店而奋斗；有了自己的门店以后，父母忙得连吃饭都没有时间，从不过任何一个节假日；除了为自己的劳务收入忙碌之外，聪明的父母接着通过投资，乘上了实物资产增值的东风，完成了家庭的经济积累。财富的背后是心怀梦想敢于冒险的“温一代”父母，黄冰茹同学感叹着父母“为这个家所携手共进的美好岁月”。

黄冰茹同学的父母完全符合媒介中对温州人形象的呈现：四海为家、艰苦奋斗，四海为家、坚韧自立。这个靠小小柜台开始的家，也简直就是一个“温州一家人”的现实案例。也许他们的平凡过往并不是电视剧《温州一家人》(2012 年)中的周卖狗一家人或是《温州两家人》(2015 年)中的侯三寿一家一般跌宕起伏的“平民史诗”，但黄冰茹的家同样承载了“温一代”精神，同样通过以往的艰辛慢慢蜕变为当下的成长。相信这种温商精神会在像黄冰茹同学一样的千千万万的“温二代”中得到传承。

(浙大宁波理工学院传媒与法学院副教授，博士)

故事

温州

黄冰茹(新闻学专业 202 专升本班)

爸爸的柜台

爷爷常说现在的小孩不懂得珍惜,他们十几二十岁那会儿,哪有我们现在这样吃得饱穿得暖。

我的家得先从我的爷爷说起,他是温州乐清一个再普通不过的农民。1990 年是爷爷的不惑之年,那时的他一个人承担着家里所有的费用。除了帮别人搬运货物之外,每天还要跟奶奶一起去距家 5 公里的农田种各种各样的农作物。

水稻用来酿酒出售,瓜类和蔬菜由奶奶拿到市场上去卖,留给全家人自己吃的通常都是卖剩下的蔬菜。一个我们现在随随便便就能吃到的梨,在当时也要切成四片,全家分着吃,日子着实辛苦。好在爸爸总是很懂事地帮着爷爷奶奶分担着地里的农活,姑姑在本该享受童年欢乐的年纪,也已经学会做起了家务。

1998 年,那年爸爸 22 岁,他考上了大学,可能是为了缓解家里的经济压力,也可能是少年壮志想改变整个家庭,他对全家人说:“我要赚大钱,我不想再读什么书了。”

现在来看虽然爸爸当时的决定可能不是最明智的,但无疑,这看似玩笑的话语后,却是爸爸想将家庭担起的责任心。

江苏昆山游方弄,是爸爸开始“赚大钱”的地方。

爸爸的舅舅在那里经营一家电器生意的店,爸爸就在他店中帮忙打杂。虽说是舅舅,但爸爸时常要做的甚至比普通员工更多。住仓库,每天吃着 3 块钱的盒饭,领着一点点的工资,那时候的爸爸只是一个替别人卖东西的打工者。

在那里的第二个年头,爸爸毅然决然地拿出攒了一年的工资,自己当起了老板。第一次,他租了属于自己的两个小小的柜台,在上面摆上了一个红白字体,面朝门外的定做标语:“电器批发”“厂家直销,螺丝批发”。

透明玻璃的展柜里,摆放着他谋生活的电器。爸爸说他每天起来后就会用布擦擦那两个小柜台,仿佛擦亮了些,生意就会更好些似的。那一方小天地,正是爸爸为之奋斗的战场。白天卖货、送货,吃饭,算账,清点货物,都在这崭新的玻璃上有条不紊地进行着。到了月亮爬上树梢时,他依旧回到那个冰冷的小仓库里。所有的时间都被禁锢在了这小小的空间里，苦涩却又幸福。

“当时的我每晚都精疲力竭，躺下就睡着。但是只要一觉睡醒，一想到能赚钱，就又充满了无限的能量。”

2000年初，可是个重大的日子。正月里，爸爸结婚了，他有了另一半。

从此，那个小仓库里，多了一个人；那租的两个小小柜台前，是一对为美好未来而一起奋斗的新婚夫妻。生活很快发生了转折，没过几个月，爸爸妈妈发现有了我这个小生命。当下爸爸就决定，不能再带着妈妈住在那个小仓库里了，经过多日问价和看房的东奔西走，这对小夫妻终于租下第一个属于自己的60平方米的小房间。

2001年，因为生意，爸爸妈妈无暇照顾我，就把我放在了爷爷奶奶身边。在爷爷奶奶带我回去前的那个晚上，爸爸说妈妈哭花了眼，舍不得那么小的一个孩子一出生就不在自己身边。可是我知道，爸爸妈妈最后的决定也是为了能给我的以后创造一个更好的生活。

“那时候呀，我跟你爸最大的心愿，就是一定要赶紧有一家属于自己的店面。”妈妈在跟我讲述以前的事时，老这样念叨。他们也用辛勤的汗水实现了他们的念想。

每天早出晚归，白天做生意，不放过任何一个客户。晚上则留在店里核对每日的账单。为了省钱买店面，他们不再买盒饭，选择自己做菜。将近中午11点时，妈妈回去做饭，吃完回到店中，爸爸再回去吃饭。赚钱，省钱。最大可能地赚钱，最大可能地省钱，就这样夜以继日着。终于，在2001年的年底，这对小夫妻用行动把想法付诸了现实。爸爸终于从那两个小小的柜台搬进了一整个40平方米的店面。

“搬电器产品的时候，东西很杂很多，也没个什么人来帮忙，这边还要兼顾着生意，但我和你妈开心啊，每天脸上乐滋滋的，觉得那些辛苦都值了。”

这店面一搬，就是十几个年头。

那10年，妈妈说他们也一直每天忙到边做饭边忙生意，从来不在任何一个节假日休息，生怕失去一点点客户。所有的钱都不会被用作娱乐和犒劳自己，而是存进银行卡。只要攒到一个数，他们就开始付房子的首付，然后分期还房贷。就这样，生意越来越好，顾客越来越稳定。

2008年，我8岁。爸爸从外面寄回老家一张照片，他和妈妈站在一辆车子旁边开怀大笑。小时候的记忆，我并没有多少，记得最清楚的，就是当爷爷奶奶把那张照片拿给我看时，我们家三代人脸上洋溢的幸福。

在2010年之前的那些年头里，爸爸妈妈陆陆续续买了10多套房子，在2012年时，把房子的贷款全都还清了。

2012年之后到现在的日子里，爸爸妈妈逐渐开始有了自己的生活，不再像原先那么忙碌。住进了自己买的房子里，可以慢慢地坐下来吃完一顿饭，可以在晚上6点店铺关门后在河边散步，在商场漫无目的地闲逛。也偶尔可以有一两次自己的小旅游，会给爷爷奶奶寄钱在老家盖房，也会经常回来陪我。

那个小小的仓库到两个柜台再到一整个店面，那就是爸爸妈妈为这个家所携手共进的美好岁月。

Wenzhou
Huang Bingru (Class 202, Majoring in Journalism)

My Father's Counter

My grandfather often says that kids nowadays do not appreciate the life they are having now. When he was young, people were still struggling for basic needs.

The story of my family starts from my grandfather. My grandfather was a farmer from Yueqing, a town in Wenzhou city, southeastern China's Zhejiang province. In 1990 when he was 40 years old, he was supporting the whole family all on his own. Besides carrying goods, he was also farming with his wife in the fields 5 kilometers away from home.

They sold wine made from the rice they grew. My grandmother sold the melons and vegetables they grew in markets. The food they had at home were mostly those left unsold and taken back from the markets. They did not have much to eat. Sometimes the family of four even had to share one pear. Those days were difficult. My father was a good kid and helped with the farm work in the fields. His little sister also started to help with house chores when she was supposed to be a carefree and happy kid.

In 1998, my father was 22 years old. He could have gone to university that year since he passed the entrance examination for university, but he did not. Maybe it was because he did not want to stress the economic situation in his family, or maybe it was because he thought that he could make a change to his family. Anyway, he told his family, "I don't want to go to school anymore. I want to make a lot of money."

Looking back from now, it might not seem to be the most sensible decision my father has ever made, but there is no doubt that behind what seems to be a joke is his determination to take up the responsibility for his family.

He set off on his way to "make a lot of money" in Youfang Lane in Kunshan city, southeastern China's Jiangsu province.

My father worked in his uncle's home appliance store there at first. Although it was his uncle that he was working for, he had to do more work than the other staff. He was only a salesman there who was making little money, sleeping in the warehouse and having cheap packed meals every day.

The next year, he pulled out the savings he made in the first year and started his own business. He rented two small counters and placed a sign for his home appliance and screw wholesale business on the counters.

He put a few appliances in the glass showcase of the counters. He used to wipe the glass with a piece of cloth every day as if it could help with his business. Behind those two little counters was where he fought for a better life. During the day, he sold and delivered products. Eating, accounting and checking goods were all done behind the counters. At night, he would go back to the cold warehouse. Those were the only two places he spent his time in. It was difficult, but my father was content.

"Every night I would be so exhausted that I would fall asleep the minute I lay down. But in the morning, as soon as I woke up and thought of the money I was going to make that day, I would be full of energy again," he said.

A big event happened in early 2000. The year 2000 was a special year. During the lunar new year, my parents got married.

My mother moved into the warehouse, and behind those two counters were then newlyweds who were fighting for a better future together. A few months later, my mother became pregnant with me. My father therefore decided that it was time for his family to move out of the warehouse. After many days of searching, they finally found a 60 square meters room to move in.

The next year, my parents left me in their hometown with my grandparents because they were too busy to take care of me. The night before my grandparents took me back to their hometown, my mother cried her heart out, and that was according to my father. She was so sorry that she had to leave me so soon after I was born. However, I know that they did it to bring me a better life.

My mother told me that all they wanted at that time was to have their own shop as soon as possible. They did achieve it in the end through hard work.

At that time, my parents left home early and came home late every day. They worked very hard during the day trying to win every customer. At night, they stayed in the shop and did the accounts. They cooked their own meals instead of having packed meals to save money. At lunchtime, they took turns to go home and have lunch. They made every effort to make and save as much money as possible, day and night. Finally, in the end of 2001, they realized their dream. My father finally moved from behind his two little counters to a shop that was 40 square meters in size.

My father said, "Moving all the appliances to the new shop is exhausting. Nobody comes to help us, and we have to take care of our business at the same time. But we are so happy, because we know it is all worth it."

They have been running that shop for over 10 years now.

My mom said that they were still very busy in the new shop in those years. They barely had time to eat. The shop was open all year round so they would not lose any customer. All the money they made those years was spent on down payments and mortgages for houses. They never had any entertainment or treats for themselves. In this way, their business kept getting better and they had more and more regular customers.

In 2008 when I was 8 years old, my father sent us a picture in which he and my mother were smiling from ear to ear standing next to a new car. That is one of the few memories I have from my childhood. I remember when my grandparents and I saw the picture, we laughed happily with them.

By 2010, my parents had already bought over 10 houses. They paid off all the mortgages in 2012.

Now not as busy as they used to be, my parents finally have the time to enjoy their life. They are now living in the house they bought where they can sit down to enjoy their meals. After closing the shop at 6 in the evening, they will take a walk by the river or stroll in the malls. They even go traveling sometimes. They are sending money to my grandparents to build a house in my hometown, and are spending more time with me now.

From those two little counters to a whole shop, my parents have built a wonderful life together.

家庭记忆的载体书写

郭　鉴

家庭是社会的基本组成单位，像其他的共同体一样，都有着属于自己的历史。每个个体都属于家庭这个群体无法分割的一部分。在这个全球一体化的时代，我们总是认为新的事物好过于旧的事物，一味地向前追赶，却忘记回看过去，总是急于放眼全球认识世界，却不曾珍惜中国的文化精髓。泛娱乐化时代，《奔波在东栅塘汇之间》通过巧妙的议程设置很好地引导现代人的家庭观念和一脉相承的家庭责任感，更好地巩固了以家庭为基本单位的传统文化，通过阐释个人的寻根和家庭的记忆，以及由家庭记忆映射出的国家历史，它能够复原我们的故土牵挂、追思念旧、家园情怀的精神线索。

一个家族见证着现时与过往，是旧时与新近事物的混合。随着社会的变迁，很多历史场景都已不复存在、无法还原，后辈无法身临其境、切实感受到过去的存在。过去虽已不在，但过去所留下的痕迹依然存在，家庭记忆需要得到保存与传承。皮埃尔·诺拉在其著作《记忆之场》中对"记忆之场"做出了明确的定义和深刻的剖析。"记忆之场"的内涵是承载着象征化的历史现实，狭义的概念为"集中于从纪念碑到博物馆、从档案到口号再到纪念仪式等纪念物，与现实具有可触可感的交叉关系"。记忆之场是记忆残留物的场域，家谱、祖居、庙堂等就都成为人们从历史中寻找记忆的切入点，影像、遗物、信件成为连接历史与现在的桥梁。

陆宇婷同学的《奔波在东栅塘汇之间》一文中，房子、香烟、糖、水果摊等成为话语分析的工具，让每位读者以这样的方式来接近她的家庭，这往往也是我们作为普通人记忆中最具象征意义的对象。正是有了这些有形的标志物的支撑，才使得记忆的内在体验更为丰富，而记忆的需要就是历史的需要。在追寻家庭记忆的过程中，需要这些载体来牵出一份家的记忆，一则是能够重返历史场景，一则是能够凝固历史记忆。

我是谁、我从哪里来、要到哪里去，这是一个古老的哲学问题，也是人类行进道路上的自我探寻。如今我们处在社会的转型期，被高速发展的社会大潮不断推着向前走，忽略了中国传统文化中的精髓，价值观念和信仰缺失，因此现代生活中的人常常处于“无根”状态，人们无法找到自己的身份认同和文化认同，寻求精神家园的富足在这时显得尤为重要。而人们寻找家庭奋斗的过程也就是认识自我的过程。《奔波在东栅塘汇之间》追寻爷爷奶奶的足迹，揭开真实的人物命运和人物情感，不仅仅只是表层意义的寻根，而是具有文化意义的寻根，是用苦难和光荣的记忆熔铸出坚韧不拔的民族精神。

（浙江万里学院副教授，博士）

故事

嘉兴

陆宇婷(新闻学专业191班)

奔波在东栅塘汇之间

1950年，我的爷爷出生在浙江嘉兴东栅。1957年就读东栅小学，1962年小学毕业。家里穷，爷爷就没有继续念下去。奶奶是嘉兴塘汇人。奶奶的日子过得也很苦，平常吃饭只就着腐乳、什锦菜、酱萝卜。

1964年爷爷14岁，从东栅到塘汇，当锻工学徒。当学徒是很苦的，刚进去的时候在厂里搞搞卫生，每天给工人们烧开水，每天做好了工作还要清理炉子。

1970年，爷爷认识了奶奶。爷爷在厂后门边上干活，奶奶在对面的棕麻厂当临时工，一来二去，爷爷奶奶就熟悉起来了。

1972年，爷爷奶奶结婚了。爷爷买了一条香烟，20斤糖，和家里人办了顿喜酒。那个时候爷爷的工资是27块钱一个月。结婚之前，用奶奶家原来住的小房子和室友换了一下，爷爷奶奶和奶奶的妈妈住到了爷爷厂里的宿舍里。爷爷奶奶就是在这个宿舍里结婚的。

1973年，姑姑出生了。一家4口人就生活在爷爷的宿舍里，有一个客堂间和一个里间，厨房什么的也挤在客堂间，在客堂间搭了一个铺子给奶奶的妈妈住，爷爷奶奶和姑姑睡在里间。说是换了一个大一点的房子，实际上也不大。而且也没有卫生设备，晚上马桶就放在床底下。

爷爷奶奶还养了两只鸡，用母鸡下的蛋来改善伙食。因为生活不便，再加上爷爷奶奶还想生老二，这间小房子就不够住了。所以爷爷奶奶想着要再换套房子。

爷爷去了七八次房管所，终于"磨"来了一套大一点的房子，一个月房租 17 块钱，那个时候爷爷的工资也只有 27 块钱，房租也是一笔很大的开销了。这间房子可以划分出里间外间，外间吃饭，里间睡觉，上面有一层阁楼，还有一个大的阳台。这个房子在当时算好的了，虽然仍旧没有卫生设备，但是有自来水。然后就有了我爸爸。姑姑和爸爸的童年，基本上就是在这里度过。

奶奶没有正式的工作，一直在打零工。奶奶做过很多活，轧棉花，做鞋帮，在社办的大饼店里卖大饼。1982 年，家里的几个小孩都长大了，上学了，奶奶的妈妈腾出了时间，又开始做生意。奶奶的妈妈有个体户的执照，开了个水果摊。因为没有店面，就在路边摆摊，搬块板摆两个凳子，就是水果摊的样子。

上午爷爷在厂里打铁，中午的时候就去水果摊进水果卖水果，下午再去厂里干活。奶奶在大饼店里干活，干完活了也去水果摊帮忙。爷爷骑着三轮车到水果市场进了满满一车的货，赶十几公里的路拉到塘汇。

1983 年一次偶然的机会，嘉兴很多中学都在招工，其中包括了塘汇中学、东栅中学，塘汇中学的名额满了，东栅中学的名额还有，但是要求必须得是东栅户口，奶奶是塘汇户口，去不了。爷爷不管三七二十一把奶奶的户口迁到了东栅，迁到了爷爷家里。终于，奶奶在东栅中学拿到了稳定的工作，一个月赚 25 块钱。

奶奶在东栅，爷爷在塘汇，又要上班又要带两个小孩，还要管水果摊。奶奶在学校里分到了一间集体宿舍，陆续将姑姑和爸爸接到东栅。宿舍也是很挤的，还要和其他老师住在一起。因为奶奶带着两个小孩，还要烧饭，地方也不够，很不方便。

1985 年刚好有一个退休老师分到了房子，老教师原来住的房子就空了出来。学校的领导照顾奶奶，让奶奶住到老教师原来住的地方。拿到这套房子，全家人都很高兴。爷爷也从塘汇搬过来，一家人住在一起。这是套老房子，是和西塘、月河那样的古街民居差不多的房子。厨房间和卫生间在楼下的弄堂里，睡觉在楼上。

爷爷每天骑车从东栅到塘汇去上班，下班再从塘汇回到东栅。

后来爷爷开始卖蔬菜，爷爷做生意的理念是薄利多销，平价把水果、蔬菜卖出去，这也为爷爷带来了不少生意。后来生意做大了爷爷还雇人拉三轮车，拉一趟两块钱，一次拉五车蔬菜水果。赚了钱爷爷把钱存到银行，以前银行的利息高，有十六点几。本金生利息也拿了不少钱。

1988 年，城市经济体制改革，实行承包经营责任制。爷爷是单位的工会主席。厂子由三个人承包，厂长、爷爷和会计。1994 年，厂里的经济效益实在不行了，就被人家兼并了。爷爷在新的精工粉末冶金厂里当车间主任，做到 2004 年退休。

1994 年，奶奶在单位里分了一套福利房，自己出了一万两三千元。一室两厅的房子，在三水湾，爷爷奶奶一直住到现在，从工作住到退休。

爷爷骑着自行车去塘汇上班，奶奶骑着自行车去东栅上班，从三水湾出发。

开始的时候爷爷奶奶住在大房间，姑姑住在小房间，爸爸那个时候当兵去了不在家里。后来姑姑出嫁了，离开家，爸爸退伍回来就睡在了小房间。姑姑结婚用了一大笔钱，爸爸结婚也是一笔大花销，爷爷奶奶贷款两万给爸爸买了新房。不过还好，房贷很快就还完了。

姑姑又给爷爷买了一辆助力车，加汽油的，爷爷就开始开着助力车从三水湾赶到塘汇了。

2001 年奶奶从学校退休，半年后我出生了。我的童年很长一段时间是在奶奶家度过的，爷爷还在上班，早上爸爸妈妈上班的时候把我送到奶奶家，奶奶一个人带着我。

2004 年爷爷退休，退休工资只有 900 多块钱，爷爷又去别的小区当保安，那是一个只有 6 幢楼的小区，爷爷和小区里的人关系都处得很好。又过了一阵，爷爷去家对面的饭店找了一个保安的活。再到后来，爷爷在所住的小区当起了保安，在爷爷的努力下，小区的居民基本上都交齐了停车费。

爷爷说，既然做了一件事，就要干到最好。现在啊，爷爷还做着小区的保安工作，上一天休两天。爷爷说，再做一阵就不做了。奶奶去打打拳舞舞剑，空闲时候到门卫室坐坐陪陪爷爷。

这样的生活也很好。

爷爷奶奶一路奔波携手走到今天，奔波在东栅和塘汇之间，奔波在春风下，也奔波在幸福的道路上。

Jiaxing
Lu Yuting (Class 191, Majoring in Journalism)

The Busy Life Between Dongzha and Tanghui

My grandfather was born in Dongzha, Jiaxing, Zhejiang Province in 1950. He studied in Dongzha Primary School in 1957 and graduated in 1962, but he didn't continue his study because the family was poor. My grandmother was from Tanghui of Jiaxing City. My grandmother also led a hard life, so the meals which she had at that time were usually preserved tofu, assorted vegetables and pickled radish.

In 1964, my 14-year-old grandfather was apprenticed as a blacksmith in Tanghui. Being an apprentice was very hard. When he first entered the factory, he did some cleaning and boiled water for workers there every day, and he had to clean the stove every day when finishing all his work.

In 1970, my grandfather met my grandmother. He worked at the back door of the factory while she worked as a casual laborer in the palm hemp factory. Gradually, they got to know each other.

In 1972, they got married. My grandfather bought a carton of cigarettes and 10 kilograms of candies for their wedding. At that time, his salary was 27 yuan a month. Before they got married, my grandfather changed my grandmother's small house with his roommate's. Then my grandparents and my great-grandmother moved to my grandfather's dormitory in the factory where they held a wedding ceremony.

In 1973, my aunt was born. The family of four lived in the dormitory where there was a guest room and a back room; the kitchen was also in the guest room. They put a mattress in the guest room for my great-grandmother, and my grandparents and my aunt slept in the back room. It was said to be bigger than the previous house, but it was still very small. There was no bathroom, so they had to put a nightstool under the bed at night.

My grandparents also raised two chickens. With eggs that the hen laid, they could improve their diet. The small house was not big enough to live in. It was inconvenient to live there and since they wanted to have a second baby, the small house was not big enough to live in. Therefore, they wanted to get a new house.

My grandfather went to the housing management office for seven or eight times and finally got a bigger house whose rent was 17 yuan a month. It was a big expense because his salary was only 27 yuan at that time. The house was divided into an outer room for eating and an inner room for sleeping; there was an attic above and a large balcony. Though there was still no bathroom, at least they had tap-water, so it could be said to be a good house at the time. Then my dad was born. It was the house where my aunt and my dad spent their childhood.

As my grandmother had no full-time job, she had been doing odd jobs. She did a lot of work, such as ginning cotton, making shoe uppers, and selling pancakes at the commune's shop. In 1982, as all the children grew up and went to school, my great-grandmother found time to start a business again. Having a license for individual business, she opened a fruit stall. Since there was no storefront, she set the stall by the roadside. With a piece of board and two benches, she made a fruit stall.

In the morning, my grandfather forged iron in the factory; at noon, he went to the stall to sell fruit; in the afternoon, he would go back to the factory. My grandmother worked in the pancake shop, and she would help out at the fruit stall when her work was done. My grandfather rode a tricycle to the fruit market to purchase a load of fruits, then delivered the fruits to Tanghui which was more than ten kilometers away.

In 1983, many middle schools in Jiaxing were recruiting workers, including Tanghui Middle School and Dongzha Middle School. The quota of Tanghui Middle School was full while the quota of Dongzha Middle School was still available, but it was required that the applicant should have a permanent residence registration in Dongzha. My grandmother could not apply for it as she was a Tanghui resident. Despite the situation, my grandfather managed to transfer her permanent residence from Tanghui to Dongzha. Finally, my grandmother got a steady job at Dongzha Middle School, earning 25 yuan a month.

My grandmother lived in Dongzha and my grandfather lived in Tanghui, so my grandfather had to take the responsibility of taking care of two children while working at the same time. In addition, he also had to manage the fruit stall. Luckily, a school collective dormitory was assigned to my grandmother, and she took my aunt and my father to Dongzha one by one. The dormitory was also very crowded, because she lived there with other teachers. Since my grandmother lived with two children, she had to cook for them. so it was inconvenient to live in such a small place.

In 1985, a house was assigned to a retired teacher, so the house where she used to live was available. The school leaders paid special attention to my grandmother and let her move into the house where the retired teacher had lived before. The whole family was delighted at this news. My grandfather also moved to Dongzha from Tanghui and the whole family lived together finally. This was a set of old houses, just the same as the ancient street houses in Xitang and Yuehe. The kitchen and the bathroom were in the alley downstairs, and people slept upstairs.

Every day, my grandfather would ride his bike from Dongzha to Tanghui for work and back to Dongzha from Tanghui after work.

My grandfather began to sell vegetables afterwards. He believed that the way of doing business was small profit and quick turnover, so he sold fruits and vegetables at a fair price, which brought him a lot of business. Later, when the business became bigger, he hired people to pull the tricycle. He would pay two yuan for a trip. There was a time when they pulled five carts of vegetables and fruits. After earning money, he would bank the money. The interest rate of the bank was high before, which was at a rate of sixteen percent. Therefore, he made lots of money from the interest.

In 1988, the urban economic system was reformed and the contractual management responsibility system was implemented. The factory was contracted by three people: the factory director, my grandfather and the accountant. My father served as chairman of the trade union. In 1994, the economic benefit of the factory was really not good, so the factory was merged. My grandfather worked as workshop director in the new precision powder metallurgy plant till he retired in 2004.

In 1994, my grandmother was assigned a welfare house in school, and she only paid about 12,000 yuan for it. It was in Sanshui bay and had two living rooms. My grandparents have lived there till now; in other words, they still live there after their retirement.

My grandfather rode his bike to Tanghui for work, and my grandmother cycled to Dongzha for work, both of them setting out from Sanshui Bay.

At the beginning, my grandparents lived in a big room, and my aunt lived in a small room. My father was not at home at that time because he was in the army. My aunt got married later and left home. My father was discharged from the army just then, so he came back home and slept in that small room. A large amount of money was spent on my aunt's wedding while my father's marriage was also a big expense. Thus, my grandparents loaned 20,000 yuan for my father to buy a new house. Fortunately, the housing mortgage was soon repaid.

My aunt bought a moped fueled by gasoline for my grandpa. My grandfather started driving the moped from Sanshui bay to Tanghui.

My grandmother retired from school in 2001 and I was born six months later. For a long time, I spent my childhood in my grandmother's home. My grandfather was still at work. When my parents went to work in the morning, they would send me to my grandmother's home where my grandmother took care of me alone.

In 2004, my grandfather retired, and his retirement salary was only about 900 yuan. After the retirement, he worked as a security guard in another community. It was a community with only six buildings and he got on well with people in the community. After a while, he found another job at the restaurant across the street as a security guard again. He worked as a security guard in the community where he lived later. With his efforts, the residents of the community all paid the parking fee.

My grandpa told me that as long as he decided to do a thing, he should accomplish it to the best of his ability. Now, my grandfather is still working as the security guard of the community and he works in two day intervals. He said that he would quit the job in a short period of time. My grandma does shadow boxing and performs sword dancing. She would sit in the janitor's room to accompany my grandpa in her spare time.

Such a kind of life is quite good.

My grandparents have been working for the better life hand in hand all the way.

They are striving from Dongzha to Tanghui; they are striving in the warm spring; they are striving on the road towards happiness.

看似寻常最奇崛

包丹虹

21年，两代人的不同。题目切口大，写好不容易。然而，张诗雅一开场便以蒙太奇手法，推出很有年代感的井，通过母女间的日常对话，自然而又直接地呈现了两代人不同生活的时代背景，并顺水推舟带出“妈妈的二十一年”。

行文笔调客观、生动、内敛。对于人生片段的截取，叙述角色的转换，情境细节的描写等，透露出作者的文学创作潜力。美国记者富兰克林说：“用故事化手法写新闻。就是采用对话、描写、场景设置等，细致入微地展现事件中的情节和细节，突现事件中隐含的能够让人产生兴奋感、富有戏剧性的故事。”在喧嚣的网络时代，想要求得传播效果和影响力，掌握运用写作技巧来提升作品的可读性，无疑是一种策略。

读《不同的“二十一年”》，如行云流水，作者没有刻意炫技，谋篇布局仿佛浑然天成。有诗道“看似寻常最奇崛”，所写人生故事也如此。原以为父母离异的孩子多少会有些不堪，可读完此文却感到温情与宽慰。其实，人生状况大都五味杂陈，全凭自己咀嚼。母亲19岁嫁人，女儿19岁读大学，前者懵懂成婚，后者读书求知，这是很大的不同。但女儿似乎禀承了母亲向阳而生的基因，她更愿缩小人生阴影，求得光亮最大面。

“沿路崎岖不平，全程起起伏伏，像极了我揣着的心情。”那还只是儿戏造成的忐忑不安，当宠爱她的奶奶去世时，对她而言无疑是一场心灵地震，可她并没有着墨痛苦。悲欢离合，生老病死，使她明白人生变数是常态，于是更珍惜身边的人。“冬至花败，然后春暖花开。”张诗雅一个转折，以细腻的笔触描写爸爸的温情。

漫漫人生长路，难免波折坎坷。当心灵遭受雨雪风霜侵蚀时，如何走出泥泞的沼泽而面向阳光？当婚姻选择错误时，离异的父母如何让孩子回忆起他们的爱来却是丝丝入骨？这是此文内涵值得大家思考的一方面。

（宁波市鄞州区融媒体中心，主任编辑）

故事

宁波

张诗雅(新闻学专业 201 专升本班)

不同的“二十一年”

“妈妈,外婆院子里的井养了一条鱼。”

“现在没用了,你外公就用来养鱼了。”

“以前是用井的吗?”

“当然了,以前可没有自来水,要用水的话都得去井里打。”

妈妈的“二十一年”——

浙江省宁波市奉化区岩头村,这是妈妈出生的地方,它的美用山清水秀、古色古香等辞藻来修饰都不为过,大概“绿树村边合,青山郭外斜”也不外如是吧。

“本来就是来这里看看没想到一来就再也没回去。”每每听外婆讲到这,外公总是憨然一笑,慢悠悠地拿起桌上的烧酒轻轻抿一口,开始和我们讲述以前的事情,那是我从未体会过的生活。其中提的最多的就是妈妈和舅舅小时候的故事,这也是我和妹妹听得最津津有味的部分。

“现在享福了,以前很穷的,书也读不起,常常因为买不起雨靴就光着脚去上学。”外公一边咂吧着嘴一边夹着花生米,妹妹忽闪着眼睛听得很认真,时不时还发出惊奇的感叹:“妈妈的小时候是这样的啊!”

1990 年,那年妈妈 12 岁,当清晨的第一线光亮洒进窗口,随之而来的是外婆和外公的呢喃细语,他们正在商量一天应该做的事情,这已经成了他们多年的习惯。而妈妈则在这片轻声话语中缓缓醒转,拿着外婆给的一张半两的粮票和三张一分的纸钱去买了一根油条,开心地去上学了。

那个年代每家每户都要上交公粮,如果有多余的米则可以去换取粮票。

听妈妈提及,放学后最开心的事莫过于花 1 分钱在校门口的婆婆那里买 7 颗炒蚕豆,然后与舅舅相携着去拔野草喂猪。

1993 年,那年妈妈 15 岁。我的妈妈并不是一个聪明的妈妈,对于学习她一窍不通,又迫于学费的压力,她退学了,毅然决然地走上了打工的道路。

妈妈在衬衫厂工作,一个月有 100 多元的工资,自己花 20 元的零用钱,剩下的就上交给外婆,因为打工的地方离家很近,所以也没有其他的开销。

1995年，那年妈妈17岁，出去做了五金，白班夜班两不误，工资涨到了400元，自己花50元的零用钱，剩下的照例上交给外婆。

这些事情妈妈说得很少，几乎是匆匆掠过。

1997年，那年妈妈19岁，也就是在那年遇到了爸爸，两人共同拥有了一个家。那时并不是买房而是自己建房，叫上亲朋好友以及左邻右舍共同出力，建造了一间粗糙的三楼落地房，虽然不精致，家具也不甚齐全，却足以遮风避雨。

1999年，那年妈妈21岁，那是妈妈第一次当母亲，没有人教她如何成为一个好的母亲，可我却觉得她做得很好，她是世间最好的妈妈。

我的“二十一年”——

1999年3月，天气已渐渐转暖却还是带了丝丝寒气。一天晚上8点溪口镇的一家医院里传出一声啼哭，我出生了。或许是冥冥之中的安排，那天是奶奶的六十大寿，因此我深受奶奶的喜爱，也从小被奶奶带在身边。

2002年，那年我4岁。父母在短暂的温情后就是无数的争吵，在这一年他们最终还是走上了离婚的道路。我被寄养在了奶奶家，每逢周末爸爸都会过来看我，街坊邻居总是笑称我奶奶多了个小女儿。

2005年，那年我7岁，在班溪村上小学，也开始记事了。

那个时候没有空调，夏天降温的方式就是奶奶搬出一把竹椅放在门口的小河里，我坐在竹椅上，手上拿着一把蒲扇摇啊摇，两只白白的小脚从宽大的裤管下露出来，没进河里让清爽的河水流淌过脚丫，别提多惬意啦。

当时的家庭条件不允许家里安装热水器，当然也没有取暖器。奶奶就会挑太阳旺盛的日子煮好多壶热水，在正中午时给年幼的我洗澡。

而妈妈则为了可以时常看到我，在我们学校门口不远处租了一间十分狭小又阴暗的房子，在我印象中那间房子的门并不是开关的，而是用一条生锈的铁链锁起来。妈妈会经常带我去她那里小住，一到家里我就会待在床上，因为房间内压根没有坐的地方，煤气灶、桌子、挂衣架都是挨着床排列的。

妈妈住了段时间后就搬走了，和现在的叔叔组成了一个新的家，可每每有时间妈妈总会来学校看望我。奶奶总是念叨我惹人疼，可我不觉得，爸爸和妈妈本身就是两个个体，他们还有长长的一生，不能因为我而葬送幸福。其实他们都很爱我，只是不住在一起罢了，我很庆幸现在的他们都很幸福。

2007年，那年我9岁。对于小时候的我来说去趟镇上就已经是极其遥远的了。当时三个村合并起来就只有一个乘车点，不过只要能出去费些脚程也不以为意。和三五个小伙伴约好后，我就偷偷摸摸地坐上了1路公交车，沿路崎岖不平，全程起起伏伏，像极了我揣着的心情。可是大人仿佛总能察觉小孩子的调皮捣蛋，不意外的在回来路上我被抓包了，奶奶大发雷霆，不容置喙地罚我在菩萨面前跪了一小时，对此我哭闹了好久。

2009年3月，这天是我奶奶七十大寿，可也是在这天我奶奶被确诊为胃癌中晚期，自那后我被爸爸接回家住。奶奶卧病在床时，时而清醒时而糊涂，有时会像个孩子直嚷着疼，有时又摸着我的手说要带我去乘凉，我不时替奶奶揉下肚子，不时用棉签蘸水给奶奶润唇。次年7月，奶奶去世了。

2011年，我步入初中，学业也渐渐开始繁忙，爸爸为了就近照顾我便在中学周围租了一间房子。

冬至花败，然后春暖花开。

2014年，我家拥有了第一台小轿车，家里也迎来了大翻新，原本的水泥地变成了大理石，院子围上了泥墙，造了大门，拥有了更敞亮的阳台和浴室，而二楼的阳台则改建成了另一个卧室，一切都在往好的方向发展。

2017年，我19岁，第一次收拾行囊离开家门，所幸我就读的大学离家不过两小时的车程。因为我不在身边，爸爸离开出租屋回到了我们那间三楼落地房。每逢我回家爸爸总会备好丰盛的饭菜，房间的被子也总有股太阳的味道，我知道那些饭菜爸爸平时都不会去做，对自己他是一贯敷衍，那些被子是爸爸在我来之前特意挑个大晴天晒的，好让我在晚上睡得热乎乎。

父母的爱虽然悄无声息，却丝丝入骨……

2020年，此时21岁的我正坐在电脑面前，述写着我和妈妈同段年龄岁月却不同的21年。

Fenghua
Zhang Shiya (Class 201, Majoring in Journalism)

Different "Twenty-One Years"

"Mom, there is a fish in the well in Grandma's yard."

"Your grandpa now raises fish in it because it is no longer used."

"You mean the well was used before?"

"Of course, there was no running water before. You had to fetch water from the well."

Mom's "twenty-one years"—

Yantou Village, Fenghua District, Ningbo City, Zhejiang Province, is the place where my Mom was born. Its beauty cannot be overstated with terms such as picturesque scenery or antique beauty. Perhaps just as the poem says, *Green woods surround the village; Blue hills slant beyond the city wall.*

"I had come here for a visit but never expected that I would never leave." Whenever Grandma mentioned this, Grandpa always showed a silly grin on his face, picked up the liquor from the table and took a sip slowly. Then he would begin to tell us about the past, which was a life I have never experienced before. One of the most mentioned stories was my Mom's and uncle's childhood, which was also the most interesting part for me and my sister.

"We are much happier now. In the past, people couldn't attend school because of poverty. And they often went to school barefoot because they couldn't afford rain boots." Grandpa sucked on his lips while reaching for peanuts. My sister listened very carefully with her eyes blinking and exclaimed in surprise from time to time: "Mom's childhood was like this!"

In 1990, Mom was 12 years old. The first ray of light came through the window in the morning, followed by the murmurs of Grandma and Grandpa discussing what to do for the day, as they had done for years. Mom woke up slowly to the soft voice. She would take one food coupon of 0.5 tael and buy a stick of youtiao (deep-fried dough stick) with three banknotes of 1 fen (0.01 yuan) given by Grandma and then went to school happily.

In those days, every family had to deliver grain tax to the state. And if there was any extra rice, you could exchange it for food coupons.

Mom mentioned that the happiest thing after school was to buy seven fried broad beans from the old woman with 1 fen at the school gate, and then she would go to pull up weeds to feed pigs with my uncle.

In 1993, Mom was 15 years old. She was not very smart and knew nothing about learning. Thus, she dropped out of school under the pressure of tuition fees and resolutely started to work.

Mom worked in a shirt factory and earned more than 100 yuan a month. She kept 20 yuan as her pocket money, and gave the rest to Grandma. There were no other expenses because she worked near home.

In 1995, Mom was 17 years old. She went out to do hardware work on both day shifts and night shifts. Her salary rose to 400 yuan. And she kept 50 for herself and the rest was handed over to Grandma as usual.

Mom said very little about these things, if any, skipped it over hurriedly.

In 1997, Mom was 19 years old. It was that year that she met Dad and they started their family. At that time, people didn't buy a house but built one on their own. Relatives, friends and neighbors were all called on to build a rough three-story house together. Although it was not exquisite and the furniture was not equipped, it was enough to shelter from wind and rain.

In 1999, Mom was 21 years old. She became a mother for the first time. No one ever taught her how to be a good mother, but I think she did a good job. She is the best mother in the world.

My "twenty-one years"—

In March 1999, the weather was getting warmer but it was still chilly. A piercing cry came out from a hospital in Xikou Town at eight o'clock one evening. And I was born. Maybe it was destiny. That day was also Grandma's sixtieth birthday. Therefore, I was deeply loved by Grandma and was taken care of by her since childhood.

In 2002, I was 4 years old. After a short period of sweetness, there were countless quarrels between my parents. They finally got divorced that year. I was fostered at Grandma's house, and Dad would come to see me every weekend. The neighbors always joked that Grandma had a little daughter of her own.

In 2005, I was 7 years old. I went to primary school in Banxi Village and started to memorize many things.

There was no air conditioning then. The way to cool down in summer was that Grandma took out a bamboo chair and placed it in the small river at the door. I sat on the bamboo chair, and shook with a cattle leaf fan in my hand. My two little white feet came out from my wide pants and then down into the river, letting the refreshing water flow over the feet. You couldn't imagine how comfortable it was.

Our home conditions at the time did not permit the installation of water heaters, and of course there was no such thing as a heater. Grandma would boil a lot of hot water on sunny days and give me a bath at noon when I was young.

In order to see me from time to time, Mom rented a narrow and dim room not far from our school. In my memory, its door was not opened and closed, but locked with a rusty iron chain. Mom would often take me there to stay with her, and I would stay in bed as soon as I got there. Because there was no place to sit in the room at all. The gas stove, the table, and the coat hanger were all lined up next to the bed.

Mom moved away after living for a while, and formed a new family with my current stepfather. But she always came to see me at school whenever she had time. Grandma always said I was adorable, but I didn't think so. Dad and Mom are two individuals. They still have a long way to go, and cannot sacrifice their own happiness because of me. In fact, both of them love me very much, and they just don't live together. I am so glad that they are both very happy now.

In 2007, I was 9 years old. A trip to town was a long way for me as a child. At that time, there was only one bus stop for three combined villages, but walking didn't bother me if I could get out. After making an appointment with a few friends, I secretly got on the No. 1 bus. The road was rugged and uneven with ups and downs throughout the journey, just like my heart. But the adults always seemed to be able to detect children's mischievous behaviors. Unsurprisingly, I was caught on the way back. Grandma was furious and punished me by making me kneel down in front of the Bodhisattva statue for an hour, not allowing others to put in a word. And I cried for a long time.

In March 2009, it was my grandma's seventieth birthday, but it was also on this day that Grandma was diagnosed with advanced gastric cancer. Since then, I was taken home by Dad. When Grandma was sick in bed, she was sometimes awake and sometimes muddled. Sometimes she would cry in pain like a child. Sometimes she touched my hand and said that she would take me to enjoy the cool. From time to time, I massaged her belly or moisturized her lips with a swab dipped in water. Grandma passed away the next July.

In 2011, I entered junior high school and gradually became busier with schoolwork. Dad rented one room near the middle school to take care of me. Flowers withered in winter and bloomed in spring.

In 2014, we got our first car. The house also got a big renovation. The concrete floor was turned into marble. Mud walls and the gate were built around the yard. We had a brighter balcony and bathroom. The balcony on the second floor was converted into another bedroom, and so on. Everything was going well.

In 2017, I was 19 years old. I packed up and left home for the first time. Fortunately, the university I attended was only a two-hour drive away. Without me around, Dad left the rented room and went back to our three-floor house. Whenever I go home, he will always prepare a big meal, and the quilts in my room always smell like the sun. I know that Dad doesn't cook the dishes usually. He always treats himself carelessly. Dad airs those quilts specially in a sunny day before I come back so that I can sleep warmly at night.

Although the love of parents is silent, it is so tender...

In 2020, I'm 21 years old. Now I am sitting in front of the computer, writing about the different twenty-one years between my mother and I at the same age.

致敬父辈

包丹虹

2020年五四青年节，bilibili网站发布了一个叫《后浪》的短视频，整篇演讲充满对年轻人的羡慕、欣赏与敬意，结果在种种争论声中，也引来了一些“后浪”对“前浪”刻苦耐劳、拼搏担当精神的赞美。《闯出个名堂》这篇文章，可以说是“后浪”致敬“前浪”的真诚表达。

蔡盈盈以纪实的笔法回顾了父母的创业过程，目睹前辈一路走来的艰辛曲折，以及他们成功得失之经验，于后者无疑是宝贵财富。尤其年近六十的父亲，依然老骥伏枥，那每天精神饱满的工作状态，令后辈的“我”感到敬佩。

人事有代谢，往来成古今。在长江后浪推前浪的过程中，代际冲突是不可否认的客观存在。想起鲁迅笔下“九斤老太”的哀叹：世风日下，一代不如一代。如今也有不少人抱怨90后、00后吃喝玩乐花钱如流水。确实，独生子女的特殊背景使得他们的消费观念与上代人的节俭相比，普遍显得更为潇洒豪放。但现代年轻人背负的生活压力也大，职场竞争梦想与现实落差也使他们焦虑与挣扎。然而，正如视频中所讲的那样：“你们有幸遇见这样的时代，但时代更有幸遇见这样的你们。”在信息发达的当今世界，见多识广具有无限创造力的年轻人，他们搭建施展自己才华的舞台异彩纷呈。有评论说“李子柒的油管频道对外文化影响力，可以说抵得上1000个CGTN(中国国际电视台)”。

蔡盈盈的母亲说他们：“那是一个能吃苦就能闯出名堂的年代，跟现在不一样，现在还是得好好读书才有前途。”虽然时势背景不同，但勤劳奋斗的精神没过时，因为没有人能随随便便成功。其父亲花甲之年仍意气奋发的工作热情，让我们想起了85岁获诺奖的屠呦呦，想起了耄耋之年亲自挂帅奔赴抗疫一线的钟南山……他们是时代大潮中涌现出来的最耀眼的身影，他们是“后浪”们滚滚向前的精神导航！

（宁波市鄞州区融媒体中心，主任编辑）

故事

宁波

蔡盈盈(新闻学专业192班)

闯出个名堂

雨雾中,青石板路冒着湿气,三轮车轻颤着碾过凹凸不平的青石板,行人踏过坑洼,溅起泥泞的雨水。街边的小店玻璃门上贴着醒目的店名,透过雾蒙蒙的玻璃,可以看见形形色色的人,窥见不同的人生。古朴的平房错落有致,拐进一个小道,就是热闹的邻里。一条小河缓缓淌过小镇,端午佳节有赛龙舟,小镇的人便都挤在河边、靠在桥头看。勤劳的妇女们在河边的小台阶上洗衣服,棒子打在衣服上,敲出有节奏的韵律。这就是我印象中的下应镇,母亲出生的地方,我最熟悉的地方。

妈妈出生于1965年,有两个姐姐和两个妹妹。妈妈在村里的学校上学。在学生时代,妈妈就需要帮家里分担农活。每天放学之后,她要和姐妹们到水稻田里去插秧。这样的生活一直持续到妈妈初中毕业去五金厂工作。妈妈20岁去了家具厂当发货员。

到了谈婚论嫁的年龄,妈妈经爸爸的姐姐介绍,认识了爸爸。爸爸是羽绒厂的销售员,工作稳定,为人踏实。据阿姨所说,那时候妈妈是村里数一数二漂亮能干的女孩子,追她的人很多。以前问过爸爸妈妈是怎么相遇的,爸爸说是他少年时在街上卖棒冰认识的妈妈,这与《功夫》有些相似的桥段曾让我深信不疑。实际上,爸爸少年时卖过棒冰是真的,他们的相知相恋却并不浪漫,更多的是细水长流。

结婚之后,妈妈和爸爸一起创业,这是一段极其艰辛曲折的过程。他们起先做羊毛衫生意,买毛线,雇人织毛衣。后来做鸭饲料,进货原料,雇人加工,再卖给养鸭场。做的最长久也是最后的生意是石材。进货是很奔波的环节,爸爸首先要去各地考察、挑选石材。石材种类很多,爸爸需要透彻了解每种石材的花色和硬度等。花岗石的天然花色不尽相同,需要挑选成色好的才能让顾客满意。爸爸去过河北、内蒙古、四川等地方,被挑选的石材会通过卡车运回宁波,广东的原料则用轮船运回来。切割过的石板不仅厚重,而且边缘锋利。爸爸曾经在翻石板的时候,不慎被石板压住手,左手中指的指甲直接被压碎,到现在那根手指都是光秃秃的。

后来爸爸终于不用亲自跑到天南海北挑选石材原料，也不用自己动手切割石板了。家里也买了第一辆桑塔纳新车。妈妈是公司里的会计员，负责核算账目，也要跟爸爸一起去谈生意。在做生意的同时，妈妈还要兼顾家庭，做家务活和带孩子几乎都是妈妈一手包揽，既是商人也是家庭主妇，个中辛苦自然不必多说。

爸爸妈妈经商几十年，也遭遇过很多困难。

“有过什么困难我记不得了，但是能解决的，就不是困难。”爸爸这样跟我说。在我记忆中，有一次已近年关，公司遭贼，第二天我跟着妈妈去公司，门开着，里面好几台电脑一夜之间被盗走。年关将近是很忙的时候，需要结工资、核对账目等等，很多事情需要安排。突遭变故，爸爸妈妈很冷静，报了警，办了相关手续。后来小偷还是没有抓到，公司又购置了更好更新的电脑。但目睹了全程的我忽地感到非常安心，好像天塌下来他们也只会说没有关系，然后平静地处理。

妈妈 35 岁的时候，想让姐姐有个伴，就选择再要一个孩子。当时 12 岁的姐姐极力反对，妈妈还是说服了姐姐。妈妈 35 岁生产，是高龄产妇，硬是顺产生下了足有 8 斤重的我。那时还在计划生育，生二胎被罚了几万块钱。生下我之后，爸爸妈妈工作还是很忙，我的哥哥姐姐们在一所寄宿学校读初中高中，他们就也把我送到了同一所学校念小学，让哥哥姐姐们多照顾我。

日子都在变好，爸爸众望所归，当选了村书记，上任后第一件大事就是负责村里的拆迁任务。要做好繁复的工作，把房子落实到每一户，也要让村民心服口服，不是容易的事情。那时候爸爸很忙，基本上是早出晚归。历时几个月，拆迁任务终于顺利完成。爸爸没有停下脚步，而是努力完善了村里的公共设施，把村子规划得更加整齐干净。

为了提高生活品质，爸妈决定再买一套房子。爸妈对新房子的装修十分上心，古色古香的红木家具，大面积的花岗石，精巧的小庭院，中式风格让爸妈非常满意。

妈妈 50 岁的时候，决定退休在家过清闲的日子。当时爸爸的朋友想要聘请爸爸去建筑公司当董事长，这也就意味着要重新开始另一份事业。

妈妈说这个公司一开始相当于是个烂摊子，只有好看的空壳。爸爸投入了很多资金，一心一意经营这个公司，在大家的努力下，公司越变越好。现在爸爸快六十了，还是每天充满精力地穿着西装早出晚归，认真工作，以前奋斗是为了养家糊口，过更好的生活，现在则是为了做更多的贡献，实现自己的人生价值。每次看到因为中标或者谈成一笔生意的爸爸喜上眉梢的样子，我都会由衷为他高兴，感到敬佩。爸爸妈妈和朋友们一起开了一个山庄，山庄上有一片果林，种了桃树杨梅树等,种了有机蔬菜,还养了很多鸡。几个人各司其职,妈妈负责会计事务。水果成熟的季节,妈妈会带上外孙女,和朋友一起去山庄采摘水果。

爸爸妈妈能够创业成功,不仅是自身肯吃苦够能干,还得益于这个时代。改革开放为人们带来了很多致富的机会,让勤恳努力的人可以用自己的双手创造美好的未来。改革开放使中国发生了巨大的变化,它对个人的影响也是非常大的。

妈妈说:"那是一个能吃苦就能闯出名堂的年代,跟现在不一样,现在还是得好好读书才有前途。"

Ningbo
Cai Yingying (Class 192, Majoring in Journalism)

To Make Achievements

The bluestone road was damp in a rainy and foggy day. A tricycle throbbed quietly over the uneven bluestone; passers-by stepped over the puddles, splashing the muddy rainwater. The glass doors of the small shops on the street were affixed with eye-catching shop names. Through the misty glass, you could see all kinds of people and caught a glimpse of different lives. The quaint bungalows were well-spaced. Turning into a small path, there appeared a lively neighborhood. A small river flowed slowly through the town, and there was a dragon boat race during the Dragon Boat Festival. People in the town crowded the river and leaned on the bridge to watch. The industrious women washed clothes on the small steps by the river by beating the clothes with a stick, which made a rhythmic sound. This was the town of Xiaying in my impression, the place where my mother was born and the place I was most familiar with.

My mother was born in 1965 and had two older sisters and two younger sisters. My mother went to school in the village. When she was a student, she needed to help the family share the farm work. Every day after school, she and her sisters went to the paddy fields to plant seedlings. Such life continued until my mother graduated from junior high school and went to work in a hardware factory. At the age of 20, my mother went to a furniture factory and worked as a consignor there.

At the age of marriage, my mother made acquaintance with my father through my father's sister and got to know my father. My father was a plain-looking salesman in a down factory. He had a stable job. According to my aunt, my mother was one of the most beautiful and capable girls in the village at that time, and there were a lot of people who were after her. I asked my parents about how they met before, and my dad said he met my mom when he was a boy selling popsicles on the street. This was somewhat similar to the movie named *Kung Fu*, which impressed me deeply. In fact, it was true that my father sold popsicles when he was young, but their love and acquaintance were not romantic, but they loved and accompanied each other forever.

After getting married, my parents started business together, which was extremely difficult and tortuous. They began with the business of woolen sweaters. They bought wool and hired people to knit sweaters. Later on, they made duck fodders, purchased raw materials, hired people to process, and sold them to duck farms. The stone business was the longest and the last one they ran. Purchasing was a part that cost them a lot of energy. My dad traveled many places to inspect and select stones. There were many types of stone, and my dad needed to thoroughly understand their color and hardness. The natural colors of granite were not the same, so he needed to find out the best one to satisfy customers. My dad had been to Hebei, Inner Mongolia, Sichuan and other places. The selected stones would be delivered back to Ningbo by trucks, and the raw materials would be shipped back from Guangdong. The cut stone slab was not only heavy, but also had sharp edges. Once, my dad accidentally crushed his hands by the slate when he turned it over, and the nail on his left middle finger was smashed to pieces. Up to now, there is no nail on this finger.

My father didn't have to travel different places to select the raw materials of stones later, and he didn't have to cut the slate by himself. My family also bought the first new Santana car. My mom was an accountant in the company, who was responsible for checking accounts and had business talks to customers with my dad. While doing business, my mother also had to take care of the family. She undertook almost all the housework and child care. She was both a businessman and housewife, so what she had suffered and endured was beyond words.

My parents went through a lot of difficulties during decades of years when they engaged in business.

"I couldn't remember those difficulties I had before, but what could be solved shouldn't be considered as difficult," my dad said to me. In my memory, the company was once ransacked at the end of a year. I followed my mother to the company on the next day, and the door was found open. Several computers were stolen overnight. It was the end of a year when they were very busy, and they needed computers to calculate the wages, check accounts and so on. There were so many things to be arranged. Meeting such an unexpected misfortune, my parents kept calm and reported to the police to complete relevant procedures. The police failed in catching the thief, so the company bought some better and new computers. As a witness of their handling of this unforeseen event, I suddenly felt reassured. Even if it was the end of the world, they would just calm down, and then deal with it without panic.

When my mother was 35 years old, she wanted my sister to have a companion, so she chose to give birth to another child. At that time, my 12-year-old sister strongly opposed, but she was persuaded by my mother. My mother gave birth at the age of 35. As an older pregnant woman, she chose to give a natural childbirth to me who weighed 4 kg. At that time, birth control policy were adopted, so my parents were fined tens of thousands of yuan. After giving birth, my parents were still very busy at work. My brothers and my sisters attended middle school and high school in a boarding school, and my parents also sent me to the same place to attend the elementary school so that my brothers and sisters could take care of me.

Our life was getting better. As many people expected, my father was elected as village secretary. The first important thing after he came into office was to be responsible for the demolition of the village. To do this complicated work meant convincing every villager to move out and making sure that every household was sincerely convinced, which was not an easy task. Therefore, my dad who was very busy at that time always left early and returned late.

After several months, the demolition task was finally successfully completed. However, my dad did not stop but worked hard to improve the public facilities in the village and to plan a neater and cleaner village.

In order to improve the quality of life, my parents decided to buy another house. My parents were very attentive to the decoration of a new house, and they were satisfied with the antique mahogany furniture, granite over a large area, the exquisite small courtyard, and the Chinese style.

When my mother was 50 years old, she decided to retire at home and lived a leisurely life. At that time, my father's friend wanted to hire him to be the chairman of a construction company, which meant that he had to start another career.

My mom said that the company was a mess at the beginning, which had nothing but window dressing for show. My dad invested a lot of money to run this company wholeheartedly. With everyone's efforts, the company was getting better and better. Now my father is almost 60 years old, and he is still full of energy. Wearing a suit every day, he goes out early and returns late. In the past, he struggled to support his family so as to live a better life. Now he is to make more contributions to realize his life value. Every time I saw the happy look of my dad who had won the bid or negotiated a deal, I was sincerely happy for him and admired him. My parents opened a mountain villa with their friends. There was a fruit forest in the villa. There were peach trees, bayberry trees and so on. They planted organic vegetables and raised a lot of chickens. They were in charge of their own duties respectively, and my mother was still responsible for accounting. When it came to the season that the fruits were ripe, my mother, together with her granddaughter and her friends, would go to the villa to pick fruits.

My parents are able to succeed in their business, not only because they are willing to endure hardships and are capable, but also because they live in a good era. The reform and opening up has brought many opportunities for people to get rich, so that diligent people can create a better future with their own hands. The reform and opening up brings about many opportunities for people to get rich, so the diligent and hard-working people can create a beautiful future with their hands. The reform and opening changes China greatly and its influence on individuals is also very significant.

My mother said: "that was an era that you could make achievements if you were hardy. Unlike nowadays, you have to study hard to have a bright future."

不屈与梦想

李义杰

阅读《浙里是我家》中的一个个鲜活故事，会激发出关于这个时代个人、家庭、国家等命运变迁和生存状态的诸多感想、思考，翻阅《从船夫到店主》《从打工到创业》等故事，我能深深地感受到每个家庭(父母)于命运、生活的那种顽强与拼搏，他们以此挣得自己在这个时代的一席生存之地，或者“向往的美好生活”。于是我认识到，这个时代也是属于他们的——千千万万的平凡的普通人、小人物，时代不仅仅属于英雄或叱咤风云的精英。但时代是如何眷顾他们的呢？亦或说，小人物如何争取到大时代中的自己的“时代”？追求幸福美好的家庭的目标是相同的，但每个家庭奋斗方式和经历各有不同。

在《从船夫到店主》中，作者洪莹莹的父亲出生于温州洞头一个小岛上，14岁继承爷爷的小渔船成为一个“船夫”；16岁因船触礁损毁而离开小渔村，去江西饺子店打工，激发出“做饭”的浓厚兴趣，做学徒，学手艺；1998年，24岁在外婆资助下开起了自己的第一家面馆，之后几经辗转，挫折失败，以30万贷款成功经营了自己的第四家“大饭店”，先后购入两台车、两套房子，让自己的家庭过上了小康生活。而未来，更是满怀豪情与希望地开一家分店。“这时一阵湿咸的海风把他掺着不少白发的头发吹得分了叉。他向后撸了一把，我仿佛看到30年前意气风发目光坚定的小小船夫……”

从小小船夫到“大饭店”店主、美好生活的创造者，作者的父亲是如何创造属于自己的“时代”的呢？那就是对生活的不屈和对梦想的坚持。作者写道，在父亲24年的创业生涯中，并不是一直能够追寻自己的梦想，很多时候，不得不暂时搁下，屈从现实，但千转百回，最后还是回归自己爱好、梦想，“没别的，就是喜欢。只要抄起锅子勺子在大火上颠炒，看着一道道喷香饭菜端到客人的桌上，我就高兴。”这段如作者所说的“出奇的简单”的话，可能却道出了小小船夫争取自己时代的秘密，在不屈和坚持中，寻找到了自己的价值定位，我们能感受到话语中的那种乐观、积极向上和利他的精神。

(浙大宁波理工学院传媒与法学院副教授，博士)

故事

温州

洪莹莹(新闻学专业201专升本班)

从船夫到店主

1974年父亲出生在温州市的一个叫洞头的小岛上,他是家里最小的儿子。问起爸爸的童年,他说,每天最开心的事就是日落时分在岸边等着渔船归岸,眯着眼找到爷爷的船,跑到跟前等着爷爷打开渔网,看鲜活的鱼虾挟杂着海腥味蹦跳到脚边、甲板上、海岸边。

爸爸14岁时,爷爷病逝。爷爷把这艘小船送给了他心爱的小儿子,于是爸爸便开始做起了船夫。每天5点天蒙蒙亮爸爸就要在岸边等着,他要送村上的人去镇里买最新鲜的菜。每将一位乘客送到对岸就可以赚2分钱,小小的船夫就这样在这片海上晃来又荡去,赚着微薄的收入。没有船客的时候,爸爸就独坐在船舷边,把脚搭入海水里,撸一把被海风吹乱的头发,一边看着远方的海平线一边想象着遥不可及的远方。这样的日子过了两年,直到一个雨天,爸爸的船在行驶过程中不慎触礁损坏,无法修复。也就是这个契机,海风挟着海腥气推着16岁的爸爸离开了这个小渔村。

离开海岛的爸爸随着大伯和伯母去了江西开了间饺子店。在那里,爸爸做着一名服务生。爸爸在打工中,突然对做饭生出浓厚的兴趣。他一有空就跑到后厨和大伯学怎么和面,如何调馅,怎样把握火候。在江西的两年里爸爸学了一点技能也存了一些钱,19岁这一年他决定返回家乡。

父亲回到温州后,去到一间厨师学校,经一年的学习后考取了三级厨师证书。随后就面试进入了一间酒店,在酒店后厨做粗加工厨师,做着清洗、宰杀、改刀等粗加工基础工作。这份工作的工资待遇和环境条件在那个年代都算还不错,可是爸爸觉得如此下去根本无法一展抱负,一年后他离开了酒店。

于是他的创业人生正式开始了。20岁的爸爸一定想不到,就算不再划船,前方还是会有更飓的风,更猛的浪。

1998年,外婆借给了爸爸5000块钱让24岁的爸爸以此为起始资金,在温州市鹿城区开起了自己的第一家面馆。面馆面积总共也就20平方米,开餐馆需要的最基础的设施——煤气炉灶已经算是全店最值钱的家具了。几张桌子,几把凳子,就已经是店里全部的摆设。店面装修更是简陋,爸爸买了些白水泥,随便掺和了一下把墙刷白就算完工了。尽管店面小,装修差,可面馆的生意却意外地不错。附近的居民都认可爸爸的手艺,家庭积蓄也在2元一碗的青菜面、5元一碗的排骨面里慢慢地积攒起来。但随着面馆的生意越来越好,麻烦事也随之而来。整日轰隆不停的油烟机把噪音和油烟持续不断地输送到上层居民的家中,被投诉了整整一个月后,爸爸妈妈最后只得关店转让。

下一年,爸爸决定搬址重开。商业街人流量大,店面周围也没有居民楼。可是租金却是上一个店铺的3倍那么多,这一年我出生了。顶着各种开销的压力,思虑再三,最后爸爸还是决定筹钱搬去商业街。在开上一个店铺时购入的桌椅碗筷,只要还能用,就全都搬来继续用。墙壁也依然还是爸妈亲自手工刷白的。除了多了两台电扇,店里的陈设和以前相比几乎就没有什么变化。令大家惊喜的是,生意异常火热,比上一家店还要火热。这间看起来简陋的小面馆甚至比同街精装修的大饭店还要热闹。在1999年,店里的月收入可以达到1万多。但好景总是不长,3年后店面所处的街道需要拆迁重建,爸爸的店又被迫关门了。

2005年,政策原因我需要回户口地念小学,于是我们一家人又回到了洞头。他们在刚规划建设完成的新城区盘下了一间150平方米的门店,精心装修,准备开一间海鲜餐馆。但规模变得比以前大后,运营成本也大得超出了爸爸的想象。而且岛上的居民,本就天天吃海鲜,一间海鲜餐馆无论规模多大对他们的吸引力终究还是不够的。店面冷清萧条,父亲用以前的积蓄,让这家店勉强运营了一年。最终这间餐馆还是破产停业,店铺转让。先前所存的积蓄一败而空。

在经历这么大一场失败后,爸爸挫败感极深。接下来一直到2010年爸爸36岁,身边的朋友个个事业有成,家庭美满。而爸爸因为生意失败,积蓄亏败一空,与妈妈的矛盾也日渐加深。身处低谷的他做了个极其冒险的决定——向银行贷款30万,开起自己的第四家饭店。于他而言,没有任何退路,一旦失败之后的日子便是艰难的负债生活。但他决定冒险。这次他将饭店选址在了温州鹿城区的一条餐饮街上,餐馆的面积足有360平方米,两层楼这么大。餐馆主营海岛海鲜,每日他驾车从海岛购入刚出海的最新鲜的海鲜,第一时间运入内陆,当天晚上做给顾客吃。这一次,他终于成功了。每天客人络绎不绝地把楼上楼下的大堂、包间都塞得满满当当,店门口等位区也几乎没空过。顾客的回头率极高,店里的老顾客都能熟到和爸爸称兄道弟。这家店开到今年已经整整10年,中间翻修整新过,生意一直都算火热。靠着这家店的经营,爸爸先后购入了两台车、两套房子。

同爸爸聊起这一切的时候,我们正在岛上的沿海公路上散步。谈到未来的打算,他说他盘算着继续开一家分店,这时一阵湿咸的海风把他掺着不少白发的头发吹得分了叉。他向后撸了一把，我仿佛看到30年前意气风发目光坚定的小小船夫……

在父亲24岁就开始的漫长创业生活中，其实不是一直地追寻着自己的梦想。多个时间段，父亲其实都暂时搁下了自己的梦想，屈从现实，做了许多在他人眼里看起来稳定踏实的工作。他做过销售员、业务员，甚至远赴北京、郑州寻求一个心仪的工作，但他最后还是决定做回餐馆小老板。向他问道为何最终还是决定回归餐饮，他的回答却出奇的简单："没别的，就是喜欢。只要抄起锅子勺子在大火上颠炒，看着一道道喷香饭菜端到客人的桌上，我就高兴。"

Wenzhou
Hong Yingying (Class 201, Majoring in Journalism)

From Boatman to Shop Owner

In 1974, Dad was born on a small island called Dongtou in Wenzhou City. He was the youngest son in the family. Speaking of his childhood, Dad said that the happiest moment every day was to wait for the fishing boat to come back to the shore at sunset. He always squinted to find Grandpa's boat, and ran up to wait for Grandpa to open the fishing net. Fresh fish and shrimps would jump at his feet, on the deck and near the shore with the fishy smell of the sea.

Grandpa died of illness when Dad was 14. And he gave the boat to his beloved youngest son, so Dad started to work as a boatman. Dad had to wait on the shore at 5 o'clock every day when dawn was just breaking to send the villagers to the town for the freshest vegetables. Every time one passenger was sent to the opposite bank, he could earn 2 fen. The little boatman wandered on this sea for a meager income. When there were no passengers, Dad would sit alone on the side of the boat, put his feet into the sea water and fix his hair carelessly, which had been rumpled by the sea wind. He watched the horizon while imagining its unreachable distance. Such days passed for two years until one rainy day. Dad's boat accidentally hit a rock in sailing and was damaged beyond repair. It was at this moment that the sea breeze mixed with the fishy smell of the sea pushed my 16-year-old Dad out of this small fishing village.

Then Dad followed my great uncle and aunt to Jiangxi to open a dumpling shop where he worked as a waiter. During his daily work, he suddenly developed a keen interest in cooking. As long as he was free, he would run to the kitchen to learn how to knead dough, mix the stuffing, and calculate the cooking time from my uncle. Dad learned some skills and saved some money during the two years in Jiangxi. At the age of 19, he decided to return to his hometown.

After Dad returned to Wenzhou, he went to a chef school and got the third-level chef certificate after one year's study. Then he found a job in a hotel through an interview as a junior chef in the hotel kitchen. Dad was responsible for basic rough processing tasks such as cleaning, butchering, and changing shapes with a knife. The wage and working conditions of this job were pretty good at that time, but Dad felt that it was impossible for him to live up to his ambition. He left the hotel a year later.

Then he truly started his own business. My 20-year-old Dad could never have imagined that even if he stopped rowing, there would still be more hurricanes and more violent waves ahead.

In 1998, my grandmother lent 24-year-old Dad 5,000 yuan as his start-up capital to open his first noodle shop in Lucheng District, Wenzhou City. The whole noodle shop only covered 20 square meters and the basic facility needed, a gas stove, was the most expensive thing in the shop. A few tables and stools were all the furnishings in the store. The decoration was even more humble. Dad only whitewashed the wall with some mixed white cement. Although the shop was small and poorly decorated, the business was surprisingly good. The nearby residents all thought higgly of Dad's cooking. A bowl of green vegetable noodles sold for 2 yuan and pork rib noodles 5 yuan. Thus, our family savings were increasing little by little. But as the business got better, troubles followed. The upper-level residents were bothered by the noise and cooking fumes the range hood made, which was booming all day long. After being complained about for a full month, my parents had to close and transfer this shop.

The next year, Dad decided to relocate the shop. There was a high flow of people and no residential buildings around the store on the commercial street. But the rent was three times that of the last one, and I was born that year. Under the pressure of all kinds of expenses, Dad still decided to raise money and move to the commercial street after thinking over and over again. The tables, chairs, bowls and chopsticks purchased before would be used again as long as they were still usable. The walls were still whitewashed by my parents themselves. Except for two electric fans, the furnishings in the shop were almost the same as before. To everyone's surprise, the shop was extremely popular, even better than the last one. This humble noodle shop was even more bustling than the well-decorated grand hotel on the same street. In 1999, their monthly income could reach more than 10,000. But the good times didn't last long. Three years later, the street where our shop was located needed to be demolished and rebuilt. Dad's store was forced to close down again.

In 2005, I had to go back to my permanent residence to go to primary school for policy reasons, so my family went back to Dongtou. They set up a 150-square-meter shop in the newly planned and constructed urban district and then carefully decorated it as a seafood restaurant. But the operating cost grew bigger than Dad had ever imagined as the restaurant was larger. Besides, the residents of the island ate seafood every day. Thus, no matter how large a seafood restaurant was, its attraction was not enough. Despite the languishing business, Dad managed to run the restaurant for a year with his savings. But in the end, it went bankrupt and had to be transferred. The previous savings totally ran out.

After such a big failure, Dad felt extremely frustrated. From then on until 2010, when Dad was 36 years old, all his friends had successful careers and a happy family. But he lost all his savings and the conflict with Mom was deepening day by day because of business failure. At the bottom, he made an extremely risky decision to borrow 300,000 yuan from the bank to open his fourth restaurant. There was no retreat for him because failure would be followed by a hard life of debt. But he chose to gamble. This time he located the restaurant at a food court in Lucheng District, Wenzhou. It covered an area of 360 square meters and was as large as a two-story building, which specialized in island seafood. Every day he drove to the island for the freshest seafood, transported it to the inland as soon as possible, and cooked for customers in the evening. This time, he finally made a hit. Every day, a continuous stream of guests filled up the lobby and private rooms upstairs and downstairs. Even the waiting area at the entrance was almost filled without vacancies. Returning customers came to eat at a high rate. The regular customers were familiar enough with Dad to call each other brothers. This restaurant has been open for 10 years, and was once renewed. The business has always been brisk. Relying on this restaurant, Dad has bought two cars and two houses.

We were walking along the coastal road on the island as I talked about all this with Dad. Speaking of his future plans, he said that he was thinking of opening another branch. At this time, the salty sea wind rumpled his greying hair. He fixed it backwards carelessly. I seemed to see the little boatman who had been in high spirits, with his eyes shining with determination 30 years ago.

Dad started his lengthy business at the age of 24 but he was not always on the way to follow his dream. He actually put aside his dream, succumbed to reality, and did a lot of work that seemed stable in others opinion for many periods of time. He once worked as a salesman and even went to Beijing and Zhengzhou for a suitable job, but he finally decided to run a restaurant. As for why he finally returned to dining, his response was surprisingly simple: "Nothing but love. I love it as long as I can just hold the wok and scoop, stir-fry the dishes over the fire, and watch the spiced dishes served on the table for guests."

大时代需要这样的人

李义杰

在《从打工到创业》中,我们看到了相似却又不同的故事,作者温纯的父亲和母亲都是20世纪90年代“打工潮”中的一员,分别来自江西和浙江衢州的小山村,在杭州相遇而组成家庭。其父亲先后到衢州砖瓦厂做过拉砖小工,到杭州做学徒学习装修、做项目经理等,2014年在湖州开起了自己的装修公司。而其母亲则主要在饭店当服务员和在服装店打工。可以说都是大时代下芸芸众生中最普通的“小人物”,但他们家庭、命运轨迹的变迁,又让我们看到了他们并没有被时代抛弃,或者说,他们一直在这个时代中追求着自己的幸福和位置。

作者写道:2014年,爸爸从原公司辞职,与朋友合伙开起了装修公司,爸爸为人正直,一直秉承着对客户负责的态度,靠着口碑与质量在湖州收获了许多忠实客户,打响了“以德为美,品质典范”的口号,在装修市场打下了自己的一片天地。而至此,作者的家庭生活也发生了翻天覆地的变化:“三十年来,我们家的房子从出租屋到老小区再到小高层,房子的变迁也代表着我们的生活越来越好。”作为小山村出来的打工者,作者的家庭在湖州拥有了两套房子。

这种变化对于小山村出来的人来说,已经是很了不起的事情了。经历了早年打工的苦累,最终迎来了美好小康生活,而这些靠的又是什么?我想,或许就是作者多次提到的她父亲的正直、秉承的为客户负责的理念,形成的“以德为美,品质典范”的口号和价值观念,大时代需要这样的人,需要这样做事。

(浙大宁波理工学院传媒与法学院副教授,博士)

故事

湖州

温纯(新闻学专业192班)

从打工到创业

20世纪90年代,改革开放已有十数年,全国各地掀起一阵“打工潮”,青年男女纷纷离开家乡,去外面的世界闯荡。我的父母也不例外。爸爸来自江西上饶的一个偏僻小山村,妈妈则是来自浙江衢州一个县城下的小村庄,两人都从家庭并不富裕的农村、山里走出来,在杭州相遇后组建了家庭。

爸爸妈妈经常对着我说:“在你这个年纪啊,我都在打工了。”

19岁时,爸爸走出了大山,到了衢州的一个砖瓦厂里工作。拉一车砖头一毛七,爸爸正是年轻有力气的时候,他一天能拉许多趟小车,几乎每天都是第一名。再过了一年,爸爸去杭州做学徒,学习装修知识,自己学着给别人装铝合金窗,再后来开了一家玻璃店。妈妈年轻时的人生轨迹和爸爸相同,高中毕业时离开了家,到了杭州打工。一开始,妈妈给一家饭店当服务员,工资是400块一个月,餐厅的一位经理看妈妈开朗外向,人也活络,就建议妈妈去当迎宾,工资也会有所提高。可是当迎宾需要喝酒,妈妈便拒绝了这个提议,之后又去了另一家饭店当服务员。可惜好景不长,该饭店没过多久就倒闭了,连工资也没有给妈妈。没有工作,便失去了生活来源,妈妈不好意思问家里要钱,硬着头皮去向饭店老板讨工资,饭店老板给不出钱,妈妈只好问朋友借钱,捱过了那艰难的一个月。后来,妈妈又去了西湖旁边的一家服装店打工,从早上9点站到晚上10点,做一休一,月工资是五百五。为了多挣些钱,妈妈每天都去上班。西湖边的服装店的衣服大多是奢侈品,一件衣服就要上千,妈妈在那家服装店打工,见过了形形色色的人。

如果说早年是为了自己,为了生计奔波,那么在我出生之后,两人则是为了孩子、家庭奔波。那时爸爸在杭州的一家装修公司当项目经理,不久后,这个装修公司要在湖州开设分公司,爸爸调去了湖州,于是我们也举家搬去湖州。有一年春节回老家,买不到车票,爸爸妈妈便打算骑摩托车回去。从湖州到江西400多公里,路途颠簸,两人愣是拖着我和行李回了家。打工的阶段,这样辛酸的日子不知有多少,个中滋味,也只有爸爸妈妈自己知道。

2014 年，爸爸从原来供职的装修公司辞职，与自己的一个朋友合伙开了装修公司。爸爸为人正直，靠着口碑与质量在湖州收获了许多忠实的顾客，他们自己的房子装修完毕后，还会把爸爸的装修公司推荐给身边要装修的朋友们。从事装修行业这么多年，不免会碰到许多难搞的客户。有一次，一家客户的地暖已经铺好，到了铺地板的阶段，客户表示地板由自己提供，同时，客户应拿出地板的质量保证书，以应对后续的材料问题。可是客户不愿意提供质量保证书。爸爸就拒绝铺地板。后来，客户拿了另一份质量保证书，爸爸看那并不是那批地板的保证书，仍拒绝铺设地板。客户认为爸爸在刁难他，找了朋友与爸爸理论，爸爸认真地分析了利弊关系，最终说服了客户。爸爸一直秉持着对客户负责的态度办事，靠着他的努力，打响了“以德为美，品质典范”的口号。开装修公司到现在，已有 6 年，自己开店与打工相比，有着更多的自由。同时，自己开店的营业额并不稳定，这时候，爸爸需要付出更多的精力去维持与客户、合作厂商的关系。一周中，爸爸常常有四五天不在家吃晚饭，不是在外面应酬，就是在办公室跟客户签单。

30 年来，我们家的房子从出租屋到老小区再到小高层，房子的变迁也代表着我们的生活越来越好。

据妈妈回忆，早年打工时，两人住在十几平米的出租屋里，狭小逼仄，从床上坐起甚至几近碰到天花板上的吊扇。夏天酷热难耐时，两人便跑到天台上去睡觉。生了我之后，因为我身上长痱子，爸爸这才添置了空调。在我的记忆中，我幼儿园时期便是辗转在不同地方的。在湖州时，爸爸在装修公司当项目经理，妈妈在商场里开店。两人那时听说衢州房价便宜，东拼西凑了 4 万块钱付了房子首付，在衢州买了房子，于是妈妈带着我又去衢州生活了两年。本打算在衢州安定下来后，让爸爸也过去，可后来因为在衢州做生意亏大于盈，妈妈又带着我回了湖州。至此，我们便一直生活在湖州了。2010 年，爸爸妈妈在湖州的一个老小区买了房子。房屋面积不是很大，车库却不小。爸爸把车库改造成了厨房。就这样，我们家厨房在一楼，住在四楼。一楼车库前有很大一片空地和草坪，夏天吃晚饭时，爸爸会把桌椅搬到门前的空地上，我们一家人趁着夏天的风，在暮色中有说有笑着吃饭，常常会引来一群老爷爷老奶奶加入我们的谈话。我们在那里生活了将近 7 年。房子虽小，五脏俱全。老小区的外观虽破旧，但邻里之间其乐融融。2011 年，弟弟出生了，我们家中又添新成员，热闹非凡。我初中毕业时，爸爸妈妈想要给我和弟弟更好的生活，又商量着买房子。2016 年，爸爸妈妈把衢州的房子卖了，又在湖州的一个新小区买了房子。我们便在这个房子里生活到现在。

从打工到创业，我们家的生活水平越来越好。到了现在，爸爸妈妈仍在为着有更好的生活在外奔走。

Huzhou
Wen Chun (Class192, Majoring in Journalism)

From Employment to Start-up

In the 1990s, the reform and opening up made remarkable achievements. There was a tide of rural workers across the country, and young men and women left their hometowns for cities, hoping to make a living away from home in the outside world. My parents were no exception. My father came from a remote mountain village in Shangrao City, Jiangxi Province, and my mother came from a small village in Quzhou City, Zhejiang Province. They both came out of rural and mountainous areas where their families were not well-off. They met in Hangzhou and started a family.

My parents always told me: "At your age, we already worked for others."

At the age of 19, my father left the mountains and began to work in a brick and tile factory in Quzhou. Pulling a cart of bricks could earn seventeen fen. When my father was young and strong, he was able to pull a cart several times a day, almost ranking the first every day. A year later, my father went to Hangzhou to be an apprentice, learning about decoration. He learned how to install aluminum alloy windows by himself, and then opened a glass shop. My mother had the same life experience as my father when she was young. When she graduated from high school, she left home and went to Hangzhou to find a job. In the beginning, my mother worked as a waitress in a restaurant, and the salary was 400 yuan a month. A manager of the restaurant considered that my mother was outgoing and lively, so she suggested that my mother should be a restaurant greeter, and the salary would be increased. But when my mother was required to accompany the guests to drink, she refused the offer. After that, she worked as a waitress in another restaurant. It's a pity that the good times didn't last long, because the hotel closed down soon, and my mother even didn't get the salary. Without a job, she lost her source of income. My mother considered it embarrassing to ask her family for money, so she went to the restaurant owner to demand the unpaid wages. The restaurant owner had not enough money to pay, so my mother had to borrow money from her friends so as to go through that difficult month. Later, my mother found a job in a clothing store next to the West Lake. She worked from 9 a.m. to 10 p.m. every alternate day, and the salary was 550 yuan a month. In order to earn more money, my mother went to work every day. Many clothes in the clothing store by the West Lake were all luxury goods, and one piece of clothing would cost several thousands yuan. My mother met all kinds of people when working in the clothing store.

If my parents had been busy with their work for themselves and for their livelihood in the early years, they were striving for me and the family after I was born. At that time, my father was a project manager of a decoration company in Hangzhou. Soon, the decoration company decided to set up a branch in Huzhou. Then, my father was transferred to Huzhou, so we moved there. I remembered one year when we intended to return to our hometown for the Spring Festival, unluckily, tickets had been sold out. Therefore, my parents planned to go back by motorcycle. It was more than 400 kilometers from Huzhou to Jiangxi, and the road was bumpy, but they, taking me and the luggage, insisted on going back. During the period of being employed, there must have been a lot of such bitter days, and I was sure my parents were the only two persons who felt it deeply.

In 2014, my father resigned from the decoration company, and started a decoration company in partnership with one of his friends. My father is an upright person, so he won the heart of many loyal clients in Huzhou through good reputation and quality. After their own houses were renovated, those clients would recommend my father's decoration company to their friends who wanted to decorate their houses. Having been in the decoration industry for so many years, my father inevitably encountered many difficult clients. Once, the floor heating in a client's house had already been well-laid, and it came to the time that the floor should be laid. The client told my father that he would offer the boards to my father. At the same time, it was necessary that the client took out the floor quality assurance certificate for the sake of subsequent material problems, but the client was unwilling to provide the quality assurance, so my father refused to put down the boards for him. Later, the client showed my father another quality guarantee, but that was not the guarantee for that batch of flooring. Therefore, my father refused to put down the boards again. The client thought that my father was making things difficult for him, so he, together with his friend, argued with my father. However, my father carefully analyzed the pros and cons to them, and he convinced them at last. Upholding the principle of being responsible for his clients, my father's company had been well-known for its slogan, which was "morality comes first, quality is guaranteed". It has been six years since he opened the decoration company. Compared with being employed, my father enjoyed more freedom from his start-up. However, the turnover of the company was not stable, so my father needed to put more energy on maintaining the relationship with clients and cooperative manufacturers. He often dined out four or five days a week, either socializing outside or signing orders with clients in the office.

Over the past 30 years, our house changed from a rental house to our own house in an old community, then to a small high-rise building, so the changes of our house witnessed the improvement of our living standard.

As far as my mother recollected, they lived in a rented house of around ten square meters in their early years. It was so small that they would bump their head on the ceiling fan if they stood on the bed. When summer came, it was so hot that they had to sleep on the rooftop. It was only after my birth that my father installed an air conditioner because of the heat rash on my body. In my memory, I spent my kindergarten time in different places. When in Huzhou, my father worked as a project manager for a decoration company, and my mother opened a store in a shopping mall. When they learned that the housing price in Quzhou was cheap, they put together 40,000 yuan to pay the down payment for the house so as to buy a house in Quzhou. Then my mother took me to Quzhou and live there for two years. We had planned to let my father come after we settled down in Quzhou, however, my mother's business didn't go well and lost lots of money, so she took me back to Huzhou. From then on, we have been living in Huzhou till now. In 2010, my parents bought a house in an old community in Huzhou. The area of the house was not very large, but the garage was not small, so my father turned the garage into a kitchen. In this way, we had meals on the first floor while we lived on the fourth floor. There was a large open space and lawn in front of the garage on the first floor. When having dinner in the summer, my father would move the table and chairs to the open space in front of the door. Our family enjoyed the summer wind, talking and eating happily in the twilight. Many elderly people were attracted and joined our conversation. We had lived there for nearly 7 years. The house was small but well-equipped. Although the old community looks dilapidated, neighbors were nice and we lived in harmony. In 2011, my younger brother was born. We were excited and delighted that we had one more family member. When I graduated from middle school, my parents wanted to give my brother and I a better life, so they decided to buy a new house. In 2016, they sold the house in Quzhou and bought a house in a new community in Huzhou where we have been living till now.

From employment to start-up, our family's living standard is getting better and better. Up to now, my parents are still working hard for a better life.

小型超市，在大变局中寻找发展空间

吴 琼

《从贵州到湖州》，吴诗雨同学讲述了父母外出创业的历程。她父母携家带口，跨越半个中国，从浙江丽水到西南的贵州从事销售工作，之后辗转苏州、丽水和湖州三地，先后经营了三家超市。吴同学的父母用半生书写了一场颇为坎坷的创业史。他们的拼闯胆魄和辛勤经营，给下一代带来殷实富足的生活。

超市，从20个世纪80年代引入中国，到现在已有40余年。90后的年轻人，无法体验到超市刚出现时对民众带来的冲击。在超市里随心挑选的购物方式带给了人们极大的愉悦感。随着中国经济的高速发展，超市行业进入快速发展的轨道。

最近几年，由于互联网技术在各行业的深入以及新零售概念的提出，超市的发展之路遇到了不少挑战。很多大型超市如家乐福、沃尔玛等纷纷出现了"关停"现象。笔者所在的城市，好几家大型超市都开通了"一小时达"的送货服务，人们只要在手机上动动手指，不一会儿就能收到新鲜的货物。作为民生保障消费的最基础行业，超市行业背后的消费需求都是刚需。因此在新冠病毒疫情初期，超市的线上订单较以往有了更大程度的增长，好多人开启半夜抢菜的模式。此外，还催生了另一种零售模式——社区团购。疫情促进中国数字经济进入新常态化的发展时期，超市的到家业务会迎来一个新的发展。在疫情过后，消费者习惯将会逐渐定式化。对传统小型超市来说，只有做好市场分析，找准消费群体，尽快调整经营模式，提供更完善的服务项目，才能在经济大变局中继续寻找到发展的空间。

（浙大宁波理工学院传媒与法学院思政讲师，硕士）

故事

湖州

吴诗雨(新闻学专业201专升本班)

从贵州到湖州

第一站:贵州。

2005年的4月,年仅6岁的我随着父母前往贵州省贵阳市的开阳县,这里是我爸妈外出创业的第一站。当时父母做的是销售产品的工作,这份工作极其辛苦,爸爸要经常外出开会以及登门拜访推销产品。夏天,烈日底下穿着公司里发的西装,看着是很体面,但满头的大汗也无法被这一份体面遮盖。寒冷的冬天,他也要穿西装外出,爸爸还常常开玩笑,说他在外面差点就要变成冰棍了。那时候为了提高业绩赚更多的钱,爸爸老是外出跑业务,脚下的运动鞋底已经用胶水粘过好几遍了,却还在用。妈妈和爸爸是在同一个公司里,但是工作没有爸爸辛苦,她是负责在公司里处理财务方面的工作。当时他们公司有一个很奇怪的现象,30岁以下的员工一般没有孩子,所以呆在贵州期间我就像一个"小秘密",只要公司有人在我没上幼儿园的时候来访问,我就会去房间里,拿着妈妈给的巧克力,边吃边看书,安安静静待上半天,等人走了才出来。后来父母有了一定的积蓄,爸爸就和妈妈商量,要不开个超市吧,自己给自己当老板,这样赚来的钱都是自己的,也不用再东奔西跑了。妈妈也同意。

第二站:苏州。

2007年,在江苏省张家港市,父母开了人生中的第一家超市,面积是200平方米,取名叫永盛超市,寓意是希望超市的生意永远红红火火。那时候我在读小学二年级,父母把我带回老家给爷爷奶奶照顾。那是我第一次离开父母,临走时我拽着妈妈的腿大哭大闹,不让她走。妈妈也泪眼婆娑,不停地和我讲道理说他们只有去赚钱才能让我买喜欢的东西呀之类的,走得时候还送给我一个小娃娃,娃娃有红红的头发,穿着黄色的公主服,带着大大的蝴蝶结,很可爱。妈妈说要是想他们了可以拿出来看看。那个布娃娃我到现在还放着,小时候奶奶说我见了娃娃就会流眼泪,哇哇哇地要往车站去,现在长大了倒也成了逢年过节遭人调侃的趣事了。2008年寒假,父母第一次带我去看超市。那一年的雪特别大,据说是好几十年才会碰上。我们那时候坐的火车,到了以后已经是深夜了,天上还一直飘着大片大片的雪花。我那时候穿了好多衣服，圆圆的像个球一样，在雪地上走得摇摇晃晃。到超市门口，因为没人来扫过雪，所以积雪很厚很深，差不多到我的膝盖。于是爸妈就一人一只手拉着我，像拔萝卜一样把我从雪里提上来，发出“咯吱咯吱”的声音，挺好玩的。这是我第一次见到这个超市，从外面看，它有四个店面的大小，边上还有一个工厂和一个小公园，现在想来地理位置还挺不错的，但对于年幼的我来说它更像一个庞然大物倒在地上，天黑黑的，看上去怪吓人的。爸爸拉开手动的卷帘门，妈妈把我抱了进去，打开灯，恍惚间整个超市像“苏醒”过来，十分亮堂，让人的心也开始安定下来。第一眼看到的是卖散称饼干的四个柜子，里面整整齐齐地按价格堆满了各色各样的饼干，看得出爸妈摆得很用心。再里面就是四排大货架了，第一排是饮料和牛奶，地上还有两箱散称的苹果和一箱橙子。第二排是各种零食小吃和方便面。第三排是日用百货。第四排是装饰品和各种酒类。看到这些琳琅满目的商品，我幼小的心里充满了激动和兴奋，我居然实现随便吃喝不用给钱的梦想了！第一次开超市的爸爸妈妈在做生意时，和客人之间的你来我往，那种游刃有余的感觉俨然是两位合格的老板了。这是第二站，我们家开的第一家超市。

第三站：丽水。

2011 年，爸爸因家里的各种原因，把苏州的超市转让了，回到了丽水老家。为了生计，他在丽水松阳又开了一家超市，占地 150 平方米，没有苏州的超市那么大，爸爸给他取名为又一家超市，因为店名奇怪，还常常会有顾客询问原因，但爸爸总是回答说是胡乱取的，没有特别的含义。超市周围都是工厂，在这些厂里上班的工人下班后都喜欢来我家超市买点东西，有时候是酱油味精、零食牛奶，有时候是被褥脸盆、衣架肥皂等物件。对于选择回归故乡，父母也是下了很大的决心的。因为当时我的外公突然中风，需要有人照顾，加上我要上初中，学习成绩不太理想，缺少人管教。那时候妈妈除了打理超市外，就是往我外公家跑，带一点菜场买的猪肉鱼肉和蔬菜，希望外公能在病后的日子里过得再快乐一点。天气越来越寒冷，外公的身体也一天不如一天，满是褶皱的面孔上是一对渐渐浑浊的眼睛，中风后的他连翻身这个小动作也无法独立完成，需要别人帮忙才行。我们去看他时，他常常拿背对着我们，说话也含糊不清了。他时常对我妈妈说自己想走得早一点，这样大家都不用为他操心了。大概在他心里想的是生病的他成了我们的负担。后来，我上初二的时候，一个冬日的午后，外公被死亡带走了。参加完葬礼的我还是不敢相信，外公真的是永远地离开我了。我甚至还会想，会不会在某天的某个时间，仍有一个慈祥和蔼的老人笑着看我，带我出去玩呢？外公的离世也成了我家第二个超市的终点，父母转手卖了它，再次背井离乡。

第四站湖州。

2015年，父母来到湖州市安吉县递铺镇，开始了第三次的超市之旅。这次选址在一座菜场边上，占地150平方米，取名一家人超市。爸爸说叫这个名字，就像把养家的责任放在了肩上，也像是带着故乡一起出发，能在异乡中也有家的温暖。这个超市的生意是三个超市里最好的，尤其是炎炎夏日，别人都嫌天热，而我爸妈就怕天不热，因为只有天热，买矿泉水和饮料的人才多，我们家的啤酒常常在饭点时能卖出去四五十箱。因为周围的菜场也带动了很大一部分的人流量，加上周围工厂较多，爸妈的生意是一天比一天红火，我们家也买上了第二辆汽车，生活也越来越好了。

我的父母大半辈子都在经营超市，他们因超市离家，也归家。在人生的旅途中，为了一份责任，一份热血，从贵州到湖州的漫长征途，于他们而言已是一场盛大的创业史了。

Huzhou
Wu Shiyu (Class 201, Majoring in Journalism)

From Guizhou to Huzhou

First stop: Guizhou

In April 2005, when I was only 6 years old, I went to Kaiyang County, Guiyang City, Guizhou Province with my parents, which was the first stop for my parents to start a business. At that time, my parents were working in sales, which was very toilsome. Dad often went out for meetings and visited people to promote products. In summer, he looked very decent wearing a suit provided by the company in the scorching sun, but the sweat on his head could not be covered. In the cold winter, Dad also had to wear a suit to go out. He often joked that he was about to become a popsicle outside. In those days, in order to improve the performance and make more money, Dad always went out for business. The soles of the sports shoes he was wearing had been glued several times, but they were still in use. Mom and Dad were in the same company, but her work was not as toilsome as Dad's. She was responsible for handling financial affairs in the company. Their company had a very strange phenomenon that employees aged under 30 usually don't have children. Thus, I was like a "little secret" during my stay in Guizhou. As long as someone from the company came to visit when I didn't go to kindergarten, I would often read a book quietly for half a day while eating the chocolate from Mom until the guest left. Later my parents had a certain amount of savings. Dad suggested opening a supermarket so that they could be their own boss and all the money earned was their own. Besides, there was no need to run around. Mom also agreed.

Second stop: Suzhou

In 2007, my parents opened their first supermarket in Zhangjiagang City, Jiangsu Province. It covered an area of 200 square meters and was named Yongsheng Supermarket, meaning that they hoped its business would always be prosperous. At that time when I was in the second grade of primary school, my parents entrusted me to my grandparents back in our hometown. That was the first time I parted with my parents. When Mom was about to leave, I grabbed her leg and cried so loudly, not letting her go. Mom was also tearful and kept telling me that only by making money could they buy my favorite things and so on. When she left, she gave me a little doll with red hair, wearing a yellow princess dress and a big bow, which was very lovely. Mom said I could take a look at it if I missed them. I still keep that doll now. Grandma said I would shed tears whenever I saw the doll, asking to go to the bus station. Now that I have grown up, it has become a fun to joke during the holidays. In the winter holiday of 2008, my parents took me to the supermarket for the first time. The snow that year was so heavy, and it was said that it took decades to encounter. We had to take the train then, but it was already late at night when we arrived. Large snowflakes were still flying in the sky. I had so many clothes on that I staggered about in the snow, round like a ball. At the entrance of the supermarket, the snow was thick and deep, almost to my knees because no one came to sweep. My parents took me by the hand, and lifted me up from the snow like pulling a carrot, making a "creak" sound, which was very funny. That was my first time to see this supermarket. From the outside, it had the size of four stores. There was also a factory, and a small park nearby. Looking back, its location was quite good. But I was too young at that time. It seemed more like a huge monster falling on the ground and could be weird in the dark. Dad pulled open the manual shutter door. Mom took me in and turned on the lights. The whole supermarket seemed to "wake up" in a trance. It was very bright, letting people's heart settle down. The first thing that caught my sight were four cabinets selling biscuits by weight, which were neatly piled up with all kinds of biscuits according to the price. I could see that my parents had laid them out very carefully. Inside were four large rows of shelves. The first row was filled with mineral water, drinks and milk, and on the floor were two boxes of apples and a box of oranges that were sold by weight. The second row was for snacks and instant noodles, the third row for daily necessities, and the fourth row for decorations and various wines. Seeing these various goods and with my young heart full of excitement, I could realize the dream of eating and drinking without paying any money! My parents, who opened a supermarket for the first time, could communicate back and forth with customers with ease, which made them look like two qualified bosses. This was the second stop, our first supermarket.

Third stop: Lishui.

In 2011, Dad transferred the supermarket in Suzhou and returned to his hometown in Lishui for various reasons. In order to support the family, he opened another supermarket in Songyang County, Lishui, covering an area of 150 square meters, which was not as big as the supermarket in Suzhou. Dad named it Youyijia Supermarket. Customers often asked about the strange name. Dad always replied that it was taken at random, without any special meaning. The supermarket was surrounded by factories. Workers in these factories liked to buy something in our supermarket after work, sometimes soy sauce, aginomoto, snacks and milk, sometimes bedding, washbasin, coat hanger, soap and other items. It was not an easy decision for my parents to choose to return to their hometown because Grandpa had a sudden stroke at the time and needed to be taken care of. In addition, I was going to junior high school. My academic performance was not satisfactory and there was a lack of parental control. At that time, besides taking care of the supermarket, Mom always went to Grandpa's house with some pork, fish and vegetables bought from the market, hoping that Grandpa could live a happier life for the remaining days. Grandpa's health was getting worse day by day as the weather got colder and colder. On his wrinkled face were a pair of muddy eyes. After the stroke, he could not even complete the small movement of turning over on his own without help from others. When we went to see him, he often turned his back to us and slurred his words. He often told Mom that he wanted to leave earlier so that no one would have to worry about him. Probably in his mind, he became a burden to us when he was sick. One winter afternoon when I was in my second year of junior high school, Grandpa was taken away by death. I still couldn't believe that Grandpa had really left me forever after the funeral. I even wondered if there would be a kind old man looking at me with a smile and taking me out to play at a certain time someday. Grandpa's death also became the end of our second supermarket. My parents sold it and left home again.

Fourth stop: Huzhou

In 2015, my parents came to Dipu Town, Anji County, Huzhou City and started their third supermarket. It was located next to a vegetable market, covering an area of 150 square meters, named One Family Supermarket. Dad said to name it One Family was like putting the responsibility of supporting the family on his shoulder, and it was like setting out with our hometown so as to feel the warmth of home in a foreign land. This supermarket has the best business among the three. Others think it's too hot in the summer days. On the contrary, my parents are afraid that it is not hot enough. Because only when it's hot, there are more people buying mineral water and drinks. Our beer can often sell forty to fifty cases at mealtime. The surrounding vegetable market also brings a large flow of people, and there are many factories around. The business of my parents is booming day by day. Our family also bought a second new car, and life is getting better and better.

My parents have been running supermarkets for most of their lives. They left home or returned home both for the supermarket. In the boundless trip of life, the long journey from Guizhou to Huzhou, just for responsibility and passion, has already been a grand pioneering history for them.

趟过乡土社会的人情河流

丁六申

《从海中岛到城中村》讲述的是一个农村家庭由乡及城迁徙发展的故事，也反映了外地人在舟山本岛的奋斗史。

传统的乡土社会是一个“熟人”社会，在每一个“村落范围”内生活的人似乎都拥有一种生来就有的“熟识感”，而对外地人突然的到来多是持打量、疏远态度，王楚琪家一开始外迁至大洋岙村时遭到村里人排挤的现象正说明了这一点。但是，扎根于此的王楚琪父亲以和为贵，微笑待人，乐于助人，与此前众人之“私”形成了鲜明的对比。村民们对这个新成员的一举一动都看在眼里，他们之间的隔阂开始逐渐消除。随着时间和岁月的沉淀，王楚琪家真正成为大洋岙村“村里人”，从第一次建房子受到监管、被“使绊子”，到从山顶搬到山脚下重建新房子时村民们纷纷给予帮助，其乐融融的生活画卷也由此缓缓展开。当2019年遭受台风灾害时，大洋岙村村干部们不畏艰险，第一时间赶到她家中实施救援，可谓雪中送炭。第二天，邻居们主动送来生活用品，言语中传递着关怀与温暖，守望相助展现了人情之美。

良好的品质是立身之本，王楚琪家庭生活蒸蒸日上，开始创业的父亲深谙真善美与人情味的重要性，以“优正”为名，寄予公司在行业里是优秀的，是公正、正直、正规代表的美好期望。

（浙大宁波理工学院传媒与法学院思政教师，硕士）

故事

舟山

王楚琪(新闻学专业 201 专升本班)

从海中岛到城中村

1973 年我的母亲来到了这个世界。农历十月初六，她出生在浙江省舟山市岱山县高亭镇渔山村的一个渔民家庭。外公出海捕鱼后，外婆便带着母亲和阿姨外出劳动，维持一家生计。8 岁时，母亲上了村里的小学。岛上没有中学，母亲走出了海岛，来到了大沙中学，开始了她的初中生活。

在这里，温文尔雅的母亲认识了调皮捣蛋的父亲。父亲早年丧父，奶奶独自抚养其长大，父亲是家中最小的孩子，上面还有三个哥哥和一个姐姐。父亲说，奶奶为了供他上学，卖掉了家中下蛋的母鸡，又因为家中供不起这么多的孩子上学，只好让二阿伯退学回家帮忙。

有一天噩耗传来，外公所在的渔船因为触礁而沉没，外公因为救人，自己没能逃出来。这对原本就不富裕的渔民之家是雪上加霜，不得已母亲只得退学回到海岛，在亲戚朋友的帮助下，在码头边开起了小店。父亲因为成绩不好，没有考上高中，只好跟着别人做起了学徒。

码头边来来往往的渔民成了母亲小店里的常客，也是店里主要的收入来源。可惜好景不长，码头因为需要维修不再允许船只靠岸，母亲的小店顿时失去了主客源，没过多久，便宣布倒闭。1992 年，母亲再次离开海岛，来到舟山定海羊毛衫工厂做女工。干了两年后，母亲逐渐掌握了技术要领，正巧大阿姨来到定海开了自己的羊毛衫工厂，邀请母亲过去当工厂的管理者。就这样，母亲顺利地成为白领，有了自己的一间小民房，虽然不大，但比起十几个人的寝室已经好得太多了，工资也上涨到了一个月 400 元左右。

母亲省吃俭用终于攒够了钱，买下了人生当中第一辆车子——海狮牌自行车。有一天母亲让父亲载着她去参加同学聚会，可是粗心的父亲忘记锁车，等到酒足饭饱后，才发现自行车早已不见了踪影。

离开学校后，父亲在亲戚的介绍下来到定海，跟着水电工师傅当起了学徒。做学徒的工资很少，一天只有 8 元，就连一碗紫菜汤都要分成两碗，中午喝一半，剩下的晚上倒点开水继续喝。为了赚更多的钱，父亲利用中午休息时间帮工地开拖拉机运沙子，每车5角钱，最多的时候能拉个10车左右。

听别人说卖棒冰很赚钱，打听清楚后，父亲果断向师傅请了两个月的假，回到大沙老家卖起了棒冰。一根棒冰卖5毛钱，买来却只要2毛5，除去租小冰箱和自行车的钱，一天最好的时候能赚50元左右。

回到定海后，在师傅的帮助下，父亲开始独自承包活计。但因为水电工行业不景气加上父亲年龄尚小，又是外地人，干完活后，有许多人拖拖拉拉地不结账，就这样第一个工程很快以亏本告终。后来父亲发现装修产业未来前景非常广阔，在朋友的介绍下，决定转行装修产业，凭借着自身的努力，父亲终于在装修产业闯出了自己的一番天地。

1997年，父亲和母亲在朋友的介绍下，终于走到了一起。第二年，我便出生了。父亲一直觉得我们要有属于自己的房子才能算真正融入这个城市。于是父亲和母亲在定海共同奋斗了三年后，决定在定海城东街道大洋岙村的山顶买下属于自己的第一幢房子。起初那是三间小平房，外面下大雨时，里面总会下起小雨，地上放满了接雨的锅碗瓢盆。母亲说，这时候刚学会走路的我总喜欢出来踩水，一不小心摔了个跟头，就变成了个小泥人，但总也不吸取教训，第二次下雨还是会继续出来晃荡。

有了一定的积蓄后，父母决定把小平房建成小别墅，父亲拿出自己所有的积蓄，又问亲戚朋友借了20万元，半年后，房屋落成，我们终于有了能够遮风避雨的家。

在建房子时，因为我们不是本村人，而是从外地迁过来的，村里人都很瞧不起我们，经常把石头等杂物扔在通往我们家的必经之路上，不让我们装材料的车通行，还每天轮流派人来监管我们，怕我们多占了他们村里的土地，外婆气不过跑去和他们争论，还被他们弄伤了手。

即使这样，父亲还总说以后大家都是邻居了，你头不见抬头见，俗话说远亲不如近邻，我们刚来要和村里的人搞好关系，才能够在这里继续生活下去。不管村里的人怎么说我们，父亲总是笑嘻嘻地和他们打招呼，还自掏腰包为村里把通往山顶的泥泞路铺成了水泥路，方便村里的老人上山耕种。

现在，我们已经从山顶搬到了山脚下，重建新房子的时候，村里的好多人都来帮忙，有的帮我们混混凝土，有的拉材料，还有的把自家的小推车借给我们运沙子。村里的老人刚种上来的蔬菜，每次都会在我们家门口放上一把，有时母亲下班回到家都不知道是谁放的呢，以至于我们家现在都不用怎么买蔬菜了。

2019年国庆，超强台风“米娜”登陆，鸿毛湾水库因没有及时放水，导致水库外泄，我们家正好在水库下面，于是成了本次险情的重灾区。洪水直接冲破了我们家的玻璃门，母亲站在门后，被玻璃划伤，割断了手筋和脚筋，血流不止，而消防部门又因为水势湍急，一时之间无法进来。村长得知消息后第一时间带着村里的干部搭着人墙走了过来，把母亲背到水势较为舒缓的一处，用村里的吉普车把母亲送往了最近的医院。

第二天一大早，有些邻居不顾自己家中也还处于洪水过后需要整理的情形，纷纷赶到我们家中，问有没有什么需要帮忙的，有些甚至直接把家里的洗衣机、晾衣架等生活用品都搬到了我们家里。看着一个个热心的村民们，听着他们一句句温暖的话语，直到这个时候，我才深深体会到父亲以前说的话。

如今，我想我们已经成为真正的“村里人”。

2014 年父亲为方便经常回家探望老人和运送货物，买下了我们家的第一辆汽车——日本铃木，当时的价格是 17 万元左右，也算是家里的一大笔开销了。提车回到家的当天，父亲自豪地对我们说从此以后我们家就又多了一名新的成员了，于是，我亲切地称呼它“大白”。

就这样“大白”正式上岗，每天父亲会开着它接送母亲上班，此时此刻的我正在读初中，对于家里的新成员也只是偶尔坐上一次，有时候还会为了抢副驾驶的位子跟母亲动足了脑筋。想起来，都是满满的幸福快乐回忆。

中考后，我来到了金塘中学。学校需要上高速才可以到，于是每个星期负责接送我上下学的任务就光荣地交到了“大白”身上。直到现在，我已经从金塘考到金华再到宁波，每次父亲都是开着“大白”送我去学校，又把我接回来。

2017 年，父亲创立了他的第一家公司——定海区优正维修中心。父亲说“优正”的“优”代表着优秀和优胜，而“正”则是公正、正直和正规的意思，父亲希望他的公司在行业里是优秀的，是公正、正规的代表。

现在，我们家的生活正蒸蒸日上，幸福快乐的画卷也在不断缓缓展开……

Zhoushan
Wang Chuqi (Class 201, Majoring in Journalism)

From a Sea Island to an Urban Village

My mom was born into a fisherman's family in Yushan Village, Gaoting Town, Daishan County, Zhoushan City, Zhejiang Province on the sixth day of the tenth month of the lunar calendar back in 1973. Whenever my maternal grandpa went fishing on the sea, my grandma would take my mom and my aunt out for work in order to make ends meet. My mom went to an elementary school in the village, after which she left the island and started her middle school life in Dasha Middle School since there was no middle school on the island.

It was in Dasha Junior Middle School that my gentle and quiet mom met my naughty and mischievous dad, who was raised up by a single mom after his father died prematurely. He was the youngest child in the family and had three elder brothers and one elder sister. My dad recalled that my grandma had to sell hens in order to send him to school. Unable to afford every child's tuition fees, my grandma had to ask one of my uncles to drop out of school.

Bad news came that my maternal grandpa lost his life when trying to save others after the fishing boat he took struck against rocks and sank, which added to the misfortunes of this already poor family. My mom had no alternative but to drop out of school and returned to the island. She then ran a small shop by the wharf with help from relatives and friends. As for my dad, he became an apprentice after failing the high school entrance examination.

Fishermen going to and fro on the wharf frequented my mom's shop, constituting a major source of income for her. But good times didn't last long. As the wharf needed to be repaired and no ships were allowed to dock there, the shop lost its major customers and was soon out of business. Therefore, my mom left the island once again in 1992 and tried her luck in a sweater factory in Dinghai, Zhoushan. She, having mastered knitting techniques after working there for two years, was asked to manage a factory newly started by her elder sister in Dinghai. In this way, my mom became a white-collar worker and had a small dormitory of her own, which meant she no longer needed to share a room with a dozen fellow workers. Her monthly salary was also raised to 400 yuan.

She scrimped and saved and finally bought her first bicycle—a Sea Lion bicycle—with 500 yuan she saved. One day, she asked my dad to take her to the alumni gathering by bike. Having enjoyed delicious food and wine, they left the gathering, only to find the bicycle was nowhere to be found—it turned out that my careless dad forgot to lock it.

Thanks to his relatives' help, my dad was apprenticed to a plumber and electrician in Dinghai. He earned a daily salary of merely eight yuan as an apprentice, so little that he had to drink half a bowl of seaweed soup and save the other half for dinner. He also helped carry sand by driving a tractor during the noon break just to make some extra money. He could make half yuan each time up to ten times a day.

During his apprenticeship, my dad asked for a two-month leave and started selling popsicles in his hometown when he learned that the business was quite lucrative. Each popsicle, with the cost of a quarter yuan, was sold at half yuan. When the business was good, he could make up to 50 yuan a day excluding refrigerator and bicycle rents.

He began independently contracting projects with his instructor's help after returning to Dinghai. Yet many clients, seeing my dad as a young immigrant worker from another city, dragged their heels in payment. Plus the sluggish industry, my dad lost money in his first ever project. He later tried his luck in the decoration industry which he believed had a promising future, and finally succeeded in carving out a career in the industry with his own efforts.

My parents, after being introduced to each other by their friends, eventually got married, and I was born the next year. Feeling that we could fit into this city only when we had a house of our own, my father decided to buy our first house which was located on the mountain top of Dayang'ao Village, Chengdong Street, Dinghai City after toiling with my mom for three years. At first, it was a bungalow with three rooms. Whenever there was torrential rain outside, it was raining inside the house, so my parents put a lot of utensils to hold rain drops. My mom said I liked wading waters after I learned how to walk, and would be covered with mud after I tumbled to the ground. But I, not learning the hard lesson at all, would hang around the house the next raining day.

Having decided to turn the bungalow into a villa, my dad took out all his savings and borrowed 200,000 yuan from relatives and friends. We finally possessed a home that could shelter us.

Villagers looked down upon us for we were not locals but moved from another place. They often threw stones and rubbles on the way leading up to our house so as to obstruct trucks carrying construction materials. They also had us monitored for fear that we should occupy more land than allowed to. My maternal grandma, arguing with them out of indignation, once got her hand hurt by them.

Even though, my father still said that those people were our neigbors, and that we, as newcomers, should get on well with them so that we could continue our life here, just as the old saying goes, "A distant relative is not as good as a near neighbor." Therefore, my dad always greeted them with a smile no matter how those villagers commented on us. He even turned the muddy road leading up to the mountain top to a cement one at his own expense so as to make it easier for the elderly to plough on the mountain.

Now we have moved from the mountain top to the foot. Many villagers gave us a helping hand when we built the new house, the closest to the reservoir, with some mixing concrete, some carrying materials and some lending us trolleys for moving sand. The elderly will lay down some fresh home-grown vegetables on our doorstep, so we barely buy any green leaves. Sometimes my mom even doesn't know who has given us those vegetables.

During the National Day holiday of 2019, our house was hit hard by the super typhoon Mitag. Hongmaowan reservoir didn't release water in time, so water overflew and our house, the closest to the reservoir was stricken by flood. My mom had her hand tendons and hamstrings cut off because she happened to stand behind the glass door when the flood smashed it. The fire department was unable to provide first aid due to torrential water. Having learned that my mom was bleeding, the village head and other cadres formed a human barricade and came to her rescue. They carried my mom over the back to a place where water flewed less turbulently and then took her to the nearest hospital in a village jeep.

Some neighbors hurried to our home and asked whether there was anything they could help with despite all the mess they had back in their own homes after the flood. Some even moved daily necessities like washing machines and clothes hangers to our home. It was not until I saw our warm-hearted fellow villagers and heard their comforting words that I related to what my dad said before.

Now, I believe we have become genuine "fellow villagers".

My dad bought our first ever car—a Suzuki in 2014 so that we could visit our elderly relatives in the hometown more often and deliver goods. The car cost 170,000 yuan back at that time, huge expense for the family. My dad told us proudly the day he got the car that a new member was added to our family. I nicknamed it "Big White".

Ever since then, my dad sent my mom to work every day by that car. I, as a junior middle school student then, was only an occasional passenger in this new family member, and tried every means possible to compete for the passenger seat against my mom. How happy and joyful memories!

I went to Jintang Senior High School after the entrance examination. As the school was only accessible by expressway from my home, "Big White" assumed the responsibility of sending me to and picking me up from the school. Later I studied in Jinhua and now I am in Ningbo. No matter where I am, it has always been my dad who drives "Big White" to send me to and pick me up from the school.

My dad started his first company—Youzheng Maintenance Center in Dinghai District in 2017. My dad said "You" represented "excellence and victory" in Chinese and "Zheng" meant "justice, fairness and standard". By so naming it, my dad wished his company could be a voucher for excellence, fairness and standard in the industry.

Now, our life is prospering with each passing day, and before us, a scroll of happiness and joy is unfolding...

012

观察

读书改变命运，母亲永远伟大

刘炳辉

姚嘉琦写的是自己外公的一生，显然外公是一位让嘉琦感到骄傲的长辈与楷模，励志故事和敬业精神也同样打动着读者的心。我为嘉琦有这样优秀的家风感到高兴和庆幸，毕竟来自什么样的家庭并不是自己能选择的，这事靠点运气。有了好运气的嘉琦，在大学里也很努力上进，积极争取为家庭再添新荣誉。

嘉琦外公一生的职业历程是非常难得的，从农家寒门子弟成为国家公务员并屡立功勋，且立功立德立言皆有，也是难得的人生圆满。而这样令人羡慕的人生，关键的转折点还是读书。1949 年新中国成立之际，嘉琦外公时年 16 岁，此时他已经是读过将近 8 年的书，这在当年可是稀缺“人才”，要知道当时全国的城镇化率不过 10%，人口中的文盲率一般认为超过 80%。虽然外公天资聪慧也有强烈求学意愿，因家庭经济条件所限未能继续读下去，但放在当时的时代背景下，读了 8 年书已经是一个了不起的成就和人生起点了，其从社会分层和教育分层的角度考虑，恐怕相当于今天的硕士生在一代人中的教育排序。

也正是这难得的 8 年读书生涯，让嘉琦外公此后的人生路走得更高更远，职业生涯走向了为人民服务的大舞台。而这个坚持求学的关键，不在于一个少年的求学之心，而是少年母亲的深明大义和含辛茹苦。嘉琦外公的母亲在本文中并非主角，但我却穿越时空看到了那个伟大母亲的坚毅和艰难。她为祖国培养了一个好干部，她为儿子铺就了一个好前程。类似这样的故事其实还有很多，但故事往往指向了一个朴素的道理：母亲，永远是最伟大的人！

（浙大宁波理工学院马克思主义学院副教授，博士）

故事

嘉兴

姚嘉琦(网络与新媒体专业 193 班)

从杭城到禾城

我的外公姓褚,名佩勤,寓意是要敬佩勤劳的人。他 1933 年出生于杭州临安於潜镇敖干村,1954 年因工作来到嘉兴。从杭州乡村到嘉兴城市,他见证了 1949 年新中国成立,见证了 1978 年改革开放,见证了 2020 年全面建成小康社会。

从小我就喜欢坐在藤椅上,外公也坐在藤椅上轻轻摇着蒲扇,诉说他的故事,透过外公深邃的眼睛仿佛可以看见从前。如今外公已进入耄耋之年,我想用笔记录下他眼中的社会变迁。

小学,外公在敖干村小学读了四年、在於潜镇中心小学读了两年,六年以来学习成绩一直是第一名。小学毕业后,外公因家里没钱交学费而辍学在家。而后,简易乡村师范学校补招 10 人,村里的人都对外公母亲说:“你们家孩子这么聪明,怎么不给他读书呢?这么一个好苗子,借钱也要给他读书啊!”于是外公母亲让外公去读书,外公一听又可以读书学习了,甚是开心。

外公在简易乡村师范读了一年半的时间,家里无法供应他继续读书,于是外公再一次辍学了。

外公艰难曲折的求学之路落下了帷幕。

随着 1949 年新中国成立,外公踏上了工作的路途。

17 岁,外公成为敖干村的村长。当时恰逢土地改革时期,他以“为人公正、办事又快又好的小村长”而闻名远近村落。土地改革结束后,各个单位因为外公出色的表现向他抛出了橄榄枝:学校请他做教师、村电影院让他放映电影、乡政府给他安排文书工作……他都一一回绝。1952 年 3 月,外公加入中国共青团,区青年团委书记让外公在区共青团做青年干部,他立即答应了。4 月,外公在县委党校学习,一个月后,被分配到县供销合作社。1953 年 10 月,外公被调到杭州市於潜县公安局。1954 年 4 月,外公又被调到嘉兴地区(包括现浙江省嘉兴市和湖州市)嘉兴县公安局预审科。外公在公安局肯干肯吃苦,年年被评为先进工作者、“五好干部”。1961 年 6 月,怀着为国家为人民奋斗一生的信念,外公加入中国共产党，成为一名党员。1963年元旦，外公与外婆结婚。1964年5月到6月，外公从全国2500多个县市的基层公安机关的干部中脱颖而出，作为全国优秀代表之一前往北京参加全国第二次预审、看守工作会议。

当时三年自然灾害刚刚结束，各种物资都很匮乏，但外公还是买了一双风凉皮鞋作为礼物送给外婆。1978年，全国检察机关陆续恢复重建，嘉兴地区重建浙江省人民检察院嘉兴县检察院，外公成为检察院重建初期仅有的9人之一，他的检察工作由此翻开了崭新的一页。1982年，全国人大通过了修订的《中华人民共和国宪法》，并相继颁布了《刑法》《民法》《行政法》等各种法律法规。外公在检察院负责批准逮捕和起诉嫌疑人。《刑事诉讼法》第224条规定："人民检察院提出抗诉的案件或者第二审人民法院开庭审理的公诉案件，同级人民检察院都应当派员出庭。"外公便成为第一批三个可以出庭的检察员之一。在检察院，外公依然忠于职守、兢兢业业，被评为浙江省级检察系统的先进工作者，成为当时嘉兴唯一一位获得浙江省奖励晋升一级工资的干部，在1989年"刑打"斗争中成绩显著，荣立二等功。

除了工作上敬业严谨，外公也十分热爱写作，经常在报刊上发表文章。外公仍清晰地记得，某天晚上11点，他还在办公室里工作，接到大桥镇粮食管理所的电话，举报有人贪污，他马上报告检察长，当天夜里出发前往大桥镇粮食管理所。他写下一篇名为《国徽在寒夜中闪光》的文章，刊登在《浙江日报》上。身着藏青的制服、胸佩鲜红检徽的检察官们秉持着公平正义的利剑，开展严打斗争，惩治腐败，打黑除恶，在夜晚的寒光中衡定世间的不平。

即使只做一颗小螺丝钉，也要做最物尽其用的那颗，发挥最大的光和热。

1993年12月，外公正式退休。退休后，外公也不闲着，发挥余热，作为力协律师事务所的特邀律师继续工作了10年，经常帮助穷苦农民免费辩护。"做辩护人一定要以理服人，站在公正的角度上，以法律为准绳，不能一味地为被告说话。"这是老法律工作者的感悟。外公仍记得，有一位农村私人企业负责人贪污受贿，他仔细研究案卷，发现委托人主动投案自首并且情节较轻可以减轻处罚，于是外公就这一点为其辩护，被法院采纳，结果被告人被判处罚金没有被拘役。

看报纸、看新闻也成为外公日常生活必不可少的一部分，他时时关注国家发展动态，经常教育子孙们要爱国、勤奋、努力。外公的一言一行能够在潜移默化中给我以人生启迪、智慧光芒和精神力量。

七十年物换星移、岁月如歌，七十年砥砺奋进、铸就辉煌。外公在艰苦岁月中度过童年，在逆境中顽强成长，最终迎来幸福美好的新生活，见证了从新中国成立到改革开放再到今天，见证了新中国的繁荣昌盛。从曾经衣服"新三年，旧三年，缝缝补补又三年"，到现在服饰不仅御寒更展示个性；从曾经找粮食，挖野菜，吃树皮充饥，到现在吃饱吃好，营养均衡，健康饮食；从曾经住在破旧的砖瓦房，到现在住在漂亮的小区公寓、家具齐全；从曾经步行、自行车出行，到现在家家都有汽车，随着高铁、飞机覆盖全国、全球，出去游玩都方便了许多。看到祖国日新月异的变化，人们生活越来越美好，外公的脸上洋溢着满满的幸福。

出生在嘉兴南湖边的我流淌着红色基因，从小外公的言传身教给我留下了不可磨灭的印记，他引领我树立正确的世界观、人生观、价值观，告诉我不忘本、不变质，要珍惜来之不易的美好生活，用自己的辛勤劳动，肩负起振兴中华民族的历史使命，让红船精神继续传递下去。

Jiaxing
Yao Jiaqi (Class 193, Majoring in Network and New Media)

From Hangzhou to Jiaxing

My grandfather's surname is Chu and his first name is Peiqin, which means to admire hard-working people. Born in Aogan Village, Yuqian Town, Lin'an, Hangzhou in 1933, he came to Jiaxing for work in 1954. From the villages of Hangzhou to the cities of Jiaxing, he witnessed the founding of the People's Republic of China in 1949, the reform and opening up in 1978, and the building of a moderately prosperous society in all respects by 2020.

Since I was a child, I have liked to sit on the rattan chair. My grandfather also sat on the rattan chair, gently waving the cattail leaf fan and telling his stories of the past. Through his brooding eyes, it seemed that I was able to see the past. Now that my grandfather has become an octogenarian, I want to write about what he sees as social change.

My grandfather studied in Aogan Village Primary School for four years and in Yuqian Town Central Primary School for two years. His academic performance ranked first for six years. After graduating from primary school, my grandfather dropped out of school because the family had no money for school fees. Then, simple village normal school wanted to recruit ten more students. The villagers all said to my grandfather's mother, "Your child is so clever. How could he be prevented from continuing his studies. He is such a good young man, and you should let him continue his study even if it means you need to borrow money!" So my grandfather's mother asked him to continue his studies. My grandfather was very happy when knowing this news.

After the founding of the People's Republic of China, my grandfather spent a year and a half studying in simple village normal school. The family could not afford to let him continue his study, so my grandfather dropped out of school again.

My grandpa's difficult and tortuous road to study came to an end.

With the founding of new China in 1949, my grandfather began to work.

At the age of 17, my grandfather became the head of Aogan Village. During the land reform period, he was known as "a fair, and effective young village head". After the end of the land reform, various organizations held out an olive branch to him for his excellent performance. The school asked him to be a teacher; the village cinema let him play movies; the township government arranged a clerical post for him. However, he turned them all down. In March 1952, my grandpa joined the Communist Youth League of China. When the district Youth League committee secretary let my grandpa be a youth cadre in the district Communist Youth League, he accepted the offer immediately. In April, my grandfather studied in the party school of the county Party Committee. After a month, he was assigned to the county supply and marketing cooperative. In October 1953, my grandfather was transferred to the Public Security Bureau of Yuqian County in Hangzhou. In April 1954, he was transferred to the Preliminary Examination Department of Jiaxing County Public Security Bureau in Jiaxing (including today's Jiaxing and Huzhou, Zhejiang Province). My grandpa was willing and hard-working in the bureau, so he was awarded the title of "Model Worker" and "Cadre Excelling in Five Aspects" every year. In June 1961, with the belief of fighting for the country and people, my grandfather joined the Communist Party of China and became a party member. On New Year's Day of 1963, my grandfather and my grandmother got married. From May to June in 1964, my grandfather stood out from the cadres of grassroots public security organs in more than 2,500 counties and cities across the country, and went to Beijing to attend the second national pre-trial and guarding work conference as one of the national outstanding representatives.

At that time, the three-year natural disaster had just ended and all kinds of materials were scarce, but my grandfather still bought a pair of leather shoes as a gift for my grandmother. In 1978, the national procuratorial organs were successively restored and rebuilt, and the People's Procuratorate of Jiaxing county of Zhejiang Province was rebuilt. My grandpa was one of only nine people in the initial reconstruction of the procuratorate, and his procuratorial work was thus turned to a new page. In 1982, the National People's Congress adopted the revised Constitution of the People's Republic of China, and successively promulgated the Criminal Law, Civil Law, Administrative Law and other laws and regulations. My grandfather was in charge of approving the arrest and prosecution of suspects at the procuratorate. Article 224 of the Criminal Appeals Law stipulates, "The people's procuratorate at the same level shall dispatch officers to appear in court in cases protested by the people's procuratorate or in cases of public prosecution tried by the people's court of second instance." Grandfather became one of the first three prosecutors to appear in court. In the procuratorate, my grandpa was still devoted to his duties and his work. He was rated as the model worker of Zhejiang Provincial Procuratorial System, the only cadre from Jiaxing who was entitled to the first-tier salary in Zhejiang Province, and he won the second-class merit in the "punishment and crack-down" struggle in 1989.

Besides being dedicated and rigorous in work, my grandfather also loved writing very much and often published articles in newspapers and magazines. He still clearly remembers that one day at 11 p. m., he was still working in the office when he received a call from the food administration of Daqiao Town. Hearing that someone was reported corrupt, he reported to the procurator-general at once. He then immediately set off for the food administration of Daqiao Town that night. He wrote an article entitled "National Emblem Glints in Cold Night" which got published in Zhejiang Daily. Wearing their blue uniforms and bright red badges and wielding the sword of fairness and justice, the prosecutors fought fiercely, punished corruption, cracked down on evil, and settled injustice in the cold light of the night.

Even if he was only a small screw, he would make the most of it and gave full play to his potential.

In December 1993, my grandfather officially retired. After the retirement, my grandfather gave full play to his talent instead of staying idle. He continued to work as a specially-invited lawyer of Lixie Law Firm for 10 years and often defended poor farmers for free. "To be a defence lawyer, he must convince others by reason. From the perspective of justice, he should take the law as the criterion, and cannot just speak for the accused." This is the comprehension of an old legal worker. He still remembered the person in charge of a rural private enterprise was accused of embezzlement and bribery. My grandfather studied the case file carefully, and discovered that if the client confessed his crime voluntarily and the circumstance was not serious, then the punishment could be lessened. Therefore, my grandfather defended for him from this point, which was accepted by the court. Consequently, the defendant was given a fine instead of getting detention.

Reading newspapers has become an indispensable part of my grandpa's daily life. He always follows the development of the country and often teaches his children and grandchildren to be patriotic, diligent and hardworking. His words and deeds can give me life enlightenment, wisdom and spiritual strength in a subtle way.

Over seventy years, things changed with the passing of time, and life was like a song with ups and downs. Seventy years of constant struggle and progress made a brilliant future. My grandfather spent his childhood in difficult years, grew up tenaciously in adversity, and finally ushered in a happy new life. He has witnessed the founding of the People's Republic of China, the reform and opening up and today's prosperity. In the past, "people wore new clothes for three years, then continued to wear them for another three years. After that, when the clothes were shabby, people would sew and repair them so as to wear in the following three years". Nowadays, clothes not only warm your body but also show your personality. In the past, people looked for food, dug wild vegetables and tree bark to appease their hunger. Nowadays, people don't have to worry about food but keep a balanced and healthy diet. In the past, people lived in a shabby brick house. Nowadays, people are able to live in a well-furnished apartment in a beautiful community. In the past, people went on foot or by bike. Nowadays, every family has a car. With high-speed trains and planes connecting the whole country and the world, it has become much easier for people to travel around the world. Seeing the motherland change rapidly with each passing day, and people's lives are getting better and better, my grandpa's face alights with happiness.

I was born near South Lake in Jiaxing, so I have inherited the essence of the tradition of the Communist Party of China. My grandfather's words and deeds have left an indelible mark on me since I was a child. He led me to establish a correct world view, outlook on life and values. He told me not to forget our roots and never become bad. We should cherish our hard-won life more, shoulder the historical mission of rejuvenating the Chinese nation with our own hard work, and pass on the Red Ship Spirit.

013

观察

站在老家的土地上

甄　晶

看到芷欣同学的文章时，我正站在老家的土地上，感受着这片土壤带来的温厚与踏实。很巧的是，我跟芷欣是同乡人，老家的位置在地理上也只有短短的十几分钟车程，看到她的文章感同身受，过往岁月中对老家的记忆便如同胶片一般，一张张滑过眼前，从无声到有声，从黑白到彩色，从凄苦到悠然。

我们的家乡——湖州织里，是典型的中国小城镇，却见证了改革开放40多年的历史变迁。改革开放前，老一辈人靠天吃饭、赖地穿衣，生活过得尤为艰苦。改革开放后年轻人们渴望发展，凭借“一根扁担打天下”的信念，从走南闯北销售自制纺织、刺绣产品，到以家庭作坊为主的童装制作，再到现如今的童装专业市场的形成，老百姓的生活越来越富足。人们不再满足于物质的丰富，开始追求高品质的生活方式，更加关注民生、关注教育、关注社会。芷欣的文章描述了家庭生活的变化，让我们看到了一代代人在平凡中用坚韧与岁月相伴而行的身影。家庭是社会的缩影，从每户小家庭的发展变化真实反映了整个时代的变迁。

艰苦终于过去，很庆幸，我们能生活在这个时代。而今，我站在老屋门前，望着眼前这块熟悉的土地，马上它也要因为新农村建设重新翻建，我仿佛看到不久后一个崭新的美丽乡村即将在这里诞生。土地还是那块土地，家乡还是那个家乡，中国人寻根的情愫依旧，不管我们走到哪里，我们都会在土壤中寻找力量，在寻找中静看岁月变迁，在变迁中砥砺前行，在前行中致敬祖国！岁月静好，请温柔以待！

（湖州职业技术学院宣传部，副教授）

故事

湖州

汤芷欣(新闻学专业 192 班)

从艰苦岁月走来

“那时候啊,真的很苦。”问起从前,奶奶的第一句话,总是“过去很苦”。奶奶不是个表达能力很强的人,对于过去,她说的也不多,说来说去我能记住的不过就是一个“苦”字,而每次她说起这个字,总是眼泛泪花。

我的爷爷奶奶都出生在浙江省湖州市吴兴区织里镇曹家簖村,两人的家离得很近,他们在媒婆介绍下开始了这段 46 年的婚姻生活。

1971 年,18 岁的奶奶嫁给了爷爷,生下了第一个儿子我的大伯,5 年后生下了我的爸爸。

她的一生,是真的很苦吧。“我三岁,爸爸就没了。”在那个男人是家里顶梁柱的时代,一个家里少了父亲的角色,该是如何艰难地度过。据奶奶说,她只上到小学二年级,文化程度仅限于认识阿拉伯数字和几个简单的汉字。她最大的特点就是事事节省:为了省水费,洗东西总是去河边洗;为了省电费,夏天总是很早喊我起来告诉我该关空调了;过期的酸奶舍不得扔掉;给她买的新衣服永远不穿。那时的爷爷文化水平虽不高,但总给人富有学识的感觉,他爱看新闻了解时事,他的字写得很好看,他待人真诚讲义气,他脾气不好,但处理问题大多讲道理而不是乱发脾气……奶奶做事总不太“体面”,偏偏爷爷又是个事事都要做的“体面”的人,他们可以说是两个三观不同甚至没什么地方契合的一对,为什么会在一起呢?

说来好笑又可悲,因为穷。爷爷家实在穷困潦倒,家中只剩下他和一个哥哥,奶奶家中虽不富有但比爷爷家好一些,于是两人就这样将就着在一起了。用爸爸的话来说:“是真的迫于无奈。”那时的婚姻,大多迫于无奈,乡下又几乎没有离婚这种说法,合得来自是再好不过,合不来便只能当作运气不好。这段婚姻,跌跌撞撞地走过了 46 年。

那时候的夫妻,即使两人不合,也没想过分开,强忍着过下去,说到底,是为了这个家。“刚结婚的时候,我们住的房子还很破嘞,风大一点雨大一点的时候,那个窗户就哐哐响,有时候还会漏雨。"奶奶说,"后来你爷爷放映员做得好了,家里才慢慢好起来。"结婚前,爷爷当过两年的兵,退役后下乡放露天电影,他会坐着船,去各个村上放电影,那时放映的是16毫米电影胶片,放映机是手提的,被称作"流动电影机"。后来做得好了,爷爷就在村上影院里放映,轻松了很多,慢慢地又升到了影院经理的位置,奶奶也在影院门口摆起了小摊,卖些冷饮、水果,家里条件慢慢好起来,终于在1983年造了新房子。

日子就这样一天天过去,家里从一贫如洗逐渐好转,添了许多家具物件。什么飞行牌的吊扇,菊花牌的落地扇,28吋的海狮牌自行车,26吋的飞花牌自行车……都是爷爷奶奶为这个家一点点奋斗的见证。

1976年出生的爸爸,是伴随着改革开放出生的孩子。1987年,爸爸上了初中,"我初中时不爱学习,很调皮,学校外面的小店有那种3元/小时的'卡片机',放了学就和几个小伙伴冲去店里打卡片机。所以成绩也很差,还好啊,你不像我,我们老汤家出了个大学生啊,"爸爸笑着说。在我们那个小村庄,爸爸那辈的人很少有"一定要努力念书,考上好学校"这种想法,大多就是初中、高中文化水平,然后就开始打工赚钱贴补家用。

1988年,爸爸拥有了他人生中第一辆摩托车——红色嘉陵50摩托车。"我喜欢摩托车启动时轰轰的发动机声,那时骑摩托是一件很酷的事,骑着它在乡村间的小路上疾驰,不要太爽了哦。"我这才知道爸爸骑摩托的爱好,原来是从那时开始的。后来他换了五洋本田125摩托车,1997年又换了大陆易90摩托车和三阳125踏板车,零几年的时候买了本田CB125摩托车,那也是"陪伴"我的一辆摩托车。"诶呀,那时候比较穷,忙的时候没办法,我一只手抱着你一只手骑车,有时候你就趴在我背上睡着了。"说起那段时光,爸爸脸上总带着歉疚的笑。我对那些辛苦的日子似乎没什么记忆,反而一直记得夏末初秋的傍晚,坐在爸爸的摩托车后座兜风的快乐,从镇上一路回乡下,听风吹过耳畔的声音。"男人都有一个机车梦!我最大的梦想就是骑着摩托车四处旅游。"爸爸对摩托的喜爱溢于言表。2010年,家里买了第一辆小轿车,去年又换了新车。我却始终记得爸爸那辆承载着那段艰苦奋斗岁月的摩托车。

我的妈妈也是如此,七八岁的时候就要帮家里干活,下地种田。"那个时候家里很穷啊,能吃上南瓜汤、酱油饭就觉得是'美食'了。"妈妈拿起锅铲,往锅里的红烧鱼泼了点汤汁,香味四溢,转头笑着说:"小时候最期待做清明乐果和冬至团子,做好了放着,想吃的时候可以拿一个。"将鱼端上桌,她停下来,思绪飘到了二十几年前,"那时候上学的书包是用一块一块的布缝起来的,到了初中才买的书包。你小时候我告诉你,你还哭着说'你那时候那么苦的啊',哈哈哈哈。我初三之前上学都是走路,初三才买了辆自行车。十七八岁的时候就上班了。"

1999年他们结婚了,2000年,我出生了。“你爸爸那时候被朋友骗去做传销了,去河南、山西这些地方,根本不着家。不过半年就不做了,回来上了没多久的班,他觉得太平淡了,我们就开始创业。”妈妈回忆道。我们这儿的镇是“中国童装名镇”,于是他们开始买机器,做童装加工。创业之初很辛苦,为了省下一个工人的工资,妈妈也白天黑夜地干活,他们没空照顾我,于是把我养在乡下爷爷奶奶那儿。每年过年是我最开心的时候,因为可以和爸爸妈妈待的时间长一些,他们离开后,我总要抱着妈妈的衣服才睡得着。我5岁被接回去以后,就上了幼儿园。他们很忙,爸爸又很马虎,有一次把我忘在幼儿园,直到吃饭时才想起来。2006年,家里有了第一台台式电脑,生意逐渐好起来。

新中国的开始,伴随着爷爷奶奶一生的开始;改革开放的开始,伴随着爸爸妈妈一生的开始。这几十年,一个个的“小家”在一步步走向小康,祖国这个“大家”也在一步步走向繁荣昌盛。

Huzhou

Tang Zhixin (Class 192, Majoring in Journalism)

Going Through the Hard Times

"Life was really hard in those days." When I asked my grandmother about the old days, her first sentence was always the same. "It was hard." She was not a very articulate person, and she didn't say much about the past. All I could remember was the word "hard", and whenever she mentioned this word, tears came into her eyes.

My grandparents were both born in Caojiaduan Village in Zhili Town, Wuxing District, Huzhou City, Zhejiang. They lived close to each other, and began their 46-year-marriage through a matchmaker.

In 1971, my 18-year-old grandmother married my grandfather and gave birth to their first son, my uncle. Five years later, my father was born.

I supposed her whole life was really hard. "I lost my dad when I was three," she said. In those days when the man was the only one who could support the whole family, how hard it would be for her family to live without a father. According to my grandmother, since she quit school when she was in the second grade of primary school, she only knew some Arabic numerals and a few simple Chinese characters. Frugality was her greatest characteristic. In order to reduce the water charges, she would wash things in the river. To reduce electric charges, she would always wake me up early in summer to tell me that it was time to turn off the air conditioner. She would feel sorry to throw away the expired yogurt and she would never wear the new clothes we bought for her. At that time, although my grandfather was not well educated, he always appeared as a man with knowledge. He liked to know the current affairs by reading the news and his handwriting was very good. He was sincere and loyal to others. He had a bad temper, but most of the time he dealt with problems in a reasonable way instead of losing his temper. My grandma hardly handled things in a "decent" way, while my grandpa handled everything in a "decent" way. They could be said to be a couple with different views and a couple unfit for each other. How come they got married and lived together for so many years?

It was because of the poverty, which sounded funny and pathetic. My grandpa's family was so poor that he and his brother were the only ones who survived. Although my grandma's family was not rich, it was much better than his family, so they got together. In my father's words, "it was a real last resort." Most marriages at that time were against people's will, and there was almost no divorce in the countryside. It would have been great if the couple could get along. If not, it could just be regarded as a bad luck. Anyway, the marriage of my grandparents had been stumbling for 46 years.

At that time, even if the couple didn't get along, they never thought about getting divorced but making do with it. In fact, it was for the best of the whole family. "When we were just married, the house we lived in was very shabby. When the wind was stronger and the rain was heavier, the window clanged and sometimes the roof leaked," she said, "Things didn't get better until your grandfather did a good job as a projectionist." My grandpa served in the army for two years before he got married. After his retirement, he went to the countryside to show outdoor films. He would take a boat and went to various villages to show films. At that time, what were shown were the 16 mm cine films and the projectors were portable, so they were called "mobile film machines". When the projectors were upgraded later, the films were shown in the village cinema then. It became a light work, and my grandpa was gradually promoted to the position of the cinema manager. My grandma also set up a small stall at the entrance of the cinema to sell some cold drinks and fruits. The family conditions gradually improved, and finally they built a new house in 1983.

As days passed, life gradually improved from poverty to a better condition. They bought many furniture items like a Flying ceiling fan, a Chrysanthemum console fan, a 28-inch Sea Lion bicycle, a 26-inch Flying Flower bicycle and so on. These objects witnessed my grandparents' struggle for this family.

My father, born in 1976, was a child born in the wake of the reform and opening-up. He entered middle school in 1987. "When I was in middle school, I didn't like study. I was very naughty. There were 'card machines' in the small shop outside my school which cost 3 yuan an hour and I would rush to the shop with some of my friends to play those card machines after class. Therefore my grades were very poor. But fortunately, you are not like me. Thanks to you, we have a college student in our Tang family," my father said with a smile. In our small village, people of my father's generation seldom thought of studying hard and getting into a good school. Most of them would quit school after middle school or high school, and then started working to earn money to subsidize their families.

In 1988, my father got his first motorcycle—a red Jialing 50 motorcycle. "I enjoyed the roar of the engine when the motorcycle started up. Back then it was such a cool thing to ride a motorcycle. Riding it down the country road was amazing." It was not until then that I learned about my father's love of motorcycling. Later, he changed to a WY-125 motorcycle. And then in 1997, he bought a Honda Louie 90 motorcycle and a SYM 125 scooter. In the 2000s, my father bought a Honda CB125 motorcycle, which was also a motorcycle that accompanied me. "Well, we were poor at that time. Sometimes I was so busy that I could only ride my motorcycle with one hand holding you, and sometimes you would just fall asleep on my back." Talking about that time, my father always had a guilty smile on his face. I seemed to have few memories of those hard days. Instead, I always remembered the joy of sitting in the back seat of my father's motorcycle on the evening of the late summer and early autumn. From the town to the countryside, I would listen to the sound of the wind that blew through my ears. "All men have a dream of driving a motorcycle! My biggest dream is to travel around on a motorcycle." My father's love for motorcycles was beyond words. We bought our first car in 2010 and changed for a new one last year. But I still remembered my dad's motorcycle which witnessed the hard struggle years.

Life was as hard for my mother. She had to help her family at the age of 7 or 8, such as farming in the fields. "The family was so poor at that time, and the pumpkin soup and the soy-sauce rice could be regarded as delicious dishes." My mom picked up the spatula and poured some soup on the braised fish in the pot. Then it was aromatic all around the room and she turned round and said smilingly, "When I was a child, I was looking forward to making Qingming Rice Roll① and Dongzhi Tuanzi②. I would put them aside when done, so that I could take one whenever I wanted to eat." When the fish was served on the table, she stopped, and her mind returned to twenty years ago, "Back then, the schoolbags were sewn together with pieces of cloth and I didn't have one until I went to middle school. I had told you about it when you were a child. You would always cry and said I had such a hard time. Haha. What was more, I went to school on foot before the third grade of middle school, and I didn't own my bicycle until that time. I started working when I was 17 or 18."

My parents got married in 1999, and I was born one year later. "Your father was cheated by his friends into a pyramid selling scam at that time. He went to places like Henan and Shanxi, and he wasn't at home at all. Fortunately, he stopped doing it after half a year and came back to work. But he found it so dull, so we started our own business," my mother recalled. Our town was famous for Chinese childrenswear, so they bought machines and started the business of children's clothing processing. It was hard at the beginning of their business. My mother worked day and night so that they

---

① Qingming Rice Roll is made of glutinous rice together with wormwood.

② Dongzhi Tuanzi, a food people eat on Winter Solstice, is made of glutinous rice with different sweet fillings.

didn't need to hire one more worker. They didn't have time to take care of me, so they sent me to my grandparents who lived in the countryside to raise me. For me, the Chinese New Year was the happiest time of the year, because I could stay with my parents for a longer time. I used to hold my mother's clothes to fall asleep after they left. When I was five years old, my parents took me back and found a kindergarten for me. They were still very busy, and my father was careless. He once left me in the kindergarten until meal time. In 2006, we had our first desktop computer. Their business was getting better.

The life of my grandparents began as the People's Republic of China was founded; the life of my parents began as reform and opening up was started. Over the past few decades, many "small families" have gradually moved towards a well-off life, and our motherland, the "great family", is also moving towards prosperity step by step.

014

观察

时代洪流中不断向前

王忠敬

对于一些人来说，山林也许是诗意的栖居，也许是田园的想象。但对本文作者来说，童年记忆中的大山也许并非人们想象中的世外桃源。父亲的那句“总归是把你们从山里带了出来”，也许隐含着些许如释重负，似一句历经千辛万苦后的喟叹。从山上搬到山腰最后定居在山下，作者一家看似在走地理空间上的“下坡路”，但实际上，他们正是通过自己的种种努力，一步一步走出了人生的“上坡路”。

人们常说“父爱如山”，用山来形容父爱的厚重与无言。在作者笔下，父亲年轻时也一定是朝气蓬勃、活力四射的，甚至略带一丝狡黠，用各种方式最终俘获了母亲的芳心。然而当年轻的男孩变成了丈夫与父亲时，作者笔下的父亲开始默默承担起家庭的重担，像大山一样，成为家人最坚实的后盾。

在作者的叙述中，我们可以感受到父母之爱与坚毅。我们常说中国人是不善于表达爱的，但从作者笔下，我们却能读到父母相互的扶持与爱，也许正是父母间有意无意的回忆和打趣，才能让孩子对父母的恋爱史如此熟悉；从作者笔下，我们亦能读到父母对孩子无言的庇护与爱，他们的无言给了孩子一个无忧的童年，也让退伍后的孩子更加懂得并延续了这份爱。

作者记录的，并不只是一个家庭“从山里走出来”的故事，也是千千万万个家庭在时代洪流中不断奋勇向前的故事，也许会很艰辛，也许会有起伏，但依然一往无前。

（浙大宁波理工学院马克思主义学院教师，博士）

故事

温州

潘俊(新闻学专升本201班)

从山里走出来

1994年。山西太原,代县。

一个满脸胡碴,穿着牛仔裤、白色衬衫的青年踢踏着步子,朝着一间家具店大摇大摆走去。到了门口便大喊:"老陈,你家的刨子和墨斗借我一下!"店内的女孩思索片刻,这么大个汉子又不认识,万一弄丢了我还要被骂,便说"不借不借"。随后将男子轰了出去。

男子后来和家具店的老板说:"你家新来的营业员怎么这么小气,借一下东西都不肯。"老板接茬:"那不是营业员,那是我老婆的妹妹。"本就胡子拉碴的脸上,顺着一丝上扬的嘴角,有一股狡黠的味道。

没过多久,男子在陈哥旁边另外找人合资开了一家家具店。每天变着法子送早餐、西瓜、坚果,连哄带骗,KTV,公园,电影院,终于,被误以为是营业员的女孩和男子在一起了。

那一年,男子24岁,女孩19岁。男子是我爸,女孩是我妈。

1996年,正月十六,二人订婚。1997年,正月初三,二人成婚,同年4月25日凌晨两点,一声哭啼打破了棉絮一般破碎的夜空,一个毛孩出生了,全身上下没有一处不被毛发包裹,整个人不仔细看以为哪里捡来的黑猩猩。毛孩是我。

医生告诉我妈,我是个奇迹。因为在怀孕初期,我妈是不清楚自己怀了我的,当时吃了好几个月的药,药性比较大的那种。孕检时,医生建议把孩子打掉,因为这种药对孩子影响很大,很有可能生下来是个畸形儿亦或智障。我妈很坚定,"傻就傻吧,生吧,毕竟是自己的",于是我出生了。幸运的是,畸形儿和智障我都没有占。

似乎这个世界不太欢迎我的到来,除了那个年代吃饭成问题,依据当时的计划生育政策,我妈并没有到可以生育的年龄。计生办开始到处逮我妈,准备将我妈带到医院打掉我。我的上一代,家里是有很多孩子的,我妈的家族也不例外。妈妈还有两个姐姐,我的二姨,和我妈很像,我妈坐车逃到了省外,家乡计生办的人抓到了我二姨,他们一直在质问我二姨是不是在代替我妈,但是奈何没有证据，在二姨一直否认，说自己就是我妈时，这件事终于不了了之，我也在之后以一个黑猩猩的形象在当地的中医院出生。

瓯北。永嘉县的一个镇，处在那里的群山之下。

这是我后来的家。在此之前，我辗转过许多地方，这里的山头，那里的山腰。因父母在外务工，我被托管给各个亲戚，外婆，阿姨，等等。

在这里，我试着像我父母小时候一样爬上门口的梨树。我长大的时候，梨树也在长，刚开始我快些，后来，我连它脚脖子都没到，都不等等我，一点义气都没有。

同样的，我还穿起了外婆给我妈缝的布鞋，试着像我妈一样连续走3个小时，终于看到了她小时候读书的小学，一所完全是泥土垒起来的学校。听老一辈的人说，当时只有一个教室，一个老师，一二年级坐在一起，三四年级坐在一起，五年级单独一组，老师讲完高年级的课后，就会顺着年级开始讲低年级的课。我妈的五年就是在这样一所小小的屋子里度过的。

我爸爸19岁时就离开了我奶奶，准确地说，是我奶奶离开了所有人。我也大概明白了后来揍我的奶奶不是我的亲奶奶，可是她也去世了，留下了我爷爷一个人。

我妈还读书读到了小学毕业，我爸更夸张，小学都没读完。那时候流行打纸板，早上带着一块小纸板出门，傍晚回来带来一打，问他，书包里的书呢？回答道，都扔了，用来装纸板了，四四方方的小纸板。爷爷生气，一顿毒打。以至于后来我爸打我可以这么理直气壮：你别瞪眼，你爸我也是这么被打过来的！我怎么听怎么觉得不对劲。

2002年，我们家搬到了一口井旁边。那时候爸爸已经干起了现在的行当，装修油漆工。当时住了一个落地房，二层楼，那会儿租金很便宜，偌大一幢，一年租金3000元出头。当时我爸带了一大伙徒弟一起做装修，每天吃着大锅饭。我所在的幼儿园在山脚下，我住的屋子在山上，一个4岁的孩子，屁颠屁颠地背着书包就下去了。

2004年，我家换地方了，这次终于不是山上了，每天上山下山，差点以为自己在渡劫。这一年，我爸为了工作方便，买了人生的第一辆车——一辆破旧的摩托，比脚踏的自行车跑得快，也省力。我爸不用像当初上班那么辛苦，要么走路要么骑车，到了工作地点就直接开始干活，都不带喘气的。

2007年，在家里亲戚的鼓励下，爸妈一起去了杭州。在杭州下沙区开了一家“好心情”旅馆。但好景不长，杭州房东的房租越开越高，开了两年终于还是没开下去，还亏了一些。所以从小到大，我在父母身边呆的日子很少，爸妈回来了。我妈去当了服装店的营业员，我爸又干起了老行当——油漆工。

因生意失败，我们又搬家了。这一次我们住在一个夜晚几乎伸手不见五指的小区里，好在终于不是山上了，但也还是在半山腰。房子是偏现代的一幢很破旧的平房，一下雨就会漏水，常常需要我们拿脸盆、水桶去接，不然就会面临着第二天家里“水漫金山”的场景。回家的路比较难走，要经过一条长长的巷弄，狭小得只能通过一个人，如果对面来人，必须得先退出去才能进去。爸爸有摩托车上到屋子里来还比较方便，我和妈妈的自行车先不说是亲戚们剩下的很旧，光是那一段长长的上坡路我们就骑不上去，每次到那里都需要下来推车，老妈就一直念叨，要是住的地方再矮点就好了。

这样的日子持续了很久，一直到 2013 年，家里买了第二辆车，一辆 4000 块的二手奥拓。同年，妹妹出生。然后我偶尔乘车将近 20 公里去上高中，可以偷闲一下。奈何高中不努力，2015 年毕业后我就去了部队。

我在部队的两年，家里终于买了一个安置房，虽然对很多家庭来说可能不算贵，但是我家还是贷了许多款才买下了这个屋子。还没住进去呢，爸爸眼睛开始因为工作的原因变得渐渐看不见，妈妈的身体里也长了一些东西，然后做手术割掉了，而这一切，他们都只在我退伍后才和我说。这一切，让本就不富裕的家庭更吃紧。

我妈因身体不适一直在家带妹妹，我爸做完眼睛手术后，又回去做刷油漆的工作。用他的话是：“我这辈子也就这样了，我也不会其他的。你妈身体也不好，没有什么想要你去完成的，你和你妹健健康康就好。对于我自己，我觉得已经很满足了，虽然不富裕，总归是把你们从山里带了出来，也给了你们一个家。”

Wenzhou
Pan Jun (Class 201, Majoring in Journalism)

Out of the Mountains

It began in 1994 in Dai County, Taiyuan City, Shanxi Province.

A bearded young man in jeans and a white shirt strutted towards a furniture store. At the door he shouted: “Lao Chen, let me borrow your plane and carpenter's ink marker.” The girl in the store thought for a moment: I don't know that big guy, and I will be scolded in case it is lost. Then she said,

"No way! No way!" and threw out the man.

The man later said to the owner of the furniture store: "Your new assistant is so stingy; she won't even lend me anything." The boss replied, "She's not a shop assistant. She is my wife's younger sister." A sly smile appeared on that bearded face.

Shortly afterwards, the man opened a furniture store next to Lao Chen's with others. He tried every means to court that girl by bringing her breakfast, watermelons, nuts and taking her to KTV, parks and cinemas. Finally, the girl who had been mistaken for a shop assistant fell in love with the man.

That year, the man was 24 and the girl was 19. The man is my father and the girl is my mother.

On the 16th day of the first lunar month of 1996, the two got engaged. On the third day of the first lunar month of 1997, the two got married. At 2 o'clock in the morning on April 25 the same year, a cry broke out in the night with a sky that was as tattered as cotton. A hairy child was born, whose body was all wrapped by hair. If you didn't look carefully, you would have thought it was a chimpanzee picked up somewhere. It was me.

The doctor told my mother I was a miracle because she was not aware of the pregnancy in the early stage. She had taken medicine for several months, a potent one. During the pregnancy test, the doctor said, it was recommended to abort the child because this medicine had a great impact, and it was likely that she would give birth to a deformed or mentally handicapped child. My mother was very firm, "I'll give birth to it even if it will be silly. After all, it's our own child". So I was born. Fortunately, I was neither deformed nor mentally retarded.

It seemed that I was not so welcome in the world. In those days when food was a problem, the policy was that my mother was not old enough to have children. The family planning office started to look for my mother everywhere, trying to take her to the hospital and abort me. In my mom's generation, there were many children in the family. My mother's family was no exception. My mother also has two elder sisters, and she and my second aunt look alike. My mother fled outside Shanxi Province by car. The family planning office in my hometown only found my second aunt. Even though they kept questioning whether my second aunt was pretending to be my mother, there was no evidence. When my second aunt kept denying and affirmed that she was just my mother, the whole thing finally came to an end. And I was born in the image of a chimpanzee in the local hospital of Traditional Chinese Medicine.

Oubei is a town in Yongjia County at the mountain foot there.

I lived there later. Before that, I had been moving around many places, the top of the mountain here, the mountainside there. As my parents were working outside, I was sent to various relatives, my grandmother, my aunts, etc.

There, I tried to climb the pear tree in the doorway like my parents did when they were young. I was growing up while the pear tree was also growing. At first, I was growing faster. Later, I couldn't even reach its ankle, and it didn't wait for me. It really had no sense of loyalty.

I also put on the cloth shoes my grandmother sewed for my mother and tried to walk for 3 hours like her. And I finally saw the elementary school where she went in her childhood, a school completely built up in mud. According to the older generation, there was only one classroom and one teacher at that time. Students in the first and second grades sat together, those in the third and fourth grades together, and those in the fifth grade were in a separate group. When the teacher finished the lessons for the senior grade students, he/she would start to teach the junior classes in order. My mother spent five years studying in such a small house.

My father left my grandma when he was 19, or to be more precise, it was my grandma who left everyone. I came to realize the grandmother who beat me later was not my biological grandma, but she also passed away, leaving my grandfather alone.

My mother at least graduated from primary school. It was even more shocking that my father never even finished primary school. Back then, a cardboard-flipping game was popular. My father took a small cardboard with him in the morning and brought a dozen when he came back in the evening. If you asked him where the books in your schoolbag were, he only replied that they had been thrown away so that he could put cardboard in the school bag, the small square cardboard. My grandfather got angry and beat him. Later, when my father hit me, he saild, "Don't stare at me. Your father, I, went through this situation!" The more I listened, the more I felt it didn't hold water.

In 2002, our family moved to a house next to a well. At that time, my father had already started his current job as a decorator. We lived in a floor-to-ceiling house, which was a two-story building. The rent was very cheap at that time. It was such a big building, but its rent was just over 3,000 yuan a year. My father organized a large group of apprentices to do decoration together and shared food from the same big pot every day. With my kindergarten at the foot of the mountain, and the house I lived in on the mountain, as a 4-year-old kid, I went down happily with my schoolbag on my back.

In 2004, my family moved again, no longer on the mountain. If you had to go up and down the mountain every day, you would almost wonder whether you were cultivating immortality through difficulties. This year, my dad bought his first vehicle for the convenience of work, a two-wheeled motorcycle, which was faster than the two-wheeled bicycle. Though it was dilapidated, it had a gas pedal so that my father didn't have to suffer a lot from commuting. He no longer needed to walk or ride a bicycle. And he could start to work directly without taking a rest.

In 2007, encouraged by relatives at home, my parents went to Hangzhou together. They opened a hotel in Xiasha District of Hangzhou, and named it Good Mood Hotel. However, the good times did not last long. The landlord in Hangzhou asked for a higher and higher rent. Thus, the hotel was closed down after two years with some loss. I didn't spend much time together with my parents when I was little. They finally came back. My mother became a salesperson in a clothing store, and my father restarted the old business of painting and decorating.

Because of business failure, we moved again. This time we lived in a neighborhood that was pitch dark at night. Fortunately, we were not on the mountain anymore, but it was still halfway up the mountain. The house was a modern but shabby bungalow, which would leak when it rained outside. We often had to use a washbasin or bucket to hold the raindrops. Otherwise, we would experience the scene of "water overflowing Jinshan Temple" at home the next day. The way back home was difficult to walk. You had to go through a long alley, which was so narrow that only one person could pass. If someone came from the opposite side, you had to exit first and then to enter. It was easier for my father to go home becuse he was on his motorcycle. For me and my mother, the hill was so steep that is was impossible for us go up on the old bicycles that our relatives gave us. We had to get off and walk every time we went uphill. My mother kept talking if only we could live in a lower place.

This kind of life lasted for a long time until 2013 when the family bought a second car, a second-hand Alto for 4,000 yuan. In the same year, my sister was born. Then I could occasionally snatch a moment of leisure as I could be sent to high school nearly 20 kilometers away by car. However, I didn't work hard in high school, and went to the army after graduation in 2015.

During my two years in the army, my family finally bought a resettlement house. Although it may not be expensive for many families, my family still took out a lot of loans to buy this house. Before moving in, my father gradually lost his eyesight due to work, and something grew in my mother's body, which was later removed by surgery. That all of these put even more stress on my poor family was told to me only after the end of my military service.

Because of poor health, my mother stays at home and takes care of my sister. My father has returned to painting and decorating after his eye surgery. In his words, "That's how I am gonna spend the rest of my life, and I'm unable to do anything else. Your mother is not in good health. There is nothing we expect from you as long as you and your sister are healthy. For myself, I feel quite satisfied to have brought you out of the mountains and given you a home though we are not rich."

平凡无声而幸福有望

邹赜韬

平凡者的日常生活是平淡而务实的。柴米油盐酱醋茶,平凡的大多数容易满足,却总在获得简单满足的生活中,演绎着不简单的幸福哲学。对于平凡者,幸福不是华丽辞藻的堆砌,而是卯足力气加油干的奋斗,更是无数朴素愿望汇成的美好生活交响乐。聚焦平凡者的《从未如此开心过》,透过作者外公与父亲的“幸福接力”,将“幸福是奋斗出来的”解读得有滋有味。

平凡者迈向幸福的奋斗,不是一鼓作气,而是持之以恒。在慈溪市经营早餐店的十余年间,作者父亲起早贪黑。正是这十余年间伴着鸡鸣腾起的早点油烟,让他们在历经艰辛后有积蓄搬离老屋,把梦寐以求的小轿车开进自家庭院。立志千日行千里者可贵,千日不断日行一里者更可敬!

平凡者迈向幸福的奋斗,不会一成不变,总在与时俱进。2008年,已60多岁的作者外公进城定居。本可安度晚年,却为改善家庭生活,从头学习电瓶车驾驶技术,并因此顺利谋得木材厂工作。同时,作者外公敏锐觉察到杨梅季采摘劳力的供需失衡,于是在打理好自家杨梅的同时做些“兼职”。作者外公从旧日“农民木匠”摇身变成新时代“司机零工”,工种蜕变凝聚着致富信念,传递着平凡者为爱筑梦的满满幸福。

平凡者迈向幸福的奋斗,不求逐利跃进,常常向善前行。在邻居家媳妇难产却缺手术费时,作者外公掏出辛苦挣来的“压箱底”积蓄支援,甚至慷慨地婉拒对方偿还。古人云,“积善之家必有余庆”。作者外公穷生活不穷德性,以善良温暖身边人,更让善良照亮了蛰伏于艰辛日常遮蔽的幸福本真。有善的日子,就是有希望的;有希望的日子,再难终归会尝出幸福的滋味。

平凡者在务实地生存,更在为理想而奋斗。平凡者迈向幸福的奋斗,面朝“汗滴禾下”的土地,更面朝“春暖花开”的大海。

(上海大学历史学系,博士研究生)

故事

宁波

李雨婷(网络与新媒体专业 184 班)

从未如此开心过

2000 年,我出生在浙江省台州市仙居县的一个山脚下。仙居,八山一水一分田,也正是这样的地貌特征促成了我外公和我父亲的生活变迁。

我的外公,是无数个无名的底层农民中最无名的一个。他年轻时是一名木匠师傅。木匠人从小拜师学艺,三年学徒,五年半足,七年才能成师傅。学木匠很苦很累,若无惊人的毅力和耐心,是学不到家的。如果功夫不到家,就吃不到这口饭了,因为那时候人们迷信风水,没有人会要一个半桶水功夫的木匠来修缮他们安祖立业的根基老宅。在缺少粮食的那些黑暗岁月,他为别人家凿眼锯木,自己饿到水肿。因为要长期在外奔波,连家也不常回,用劳动好不容易换来的粮食也都用来养家糊口,自己没享受到分毫,只是坐在田地上吃野菜喝盐汤。家里很多常用的木制品都是外公自己亲手做的,我小的时候,目睹我外公制作木梯、木桶和一些小玩意儿,还有我从小坐到大的木板凳。

虽然外公现在已经不知道多少年没做过木工,但他如树皮般黝黑苍老的双手上仍然留下了岁月粗糙的勒痕。村里人都知道,外公是一个有着菩萨心肠的人。每年过年杀鸡宰牛,他是不会亲自动手的,平时更是连虫子都舍不得踩死一只。在最艰难的年代,当听说邻居家的媳妇难产要送卫生所却拿不出手术费时,他拿出了自家藏钱罐,从罐子里抠出一大把一分一角的皱巴巴的纸币塞给邻居,不求偿还,只当做这未出世孩子的满月钱,但实际上这点钱是他做木匠时好不容易存下来留给儿女的学费。他辛劳一辈子,养鸡,种豆,借钱,求人,赚少到可怜的钱,拉扯我的母亲和舅舅们长大成人,而如今,他自己却像熟透了的稻穗般压弯了腰,还要榨出自己最后几分精力献给劳作终生的大地。他种南瓜、玉米、红薯、稻米,自己不曾享受却全部拿来喂鸡鸭鱼犬。每年回家,大家都劝他不要做农活了,因为农产品不仅不值钱而且还难以打理,耄耋之年的老人保养好身体才是最大的福气,况且兀兀穷年到头来却全喂给了牲畜,倒像是人累死累活地去服侍那些牲畜,最后却舍不得杀它们,这又是何苦?外公轻轻地笑,挥挥手说就当自己上辈子欠了它们的吧。在这些艰难岁月里,他从来不曾忘记参悟禅理,走正道行善事。外公曾说："家里几口人，死不起，如果自己不去攒劲做，哪里有的活？"正因为心存磐石般的希望，他才能生生地承受住这生命的负荷。

外公是个木匠，但又不仅仅是个木匠，他也秉持着所有农民该有的技艺，那就是耕种。外公总对我们说："春不种，秋不收。人哄地一天，地哄人一年。"

2008年的时候，舅舅在城里找了工作，租了房子，把外公也接了去，但是外公辛劳了一辈子，也闲不下来，就提出想学着开电瓶车然后再去找一份工作。此时外公已然60多岁，家里人都不是很支持他这么做，总觉得太危险了，可最后还是拗不过他的倔脾气。外公最后学会了开电瓶车，在离家比较近的木材厂找了份工作。虽然在城里的生活比较方便，但是外公还是念叨着要住回山上，经常开着他的电瓶车沿着那蜿蜒的盘山路回他心心念念的家。尤其是在每年端午前后摘杨梅的时节，他不仅把自己家的杨梅打理好，还去合作社帮忙摘杨梅赚一些"外快"。在我的记忆中，我待在外公家时，外公好像每天都要上山或者下地干活，好像地里有挖不完的宝藏，山上有寻不完的山珍。可能只有每次过年舅舅和妈妈一起劝说他，他才甘心好好休息一会儿。

我的父亲，可以说是小小的身材，大大的能量。父亲和母亲的结合离不开外公。父亲家和我外公家隔了一座山头，直线距离非常近，但是实际上翻过一座山可把人累够呛。我父亲年轻时天天翻过那座名叫"十七岭"的山头来向我外公学手艺，一来二去，父亲和我母亲也熟络了起来。父亲是家里最小的孩子，也是家里唯一的男孩，爷爷去世得很早，奶奶眼睛又不好使，出生在70年代的父亲一个人扛起了家里的所有负担。小时候父亲带我去自家的田地里，他总是会望着那片田出神，我知道他一定是又在回忆那艰苦的岁月了。

父亲说生活真正开始好起来大概是在我出生以后。在2000年以前，父亲和母亲一直在江苏闯荡，凭借着和别人学的手艺开起了早餐店，一开始还稍有收入，后来由于同行竞争激烈，生意日渐惨淡，他们干脆就回了老家，母亲在家待产，父亲就靠帮别人造房子赚钱。但是这样的生活仅仅够温饱，父亲在我3岁的时候决定重拾老本行，和母亲一起开餐饮店，于是就带着我来到了宁波，在慈溪市胜山镇胜山塘路找了一个地段还可以的地方开起了店。

其实要说生活上的变化，体现在衣食住行方方面面，尤其表现在住和行上。在记忆中以前住的是两层的小阁楼，一楼的地面坑坑洼洼，都是时代的烙印，通往二楼的木质楼梯嘎吱作响，甚至有的台阶上还有一些小洞，每次刮风下雨屋顶上漏下的水总会滴下来，顺着地板上的小洞滴在坑坑洼洼的地上，就这样一直住了好些年。直到2016年的时候，因为村子里要建新农村，父亲这才东拼西凑了一些钱重新造了房子。"现在变化可大嘞，像以前你小的时候总是坐在我的自行车后面，脚被自行车轮子夹到了不觉得疼还只顾心疼自己新买的皮鞋。"父亲如是说道。

好像每谈到一个家庭生活质量的提升总是离不开车，父亲最初只有一辆破旧的自行车，2003 年由于开店需要进货，就买了辆三轮车，每次去进货我就躺在三轮车里和父亲一起去，进完货就躺在满满的货物上“满载而归”，后来有了些收入才把脚踏三轮车换成了电动三轮车。之后的几年里，父亲就一直在为买一辆小轿车而奋斗，这一奋斗就将近 10 年。餐饮行业是非常不容易的，他们往往凌晨 2 点就要起来准备食材，一天从早忙到晚。幸好这些付出终于得到了回报，就在 2019 年，父亲几经挑选，终于买了一辆小轿车。他奋斗了半生，好像从未如此开心过，“终于我们家也有车有房，这才叫进入了小康社会嘛”。也许这就是他开心的原因吧。

Ningbo
Li Yuting (Class 184, Majoring in Network and New Media)

We've Never Been So Happy Before

In 2000, I was born at the foot of a mountain in Xianju County, Taizhou City, Zhejiang Province. Xianju is well known for its land features of "eight mountains, one water and one farmland". It is the geographical feature that changes the life of my grandfather and my father.

My grandfather was one of the countless ordinary farmers at the bottom of society. When he was young, he used to be a master carpenter. Generally speaking, a carpenter learns from his master from his childhood. It takes three years to be an apprentice and five and a half years to be a real master carpenter. The process of learning to be a carpenter is very tough and tiring. One would never get the essence without impressive perseverance and patience. If you didn't have a good grasp of this skill, you were unable to seek a livelihood in this trade. Because at that time, people were very superstitious about geomantic omens, no one would want a carpenter who was a dabbler to repair their old house where they put the memorial tablet and built their career. In those days when there was not enough food, he chiseled holes and sawed wood for other families even though his hunger caused oedema. Because he had to work outside for a long time, he seldom went back home. The hard-earned food through his work was just enough to eke out a living for his family. He enjoyed nothing but just ate wild vegetables and drank salt soup in the field. Many wooden products in our family were hand made by my grandfather. When I was a child, I witnessed the process of my grandfather making wooden ladders, buckets and some small things like wooden benches that I've been sitting on from childhood to adulthood.

Although my grandpa stopped making carpentry many years ago, his hands, dark and old as the bark of a tree, still retain the rough and gnarled marks of age. Everyone in the village knew that my grandfather was a kind-hearted man. He wouldn't kill a chicken or an ox every Spring Festival, or even stamp an insect to death. In the most difficult times, when he heard that his neighbor's daughter-in-law had a difficult labour and could not afford the operation fee, he took out his money jar without hesitation, from which he took out a large amount of crumpled paper money, and gave it all to the neighbor. He didn't want his neighbor to pay him back, so he asked them to treat it as gift money that he would give to the unborn child when the child was one month old. In fact, the money was the tuition fee he had saved for his own children when he was a carpenter. He had toiled all his life, raising chickens, planting beans, borrowing money and asking for help. With the little money he earned, he raised my mother and my uncles. Now his back is bowed, bent like dropping ripe ears of rice, but still, he squeezes out his last strength for the land that he has worked all his life. He grew pumpkins, corns, sweet potatoes and rice, and he didn't enjoy them himself but fed them to chickens, ducks, fish and dogs. When we came back home, we all tried to talk him out of doing farm work anymore, because agricultural products were cheap and difficult to take care of. It was the best blessing for an old man to maintain his health. What's more, he fed all the animals with the food he had been busy growing all year round. It seemed like people were the servants of animals, and my grandfather was reluctant to kill them when they grew up. Was it worth the trouble? My grandfather smiled gently, waved his hand and said that he just assumed he owed them in his previous life. During these difficult years, he never forgot to meditate on the principles of Buddhism, walk on the right path and do good deeds. He once said, "There were several people in the family, and I had the responsibility to take care of them and I can't die. If I didn't struggle hard and work, how could we survive." It was his firm belief that supported him to shoulder the burden of life.

My grandfather was a carpenter, but he was more than that. He also had the skill that all farmers should have, that is, farming. My grandfather always said to us, "If you don't plant in spring, you won't harvest in autumn. You treat the land well for one day, and it will reward you all year round."

In 2008, my uncle got a job in the city and rented a house there, so he took my grandfather to live with him. But my grandfather was used to being busy all his life and didn't want to stay idle, so he suggested that he wanted to learn to drive an electromobile and then went to find a job. At that time my grandfather was already 60 years old and all the family members opposed because it was too dangerous, but failed to change his mind. My grandfather finally learned how to drive an electromobile and took a job in a lumber factory close to home. Although life in the city was more convenient, he still talked about moving back to the mountains. Every time he was homesick, he would drive his electromobile along the winding mountain road back to his home. Especially when it came to the season of picking waxberries around Dragon Boat Festival every year, he not only took care of his wax myrtle, but also went to the cooperative commune to earn some extra income. In my memory, when I stayed at my grandfather's house, he seemed to be in the mountains or fields every day, as if there were endless treasures to be dug in the mountains and in the fields. Maybe, only when my uncles and my mother persuaded him to rest during the Spring Festival could he be willing to have a rest.

My father was small but had great energy. My parents' marriage couldn't be possible without my grandfather. The linear distance between my father's house and my grandfather's was very short. However, it was extremely exhausting to climb over the mountain that was in the middle of the two houses. But when my father was young, he climbed over the mountain whose name was "Seventeen mountains" every day to learn skills from my grandfather. Gradually, my father and my mother got familiar with each other. My father was the youngest child in his family, and also the only boy. His father died young, and his mother's eyes were bad. My father, who was born in the 1970s, carried all the family burdens alone. When I was a child, my father took me to our own field. He always looked at the field in a daze, and I knew that he must be recalling his hard years again.

My father said that life truly became better since I was born. Before 2000, my parents had been wandering in Jiangsu Province to make a living. They opened a breakfast shop with the skills learned from others. At first, they could earn a little income. but later due to fierce competition, the business was getting worse and worse so they went back to their hometown. My mother was staying at home for my birth, and my father made money by helping others build houses. However, such a life was only enough for basic living needs. When I was 3 years old, my father decided to go back to his familiar work and opened a restaurant with my mother. He took me to Ningbo and opened a shop in a good location on Shengshantang Road, Shengshan Town, Cixi City.

In fact, the changes in life were reflected in clothing, food, housing and transportation, especially in housing and transportation. In my memory, I used to live in a small two-story attic. The ground on the first floor was bumpy because of the times. The wooden stairs leading to the second floor creaked, and there were even some small holes on some steps. Every time it rained, the water on the roof would drip down to the ground through the small holes on the roof. I had lived there for many years till the year of 2016 when the village planned to be renovated into a new one. Then my father scraped together some money to rebuild the house. "Now it has changed greatly. When you were a child, you always sat on the back of my bicycle. You even didn't feel pain when your foot was pinched by the wheel. Instead, you just paid attention to your new leather shoes," said my father.

One cannot talk about life improvement without mentioning the family cars. My father had only a worn-out bicycle at first. In 2003, he bought a tricycle because he needed to replenish his stock. Every time he went to buy more goods, I would lie in the tricycle. After getting the goods, I would lie on the goods and returned home with the tricycle full. Later, when they had some savings, he changed the pedal tricycle into an electric tricycle. My father had been fighting for a car for nearly 10 years. Running a restaurant was very difficult. They often had to get up at 2 a. m. to prepare food materials. Fortunately, these efforts had finally paid off. In 2019, after careful selection, my father finally bought a car. He had struggled for half a life time, and had never been so happy before. "Finally our family has a car and a house, and this is what you call a well-off life." Maybe that's the reason why he is happy.

绍兴文化的显现

赵　红

我与作者是同乡，其父母包括整个家庭的经历与我的七八分像，文章读来甚有感觉。绍兴人历来精打细算过日子，无论穷富，不显山露水，按着计划经营家庭，不停地想方设法赚钱近乎一种本能，为着日子越过越红火，这也成就了绍兴人低调内敛的师爷文化和坚韧不拔的性格特点。文中作者父母的辛勤打拼换来洋房新盖、家具更替、生活平淡美好正是最好的写照。文章彰显女性的力量，作者母亲小小年纪田间劳作、吃苦养家，对婚姻没有更多选择的余地，服从权威仍乐观向前，有独当一面的魄力，犹如绍兴传统名酒“女儿红”，撒下了孝的种子，也添了“敢”的味道。务农、务工、经商、手艺、读书等，改革开放早期，世人谋生的选择无非这几种。作者父亲如同其他肩负养家重任的男性一样，几乎尝试了所有谋生手段，不甘于续写祖辈“面朝黄土背朝天”的命运，试图创业填充增长的赚钱欲望，也有忽视读书带来的遗憾，经历过离家打工，最终凭着毅力找到一门适合的谋生手艺，坎坷探索谋生之路，犹如绍兴名小吃茴香豆软而又韧，彰显男性的顾家与担当。从前的日子从无到有，今后的日子将从有到好，继续诉说着苦难与美好、跌撞与觉醒，世人磕磕碰碰、热热闹闹呈现着不一样的小家生活，谱写着一样的大时代华章。

（浙大宁波理工学院思政讲师，硕士）

故事

绍兴

胡淡燕(网络与新媒体专业 193 班)

从无到有的日子

在长辈眼中,我一直是个需要被照顾、被操心的人。我敬他们是长辈,但却很少问过他们的过去。我从长辈口中开始了解当时那个年代亲历者的一点一滴,我深知,他们所经历的,是我这 20 年来没有想过也不敢想象的,我不清楚当我面临跟祖祖辈辈那样的经历时自己是否能够承受住他们的苦日子。

母亲的人生是从 1970 年的一个冬天开始的,她是家里最小的孩子。都说穷人的孩子早当家,在母亲的记忆中,从她七八岁开始就帮着家里做一些农活。每次放学回到家,母亲的第一件事不是写作业,也不是找小伙伴去哪里野,而是拿起一只背篓、一把老旧的镰刀,在田地里、在山间各处割草,饿了就自己在外边采些野果子吃,渴了就找一条小溪放下背篓和镰刀,俯身便能喝到泉水。

在分田到户几年后,两个舅舅纷纷出门打工,家里留下了妈妈帮衬外公外婆。因为农忙时节要插秧苗、喷农药,丰收季节又要收割水稻、晾晒谷物,加之当时农村人受教育意识薄弱,母亲在读了一年初中后就辍学回家帮着做农活了。母亲第一次收割水稻,就一大早跟外公出门,连早饭都没顾上吃。当时母亲也才十五六岁,走在水稻田里,一眼望去不仔细分辨很难看到她的身影。早晨的温度还算适宜,但随着晌午的到来,地表温度渐渐升高,加之周围密实的水稻丛,在这样的环境下多呆一秒或许都是一种煎熬,更别提还要劳动。母亲顶着饥饿和酷热拿着那把镰刀砍下了一垄又一垄,想着能帮一点是一点。将近午饭时间,母亲才放下手中的工具赶回家做饭,外公外婆则继续劳作着。母亲说那一年的农忙是她记忆中最吃力的一次,后来,母亲渐渐地开始适应这样的工作强度,这也成就了母亲特别能吃苦的品质。

或许人到一定年纪就喜欢回忆吧,并且乐此不疲。从母亲的字字句句中我可以体会她从小生活的不易,但也这样过来了。一旁的父亲显得有些沉默,只是偶尔应和一下母亲,为了让他也能够参与到这个话题中来,我把目光转向父亲,说到:“爸爸,你也分享一下你的故事嘛。”一开始,父亲似乎还有点放不开,在我的几番“引导”下,他慢慢打开了话匣子。

2001年我出生在浙江省绍兴市上虞区的一个小镇上，在这里开始了我的人生，同时这也是我家祖祖辈辈生活过的地方。

爷爷离开我们也有四五年了。爷爷奶奶有3个孩子(在当时那个时代，3个孩子并不算多)，我的父亲排在第二，他还有一个哥哥和一个妹妹。

相比于年长两岁的大伯，1969年出生的父亲初中毕业就不再上学了，跟着爷爷奶奶在田地里干一些农活，大夏天在我们的小镇上卖过冰棍，也开始了他的谋生之路。我有问起过父亲为什么不继续读下去，他的回答也很简单："当时考了两次也没考上干脆就不读了，当时的人读书的意识都还不是很强。"说完，我有注意到父亲叹了口气，眼神飘向远处的地面，沉默了一会儿，或许他当时也在思考为什么自己当时不坚持考高中。

在小镇上待了一段时间后，19岁那年父亲打算跟着几个朋友到外面闯闯，尝试着在外面找找有什么适合自己的工作。那段时间，他去过大连，去过上海，去过福建，10多个小时的绿皮火车是他印象最深的一段记忆。1988年是中国改革开放的10周年，尽管当时的大连、上海等地经济形势都较好，但父亲还是吃了读书少的苦，低学历只能让父亲从事一些体力活。说到这里，父亲似乎显得有些落寞。因为每天高强度的工作让父亲的身体有些吃不消，因此在外打工一年后他还是选择回到了家乡学好一门手艺。在师傅的带领下，父亲成功把握了装潢这门手艺，成了当地的一名油漆师傅。都说师傅领进门，修行靠个人。在正式成为一名油漆师傅之前，父亲为了尽量避免在工作中出现差错，给别人带去不必要的麻烦，就会在自己家周围的地上一遍又一遍地练习。一来对得起信任他的客户，二来也可以揽得个好口碑为自己招揽更多的活。父亲总说："不管什么行业，做什么都要对得起自己的良心。"就这样，父亲干了大半辈子这样的工作。我家虽然并不是一个富裕的家庭，但还过得去，至少我认为生活平淡而美好。

父亲和母亲之间并不是一见钟情，也没有轰轰烈烈的爱情，有的是柴米油盐，一起经历的酸甜苦辣。当时爷爷和外公是隔壁村的两个会计，所以平时多少也会有点交流，因此父母就在双方长辈的撮合下在一起了。可能对于当时的人来说很少会有因为爱情而组成家庭，很多时候觉得合适就在一起了。父母在相识两年后就领证结婚，不久就生下了我姐姐，时隔七年才有了我。

在7岁之前，连同爷爷奶奶我们一大家子的人是同住在一个三合院里的。回想那段日子，当时的家里还没有淋浴房，没有个正儿八经的厕所，没有空调，只是老式厨房、老式楼梯，门还吱吱作响……

2008年，也就是我7岁那年，父母用那些年一起打拼赚的钱又重新盖了一幢小洋房，离当时的老房子有一段距离，处在一个比较安静的地段。当时想让爷爷奶奶搬来一起住，但老一辈的人热闹惯了，对住了大半辈子的房子有种特殊的情结。为了两位老人想在老房子里度过晚年的心愿，父亲又把老房子稍稍翻修了一下。搬到新家后，伴随着小学生涯的开始，紧接着上初高中，我与爷爷奶奶见面的时间越来越少。每次去看望他们，他们总能翻箱倒柜地找出一堆吃的来招待我，还笑称我为“小客人”。这时候奶奶总会拉着我的手问我在学校怎么样，问爸爸最近在哪里工作。至于爷爷，我印象里是个和蔼的老人，他不愿我将来远嫁，希望我最好留在这片故土。一直想知道爷爷为什么有这样的想法，但到爷爷去世我也没来得及问。但我相信时间会给我最好的答案。当一件件崭新的家具、电器开始搬向家里的某个角落，我知道那是父母这些年来在这片土地上一点一滴奋斗的见证。

Shaoxing
Hu Danyan (Class 193, Majoring in Network and New Media)

Days from Zero to One

In the eyes of my parents, I have always been the one that needs to be protected and taken care of. I respect them as elders, but seldom ask them about their past. When I started to learn from them about their lives when they were young, I realized and understood deeply that what they had been through was something that I could never imagine in the 20 years of my life. I doubt I would be able to withstand the same kind of hardship if I were facing the same kind of situations.

My mother was born in the winter of 1970, and was the youngest child in her family. People always said that children from poor families manage household affairs early. As far as my mother could remember, she started to do farm work with her family when she was only 7 or 8 years old. The first thing she did every time she came back from school was neither doing her homework nor hanging out with friends, but heading to the fields or mountains to cut grass with a basket and an old scythe. When she felt hungry while cutting grass, she would just eat wild fruits. When she felt thirsty, she would lay down the basket and the scythe by the side of a creak, bending down to drink spring water.

A few years after the farming fields were distributed to families, both of my two uncles left home to work. My mother stayed to assist her parents with chores. Farmers were busy in the farming season when they needed to plant seedlings and spray pesticides and in the harvest season when they needed to harvest rice and dry grains in harvest seasons. Since people in the countryside at that time did not think education was important, my mother dropped out of school after one year in middle school, and came back home to help with the farm work. The first time she harvested rice was in an early morning, so she did not even have the time to eat breakfast before going to the fields with her father. She was only 15 or 16 years old, and you could barely see her in the rice fields. The temperature was agreeable in the morning, but as noon approached, the temperature rose gradually. Staying in dense rice fields in a temperature like that was torturing enough, let alone laboring. My mother, however, endured the heat and hunger and cut rice ridge by ridge with her old scythe. It was not until lunchtime that she stopped scything and went home to cook, while her parents continued farming. She told me that it was the hardest farm work she had ever experienced. Since then, she gradually adapted to the intensity of the work, and developed a quality of toughness.

Maybe people like to recall the past when they reached a certain age. From her descriptions, I learned how difficult her childhood was, and how she made it through anyway. My father, however, remained silent most of the time when my mother told her stories. To have him involved in this topic, I turned to my father and asked: "Dad, share with us your stories too, please?" He seemed to be a little reserved at first, but as I insisted, he gradually began to talk.

I was born in 2001 in a small town in Shangyu, a district in Shaoxing, Zhejiang Province. Our family has lived there for generations.

It has been four years since my grandfather passed away. He had three children (three was not many at that time—two sons and a little daughter). My father was in the middle.

He was born in 1969. Unlike his brother who was two years older, he quit school after middle school and came back home to do farm work with his parents. He also sold ice pops on hot summer days in our town. He started to make a living. I asked my dad why he didn't continue school. His answer was simple: "I gave up after failing twice in the test for high school. People didn't care so much about education at that time." He sighed, lowered his eyes, looked away, and didn't say anything for a while. Perhaps he was thinking about why he didn't insist on going to high school.

After living in the town for a while, at the age of 19, my father decided to get out of the town with a few of his friends, and see if he could find a job. He went to Dalian, Shanghai and Fujian. Long train trips lasting for more than ten hours left a deep impression on him. It was 1988, 10 years after the reform and opening-up. The economic situations in Dalian and Shanghai were optimistic. However, due to lack of education, he could only find manual labor jobs. Speaking of it, my father seemed a little downhearted. My father could not stand doing hard physical work everyday, so one year later, he decided to come back to his hometown and learned a trade. He learned from a master craftsman to paint and decorate. People always say that you can learn how to do a trade from a master, but can only do it well by practicing on your own. My father practiced his skills by painting on the floor near our house again and again so as to avoid making mistakes when he started to work. The practice he did was not to fail the trust his clients put into him, and also for a better reputation. He always said: "What ever your job is, you should always do it with your heart." My father has worked as a painter for his life. We are not a wealthy family, but still quite decent. At least I think our life has been stable and happy.

My parents didn't fall in love at first sight, nor did they have a romantic love story. All they had was living an ordinary life with each other, and going through ups and downs in life together. Their fathers were both accountants in a village nearby. Naturally, they brought their children together and arranged the marriage. People at that time seldom married for love, very often they got married simply because they thought they could be able to build a life together. My parents got married two years after they met. Shortly after that, they gave birth to my sister. Seven years later, I was born.

Before I was 7 years old, I, my parents and my father's parents all lived together in a three-sided courtyard house. I remembered we didn't have a shower room or a decent toilet room, nor did we have an air-conditioner. The kitchen and stairs we had were ones of the old types, and the doors were squeaky...

In 2008 when I was 7 years old, my parents spent the money they accumulated together throughout all those years to build a new house, which is in a quiet area that is a little far from our old house. We wanted my grandparents to move in too, but they preferred to stay in the old house which was not so quiet and they were obsessed with. Therefore, my father fixed our old house for them to spend the rest of their lives. I began to go to school after leaving our old house, which left me little time to visit my grandparents. Every time I visited them, they would always find a lot of snacks to treat me and call me "little guest". My grandma would hold my hands and ask me questions about school and where my dad was working. As for my grandpa, I remember him as a kind old man. He told me that he didn't want me to marry someone that lived far away, and wanted me to stay where I grew up. I have always wanted to know why he had wished that, but I never had the chance to ask him when he was alive. But I believe that someday I will know the answer. When seeing pieces of new furniture and new appliances being moved into our home, I know that the hard work my parents have done all these years are being paid off.

小康生活“时代样本”

王冬晓

从温州一户普通人家30年变迁中,我们看到了小康生活的“时代样本”。

为什么说是“时代样本”?因为它代表了千千万万普通人在改革开放大潮中,在国家实力上升期,通过辛勤劳动可以拥有的实实在在“获得感”。

30年前,作者的父亲是普通村民,30年后,他还在温州瓯海屏山村,但村民的意义大不一样。“吃改革饭长大”的温州,在传统轻工制造产业创下了许多“全国第一”,而鞋业是温州五大支柱产业之一,第二大千亿产业集群。

30年前的“父亲”凭手艺讨生活,从田间到车间,从地头到作坊,为产业发展做贡献,也在产业化中养家糊口,积攒积蓄。2008年“父亲”把小瓦房改建成五层小洋楼,现代化家电一应俱全,还把其余四层对外出租,从一个靠手艺吃饭的修鞋匠变成了出租生产生活资料的商人。

这其中除了“父亲”的辛勤劳作,我们还应该看到产业化发展带动城市化发展的时代红利。“父亲”的房子出租给了外卖小哥、快递人员、开网店的个体经营户等,而这些外来人员不也是跟随资本、产业、科技的流动而聚集,和“父亲”一样通过辛勤打拼,获得小康生活的“时代样本”吗?

(现代金报,记者)

故事

温州

郑佳慧（新闻学专升本201班）

从修鞋匠到房东

1973年，老爸出生在温州市瓯海区潘桥街道屏山村的一个小瓦房。这座小瓦房与其他几座小瓦房紧密相连，房子面朝一条小河，暴雨时，河水涨起来，与石头路中的泥土混在一起，变得浑浊；背靠着一片小竹林，风吹时，小竹林发出沙沙响声。小瓦房二层高，砖头砌成的房，木头做成的窗，推下窗户，还发出吱呀吱呀的响。台风来了，刮出了一个窗洞子，有时家人就拿着胶带补上透风的洞。

老爸在这小瓦房里渐渐长大。听妈妈讲，老爸从小就是个优等生，学习成绩总是名列前茅，100分是常事。初中那会儿，老爸有了一定的劳动力，一放学就要下田去干农活。渐渐地，他在学习上变得吃力，最后，只能放弃学业讨生活去了。

1990年，老爸17岁，初中毕业，和村里的老师傅学了三个月的修鞋手艺，便带上吃饭的家伙去市里打拼。

老爸和同村的小伙伴一起组成了找工作小分队，辗转在市里的各个鞋厂之间，第一天去西边的这家，第二天又去东边的这家。这些鞋厂大多是私立的小作坊，没有厂名。

据老爸说，鞋厂是按件计费的，因为鞋子的材质不同，修鞋就有难易，自然单价也会不同，有的三毛，有的五毛。修鞋拼的就是体力，钉、缝、粘，每个步骤都马虎不得，一双接一双，一天下来，手上都是鞋油味不说，还腰酸背痛。老爸的那双手满是老茧，留下了磕磕碰碰的痕迹。

“那时，我每天都要骑自行车一个小时到市里去。一个月下来，好像可以挣几百块。”老爸的眼睛微微向上抬，一边回忆着过去一边诉说。

年复一年，老爸靠着这门手艺，有了点积蓄，又因这小瓦房年久失修，成了一座危房，便和亲戚们借了点钱，商量着要和邻居们一起建新房。

2008年初，建房大队开着大卡车到达我家门口。建房工程开始了。小瓦房在工人的锤头下，瞬间倒塌，新房子又在工人的巧手里慢慢建成。

建房那会儿，老爸几乎不着家，天天在施工现场盯着，宛如一个包工头。他说:“我就担心他们会偷懒,到时候弄坏了,不就麻烦了。”为此,他还特地自学了一些建筑方面的知识,等房子建好了,他还考出了张二级建造师证。

2008年末,一座五层楼的大楼房拔地而起,屋内设施现代化,安上推拉窗,铺上洁白的地砖,屋外的墙面刷成绿漆。前门的石头路也改了旧貌,铺上一层沥青,便成了平坦的硬化路,屋后的竹林也被钢筋水泥所代替。

我们搬回家的那一天,好似村里的大喜事。同村的叔叔阿姨相约来帮忙。又是提行李,又是收东西,大家有说有笑地把我们这家子迎进新家。老爸乐呵呵地与各位朋友们道谢:“下次来我家喝酒。”大手一挥,高兴极了。

新房虽建好了,有了新屋,但当初建新房时向亲戚们借的钱又成了老爸心里的一块疙瘩。这么大一笔数目,只靠修鞋这一门手艺是远远不够还的。这时,老爸看到路边的租房小广告,心里一亮:“新房总共有五层,自家用占了一层,还有四层。”

老爸把自己的租房信息告诉潘桥的介绍所,写上自己的联系方式和房子的基本信息:每层125平方米,一月一千,水电自费,就等着房客电话来联系了。老爸起初还担心这起不了什么实际的作用。一来,屏山村地偏,很少有人愿意来。二来,除了自家的房子装修过,剩余几层楼都是实实在在的水泥房,除了装上了卫生间和大门,其余设备都要房客自己准备。

“我那时候就担心的呀,天天盯着手机看。”老爸说,当时他拧着眉,眼睛和手机长在一块了,定要把手机盯出来个洞不可。但当手机电话铃响起后,他的面部瞬间放松下来,心里的石头终于落地了。

让老爸没想到的是,这房子还挺火热的。来租房子的一般是外地来在这打拼的年轻人,有当快递员的,有当外卖员的,有自己开网店的。各色各样的人汇聚在这座楼房里。有住了个把月就走了的,也有提着大包小包来的。有些房客在这住了几年,出租屋也就成了一个家。自己买空调,买床,又不满意这房子架构,便自己动手做了个隔间。

在房客的一来一往、一进一出中,建房欠亲戚的钱也就慢慢还完了。我们家平平常常的日子也一直走到了今天。

Wenzhou
Zheng Jiahui (Class 201, Majoring in Journalism)

From Shoe Repairer to Landlord

In 1973, my father was born in a simple tiled-roof house in Pingshan village, Wenzhou City. The house was in line with other similar ones and all formed an adjacent structure, facing a river. Between the houses and the river lay a stone road. Whenever a rainstorm came, the river would rise upon the road and turn muddy. To the back of the house grew a bamboo grove, which rustled upon a gust of wind. The shabby house was two-story and made of brick, while its window frame was wooden. The windows would crack at one push, and could be even blown out in the typhoon season, so we had to patch the leaking window with sticky tape sometimes.

My father grew up in this house. He was such an excellent student from childhood that the full mark was not strange to him, according to my mother. During his middle school, however, he had to work in the fields once class was over, as he grew into a half labor force then. In this way, he had trouble in learning over time, and eventually had to drop out of school to make a living.

In 1990, after three months experience as an apprentice of a shoe repairer in the village, my father went to the city to seek his fortune, with a junior diploma, a kit of shoe mending tools, and his braveness. He was only 17 years old.

He and his fellow villagers teamed up to seek jobs, shunting around the shoe factories across the city. Today here, tomorrow there. Most of the factories were small private workshops without brands.

My father said the craftsman for the factory was paid on a piece basis and the unit price varied according to the shoe materials, as different materials posed different demands on a craftsman's skill. Some were worth three jiao, while others five. Mending shoes was literally manual labor, demanding meticulous craftsmanship in every procedure-pinning, stitching, sticking-one by one. After a day's work, one's hands were stained with shoe oil and his back arched with tiredness. I looked at my father's hands, and noted thick calluses all over them and traces of bruise were left.

"In those days, I rode to the city for an hour every morning. I could earn about several hundred yuan in a month." Eyes raised a bit, he reminisced about the past days.

Through shoe mending, my father saved up some money after years of working. He thought about building a new house, as our old tiled-roof one had fallen into disrepair. Therefore, he borrowed money from his relatives, and discussed with his neighbors about it.

In early 2008, a construction truck rumbled all the way to my front door. And then the house building began. The old tiled-roof house was toppled down under the worker's hammer, while the new modern building erected piece by piece.

During the time, my father would go to the construction site to supervise the workers every day. "I was worried about their perfunctory work. It would be a real trouble if something went wrong." For that reason, he learned about construction by himself, and even passed the national second-level examination for certified architects after the new house was constructed.

At the end of 2008, a brand-new five-story building stood upright before us. Its façade was painted green. And when walking inside upon the white-tiled floor, you could find modern appliances almost everywhere. The wooden windows were replaced by the sliding ones, from which you could see the former stone road which was also transformed into an asphalt pavement.

The relocation of my family was a big thing in the village. That day, villagers came around to my house to welcome us home. They chatted and laughed, and helped us carry luggage and put away things. My father thanked them gladly: "Come over and drink with me sometime."

After the house building, the money my father borrowed from his relatives became his major concern, as for such an amount, only by shoe repairs he could never make enough. Then he incidentally saw the rental ads around the street, and came up with an idea: "Since our family only takes up one out of five floors of the house, the rest could rented."

He thus entrusted a house rental agency in the town with this business, attached with his contact details and the basic information of the house: 125 square meters per floor; 1, 000 RMB per month, exclusive of water and electricity. Then all he waited for was a tenant. Initially he was worried that this advertisement wouldn't be helpful: for one thing, few people were willing to come to the remote village of Pingshan and stay here; for another, other than the single floor our family lived in, the house was a real cement building with no decoration and furniture. Except for the front door and toilets, tenants would have to prepare other devices by themselves.

"I was so concerned that I looked at the phone all the time, waiting for somebody's call," said my father. At that time, he frowned, and his eyes couldn't get away from the cell phone as if he would dig a hole in the phone by his gaze. When the phone was ringing, finally, his face relaxed and heart relieved.

Out of his expectation, the house of my father's turned out to be a "hot cake". Most of his tenants were young people who came from other places for jobs. They earned their living by various means-courier, food deliveryman, online shop owner and so on. All kinds of people lived in the house. Some lived and left after months, some carried with themselves much luggage, some stayed for years and made the house their own home, and some even made a compartment by themselves, after purchasing an air-conditioner and a bed, because they were unsatisfied with the structure of the house.

As the tenants came and went, my father paid off his debts little by little, and since then lasts the ordinary and harmonious life of my family.

创业艰难百战多

刘建民

大不了从头再来！耳边回旋的是上个世纪90年代内地歌手刘欢演唱的歌曲《从头再来》。那时候这句话曾经成了中国改革开放进程中的一个特殊阶段的流行语汇。

20世纪90年代中后期的中国处于无外需又无内需的经济萧条期，整个产业链条的停滞让链条上的所有企业都面临着尴尬的境地，工人失业也集中于这一时期。1998年政府提出花三年的时间解决国企裁员问题。“下岗再就业”就成了当时举国关注的重要工程。

薛佳颖同学家的故事不是这种背景里的下岗再就业故事。她家的故事讲的是一个普通的打工家庭办厂的一波三折。2017年的一场大火，烧毁了她父母辛辛苦苦办起的两个厂，几年来所有的心血在大火中被摧毁得一干二净。火焰将息，作者听到妈妈沙哑的声音从话筒中传了出来：“没关系的，家里一切都好，爸妈都没事，只是小火，妈妈很快会再开一家，你不要担心，只管好好读书，这周末先不要回家了。”看似平淡的语气，却透出一介平民百姓在创业之路上涅槃重生的坚定信念。这位妈妈如何自救，如何终结厄运，如何组织换厂地，如何重新组织生产……大家可以展开故事去读。

看完这个故事，我想把刘欢当年唱的歌再播一次给这个起死回生的家：“心若在梦就在，天地之间还有真爱。看成败人生豪迈，只不过是从头再来。”我更愿意把陈毅写的《梅岭三章》七言绝句翻出来，与所有的创业者共勉：处在危难之际，但献身革命的决心和对革命必胜的信心却矢志不移，革命乐观主义精神是中华民族的宝贵精神财富，激励着一代又一代华夏后人为中华民族的伟大复兴艰苦创业，勇往直前。

陈毅的诗是这样写的：断头今日意如何？创业艰难百战多。此去泉台招旧部，旌旗十万斩阎罗。

（浙大宁波理工学院传媒与法学院，高级编辑）

故事

绍兴

薛佳颖(新闻学专业 202 专升本班)

大不了从头再来

我在厂里住了小六年的时间,从我的初中到高中,我所有对家的记忆,都在妈妈换的几家厂里。“那有什么办法嘛,那时候给你买药都买不起。”妈妈望着我的眼神中透露着无奈。

我是个名副其实的药罐子,8 岁被检查出先天性疾病,至此父母就带着我开始了漫漫求医路,绍兴,杭州,上海,北京,城市与城市之间的反复辗转,记忆里最深的是灰扑扑的大巴和一列列长长的绿皮火车。

“你那时候吃中药,一个月要 1200 元,那些收据单,我都攒着,你长大了再来报销。”报销一直是妈妈的玩笑话,我看着手里厚厚一叠的药费单子。

家纺厂开起来,无他,为了给我治病,为了给我赚点药钱。

妈妈在过去三十几年的人生里,一直过着保守而普通的被雇者的生活。在她的固有思维里,领着一份固定的工资,过着朝九晚五的固定生活,已然成为习惯。那么这个决定,意味着打破所熟知的一切,让一个 36 岁的中年女性从头开始,可想而知的困难。

“这厂开起来的时候啊,我银行卡里的钱加起来才 1 万,其他钱都是借的,你妈就靠着这么点钱把厂搞起来了。”妈妈说这话的时候带着些许的自豪。

决定开厂后,妈妈开始四处奔波,为了找一个合适便宜的厂房。当时工业园区的房租很贵,妈妈把目光放在绍兴市柯桥福全龙尾山的废弃礼堂,那年的房租只要 4 万。接着她去二手机器市场淘了一批电脑缝纫机,再购置一些杂物,装好电线。

几天后,厂牌终于送了进来,红色的。母亲一直都没告诉我新厂的名字,说是给我一个惊喜,挂厂牌的那天我去了,我看到“乐乐家纺”那四个正正方方的大字,被工人用绳子拉着,往上抬,一直固定在厂房的最上方,我看着母亲的视线随着那一抹红色起起伏伏,她的眼中有坚定,也有迷茫。

为了少请一个门卫,减少一点开支,厂子启动后的一个月,我们就搬进了厂里,一边做着名义上的老板,一边承担着门卫的工作。

“第一年真的难呐，赚的钱只够给工人发工资的，一年到头，啥都没剩下，白忙活。”

转机出现，是在第三年，妈妈高兴地告诉我，我们接到大单子了，那是原来合作的上家，原来和我们没有什么直接接触的机会，因为我们之间的中间人搞错了订单，一批货的尺寸全部弄错了，客户投诉要求重做。也是因为妈妈之前出货的品质尚可，那家宁波外贸公司直接找上了妈妈，询问她是否可以接下这个单子。

“那批货花头多得很嘞，花型有十几种，商标有十几种，纸箱型号又都不一样，我都要看着，不能出错。”接下单子已经在10月份了，年底要出货，短短两个月时间要做完，还不能出现大的纰漏。那段时间是真的忙，有时我晚上叫妈妈吃饭，就看见她站在两辆拉边缝纫机旁边，用砖头放在踏板上代替脚，眼睛死死盯着工作中的针头，一伸一缩之间，长长的花边带飞速落下，掉在框中。匆匆扒拉两口饭，她又回到工作岗位上。

12月出了货，1月收到了货款，那是开厂后第一个富裕的新年，妈妈看着卡里的钱，笑着和我说：“以后药钱就不用发愁啦。”

做完这单生意后，妈妈突然意识到在绍兴还极少有厂专门做压边靠垫，这是一项新的商机，于是开始转型，将单子的重心放在靠垫上。但是靠垫的填充物主要是片状海绵，非常占地方，这个由废弃礼堂改造的厂子终于还是不够用了，妈妈开始物色新的地址。

新址选在绍兴福全的环岛园区里，上下两层，大约1200平方米，足够加工材料的堆放。

第二年，妈妈靠垫的生意已经做得非常红火了，缝纫机的声音一直到晚上八九点才停下，款式也由原来的单一的压边靠垫，发展为充棉靠垫。充棉的单子很多，有时外派出去又来不及，妈妈思前想后，决定自己开一家充棉厂，在给自己出货的基础上，还能接到一点别的单子。

有了之前开厂的经验，充棉厂的运营非常迅速。前后不到一个月，妈妈在家纺厂旁边租了个小厂房，设备非常简单，两台充棉机，一台压缩机，加上几个员工，充棉厂就风风火火地开了起来。妈妈一个人也终于是管不过来了，叫爸爸辞去工作，一起帮衬着。

家里的条件似乎是好了起来，爸妈也在2015年买下了第一套房，虽然不是我所期待的高层，但是带着一个小花园，妈妈指着那块花园笑着说：“回头啊，这里就给你爸种菜用，再养几只鸡，搞个农家乐。”

2017年，我很难再去回忆这一年的细节，低靡、悲痛、无奈。

一场大火，烧毁了两个厂，爸妈这几年来所有的心血也在大火中被摧毁得一干二净。

5月30号早上7点，爸妈照常起床开工，一同往日的平静。8点，靠墙的女工们都开始觉得越来越热，空气里弥漫着一股看不见的热浪，爸爸上去查看，透过铁皮之间的缝隙，看见隔壁的仓库里一片红色，是火，火在燃烧……大火持续了一个多小时，消防车赶来时，现场已经和废墟别无两样了。

家族群里那段视频我反复看了十几遍，我也从未想过我的眼泪能流得那么快，那么多，多到止也止不住。

给妈妈打电话的手一直在抖，电话只响了两声，接得很快，我听到妈妈沙哑的声音从话筒中传了出来，妈妈告诉我："没关系的，家里一切都好，爸妈都没事，只是小火，妈妈很快会再开一家，你不要担心，只管好好读书，这周末先不要回家了。"

"全烧光了，要赔的钱这么多，没办法啊，有什么办法能赚这么多钱去赔偿那些货啊，只能重新再把这个厂开起来。"那是我再一次见识到妈妈女强人的一面。就在意外发生的第三天，妈妈就开始强迫自己振作，和爸爸一起找起了新工厂址。一个星期后，当我从学校回家时，又看到了一个简易的临时工厂，在绍兴富强的一个新的园区里。

那是家里起伏最大的一年，火灾后，后续很多事情要处理，重新开厂，赔偿订单损失，打官司。直到年末，房东又突然来联系妈妈说，这临时工厂要拆了重建，需要我们搬走，接二连三的麻烦事仿佛都在这噩梦一般的2017年发生了。

年末，终于又搬好了厂，这是第四次换地了，妈妈坚决地换到了安全系数相对高的标准化工业园区，也给厂子买了保险。下半年一直在补被烧的订单，也都在年末全部赶完出货了。妈妈的生意伙伴大都是和气人，对我们一家的遭遇表示同情，承担了小部分的损失。厄运应该是被终结在了2017年。

此后，日子倒也算是顺风顺水，法院的批文终于下来了，虽然赔偿的结果不尽人意，但总归也给了妈妈一个交代。家里也装修了新房，爸爸买了一直以来都心心念念的爱车，我也考上了心仪的学校，一切都在朝着更好的方向发展。

今年，我也完成了一直以来的一个小心愿，拉着爸妈一起去拍了第一张全家福，照片打印出来放在爸爸的茶室里。家呐，只要人在，家就在。

Shaoxing
Xue Jiaying (Class 202, Majoring in Journalism)

Start All Over Again at the Worst

I lived in factories my mom worked in for nearly six years, so my memory of home from the junior high school to the senior high school was all about those factories. "I had no other options. We even couldn't afford your medicine at that time," said my mom, looking at me with resignation in her eyes.

I, diagnosed with a congenital disease at eight, was a chronic invalid. Ever since my diagnosis, my parents and I embarked on a long journey seeking treatment, shuttling between cities like Shaoxing, Hangzhou, Shanghai and Beijing. Grey coaches and long green trains were deeply imprinted on my memory.

"The traditional Chinese medicine you took then cost 1,200 yuan every month. I have collected all those receipts and have been waiting to get reimbursement from you once you grow up." Seeing a pile of medical bills in my hands, I know reimbursement is meant only as a joke.

The only purpose my mom started a textile factory was to earn money to pay for my medical bills so that I could be cured.

My mom had led a conventional and conservative life in the three decades of her life. She had much accustomed to getting a fixed and stable monthly income by doing a nine-to-five job. It was naturally very difficult for a 36-year-old woman to get out of her comfort zone and make a fresh start.

"With savings of only 10,000 yuan and some borrowed money, I started the factory from scratch," said my mom, with pride.

My mom started rushing about in order to find an appropriate and inexpensive factory site. Seeing the high rents in industrial parks, she turned her eyes to a deserted assembly hall in Longweishan Village, Fuquan County,

Keqiao District, Shaoxing City, Zhejiang Province, the annual rent of which was only 40, 000 yuan. She then purchased several computerized sewing machines from second-hand household appliance markets and some miscellaneous items, and wired up the whole building.

A few days later, the signboard of the factory finally arrived. It was a red signboard. My mother didn't tell me the name of the new factory, saying it was a surprise. I was there on the day when the signboard was put up. The name, "Lele Home Textiles", was printed on it. As the board was slowly pulled upwards by the workers with rope and then fixed at the top of the factory, my mother kept staring at the red board, with a confused yet firm look in her eyes.

One month after the establishment of the factory, we moved into the factory so as to save the cost of hiring janitors. We were bosses in name and janitors as well.

"It was extremely difficult in the first year. Excluding money to pay for salaries, your dad and I barely earned anything."

Our luck finally came in the third year when my mom told me excitedly that we clinched a big order from an indirect buyer, with which we couldn't have had any direct contact at all if the middleman hadn't got specifications wrong. Wanting the goods to be remade and thinking highly of the quality of previous goods, that Ningbo-based foreign trading company approached our factory and asked whether we were willing to accept the order.

"I had to supervise every step to avoid mistakes since there were over ten patterns and trademarks. Besides, even the specifications of cardboard boxes varied." It was an extremely busy period for we only had two months of lead time before delivering goods at the end of the year. Sometimes when I called my mother for dinner in the evening, I saw her standing next to two top-rolling sewing machines, with a brick placed on the pedal as her foot and her eyes fixed on the needle. As she leant her body back and forth, long strips of lace kept falling in the basket. After two quick bites of food, she returned to her work again.

We delivered goods on time in December and received payment the very next month. That was the first prosperous New Year for us since the factory opened. Seeing figures on the passbook, my mom said to me with a smile on her face, "We will no longer worry about your medical bills."

After that deal was wrapped up, it dawned upon my mom that there were very few factories dedicated to making beaded cushions in Shaoxing, which was a niche market. Therefore, my mom decided to shift the business focus onto cushions. However, flaky sponge—the cushion fillings—occupied so much space that the original deserted assembly hall no longer sufficed. My mom had to look for another site.

The new two-story factory, located in the roundabout industrial park in Fuquan County, occupied an area of 1,200 square meters, enough to stack processing materials.

The cushion business was booming the next year, with sewing machines operating until eight or nine at night. My mom also expanded the business scope to cover cotton-quilted cushions. She, considering huge demands for cotton-quilted cushions and occasional tight lead time, later decided to set up a cotton-quilting factory so as to ensure raw material supply while selling the rest to other buyers.

Based on previous experience, my mom, having rented a small factory next to the original textile mill, bought two cotton-quilting machines, one compressor, hired several workers and set up the cotton-quilted cushion factory within a month. Having two factories to attend to, my mom had her hands full and had to ask my dad for help. Therefore, he resigned and joined the factory.

Life seemed to become better, and my parents bought our first house in 2015, not the high-rise type I had always dreamed of, but a bungalow with a garden. "Your dad could grow vegetables and keep some chickens here—a perfect place for agritainment," chuckled my mom as she pointed to the garden.

Everything changed in 2017 and it is still heart-breaking to recall that year. All I remember was how depressing, painful and hopeless 2017 was for my family.

A blaze burned into ashes not only two factories but my parents' years of effort.

Everything seemed as normal when my parents got up for work at 7 am on May 30. At eight, female workers sitting near walls felt the temperature go up and invisible heat waves were in the air. My father peeped through chinks in the iron walls and found out the warehouse next door was on fire... The blaze raged on for over an hour and burned almost everything into ashes when the fire engines finally arrived.

I replayed the video clips which were shared in the family group chat many times, and never before had I realized that I was able to shed so many tears so quickly.

As I called my mom, my hands shook terribly, and soon I heard my mom's hoarse voice as she picked up the phone and said, "Never mind. It was just a small fire, and everything is all right with your dad and me. I will soon start again. There is nothing for you to worry about but your own study. Just stay at school for the upcoming weekend."

"I had no better idea to make up for the destroyed goods than to rebuild the factory." In handling the terrible situation, my mom once again demonstrated her perseverance and tenacity. The third day after the accident, my mom put herself together and started seeking for another factory site together with my dad. When I returned home one week later, I saw a makeshift factory in a new industrial park in Fuqiang Village.

The year of 2017 brought the most dramatic twists and turns to my family. There were so many follow-up things to attend to, like restarting the factory, compensating for clients' losses and going through legal procedures. To make things worse, the landlord asked us to move out at the end of the year since the makeshift factory needed to be demolished. All sorts of troubling and upsetting things happened in that nightmarish year.

We finally completed the fourth relocation and settled our factory in a standardized industrial park with safety guarantees as strongly insisted by my mom. We also insured the factory. Pooling all resources to make up for the destroyed goods in the second half of the year, we finally delivered all products before the year ended. Our business partners, kind and considerate, related to our encounters and offered to bear a small proportion of the loss. Misfortune was finally left in 2017.

Things have gone smoothly ever since. Court rules, though not satisfying enough, at last brought the whole thing to an end. Our new house was decorated, my father bought his favorite car and I was admitted to the ideal school. Everything was moving on the right track.

This year, we took our first family photo at my request and a photo copy has been put in my dad's teahouse. Home is such a magic place: it's always there as long as family members get together.

019

观察

“千万工程”打造农村新家园

吴　琼

房子对于中国人来说意义重大。人们将房子作为安身立命的场所，有了房子才有在这个世界上的归属感。《汉书·元帝纪》提到：“安土重迁，黎民之性；骨肉相附，人情所愿也。”故房子于中国人而言，是依靠，是保障。从一定意义上来讲，房子就是家的缩影。人们生活的幸福指数，很大程度是和房子有关。

居住在湖州市吴兴区环渚乡欣安村的沈静一家，通过她的《房屋的变迁》向我们展示了最近十年她家房屋翻天覆地的变化：从平房到自建的双层小楼，到目前安居的小区多层楼房。她一家的家居环境变化，正是浙江省“千万工程”造就的万千美丽乡村中的一个缩影。

湖州是习近平总书记“绿水青山就是金山银山”理念的诞生地，是中国美丽乡村发源地。2003 年，浙江省启动“千村示范、万村整治”工程，通过全面推进村内道路硬化、垃圾收集、卫生改厕、河沟清淤、村庄绿化和房屋拆迁改建等，对农村人居环境进行大改建。据了解，浙江 5 年内建成了 1000 多个全面小康示范村和上万个环境整治村。

身处浙江的我们，深切地感受到这些变化。之前，农村人羡慕城里人，有车有房，上班方便。如今，浙江的新农村不仅道路干净，空气清新，大多数村民住上了现代化的排屋。每到节假日，城里人更乐意跑到农村去放松，亲近大自然。美丽乡村不仅成为农民美好生活的幸福家园，也成为城里人休闲旅游的“大花园”。

（浙大宁波理工学院传媒与法学院思政讲师，硕士）

故事

湖州

沈静(新闻学专业191班)

房屋的变迁

我家的房屋在改革开放的40多年里发生了不可思议的变化。从一层平屋再到小楼房再到现在的多层房屋中的一层,它可以被看作我们家生活水平变化的标志,也可以被看作万千户湖州人民生活水平提高的缩影。

我出生于湖州市吴兴区环渚乡欣安村西南湾的一栋双层小楼房。楼房的南面有一片宽阔的稻场,在水稻丰收的季节它被用来晒谷子,这时,我的太爷爷会使用一把像猪八戒的武器般的农具把稻谷翻来覆去,金黄色的稻谷十分好看。我曾经快乐地往上一躺,结果爬起来时后背扎满了稻谷。当没有被稻谷占领时它可以被用来看星星。小学的时候我学习到关于张衡和星星的课文,脑海中出现的就是张衡坐在我家的稻场上观看星星的画面。稻场的南边,有两个平屋从地上生长出来。现在的城市里没有水稻,也没有稻场,有时候连星星也没有。

据我奶奶说,在我出生前,靠东的那间曾经被用来织机。织机在我的印象中,就是把一根根线变成一块块布的行动。我没见过自己家织机,但是我见过别人家织机。我小时候,乡下千家万户都在织机。每家每户都有一间神秘的房屋被用来织机,但我非常不喜进入织机的场所。我曾经潜入过姑姑家织机的场所,织机的声音震耳欲聋,假如你要和正在织机的人说话,实在是要使出吃奶的力气。现在回想起来,我发觉这真是一个巨大的产业,每村每户都在织机,这个产量真是惊人,现在却像人间蒸发一样,不知道那些机的踪影了。

湖州现在有一个有名的公园叫西山漾,它是最近几年才建设起来的。为什么要提它呢?因为据我奶奶说,在楼房之前我们家只有一排平屋。我爸爸小时候,也就是改革开放没多久,我爷爷和奶奶要建造楼房,他们就去西山漾上弄石头来建造我们家的房屋。

我现在实在想象不出他们去西山漾弄石头的画面。在我的印象中,建造房子会有专业的团队拉来一车车建筑材料开始一点一点建造房屋。我也实在想象不出生活在平屋里是多么凄惨。我奶奶这边的太爷爷和太奶奶的房子是我印象中唯一住人的平屋。他们的地上没有瓷砖和地板,只有硬梆梆的泥土,虽然如此,他们仍然生活得十分愉快,毕竟是经历战争年代和新中国成立这些大事件的人,吃苦耐劳、勤俭持家是他们的宝贵品质,但是假如叫我生活在这样艰苦的条件中,我必定会逃之夭夭。可以说多亏了改革开放,我才不至于沦落到住平屋。

我对于造房子的印象来源于我们家的另一栋楼房。它出现在我妹妹出生后,据说我爷爷花了10万元来建造它。对于当时的10万元我没有概念,只感觉是一个虚无缥缈的天文数字,谁知道它现在只能在市区里买一个厕所呢。楼房取代了两间平屋,霸占了一大半稻场。我爷爷请了一个姓杨的师傅来统领房子的建设。我当时正在读小学,只记得它一点点地拔地而起。我亲眼看到了楼的建造,看到了它从无到有的过程。

现在湖州农村造小洋房都十分讲究,不像以前那样粗糙,精致得可以被称作中国农村的城堡。以前除了光滑的地砖和雪白的粉刷就别无他物了。我们新房子没有精致的装修,显得很空旷,我甚至可以在家里面溜旱冰。新楼房一共有3层,实际上第三层没有什么用处,下雨的时候还漏水。唯一的有用处是南面的阳台,它可以被用来观看风景,假如有幸遇上下雪还能堆雪人。建造了新的房屋之后我的爷爷奶奶仍然住在以前的房子里。

快拆迁的时候,我爸爸给我妈妈买了一个iPhone 4,我感到梦幻和不真实,然后和妹妹抢着玩她手机上的神庙逃亡。我用iPhone 4拍了我们家的角角落落,免得我以后想到在农村的生活连个记忆碎片也没有。以前用手机拍出来的照片,和现在的简直没法比,但是在我以前看来,用手机拍出那样的照片是一件非常神奇的事情。

拆迁是为了顺应整个城市的发展,我们村拆迁之后我曾回到我的老家。那里已被用作工业用地,简直可以用断壁残垣来形容。拆迁之后,太湖流域的一部分肥沃的水稻田被水泥地取代了。这多亏了生产力水平的提升,否则生产的粮食不够多我们将饿死。种田实在不是一件悠闲的事。太湖流域的水稻种植水平一直可以的,但是农民仍然要吃苦。长江中下游到了七八月份的伏旱天气,干农活热得要死,我的太爷爷种了一辈子地,整个人都晒成了古铜色,到了夏天,瘦骨嶙峋的他就穿着一个短裤在家里晃悠。

拆迁之后我们得先到别的小区租房子过渡。我爸爸很嫌弃过渡的地方,因为以前两栋楼房里的东西全部塞进了150平方米的空间,又挤又破。现在我居住在建造好的新小区里面,假如叫我再去住过渡时期的房子,我是万万不愿意的。

我奶奶现在仍然对我们家拆迁的时机不好耿耿于怀。我那时候15岁,能分到50平方米的房屋,但是假如16岁,就可以分到100平方米,她说我要是早点出生就好了。我太爷爷在拆迁前的几年里去世了,假如他没有去世,我们家就可以再分到100平方米的房屋,他也可以过过城里人的生活。

过渡了4年,我们新小区里的房子装修好了,装修房子花掉的钱可以在以前的农村建一栋小楼房。我像模像样地过上了印象中城里人的生活。

我发觉我们的生活就像政治书上说的一样,是一个螺旋式上升的过程,它在这个过程中发生了惊人的变化。

当我住在农村里的时候,我是绞尽脑汁也想象不出现在的我会生活在这样美好的环境。而这样惊天动地的变化竟然只发生在10年间。农村的人们舍弃了水稻田和一排排的织机,把自己土生土长的农村变成了城镇,假如没有社会财富的增加,这是很难实现的。我从出生起搭上国家快速发展的列车,过上了以前的人们梦寐以求的生活,更是可以有机会去千里之外的城市上学。能过上这样幸福的生活,我真得感谢改革开放中的每一颗螺丝钉。

Huzhou
Shen Jing (Class 191, Majoring in Journalism)

The Changes of the Housing

My family's house has undergone incredible changes in more than 40 years since the reform and opening up. From a bungalow to a small house, and then to a floor of the current multi-storey building, it can not only be regarded as the symbol of the change of living standards of our family, but also as the epitome of the improvement of living standards of thousands of Huzhou people.

I was born in a small double-storey house in the countryside of Huzhou. There was a wide threshing ground on the south side of the house which was used to dry grain during the rice harvest season. At that time, my great-grandfather would toss the rice over and over with a farm tool like Pigsy's spike-tooth harrow. The golden rice was so charming. I used to lie on it happily, but got up with my back full of rice. If there was no rice on the ground, I would be there to watch the stars. When I learned a text about Zhang Heng and the stars in primary school, what came to my mind was the picture of Zhang Heng sitting on the threshing ground of my house to watch the stars. On the south of the threshing ground, two bungalows were built from the ground. But now, there is no rice, no threshing ground, and sometimes no stars in the city.

According to my grandma, the bungalow to the east had been used as a loom room before I was born. The loom, in my mind, was the action of turning threads into cloths. I never saw a loom at home, but I saw looms at others' home. When I was a child, there were looms in thousands of families. At that time, every house had a mysterious room which was used as a loom room, but I really didn't like entering such a place. Once I sneaked into the loom room of my aunt's house, and the sound of the loom was so deafening. If you wanted to speak to someone who was working on it, it would take all your strength. Looking back on it, I found it was really a huge industry that every household in village was engaged in it and its output was really amazing. But now, the looms suddenly disappeared. I didn't know where all those machines had gone.

There is a famous park in Huzhou called Xishanyang Park, which was built several years ago. Why should I mention it? Because according to my grandma, our house was just a bungalow before we moved into a small house. When my father was a child, that was not long after the reform and opening up, my grandparents wanted to build a house, so they went to Xishanyang Park to find stones to build our house.

I can hardly imagine the scene that they came to Xishanyang Park to bring stones. In my impression of building a house, professional teams would bring in loads of building materials to start building the house bit by bit. Similarly, I can't imagine how miserable it was to live in a bungalow. My great-grandparents' bungalow was the only place where we could live in my memory. There were no ceramic tiles and floor boards but only hard earth. In spite of this, they lived a contented life. After all, they were the people who had experienced such great events as the War of Resistance against Japan and the founding of the People's Republic of China, and their precious qualities were their willingness to bear hardships and their diligence and thrift in running the household. But if I had lived in such hard conditions, I would definitely have run away. Thanks to the reform and opening up, I don't have to live in a bungalow.

My impression of building a house came from another house in our family, which was built after my younger sister was born. It was said that my grandfather spent 100,000 yuan to build it. At that time, I had no idea about such a large sum of money. I just felt it was unreal and huge. No one could have imagined that all that money could only buy a bathroom in the city nowadays. The house replaced two adjacent bungalows and occupied more than half of the threshing ground. My grandfather hired Mr. Yang, a master, to organize the construction of the house. I was in primary school at the time. All I could remember was it rose up little by little. I saw the whole progress of how it had been built from nothing.

Now, the construction of houses in the countryside of Huzhou is very particular, which is not as humble as before. It is so delicate that it can be called China's rural castle. By contrast, there was nothing precious except the smooth floor tile and white paint in the past. Since there was no large pieces of furniture, our new house looked very spacious, and I could even roller-skate inside. The new house had a total of three storeys, but the third floor was actually useless and leaked when it rained. The only advantage was that the south balcony could be used to view the scenery. If I was lucky enough to meet a snow day, I could make a snowman there. Although the new house had been built, my grandparents still lived in the old house.

When the house was about to be pulled down, my father bought an iPhone4 for my mother, which made me feel dreamy and unreal. And then my sister and I scrambled to play the Temple Run on the phone. I photographed everywhere of the house with the iPhone 4, just in case I did not have a shred of memory when I thought of life in the countryside. There is no comparison between the photos taken in the past and those taken nowadays, but in my eyes at that time, it was an amazing thing to take such photos with a mobile phone.

The demolition was in response to the development of the whole city. After the demolition of the village, I went back to the site of the old house, which could be described as ruins. Now, the site has been turned into industrial land. Part of the fertile rice fields along Taihu Lake Basin was replaced by concrete. Had it not been for the productivity increase, I would have starved to death. Farming is really hard work. The rice production in the

Taihu Lake Basin has basically been sufficient, but farmers still have to endure hardship. In July and August, the middle and lower reaches of the Yangtze River entered the drought season and it was very hot to do farm work. My great-grandfather did farm work all his life, so his whole body became bronzed. When summer came, he wore a pair of shorts and wandered around the house.

After the house was demolished, we had to rent a house in another community before moving into a new one. But my father disliked this place, because everything in the previous two houses was crammed into this house of 150 square meters, which was crowded and dilapidated. If you ask me to live in that kind of house now, I will definitely be reluctant.

According to my grandmother, she is still bitter about the timing of our house dismantlement now. She said that it would have been better if I had been born earlier. I was 15 years old that year, so I could only get an apartment with an area of 50 square meters. But if I had been 16 that year, I would have got a house of 100 square meters. My great-grandfather died a few years before the demolition. If he had been alive, our family could have got another house of 100 square meters, and he could have lived in the city as well.

Four years later, our new apartment in the new neighborhood was well-decorated. The cost of decorating the apartment was equivalent to the cost of building a small house in the countryside before. From then on, I lived the city life as I expected before.

I think our life moves in a spiral way as the politic book says, which has undergone amazing changes.

Today, I live in such good conditions that I could never have imagined when I was living in the countryside. What surprises me even more is that such an amazing change only takes 10 years. People who once lived in the countryside abandoned rice fields and rows of looms to turn countryside into towns, which would have been difficult to achieve without the increase of social wealth. From the time I was born, I experienced the rapid development of the country and lived the peaceful life that people dreamed of before. Moreover, I had the opportunity to go to school in a city far away. Thus, I must express my gratitude to the people who have contributed to the reform and opening up, making it possible for me to live such a happy life.

变与不变中的奋斗画面

陈　辉

房屋承载着家的记忆。每一代人都有每一代人关于房屋的记忆。房屋的变迁，见证了一个家庭的时代际遇，陪伴了一个家庭的成长。在房屋中，既有欢声笑语，也有同甘共苦。房屋既是家庭回忆的承载，也是家庭改变的缩影。房屋在不断地变化，而我们对美好生活的向往和追求不变。

家是最小国。每个家庭的房屋从茅草屋变成砖瓦房，从平房变成了商品房，房屋变化了，我们的生活条件逐渐变好了。房屋的变化，让我们每个家庭感受到了幸福，房屋的变化，使每个家庭更加坚信，只要通过辛勤劳动，就能换来幸福生活。能看到希望，是生活的最大希望，能看到幸福的可能，是最大的幸福。

国是千万家。房屋的变化，描绘了一幅幅人们勠力同心的奋斗画面，家庭的变化，折射出了千千万万的人在推动社会发展中的作用。房屋的变化，对一个社会、一个国家的变化来讲，是一个缩影，在房屋变化中，我们感受到了经济的腾飞、社会的和谐和文化的繁荣等。在房屋变化中，我们更感到了时代的美好、幸福的可靠和生活的希望。

（浙大宁波理工学院马克思主义学院教师）

故事

嘉兴

徐淳迪(网络与新媒体专业192班)

房屋进步史

最能见证和记录几十载岁月变迁的就是住房了，我见证的住房改变只有一次——前两年对桐乡市高桥街道湘庄村老家宅基地上旧房的推倒重来，事实上我也参与了部分工作——清理旧房的砖头，找出成色不错的再利用，因而记忆深刻。

记忆里的老家房子其实已经建成有30多年历史，并且在20世纪90年代经历了一些改造——把后面的平房改造成两层洋房作爸爸的婚房。现在回到乡下，已经没有了原来童年暑假住所的痕迹，取而代之的是一座三层农村小排屋，也算是父母一代辛劳一生的有力见证。

时光机拨动齿轮回到上世纪50年代，爷爷奶奶那一辈人居住的房子还很简陋，只是一层的几间平房，用的是制作工艺简单、质量不高的泥砖，地基用的也只是石头，屋顶是前后都有黑瓦覆盖的两个斜面——就类似乌镇那些历史悠长的旧居。除了墙壁外，大多使用木质结构，包括房梁、大门、窗户等。

“那时候家家户户都很穷，所以房子都是很粗糙，能避雨、能遮阳就行了。”爸爸讲道。

爷爷奶奶就是生长在这普普通通的黑瓦白房中，度过了他们饥饿困顿的童年、青年。虽然简陋，却毕竟是个家，免去了风餐露宿。每天早出晚归忙忙碌碌，还能记得有一处休憩的住所，能安安稳稳地睡一觉洗去一身疲惫，也是一种幸福——简单、安逸、知足。

值得一提的是那时的房子都是亲戚邻里互相帮忙盖起来的，这家派个男人来搬砖，那家派个汉子来做木工，而专门的泥瓦匠也是有的，靠师傅徒弟代代相承的技艺谋生，那些杂活则都交给了邻里乡里的男人们。今天你家盖房我来帮，明天我家盖房你来帮。爸爸回忆道：“那时候房子结构也简单，不需要工程师画图纸，大家互相帮帮忙，一座新房子就盖起来了！”

农村电力普及是很晚的事，爸爸幼时家中夜间还在使用煤油灯、蜡烛等照明，那时的生活也很接近于“日出而作，日落而息”。80年代盖的新房才第一次配备了老式黄光的电灯，而且非常简陋，并没有把电线隐藏在墙体内部，而是很不雅观地用钉子固定在墙面上，甚至直接垂下来，连开关也和现在习以为常的白色按键大相径庭——仅仅只是一套滑轮组，靠手拉绳子实现开、关。这种开关的直接缺陷就是容易坏，经常需要更换绳子，好在零件也很普通，倒也锻炼了男人修修补补的技术，基本家家户户都能自己解决问题。

爸爸上学那会儿就是靠着微弱的黄光读书、写字，虽然简陋却实现了一个质的飞跃——农村的夜晚不再一片漆黑，家家户户的微弱黄光汇聚起来，点亮了农村学子们的璀璨前程。

转眼到了80年代，改革之风席卷了整个中国大地，经济的腾飞终于带动着农村地区人们的日子好了起来！又到了盖新房的时候了。

这次盖房是爷爷奶奶结婚的需要，而爷爷做木工攒下的一些钱刚好派上用场。“结婚都是要再盖新房子的，那时候基本都是这样，算是准备结婚的一件大事了。”爷爷讲道。

很快，一间两层的崭新泥瓦房诞生了，结构还和原来一样——黑瓦白墙，只是多了些装饰——二楼走廊的栏杆用水泥做出了曲线的形状，最西面的外墙上用水泥做了个多菱形组合的图案等。

这间房子的前半部分一直没变，我的童年也是在那里度过的，只是在九几年我爸妈结婚那会儿拆去了后半部分，造了第一个配备两个卫生间、平面屋顶、彩色瓷砖装饰的新式洋房，去集市买了沙发、抽水马桶、彩色电视机等新鲜玩意，爸爸妈妈的生活条件获得了极大改善。

“那个时候听说过城里的卫生间用的是抽水马桶，但是真正去买的时候才第一次亲眼看见，觉得神奇得不得了。”爸爸露出喜悦的神色。

这次造房子变的地方很多，而一直没变的是农村家家户户必须配备的灶台——烧柴做饭、迎灶神的地方，即便是新式洋房以至于如今的三层小排屋也不例外，那是真正农村住房的内核所在，而在如今的城市现代化建筑中，灶台早已被淘汰了。

后屋新建的改造方式在那会儿是非常盛行的，改造一半既节省了金钱，也不影响在前面继续居住，值得一提的是当时流行绚丽的外瓷砖颜色，农村里一时间拔地而起一间间绿的蓝的红的紫的双层洋房，原本非黑即白的农村建筑骤然多了花样。

“本来大家都是黑色的瓦片白色的墙体，突然流行起了彩色的瓷砖，大家都觉得亮闪闪的很好看，我跟你爷爷那时候也随大流用了天蓝色的外瓷砖，别看后来褪色了，当时漂亮着呢！”爸爸难掩自豪之情。

随着改革开放推进，农村老百姓的眼界也逐渐随之开阔起来，纺织厂、服装厂的涌现带动了农村青壮年的多元化就业，种地不再是年轻人的唯一出路，更多毕业生选择去工厂上班，逐渐过渡到“新城里人”。我父母也跟随潮流，找了一份城里的工作，勤勤恳恳地打拼买房。

以现在的眼光看，当时即便全额付款一套商品房也才10来万元接近20万元，可在零几年的农村，这无疑是一笔巨款。

“当时真的很穷很穷，本来也买不起房，上班都是开摩托车从乡下骑到城里去的，主要还是2001年出了车祸，觉得还是应该买套房子上班近一点。当时很不容易，你爷爷奶奶拿出家底出了几万，我和你妈妈那几年攒下的工资根本没多少钱，差很多，就跟亲戚朋友家借了好多钱，最后还是贷款了整整5万才住进去的。”爸爸谈到这套商品房。

“是的，5万的贷款还有好几万的借条，真的是很大的负担，我和你老爸那时候每天都是胆战心惊的，只恨加班时间不够长，工资太少，吃的用的也很朴素，能不买就不买。”妈妈在一旁补充道。

最终，在2003年我们家在嘉兴市桐乡市梧桐街道西门小区成功买房，拥有了属于自己的城里住所，改变了爸爸妈妈在农村守着宅基地做一辈子农民的命运。

Jiaxing
Xu Chundi (Class 192, Majoring in Network and New Media)

The Changes of Houses

The housing is what can most witness and record the changes over the decades. The housing change I have witnessed was only once. Two years ago, the old house on the homestead of Xiangzhuang Village, Gaoqiao Street, Tongxiang City was overthrown. In fact, I also participated in part of the work. I cleaned up the bricks of the old house and found the ones with good condition for reuse, so I had a deep memory.

The old house in my memory has actually been built for more than 30 years, and it had undergone some transformations in the 1990s. The bungalow at the back was transformed into a two-story western-style house as my father's wedding house. Now back in the countryside, there are no traces of the original childhood summer residence which was replaced by a small three-story rural townhouse. It could be regarded as a powerful testimony to the hard work of my parents.

Let's move the gear of the time machine back to the 1950s, the houses of the grandparents' generations were still rough and shabby. There were just a few one-story bungalows which were made of simple, low-quality mud bricks. Stones were used for the foundation. The roof was two slopes covered with black tiles on the front and the back, which was similar to the old houses in Wuzhen which had a long history. Except walls, wooden structures were mostly used, including beams, doors, windows, etc.

My father said, "At that time, every family was very poor, so the houses were very rough, and we merely needed a place as a shelter from rain and sun".

My grandparents grew up in these ordinary and white houses with black tiles on the roof, and it was this place where they spent their hungry and troubled childhood and youth. Rough as it was, it was still home, which protected us from eating and sleeping in the open. They went out early and came back late every day, but still remembered there was a place to rest. Being able to have a sound sleep to get rid of the fatigue was also a kind of happiness— simpleness, comfort and contentment.

It is worth mentioning that the houses at that time were built with the help of relatives and neighbors. A family sent a man to move the bricks, and the other sent a man to do carpentry. There were also some specialized masons whose skills were passed down by masters to apprentices to earn a living. Then, all the chores were given to the men in the neighborhood. They hepled each other to build houses. My father recalled: "At that time, the structure of the house was simple, so it did not need engineers to draw sketches. Everyone helped each other and a new house was built!"

It was very late to popularize electricity in rural areas. When my father was young, he still used kerosene lamps and candles for light at night in the house. Their life at that time could be better described as "working at sunrise and resting at sunset." The new house built in the 1980s was equipped with old-fashioned yellow electric lights for the first time, and the quality was not good. In addition, the wires were not hid inside the wall, but were unsightly fixed on the wall with nails, or even hung down directly. Even the switch was very different from the white button being used nowadays. It was just a set of pulleys, which could be switched on and off by pulling a rope. The obvious defect of this kind of switch was that it was easy to malfunction, and it was often necessary to replace the rope. Fortunately, the parts were also very easy to find, so men could learn repairing skills, and every family could solve the problem by themselves.

When my father went to school, he read and wrote under the dim yellow light. Although the condition was poor, there was a big change. That is, it was no longer dark at night in the countryside. The dim yellow light from every household gathered together, lighting up the bright future of the rural students.

The 1980s was coming before we knew it. The reform and opening up was carried out all over China. The economy developed rapidly, and it led to a better life for people in rural areas! It's time to build a new house again.

The reason for building a house this time was because of my grandparents marriage. The money saved by my grandpa when he did carpentry just came in handy. "It was common to build a new house when people got married. It was an important thing when people made preparation at that time," said my grandpa.

Soon, a two-story brand-new mud-tile house was built, and the structure was still the same as before——black tiles and white walls, but with more decoration. For example, the railings of the corridor on the second floor were made of cement in a curved shape and a multi-diamond combination pattern was made on the westernmost exterior wall with cement.

The first half of this house had not been changed. I also spent my childhood there. In the 1990s when my parents got married, they removed the back part of the house and built the first new western-style house with two bathrooms, a flat roof and colorful tiles. They went to the market to buy sofas, flush toilets, color TV sets and other new things. Therefore, the living conditions of my parents had been greatly improved.

"At that time, I had heard that the flush toilet was used in the bathrooms in the city, but it was the first time I saw it in person when buying it. It was amazing." There was a lively delight on his face.

There have been many changes to the house this time, but what did not change was the wood-burning stove with which every household in the countryside must be equipped. That was where people burnt wood to cook and welcomed the kitchen god. Therefore, even the western-style house and the three-story small townhouses today are no exception. It is the essence of real rural housing. But in today's urban modern buildings, the wood-burning stove has long been obsolete.

The renovation method to rebuild the back part of the houses was very popular then. The renovation of this kind not only saved money, but also did not affect living in the front of the house simultaneously. It should be noted that the gorgeous exterior tile colors were popular at that time. Consequently, many western-style houses in green, blue and purple rose up from the ground at the same time. The buildings that used to be black and white became more colorful in the countryside.

"Originally, everybody's house had black tiles and white walls. When colorful tiles became popular, everyone thought they were shiny and beautiful. My grandpa and I went with the flow to use sky blue exterior tiles. Even though the color began to fade, it looked pretty at that time!" My father couldn't hide his pride.

With the enforcement of reform and opening up policy, the horizons of the rural people have been gradually broadened. The emergence of textile factories and garment factories had promoted the diversified employment of young and middle-aged rural people. Farming was no longer the only way for young people. More graduates chose to go to work in the factory and gradually become a "new city resident". My parents also followed the trend, found a job in the city, and worked diligently to buy a house.

From the current perspective, even if the full payment for a commercial house was more than 100,000 yuan or close to 200,000 yuan at that time, this was undoubtedly a huge sum of money in rural area in the 2000s.

When my father spoke of this commercial house, he said, "I was really poor at the time. I couldn't afford to buy a house. I used to ride a motorcycle from the countryside to the city to work. The main reason was that there was a car accident in 2001. I knew I should buy a house so as to be closer to the working place, but it was not easy. Your grandparents also paid out about tens of thousands yuan which was all their savings. Your mother and I didn't save much in those years. It was far from enough, so we borrowed a lot of money from relatives, friends, and your aunt. In the end, I took out a bank loan of 50,000 yuan to buy it."

"Yes, a loan of 50,000 yuan and IOUs of tens of thousands were really a huge burden. Your father and I were terrified every day at that time. We were afraid that the time for extra work was too short; the salary was too low; we didn't demand much on food and clothes, and we spent money as little as possible," my mother added.

In the end, in 2003, our family successfully bought a house in Ximen Community, Wutong Street, Tongxiang City, Jiaxing City. We had our own urban residence, which changed my parents' destiny as farmers for a lifetime on a rural homestead.

人生的拼搏与浮沉

张文祥

作者讲述了自己父亲二十年来打拼生意、谋生发展的过程，其中有赚了钱的高兴和轻松，也有因为各种主客观因素造成投资失利、资金被骗、辛苦白费，甚至于觉得无路可走，失去前行的动力和信心的困窘和无助。作者用细腻的笔触，讲述了小学时看到父亲酒醉哭泣的场景，记录了父亲人生中最艰难的半年光景。从文中可以看出，父亲在“浮沉二十年”中，先后走过河北、安徽、西藏，以及越南、缅甸，做过的生意包括开编织袋工厂、做海鲜排档、开童装店、承包水泥厂、淘金、做塑料和管道……可以想象，这二十年，父亲一定是遍尝人间苦，做过千般难，是很不容易的二十年。好在终于是坚持下来，让家人看到希望，“带领我们家这艘小船在时代的大浪里摇摇晃晃地前进”。

人生确实无坦途。生意场也是人生路，注定会曲曲折折，可能柳暗花明，也可能山重水复。决定成功或失败的因素是很多的，但成功绝不可能是偶然的。想当年，晋商的驼队从福建、浙江贩卖茶叶到遥远的蒙古、俄罗斯，再从荒蛮北地带回皮毛贸易，继而诞出现代商业银行雏形之“票号”。今虽只能从一串串山西大院遥想当年辉煌，但我们知道，晋商的“人前光鲜”是无数的“人后作难”所换来。如今名动天下的浙商，何尝不是如作者笔下的父亲一样，在几十年的浮沉打拼中所点滴垒成？因此，我们应当致敬每一个不畏艰难、不轻言放弃的创业者，因为他们给我们以启迪——人生的意义就在打拼！

（浙大宁波理工学院传媒与法学院，教授）

故事

温州

蒋明瑜(网络与新媒体专业183班)

浮沉二十年

1976年8月11日,温州市苍南县沪山的一间小房屋中,母亲诞生了。母亲16岁时,由于家庭经济情况紧张,加上距离初中的路程太长,放弃了学业,随外婆一起进工厂做编织袋。

相比于母亲艰难的童年时代,父亲的童年要轻松不少。爷爷和阿公们通过生产冰棍里面的小木棒挣了不少钱,家庭也逐渐宽裕起来。但是长辈们的溺爱也让父亲无心于学业,在初中毕业之后,父亲也结束了他的学业,跟着我的爷爷一边工作一边学习如何做生意。

父母命运的交汇点在河北武安一个小小的编织袋工厂,母亲作为技术工在工厂里工作。而工厂主是我的阿公们,因此父亲也一边学习技术一边作为管理者在工厂中给我的阿公们帮忙。母亲说虽然头一年他们就认识,但是在工厂的前两年他们几乎没有说过话,直到第三年才经人介绍谈起了恋爱。他们的相遇开启了这个家庭的故事。

母亲和父亲在一年恋爱之后回老家结了婚。因为不甘心一直为他人打工,两个人都辞去了工厂里的工作,在镇上做起了海鲜排档的生意。但是一年下来也没能挣到什么钱,幸福的曙光还远远没有进入他们的视野,因此父亲和母亲果断决定结束这段不大成功的日子,再去寻觅新的机会。

经过一番考虑,他们决定在镇上开童装店,于是两人坐着渡轮一起来到上海寻找可以代理的品牌。虽然成功拿到了一个童装品牌的代理权,但是受困于当年经济的不利形势,两人还是没能让家庭的经济情况走上正轨。

两人一番计议之后,父母带着年幼的我来到了安徽,跟着我的阿公一起合资开起了编织袋工厂。一家人就搬进了工业园区,我们住在一间员工宿舍里,隔壁的邻居们就是工厂里的工人。宿舍的对面就是工厂。家里的家具只有一张床、一台电视,还有一张餐桌和几个椅子,晚上3个人就挤在一张单人床上入睡。

虽然父亲经常忙于工作,但是想见到父亲却是一件非常容易的事情。因为我们的小房间就在工厂的对面,而父亲常常会在生产线上和技术师傅讨论产量、速度等事情，所以每次我跟小伙伴跑进工厂就能看到父亲，父亲在工厂的生活作息与普通工人没有什么区别，这也让他很快了解了整个编织袋工厂的生产流程和许多技术细节。这段跟工人们共同生活、工作的经历对于父亲之后的创业产生了很大的影响。后来在缅甸淘金时，父亲也总要住在环境恶劣的矿山旁边以最快地了解工作进度。

在到安徽的第二年，工厂的生意逐渐有了起色，而这一年也使父亲积累了许多管理工厂的经验。父亲管理的编织袋工厂的主要客户是一家水泥厂，一年的合作让父亲接触到了许多关于水泥行业的信息与人脉。在第二年的时候，那家水泥厂由于效益下降，工厂老板想要把工厂承包出去，于是凭借着一年的积累父亲承包了这家水泥厂，从阿公们的编织袋工厂腾出手来经营自己的工厂。"当时承包水泥厂确实赚了点钱，然后就买了房子。"母亲在说这句话之前长长地出了一口气。仿佛之前的所有努力最终让家庭看到了一点希望。

在有了一些积累之后，我们终于在老家的灵溪镇上有了自己的房子，父亲和母亲也稍微感到安心了。在过年回老家的时候，我不停地嚷嚷着要去新家看一看，虽然几次去都是在装修工地，但是对于我来说，对于新家的期待也逐渐强烈了起来。我们怀着对新家的期待回到了安徽，艰苦的生活似乎逐渐步入佳境。

但是好景不长，来到安徽的第三年，工厂主不再允许父亲承包，因此刚刚看到了希望的父亲又回到了编织袋工厂继续之前的生意，而母亲则将重心逐渐转到了家庭。

在安徽的工厂关停之后，父亲又辗转各地寻找做生意的机会，我的记忆中父亲似乎除了过年回家，其余时间都是在外地做生意。

然而做生意总是有风险的，努力也并不一定就能取得回报，特别随着时代的发展，父亲熟悉的编织袋产业等轻工业的效益不再像上世纪那个野蛮生长的时代一样高了。尽管放弃了和家人在一起的时光，父亲的生意还是没能看到起色。一点一点的失望与气馁在父亲的心头累积起来。"那几年做什么都没赚到钱，还被人骗了好多。那半年又没什么好做的，只能在家里闲着，当时实在是想不到办法了。"还记得上小学时，一天父亲竟然白天喝得大醉，很安静地躺在床上，抹下一把又一把的眼泪，却一点声音也不出。父亲不是个软弱的人，那是我第一次也是唯一一次见到他哭。我站在床边也不知道该怎么办，只是看他一点一点地擦眼泪。

父亲骨子里是个强硬的人，虽然失败了很多很多次，但是一点点的希望和机会就能让他振作起来。在家里失落了大约半年后，父亲又一次离开了。这次他去往邢台，将目光从自己熟悉的编织袋产业转向了更广阔的领域，例如塑料、管道等等。我们的房子又只剩下了母亲、姐姐和我 3 个人。虽然父亲在外工作让我们长时间无法见面，但是看到父亲逐渐振作起来，一家人又安心了下来。

之后的几年中，父亲又去了西藏，还有越南、缅甸等地，每次从外地回家，他总会和我说说他在外地的见闻和有趣的经历，介绍当地的一些生活习惯和习俗。跟过去的十几年一样，他仍然在失败与成功之间不断徘徊，但是他再也没有像早先那么垂头丧气过，他总能让我们的小家安心，让我们看到一点点的希望。父亲像是一个可靠的船长，凭借着他不太跟得上时代的技术带领我们家这艘小船在时代的大浪里摇摇晃晃地前进。

Wenzhou
Jiang Mingyu (Class 183, Majoring in Network and New Media)

Twenty Years of Ups and Downs

My mother was born in a small house in Hushan, Cangnan County, Wenzhou City on August 11, 1976. Due to the poor situation of the family and the long distance to school, my mother dropped out of school when she was 16 years old. Then she went to the factory to make woven bags with my grandmother.

Unlike my mother's tough childhood, my father's early days were much easier. My grandpa and his friends made a fortune from selling wooden sticks in popsicles, so family became better off gradually. Spoiled by the senior members of the family, my father lost his interest in studying. After graduating from middle school, he didn't continue his study and started to do business with my grandfather.

The paths of my parents crossed in a small woven bag factory in Wu'an, Hebei Province, where my mother worked as a technician. The factory was owned by my grandfather and his relatives, so naturally, my father helped in the factory as an administrator as he learned weaving techniques. According to my mother, they had barely spoken with each other for the first two years even though they had known each other in the first year, and it was not until the third year that they were introduced to each other and started dating. It was their encounter that started the story of this family.

After being in love for a year, my mother and father returned to their hometown and got married. Since both of them were not willing to work for others, they quit their jobs at the factory and started a seafood diner in town, but they did not earn much in that year. The happiness they was expecting was far out of sight. My parents immediately decided to stop this unsuccessful business to look for new opportunities.

After due consideration, they decided to open a store selling children's clothing in the town. They boarded a ferry to Shanghai in search of a brand that they could take the agency. Even though they were successful in being granted the dealership for a clothing brand, the troubled economy of that time failed to get the family's financial situation back on track.

After a detailed discussion, my parents took me to Anhui where they opened a joint venture woven bag factory with my grandfather. The three of us moved into the industrial park. We lived in the employee dormitory, and our neighbours were factory workers. The factory was opposite our dormitory building. The furniture in the dorm were just a bed, a TV, a dining table and a few chairs. At night, the three of us had to share a single bed.

My father was often busy with work, but it was not difficult to see him, because our small room was just opposite to the factory. He would often discuss production quantity, speed and things the like with the technicians, so I could see him every time my friends and I ran into the factory. His daily routine in the factory was no different from that of an ordinary worker, which allowed him to quickly understand the production process as well as many technical details of the entire woven bag factory. The experience of living and working with the workers had a great influence on my father's entrepreneurship afterwards. When he was panning for gold in Myanmar several years later, my father also chose to live next to the mine in a harsh environment to understand the process as soon as possible.

The second year in Anhui, the factory business gradually got better, and it was also in that year that my father accumulated a lot of experience in factory management. We sold woven bags mostly to a cement factory, so my father had a lot of connections with people from the cement industry. During the second year, the cement factory owner wanted to contract the factory out because of the declining profits, so my father took over the factory with years of savings. "We did make some money with that cement factory," said my mother with a long breath, "and that was why we could afford to buy a house later." All their previous efforts finally paid off. The family finally had something to hope for.

After saving some money, we had a house of our own in our hometown, Lingxi Town. My parents felt a little bit assured. I keep clamouring to have a look at the new house when we spent the Chinese New Year in the hometown. Although what we saw was just a construction site, for me, I had greater expectations for our new house. We returned to Anhui with the expectation of our new home, and our tough life seemed to get better and better.

However, good things didn't last long. During our third year in Anhui, the owner of that cement factory stopped the contract with my father, so my father who just found hope had to pick up his own business in the woven bag factory. My mother, subsequently, shifted her focus to the family.

My father had to look for business opportunities everywhere when the factory shut down. In my memory, my father would only come home for Chinese New Year. The rest of time, he did business in other cities.

However, there were always risks involved when doing business, and your efforts would not always pay off. With the advancement of the times, the benefits of light industry like woven bags was not as immense as it was during the last century which was an ear of barbarian growth. So the business of my father did not improve for a bit even though he had given up a lot of family time. Over the years, my father was disappointed and discouraged. "In those years, I earned nothing no matter what I did, and I even lost quite a lot money because of scammers. For six months, I had nothing to do but idle at home. At that time, I couldn't think out any solution." I still remembered one day when I was in primary school, my father was completely drunk in the daytime. He lay on the bed quietly, wiping his tears in silence. My father was not a coward, and that was the first and only time that I had seen him cry. Standing by the bed, I didn't know what to do but watch him wipe his tears again and again.

My father has been a tough person by nature. Although he had failed many times, a little bit of hope and opportunity were all he needed. After a sense of loss at home for about half a year, my father pulled himself together and left home again. This time he went to Xingtai, and he diverted his attention to such broader fields as plastics, pipes and the like from the woven bag industry which he knew well. The house was left to three people once again: my mother, my sister and me. Although we were unable to see my father for a long time as he was working in the other city, we were relieved to see that he could cheer himself up.

In the following years, my father went to Tibet, Vietnam, Myanmar and other places. Every time he returned home, he would always tell me about his interesting experiences and introduced to me their local habits and customs. Like the past decade, his business was still on and off from time to time, but he had never been discouraged as he was at that time. He would always assure our small family and let us see a little of hope. My father was like the captain of the ship of our family. He would lead us to stagger forward in the waves of the time with his rusty and outdated technology.

科技发展中渔民精神的传承

丁六申

《海边人家》刻画了舟山六横岛一个渔村家庭在改革春风沐浴下的生活变迁,这也是千千万万舟山渔民生活的缩影。

85 公里的海岸线为舟山六横带来了无尽的美景和宝藏,渔民们仅凭一舟一楫,一身智慧与勇敢,书写了动人的篇章。史铃妮的家庭一直在这片土地上临海而居、依海劳作,因为家中没有渔船,史铃妮爷爷和当时许多农民一样,只能以种植庄稼为生,在改革开放后也曾到青岛做过舟山虾米的生意,但在那个技术与交通落后的年代,虾米自然是没法贮藏完好运送到目的地。随着海洋科技发展,上世纪 80 年代有了木船和机器船,90 年代有了铁壳船,诸如史铃妮爸爸这样的年轻渔民不再局限于近海捕鱼作业,开始可以投资船只、通过考证进行远洋捕捞作业等,渔民收入增加,但条件仍旧艰苦、充满危险。再后来,卫星电话和定位系统帮助渔民们可以更长时间、更远距离、更安全地出海,在 2015 年,史铃妮爸爸便选择到为期两年的南太平洋船舶上出航。

20 多年的时间,史铃妮爸爸一直过着海上漂的日子,从文字中我们看到岁月在他身上留下了海的烙印,看到普通渔民家庭一直过着聚少离多的日子,看到了一份深沉的父爱,也见证了新科技、新设备的运用助力渔民丰收,但最为重要的是要去体会和传承那份吃苦耐劳、敢于担当、永不言弃的渔民精神。

(浙大宁波理工学院传媒与法学院思政教师,硕士)

故事

舟山

史铃妮(网络与新媒体专业 184 班)

海边人家

一座被山和海包围的小村庄——舟山市六横岛上的涨起港渔村,就是我出生成长的地方。小村庄被山与岛中心隔离开来,由于海文化和江南文化的交融,在我看来村民们的骨子里却既透露着波澜起伏的凌云壮阔又缠绵着情义绵长的闲情雅致。

爷爷是农民,因为家里没有渔船,庄稼就是我们家的根本,多数时候他就喜欢呆在农田里研究怎样把水稻种得颗颗饱满,怎样把瓜果种得香甜。从 1999 年开始爷爷因为爸爸的生意失败扛不住经济压力出门打工了,但是也心心念念他的田地,一打电话回来就是催促奶奶什么东西要种下去,什么要浇水施肥了。奶奶多数时候能听,说得多了,烦了,就大骂一声“就田最重要”,我还没来得及说爷爷再见,电话就被掐断了。

可他偏不会让我们碰锄头,他常说“读书人就好好读书”,我们家里没出过大学生,爷爷就把教育看得特别重。

爷爷自然也曾做过生意的,但是奶奶总是说我们史家缺根做生意的筋,爷爷表面长得精明,内心却憨厚老实。1985 年左右他带着舟山的虾米去山东青岛做生意,一路北上,却基本没卖出去过,心里却还道,到了目的地应该就会好了。没想到到了青岛,虾米都快烂得差不多了,他着急卖出去拿回本,价格更是被当地商贩压得死死的,最后连回家的本都丢在那里了。分文不剩,他就去工地上搬了一个月的砖,终于凑够了回舟山的钱。灰头土脸回来,爷爷从未向别人提起过,直到我上了大学,爷爷回忆往事才不好意思地讲给我听。

母亲和父亲在 1998 年准备结婚,爷爷奶奶动作更是利落,立马敲好了盖新房的章,叫来了村里人建好一套洋气的新房。在此之前,他们一直住在平顶房里,那是顶多 60 平方米的房子,冬天漏风夏天又不通风,小小的院子里还养了鸡鸭,对于爸爸妈妈来说简直是噩梦。

经过多年的努力,终于在我和姐姐出生的前一年,他们从平顶房里搬了出来。家里人对装潢甚是上心,客厅里装了那种五颜六色的小彩灯,中间的大灯富丽堂皇，地砖铺了能买到最贵的，马桶和浴缸更是准备齐全，在爷爷奶奶眼里，这栋房子就是用来享福的。这样顺顺溜溜无大风大浪的日子在爸爸从事远洋船舶行业之后戛然而止，本来在两代人努力下还算宽裕的小家第一次承受了巨大挫折。

爸爸因为学历不高，年轻时经常换工作，但是他人机灵，差不多在1995年左右开始跟船，之后又顺利考取了相关证书，准备去远洋钓鱿鱼。妈妈年轻时就跟着一位理发师傅学习手艺，出师以后在码头附近开了一家理发店。妈妈为人好相处，村里的人都愿意去她那里理发，生意一直不错。

爸爸经历了几年的海上生活，手头有了些积蓄，就毫不犹豫投资了一艘船。可就在我和姐姐出生的那一年，爸爸投资的船出了问题，因为船板没被钉牢，海水倒灌，船沉没了，所幸没有人员伤亡，但是作为投资方，我们家还没挣钱就赔得血本无归。

妈妈还在孕期，爸爸更是不能休息，仍是出门挣钱了。家里负债累累，爷爷放弃了他的一亩三分田，出门务工了。奶奶不但要在生产大队里工作，还要和妈妈轮流去公交车里当售票员才能勉强维持生计。我和姐姐因为早产体质弱，经常感冒发烧，最穷困的时候家里甚至连5块钱都拿不出来看病。

妈妈后来回忆起那段艰难岁月对我说："我还记得有次我在理发时，你和姐姐就在旁边玩，我嫌烦了，踢了一脚，你一下子摔在头发堆里。"我听完哈哈大笑，妈妈也跟着笑，但是她的眼里更多是心酸和怜爱。

好在靠着爸爸在海洋上的坚持，几年之后我们家从那场灾难里熬过来了，日子又平稳过了几年。直到2007年政府要修建隧道，家里拆迁了。这对于我们家来说确实是个好消息，我们可以拆迁进镇中心去了。虽然有了地基，可手里没有存款，直到那个小区其他的房子基本都建造完成了，喝了两三次上梁酒，我们家那块儿仍然是光秃秃的，妈妈心里日日盼着新房子建成。又过了两年，我们家的房子终于开始动工了，妈妈比谁都开心，整日和奶奶忙里忙外，为自己的房子添砖加瓦。

到我升学要上初中，妈妈一狠心把我送去舟山城区的学校。这下，刚建好的新房都没住上几年，我们又开始了离家在外的旅程，背上行囊从六横岛跑向了舟山本岛。

2012年，父亲考取了船长证书，这对于父亲来说分外开心，妈妈也更是支持，即使上次的投资失败，他们仍然决定入股父亲的那条船。2015年我初三，爸爸为了挣更多的钱，决定不再行驶半年的船，而是去了为期两年的南太平洋船舶出航。

小时候的我其实已经习惯父亲常年不在家的状态，所以对于父亲的长时间离别并没有多少伤感。直至妈妈带我去码头为爸爸送行，爸爸向来不是很沉稳，年轻时的痞气直至现在也没消退，可是那日他话却格外少，点了一支烟，安静地抽着，时不时看一眼我们和妈妈，时不时又看一眼船。夏日炎炎，船员们个个都被晒得皮肤黝黑，在船甲板上跳上跳下，开始最后的准备工作。

"船长，准备开船了！"一声呼喊让爸爸回过神来，他跟我们招呼一声"走了"，急忙跳上了船跑进了船长室。船只嗡嗡嗡发动了，岸上的人跟船上的人挥手分别，爸爸却没有从船长室里跑出来再看我们一眼，直接离开了。船渐行渐远，即使爸爸看不见，妈妈的手也在高高挥举着，而这样的离别她已经历数次。

2017 年爸爸回家了，时过多年，我依旧记得打开家门的那一刻，爸爸喜悦的笑容以及黝黑的脸庞，因为没有理发师，他们的头发都是自己剃的，已经杂乱无章。巨大的变化，让我一瞬间没有认出来，还以为自己敲错了家门。

2017 到 2019 年间，我们家终于被幸运之神眷顾，父母亲的投资明显有了回报，家里的经济条件一下子好转起来。仿佛所有的努力在一夜间开花结果，母亲现在可以不用开理发店，而我们也已经上了大学，所有的量变终于质变，风风雨雨 20 年，所幸我们家一个都没缺。

Zhoushan

Shi Lingni (Class 184, Majoring in Network and New Media)

The Seaside Family

I was born and grew up in a fishing village of Zhangqigang Village on Liuheng Island, Zhoushan City, which was surrounded by mountains and sea. The small village was separated from the center of the islands by mountains. In my opinion, due to the integration of sea culture and culture in the south of the Yangtze River, there were uneventful ambitions and elegant leisure in the villagers' heart.

My grandfather used to be a farmer. Because there was no fishing boat at home, the crops were what we lived on. Most of the time he would love to stay in the farmland to study how to grow bumper rice and how to plant sweet fruit. Since 1999, my grandfather could not bear the economic pressure which resulted from the failure of my father's business, so he went out to work. However, he always worried about his fields. Every time he called home, he would urge my grandma to plant, water or fertilize. Most of the time, my grandmother followed his words, but when she was impatient, she would complain that my grandfather cared nothing but the fields. Then the phone was hung up before I could say goodbye to him.

However, my grandfather never allowed us to touch a hoe. He always told us that students should focus on nothing but studying. As there was no university student in our family, he paid much attention to our education.

In fact, my grandfather had done business before. However, my grandmother thought our family didn't have a head for business. My grandfather looked shrewd, but he was honest and kind. In 1985, he once ran a business by selling shrimps from Zhoushan to Qingdao. On his way north, he sold nothing but he always felt hopeful and expected the shrimps would be sold out as soon as he arrived the final destination. It didn't occur to him that when he arrived in Qingdao, the shrimps had rotted already. He was so worried to get the capital back that the price was forced down by the local peddlers without mercy. Finally, he lost so much money that he had no money to go home. Thus, he went to the construction site to move bricks for a month. Finally, he earned enough money to go back to Zhoushan. Ashamed and embarrassed, he went home and never mentioned it to anyone. Not until I entered university did my grandpa tell me this experience when he recalled the past.

My parents prepared to get married in 1998. My grandparents were so deft that they immediately got the official permission of building a new house and called for the neighbors to build a new stylish house. Before that, they had lived in a bungalow, no more than 60 square meters, which was leaky in winter and pooly-ventilatied in summer. They raised chickens and ducks in the yard, which was totally a nightmare for my parents.

After years of efforts, my parents finally moved out of the bungalow one year before my sister and I were born. They paid much attention to the decoration. The living room was decorated with tiny multicolored lights and the overhead light in the middle was gorgeous. We bought the most expensive floor tiles, and the closestool and the bathtub were well equipped. In my grandparents' eyes, this house was for enjoyment. However, the smooth and peaceful life came to an end when my father engaged in ocean shipping business. The family which used to be relatively well-off under two generations' efforts suffered a huge setback for the first time.

As a result of low education, my father always changed his job when he was young. However, he was clever and started to work in the ship in 1995. After that, he successfully obtained some certificates and sailed away to catch squid. As for my mother, she learned some skills from a barber when she was young. She opened a barber shop near the wharf after her apprenticeship. She was so easygoing that villagers liked to get a haircut at her barber. Therefore, her business was always good.

After a few years living at sea, my father had some savings and didn't hesitate to invest in a boat. But in the year we were born, the ship met some trouble. The boards were not nailed down and the seawater overturned the ship. Fortunately, there were no casualties. But as an investor, our family lost everything before making money.

As mother was in pregnancy, my father hardly stopped working but went away from home for money. Meanwhile, the debt was so heavy that grandpa gave up his fields and went out for work. As for my grandma, she barely made ends meet by not only working in the production brigade, but also taking turns with my mother to work as a bus conductor. Moreover, my sister and me had weak constitutions because of premature birth, so we were given to have a fever. We could hardly take out 5 yuan to see a doctor when we were in the hardest period.

Mother once remembered those suffering times and said to me, "I still remembered there was a time when I had my hair cut, and your sister and you were playing by my side. I was so impatient that I kicked you. You just fell to the hairs!" I burst into laughter and so did my mother. But in her eyes, I saw sadness and compassion.

Luckily, with my father persisting in working at sea, we finally got through the sufferings after several years. Life was good in the following years until a tunnel was to be constructed by the government in 2007. We had to resettle. It was actually a good news to us because we could move into the town center. However, even though we had the foundations, we didn't have any savings. Therefore, all the other houses in the neighborhood had been built, but our house still hadn't started building after we had held several times of Shangliang wine, which was a Chinese tradition to celebrate the completion of the house by putting the last beam on the roof. Every day my mother longed for the completion of the new house. Two years later, it eventually began. My mother was happier than anyone else. She was busy around the house with my grandmother, doing whatever they could do to build it up.

When I was ready for middle school, my mother determinedly sent me to the school in Zhoushan. Thus, we just lived in the newhouse for a few years, then we left the new house and began a journey away from home. We packed our bags and left Liuheng Island for Zhoushan Island.

In 2012, my father obtained a captain certification, which was extremely satisfying for my father and highly supported by my mother. Though the previous investment failed, they still decided to put money into my father's ship. When I was in Grade Three of middle school in 2015, to earn more money, he decided to set out on a two-year south pacific sailing instead of the half-year one.

When I was little, I was actually used to my father being away from home all year round. I didn't feel very sad when father was away for a long time, until my mother took me to the dock to see him off. My father wasn't a mature man and the sense of ruffian he had when he was young didn't fade away. However, that day he said little, lighting a cigarette and smoking quietly. He looked at us and then looked at the ship. It was a hot summer, the crew were greatly suntanned. They jumped up and down on the deck of the ship to do the final preparation.

"Captain, we are ready to sail." The call got my father's attention. He said to us, "I am leaving." Then he jumped on the ship with hurry and ran to the captain's cabin. The ship hummed and started to sail. People on the shore waved their hands to say goodbye to the crew on board. My father didn't go out of his room again but left directly. The ship sailed away further and further. Though my father could not see us, my mother still waved her hands above her head. Actually, for her, such separation had happened many times.

My father came back in 2017. I still remembered the joyful smile on his swarthy face the moment he opened the door after a lapse of many years. Because there was no barber on the ship, he shaved off his hair by himself, so his hair was really a mess. I even thought I knocked at the wrong door because his change was so big that I could hardly recognize him.

Between 2017 and 2019, our family had been blessed by the God of luck at last. My parents' investment has greatly paid off and our family's financial situation suddenly improved. Every effort got paid overnight. After that, my mother didn't need to run the barbershop anymore and we entered the university. Every quantitative change has begun to make a qualitative change. Though there have been 20 years of ups and downs, fortunately we are alawys together.

023

观察

原来我们的梦想不必是当大富豪

王元涛

读《轰鸣中成长》，最强烈的感受就是，短短一篇文字，却蕴含了改革开放大潮下普通人创业如何才算成功的深刻道理。

在这个问题上，我也曾有很真切的体悟。比如在深圳从事记者工作多年，采访过数十位成功的企业家，其中最让我信服和敬佩的一种类型，就是他们从打工仔打工妹做起，从没想过自己要创业，要发大财，要当大富豪，他们只是拼尽全力在自己的行业里努力工作，认真积累而已。

在此过程中，很自然的，他们就把所在行业的各种运作细节摸熟摸透了，往往是出于偶然，他们得到机会，可以在行业的某一个节点上，做点自己的事情，也就是独立创业。起初一定是小打小闹，但他们不嫌小，一直稳扎稳打，步步为营，最后，在他们自己看来，几乎就是意外地获得了成功。

在《轰鸣中成长》中，作者的父母其实也属于这种类型，只不过，他们中间走了一段弯路，放弃了自己熟悉的毛衣加工业，转行进入了外贸领域。是有了一定资金积累之后，有点看不起简单的加工业了？还是觉得加工业太辛苦，获利太少？总之，他们拐了一个大弯转行，结果却遭遇失败，家庭生活都一时出现了困顿。

他们为什么会失败？当然谁都可以简单地总结，说他们能力不行。但实际上，最真实的原因在于，他们所拥有的资源不足。在外贸领域，他们还是白丁。市场最精明最无情，它从来不理会你的良好愿望，它只看你所能支配的真实资源。无本之利，在市场上是不存在的。说句难听话，哪怕是诈骗，也有坐牢的风险在后头跟着充当着你的潜在成本啊。

幸好，作者父母及时勒马止损，重回毛衣加工这个自己完全可以掌控的领域，于是轰鸣声重新在作者家中响起，持续成为她健康成长的美好背景。可以说，这才是生活最本真的样貌。相比之下，我们的时代文化，是不是太热衷于鼓动年轻人走捷径、赚快钱了？其结果，就是钱没赚着，却集体陷入了浮躁。

在浮躁的大潮下，我们可能一度都忘记了，原来，我们的梦想，可以像作者的父母一样，不必一定要当大富豪，而是在自己资源和能力的边界之内，实现收益的最大化，从而实现殷实与体面的生活。这不就是我们普通人创业最牢靠的根基吗？

（资深媒体人，居深圳）

故事

嘉兴

沈晓琳（新闻学202专升本班）

轰鸣声中成长

自我记事以来印象最深的，便是一刻也不停的轰鸣声，白天也响着，晚上也响着，吵得人头脑发昏，却又是我归属感和安全感的来源。

我的家位于嘉兴市秀洲区洪合镇，是一个几乎家家户户都与毛衣形影不离的小镇，我们家从事的就是毛衣产业链的第一步。而那轰鸣声，便是我们所有机器努力工作时的响声，我们家的悲喜，几乎全部来源于此。

一根细细小小的钩针，一枚亮闪闪的针线，在妈妈的手里轻快地舞动着。手腕稍一用力，手轻轻一钩，准确地找到多余的线头，圈在钩针里，再往回收手，这一来一回间，小小的线头便隐藏在毛衣中。这是最简单的一项技术，但在当年还是让妈妈琢磨了很久。

1989年妈妈只有15岁，因为成绩不理想所以就想早早去外面打工挣钱。一开始妈妈先去厂里上班，帮他们做一些毛衣上的手工活。妈妈那时候年纪小，连什么是做手工都还不知道，甚至是最简单的缝线针都还不会拿，而工厂里的老人又没功夫教妈妈技术，“做什么事情都得靠自己，别人想教你也只是教一个大概，只有自己实践，慢慢琢磨出来的，才是长长久久的”。凭着自己的一针一线，妈妈终于在工厂里安定了下来。

一年后，妈妈16岁，为了更高的工资，又开始学习手摇横机的技术，成为一名“挡车工”。在当时，挡车工算是一线的技术人员，不光意味着更高的工资，也意味着当时还十分年轻的妈妈迈上了职业生涯的又一个台阶。

1993年，妈妈19岁，当时的洪合镇毛衫市场渐渐发展起来，羊毛衫的生产开始从工厂承包生产慢慢转变为私人化的产业链，很多有技术的人开始自己着手买机器来生产。妈妈也用先前几年的积蓄买来了一台属于自己的手摇横机，并且接了一家私人的订单。白天，妈妈在工厂里上班，晚上回家后再自己生产。这时候的妈妈已是早晚都处于机器的轰鸣声中了。

再后来，随着洪合毛衫市场的愈发壮大，私人小作坊式的羊毛衫生产越来越多，妈妈就开始全心全意地在家自己生产羊毛衫。

“在家里做羊毛衫的这几年我很开心的，一年能有1万多元的收入，在当时已经算是挺多的了。”说起那段时光，妈妈的语气里满满都是愉悦。

1997年年底，爸爸妈妈结婚了。爸爸妈妈决定放弃以前的工作，自己创业当老板卖羊毛衫，于是，那时候还没有做生意经验的爸爸妈妈开始与我的干奶奶一家合伙做羊毛衫的外贸生意。那时的他们满怀热情，一心想把生意做好，然而好景不长，做生意的第一年就被一个老外骗了五六万。在当时五六万可是一个大数目，这样的打击对爸爸妈妈来说如同晴天霹雳，当时的他们连工人的工资都已经支付不起了，走投无路的他们只好向银行贷款，才最终度过了危机。

1999年8月，我出生了，因为要在家里照顾我，只好让爸爸一个人在外面做毛衣生意。许是没有头脑，或者是运气不好，我们家的创业之路十分艰难，几乎一直处于亏钱的状态。到最后爸爸妈妈实在是坚持不住了，便放弃了做生意的想法，改变规划，开始一心一意地做起了羊毛衫加工。

2001年，我两岁，那是我们家最艰难的时候。前些年做生意亏了太多钱，而加工羊毛衫的钱又还没有拿到，再加上我每天的奶粉钱更是给家里带来了一笔大开销。有一次，家里实在是没有钱给我买下个月的奶粉了，爸爸只好去外面当水泥工，留妈妈一个人在家管理机器。那时候做一天的水泥工有30块钱，刚好能给我买一袋奶粉。万幸的是，爸爸在外辛苦的那一段时间，终于让我们家度过了这个难关。“还好你爸爸有这个技术啊，这才顺利地把你养活了！”

在我3岁的时候，爸爸妈妈一共买了3台小电动横机，每天清晨我吃过早饭后，妈妈便会把我领到车间去，一边看管机器，一边看管我。妈妈干活很麻利，机器产出毛衫零件的速度很快，往往两三个小时就要去清理一台机器产出的毛衫。妈妈就总是坐在机器前的小凳上，把产出的一长串毛衣零件放在腿上，剪刀一下下挥舞，把不要的废弃毛纱全部剪掉，然后再抽走连接两只毛衫零件的细线，这样一来，原本连接紧密的毛衫便分离了开来。剪完所有的毛衫后，再把他们一只只地叠好，放在一边，妈妈好像总是有让一切井井有条的能力，在妈妈手里，那一堆堆的毛衫，像城墙砖石一样整齐。

爸爸则会每天雷打不动地在早晨时把前一天生产的毛衫附件送到市场的店铺里，然后回家帮着妈妈一同照看机器。有时遇到机器出故障了，爸爸便一手拿着工具，一手在机器上摸索着，奇怪的是无论多么古怪的问题，都能在爸爸手中一一解决。爸爸往往还包了去菜场买菜这一工作，每天的几个小菜，几袋零食，有时还有一杯美酒，我们就这样，在轰鸣声中度过了一个个平凡而快乐的日子。

时间就这样有条不紊地流逝着，后来的几年间，爸爸妈妈都靠着前一年努力得到的积蓄再多添几台机器，直到我 12 岁那年我家已经有了 25 台机器了。为了放下这些庞然大物，爸爸和爷爷还将我们屋子前的小池塘填了起来，重新造了一间大大的车间，将这些机器全部容纳在里面。这些大家伙在里面一列列整齐排开，威风凛凛。

在那一声声轰鸣中，我学会了说话，学会了自己吃饭，学会了写字；而我们的家庭也在这轰鸣声中逐渐步入正轨，慢慢成长。

2013 年，我们搬了新家，借着这个契机，爸爸妈妈把原先的电动机器全部低价卖出了，虽然原本几千元的机器每台只能换得几百元，但我们还是向这些陪伴了许久的老伙计说了再见。后来爸爸妈妈拿着家里的积蓄买了更加先进的全自动电脑横机，这些新的机器比以前更加大一些，但也更加聪明，他能生产更多更漂亮的毛衫附件，也让我们家迈上了一个新的征程。

每天不停的轰鸣声持续得越来越长，几乎昼夜都没有停歇，交货、拿毛纱、接生意等总是让爸爸妈妈忙得焦头烂额，但在这一刻不停的轰鸣声中，我们也渐渐找到了忙碌和快乐的平衡点，虽然有时会有厌倦，但大多数都是充满斗志和希望。

“想当年我小的时候，家里可只有三间破瓦房啊，连写个作业都要常常断电。”每当妈妈讲起从前的事情，总会发出这样的感慨，“现在我们的生活可真是越来越好啦！”

每当回到家，我还能远远地听见车间里传来的不停歇的轰鸣声。

“啊，女儿你放假回来了啊，要不要帮帮我们理理毛衫啊。”爸爸妈妈总会这样说，那就让我也来会会这些大家伙吧，我想。

Jiaxing
Shen Xiaolin (Class 202, Majoring in Journalism)

Growing up Amid Machine Noises

What has impressed me most since I was old enough to remember things is incessant roars of machines which rumble day and night. Though causing dizziness, they also give me a sense of belonging and security.

My family live in Honghe Town, Xiuzhou District, Jiaxing City, a town closely related to sweaters. We are engaged in the first step of the sweater-making industry. Roars are the sound from the machines operating in our family factory, and that is where the sorrows and joys of our family come from.

With a tiny bearded needle in one hand and a shiny thread in another, my mother moved her fingers nimbly. She accurately found the excess thread and hooked it into the needle by the wrist, and then drew the hand back. After doing so again and again, small thread was hidden in the sweater. This was the simplest sewing techniques, but in those days it still took a long time for my mother to figure it out.

In 1989, my 15-year-old mom made up her mind to drop out of school and start working early because she didn't do well at school. At first, she helped with manual work in a sweater factory. She was so young that she knew nothing about manual work, including how to hold a needle, yet senior workers in the factory didn't have spare time to teach her how to sew. "You could depend on nobody but youself. Even if others were willing to teach you, they couldn't teach you everything. Only skills learned by practicing and pondering on your own can be remembered for a lifetime." My mom finally settled down in the factory with her superb sewing skill.

A year later, when my mother was 16 years old, she started to learn how to operate the hand-cranked flat knitting machine for a higher salary. A knitter was a first-line technician at that time. The job did not only promise my mother higher wages, but also marked the first step of another career, though she was still very young.

In 1993, the sweater industry in Honghe Town developed gradually, and witnessed a transition from a contract-based manufacturing model to a private industrial chain. My mom started taking private orders, just like many others did at that time, by using a hand-operated flat knitting machine she bought with her savings. She, after finishing the factory work at daytime, would attend to her private business at night. Thus, she was completely engulfed by machine roars all day long.

With privately-owned sweater workshops taking off against the backdrop of an ever-flourishing sweater industry in the town, my mom immersed herself in the sweater-making business.

"I enjoyed making sweaters at home, for I could make over 10,000 yuan a year, which was quite a lot at that time," said my mom joyfully.

At the end of 1997, my parents got married. They decided to give up their previous jobs and start their own business, that is, selling woolen sweaters. With no experience in business, they set foot in the foreign trade business in woolen sweaters in partnership with my god-grandmother's family. They were full of passion and devoted to the business, but unfortunately, they were cheated by a foreigner in the first year and lost nearly 60,000 yuan. It was a huge loss back then and a very hard blow to my parents too. They couldn't even pay the workers. They had no choice but to apply for a loan from the bank. At last, they tided over the crisis.

My dad was left alone to attend to the sweater business since my mom needed to take care of me after I was born in August, 1999. Our family business was extremely hard and always made a loss, presumably because my parents lacked business acumen or luck. They finally gave it up and focused on the sweater processing business.

The year of 2001 was the hardest time for my family. I was two years old then. My parents were faced with a massive expense due to the business lost in previous years, the failure to collect the money for processing woolen sweaters and my demand for milk powder every day. My dad had no choice but to work as a plasterer, leaving my mom alone to take care of me and machines. just because they had no money to buy the milk powder for the next month. He earned 30 yuan a day as a plasterer, just enough to pay for a bag of milk powder. We finally tided through this crisis thanks to my dad's hard work. "But for your dad's skill, we couldn't have raised you up."

They bought three small electric flat knitting machines when I was three years old. My mom would take me to the workshop every day after I finished my breakfast so as to take care of me while attending to machines. My mother worked very fast. The machine produced sweater parts quickly and it was often the case that a worker had to clean up the finished sweaters every two or three hours. My mother always sat on a small stool in front of the machine and placed a long string of sweater parts on her lap, using the scissors to cut off all the unwanted yarn and then the thin thread connecting the two sweater parts to separate the tightly knitted sweaters. After handling all the sweaters, she folded them one by one and put them aside, piling up neatly just like the bricks on the city walls. It seemed that my mother could always keep everything in order.

My father sent the sweater accessories produced the day before to markets every morning, and then went home to help my mother take care of the machines. Whenever something went wrong with machines, my dad would try to find out the crux with tools in one hand. It was incredible that my dad was able to fix the machines no matter how difficult the fault was. He also took over the task of buying food. With home dishes, some snacks, and an occasional glass of wine, we spent so many simple but happy days amid machine roars.

Time went by smoothly. In the following years, my parents bought more machines with savings from the previous year, and there were 25 machines when I was 12 years old. My paternal grandpa and my dad, in order to put down those huge machines, filled the small pond in front of our house and rebuilt a large workshop to accommodate them. These majestic giants were lined up in rows there.

Accompanied by machine roars, I learned to speak, to eat by myself, and to write; and accompanied by machine roars, our life was put back in order and became better.

My parents sold off all the original electric machines after we moved to a new house in 2013. Although those machines of several thousand yuan only sold at several hundred yuan, we bade farewell to those old friends which depreciated by almost ten times. My parents later bought more advanced automatic computerized flat knitting machines with their savings. Thanks to those bigger and smarter new machines, we were able to produce more sweater accessories with more intricate and beautiful patterns, and consequently embarked on a new life journey.

Every day, the deafening noise of the machine lasted longer and longer, almost around the clock. My parents were totally tied-up with delivering goods, buying woolen yarn and negotiating deals. It was amid the persistent roars that we gradually struck a balance between business and happiness. We stayed ambitious and hopeful for most of the time despite being tired of work occasionally.

"Three dilapidated tile-roofed houses were all we got when I was a child and there was always a blackout when I did homework. And now our life is really getting better," said my mom when she recalled the past.

Now every time I get back, I can still hear incessant machine roars coming out of workshops in the distance.

"Sweetheart, you are on your vacation now. Would you like to help us with the sweater?" That's what my parents would always say. Well then, I would have a try on these advanced computer machines, I thought.

温州人奋斗精神的传承

赵庆远

这个故事显然不是什么宏大叙事，只是浙江温州无数农村青年为生活而打拼的一个缩影，但如果放到改革开放时期浙江特别是温州地区飞跃式发展的大背景下，这个故事和千千万万个小故事一起，成为改革大潮中的一朵浪花。

家庭工业是温州模式的核心。温州模式又被称作“小狗经济”，贴切形容了温州遍地的小企业、小家庭作坊的场景。作者的父亲正是从亲戚的家庭企业开始学徒，逐渐独立出来创办了自己的家庭企业。温州的家庭企业也正是这样开枝散叶、遍地开花，如雨后春笋一般快速生长，又如同春天的草原一样，瞬时就染绿了整个温州地区。小微企业支撑了温州地区庞大的市场体量，广大农民因此而摆脱了传统的农业生产方式，迈上了小康之路，而条件适合的很多农村地区也就地实现了城镇化和工业化，温州地区在短短20余年的时间里实现了社会经济发展的巨大变迁，成为改革开放的排头兵。作者的家庭无疑是温州模式的受益者，是改革开放的受益者。发生在作者家庭里的故事，显然已经成为民间口头文学的一部分，无数个这样的小故事又构成了温州传奇，不光流行于本地区，同样也流行于长城内外、大江南北。文化的积淀是一个地方人文精神的根源，温州人的奋斗精神可以说是“与生俱来”的，生长在这样的文化氛围中的温州人在潜移默化中把这种自强不息的精神一代又一代传承下去，这也是这篇文章里所显示出来的文化之根。

作者的母亲初中毕业后，用自己单薄的肩膀扛着小小的家当来到北方城市太原做工，而作为读者的我当时也正在太原的国有单位工作。我亲身经历了20世纪90年代国企改革的浪潮，目睹了其中的各式各样的悲喜剧。

温州的农民依靠自己的双手去打工、创业，而北方一些城市的工人们却固执地期待着单位能为自己解决生存大计。这种对比和差异只有亲身经历过的人才能感受得到。温州模式已经被证明了是一种具有强大生命力的发展模式，但归根到底，它靠的是人的观念来支撑的。

从文章中，我看到的是观念和文化的传承，看到的是温州人把奋斗精神已经很好地传给了新时代的年轻人。我希望，这种精神在新时代的背景下能够得到新的发展和提升，在时代大潮中以新的面貌展现出来。我相信，新时代的青年人一定会做得比老一辈更好。

（宁波甬安社会评价研究院）

故事

温州

胡露敏（新闻学专业 192 班）

虹桥镇上那点事

我的父母出生于浙江温州乐清虹桥镇，农村出身的他们没有优越的家庭环境，今日的生活靠的全是他们的打拼。

母亲的家庭是当时农村家庭的普遍例子——多女一子，母亲有三个妹妹一个弟弟，作为家中长女的母亲，自是早早地懂事。初中一毕业她就去了家附近的裁缝店学手艺，学习设计图纸、裁剪、做服装，总共学了三个月。和镇上的许多人一样，三个月后，年仅 16 岁的母亲就跟着表姐远去太原帮人做服装，这是母亲人生的第一场远行。瘦弱的臂膀扛着大包小包的行李，从汽车到绿皮火车，1490 公里的路，从南方到北方，两天两夜的行程，餐餐泡面，两个女孩只有相互依靠。然而旅途的艰辛远比不上呆在太原的日子。

昏暗的灯泡泛着黄白的灯光，深夜里只能听到缝纫机吱吱啦啦的声音，偶有狗吠与猫叫，做工的夜晚是漫长又难熬的。曾有一次，母亲凌晨仍在做衣服，她困得不行，眼皮欲合，一时疏忽下，缝纫机的针直插手指，母亲瞬间清醒了过来，被针扎的手指滋滋冒着鲜血。那是不眠之夜，流血的手指，未做完的衣服，都是 16 岁少女在外乡打工时咽下的苦楚。

16 岁的母亲，独身在外乡打工，谈起她人生赚的第一桶金，母亲不由自主地嘴角上扬："那会儿干了三个来月吧，到年底也只有 1000 块，虽然挺辛苦的，但当时也觉得很幸福，因为是自己第一次赚的钱。"

后来母亲还打趣道："从太原回来后，说以后一定不要嫁个做生意的，太辛苦了，于是就和你爸结婚了。"

我的父亲，同样也是初中毕业后便同舅舅远赴内蒙古做生意，这也是父亲的第一场远行。父亲在内蒙古呆了半年，帮他的舅舅在乌审旗（内蒙古称县城为旗）的门市部（内蒙古商店的称呼）卖百货。据父亲的描述，当时的店名为五一商店，商店店面有150平方米左右。五一商店是那个县城第二大的商铺，售卖各类百货，如服装、生活用品和玩具等。

那时候条件不好，父亲和他的舅舅是住在商店里的，没有单独的房间，店里只有一张小小的折叠床，只在晚上睡觉时再搬出来。而且作为一名南方人，刚来到北方，多少有些不适应的地方。内蒙古常刮风沙，空气中常是沙尘的味道，眼前也常常只有茫茫的黄色，几米外看不清人。有时候风沙一刮，店里便布满了沙尘，玻璃柜台、地上全被沙尘覆盖，所以每回刮起风沙，父亲就得重新清理商铺。还有一点令父亲不适应的就是内蒙古的冬天，零下的温度加上刺骨的寒风，还有下雪，在南方呆惯了的父亲，没有穿大棉袄的习惯，自是受不了。

母亲17岁那年又辗转去了南京，帮一个表哥做服装，因为当时很多的温州人在南京做服装，那时候母亲在同一个院子里认识了一个同龄的温州女生，那个女生在南京读高中，母亲和她常在周末一同游玩，中山陵、公园、她的学校。母亲谈到她们的校园生活时，语气中满是羡慕。

我问母亲为什么当时不去读书。她笑着说："那时候想读书啊，但是家里没钱。如果当时条件好一点的话，应该也会去上学的，初中毕业那会你外婆给了我40块报名费，她说'如果你能考上普高就给你上学，如果考上职业中学就别读了，家里负担太重了，家里那么多人，负担太重了'。以我当时的成绩，我觉得普高有一点难度，于是就没去试，想想还是很遗憾的。"

曾与外婆聊天时，外婆还感叹："你妈妈当时就是想读书的，但是她懂事，很早就出去打工了。唉，当时就是没钱啊！"

在内蒙古呆了半年的父亲，最终还是选择回到温州学习手艺。那个时候虹桥镇上学习模具手艺的人很多。父亲向他的姑父学习做模具，那时候没有学费，只是买了烟酒赠予姑父。刚学模具，学的是最基本的钳工，像是挫切、打光、钻等基础手艺。因为以前的机床设备少，在外加工工件还需要排队等待，光是基本功就学了有整整一年，然后再是学习模具装配、画纸质图设计。

父亲学习做模具大概花费了两年的时间。在做学徒期间是没有工资的，学成之后他跟着姑父做了一年，一个月大概也只有七八百元。即便学习的时间长，刚开始工作时的薪水也并不高。但父亲并不是一个急躁的人，他能够沉下气来，他认为只要掌握好一门技术就不愁没钱赚。

在1996年，父亲来到本地工业区的一个电子厂上班，刚进厂时工资也只有1000块一个月。当时所在的公司并不是很忙，接的单也不多，工作虽然不是很辛苦只是工资也没有明显的上涨。

于是在 1998 年，不甘止步于此的父亲，选择跳槽到另外一家公司，刚跳槽新公司时的工资也只有 1000 块一个月，但年终奖有 8000 块，相比于原来的公司也更有上升空间。在新公司期间，父亲带了许多的学徒，后期又利用晚上的空闲时间在家中自己接活干。

2004 年，父亲从公司出来，选择单干，买了模具的设备，自己接模具单，同时收了两个学徒。在此期间，父亲还自学了电脑绘制模具图，自己琢磨研究，在网上查找资料，捣鼓软件。

2005 年，因为原来工作的公司变忙，老板重新聘请父亲回去工作，并以承包车间的方式让父亲管理整个车间。

父亲的工作生涯并非一帆风顺，但他肯下功夫与精力，正是他一点一点踏踏实实地干，让我们家的生活越来越好。

1999 年，在浙江温州乐清的虹桥镇上，同许多人一样，我的父亲与母亲经媒人介绍相识。1999 年 9 月 29 日，父亲骑着自行车载着母亲来到镇上领结婚证。

2000 年订婚时，母亲家花了 3 万块钱买了一辆日本进口的摩托车作为嫁妆。2001 年和 2007 年我与弟弟分别出生了。2008 年在母亲和父亲的共同努力下家里买了一辆价值 14 万元的日产尼桑。2011 年我们家开始翻新盖房，耗时一年后入住。2019 年 6 月我们家又新购置了一辆车。生活在小镇上的我们一家，生活虽比不上大城市里的优质，但父母有着相对稳定的收入，没有房贷的压力，有车有房，养育着两个孩子，

我们家的故事看似平淡，但也是虹桥镇上许多家庭走向小康的一个缩影。

Wenzhou
Hu Lumin (Class 192, Majoring in Journalism)

A Story in Hongqiao Town

My parents were born in Hongqiao Town, Yueqing, Wenzhou, Zhejiang Province. Born in rural areas, they did not have a good family environment. It is their struggle that has brought them a happy life today.

My mother's family was a typical rural family at that time where several daughters and one son were raised. My mother has three younger sisters and a younger brother. As the eldest daughter of the family, my mother was sensible at an early age. As soon as she graduated from junior high school, she went to a tailor shop near home to learn craft. She studied drawing design, cutting and making clothes for three months in total. Like many other people in town, my mother, a 16-year-old girl, followed her cousin to Taiyuan three months later to make clothes. It was her first long journey. Bags of luggage on their thin arms, they travelled 1490 kilometers from south to north by taking buses and the green train. Spending two days and nights travelling, they only had instant noodles to eat. The two girls relied on each other. However, the journey was far less difficult than the days in Taiyuan.

The dim light from bulb was yellow and white. There was only the sound of the sewing machine in the wee hours of the night with dogs and cats' barking occasionally. Working at night was long and oppressive. Once, my mother made clothes in the early morning, but she was so sleepy that her eyes were half closed. The needle of the sewing machine pricked her finger through a moment's inattention, and the finger was bleeding freely. The pain woke her up immediately. The bleeding finger and the unfinished clothes were the sufferings she had to swallow when working far away from home.

When my mother who worked alone in the other city at the age of 16, talked about the money she first earned in her life, she smiled involuntarily and said, "I worked for three months, and only earned 1,000 yuan by the end of the year. I felt really happy at that time although it was very hard, because it was the first time that I earned money."

Afterwards, my mother joked, "After I came back from Taiyuan, I told myself not to marry a businessman because it was too hard. However, I didn't expect to marry your father."

My father went to Inner Mongolia to do business with his uncle after graduating from middle school, which was his first long trip. My father spent half a year there, helping his uncle sell groceries in the sales department of Wushenqi county. According to my father, the store was called Wuyi Shop, which had an area of about 150 square meters. It was the second largest shop in the county, selling all kinds of merchandise such as clothes, daily necessities, toys and so on.

The condition was not good at that time. My father lived in the shop with his uncle. There were no separate rooms but only a small folding bed for them in the shop. The folding bed would only be taken out at night when they were going to sleep. As a southerner who just came to the north, he was somewhat not used to the weather there. It was usually windy and dusty in Inner Mongolia, and the air was mixed with sand and dust. What they could see was a vast stretch of yellow, and it was hard to recognize people a few meters away. When a sandstorm came, sand could be found everywhere in the shop. There was sand and dust on the glass counter and the floor. Therefore, every time sandstorm came, my father had to clean up the shop again. The winter in Inner Mongolia was what my father found hard to get used to. The temperature was below zero and there was freezing wind and snow. Growing up in Southern China, my father could not bear the coldness of the winter in Northern China for not having the habit of wearing a cotton-padded jacket.

At the age of 17, my mother left for Nanjing to help her cousin make clothing. There were a lot of Wenzhou people making clothing in Nanjing at that time. My mother met a Wenzhou girl of her age in the same yard. That girl was studying at a high school in Nanjing. My mother often played with her at the weekend, visiting places like Sun Yat-sen's Mausoleum, or her school. When talking about their campus life, my mother was really envious.

I asked my mother why she didn't go to school. She smiled and replied, "I wanted to study at that time, but my family had no money. If the condition had been better at that time, I would have gone to school. When I graduated from middle school, your grandmother gave me 40 yuan as registration fee. She told me that I could keep studying only if I could pass the examination and be admitted by a high school. However, if I could only reach the admission score for a vocational school, then I had no choice but quit school, because it was a really heavy burden to support so many people in our family. It was a bit difficult for me to enter high school with my exam results, so I didn't give it a try. What a pity."

Once when I chatted with my grandma, she sighed: "Your mother wanted to study at that time, but she was so sensible that she chose to work early. We really couldn't afford it at that time!"

My father, who spent half a year in Inner Mongolia, returned to Wenzhou to learn craft. At that time, there were a lot of people learning the mould craft in Hongqiao town. My father learned mould crafts from his uncle. At that time, there was no tuition fee, so he just bought cigarettes and alcohol as gifts for his uncle. When he first studied moulding, what he learned was the basic bench work, which was work like mould cutting, polishing, drilling and other basic skills. Because there was little mechanical equipment in the past, he had to wait if he wanted to process the workpiece outside. It took him a whole year to learn basic skills, and then he learned mould assembling and paper-drawing design.

My father spent two years learning how to make moulds and there was no salary during the period of apprenticeship. My father worked for his uncle for a year after apprenticeship, about 700 or 800 yuan a month. The salary was not high even for one who had been learning for a long time, but my father was not in a rush. and he was really patient. He thought he would have no trouble making money as long as he mastered a skill well.

In 1996, my father worked in an electronics factory in the local industrial area. His salary was only 1000 yuan a month when he entered the factory. The company was not very busy, and didn't have many orders. The work was not very toilsome, and his salary did not increase significantly.

In 1998, my father chose to charge his job to another company. At the beginning, his salary was only 1000 yuan a month, but his year-end bonus was 8000 yuan, which had more potential to be raised compared with the previous company. During the time in the new company, my father took many apprentices with him. Later, he did part-time jobs at home in his spare time in the evenings.

In 2004, my father quit his job from the company to work on his own. He bought mould equipment and took the mould orders by himself. At the same time, he accepted two apprentices. During this period, my father learned how to draw mould designs on computer by himself. He searched for information on the Internet and learned about software.

In 2005, as the company that he had worked for before became busy, the previous boss hired my father back to work and let him manage the whole workshop by contracting the whole workshop.

My father's career life didn't go smoothly, but he was willing to work hard and devoted a lot of effort to it. It was because of his earnest work that made our family's life better and better.

In 1999, like many other people, my parents were introduced by the matchmaker in Hongqiao Town, Yueqing, Wenzhou City, Zhejiang Province. On the 29th of September in 1999, my father, riding a bicycle, took my mother to town to get a marriage certificate.

When they got engaged in 2000, my mother's family bought a motorcycle which was imported from Japan for 30,000 yuan as a dowry. I was born in 2001 and my brother was born in 2007. In 2008, my parents worked together to buy a Nissan car which was worth 140,000 yuan. In 2011, our family rebuilt the house, and we moved in after one year. In June of 2019, our family bought a new car. Although we live in a small town and our life is not as good as those people living in a big city, our parents have a relatively stable income. Without a mortgage to pay, they have cars, a house and two children.

The story of our family seems to be ordinary, but it is a microcosm of many families struggling for their well-off life in Hongqiao Town.

此生结缘此屋中

孙懿琳

从古至今，房屋对于中国人来说意义非凡，没有一个国家会像中国人那样，如此地重视自己的住宅。中国人注重家的概念，而承载家庭最基础的并且最具有象征性的就是房屋。《汉书·元帝纪》里说到："安土重迁，黎民之性；骨肉相附，人情所愿也。"其中前半句就说明了百姓安于本土本乡，不愿意轻易迁移。其中原因之一是房屋本是不动之物，无法随人携带；当然原因之二是房屋内设所承载的是一家几代人的记忆，一砖一瓦、一花一木，从朝阳初升到日暮黄昏，房屋也见证了于它之内的各种变化。从一个人牙牙学语、蹒跚学步时期，到坚定创业、明确方向时期，再到年入古稀、儿女承欢时期，无论是幼年、中年，还是暮年，离不开的就是房屋住所。金家祖孙三代与花屋的情缘便是如此，这份情，是动不得的。

从安定的房屋住所，到流动的城市变迁，为了顺应大环境的变化，守护金家三代的花屋不得不接受它最终的宿命——拆迁。从那一刻起，花屋被永远地封印在了金家人的记忆里，除了他们，可能再无人知晓、无人提起这花屋里的欢声笑语、悲欢故事。所以当提起房屋对于中国人的意义的时候，我仍然觉得：与其说是我们住在了屋子里，不如说是屋子给予了我们相识，房屋是一份情，而不是冰冷的四方体。

（浙大宁波理工学院新闻学专业181班学生）

故事
湖州
金颐宁(新闻学专业202专升本班)

花屋下的三代人

嘀嗒,嘀嗒,嘀嗒,雨中的世界总是不太宁静的。耳边那雨水碰撞的曲音渐渐模糊,时光将我倏然拉扯回我的家,那个充溢着花香的家。湖州市吴兴区小西街29号,一个再普通不过的坐标,却埋下了我们祖孙三代与花屋数十载的缘。

我家的屋子嵌在江南水边的一条弄堂里,邻居们总喜欢亲切地称它为"花屋"。说它是花屋,可丝毫没有夸张。从远处看,它是被花裹挟着的,整个弄堂的颜色仿佛皆浓缩在了这一间屋内。而走近,那四溢的清香便会沁入人的心脾,融化所有的愁闷。有人说,透过一朵花便可看及整个世界。我虽无此种格局,却深谙从花屋里确是足以味遍我整个家的。

1972年爷爷33岁,正值壮年。在湖州著名画家、茶学研究者寇丹家做客时,爷爷偶然间被书桌上的一盆仙人球勾住了眼球。只见其三岔直立,怒发冲冠,尖锐之刺直指苍穹,着实有趣。爷爷问后才知,那仙人球名为"三箭齐发",爷爷体悟到了植栽的乐趣,由此,便开始了养花之路。

于是,爷爷便开始四处搜罗各种养花宝典,向各处取经,月季花成了栽培重心。渐渐地,家里的整个院子都被爷爷铺满了各式的月季花。

几近疯狂地,爷爷对花的热爱一发不可收。不仅院墙内、台阶上,即便是屋顶上,也被爷爷搭满了铁丝架。奶奶说:"你爷爷把花看得比什么都重要,每次从外面回来,他先上屋顶浇花,不浇完不吃饭。一到周末,他就跑到花鸟市场去买花,那时候上班一个月能挣25块,他把厂子里挣来的钱都用在养花上了。你爸爸那时候上小学,起居、作业都是我管的。"爷爷笑回道:"坚持一件事,就要做到尽善尽美,中途放弃可不行。"

"你爷爷不管晴天雨天,对养花的热爱从来就没减少过。所以他告诉我,要我学得精,学得专,对一件事要持之以恒,决定了就算走岔路也是一种精彩。"爸爸回忆道。

养着养着,爷爷种月季花渐入佳境,很多心得也随之产生。1979年,上海青浦一个交通站的站长对月季颇有兴趣,便通过朋友的介绍来湖州拜访爷爷。"当时我对他说，别人种月季花总喜欢用大的紫砂盆，但是我说用小的泥盆就行了。月季花喜欢干燥的环境，太潮湿了就容易得黑斑病，我把月季养在小的花盆里，还就只放一半的泥，就是为了让泥里的水分快速排走，预防黑斑病。你爷爷有个特质，就是爱钻研，我发现有时候书上说的也不一定对，所以我喜欢通过自己的经验，来研究一些新的培植方法。”

在爷爷的熏陶下，爸爸也渐渐能够帮衬着干些院里的活儿。一到周末，他便拿着又大又沉的工具，从困水、浇水，到修枝、剪叶，一些基础的活计都逐渐变得得心应手起来。在这一方小院里，那两个忙碌的身影常常是花屋里一道独特的风景线。也正是在一次次与花交往的过程中，爸爸的心里也渐渐埋下了爱花的种子。

就这样，在爷爷的培育下，原本单调的老屋成了远近闻名的花屋。街坊邻居总时不时地串门，坐在院子里话话家常，爷爷的花园成了这条弄堂里最热闹的地方。

1986年，17岁的爸爸辍了学，决定将养花作为他终身的事业。爷爷爱花，却也懂得，养花虽可陶冶志趣，但只能作为闲适时的一类爱好。而在奶奶的观念里，以养花为业更是痴人说梦。因此，爸爸与爷爷奶奶大吵了一架，一气之下搬到了朋友家暂住了一段时间。

“你爸遗传了你爷爷的犟脾气，一下决心，十头牛都拉不回来。”最终在大家的解劝之下，爸爸才与爷爷奶奶达成和解，重新搬了回来。

那时，山茶花、杜鹃花可谓花界新宠，红极一时。爸爸便用在石粉厂打工挣的钱添置了5盆绯爪芙蓉，5盆皇冠，10盆大玛瑙，20盆西洋杜鹃，并在屋顶植满了凌霄花。在这些花儿的装点下，旧日的花屋又重焕了新色，爷爷的脸上也重展了笑容。

1991年，经过5个年头的经验积累和资金拼凑，爸爸的花卉行终于在城西开业了。“当时为了筹钱，几乎把朋友亲戚借了个遍，最后还是你奶奶把藏着准备给我结婚的钱拿出来了。”经营初期，百废待兴，年仅22岁的爸爸却对未来充满了希望。“当然是想把花行越做越大，一来是好早点还清家里的债，二来是多攒一些钱好给你爷爷奶奶养老，养儿防老嘛。”

就这样，爸爸本着踏踏实实的生意经，拿到了一手的货源。而更为重要的是，爸爸的人脉也因此迅速扩充。此后花行的生意可谓蒸蒸日上。

1995年，爸爸在朋友的介绍下认识了妈妈。那时妈妈在城南的丝织联营厂工作，而每天下班不论早晚，总能在路口看到倚靠在电灯柱旁的爸爸。“你爸爸每次都会带着一朵小白花给我，我那时不知道那是什么花，只知道那花香喷喷的很讨人喜欢。”在我的印象里，妈妈总喜欢坐在花屋一角的一棵树下洗衣服，她告诉童稚的我，那小花叫做含笑，象征着她和爸爸纯真而羞涩的初恋爱情。

1998年，我出生了，这个花香四溢的屋子又迎来了新的声音。我笑着、哭着、喊着、闹着，花屋下的家人们忙碌在我的周围，时刻为我的一举一动所牵动着。我成了花屋的中心，也成了这个家的中心。或许是因为我在这和着花香的爱中长大，我对花与家也有着特殊的情愫。不论在哪儿，一看见花，我的心头总会浮现出家人们的一颦一笑；不论何时，一闻到花香，我的血液总会汹涌起家的暖流。

2013年，依城市发展的需求，花屋被纳入了拆迁范围，爷爷与爸爸只能在匆忙间将花悉数赠予他人。这历经41年的花屋，终于被永远地印在了一卷卷胶片上，成了我们三代人再也无法触摸到的记忆。

如今，爸爸的两鬓渐霜，已看不到年轻时的傲气，却仍为了我们的家而奔波操劳着。爷爷也已81岁高龄，再没有攀上爬下的力气，走路时也只能是伛偻着。他与奶奶在僻静的小楼里租了一间房，在那小小的阳台上养了一盆水仙。在和爷爷谈起年轻时养花的经历时，我清楚地看到他几近失神的眼里又重燃起了热情的光芒。我倏尔瞥向那角落里蓄势的水仙，仿佛恍惚中又看到了花屋屋顶上爷爷那宽厚而忙碌的背影。无言地，我只觉一阵鼻酸，接着便任由泪水模糊了我的视线。

嘀嗒，嘀嗒，嘀嗒……

窗外雨的曲音仍在继续，这就是花屋的故事，以及花屋下我们祖孙三代的故事。

Huzhou
Jin Yining (Class 202, Majoring in Journalism)

The Three Generations in Flower House

Tick, tick, tick, tranquility was always disturbed on the rainy days. The melody played by the rain gradually faded and time suddenly pulled me back to my home—the one full of flower fragnance. Despite an ordinary coordinate in a map, No. 29 apartment on Xiaoxi Street, Wuxing District, Huzhou City, has made a bond between the three generations of my family and the flower house for decades.

My home was embedded in a lane by the river south of the Yangtze River. Neighbors always liked to call it the "flower house". It is not an exaggeration to say so. Seen from a distance, it was surrounded by flowers, and the color of the entire lane seemed to be concentrated here. Up close, the overflowing fragrance would gladden people's hearts and drive away all the depression. It's said that the whole world can be seen through a single flower. Though I cannot reach this level, I know well that it is enough to see my family through the flower house.

Grandpa was 33 years old in 1972, just in the prime of his life. When visiting Kou Dan, a famous painter and tea researcher in Huzhou, he was attracted by a pot of cactus on the desk. Its three branches stood upright with anger, and the sharp thorns pointed directly at the sky, which looked really interesting. Grandpa later learned that it was named "Three Arrows Shot at Once". He realized the joy of planting, and thus began growing flowers.

Grandpa searched for various secrets about growing flowers from everywhere. Chinese rose became the focus of cultivation. Gradually, the whole yard was covered with all kinds of Chines roses by Grandpa.

Grandpa's love for flowers became almost crazy and unstoppable. The courtyard walls, the steps, and even the roof, were also covered with wire frames by Grandpa. Grandma said, "Your Grandpa valued flowers more than anything else. Every time he came back from outside, he first went to the roof to water the flowers, and wouldn't eat until finishing watering. On weekends, he went to the flower and bird market to buy flowers. At that time, he could earn 25 yuan a month at work. He spent all he earned from the factory on growing flowers. When your father was in elementary school, I was in total charge of his daily life and homework." Grandpa laughed and said, "When you insist on one thing, you have to make it perfect and cannot just give up halfway."

"Whether rainy or sunny, your Grandpa's love for growing flowers has never faded. Since I was a child, he has told me to be good at what I learn and be an expert at what I do. You should persist on one thing. It's a different scenery in your life even if proved to be wrong finally," Dad recalled.

As time went by, Grandpa grew Chinese rose with higher proficiency and gained more experience. In 1979, the stationmaster of a traffic station in Qingpu District, Shanghai was interested in Chinese rose, so he came to Huzhou to visit Grandpa under the introduction of his friends. "I told him that others used to grow Chinese rose in big purple clay pots, but if you ask me, a small clay pot would do. Chinese rose likes dry atmospheres. Otherwise, it's easy to get black spot. Keeping Chinese rose in a small pot and only putting in half of the clay are to quickly drain away the moisture in the clay, and prevent black spot. I have a trait that I am keen on studying. I find what the books say is not always true, so I like to study some new methods of cultivation through my own experience."

Under the influence of Grandpa, Dad was gradually able to help with some work in the courtyard. At the weekend, he usually held large and heavy tools. Some basic tasks, such as regulating water quality, watering and pruning gradually became handy for my dad. Two busy figures in this small courtyard often made a unique scene at the flower house. It was also in the constantly interacting with flowers that the seeds of love for flowers were gradually sowed in Dad's heart.

In this way, under the cultivation of Grandpa, the old dull house became a well-known flower house. The neighbors would drop by from time to time and sit in the yard chatting with each other. Grandpa's garden became the busiest place in the lane.

In 1986, Dad quit school at the age of 17 and decided to make growing flowers his lifelong career. Grandpa loved flowers, but also knew that flower cultivation could edify sentiment, and should only be taken as a hobby at leisure. In Grandma's opinion, this was no more than a fool's talk. Therefore, after a big quarrel with my grandparents, Dad became angry and moved to a friend's house for a while.

"Your father is as stubbon as your Grandpa. Once he was determined, nothing could change his mind." Finally, after everyone's persuasion, Dad reached a settlement with my grandparents and moved back.

At that time, camellia and rhododendron could be said to be new favorites in the flower world and enjoyed popularity for a time. With the money Dad earned in the stone powder factory, he added five pots of Feizhaofurong (one kind of Hibiscus), five King's Cup, ten Cornelian and twenty Rhododendron hybridum, and filled the roof with trumpet creepers. With the decoration of these flowers, the flower house regained its new color, and the smile on Gandpa's face was restored.

In 1991, after accumulation of experience and fundraising for five years, Dad's flower shop finally opened in the west of the city. "At that time, I almost borrowed money from all our friends and relatives. In the end, your grandmother took out the money that was saved up for my marriage." In the initial stage, thousands of things waited to be done, but 22-year-old Dad was still hopeful for the future. "Of course, I wanted to make the flower business bigger and bigger to pay off the debt of our family as soon as possible, and on the other hand, to save more money so that I can support your grandparents for their old age. Just as the saying goes, people raise children to provide for old age."

Dad got the first-hand supply of goods in a down-to-earth way. And more importantly, his social network also expanded rapidly. After that, the flower business had been thriving.

In 1995, Dad met my mother under the introduction of a friend. My mother was working in a silk weaving joint venture, south of the city then. Whenever she got off work every day, she could always see Dad leaning on the light pole at the intersection. "Your father always brought me a small white flower I didn't know at the time. I could only tell that its fragrance was so pleasant." In my impression, my mother always liked to sit and do the laundry under a tree in the corner of the flower house. She told me that the little flower was called Michelia figo, which symbolized their pure and shy first love.

In 1998 when I was born, a new voice appeared in this fragrant house. I was laughing, crying, shouting, and making noises, surrounded by my busy family members. They were always being affected by my every move. I became the center of the flower house, and also the center of the whole family. Perhaps because I grew up in love with the fragrance of flowers, I have a special affection for flowers and home. Wherever I see the flowers, the smiles of my family members are always vivid in my mind. Whenever I smell the flowers, the warmth of home always wraps me.

In 2013, according to the needs of urban development, the flower house was included in the scope of demolition. Grandpa and Dad could only give all the flowers to others in a hurry. This 41-year-old flower house was finally printed on rolls of film forever, and became the memory that the three generations of my family could never touch anymore.

Now, the hair on my Dad's temples gradually became silver, and the pride of his youth cannot be seen. But he is still working hard for our family. Grandpa is already 81 years old and no longer has the strength to go up and down. He can only walk with his back bent. He and Grandma rented a room in a small secluded building and kept a pot of daffodils in that small balcony. When I talked to him about growing flowers when he was young, I clearly saw the light of enthusiasm rekindled in his almost faded eyes. I glanced at the budding daffodils in the corner, as if I had seen Grandpa's generous and busy figure on the roof of the flower house in a daze. Silently, a burst of tears strunk me and blurred my eyes.

Tick, tick, tick...

The melody of the rain still goes on outside the window. This is the story of the flower house and also the story of the three generations of my family.

在水的隐喻中品塘栖叙事

周盼佳

《家在塘栖》这篇文章用叙事的手法讲述了一户小镇人家自20世纪60年代以来的变化。叙事（narrative）是一种故事化的叙说言谈形式，既是认知或表达模式，也是生活或行为模式，普遍存在于生活原貌之中。简单来说，就是讲故事。学者刘渼认为叙事的基本结构是由故事（story）、言说（discourse）和叙述行为（narration）所组成。在文中，作者讲述了父亲和母亲的创业历程，从国营企业到自己开公司，从哑巴英语到开英语教育机构。平铺直叙的语言娓娓道来。虽然没有华丽的词藻，但让读者很快能明白作者家庭生活的变化紧跟着时代的变革。

塘栖的水是故乡的隐喻，是生活的缩影。塘栖，一个古色古香的小镇，坐落在京杭大运河畔。水是这个江南小镇的生命。文中，关于水的隐喻贯穿了整篇文章，比如说井里的水和父亲培训时的汗水。理查德斯在1936年的著作《修辞的哲学》一书中指出，隐喻的组成有三部分：1.喻体，指作者想要描述之主题；2.喻依，指的是用来描述意义的凭借；3.喻词，指用来连结喻体和喻依的补助词。在这篇文章中，喻体是生活，喻依是水。流动的水就像流动的生活，随着时间的延展而缓缓地变化。这种变化是美好的，就像京杭大运河最终随着甬江流向东海，流动的生活业也奔向美好的未来。

（宁波诺丁汉大学国际传播学在读博士）

故事

杭州

沈雨清(网络与新媒体专业 193 班)

家在塘栖

我出生于塘栖,杭州的一个普普通通的小镇,京杭大运河穿镇而过。这个古色古香的小镇,是我爸爸妈妈出生的地方,也是我儿时成长的地方。

塘栖奶奶家的后面仍有一口井。这口井在我儿时就有了,并且一直被使用到现在,奶奶说,这口井已经很老很老了。我依稀听见了水桶和井壁碰撞发出的声音,时间在井边变得很慢很慢。

20 世纪 60 年代末,我的父亲出生于塘栖。

高中毕业之后,他应聘到一个 1985 年建厂的老牌国营企业,在精工车间中做钳工,工作一段时间后,企业送他到绍兴轧钢厂培训。几百度高温的铁条在头顶上方的机器中飞过,闷热的车间里,汗水浸湿一件又一件的衣服。培训不仅是艰苦的,更是一次磨练。

三个月的辛苦培训结束后,由于表现优异,父亲有了更多展示自己的机会。父亲被领导安排到了企业的各部门轮训,在这个过程中,他不仅学到了更多的技能,也对一个企业的运作有了更多的了解。

1989 年后,在改革开放的大背景下,对外开放有了新的进展,中国的对外贸易也进入了一个新的阶段。机缘巧合下,外国企业来收购工厂的出口业务,父亲的英语水平不错,1990 年便组建了浙江省冶金行业的第一家中外合资企业。

当时工厂所生产的钢丝绳是国家所限制的出口产品,父亲便开始往返于北京和杭州,去北京国家对外经济贸易部审批出口商品的许可证,一年中跑了数十趟北京才办下来。

企业运作初期,所有的出口渠道都被外方所垄断,产品价格被恶意压低,父亲在很多进出口公司中寻找出口的办法。这个过程中遇到许多的困难,苍天不负有心人,父亲找到了出口的渠道,使得企业的销售额极速上升,钢丝绳的生产从原来占企业产量的 5%涨到了 40%。

由于能力突出,父亲赢得了一个去浙江大学经济学院学习 2 年的机会,而后也从一个外贸部的经理被提拔成了负责整个销售部的副总经理。

后来国营企业转制，父亲便跑到上海去开了一家属于自己的公司。2000年我出生后，家庭的条件也越来越好。

1972年，我的妈妈也在塘栖出生了。她5岁那年，高考制度的恢复，使得全国上下都掀起了爱教育的狂潮，我妈妈也成为小镇里为数不多的女大学生之一。20世纪80年代，外婆进入了钢厂工作，外公在超耐厂也有了稳定的工作。改革开放后，外公家的经济状况也好了很多，有了第一台电视机，也让独生的女儿有了更好的生活。

从大学毕业后，妈妈成为一名财务，在一次海外出差的经历中，她发现她们那个年代的毕业生都存在一个共性难题——口语不行，“考场上的学霸”一到了国外就变成了“哑巴”。从小的教育经历让妈妈对“科教兴国”有着深刻的认知。本来就有创业打算的妈妈回国后，经过与爸爸的商量决定开办一家英语口语辅导机构。

创业，注定是一条筚路蓝缕的征程。在大众眼中，很多身披铠甲的创业者都是无所不能、刀枪不入的强者，但表面的云淡风轻背后，苦涩和心酸只有创业者自己能懂。没有相关经验的妈妈一开始步履维艰，为了加强自己的说服力和沟通能力，她不惜花大价钱学习教学技能和方法。很快她就从一个新人老师，变成了一个对孩子们了如指掌的老师，不仅能记住机构里200多个孩子的名字，还清楚了解每一个孩子的英语水平、性格特点、优势和劣势等。

创业之路荆棘满满，是一个充满挑战与困难的过程，但是妈妈作为一名90年代的女性创业者，诠释了一代人的拼搏奋斗精神，演绎了当代女性的独立自强。同时她也用匠心传承了教育精神，让知识惠及更多的下一代。

2000年我出生在塘栖，享受着长辈所创造的美好生活。在这个经济腾飞、技术发展的年代，我们碰到了最好的时候。有书读、吃饱饭、有衣穿的我们从小在全家的呵护与照顾下成长。

我在塘栖读完幼儿园后，爸爸在杭州市区买了房子，举家搬进了大房子，我有了更好的读书机会。如今的城市，甚至乡村，也很少再见到黄土路，取而代之的是整齐宽阔的柏油马路。我谨记长辈的言传身教。

我小时候的那个京杭大运河，还不是世界文化遗产，那条河是一代代人的生活内容之一，它见证着这里很多家庭的兴衰变革，见证了新中国70年、改革开放40多年来日新月异的发展和社会进步。

以前奶奶便是在塘栖的大运河边留下了许许多多的生活印记。以前爷爷奶奶住得离广济桥很近。

今天我又走在桥上，走在河岸两边的“美人靠”边上，依然能感受到这份历史沉淀的美。我小时候也会在上桥和下桥时认认真真数台阶，今天我不数台阶，我要数的是桥上桥下像流水一样美好的未来。

Hangzhou
Shen Yuqing (Class 193, Majoring in Network and New Media)

My Hometown in Tangqi

My birthplace Tangqi is an ordinary town in Hangzhou with Beijing-Hangzhou Grand Canal running through it. This ancient town was not only my parents' birthplace but the place where I grew up during childhood.

There's still a well behind grandma's house in Tangqi. It had been in use since I was a child. She told me that it was a well with a long history. Vaguely, I heard the sound of a bucket colliding with the wall of the well, while time seemed to slow down at the edge of it.

At the end of the 1960s, my father came to this world.

Graduating from high school, he was employed by an established state-owned enterprise founded in 1985 as a fitter in a workshop. After a while, the enterprise sent him to Shaoxing Rolling Mill for training. With iron bars of several hundred degrees shuttling in the machines overhead, he sweated countless clothes in the stuffy workshop. The professional training is tough indeed, but it's also a process to harden himself.

After that, my father was given more opportunities to show his talents because of his excellence in the three-month training. Soon after, he was arranged by leaders to various departments of the company for rotation training. In the process, he not only learned more skills, but also had a better understanding on the company's operation.

Since the year of 1989 when the reform and opening-up policy was implemented, China has witnessed a brand-new surge in foreign trade, with many foreign enterprises coming to purchase export business of factories. My father, with a good command of English, set up the first Sino-foreign joint venture of metallurgical industry by chance in 1990, in Zhejiang Province.

At that time, policy regulated that steel wire ropes produced by factories were restricted from export, so my father began to travel back and forth between Beijing and Hangzhou to apply for the exporting approval licensed by the Ministry of Foreign Economics and Trade. Dozens of trips within one year made it possible for him to get the license.

At the beginning of father's startup, all export channels were monopolized by foreign companies, with the price being maliciously cut. Therefore, my father looked for ways to export in many import and export companies. Finally, his hard work paid off. Despite so many difficulties, he not only found access for export, but also lifted the sales volume rapidly: the production of steel wire ropes increased from 5% to 40% of the original enterprise output.

Witnessing his excellent capacity, my father's superiors gave him an opportunity to further his study in the School of Economics of Zhejiang University for two years, and then he was promoted from a manager of the foreign trade department to deputy general manager of the whole sales department.

Afterwards, as the state-owned enterprise transformation failed, my father set up a company of his own in Shanghai. After 2000, I was born, and living standards for our family got better.

My mother was born in 1972, also in Tangqi. When she was five years old, the resumption of the College Entrance Examination System (Gaokao) made education trending all over the country. Undoubtedly, Mom became one of the few female college students in the small town. In the 1980s, both of my grandparents got stable jobs in a steel plant and a superduty refractory manufactory. The reform and opening-up improved their economic situation, bringing them the first TV set and higher-quality life for their only daughter.

Graduating from university, Mom started to work as an accountant. An overseas business trip made her realize the common problem that all graduates at her times had: their spoken English was so poor because of the examination-oriented education. Her education experience during childhood left her a deep understanding of "rejuvenation the country through science and education". She was determined to start her own business. After coming back to her motherland, Mom decided to set up a tutorial center for English speaking training through negotiation with father.

Starting a business is destined to be a long journey. Many ordinary people think that entrepreneurs are like soldiers in armor, who are undefeated and invulnerable. However, under the surface, the bitterness and sadness can only be understood by entrepreneurs themselves. Unexperienced as Mom was, she still took on everything on her own. In order to improve her persuasiveness and communication skills, she spent a huge amount of money and time on teaching skills and methods. Soon, she grew into an experienced teacher who had a comprehensive understanding of kids from a green hand. She could memorize more than 200 kids' names in the tutorial center and knew exactly their English proficiency, personality, advantages and disadvantages.

The road of managing a startup is full of thorns. It's a process full of challenges and difficulties. However, as a female entrepreneur in the 1990s, Mom interpreted the unshakable spirit, the independence and self-discipline of women of her generation. At the same time, she inherited the spirit as an educator with ingenuity, spreading knowledge to the next generation as much as possible.

Since I was born in the year 2000, I've been enjoying the wonderful life created by my elders. In the era of economic take-off and technological development, it's the best time. With sufficient books, food and clothing, I was taken good care of by my family.

After I finished kindergarten education in Tangqi, my father bought a house in downtown Hangzhou and we moved into a big house. Besides, higher-quality education became accessible for me. Nowadays, loess paths, rare in cities and even rural areas, have been replaced by neat wide asphalt road. Instructed and influenced by the words and deeds of the elderly in my family, I've never forgotten their earnest teachings.

The Beijing-Hangzhou Grand Canal wasn't a world cultural heritage then, but it's a crucial part of life for generations. It has witnessed the rise and fall of many families here, and the soaring development and social progress since the founding of China 70 years ago and the introduction of the Reform and Opening-up policy 40 years ago.

My grandmother left many marks of her life by the Grand Canal in the Tangqi basin when she and grandfather lived near the Guangji Bridge, the bridge above the Grand Canal.

Today, as I walk across the bridge and wander along both sides of the river, I can still appreciate the beauty of its long-gone history. I used to count the steps with heart when walking up and down the bridge, but now, what I want to count on instead is the brilliant future like the non-stop flowing river.

幸福都是奋斗出来的

董亚钊

张唯佳在《将故事写给我们》一文中重点提及了父母的创业经历，从1995年创立服装厂到印刷厂，再到油墨厂，直至2019年村子拆迁，他们用拆迁款买来新的厂房继续创业，向我们描绘了一个小家在20多年间的发展变化并逐步走上幸福小康之路的图景，同时也在一定程度上折射出中国社会经济在这20多年间的发展历程。

改革开放以来，我国的经济社会发生了翻天覆地的变化，从邓小平提出“小康社会”的战略构想，到20世纪末基本实现“小康”，再到党的十八大报告中明确提出“全面建成小康社会”，直到党的十九届五中全会高度评价决胜全面建成小康社会取得的决定性成就，我国的发展改革成果真正惠及了十几亿人口。当然，一个家庭的幸福生活一方面得益于社会发展变革带来的红利，另一方面与个人的努力奋斗密不可分，正如文中写的那样，“厂越来越大之后，管理就成了很大的问题，妈妈已经在厂里忙得不可开交了……但爸爸依然很忙，要不停地跑各个地方接单子，所以在我小时候的记忆里，爸爸总是留给我匆忙的背影”。

社会经济发展的滚滚洪流，奔流着，前进着，身处这洪流中的每个人、每个家庭也被裹挟着，发生着翻天覆地的变化，只要抓住机遇，努力奋斗，美好生活总有一天会来到！

（浙大宁波理工学院传媒与法学院，讲师）

故事
嘉兴
张唯佳(网络与新媒体专业193班)

将故事写成我们

爸爸出生于1968年,是家里的幺儿,上头有五个姐姐。

爸爸小的时候因为爷爷在嘉兴乍浦镇张家桥桥边经营着小卖部,家庭条件还算不错,所以爸爸在那个乡下思想还不是很先进的情况下,被爷爷送进了学校。爸爸心思没有放在学业上,高中便辍学开始了学徒工生涯。

爸爸当过很多种学徒工,其中做的时间最长的就是木工和渔夫。

1980年,爸爸开始学习木工,慢慢靠着他的木工手艺穿梭在小镇的条条小巷中,用双手赚着一份份来之不易的钱。几年之后,爸爸也称得上是木工师傅了,但小镇上的木工师傅也越来越多,再三权衡之后,他决定放弃木工,另谋出路。

1986年,爸爸漫无目的地来到乍浦镇的海边,岸边搁浅着出海船只,船上的号角声一下一下敲在爸爸的心上,一个新的想法就这样诞生了,爸爸决定出海打渔。爷爷并不同意,吵架的结果就是爷爷在爸爸再三保证会注意安全下妥协了,于是爸爸便一如当初开始学习木工时那样,怀着满腔热血跟着镇上的大船长踏上了出海的路。在后来打渔的时候,爸爸结识了我同为渔夫的舅舅——我妈妈的哥哥,也才有了更多的故事。后来爸爸的身体情况变得有些糟糕,爷爷在这时就更加不同意爸爸继续从事这个职业了,这次轮到爸爸妥协了。

妈妈出生于1969年,是家里的老幺,上头有一个哥哥。

妈妈很早就开始帮着外公外婆做事了。小学毕业之后,妈妈没打算继续念书,彼时正好她的哥哥也就是我的舅舅开始外出做工赚钱了,妈妈也想着自己作为女孩子,针线活总不在话下,便去了服装厂上班。妈妈是一个很机灵的人,很快就上手了,裁剪、缝纫之类的活做起来都得心应手。后来,妈妈又去了一家印刷厂工作,同样也上手很快。妈妈直到结婚之前才结束在印刷厂的工作,后来就到了属于自己的厂里。说来也巧,妈妈做的这两份工作恰好就对上了爸爸妈妈后来自己创办的两个工厂。

爸爸妈妈在18岁时相遇,但后面的桥段并没有立刻上演,原因就是我的外公外婆不愿意妈妈这么早就定下人家，所以这段故事就这么被“扼杀”在了摇篮里。然而缘分这个东西，有时候就是这么不可思议，兜兜转转8年后，他们又再次相遇，男未婚女未嫁，一切都是那么顺其自然，爸爸妈妈还是走到了一起。

1995年，爸爸妈妈走进了婚姻的殿堂，那时候的爸爸因为早早开始工作有了点积蓄，所以和妈妈的婚礼称得上隆重。因为两家人离得太近了，只单单从娘家把妈妈接过来就太快了，所以他们绕着整个小镇走了一圈，收获了很多乡亲的祝福。

爸爸妈妈成了一家人，想到以后还会有孩子，要承担的责任就更多了。爸爸妈妈再三商量之后决定自己开厂创业。爸爸在跑了几趟工商局之后办好了名为“正大”的服装厂的营业执照，和乡亲借了土地之后在离家不远的长安桥村开了工厂。工厂员工最多的时候达到200人。厂越来越大之后，管理就成了很大的问题，妈妈已经在厂里忙得不可开交了，于是爸爸便请了四姑妈和四姑父到厂里帮忙。但爸爸依然很忙，要不停地跑各个地方接单子，所以在我小时候的记忆里，爸爸总是留给我匆忙的背影。

服装厂的好光景让爸爸萌生了搞副业的想法，因为服装的吊牌还是外包的，所以爸爸就想着自己做以减少开支，于是“正大”印刷厂就这么在八字村创办了。这样的安排让爸爸变得更加忙碌了，不过还好有妈妈在旁边帮衬着。这样和谐的日子过了很久，本以为服装行业能一直继续下去，但是谁曾想地区的服装业开始走下坡路，一些外来务工人员接收到家乡改革的消息也陆陆续续离开了，爷爷又在这个时候病重去世，厂里和家里的气氛一下子都变得凝重了起来。爸爸作为一家之主，势必要承担起更多的东西。

服装厂难以维系，让爸爸在这个时候开始担心起会亏损，单凭刚刚起步的印刷厂似乎不足以支撑家里的花销。爸爸在和朋友的聊天中发现了水性油墨的商机。在经过多方打听之后，爸爸决定在服装厂原址上将印刷厂迁入，再购入生产油墨的机器，开设油墨厂。水性油墨生产前期的投入是很大的，再加上可能存在污染水环境的情况，所以爸爸这次的营业执照办得相当艰难，加之机器非常的昂贵和繁多，妈妈甚至怀疑过这个做法是不是正确的。但所幸后期慢慢走上正轨，成功拿到营业执照，“正大”墨产正式成立，并获得了很多订单，我们一家人的生活也随之不同了。

在爸爸创办三厂的过程中，我们的家庭成员也发生了变化。

1996年，姐姐出生了。姐姐的名字是“唯一”，意义可想而知。在2001年，作为老二的我出生了，于是便是这个家里加上来的一份子，名为“唯佳”。爸爸在取名这一块倡导简单，事实也确实如此。我们两姐妹的出生让这个家变得更加的完整，爸爸也为了我和姐姐更加努力工作，争取给我们创造更加良好的生活环境。

2013年，爸爸的生意做得已经不错了，他拿出一部分钱把长安桥村的房子翻新，要知道这个房子还是爷爷之前建的。新房子住了有6年，我们村宣布拆迁，我们一家人在不舍中收拾行李离开这个充满记忆的地方，去寻找另一个储存记忆的地方。

爸爸把拆迁款用来在嘉兴港区买了住房和厂房，他说他和妈妈要为我和姐姐再工作10年。爸爸妈妈今年都已过50岁，10年之后便到了退休的年纪。10年很长啊，不知道会发生什么，但我们都知道只要我们像之前那样互相陪伴，总能走完这看似漫长的10年，而我们的故事也未完待续……

Jiaxing
Zhang Weijia (Class 193, Majoring in Network and New Media)

Write a Story About Us

My father, born in 1968, was the youngest child in the family, and he had five elder sisters.

When my father was young, my grandfather's small shop by Zhangjiaqiao Bridge in Zhapu Town, Jiaxing ensured a good family condition, so he was sent to school even though people weren't open-minded in the countryside at that time. However, my father didn't concentrate on his study; instead, he dropped out of high school to begin an apprenticeship.

My father had been an apprentice of many different kinds, among which carpentry and fisherman lasted the longest.

In 1980, my father began to learn carpentry. Relying on his carpentry skills, he shuttled back and forth in the alleys of the town. Every sum of money he earned never came easy. After a few years, my father could claim to be a master carpenter, but there were more and more carpenters in the town. After weighing again and again, he decided to give up carpentry and look for another job.

In 1986, my father came to the seaside of Zhapu Town aimlessly. A ship stranded on the shore and the sound of the horn on the ship struck my father's heart. Then he came up a new idea. He decided to go out to sea to fish, but my grandpa did not agree with him. The result of their quarrel was that my grandpa compromised when my father promised that he would be careful. Therefore, my father followed the big captain of the town to fish with full enthusiasm, which was like the time when he began to learn carpentry. It was also in the fishing days that my father got to know my uncle who was also a fisherman and my mother's brother, which was the beginning of the following story. Afterwards, my father's health got worse, so my grandpa prohibited him from pursuing his fishing career. This time it was my father's turn to compromise.

My mother was born in 1969. She was the youngest child of the family and she had an elder brother.

My mother helped my grandparents at an early age. After graduating from primary school, my mother did not intend to continue her study. At that time, her brother happened to work outside to earn money, and my mother also thought that needlework was not a problem for a girl, so she found a job in a clothing factory. My mother was very clever, so she quickly mastered such works as cutting and sewing. Later, she went to work in a printing factory and turned out to be a quick learner. She didn't quit her job in the printing factory until she got married, and later she set up her own factory. It was such a coincidence that the two jobs my mother did before had something in common with the two factories that my parents established later.

My parents met at the age of 18, but their love story didn't start immediately. Because my grandparents didn't want my mother to be engaged so early, their love was "stifled" in the cradle. However, fate was incredible. After eight years of going around, they were single when they met each other again. The following things happened naturally, so my parents finally start dating.

In 1995, my parents got married. At that time, as my father had saved some money from his early work, the wedding was somewhat grand. Since the distance between two families was too short, picking up my mother from her family would end quickly, so they walked around the whole town and ended up with the blessings of many villagers.

Considering that they would have children after they formed a family and the responsibility for my father would be greater, my parents were determined to establish their own factory after repeated discussions. After several trips to the Industrial and Commercial Bureau, my father finally got a business license for his Zhengda Clothing Factory. After borrowing the land from the villagers, he opened the factory in Chang'anqiao village which was not far from home. The factory had 200 employees at its peak. As the factory grew larger and larger, management became a big problem. Owing to the fact that my mother was as busy as a bee in the factory, my father asked the fourth aunt and her husband to help in the factory. However, my father was still very busy, because he had to run around to take orders, so the sight of his back was deeply rooted in my childhood memory.

The prosperity of the clothing factory let dad germinate the idea of the sideline. As clothing tags were still outsourced, my father thought of making their own clothing tags to reduce expenses. That was how Zhengda Printing factory was founded in the Bazi village. My father became busier because of that. Fortunately, my mother was a great helper. Such a harmonious day lasted for a long time. They had thought that the clothing industry could develop well, but nobody could predict that it would be in decline. Some migrant workers who had learned the news about the reform of their hometown also left one after another. My grandpa died of a serious illness at that time, so the atmosphere in the factory and at home suddenly became serious. As the head of the family, my father was bound to take on more responsibilities.

It was extremely difficult to maintain the clothing factory, which made my father worry about the situation that the loss might be greater than the profit. Meanwhile, the newly-found printing factory was unable to afford the family's expenses. Then, my father discovered the business opportunity of water-based inks when chatting with friends. After many inquiries, my father decided to move the printing factory to the site of the clothing factory. He bought the ink-producing machines to open an ink factory. The investment in the early stage of water-based ink production was very large, and there might be the risk of polluting the water environment, so it was very difficult for my father to obtain the business license this time. Coupled with the fact that the machine was very expensive and varied, my mother even doubted whether this decision was right or not. Fortunately, we gradually got on the right track and successfully obtained the business license. Zhengda Ink Industry was officially established and many orders were obtained, so our life improved a lot.

During the process to establish the third factory, the family had a new member.

In 1996, my sister was born. Her name was "Weiyi", which had a significant meaning of being the only one. However, I was born as the second child in 2001. As an added member of the family, I was named "Weijia". As the facts showed, dad advocated simplicity in naming. The birth of my sister and me completed this family, and my father also worked harder for us to create a better living environment.

In 2013, my father was doing well in his business. He spent a portion of the money to renovate the house in Chang'anqiao Village, which was built by my grandpa before. After living in the new house for 6 years, our village announced the demolition. My family packed up and left this place full of memories in reluctance to seek another place to store memories of our life.

The demolition compensation was used to buy houses and factories in Jiaxing Port District. My father told me that he and my mother would work for my sister and me for another ten years. They are over 50 this year, and will retire in ten years. Ten years is so long that nobody knows what will happen, but we all know that as long as we accompany each other as before, we can always go through this seemingly long ten years, and our story will continue.

用文字摄取真善美而见象

吕厚龙

行走世界，用眼睛观察社会、体会自然。

驻步心灵，用文字记录所见、沉淀所思。

文字，不是文字，是真善美的如实遇见，如是感知。

对于行走的观察者而言，把眼睛变成摄影机，把文字变成真善美的现象记录乃至心象记述，是一个很重要的基本功，很可能须要下一辈子的苦功夫。

中国文化里有个著名的"诗中有画""画中有诗"论，是个极其博大精深的美学命题，也是中国文化一直的意境追求。诗是文字浓缩型文体的一种表达，再浓缩也是文字。好文字，必具真善美之大象，或流动的，或定格的，或艺或技，或道或本。

李瑶琼的《金塘兄弟情》，文字运用与文章构成尚需继续磨炼，但是文章里那些真善美充盈的动人景象，让人读后感觉到一股清风拂面的愉悦。

比如对"大爷爷"的描述，由"背着一个帆布包，拎着一个旅行袋，手上拿着那个常年不离手的保温杯，一头银发，一直都是笑呵呵的"，到作者随爷爷探望时所见憔悴反差，再到"帆布包、旅行袋、保温杯、银白色寸头"，几乎生离死别的74岁老李和77岁老虞又一起喝起了白酒，笑呵呵地讲着他们年轻时代那些纯朴的故事——动静画面都有很强的视觉冲击力。纯朴不饰的形象，情亲无间的意象，善缘乐聚的具象，无不是凝聚真善美的实象，引人突破文字束缚而入其中。

真善美是人的根本也是基本，有真才具善，心善才能美。较之于文字之好坏善恶，分水岭在于是使人趋善、向美、归真，还是发人恶习、仇念、嗔心。

能把摄取到的真善美，定格成美好的意象或者流动的心象，文字的生命力就强大了。

（学者、诗人，现居北京）

故事

舟山

李瑶琮(网络与新媒体专业191班)

金塘兄弟情

"我们俩可是认识了几十年的好兄弟啊!"爷爷经常把这句话挂在嘴边,神情透露着自豪,每次提起他和大爷爷的事情就能讲上好几个小时……

在浙江省舟山群岛新区的西南部有个叫做金塘的小海岛,那里就是我们祖祖辈辈生活的地方。

听爷爷说,我的曾祖父去世得早,曾祖母身体也一直不好,那时家里穷,他靠着自己的本事一来二去就把当时家境比较好的奶奶给"骗"到了手。"那时候可没像你们现在还有求婚呢,他当时对我说,虽然我家里穷,但是我会努力赚钱的,让你跟着我享福,不会让你出去工作辛苦。就凭着这句话我就嫁给他了。"奶奶笑呵呵地讲着,眼睛还不忘看着爷爷。爷爷的这句承诺,已经兑现了50多年,奶奶嫁给他后,真的没有出去工作过,爷爷也靠着自己一双手踏踏实实工作,在上世纪80年代就在村里盖起了楼房。

爷爷和奶奶有两个孩子,一儿一女,爸爸是小的那个,还有个大他3岁的姐姐,也就是我的姑妈。爷爷奶奶都很开明,没有农村人重男轻女的传统思想,反而在家里奉行女儿富养儿子穷养的理念。爸爸也不是一个很爱读书的人,读完高中就出来工作了,听他说,他的工作经历很丰富,开过超市、做过电工、卖过门窗、也曾在北京漂过……最后他还是决定定下心跟着爷爷一起开厂,这么一做一直做到了现在。

妈妈当时在爸爸的舅妈开的纺织厂工作,一次爸爸因为有事去找他舅妈时看到了在工作的妈妈,一见钟情,开始了对她的追求,两人很快就在一起了,差不多一年后他们结了婚,后来有了我。

爷爷年轻时在定海的一家微型电机厂做销售,因为业务的往来经常会和镇海的一家电机厂有联系。1986年4月,因为业务往来,爷爷认识了镇海电机厂一位与他对接的销售员老虞,他就是在我记事起爷爷口中时常牵挂的好兄弟。

我问爷爷当时一起工作的人那么多,怎么偏偏就和大爷爷成了好兄弟呢,"可能因为性格比较合得来吧",爷爷笑着说,脸上的皱纹都舒展开来。每次提到他这个好兄弟，满脸掩不住笑意。他们两个人由对接业务相识，由性格相投相知，成了一辈子的朋友。

因为住在海岛，在有大桥之前，我们出行是非常不便的。要出岛就要坐船。回忆起坐船，记忆里最多的就是一股咸咸的海水味和轮船呜呜的鸣笛声。

大爷爷的家在宁波镇海，爷爷说："每次去串门都得挑个好天气，免得遇到刮风下雨，那坐船就是活遭罪啦。"对大爷爷家的印象我只停留在小学一年级，那年我们全家带着悲痛的心情去了他家，是去送大奶奶的，她因为生病离开了大家。后来，大桥开通了，出行变得容易了许多，爸爸也买了车，但是因为要上学、爸妈工作又忙，我就再没有去过大爷爷家。

小学初中时，大爷爷来爷爷奶奶家的频率变高了，一年有时会来上五六趟，每次住上个四五天。在我的印象里，他每次来都背着一个帆布包，拎着一个旅行袋，手上拿着那个常年不离手的保温杯，一头银发，一直都是笑呵呵的。

爷爷奶奶的恩爱是我们村子里出名的，和他们年龄相仿的邻居总是羡慕他们的感情，常常能听到邻居奶奶在抱怨自己丈夫时说的话，你看看人家老李，对他老婆多好，再看看你。

时间在流逝，爷爷奶奶的年纪也大了，大爷爷的身体也没有那么硬朗了，近几年来家里的次数明显少了，有时一年都不会来上一次，和爷爷奶奶的交流联系更多地停留在了电话上。

去年春节，大爷爷得了直肠癌，切除了一部分直肠，出院在家休养。我们都很担心他的身体，便决定去看望。第二天在亲戚家吃完饭，买好礼品出发去镇海。

那是我时隔十多年再次去大爷爷家，走进他家，记忆里的碎片被牵扯出来，既模糊又熟悉。看到大爷爷的时候，他满脸憔悴躺在床上，这是我第一次看到他那么虚弱，记忆里的他是一个有着一米八大高个、留着大平头的精神老头。爷爷是个乐观的人，拉着大爷爷的手说："老虞，你可要好好养身体啊，好了以后去金塘，我还等着你陪我喝白酒呢。"他的话让大爷爷笑了起来，直说："一定，一定。"后来的一次通话中，大爷爷透露了自己和照顾他的护工在一起的消息，还说过段时间把她带来给爷爷奶奶看看。这可把奶奶的好奇心给引起来了，每次爷爷在打电话时总要问问他们什么时候来。

因为疫情，大爷爷来金塘的行程被一拖再拖。今年暑假，大爷爷突然打电话给爷爷说7月10号要带着他的新老伴来家里做客，这可把爷爷高兴坏了，上街买菜，亲自下厨，准备好酒迎接他们。大爷爷来的时候，又是我记忆里的那个样子，帆布包、旅行袋、保温杯、银白色寸头，只是这次，他的身边多了一个人——他的新老伴。这个奶奶带着和善的笑容，给人一种很好相处的感觉，果不其然，一会儿工夫就和奶奶聊到一块儿去了。

看得出来，大爷爷的气色好了很多，又回到了之前精神老头的样子。在饭桌上，看着74岁的老李和77岁的老虞又一起喝起了白酒，笑呵呵地讲着他们年轻时代那些纯朴的故事，好像讲不完讲不厌似的，那是属于他们两个之间美好的回忆。

小时候，我和爷爷奶奶一起生活，对他们的感情很深。记忆里，爷爷每次吃饭会耐心地给我剥虾、剥螃蟹，会帮我把鱼刺挑掉；每天会送我去幼儿园、给我绑头发。他对我的要求几乎是有求必应，一直以来，他在我心里是个无所不能的人。

原以为爷爷不会老，永远是那个我要什么他就能给我的人，殊不知，我在长大，他在变老。看着他的背变得弯曲，走路变得迟缓，头发变得花白，我才意识到那个能把我举起来坐在他肩膀上的人已经老了，他需要我们的陪伴与关心。

Zhoushan

Li Yaoqiong (Class 191, Majoring in Network and New Media)

Jintang Brotherhood

"We have been bosom friends for decades," my grandfather always said with pride. He could talk for hours about the story between he and his soul mate "Dayeye".

There is a small island called Jintang in the southwest of Zhoushan Archipelago New District in Zhejiang Province where our family has been living for generations.

My grandfather said that my great-grandfather died at a young age, and my great-grandmother had been in poor health. At that time the family suffered from financial difficulties, but my grandfather, by virtue of aptitude, won over the heart of my grandmother, whose family was better off. "There was no such thing as a proposal at that time. Your grandfather promised me that he would work hard to make money to let me live a happy life and I needn't go out and work for a day. On hearing that promise, I made up my mind and married him," my grandma said with a smile while looking at grandpa. For 50 years, my grandfather had been working hard to live up to his words. After the marriage, my grandma never worked for a day. My grandpa worked day and night, and he built a house in the village in the 1980s.

My grandparents had two children, a son and a daughter. My father was the younger one. My aunt was three years older than him. My grandparents were very open-minded, so they did not hold on to the timeworn ideas that sons were more valuable than daughters. Instead, they adhered to the parenting strategy that sons should be raised in fruglity and daughters in abundance. My father didn't like studying, so he went to work after graduating from high school. My father claimed that he had many work experiences. He had run a supermarket, worked as an electrician and a door salesman; he even had been a Beijing drifter before. In the end, he decided to run a factory with my grandfather till this day.

My mother was a worker in a knitting factory which was run by my father's aunt. He fell in love with her at first sight during a visit to the fatory, so he started pursuing her. They got together and married after about a year, then I was born.

My grandfather worked for a micro-motor factory as a salesperson in Dinghai when he was young. He would often visit a motor factory in Zhenhai. On the April of 1986, my grandpa made the acquaintance of Mr. Yu, who was a salesman of Zhenhai Electric factory. They quickly became as close as brothers, and Mr. Yu was the good friend my grandfather always talked about.

I asked my grandfather that how come he made good friends with Grandpa Yu instead of other people he did business with. "Maybe it was because we had the same congeniality." he said with a smile and his wrinkles relaxed. He couldn't hide a smile at the mention of his good friend. They got to know each other by business connections, and became lifelong friends because of congenial personality.

We lived on an island, so it was very inconvenient for us to go to places before a bridge was built. If we wanted to leave the island, we would have to take a boat. The smell of salty seawater and the sound of the ship's horn were what I remembered most when recollecting the experience of taking a boat.

Grandpa Yu lived in Zhenhai, Ningbo. My grandpa said, "Every time I went to visit, I had to pick a fine day for fear of the wind and rain. Otherwise, taking a boat was a living hell." The only memory that I had about Grandpa Yu was my first year in elementary school. That year, the whole family visited him to say goodbye to his wife who passed away because of illness. Afterwards, the bridge connecting cities opened. My father bought a car, but we never visited Grandpa Yu since we were so busy.

During my primary school and middle school years, Grandpa Yu paid more frequent visits to my grandparents. Sometimes he would visit five or six times a year, and he would stay for four or five days at a time. In my impression, he is a jolly old man with silver hair. Every time he visited, he would carry a rucksack with a traveling bag and a thermos that he always held in hand all the year round.

My grandparents' conjugal love was well known in the village. Neighbors of their age were always envious of their affection. I often heard neighbors complaining to her husband, "Look at Lao Li, how nice he is to his wife, and what about you?"

As time went by, my grandparents were getting older and older. Grandpa Yu's body was not as strong as it used to be. In recent years, his visits to us became less frequent. Sometimes, he would not visit us for the entire year. My grandparents had to rely on the phone to get in touch with him.

Last Spring Festival, Grandpa Yu was diagnosed with rectal cancer and had to have a part of his rectum removed. We all worried about his health and decided to visit him when he was discharged from the hospital. The next day, after dinner at my relatives' home, we bought gifts and set out for Zhenhai.

It was more than ten years since I had been to Dayeye's home. Upon entering his doorway, the memories about him flooded my mind. They were blurred but familiar. When I saw Grandpa Yu, he was lying on the bed with a gaunt face. This was the first time I saw him so weak. In my memory, he was an energetic man with a big crew-cut and a height of 1.8 metres. My grandpa is an optimistic man, and he took Grandpa Yu's hand and said, "Lao Yu, you should take good care of your health! When you recover, let's go to Jintang together. I'm waiting for your coming to have a drink!" His words made

Grandpa Yu laugh, and he replied, "It's a deal." Later, in a call, Grandpa Yu revealed that he fell in love with his carer and he would bring her to visit my grandparents, which raised my grandma's curiosity. Every time my grandpa called, she would ask when Grandpa Yu would come.

His trip to Jintang was delayed again and again because of the epidemic. This summer vacation, Grandpa Yu called my grandfather out of the blue and mentioned that he would bring his new wife and pay a visit on July 10. My grandpa was so excited that he bought food and cooked in person, and prepared white wine to greet them. When he came, he was the same person as in my memory: canvas bags, travel bags, thermos cup, silver buzz-cut. However this time, he had a new person by his side—his new wife whose kind smile gave people a feeling that she was approachable. Sure enough, it wasn't long before that she chatted happily with my grandmother.

I could see that Grandpa Yu was much better and he was back to the spirted man whom he used to be. At the dinner table, Mr. Li, 74 years old, and Mr. Yu, 77 years old, drank white wine together and talked smilingly about the simple stories of their youth. They would never get tired of telling them, because it was the happy memory between them.

When I was little, I lived with my grandparents and was quite dependant on them, so I had a deep affection for them. In my memory, my grandfather would patiently remove the shell of shrimps and crabs every time we had a meal, and he would help me pick out the fish bones. Every day he would send me to kindergarten and tie my hair. He could deny me nothing, and he had always been omnipotent in my heart.

I had thought that my grandpa would never get old; he was always the man who gave me whatever I wanted. It never occurred to me that he would get old as I grew up. Seeing that his back became hunched, his pace became slackened, and his hair became grey, I realized that the man who lifted me up on his shoulders was getting old and needed our company and care.

“物”解唯物史观的青年视角

李　炜

唯物史观是马克思主义哲学的重要组成部分，为人类观察和探寻社会规律提供了科学的历史观和方法论的理论基础。在我个人的理解里，对于唯物史观的认识和运用，与个体的成长阶段、成长经历是密不可分的；除了生产力和生产关系、物质基础和上层建筑辩证统一的哲学层面，很难否认还有“物”与“情感”的精神存在。毫无疑问，精神存在也是历史唯物主义的范畴，因为精神存在的背后是“物”的存在，是隐藏在“物”之中历史、故事、文化的存在，通过对“物”的阅读和理解，从本质上内化对历史的认识，对规律的把握，对未来的预策，根本上也是唯物史观在方法论上的应用；特别是青年朋友，在世界观、价值观、人生观逐步成熟的重要阶段，观察并提供判断基础的就是“物”，这一结论本身也是唯物史观作用的结果。

作为这一结论的支撑，江薇同学对旧物、旧屋的考察、审视及其背后的思考就是例证。从中，我们不仅可以回溯她父辈祖辈所经历的社会情景，感察到当时的社会状态与人们的精神生活，而且可以直接地进行现实对照，揭示出社会演进所内藏的规律，人们对于美好生活的追求归根结底是要寄付于和祥安宁的环境、寄托在日出而作的勤勉与艰辛，这也正是我们这个民族最质朴的精神存在与传承；更难能可贵的是，我们还可以读到青年朋友在读懂“物”的同时，已经逐渐掌握了用唯物史观解答社会课题和人生命题的方法，这或许才是对一个人以及一个群体最大的价值，即使这份读懂还是浅显的，或是稚嫩的，但无论如何这已经是一个真实的启蒙，一个良好的开端；这样的青年观察与思考越来越多，越来越澎湃，我们的民族和国家就能延绵生长，历久弥新。

（浙大宁波理工学院党委宣传部常务副部长）

故事

杭州

江薇(新闻学专业 201 专升本班)

旧物屋

一楼的楼道里，有一面白色的斑驳的墙，脱落的墙皮沿着墙底，零碎地铺在灰色的水泥地上，抬头看墙面，我看到了孩童时期留下的“大作”，顺着墙往里走，有一个小小的旧物间，里面锁着过去的时光。

我拿着钥匙，对准锁眼，手腕微微转动，只听“咔哒”一声，锁——开了。

打开门最先看到的是左面墙上挂着的军用水壶，爷爷年轻的时候，曾被选为义务兵，这水壶就是当兵那年领的。

1949 年 4 月，浙江省衢州常山县解放了，江源村作为常山县里的一个小村庄，也开始组织民兵、建立儿童团组织，那时候的爷爷尚且只有 13 岁，还不满足民兵的年龄要求，所以他只能将心中的“当兵梦”掏出来团了团，又放回心里。虽然不能参军，但爷爷参加了儿童团组织，儿童团组织的任务是保护粮仓。

“我们当时保护得可好啦，区政府和村领导都表扬过我们。”爷爷和我提起这事的时候，上身稍稍地抬起，离开了椅背，侧头看着我，眼神亮晶晶的。

1955 年，爷爷终于等到了他的 18 周岁，“当兵梦”随着时间的流逝，也变得枝繁叶茂，他怀着满腔的热血和期待，参加了义务补充兵役选拔，很幸运，兵检结果及格，于是爷爷胸前挂着象征成功的大红花，“大摇大摆”地回县里集合。入伍后的日子很清苦，离开家乡，离开母亲，每天在晨光吐露前就开始训练，不论冬夏，十几个小时的强度训练使他每次碰到床，都恨不得一睡不起。那时，身体虽然疲惫，但内心的满足感却是真真切切的。

但无论是什么梦，总有破碎的一天，在一次身体复查中，检查人员发现爷爷身上存在严重的陈年疮疤，因此他无法继续服役。尽管万分不愿，但爷爷只能离开，回到乡政府，退还了军装。

“虽然当兵时间不长，但是我思想上得到了很大的进步。”爷爷像孩子一般仰着脸，骄傲地说，他为曾为党和人民作出贡献而自豪着，爷爷似一盏杯杓，家国情怀在杯中醇香四溢。

墙上的水壶很旧了，可能已经不能装水，但它还装着 1955 年一位少年的一腔孤勇。

水壶的右下方，是两辆自行车。

一辆高高大大的自行车是我爷爷50岁那年因为上班路远而买的，130多元，四处凑钱才付清。旁边挨着的那辆车是我12岁的时候买的，更贵，240元，却是一次性付清的。

爷爷的自行车对我来说，就像是《一千零一夜》中的飞毯，能快速地带我去想去的地方。

我六七岁的那两年，爷爷的单车后面一直挂着两个铁框。每天早晨六七点，爷爷会分别在框里放一个乳白色的塑料桶，骑上单车，慢悠悠地骑上几公里，就到了山下。山坡裸露的山岩上搭着一段四五米长的半截空心竹，山泉水就顺着空心竹流入了另一截平行于地面的空心竹，地面的空心竹被挖空了几个缺口，干净可口的泉水顺着各个缺口徐徐流出。即使是早晨六七点，这儿的人也不少，每个缺口处都站满了来打水的人。等回去的时候，自行车的速度就慢了下来，老牌的自行车不堪重负，发出了吱呀吱呀的声音，我就坐在后座，抓着爷爷的衣衫，看着大片的田野向后奔跑。

可是后来，水龙头里的水变得干净了，山上的泉水却变得污浊，铁框就被取下，渐渐闲置了，而那些和蔼可亲的叔叔们，也很难再见到了。

向右边看，有一个巨大的衣柜。

衣柜里有很多旧毛衣、旧围巾，小孩穿的袜子、手套。其中有部分是奶奶织的，厚实温暖。1972年，奶奶从浙江衢州常山出来谋生，经过十几天的摸索求职，终于有一家林场因为她曾经在乡里做过出纳而接纳了她。于是奶奶开始做起了零工，理财、拔草、栽树等等。在那里，她还发展了她的爱好——织毛线，奶奶会织各种小东西，袜子、手套、围巾。后来林场办了一个幼儿园，奶奶很喜欢小孩，这些用毛线织起来的小物品就更多了，各种款型，各种花色，奶奶会把它们当作奖励送给当天最听话的小孩。1999年，我出生以后，爷爷每次抱着我去找奶奶的时候，我总会有“撞衫”的困扰。

奶奶这辈子，给很多人织过衣服，但唯独漏了她自己。林场并不是一个很有秩序、很干净的地方，地上随处可见丢弃的工具和木屑，伐木修林的噪声就像七月的蝉鸣，连绵不息，奶奶就坐在门前的一个小木凳上，目光柔和，后脊微驼，深色的衣裤仿佛要和墙上的斑驳融为一体，她永远穿着素色的衣物，织着亮色的衣物，身边伴着几个小孩，像是刚长出绒毛的小鸡仔，叽叽喳喳地说着话，奶奶微笑地听着，时不时回两句，再摸摸他们的头。

后来林场没落、荒废了，多余的没送出去的毛织物就堆在了那个深红色的大衣柜里。

衣柜和衣柜里的衣服都旧了，但奶奶的心意永远熠熠生辉。

衣柜的上方堆放着一个折叠货架。

我小学期间，父亲在东昌南路开过一家卖男装的服装店。因为白天要看店，所以进货的时间往往在天黑之后，等到夜深人静，家里的呼吸声都趋于平稳时，门悄悄开了，外面橙色的灯光悄悄钻进来晃悠一圈，没有发现玩伴，又悻悻地出去了，家里就多了一个两手提着黑色大袋的男人，他就是我进货回来的父亲。父亲是一位细心的人，每次回来都是轻手轻脚的，生怕吵醒睡着的家里人，他慢慢地把袋子放在客厅沙发的旁边，蹑手蹑脚地洗漱完才回屋睡觉。第二天，天还是乌黑的时候，父亲就会用摩托车载着这些巨大的黑色塑料袋出发，到了店里就撑开靠在墙边的折叠货架，解开黑色袋子上的结，取出里面被塑封好的衣服，将其分类放置，两个小时的分类结束后，营业的一天就开始了。

开始，店里还是很热闹的，也许是新店的缘故，镇上的人们总会进来逛逛，但时间久了，人们渐渐地就失去了兴趣。几个月的深思熟虑后，父亲还是选择关闭了服装店，货架也就被闲置了。

在我看来，这个折叠货架并不代表着失败，而是一段成长。

旧物屋里装着的是换下来的旧东西，里面的每一样东西，都是一段回忆、一段过往。而我，就像打开了时间机器，跟着这些旧物，回到了祖辈生长的那个年代，见到了我未曾参与的他们的过往与成长。

旧物，或破损，或蒙尘，哪怕再不起眼，它的背后都深藏着一段已经消逝的时光。

Hangzhou
Jiang Wei (Class 201, Majoring in Journalism)

The Storeroom for Old Stuff

In the corridor of the first floor, a mottled white wall stands a long time, so long that the peelings of the plaster have fallen off and scattered in the grey concrete ground. Looking upon the wall, I can still see my childhood "masterpieces". And then I walk along the wall, knowing that a small storeroom is awaiting me there, where is locked not only the old stuff, but also the past days.

I insert the key in the lock and turn it. With a click, the door is open.

The first thing I see is the military canteen hung on the left wall which belongs to my grandfather. When he was young, my grandfather was drafted as a conscript, and the canteen was given out by the military that year.

In April 1949, Changshan County in Quzhou City, Zhejiang Province was liberated. Jiangyuan Village, as a part of Changshan county, started to build the local militia and children group like other places across the country. Despite his cherished dream of being a soldier, my grandfather was merely 13 years old then and failed to reach the minimum age limit. Though reluctant, he had no choice but let go of his dream temporarily. While the good news was that he succeeded in joining the children's group, the task of which was safeguarding the local barn.

"We did a great job, and even won the praise of the village and district officials." When mentioning this to me, my grandfather leaned up and forward a little and tilted his head toward me, eyes gleaming.

In 1955, my grandfather finally embraced both his eighteenth birthday and his dream of serving the country. Ached with passion and expectation, he signed up for the compulsory military service and fortunately passed the body examination. Then he strode all the way to the county for muster. The military days were rather hard: he had to start his daily training in the dawn, winter or summer, away from home and his mother. Every day, after the intensive training of ten-odd hours when he finally lay down, he even wished that he could have a life-time sleep. However, despite his physical exhaustion, his mind was filled with the sense of contentment.

However, my grandfather's dream was broken at last. Once in a health re-examination, a serious old scar was detected and he was unable to continue his military service. Unwillingly, he returned his uniform to the village government.

"Although my service wasn't long, I learned a lot about the love for the Party, the country and the people," said my grandfather proudly, face upward like an innocent child. He was proud of his contributions for the Party and the people. Like a wine cup, his bosom was filled with the mellow patriotism.

The canteen on the wall is too old to hold water, but still the braveness of a young man.

At the bottom right of the canteen lies two bicycles.

The bigger one belongs to my grandfather. He bought it when he was 50 because of the long way between home and workplace. The price was up to over 130 yuan, which he barely made by borrowing around. The other bike was bought when I was 12, with a much higher price of 240 yuan, yet paid in a lump-sum.

During the two years when I was six and seven, two iron frames were fixed at the back of my grandfather's bike. At six or seven o'clock every morning, he would put a white-milk bucket in the frames respectively, and then pedaled his bike downhill for miles. Our destination was the water supply somewhere on the mountain: the spring water was flowing through two large hollow bamboo stems and out of the artificial holes made on the lower stem. Though it was only six or seven o'clock, in front of every hole lined up villagers awaiting to fetch the water. On our way back, the riding slowed down, and the old bike groaned under the weight of the water. I sat at the back, clenching the clothes of my grandfather, and watched the stretches of fields receding fast.

But later the tap water grew clean, while the mountain spring dirty; the iron frames therefore were taken off and gradually lay idle. And I barely had a chance to meet those genial villagers again.

At the right side of the room, a wardrobe occupies a large space.

It contains various old sweaters, scarves, toddler-sized socks and gloves, part of which were knitted by my grandmother, warm and thick. In 1972, she went out of Changshan County in Quzhou City, Zhejiang Province to make a living. After ten-odd days of job searching, she finally got one in a forest farm with her former working experience as a cashier in the village. In the farm, apart from doing odd jobs such as financing, weeding, and planting, my grandmother also developed her hobby during the break-knitting. She was adept at knitting miscellaneous small stuff, especially after the farm opened up a kindergarten, her skill was developed perfectly. Socks, gloves, scarves, in all sizes and colors. She would grant those small stuff as a prize to the child of the best behavior of the day. She was in nature fond of children.

In her whole life, my grandmother knitted clothes for many people, exclusive of herself. The forest farm was not an ordered, clean place, where you could see tools and sawdust almost everywhere. It seemed that the sound of logging, like the song of the cicadas, would last forever. My grandma always sat on a small wooden stool, stooped slightly, in front of the door. Dressed in her typical dark and plain, she was knitting bright-colored clothes for children, eyes soft. Several kids were chatting around her, like newly feathered chicks. Grandma listened with a smile, and occasionally responded and petted them.

Later, as the forest farm declined and became deserted, some of the clothes were left over and she never had a chance to give them out, which were therefore all piled in the crimson wardrobe.

The wardrobe and the clothes inside are all faded, but never will the beauty of my grandmother' gentle heart.

Upon the wardrobe places a folding store shelf.

When I was in the primary school, my father used to operate a men's clothing store. He worked at the shop in daytime, and purchased from the supplier at night. At midnight, when all of us were sleeping, the door would open quietly, with an orange street lamp light slanting through in a moment and then shut outside. The man who entered with big black bags in both his hands was my father. Careful and considerate, he would place the bags near the sofa and get washed without a slight sound, then tiptoed towards his bed. The next day, before the sun rise, my father would carry those bags to the store by motorbike. At the store, he took out the folding shelf leaning on the wall, opened the bags, sorted the clothes and placed them on the shelf in the next two hours. After all these, a new day of working started again.

The store was busy at first. In its inception, people in the town often came in and browsed out curiosity. However, their interest faded away over time. After months of consideration, my father decided to close the shop at last, and the folding shelf therefore was laid away.

In my view, the folding shelf is never a symbol of failure, but a valuable experience in his life.

The storeroom contains the spare old stuff-each is an embodiment of an old memory, of the past days. I feel like I have sat on a time machine, and gone back to the times of my grandparents and parents, and witnessed their past and growth that I never partook.

The old stuff, however plain, dusted, and worn-out, all enclose a good lost time.

一个普通浙江人的创业史

张文祥

2002年，当时还是记者的我，作为济南市民营经济采访团一员，赴江浙六个城市采访报道民营企业取得的辉煌成就。而在这之前，我还曾阅读过一本书，书名大概是《8个农民20年》，讲述的是鲁冠球、徐传化等老一辈浙江农民克服艰难险阻、艰苦创业的动人故事。我们采访的对象就包括其中多位昔日农民、如今的市场经济弄潮儿。而现在，我们的同学又记述了自己的舅舅：从高考落榜，到艰辛创业，几经沉浮，终于得以成功。这样的故事，在浙江或许并不稀奇罕见，但每一个故事读来，都让人感动和振奋。脑瓜灵、能吃苦、不服输、天生喜欢创业，这些特质似乎已渗入每一个浙江人的血液，成为浙江人的精神。还记得读过的那本书里讲到，在"割资本主义尾巴"的威压下，鲁冠球都没有放弃做小生意，始终想着要赚钱过好日子。所以，舅舅遭遇生意挫折又有什么可怕呢？找准机会，大胆去闯去试，失败了，爬起来，吃一堑长一智，总没有被打趴下的时候。中国民众的创造力是最宝贵的。农村的联产承包是没饭吃的安徽农民创造的，市场经济则可以说是无数浙江人摸爬滚打闯出来的。舅舅就是这样的创造者之一。改革开放40多年来的辉煌成绩，就是舅舅等无数普通民众的创业故事汇成的。这个故事的真谛就是：人民的创造力和发展冲动应该得到充分尊重。把浙江人的创业精神弘扬开去，让更多国人拥有这种精神，中国的未来必更有希望！

（浙大宁波理工学院传媒与法学院，教授）

故事

金华

马旭灿(新闻学专业201专升本班)

舅舅与他的厂子

外公是一名人民教师,在金华市东阳的南马镇教过小学、初中、高中,民主五七中学是高中,林甘、岭脚和大路都是初中,也可谓“桃李满天下”了;外婆则出身当地名门,又是家里的独女。而舅舅作为三个孩子当中唯一的男生,被寄予了更大的厚望。所以在1987年高考仅差4分上线时,家里人选择让舅舅复读,可是苦读一年换来的反而是离上线分更远了。当时外公的意见仍然是继续读继续考,想要让舅舅也从事和他一样的工作。但舅舅辛苦复读两年仍失利,再加上当时浙商涌动,人人都出去做生意,舅舅也耐不住了。

在自己姨夫的介绍下,舅舅从别人手里买了一台废弃的机器开始做小刀。没有资金,租不起场地,就把机器从永康五金城拉到乡下的家里。对五金技术一窍不通,边学边做,舅舅联想到了永康的“大云东”废旧磨具场,那里的磨具虽都是些废弃东西,但至少也成型,可以看出制作工艺。于是舅舅三天两头地往那里跑,后来几乎每一家商铺都和他成了老朋友,他在这里“淘宝”,边看边学,有时拿来研究把玩,认为能利用就低价买回去。

就这样,学一点技术干一点活,一窍不通的舅舅请了磨具师傅装好之后,生产出了第一批产品。

有了产品,关键还得卖出去。舅舅开始往全国各地推销,最北到过辽宁大连,也正是这一份经历使舅舅迅速成长。我曾以为体面、幽默的舅舅原来爬过火车,进过拘留所,住过桥底。

1987年,20出头的舅舅到新安江销售,在火车站遇到两个人问路,因为他也说不清楚,所以被人断定是外地人。于是一名收购银元的“小贩”登场了,银元骗局上演了。当时单纯的舅舅把身上仅有的两百元给了他们,结果天亮了,那几个人也没再回来。看着眼前匆匆而过的行人,凛冽的冷风打在脸上,舅舅紧紧拽着兜里那仅剩的还温热的3块钱。

3块钱哪够买票?但也要回家啊。上世纪90年代的火车站与现在不同,只是由一排排铁栅栏围着,于是舅舅拎着销售包,手脚并用爬过铁栅栏,逃票搭上了火车。他在一个空位坐着，因为没钱吃饭，只好一个劲儿地问乘务员要水。原以为上了车就可以平安到家，但没想到中途遇到查票。舅舅急得面红耳赤，说不出一句话，他不知道该如何开口解释自己的逃票行为，他被骗的经历又能否获得乘务员的同情。正当他不知所措的时候，一只捏着两张纸币的大手出现在大家眼前，没有说一句话，替他买了票。

这一趟出行，让初出茅庐的舅舅尝到了人间险恶，同时也让他感受到了人性的温暖。

舅舅工厂起初的小刀是由刀片和铁壳做成的，为了美观，铁壳外面需要喷漆绘色。但这种铁壳极易生锈，且对人体健康有害。所以在起初的一年多时间里，舅舅的生意不如意，虽说没有亏损，但也只是收支平衡，勉强度日。于是舅舅开始思考有没有其他的材料和工艺可以代替。有一次，他在用开水壶倒水时，看到了开水瓶外面的这一层铁皮，图案漂亮又不生锈，于是他想能不能用这一种材料来做小刀的外壳呢？他把水杯一放，连开水壶的盖子都顾不上塞回去，马上跑到永康五金城去寻找这种材料。很快，这种铁皮替换了原来的材料，减少了喷漆这一道工序，效率提高了，工人的健康得到了保障，舅舅的小刀成了市场的香饽饽。

然而好景不长，1990 年，越来越多义乌的小刀制造厂纷纷转型。舅舅小作坊的生产效率不及他人的大工厂，他觉得小刀利润薄，于是也开始转型，拿着做小刀赚的 20 万元改行做铁皮铅笔盒。因为之前也没有工厂在铅笔盒上印过花，所以舅舅找了一个在罐头上印花技术较成熟的工厂印了第一批铅笔盒。由于铅笔盒的四个角较锋利，需要将铁皮拉伸、往下压，铁皮一拉印花就容易变形、掉色。这一批货低价处理出售，亏损六七万元。第二批货，舅舅跑到温州苍南找了一个专门做铅笔盒的公司，买了原材料，拉到金华继续印，没想到又失败，亏损十几万元。

就这样，年轻时所赚的钱亏空。没有更好的想法，又回去做起了小刀生意。但此时的市场已经不再是当初那个刚被打开的样子，而舅舅做小刀的技术已经停滞三四年，很难跟上新技术的发展。

就在舅舅一蹶不振的时候，永康五金城的又一个项目兴起——箱包扣。当时有两种扣子，一种塑料扣一种铁扣，因为有冲床等机器做基础，于是舅舅决定做铁扣子。虽说都是铁产品，但小刀、铅笔盒和铁扣当然不一样，由于前期的亏损，此时已没有余钱买机器。舅舅就去五金城里看机器，看了几眼回来自己改装。凭借几眼的记忆就能将机器改装成功已经非常了不起了，但舅舅说当时最难的可不是改装机器，而是创造出做铁扣的磨具，磨具才是做扣子的关键。镇上有位师傅，做了十几年的五金，才做出一个又大又笨重的磨具，每次出工时都需要两个人扛，很不方便。于是整整大半年，几乎没出一步家门，舅舅就呆在房间里画图纸,不断地揣摩思考。终于,第一套半圆、三档扣的轻便磨具成型了。

有了冲床、磨具,设备都已齐全,在姨夫的介绍下,很快就有了第一个单子,紧接着就投入生产,走上正轨,开始盈利。

现在,舅舅的工厂已经发展得越来越好,但他仍然不忘创新。前几个月,他又给我看了一项他的发明——自动包装器,往机器里投入25个扣子即可自动包装成一袋。他说他还在继续创新,想要使他变成全自动化,连"扔"这个动作都由机器完成。

我心中对他满是佩服,高中毕业,并没有经过技术培训的舅舅,居然对机械如此敏感,看过一眼便可自己揣测创造。然而这也是他心中的遗憾之处,他后悔当初没有进入一所大学去学习机械制造。

但,这就是人生啊。起起伏伏,跌跌撞撞,尝遍酸甜苦辣咸,但只要你一直往前走,最好的总会在不经意间出现。

Jinhua
Ma Xucan (Class 201, Majoring in Journalism)

My Uncle and His Mills

My grandfather was a teacher. He had taught in primary school, junior high school and senior high school in Nanma Town of Dongyang, Jinhua City. Among them, Minzhu May Seventh Middle School was a senior high school, while those in Lingan Village, Lingjiao Village and Dalu Village were junior high schools. My grandfather almost has "pupils everywhere". My grandmother is the only daughter of a prestigious local family. Therefore, my uncle, as the only boy among their three children, was given greater expectations. After the college entrance examination in 1987, my uncle's score was only 4 points short of the admission score. The family encouraged my uncle to take the exam the next year, but after a year of hard study, his score was further away from the admission line. At that time, my grandfather hoped my uncle would continue studying and take the exam again, because he wanted my uncle to work in the same unit. But the exam failures after hard study for two consecative years, coupled with almost everyone in Zhejiang going out to do business, drove my uncle to do business.

Through the introduction of his brother-in-law, he bought an abandoned machine from others to make knives. My uncle couldn't afford to rent the site, so he moved the machine from Yongkang Hardware City to his home in the countryside. Knowing nothing about hardware technology, my uncle taught himself while making knives. One day he thought of the "Dayundong", an abrasive tool plant in Yongkang, where the abrasive tools were all discarded but at least shaped and the manufacturing processes could be learned. So my uncle went there frequently, and then almost every shop's owners became his friends. He "hunted useful things", observed and learned manufacturing processes there. Sometimes he studied the products with interest, and bought those that could be reused for a low price.

In this way, through learning and practicing, my uncle produced the first batch of products after he had hired an abrasive tool master.

The key was selling these knives, so my uncle began to sell the products all over the country, even to Dalian, Liaoning Province in the north. It was this experience that made my uncle grow rapidly. My uncle, who I thought was decent and humorous, had stole a ride in the train, was put into the detention center and lived under a bridge for his business.

In 1987, my uncle in his early twenties went to Xin'anjiang to sell his knives, and met two people who asked for directions at the railway station. He didn't know that place and couldn't say clearly, so people knew he was a stranger. Then came a peddler who bought silver coins, and the silver scam clutched. My simple uncle gave them two hundred yuan. However, at dawn, the peddler and his accomplices did not come back. Looking at people passing by in a hurry, my uncle clutched his last three yuan in his pocket that was still warm with cold wind blowing his face.

How could three yuan be enough for a ticket? But he had to go home. The railway station in the 1990s was different from today's station, only surrounded by a row of iron fences, so my uncle took the sales bag, climbed over the iron fence on his hands and knees to get on the train without paying fare. He sat in an empty seat, and kept asking the steward for water because he had no money for food. My uncle thought he would get home safely after getting on the train, but didn't expect a ticket check on the way. He was so anxious that he couldn't say a word. He didn't know how to excuse his ticket evasion and whether his experience of being cheated could win the sympathy of the steward. Just when other passengers were looking at him, a big hand holding two pieces of banknotes appeared in front of everyone. Without saying a word, that man bought tickets for my uncle.

This trip made my fledgling uncle experience the dangers of the world, but also felt the warmth of human nature.

The knife in my uncle's mill was made of a blade and iron shell at the beginning. For the sake of beauty, the outside of the iron shell needed to be painted. But this kind of iron shell easily rusted, and was harmful to human's health. So for more than a year at first, his business was not satisfactory. There was no loss neither. He was just making ends meet and barely made a living. Then my uncle began to think whether there were other alternative materials and crafts. One day, when he was pouring water from a kettle, he noticed the iron sheet outside the kettle which had a beautiful pattern but did not rust. So he wondered whether this material could be used to make the outer shell of the knife. Putting the cup down, without even putting back the lid of the kettle, he immediately went to the Yongkang Hardware City to look for this material. Soon, with the material replaced, the painting process could be skipped and the efficiency improved, which guaranteed workers' health. My uncle's knife became a "sweet pastry" in the market quickly.

However, good times didn't last long. In 1990, as more and more knife manufacturers in Yiwu transformed, my uncle's small mill was less efficient than other large factories. With thin profit, my uncle began to transform his business into a tin pencil box with two hundred thousand yuan earned by making knives. Since no factories had printed patterns on the pencil boxes before, my uncle found a factory with more mature printing crafts on cans to print the first batch of pencil boxes. Because the corners of pencil boxes were sharp, the iron sheet needed to be stretched and pressed down, which made the pattern easily deformed and faded. This batch of goods was sold at a low price, with a loss of sixty to seventy thousand yuan. For the second batch of goods, my uncle went to Cangnan County of Wenzhou, and found a company specializing in manufacturing pencil boxes. He bought the raw materials and took them to Jinhua to continue printing. Unexpectedly, he failed again and lost more than ten thousand yuan.

In this way, the money earned when he was young was lost. Without a better idea, my uncle went back to the knife business. But the market was no longer the same as it was before, and my uncle's technology of making knives had been stagnant for three or four years, so it was hard to keep up with the development of new technology.

Just when my uncle was depressed, another project of Yongkang Hardware City rose—luggage buckles. At that time, there were two kinds of buckles: plastic buckles and iron buckles. My uncle decided to make iron buckles with the punch press and other machines as the foundation, although all were iron products, but knives, pencil boxes and iron buckles were of course not the same. There was no spare money to buy the machine at that time due to the early loss. My uncle went to the Hardware City to observe the machines, and modified his own machine successfully by memory, which was incredible. However, my uncle said that the most difficult part at that time was not to refit the machine, but to create an abrasive tool for making iron buckles, which was the key. There was a master in the town who had been making hardware for more than ten years. The master made a big and heavy abrasive tool, which turned out to be very inconvenient and needed two people to manage it every time it worked. So for more than half a year, with hardly a step out of the house, my uncle stayed in the room, drawing and thinking. Finally, the first set of semicircular and three-bar adjusters of the portable abrasive tool took shape.

The equipment was complete with the punch press and abrasive tool in place. Under the introduction of his brother-in-law, soon there was a first deal, and then the equipment was put into production and the business was on the right track. My uncle began to make profit.

Now, my uncle's mill has developed better and better, but he still does not forget innovation. A few months ago, he showed me another invention of his automatic packer, which could automatically pack buckles into a bag by throwing 25 buttons into the machine. He said he was still innovating, trying to make the machine fully automated with even the action "throwing" done by the machine.

I admire him very much. My uncle, who graduated from high school and did not receive technical training, is so sensitive to machinery that he can make his own creation through speculation after a glance. But it is also a pity for him that he has not entered a university to study mechanical manufacturing.

But this is life, full of ups and downs and with sweet and bitter experience. As long as you keep going, the best will always appear inadvertently.

生活观察与形象记忆的诗性表达

朱滢滢

“生活是写作的源泉，源头盛而文不竭”，“行走的新闻”系列中年轻一代自下而上的观察与上一辈人的口述历史记录，都印证着叶圣陶先生所认为的写作源自于生活。随着口述、图像等记录形式出现，越来越多人不仅看到了宏大的社会脉络，还看到了社会中一个个小家的日常生活，文稿亲历者的切身感受、民众真实的生活记录，都在向后来者诉说那些部分人无法忘却的普遍记忆。

在文稿的写作当中，诗性表达是深描和阐述的必然产物。参与记录的他者通过对比、隐喻等方式构建真实，能使读者保持较高的参与度，实现情绪引导与叙事内核的引出。文章以江南的雨季展开，湿漉漉的空气包裹着作者父亲丝丝缕缕的情怀与记忆：“帮忙种菜、采桑叶、钓鱼、喂养放羊、给兔子剃毛……”这些让大多数都市人感到陌生的事物，对于作者来说也已经逐渐变得遥远，这使作者以一个他者的身份，天然地带着陌生感接触了“以前的生活”，并在纯粹的口述历史中辅以过去和现在的生活对比，这使其父亲对于生活的观察和形象记忆呼之欲出。文章题为《开过火车的父亲》，文中关于火车的部分却寥寥，也许火车只是一个意象，代表着流动的时间，或者是现在难以交集的过去。这些都诗意地点明了“家、时间、自然”等主题，引起读者对社会变迁的思考。

在自下而上的观察、聆听的过程中，不仅应该看到、听到一段记忆里的故事，更应体会讲述者言外交织的情感。在诗意的表达中，过去的时间可以被无限延长，每个细节都能散为引人共鸣的意象。

（浙大宁波理工学院新闻学专业 2018 级学生）

故事

杭州

顾笑笑(网络与新媒体专业 182 班)

开过火车的父亲

江南的雨季,潮湿而漫长。窗外湿润的水汽,为一切景色披上了朦胧的外衣。此刻突然失去了交流声的房间格外寂静。在杭州江干区闸弄口的家里,父亲抬起头望了眼天花板,又再次看向我,眼神逐渐明亮起来。

提起童年,父亲的脸上洋溢着幸福,甚至不惜用能想到的最美好的形容词去描述:“和你们现在的生活可是完全不一样啊。”

父亲出生在海宁市的黄湾镇尖山村,是家中的老小,有一个哥哥和两个姐姐。帮忙种菜、采桑叶、钓鱼、喂养放羊、给兔子剃毛……这些童年的趣事,父亲如数珍宝般一件件列举开来。

“记得奶奶家的鱼塘、羊圈、养蚕架吗? 还有小兔子呢,记不记得了?”

我使劲回忆着,小兔子怎么也无法从脑海里蹦出来。我在城市里出生,也在城市里读书和生活,初高中以后回奶奶家的频率越来越低,在奶奶家生活的日子也越来越短。养蚕架早已不见了踪影,羊圈里也没有了咩咩的叫唤和熟悉的味道,橘子林也被卖给了别的生意人。

“以前的生活虽然值得怀念,却也要老是为吃饭和穿衣发愁,还记得我十几岁就帮忙挑很重的担呢!”父亲又谈起以前童年时期帮家里人干活的情景。“以前不是抓着孩子学习,是抓着孩子干活。”每天的功课结束就要帮家里人干活,饿到晚饭恨不能吃下两大碗。

“我学习还是很认真的。不过我英语太差了,没有好好学。”

父亲回忆起学校的老师。说那个时候英语老师喜欢拿着一个收音机在教室前面放英语听力,他老是坐在后面和别人一起偷偷看武侠小说。奶奶家的木头柜子里还留着一柜子当时的书,金庸的、古龙的,纸张硬硬脆脆的,我不敢使劲翻动,生怕碰坏,纸页因为年代而泛黄,一股子老底子旧书的味道。

“金庸可是袁花(海宁的一个镇)人,不过我最喜欢的还是古龙。”古龙作品里的爱和侠义老是能感染别人,古龙的话挺糙的,但作品就是看不腻。

父亲还八卦地告诉我英语和数学老师是一对夫妻。数学老师特别凶,他害怕数学老师，所以对待数学的态度特别认真，后来也渐渐发现学习数学的乐趣，他的数学就特别好。“满分100分基本都能考96、97分呢。”所以毕业以后，父亲就在爷爷的帮助下去供销社做了两年会计。

“那个时候政策不一样。”计划经济时代，国家包办一切经济生活，生产统一安排、产品统一分配，农民要买东西只能去供销社买。

“爷爷以前就是在供销社的。”爷爷在年轻的时候更是穷，在供销社帮忙卖卖东西。后来抗美援朝征民兵，爷爷年轻力壮就和其他年轻人一起坐着火车赶往前线，但去了之后战争已经结束了，于是回来在国家的安排下进入了铁路部门工作。

在供销社干了两年的会计工作后，父亲便被爷爷“赶出”海宁了。

“男孩子嘛，多闯闯。”这一直是我爷爷的态度。于是我的父亲便一个人前往杭州打拼和闯荡。父亲的哥哥则选择了留在海宁创业。

来到杭州最初的几年，从基层做起，每天做一些基础的工作，要搬运很多的重物，后来又在铁路开了一年的火车。问到父亲为什么只开了一年，父亲指了指眼睛。因为经常看小说，视力本来就不太好。小的时候因为调皮，从台阶上摔下去，视网膜就受损了。

“视力检查不过关啊。”父亲感叹道，于是他继续留在上海铁路局杭州机辆段从事检测工作。“铁路是铁饭碗。”虽然不像部分创业的人拥有更多的财富，可是这份稳定、舒适的生活也同样叫人安心。

父亲还提起了我的伯父，伯父做生意的过程也很辛苦，创业往往需要机遇。现在的伯父拥有自己的一个小厂子，也顺应潮流进入了电商行业，主要由我堂哥在打理。

“你一定想不到我以前每个月的工资只有70块。我当时还花了整整一个月的工资去买了迈克尔·杰克逊的CD专辑。”我的父亲在那时不仅关心温饱，也很享受小说和音乐这些娱乐活动。父亲的这些兴趣给了我很大的影响，在我很小的时候父亲便给我“安利”各种他喜欢的书、喜欢的音乐。

收音机更是我童年里最深的回忆，直到现在，我们家还有收音机，只不过已经不再是需要天线的笨重款式，更轻便也更智能。

“现在谈起几十块的工钱特别感慨，不知道翻了几倍，现在连5000元的工资都算一般水平吧。”的确，父亲甚至外公都给我讲过几毛钱能买好多东西，一根棒冰几分钱也就够了，现在的东西却都已能用千和万来计算。

“生活水平也不一样了吧。以前出家乡都是打工，现在是旅游。”

仔细算了算我家一年的开销，用在吃上的基本只占很少一部分，现在也不是有衣服穿就行了，要追求好看的、时尚的。教育投入也变大了，电子产品也非常普遍。人均一样。“现在充实每天生活的可能是刷手机。”父亲笑道,“真的想不到科技变化那么大。”

除了生活方面,父亲还谈起以前和现在的工作方式。

以前火车维修需要消耗很大的人力。需要有人去一个个地方检查,于是经常需要攀爬火车头。现在很多操作都可以由机器代劳。“效率变高了,精确度也变高了。”父亲就曾经受过工伤。一些危险的工作或者是消耗大量体力的任务由机器代劳,是父亲认为科技社会最大的优点。

“那你呢,以前的日子你还有印象吗?”父亲突然反问起我来,其实我的生活变化也是我们家的奋斗史。

“我印象最深的是住出租房的时候。”

我们家是在我小学的时候正式拥有了自己的一套小屋。我的幼儿园回忆都在出租房里度过。可能只有三四十个平方吧。没有那么多的房间,只有一个和餐桌一起的厨房,一个卫生间和一个紧挨着摆了两张单人床的卧室。甚至没有阳台。

以前只有一个小电视机摆在卧室,是那种特别厚的老式电视机,又重屏幕又小。我特别喜欢那时父亲给我买一堆碟片,一部一部放过来。现在屋里的电视机换了好几次,屏幕越来越大也越来越薄,画质从标清到高清到超清,片库里有各种各样的片子可以选择。

雨点“滴答滴答”落在雨棚上,似乎在一点一点将一切思绪和记忆拉至10年前、20年前、甚至是40年前。

Hangzhou
Gu Xiaoxiao (Class 193, Majoring in Network and New Media)

Father Who Drove the Train

The rainy season in regions south of the Yangtze River is humid and long. The steam outside the window cloaked all the scenery in a haze. The room was extraordinarily silent at this moment when the sound of conversations suddenly died out. At his home in Zhanongkou, Jianggan District, Hangzhou City, my father looked up at the ceiling and then looked at me again, his eyes gradually lit up.

Talking about his childhood, my father was alight with happiness. He even used the nicest adjectives he could think of to describe it, saying "It was completely different from the life you have now."

Born in Jianshan Village, Huangwan Town, Haining City, my father was the youngest in his family, with one elder brother and two elder sisters. Helping grow vegetables, picking mulberry leaves, fishing, feeding and herding sheep, shearing rabbits… These childhood anecdotes were listed by my father, as if they were treasures waiting to be opened.

"Do you still remember the fish pond, sheepfolds, and silkworm racks at your grandma's? And the bunnies? Do you remember any of those?"

I tried to recall them, but the bunnies could not pop out in my mind. I was born in the city, also studied and lived in the city. After junior and senior high schools, I went back to my grandma's home less often and stayed there for shorter time. The silkworm racks had long gone, the sheepfolds were devoid of the bleating and the familiar smells, and the orange groves were sold to other businessmen.

"The old life was memory-making, but we always had to worry about food and clothing. I remember when I was a teenager, I had to help shoulder heavy loads!" Father was talking about his childhood when he used to help his family with their daily work. "Back then, we children were dragged to work outside instead of to study. Every day after school, I had to help my family, and I was so hungry that I could eat two big bowls of rice."

"I studied hard. But I was so bad at English because I didn't pay much attention to it."

My father recalled his teachers at school. He remembered while his English teacher put on English recordings by radio in the front of the classroom, he would always sit at the back with others to secretly read martial arts novels. Some of those books written by Jin Yong and Gu Long, with hard and brittle pages, were still put in the wood cabinet at grandma's. I dared not turn the pages with too much strength for fear that they should fall apart. Those time-honored classics were yellowed, with a smell of the old books.

"Jin Yong was a local here. He was from Yuanhua (a town in Haining). But my favorite is still Gu Long." The love and chivalry in Gu Long's works were infectious with his relatively simple words. Still, people just wouldn't get tired of reading them.

My father also told me gossip that his English and math teachers were a couple. His math teacher was particularly strict. My father was afraid of him, so he took math seriously. It turned out he gradually found joy in learning math, and his math grade was outstanding. "I could have 96 or 97 out of 100!" After graduation, my father went to the supply and marketing cooperative with my grandpa's help as an accountant for two years.

"Policy was different at that time." In that era of the planned economy, the state took care of all the economy, with unified production arrangements, unified distribution of products. Farmers could only buy things from the supply and marketing cooperative.

"Grandpa used to work at the supply and marketing cooperative." Grandpa's life was even poorer when he was young, and he helped sell things there. Later, when the militia was drafted for the war to resist U. S. aggression and aid Korea, grandpa took the train to the frontline together with other young people. The war was over when he arrived. After he came back, he joined the railroad department under the arrangement of the state.

After working as an accountant in the supply and marketing cooperative for two years, my father was "forced" out of Haining by my grandpa.

"Boys should take some adventure" was always my grandfather's motto. So, my father went to Hangzhou to work and make a living on his own. My father's elder brother chose to stay in Haining to start his own business instead.

For the first few years in Hangzhou, my father started by doing basic jobs, such as carrying heavy things. Later, he drove trains for a year. I asked my father why he drove trains only for a year, and he pointed to his eyes. When he was young, he fell down the stairs while playing around, which damaged his retina. Besides, he read novels too often, which didn't do any good to his eyesight too.

"I failed my vision test," my father sighed, so he stayed in the Hangzhou locomotive section of Shanghai Railway Bureau to engage in inspection work. "Working for the railway department is a 'iron bowl', or a permanent and stable job." Although it was not as profitable as some entrepreneurial jobs, its stability and comfort were quite reassuring.

My father also mentioned my uncle, who had a hard time with his business because it often depended on opportunities. My uncle had a small factory of his own and had been engaged in the e-commerce industry in line with the trend, which was mainly managed by my cousin.

"You couldn't have imagined that I used to have a monthly salary of only 70 yuan. I once spent a whole month's salary at that time to buy a Michael Jackson album." My father was concerned with food and clothing, but enjoyed entertainment such as novels and music at the same time. My father's interests had a significant influence on me. At an early age, I was immersed in his favorite books and music recommended by him.

The radio was one of my fondest childhood memories, and up till now, I still had radios in our house. They were no longer the bulky models that required antennas, but lighter and smarter.

"It was particularly emotional to talk about the fewer-than-a-hundred monthly salary. The salary now had multiplied numerous times, even 5000-yuan salary is considered average now." Indeed, my father and even my grandpa had told me that a few cents could buy a lot of things in the old days, and a popsicle would only cost a tenth of a cent. But it cost several thousand yuan to buy only a few things now.

"The living standard had changed, right? In the past, we left our hometown to find jobs, but now we leave to travel."

I calculated my family's annual expenses, only a tiny part of which is spent on food. Now we are not satisfied with merely putting clothes on, but to pursue good-looking and fashionable clothes. The investment in education has also increased. Everyone has some electronic devices in their hands. "Now we enrich our daily lives by browsing our phones," my father laughed, "I really couldn't have imagined the developement of technology would be so impressive."

Other than daily lives, my father also talked about the differences in working.

Train maintenance used to be labor-intensive. It required people to go from place to place to inspect, so they often needed to climb the locomotives. Now many operations can be done by machines. "It was more efficient and more accurate." my father once suffered work-related injuries. According to my father, some dangerous jobs or tasks that consumed a lot of physical strength are done by machines now, which has been the most significant advantage of the technology-based society.

"What about you? Do you still remember the old days?" my father suddenly asked me. In fact, changes in my life reflected the history of our family's struggle.

"What I remember most is when we lived in a rented house."

Technically speaking, our family owned a house when I was in elementary school. I spent all my kindergarten life in a rental house. It was probably only 30 or 40 square meters. There weren't that many rooms, just a kitchen with a dining room table, a bathroom and a bedroom with two single beds right next to each other. There was not even a balcony.

We only had a small TV set in the bedroom, an old-fashioned bulky one with a small screen. I liked it when my father bought me a bunch of discs and played them one by one. Now the TV in our home has been upgraded several times. The screen is getting bigger and thinner, the picture quality improves from SD to HD to Ultra HD, and there are all kinds of movies in the library to choose from.

The rain dripped on the canopy, which gradually yanked all my thoughts and memories back to 10 years ago, 20 years ago, or even 40 years ago.

小人物的浮沉折射时代大潮

马利文

大山里的老百姓怎样摆脱贫困？邹姗姗同学的爸爸妈妈，从最初因生活所迫，走出大山，找出路，从湖南省一个小山村辗转到广州、株洲、深圳、义乌等城市打工谋生，最后全家脱贫致富，走上幸福路，还把浙江义乌人"鸡毛换糖"勤劳致富经带回到湖南老家，带动当地百姓一起走向了富裕的道路。《开往义乌的绿皮火车》用朴实的文笔，告诉我们只要开动脑筋、实干肯干，积少成多，摆脱贫困，走向富裕的道路就不止一条。这不仅仅是一趟开往义乌的绿皮火车，这更像是一趟开往脱贫致富的幸福火车。

苦难是一种伤害，也是一笔财富。如果没有苦难，就不会毅然决然走出大山，如果不走出大山，就不知道外面的世界，如果不经历外面世界的精彩和无奈，就不会找到幸福之门。一个人贫穷不可怕，可怕的是甘于贫穷、不思进取。在那个物资匮乏的年代，浙江义乌人没有"等靠要"，用"鸡毛换糖"，毫厘争取，完成了资本的原始积累，走村串巷，用双脚脱贫，用双手致富，逐步成长为中国商界的传奇，义乌成为国际小商品之都，"鸡毛换糖"成为浙商的生意经。

2020年，中国全面建成小康社会取得伟大历史性成就，决战脱贫攻坚取得决定性胜利。历经8年，全国现行标准下近1亿农村贫困人口全部脱贫，832个贫困县全部摘帽。这是令全世界刮目相看的重大胜利。脱贫摘帽不是终点，而是起点，是新时代中国人开启新生活的起点。"天行健，君子以自强不息。"无论是国家的发展，还是个人的梦想，都离不开艰苦奋斗，历史的接力棒交到了我们手中，辉煌的未来需要我们用智慧和勤劳去创造。

（浙大宁波理工学院党委宣传部）

故事
金华
邹姗姗(新闻学专业 201 专升本班)

开往义乌的绿皮火车

我们家位于湖南省娄底市新化县奉家镇上团乡下面的一个贫困小山村——莫西村,那里群山环绕,空气清新,环境优美,但地理位置偏僻,交通不便。改革开放之前,从来没有人想过离开那里。

1970 年,我的爸爸就出生在这个贫困而优美的小山村。1974 年,妈妈出生在湖南省怀化市溆浦县下的一个小镇上。改革开放之后,爸爸妈妈那一代人成为他们贫困山区外出务工的第一批农村青年。爸爸初中毕业,妈妈小学毕业,他们十几岁的时候,就跟着稍微大一点的朋友们,在广州、株洲、深圳、义乌等城市打工。

由于文化水平低,爸爸妈妈能挣的钱少之又少,又加上当时农村合作社取消了,爷爷奶奶欠了 8800 多块钱的债。妈妈说:"那时刚刚嫁过来,到处都是来家里要债的。出去打工一天也才 14 块,当时欠的这么多钱到现在都不知道翻了几倍了。"生活还在继续,爸爸妈妈什么也没有说,每年都外出打工慢慢还债。

2001 年,也就是我出生一年左右,爸爸妈妈把我留给了爷爷奶奶,一起去了广西打工。爸爸在工地当建筑工人,早上 5 点起床,晚上 11 点下班,一天 29 块钱的工资。爸爸 162cm 的身高,瘦得宛如竹竿一般,每天要运比自己还要重得多的钢筋水泥,爸爸说那是他最累的一年。

妈妈心疼爸爸,在附近租了一个小房子,每天下厨烧点好吃的,送到爸爸工地上去。除此之外,妈妈开始做自己的小本生意——贩卖水果。妈妈花钱买了一辆二手三轮车,每天天不亮就踩着三轮车,跟着那些卖水果的小摊贩,去两个小时以外的水果市场进货,然后再骑车回来摆摊,把水果卖出去,挣个差价。

妈妈说,那也是她觉得最苦的一年。她清晰地记得,8 月 15 日那一天,她挣了 39 块钱,爸爸一天工资才 29 块。他们省吃俭用,过年回来,挣的钱也都拿去帮爷爷奶奶还了债。我的爸爸妈妈,他们什么也没有说,默默地撑起我的小家。

2002 年,妈妈决定不去广西了,和爸爸去浙江义乌打工。后来他们也把我从老家接了过去,这一去,就是十几年。

他们一开始去了义乌上溪一家加工厂，那是一家小小的私营企业，老板租了一个面积不大的农民房作为车间。再雇几个员工帮忙做货，做的是饰品类，耳环、手链等。工人们需要右手拿火枪，左手拿焊锡丝，用高温的火枪对准焊锡丝，在特定的地方让焊锡丝融化，融化后焊锡丝又凝固，这样饰品就定型了。老板负责把这些货拿到大型电镀厂，电镀成银色、金色的小首饰，再送给下订单的老板验收。

当时的义乌，迎着改革开放的巨大浪潮，大力弘扬“鸡毛换糖”的精神。义乌遍地都是这种小作坊，到处都是和我爸爸妈妈一样的外来务工人员。爸爸妈妈刚去时住的地方是老板租的，是墙上泛起白皮的小平房。房间很小，刚好可以放下两张床。房子阴暗，潮湿，床下还堆满了妈妈要做的手工活。

晚上下了班，妈妈还要跟爸爸干一点手工活，手工活是记件结算工资的，虽然才几厘钱一个，可当时爸爸妈妈想的是能挣一点是一点。之后三年，爸爸学会了设计不同种类耳环，也开始帮老板给各订货商送货，每月给员工们结算工资。

2007 年，爸爸妈妈在义乌开了第一家饰品加工厂。爸爸回忆说，那时候厂里几个人合资，每人出 2000 元，从老板那把办厂的材料、房子租金等都接了过来。大家合伙一起重新经营，还买了一台三轮车，爸爸负责每天踩着三轮车送货。再后来，爸爸妈妈自己接手了这个小加工厂，从此有了他们自己真正意义上的第一家厂。

我 7 岁那年春节，也就是爸爸妈妈开厂的第一年。这一年，爸爸妈妈没有回家过年，那是他们唯一一次没有回家过年。妈妈说，那年刚开厂，根本就没有挣钱，就连回家的车票也买不起。第二年的初夏，妈妈一个人带着弟弟回家，把爷爷奶奶欠下的最后几千块钱的债给还清了，顺便把刚断奶的弟弟留给了爷爷奶奶。趁弟弟开心的时候，妈妈偷偷地溜出了他的视线，眼里含着泪水，悄悄拎着提前准备好的行李，默默上了开往义乌的绿皮火车。

2009 年的时候，爸爸妈妈小厂的生意慢慢开始变好，工人们从一两个变成了十几个。为了送货更快一点，爸爸买了一台二手助力车。渐渐地，厂里的工人越来越多，从十几个变成了几十个，原来的小厂空间不太够了。于是爸爸妈妈就把厂搬到义乌城西街道的横塘村，租了一个稍微宽敞的平房作为车间，一栋两三层的农民房作为工人的宿舍，房租是 7000 块一年。专门请了小姨来给工人们做饭。这年我也去了义乌，开始在那里念小学，后来一直在那里念初中、高中。

2010 年，爸爸妈妈买了一台五菱宏光面包车，这是我们家的第一辆面包车，也是我们那个贫困小山村的第一辆面包车。与此同时，妈妈也是我们村第一个考出驾驶证的农村妇女。

我上高中时候，互联网经济的蓬勃发展对线下传统行业、实体店铺的冲击越来越大。义乌的传统生产行业，如果不转型，最终会被时代淘汰。因为没有什么文化水平，爸爸妈妈的生意一年比一年要难做，工人们也慢慢地减少。

2016年，爸爸妈妈把小厂迁回湖南老家。利用日益发达的物流行业，把原材料寄回湖南老家，再利用老家相对廉价的劳动力、农村便宜的房价来降低成本，提高单个产品的利润。就这样，爸爸妈妈分隔两地，爸爸继续在义乌，妈妈则留在湖南老家，一方面照顾弟弟上学，一方面和爸爸两边配合，办起了在湖南的第一家小厂。这样的状态一直持续到了现在。小厂生意一直不温不火，但爸爸妈妈十几年都兢兢业业地经营着它们，撑起了我们的小家。

爸爸妈妈去年在老家承包了政府出资扶持的鱼塘。疫情期间，爸爸妈妈整天都在鱼塘边上种植鱼草。爸爸说："等你们都读书出来了，我就不去义乌了，在家搞搞农业，养养鱼，也不用你们负担什么，你们把你们的日子过好，有空多回来莫西村住住就好了。"

今年，我们家盖起了莫西村的第一栋小洋房，同时我也是莫西村的第一个大学生。

Jinhua
Zou Shanshan (Class 201, Majoring in Journalism)

Green Trains to Yiwu

My family lived in Moxi Village, a small poverty-stricken village in Shangtuan Township, Fengjia Town, Xinhua County, Loudi City, Hunan Province. It is surrounded by mountains with fresh air and a pleasant environment, but it's remote and the traffic is inconvenient. Before the reform and opening-up, no one ever thought of going outside.

In 1970, my father was born in this poor but beautiful mountain village. In 1974, my mother was born in a small town in Xupu County, Huaihua City, Hunan Province. After the Reform and Opening-up, people of my parents' age became the first group of rural youth flooding out of poor mountainous areas for work. My father graduated from junior high school and my mother from primary school. As a teenager, they worked in Guangzhou, Zhuzhou,

Shenzhen, Yiwu and other cities with friends just a few years older them.

However, they earned a limited salary because of the lack of education. At that time, the Rural Cooperation System was abolished, and my grandparents were in debt of more than 8800 yuan. According to mom, "The earliest years after we got married, many people came to our family for debts. At that time, we could only earn 14 yuan at most at work, and really I didn't know how we could make it." But life goes on, my parents left the village to seek a fortune without any complaints.

In 2001, one year after my birth, my parents left me with my grandparents and went to Guangxi for work. Dad worked as a construction worker, so he had to work from 5 a.m. to 11 p.m. with a salary of 29 yuan per day. My father was 162cm tall, but he was as thin as a bamboo pole, because he had to transport the steel and concrete much heavier than himself every day. It was the most tiring year for him.

My mother loved him deeply, so she rented a small house nearby. In this way, she could cook some delicious food every day and sent to my father's construction site. In addition, mom started her own business of selling fruit. She bought a used tricycle and started her business. Every dawn, she would pedal her tricycle to the fruit market with other vendors to purchase. It was a two-hour ride to and forth. Then she would set up a stall and sell the fruit to earn some profit from the meager price differences.

According to Mom, it was also the hardest year for her. Her memory of that time is still clear: on August 15th, she earned 39 yuan, and father's salary was only 29 yuan. They lived frugally. When they returned to their hometown for the New Year, they paid back the debts of grandparents with all of their yearly savings. They supported the whole family without any complaints.

In 2002, my mother decided to leave Guangxi and went to Yiwu, Zhejiang Province, with my father. Later, they picked me up from their hometown. Since then, we've been there for more than a decade.

At the beginning, they worked in a processing factory in Shangxi of Yiwu, which was a small private enterprise. The employer rented a small house as a workshop. A few workers were there to make accessories, including earrings, bracelets and so on. They melt the solder wire in a specific place with a torch in their right hand and solder wire in the left, aiming the torch at the solder wire with high temperature. Then, the melting solder wire solidified, which was how an ornament was shaped. The employer would take these goods to electroplating factories to electroplate them into silvery and golden ornaments, and then deliver it to clients with orders.

Yiwu was one of the pioneering places in the huge wave of Reform and Opening-up, vigorously carrying forward the spirit of favoring commerce. The situation also made Yiwu a home to small workshops and migrant workers. When my parents got there, they had to live in a small bungalow with peeling walls rented by their employer. The dark and damp room was small to accommodating two beds, under which was full of mother's handiwork materials.

After getting off from work, my mother continued to do some manual work with my father. It was paid by quantity. Although it worth only a few li per piece(one li equals to a thousandth of one yuan), my parents tried to earn as many as they could. Three years later, my father learned to design different kinds of earrings, and began to assist delivering goods to their clients and settling salaries for the employees every month.

In 2007, my parents started their first ornaments processing factory in Yiwu. As dad recalled, some colleagues in the factory invested 2000 yuan each, and bought materials and houses from their employer. They ran the business together, and they bought a tricycle in partnership. My father rode it to deliver products every day. As time passed by, my parents could manage the factory on their own, which made it their own first factory.

In that year, I was seven years old. My parents didn't return to our hometown for that Chinese New Year, and that was the only time. My mother said that when the factory opened that year, they didn't earn any money at all, so they couldn't even afford the ticket to go home. In the early summer of the second year, my mother took my brother home, and paid off the debts for my grandparents. She left the newly weaned son with my grandparents and sneaked out of his sight with tears in her eyes. After that, she stepped on the green train to Yiwu with her luggage which was packed up in advance.

In 2009, their business started to thrive, and the number of workers also increased from two to more than a dozen. Dad bought a used bicycle in order to deliver products faster. Gradually, more and more workers appeared in the factory, from a dozen to dozens. The space of the small factory became limited, so mom and dad moved the factory to Hengtang village on the West Street of Yiwu, and rented a more spacious bungalow as a workshop, and a three-floor house as workers' dormitory, charging them 7000 yuan a year for rent. They also hired my aunt to cook for the workers. At the same time, I entered primary school in Yiwu and furthered my study since then.

In 2010, my parents bought a Wuling Hongguang van, which was the first van in our family and the first van in my poor village. Mother also became the first rural woman in our village to get a driver's license.

When I was in high school, the vigorous development of Internet economy left an increasing impact on traditional industries and physical stores, especially on production industry in Yiwu. A company was destined to fail if it didn't transform. Due to limited education, my parents' business became more and more difficult year by year, and the number of workers gradually decreased.

In 2016, mom and dad moved their factory back to their hometown in Hunan. By taking advantage of the increasingly developed logistics industry, they could send raw materials back to their hometown in Hunan. They made use of the relatively cheap labor force and the cheap house price in rural areas so as to reduce costs and improve the profits of individual products. In this way, they had to separate from each other, with father remaining in Yiwu, while mother went back to Hunan. She could take care of my younger brother and cooperated with father to set up their first factory in Hunan. Till now, their small factory business has been tepid, but my parents have been running them conscientiously for more than a decade, supporting the whole family.

Mom and Dad were in their hometown last year and contracted the fishpond funded by the government. During the epidemic, they stayed by the pond, planting fish grass. Father once said to me, "After you all graduate, I won't go to Yiwu anymore. I'd like to do some agricultural business and raise some fish. We won't give you any burdens. All I wish is that you two can live a better life and visit us more often."

This year, my family built the first villa in Moxi village, and I also became the first college student.

有多少新浙江人为浙江打拼?

刘建民

几年前浙江省政府办公厅发出过一份《关于调整完善户口迁移政策的通知》。其中,“优秀农民工可以申请常住户口”备受外界关注。“优秀农民工”又有哪些标准?当年澎湃新闻查阅相关资料发现,相较于庞大的农民工群体,真正有资格落户的并不多。

故事的作者一家最终还是落户在了浙江,但他的家估计不是“优秀农民工”之家。作者说:“我们不是地道的浙江人,但我们一家从组成就在这里漂泊,在这里生根发芽,在这里为美好生活而奋斗。‘浙’也就成了我们的第二故乡。我的家庭可以是好多从外乡迁来浙江的打工者的一个缩影。”

就当代中国而言,农村劳动力进城打工,是改革开放的成果,是当代农民获得生产力解放的程度性标志,其进步意义不可低估。因为在改革开放之前的人民公社体制下,这一切是不可能的。那时的农民被牢牢捆绑在土地上,没有迁徙的自由,也没有择业的自由,如果哪个农民私自外出居留,就是“盲流”,要被抓捕遣返。

从这个意义上说,改革开放功德无量。“我的父母来到浙江的第一个地方是北部的桐乡市,他们在这里结婚登记,在这里有了我,在这里组成‘小扁舟’,虽然还是飘无定所,但有了家,就有了为生活的安定幸福奋斗的动力。第二个地方是浙江省杭州市的余杭区,我的小学学习就是在运河旁的五杭小学完成。所以我家在这里大约待了6年左右。”人的迁徙与流动改变着世界,也改变着中国。今日之中国,迁徙与流动已然是全社会的集体体验,几乎每个个体,或至少每个家庭都被卷入其间。

作者说:我的家庭没有轰轰烈烈的创业史,有的是从无到有的平凡幸福。但这并不妨碍我为父母感到骄傲,他们用自己的双手筑建了“小窝”,为我和妹妹创造了更多可以选择的机会,我想这也是很多外来浙江的打工父母所为之努力打拼换来的。

改革开放40年,有多少新浙江人,在浙江安家落户,为未来打拼?当时买不起那张返程火车票，却坚定乘上火车，或许就是一场“赌”，这也是和故事讲述者的家庭一样的那些新浙江人和他们演绎的浙江故事的开始。

（浙大宁波理工学院传媒与法学院，高级编辑）

故事

湖州

殷吉梅（网络与新媒体专业 193 班）

来浙江，没有返程车票

我的家庭有点特别但也很普通，我们不是地道的浙江人，但我们一家从组成就在这里漂泊，在这里生根发芽，在这里为美好生活而奋斗。“浙”也就成了我们的第二故乡。

虽然翻开户口簿，户口迁移时间一栏是定格在 2013 年，但我们来到这里的时间要更久。我想我的家庭是好多从外乡迁来浙江的打工者的一个缩影。

为什么选择浙江？父亲和母亲是 70 后的尾巴，刚好是改革开放之初。他们出生于云南广南县文山的大山中，是大山的孩子，文化程度是初中。据父亲回忆，他不到 20 岁时就和母亲认识了，两个人四处打工，也四处碰壁。

母亲回忆说：“我和一些小姐妹一起摆摊卖水果，刚开始还能挣点钱，后来那些专门卖水果的店多了起来，我们的生意就不好了，水果都放烂了也卖不出去，一直亏本，吃饭的钱都快没了。后来就不卖了，跟着你爸去了浙江。”

父亲谈起这个问题，直截了当说：“我们都是农村里的，没什么文化，当时想得就很简单，就是怎么可以赚钱，怎么可以混口饭吃，那个时候，哪有什么手机，外面的一些消息听不到也看不到，村里好多年轻人都是往外面走，说去打工，听说浙江好找工作，我们也就跟着去了，当时记得很清楚，就拿了几件衣服和一些吃的，钱也只够买去的火车票，回来的车票都买不起，就这么稀里糊涂地去了浙江。”

我想，当时买不起那张返程火车票，却坚定乘上火车，或许就是一场“赌”，这也是我的家庭和浙江故事的开始。

我的父母来到浙江的第一个地方是北部的桐乡市，他们在这里结婚登记，在这里有了我，在这里组成“小扁舟”，虽然还是飘无定所，但有了家，就有了为生活的安定幸福奋斗的动力。

第二个地方是浙江省杭州市的余杭区，我的小学就是在运河旁的五杭小学完成。我家在这里大约待了6年。父母是在纺织厂里上班的，租的一间房，不大，放得下两张床和台式电视、饮水机等三两样简单的家电，可以说是“麻雀虽小，五脏俱全”。还记得一到雷雨天气，电视机就会闪屏，甚至变成灰白的，连的是天线，父亲经常去修。当时的生活条件并不好，母亲说：“那个时候就是想到要买什么，就存钱买。”比如为了方便我学习查找资料，丰富一下家里的娱乐活动，父亲就会定一个小目标：“今年买台电脑。”“夏天越来越热，要买台空调。”……向往幸福的生活，这是奋斗的动力。

2008年，我有了妹妹，她很调皮，原本的家就显得有些拥挤了，于是就有了新的目标，“要换个大一点的房子”。搬家对于打工讨生活的父母来说，是要慎重的事。从父亲那里得知，他是在过年走亲戚的时候，听到别人谈起了迁户口的事情，后来自己去认真了解了一番。加上那个时候外地子女在这边上学的手续很复杂，而且高考要回老家考，而落了户口就可以在这边高考，省去了一些麻烦。父亲是个执行能力强的人，他经朋友介绍得知在湖州的禹越镇有一处空置的房子，又认识了一位本地人家，知道他家有个亲戚是没有子女的老人，于是在经过长时间的考虑考察后，拿出积蓄买下了房子，把那位老人接过来赡养，户口也就顺理成章地迁了。有了固定的“窝”，就有了实在感，有了满足感，有了归属感。

“以后这就是我们的新家了。”还记得父母第一次带我来看这积了灰的房子，辛苦地打扫了一天，拂去尘土，他们的眼睛里是有光的，我想是对未来生活的满满期待。

我家现在在湖州德清，前面是一条河，属于太湖水系，捕鱼的季节，会常看到渔船，家门口对着的是一棵粗脖子大树，枝条常常伸到河面，夏天知了聒噪，与河水接近的地方，还常常会有水蛇出没。梅雨季节，门前的路常常泥泞，河水暴涨，逼近家门前。后来因为河道疏浚拓宽，那棵大树就被砍了，青石板也被挖走了，岸边筑起了高高的堤和栏，偶尔会有载满泥沙的大船经过，曾经的泥泞小路也变成了柏油路，随之可见的是村里有多辆小汽车驶过。村旁的公路也扩大修成了双向六车道。

2015年，家里来了一位“新伙伴”小汽车，这让我家更有了享受生活的样子。放假的日子，父亲会自驾带着我们出去旅游，西湖，乌镇，上海……有时候，幸福都是生活中那些不经意的小事情。父亲很爱护那辆车，刚开始的时候每天都冲洗一遍，周末的时候经常拉着我和妹妹一起洗，这种短暂的劳动时光惬意快乐；在朋友圈看到有人分享哪里开放了新的景点，吃完晚饭我们就会讨论，然后找一个空闲的时间去游玩；镇上在前年修了一个很大的公园，父母下班后，会常常去公园里遛弯，有时还会跳一跳舞；有时候，一顿晚饭是一家人一起做的，妹妹洗菜，我切菜，父亲和母亲炒菜，这是以往的四角平房里无法做到的。

让父母回忆一下，是从什么时候对“浙”里有了融入感，他们提到了刚搬过来那一年过年前的“打年糕”，“很有年味，很有人情味。”我回忆了一下，当时一大早是被窗外的热闹声吵醒的，走到阳台推开窗户，冬天的清晨带着雾气，朝下看，村里人把家里的长凳都搬了出来，在路上横着接连摆开，健壮的男人们在石缸旁围着，轮流交替抡起木桩打年糕。父亲也在那里，和一旁的邻居有说有笑，母亲则在一旁帮着揉打好的年糕。现在邻居们熟得很，有时候还会串串门，或靠在河旁的围栏上唠唠家常。

我的家庭没有轰轰烈烈的创业史，有的是从无到有的平凡幸福。但这并不妨碍我为父母感到骄傲，他们用自己的双手筑建了“小窝”，为我和妹妹创造了更多可以选择的机会，我想这也是很多外来浙江的打工父母所为之努力打拼换来的。

Huzhou
Yin Jimei (Class 193, Majoring in Network and New Media)

Came to Zhejiang with a One-way Ticket

My family is ordinary but special. We aren't local people in Zhejiang, but we started roving here since the family was formed. We took root and developed here; we struggled here for a better life. "Zhejiang" has become our second hometown.

If opening the household registration, you will find that 2013 was the year we migrated to Zhejiang. Actually, we came here much earlier than that. I think my family is an epitome of most migrant workers who come from other cities to earn a living in Zhejiang.

Why did we come to Zhejiang? My parents were born at the end of the 1970s, which happened to be the beginning of reform and opening-up in China. Born in the mountain of Wenshan, Guangnan County in Yunnan Province, they can be regarded as children of the mountain. They quit school after middle school. According to my father, he met my mother when he was under 20. They tried to find a job everywhere but were always turned down by others.

My mother recalled, "my friends and I sold fruits on a market stall. In the beginning, we could make some money. However, more and more fruit shops opened, so it was not easy to sell fruit. Fruits couldn't be sold if they got rotten. My parents kept losing so much money that we hardly had money to feed ourselves. Therefore, they stopped selling fruit and went to Zhejiang."

Speaking of this question, my father said frankly: "Your mother and I were from the farmer family with little education. We didn't think too much; all we wanted was to make a living and make money. At that time, there were no mobile phones, and we knew nothing about the outside world. Many young people in the village went out to work. When we heard that it was easy to find a job in Zhejiang, we followed them. We remembered very clearly that we just took a few clothes and some food. The money we had was only enough for a one-way ticket; we even didn't have money to buy one more ticket to return back. That's how we came to Zhejiang without knowing anything."

In my opinion, they got on the train firmly though they couldn't afford the ticket for coming back. Maybe it was a gamble. Actually, this was the beginning of my family and stories in Zhejiang.

The first place that my parents visited was Tongxiang which lies in the north of Zhejiang. They got married and gave birth to me here. We were like a small boat, floating around aimlessly. Anyway, having a family helped them find the drive to struggle for the happiness of their life.

The second place my family moved to was Yuhang of Hangzhou city. I completed my study in Wuhang primary school beside the Grand Canal, where my family lived for 6 years or so. My parents worked in a textile mill and rented a small room that could only hold two beds, a television, a water dispenser, and some necessary household appliances. Small as it was, it was equipped with everything we needed. As I recalled, our TV was attached with an antenna, so it would begin to splash, or sometimes turn into black and white in a stormy day with thunder. Therefore, my father always had it repaired. At that time, my family's living condition was not good. My mother said, "at that time if we wanted to buy something, we would have to save money for it." For example, for the sake of the convenience to search information and have more family recreation, my father would set such small goals as "buying a computer this year" or "air conditioner is needed when it is getting hot in summer". Our yearn for a happy life was the motivator to work hard.

In 2008, my little sister was born, and she was naughty, so our house seemed to be even more crowded. Therefore, we got another new goal, that is, "a bigger house". For my parents who made a living by working for others, moving house was a matter that we needed to think carefully about. My father told me that he heard about the transfer of hukou when visiting relatives during the spring festival. Then he got to know more about it later. At that time, the procedures for migrant children's study in local school were very complicated. Migrant children had to go back to their hometown when taking the college entrance examination. If we got the registered permanent residence, we could take the examination here, which would save a lot of trouble. My father is a man of high efficiency. With the help of his friends, my father found a vacant house in Yuyue town of Huzhou, and he also acquainted with a local family. Knowing that the old man had no child, he bought the house with family savings and shouldered the responsibility to care for the old man after a long consideration and investigation. Thus, the transfer of our household registration was settled successfully. With a fixed place to live, there came the sense of reality, a sense of satisfaction and a sense of belonging.

"Here is our new house now", said my parents. I still remember the first time when my parents brought me here to have a look at the dusty house. We spent the whole day cleaning it up. I saw the shining light in their eyes. I supposed that was hopes for our future.

We are living in Deqing County, Huzhou nowadays. In front of our house was a river, which was a branch of Taihu lake. When the fishing season came, we could see the fishing boats passing by. Facing the door of our house was a big tree with stout branches, which often extended over the river. In summer, the cicadas made buzzing and clicking noises; water snakes often showed up near the river. In the rainy season, the road in front of the door was often muddy, and the river surged to the door. Afterward, because the river was dredged and widened, the big tree was cut down, and the bluestone slabs were also dug out and taken away. The dyke and fence were built high along the riverside. Occasionally, large ships loaded with sand would pass by. The once-muddy pathway also turned into a tarmac, so more cars could drive at a time in the village. The road beside the village has also been expanded into a two-way six-lane road.

In 2015, we bought a car which brought much joy to our family. During the holiday, my father would drive us to many places, such as the West Lake, Wuzhen, Shanghai and so on. Sometimes, happiness came from the trifles in life. My father took good care of the car. In the beginning, he washed it every day. On weekends, he often invited my sister and me to wash it together. This short period of working time was very pleasant and enjoyable. When we saw someone sharing the news about the opening of a new scenic spot in the circle of friends, we would discuss it after dinner, and then we would go to play in spare time. A large park was built in town the year before last. After work, my parents would often go for a walk in the park, and sometimes they would dance. Sometimes, dinner was cooked by the whole family. My sister washed the dishes, I cut the vegetables, and my father and mother made dishes. All these were impossible in previous square bungalow.

I asked my parents to recall when they began to have a sense of belonging to Zhejiang. They mentioned the year that they just moved here, and the custom of making New Year cakes before the Chinese new year was very festive and human. I remembered that I was woken up by the bustle and hustle outside the window early in the morning. I went to the balcony and opened the window. The early winter morning was foggy. I looked down on the street. The villagers took the benches out and placed them one after another on the road. The strong men, surrounding the stone tanks, took turns to swing wooden piles to make New Year cakes. Among them, I saw my father who was talking to my neighbors smilingly. My mother was helping knead the finished New Year cakes. They were familiar with our neighbors. Sometimes they would visit our neighbors, or had a small talk while leaning on the fence beside the river.

My family doesn't have an earth-shaking entrepreneurial story. Instead, there is only ordinary happiness that we have been struggling from scratch.

However, nothing can prevent me from being proud of my parents. They have built a cozy house with their own hands, creating more choices for my sister and me. I think this is also what many migrant parents have achieved when working hard in Zhejiang.

住房变迁中融入了几代人的奋斗

史望颖

《老房翻新》开头就很吸引人，作者毫不避讳地描写了家人近期遭遇的不幸经历，从二老的"两摔"引出了老房焕新颜。记录很平实，却有一股打动人心的力量，这就是"真实"的力量。

家庭住房的变迁折射时代的变迁。文章呈现了老房翻新前后的真实场景。建于2000年左右，位于金华永康石柱镇姚塘村的房子，厨房里是烧柴火的老炉灶，作者幽默地用"家徒四壁"来形容。这次趁着房子翻新的契机，把一层重新装修，有力提升了生活水平。居住条件的改善，折射出这个时代千千万万个家庭对美好生活的期盼。

小康家庭不仅是物质的丰足，更是精神的丰盈。文章中自然地流露了亲人间的相互支持。这里有父母对子女的关爱。父亲十分节俭，但给孩子提供的生活都是按小康水平来的，用自己的节俭换来对家庭的经济保障；这里有子女对父母的感恩。这次房子翻新是年长8岁的姐姐主导的，姐姐体恤父母的不容易，想用自己的努力给父母创造更好的条件；这里也有姐弟之间的相亲相爱。姐姐疼爱弟弟，弟弟感谢姐姐。小康生活里，亲人间相互的精神支持，就像一盏明灯照亮了前行的道路。

迈向小康融入了几代人的奋斗。文章真实描述了几代人为追求美好生活而奋斗的过程。这里有父母的奋斗。爸爸开拖拉机干活，周末从不休息；这里有姐姐的奋斗。随着时代潮流做海淘代购，积累一定资金后开培训机构，添置新房。这次房子翻新也由姐姐承包；这里也有作者本人的奋斗。尽管还没毕业，他利用英语基础好的优势做了几份兼职，获得了酬劳，更收获了自信。几代人的接力奋斗，在决胜全面小康路上越走越稳。

正是这样一个个普通家庭的变迁，汇成了我国决胜全面小康社会的生动场景，展现了人们对美好生活的向往和不懈追求。

（中国教育报宁波记者站记者）

故事

金华

姚冯胜(网络与新媒体专业 181 班)

老房翻新

2019 年 12 月末,我的父亲不幸出了车祸,是对方追的尾,父亲昏迷了 30 多分钟,醒来手脚不得动弹。所幸在医生的救治后,他脱离了生命危险。老爸住院的日子,都是老妈在医院陪床护理,难得有一天老妈回家休息,第二天她早起上厕所的时候,不慎把股骨头摔裂了。当时大家庭里也有许多其他家人遇上了各种各样的毛病和不幸,有面瘫的,有划破经脉的,有眼睛动手术的等等。事后亲友都说老妈摔跤那天是因为我不在家,家里阳气不足,致使了意外更易发生。老妈摔跤,是 2020 年 3 月份发生的事了。此时老爸已经能基本自理,本来是老妈陪护老爸回医院复查复健住院,现在反过来是老爸照顾老妈了。一个被安排在了医院的骨科(一),另一个在骨科(二)。不过二老的这两摔,也把家里的房子摔出了个翻天覆地的变化。

现在金华永康石柱镇姚塘村的家里住着的房子,是 2000 年左右盖好的,当时家里的经济条件确实不景气,厨房里是烧柴火的老炉灶,各种桌子椅子及其他家具,都非常的简陋。或许当年置办的时候是新的,但 20 年过后从未换新。我的姐夫用了 4 个字来形容我家的房子——“家徒四壁”,可真是一点也不夸张。家里有 3 层,自家人都是住在 2 层的,1 层有着车库和厨房,其余空着闲置的空间都被老爸隔出来出租用了。老妈的这一摔,把自己的行走能力暂时地摔没了,起初她完全无法行走,现在已能缓慢短途行走。虽然老爸能够自己走楼梯,但毕竟是受过伤的腿,加上二老的年纪也愈来愈大(妈妈大我三轮,老爸更是已经年过花甲),已经不适合经常性地上下爬楼梯,在一番艰难的“游说”后,爸爸终于同意,将一楼好好装修一番,他和妈妈搬到一楼生活。

长我 8 岁的姐姐,是这次重新装潢的主导者。跟我的父亲聊天,基本三两句就能绕到“钱”的这个话题上来,老爸一辈子是跟“钱”磕上了。年轻的时候穷怕了,即使现在家庭条件已经比从前好了许多,他对钱的用途,还是非得花在刀刃上不可的。当然,他爱抽的烟不算。

我们先来将故事的视角放到更久远一点,我上幼儿园的时候。这时候爸爸是拖拉机运货司机，妈妈也上班。周一到周五白天我在学校，晚上我自己回家。一到周六，爸爸就会把我送到外婆家代管，周日下午再把我接回家。也可以说，我是外婆拉扯大的。爸妈在我小的时候实在是太忙于工作了，导致我现在跟外婆会更亲近。在大一点能够安全地乘坐公交车以后，我会在周五自己坐车到外婆家。再到后来，我周日也会睡在外婆家，周一早上起个大早去上学。

老爸的拖拉机，前前后后也是换了好几辆，但总是在前一辆实在开不动的情况下，老爸才会舍得花钱再换一辆，而且有时候他换的还是二手的，就是为了“截流”式地省钱。外婆也经常跟我吐槽爸爸去外婆家的时候，从来什么也不提，夏天连个西瓜都没有。真是一点不客气。外出开车，老爸的午饭自然是在外解决。多数情况老爸不会舍得去饭店吃，甚至快餐都不舍得。他会从家里带着白米饭，就着梅干菜来吃。老爸也是个宁愿享受点口福的人，有一次我发现他车上放着一整箱香肠，但我又注意到那种香肠是极其劣质的，口感也非常的差。老爸跟我说，他的午饭就是几根香肠。

我得知老爸如此节俭，内心一阵阵的酸楚。老爸就是牺牲自己，为我付出。虽然家里不阔绰，在当时也不能算是小康，但老爸给我的生活条件就是小康，该给我的零花钱一分也没有少给。不善言辞的老爸，不够细心体贴的老爸，非常大男子主义的老爸，在为家庭提供经济保障这点上，从来都没有马虎过。

现在你大概了解我的父亲是一个多么“抠“的人，可想而知劝说他同意这次的装修计划是多么难得的一件事了。在这里我真的非常感谢，也非常感恩我的姐姐。我的姐姐特别疼爱我。此次装修全部是由姐姐出的钱，虽然不用老爸自己出钱，但是老爸也不想花姐姐的钱，老爸怕姐姐的婆婆认为姐姐老是拿钱补贴娘家。事实不是这样的，姐姐的事业虽然离不开老公的支持，但是姐姐现在的收入非常可观，这次装修的钱，花的都是姐姐自己赚得的。

提起我姐，她的事业发展也是乘了一波海淘代购潮的东风。2014年刚毕业的她，原本只是一家辅导机构的作文老师，最开始的基本工资只有2000元，这比我之前做的一个私人助理兼职的薪资还低。因为她的男朋友在澳洲念硕士，我姐就渐渐开启了代购生意，后来越做越好，就把作文老师这份工作辞了。由于代购，她积累了大量的人脉。后来她自己租了房子，办自己的补习班，同时也建立了自己的仓库。现在，姐姐一边忙补习班一边也做些代购，有了十分稳定的收入，生活水平越来越好了，我也为她感到非常高兴。她和姐夫也买了一套小房子，当时是想着自己可以住，又能算作投资。不过，最近他们正考虑售出，下一步打算去杭州买房。

聊聊自己几份工作经历。这都跟我的英语基础比较好有关系。第一份我做了1年多的兼职，是给一位在澳洲开清洁公司的老板当助理，处理一些开发票、安排清洁外出、回复邮件的任务，这份工作是姐姐给介绍的，工作量不大，试用期时薪水是1800元一个月，三个月转正后2500元。第二份暑期短暂的兼职是在杭州的一家雅思托福培训机构当助教老师，工作了三个星期后有5000元，自己觉得是挺不错的收入了。这个助教也是姐姐给我介绍的。不过，无论什么工作，无论多少薪水，总是对自己能力和付出的考验与回报。

一路走来，虽然坎坷，但也有一家人其乐融融的幸福。站在今天，我想说："小康家庭，在我的小家里面已经完成了决胜。"

Jinhua
Yao Fengsheng (Class 181, Majoring in Network and New Media)

The Renovation of the Old House

At the end of December 2019, my father had a car accident. The rear-end collision left my father in coma for 30 minutes, and he was unable to move his hands and legs upon waking up. Luckily, he escaped death after some time in the hospital. During his hospitalization, my mother took such a good care of him that she barely had a chance to go home. One morning, my mother fractured her femur when using the toilet. At that time, other members of my extended family also suffered all kinds of misfortunes: facial paralysis, meridians strain, eye surgery. Many relatives attributed my mother's misfortune to my absence, saying that not having me in the house decreased the Yang Qi, the masculine energy of fengshui, which increased the possibility of having an accident. Mother's accident happened in March 2020, and my father could already take care of himself at that time. At first, it was my mother who accompanied my father back to the hospital for reexamination and rehabilitation, but now it was my father who took care of my mother instead. The two of them together occupied two treatment rooms of the hospital's orthopaedics department, and the accidents caused such a big change to our family.

Our house was located in the Yaotang Village, Shizhu Town, Yongkang

County, Jinhua. It was well-built around 2000. Back then, the financial situation at home was not good. We used a wood-burning stove in the kitchen while all the furniture was very simple. They might be brand new when being bought; however, we never replaced them even after 20 years. My brother-in-law would often use four words to describe our family: Nothing left but walls, and it was not exaggerating at all. There were three floors, two for living, and one for garage and kitchen. My father leased out every available space in the building. My mother's accident made her unable to walk for a while, but now she can walk slowly for short distances. Even though my father could climb the stairs by himself, his legs had been injured before, and they were getting older (my mother was 36 years older than me while my father was already 60 years old), it was inconvenient for them to climb up and down the stairs. Therefore, after a hard persuasion with my father, he finally agreed to move to the ground floor with my mother after giving it a total makeover.

My sister, who was 8 years older than me, was the one who took the lead in this redecoration. Every time I talked with my father, he would always shift the topic to money. He was entangled with money for his whole life, because he had serious financial difficulties at a young age. Naturally, even if the family condition got much better than before, he had become a person who would only spend money on things that were necessary, except for his cigarettes, of course.

Let's take the story a little further back in time. My father was a tractor delivery driver when I was in kindergarten. From Monday to Friday, I would spend most of my day at the school and would return home alone in the evening. On Saturday, my father would drop me off at my grandmother's house and pick me up again on Sunday afternoon. It could be said that I felt raised by my grandmother. My parents were really busy with work when I was little, so that was why I felt closer to my grandmother emotionally. After I was older and could safely take the bus by myself, I would often travel on the bus to my grandmother's house on Fridays by myself. Later, I would sleep at my grandmother's house on Sundays and get up early on Monday mornings for school.

My father's tractor had been replaced several times. He would only spend money on another tractor when his previous one broke down. Sometimes he would buy second-hand tractors to save money. My grandma also often complained to me about my father, because he had never brought a single gift to my grandmother, and he would not even spend money on a watermelon. When he was driving for work, he would not eat at a restaurant, not even fast food. Instead, he would bring rice with preserved vegetables. My father was a person who would like to satiate himself. There was one time that I spotted there was a box of sausages in his car, but I noticed that the quality of these sausages was bad and they tasted awful. My father told me that they were the only things he ate for lunch.

Knowing that my father was so frugal, a sudden sorrow and grief filled my heart. As a father, he sacrificed himself for my happiness. He gave me a well-off life, although my family was not ostentatious, not even well-off at that time. However, my father gave me a well-to-do life, because he was never thrifty with my pocket money. My father who was ineloquent, inconsiderate, and very chauvinistic had never been sloppy in providing financial security to the family.

Now you probably know how stingy my father was, and you can imagine how difficult it was to persuade him to agree to the renovation plan. I'm grateful to my sister. My sister loved me so much that she paid all the money for the renovation. My father didn't need to pay for the renovation, but it did not mean that he enjoyed using the money of my sister. My father was afraid that my sister's mother-in-law would think that my sister always used the money to subsidize her parents, which was not true. My sister's career could not be separated from her husband's capital support, but the income created by her sister was also very impressive. The money spent on this renovation was earned by herself.

Talking about my sister, she was the one who took advantage of the trend in overseas shopping purchase agent. She had been a writing teacher for a tutoring organization when she graduated from the university, and at the beginning, her basic salary was only 2,000 yuan, which was lower than the salary of a part-time personal assistant I took previously. Because her boyfriend was studying for a master's degree in Australia, my sister gradually started her purchasing business. Later, the business was booming, so my sister quit her job. She had accumulated a large number of connections and customers. Then, she rented a house by herself and ran her cram school. At the same time, she also established her warehouse. Now, my sister was busy with her cram school and purchasing business. Her life was getting better. She and her husband also bought a small house. At the time, they thought it could be well for living and investment. Recently, they are considering selling the house and they want to buy a house in a larger city—Hangzhou.

Regarding my work experience, all of my opportunities are accredited to my outstanding English. The first part-time job that I did for a year was being the assistant of a person who ran a cleaning company in Australia. My responsibility was to issue invoices, arrange cleaning and reply emails. My working language was English. The job, introduced by my sister, did not require much work. The salary was 1800 yuan per month in the probation period, and it was raised to 2500 after three months. My second job, also introduced by my sister, was to work as a teaching assistant for an IELTS training school in Hangzhou; I was paid 5000 just after 3 weeks. The payment was quite generous.

Our family has become a well-to-do family.

心里有家就不必怕浪迹天涯

樊　亮

“老家”是一个充满浓郁感情的词汇，特别是对于中国人。无论是生在南方还是北方，血液里流淌的都是一样的故土难离，脑海里萦绕着的都是相同的落叶归根。李微微的《老家印象》写了很多关于老家的记忆，初看上去有些零散，可仔细想来，老家本来也不单指一栋房子、一棵大树，恰恰就是那些铭刻在心灵深处的零散记忆。

《老家印象》里的爷爷、奶奶、爸爸、妈妈和“我”，正好是几代中国人的缩影。爷爷奶奶小的时候很穷，想通过读书改变命运，却因为没有条件，而最终窝在了乡村。但是，他们没有忘记教育的重要性，他们也尽全力去培养自己的孩子。而爸爸和妈妈这一代则彻底赶上了好时候，他们可以放心大胆地去做生意，用自己灵活的头脑去赚钱，并用这些钱去改善老一辈人的生活条件，给下一代创造一个更好的学习和生活环境，使整个家族更好地融入国家和民族的发展进程之中。这本身也是一种和谐。

随着国家和社会的不断发展，年轻人势必会离故乡越来越远。老家也必然会在越来越多的时候仅存于记忆之中。但是，老家做为一个生命的原点、生命里永远的根，点亮的不只是记忆的符号，更应该是未来景象的标识。老家，永远是我们积极向上不断追求新目标的信念支撑。所以，无论我们走到哪里，只要心里有家，就不必惧怕浪迹天涯。

（吉林长春媒体人）

故事

温州

李微微(网络与新媒体专业 193 班)

老家印象

“小学读了几年就没有再读了,不过现在很多字我都认识的哇。”奶奶自豪地说。

“你从小到大有因为什么事情而自卑吗?”

奶奶眼睛不再看我,缓缓吐出一个字:“穷。”

奶奶作为家里的姐姐,小学成绩一直是班里第一,可是为了挑起家里的担子,学业也就不了了之了。

我的老家,温州文成,坐标浙南。老家在山上的一个小镇里,有趣的是,我们那一个村的人都姓李,好像所有人都是亲戚一样,一些个嫁过来的别姓也已经很好地融入。

我老家属于比较偏僻的地方,很多孩子能读完初中就很不错了,基本上是小学毕业走一批,初中毕业走大部分,寥寥几个读高中,很少有人读大学,当然后来到现在就很多了,家人也重视教育了。现在的中年人一般男的是小学文凭,女的是初中文凭。

妈妈爸爸开店了,为了方便,八九岁就把我送到了奶奶这里,奶奶非常非常疼我。在那间平房里,有两张大床,它们床头靠着床头,前者属于爷爷,后者属于奶奶和我。我从来不敢自己先上床睡觉,总觉得从床头和墙之间的缝隙里,会伸出一只手来将我抓走或者爬出什么东西来喝我的血。

家还是土房子,有个衣橱隔开,然后有个柜子,柜子上面放着电视,大脑袋电视哈,也算是当时家里唯一的娱乐设施了。床的上边靠墙那里一块板有一张床那么长,爷爷奶奶在房间里面看电视剧,奶奶就会给我拿小凳子坐床上,然后我在那块板上面写作业,偷偷看看电视偷着乐。

另外一边是爷爷年轻时候的书房,还有案桌子,进去能闻到水墨还有老的纸的味道,墙上挂有爷爷写的字。后来这个房间不用了,奶奶就会存放一些过年别人送的东西,整整齐齐地。地还是泥地,不过是经过夯实的,基本不会起尘土。

记忆深刻的是下雨,因为下雨会漏水。其他地方倒也不会,就是厕所会。

以前厕所上面架的是塑料波浪形的黄色的瓦片，可以透光，用久了漏水哩，需要拿东西接水，所以下雨天我最讨厌上厕所，因为有时候水会溅到屁股上。

家后面是山，对应有两小块地是我家的，奶奶在那里种了常吃的蔬菜，浇的是自家的粪便，顶楼一小块地种葱、芹菜或香菜。后来条件开始好了，高中时代家里翻新了房屋，盖了砖房，分出了好几个房间，也有了水泥地、大白墙，又翻盖了楼房。村里的路很长一段时间还是土路，不下雨还好，一下雨全是各种泥水，然后一到天黑，村里全是黑漆漆的一片，整个村子也很安静。

近几年修了新路，路程变成半个小时。之前回老家只有两班去山上的公交车，放暑假我会去妈妈店里待一个暑假，坐的是长途车。

奶奶每次都会扇着扇子拉着我的行李送我去马路上等车，车来了，她总是会向司机再三强调我的目的地，说在哪个高速路口下车叫我一下，于是小学生时代我就会一个人坐 4 个小时的长途车了。

路上我也会想司机会不会忘记，时不时看一下路，也就安慰作用吧，我哪里认得路呀。暑假回来也是一样，爸爸会比较潇洒，来送我的话，换上简单的体恤(爸爸有个坏习惯，夏天很少穿上衣)，在公交车站帮我把行李放在大巴车的下面，然后等司机上车，说一声就走了。

记忆中爸爸会偷偷往我这里看。我也会偷偷看看爸爸。

不知道什么时候开始路边安装了太阳能路灯，一下子让整个农村的夜晚亮起来，各种夜生活也开始有了，有人跳广场舞，有人摆摊叫卖，还有人去镇上吃烧烤大排档，不再是那种大家天黑就回家，黑漆漆静得可怕的环境；路好了，开上电瓶车，到镇子的这 2 公里的路程基本没啥距离感。

阿姨和妈妈回老家的一大爱好就是打麻将，打到半夜才回家。

爷爷是个很抠门的人，能够不花的钱绝对不会花；奶奶不一样，奶奶是很省钱，衣服穿到不能穿，本来就很便宜的鞋，穿坏了自己修不了就花点钱去路边鞋匠那里修。家里从不曾见到爷爷做饭，奶奶则在爷爷身边料理着油盐酱醋，如果家里的电话响了，两成是找奶奶，八成是找爷爷。

这是老一辈的观念吧。

我们家是爸爸做饭多，妈妈的手艺还不如爸爸。

我做小学生时以前每个星期一有赶集，奶奶看我很想买新衣服就会带我去逛，不过我小时候的品位还真是糟糕，看中衣服奶奶砍价，回去穿起来还这么丑，奶奶说那下次赶集拿去退掉吧，就闹了笑话。

我们请认识的人吃饭的时候，一般都有个两三桌，会用锅灶烧菜，妈妈手艺不好，常常担任烧柴火的角色。

长辈会请村里经常帮别人烧锅灶饭菜而且公认厨艺好的阿婆来帮忙，其他来吃饭的阿婆也会帮忙摘摘菜,吃完了也会帮忙洗碗,不然我们一家人哪里干得完呀。

后来有了电饭锅、煤气灶,烧饭也方便了很多,但是我们还是喜欢锅灶烧出来的东西。“香!”

冬天,烧柴火的那个煤炭会被夹出来放在小火笼里,外公在上面盖一层布,出来聊天的时候会提在手里,看起来就很暖和;还可以放在脸盆里面烤烤脚,冬天的脚总是会湿或者冷冰冰的。

现在有了空调,条件就没有那么艰苦了,不过还是少了些许氛围。夏天,奶奶有两把扇子,一把经常用,也很好用,手柄被汗和手心磨成深色,光滑。老房子里面虽然没有空调,开电风扇也挺凉快。

妈妈老是和阿姨一起约好去商场买衣服。我呢,刚开始还会和她们一起,后来觉得,商场里的衣服是二货,全部堆在一起,还比网上贵,款式又比网上少。妈妈试过在网上买衣服,但是质量极差,就放弃了。

那会过年的时候手机还不会像现在这样不离手,大家聚在一起“斥巨资”买鞭炮和烟火,玩完了还会玩 123 木头人、大王小王的游戏,乱哄哄的,一不留神鞭炮还会把新衣服给烫一个洞。

现在大家也不会在意过年穿不穿新衣服,稍大的孩子聚在一起是为了打牌打游戏喝酒。送的东西也多了,尿不湿奶粉什么的以及高科技的也都有了。

怀念这一个又一个有点闹哄哄的中国式新年,最后在神明面前的祈福无非关乎家人身体健康。

这最后一个许给自己跟中国年一样很俗气也很真实的愿,希望自己再接再厉步步高升,学业有成。

我们一定在某些时刻,会怀念那个自己出生长大的地方。因为知道,回忆再也回不去了。

Wenzhou
Li Weiwei (Class 193, Majoring in Network and New Media)

My Impression of Hometown

"I discontinued my education in primary school after studying for a few years, but I can recognize a lot of words now," my grandma said proudly.

"Was there anything that made you have the feeling of inferiority when you were growing up?"

My grandma stopped looking at me and slowly uttered one word: "Poverty."

As the elder sister in the family, she had always been top of her class in primary school, but to take up the burden of the family, she had to give up her education.

My hometown, Wencheng Wenzhou, is located in southern Zhejiang. My hometown is in a small town in the mountains. Interestingly, all the people in our village shared the same surname Li, as if all of them were relatives. People with different surnames married to the people of this village, and they all found they could integrate with us soon.

My hometown is located in a remote place, so few children were able to finish the study of middle school. Some of them would stop going to school after graduating from primary schools, and others would barely make it to the end of middle school. Only a few students attended the high school, let alone studying in the university. Nowadays, villagers have paid more attention to education. The middle-aged men in our village usually just owned primary school certificates whereas ladies had middle school certificates.

My parents opened a shop and sent me to my grandmother at the age of eight for convenience's sake. My grandmother loved me very much. I remember there were two beds in my grandparents' bungalow, and they were placed side by side; the former one belonged to my grandfather and the latter one to my grandmother and me. I never dared to go to bed by myself first, always fearing that a hand would reach out from the gap between the bed and the wall to grab me away or drink my blood.

The house was an adobe house, which was divided by a wardrobe into two parts. There was a cupboard with a big television on the top. That CRT television was the only entertainment in the family at the time. On the bed against the wall lay a tabletop which was as long as the bed itself. Whenever my grandparents were in the room watching TV serials, my grandmother would provide me a stool so I could sit on the bed and write my homework on it while taking a few sneak peeks at the television.

On the other side of the house was a study for my grandfather; the room had a wooden desk, and you could smell the scent of the ink and some old papers. My grandfather's calligraphy was hanging on the wall. Later, my grandparents used this room as a storage room to keep presents given by others in the Spring Festival. The floor of that house was muddy, but it was compacted, so generally no dust would be raised.

What impressed me deeply was the rain, because the house leaked. Not every place leaked, but the toilet.

On the top of the toilet were yellow wave-shaped tiles for the house to let in the light, and the bad thing was that it leaked after using for a long time. You needed something to catch the water, so I hated going to the toilet on rainy days because sometimes the water would splash on my bottom.

There was a hill behind the house, and our family had two pieces of land where my grandmother grew the vegetables we always ate, fertilized with our own faeces. She used our rooftop for onions, celery or parsley. Our financial conditions got better during my high school. The family built a brick house with several rooms; it also came with a concrete floor and big white walls. The village still had dirt roads for quite a long time; it was fine during the sunny days, but when it rained, it was full of mud and water. After the sunset, the village would be all dark and quiet.

In recent years new roads were built in my hometown, and the time we went back home was reduced to only half an hour. Before that, there were only two bus services available, and I would go to my mother's shop for the summer holiday and what I took was the long-distance bus.

Every time I took the bus, my grandmother would take my luggage for me, and she would always fan me to make me cool. When the bus came, she would always repeat my destination to the driver; she would ask the driver to remind me at my stop. Naturally, I learned to take the four-hour bus ride alone as a primary school student.

On the way, I would wonder if the driver would forget to remind me; so I would look at the road every now and then, which was just for peace of mind, because I didn't know the path. It was the same when I came back from the summer holidays. My father had more confidence in me. He would wear a T-shirt every time he dropped me off to the bus stop (he didn't like to wear a top during summer) and saw me off without conversing too much with the driver.

I remembered my father would peek over at me. I would also sneak a look at him.

I didn't know when the solar streetlights were installed on the road, but all of a sudden the whole countryside was lit up at night, and all kinds of nightlife began to exist. There were people dancing; there were some stalls at night, and people went to town to eat at barbecue stalls. It was no longer the kind of darkness where you had nothing to do after sunset. The road was well-built, and my family bought an electromobile, so the two-kilometer distance between the village and the town was not long any more.

My aunt and my mother's big hobby back home was playing mahjong, and they would play till midnight.

My grandpa was a very stingy man and would never spend a penny on unnecessary things; my grandma was different. She was very economical; she would wear clothes until they were too shabby to put on. If she couldn't fix her own shoes which were actually very cheap, she would spend some money to go to the cobbler by the roadside to have them repaired. I never saw my grandfather cook at home because my grandmother was always the one who prepared the food for all of us. If the phone rang at home, twenty percent were for my grandmother and eighty percent were for my grandfather.

That might be the view of the old generation, I suppose.

In our family, it was my father who cooked most of the time and my mother was not as skilful as my father in terms of cooking.

When I was a primary school student, there used to be a fair every Monday, and my grandmother would take me shopping when she saw that I really wanted to buy new clothes, but my taste was really bad when I was a child. Every time I had my eyes on something, my grandmother would bargain with the seller, but these new clothes that I bought were not desirable when I tried them back at home. What a joke!

When we invited people we knew to dinner, we usually put two or three tables and would cook the food on a pot stove. Since my mother was not very good at cooking, she would often take care of the firewood instead.

The elders would sometimes hire women who often cooked for others to help us, and those who joined us for dinner would always help us pick vegetables and wash dishes; otherwise, it would be too much for us.

Then there came electric rice cookers and gas stoves, and it was much easier to cook rice, but we still liked what came out of the pot stoves. "Because it smells good!"

In winter, the coals from the wood burner would be chucked out and put in a small fire cage; and my grandpa would cover it with a layer of cloth and hold it in his hand when chatting with others outside, which seemed to be a good way to keep warm. some of the coals would be put into a washbasin to warm our cold feet, because feet always got damp or cold in winter.

Now that we have air conditioning, the life is not as hard as before, but the atmosphere is not as good as before. In the summer, my grandmother had two fans, one of which she used regularly and well, and the handle was dark and smooth because of the sweat from the palm of her hand. Inside the old house, although there was no air conditioner, it was quite cool with an electric fan.

My mother always went to the mall with my aunts to buy clothes. I would go to the mall with them at first, but then I thought that the clothes in the mall were of inferior quality. It was much cheaper to buy online, and more styles could be found online. My mother tried buying clothes online, but the quality was so bad that she gave up.

During Chinese New Year, we didn't use our mobile phones as much as we do now. We would get together and spend a lot of money on firecrackers and fireworks, and afterwards we would play the game, such as "What time is it, Mr Wolf", "Big King and Little King". The scene was so chaotic that firecracker burned a hole on our clothes before we knew it.

Nowadays, people don't care about new clothes anymore. Many children get together to play cards and games and drink. People give all kinds of things to each other as presents. Things like nappies and high-tech products are available.

I miss the Chinese New Year which was a little bit messy and chaotic. I pray before the gods for the health and well being of the family.

My last wish is as cheesy but real as the Chinese New Year; that is to wish myself the best of luck and success in my studies.

At certain moment, we are sure to miss the place where we were born and brought up, because we know that we will never go back to the same place that we keep in mind.

一个江南农家的人类学简史

李仲庆

从百年前的殷实富足的江南乡村大户人家，到社会巨变后的解体，第二代成了集体农户。

女孩的外婆从诗礼人家出嫁到一个泥草屋，成为大集体里饥一顿饱一顿的稻农。

到第三代的“舅舅”11岁的时候，改革开放开始了。家里重新拥有了自己的土地，再度开始财富之路。从开鱼塘、卖蔬果，完成了改革开放初期的积累：建起了三层楼房，开始碾米、磨豆腐。

舅舅的学艺创业颇多曲折，经营袜子厂失败后成为打工人。为了赡养老人和子女，舅舅又开始漂泊国外。

衢江边的小村庄开始了城市化，但家庭的支柱却去国离乡。

女大学生程书棋以千字文简约地记录了母亲一家四代人的生活变迁和命运遭际，是家庭历史融入家国时代变迁的微小而有益的记录。毕竟篇幅有限，我倒觉得这个家庭的小历史应该得更持久地书写，尤其是老一辈的命运。

私人史足以填补官方历史的缺憾，这当然也符合中国历史书写的传统。如果这个新闻班的学生深入一个村镇，能采写出一部大部头的村庄信史，价值远超过官方史志。

从人类学或者社会学的视角，这个家庭的简史也颇有可咀嚼之处。

中国的乡村传统是安土重迁，但到了全球化时代，家庭唯一的男性支柱“舅舅”成了国际打工人。

即便如此，其家庭纽带并未断裂，实际上去国外也是为了家庭。

家庭的小微化，将一代代缓慢消解中国传统家庭伦理。费孝通所说的“乡土性”也可能在大流动中逐步瓦解。以程书棋母亲一家几代人来看，他们从集聚土地财富到失去土地，再获得分配土地，在城市化中又失去部分土地，他们与泥土的联系逐渐消失。

凝结在土地上的家庭伦理也在变化。“土”是农民的命根，当命根不在，何处是家乡呢？

从现代性城市政治文明、特别是法治角度，以我的浅见，中国广袤的土地上依然是费孝通当年所谓的“熟人社会”，以家庭亲属为同心圆的圈子交际伦理，只不过在缓慢地变化中。

我们并不知道，祖辈的乡村诗礼人家蜗居一地，舅舅的去国打工，寻求财富，哪一个是更美好的生活方式。

从这篇家庭私人历史书写来看，亲缘、地缘、家庭同心圆依然坚固地存在，家庭的支柱一直是经济性的，也是生命延续性的。

先辈的大户府邸今安在？曾经的古玩字画都已烟消云散，空留嗟叹。

衢江边的小村，古往今来从不缺少离歌。

（吉林长春，前媒体人）

故事

衢州

程书棋（新闻学专业202专升本班）

老钱家的“支柱”

“哎，要是当时知道埋几件在土里，现在也算宝啦。”外婆和外公正用方言点评着《国家宝藏》的藏品，“那时候怎么会晓得呢……”恍惚间，时间似乎随着他们的一言一行回到过去的年代。

衢州市衢江区云溪乡西山村的吴氏府邸算是当地的大户人家，平时外高祖父有闲钱喜欢收藏些古玩字画、墨宝真迹。皇帝倒了，辫子剪了，新中国成立了，时代在改变，外高祖父也分到了自己的一份土地，家里收藏的古玩字画该扔的也都扔了，就此吴氏府邸的大门被封上了。

外婆是家中第三大的，到了谈婚论嫁的年纪，就按照父母之命、媒妁之言，和隔壁的外公结成了夫妻，在云溪乡的黄甲山村扎下了根。老钱夫妻两人住在男方准备的婚房里。房子是外公年轻的时候自己用石块和黄泥垒成的房子，房子里的东西也刚置办，一张床、两个木箱、一个衣柜。

外祖父母被安排在同一个生产队，生产队分配的工作量很多，他们每天只要听到鸡鸣就得起床,生产队的事情忙完,领到每天分配到的粮食回到家中已经是深夜。老钱家算是儿女双全,两个女儿和一个儿子,但是他们要面对的生活压力只有他们自己知道。他们经常是自己喝稀米粥,把米饭留给孩子们。孩子们也很懂事,外祖父母深夜晚归,灶台旁边就会放着小椅子,灶台里会有饭菜。这大概就应了一句老话:穷人的孩子早当家。老钱家经常会有断粮的时候,没有米没有菜,外祖父母就只能去小山上挖番薯、野菜,做地瓜粥、野菜汤,要是在路上可以看到能当柴生火的木头之类,外公总会说上一句:"今天运气不错",就丢下锄头,找旁边的枯草编成草绳把一堆堆树枝捆在一起,先扛回家,怕其他人把柴给抢走。

据外婆说,最苦的是刚生完舅舅赶上插秧的时候。她经常这么说:"现在这个腿一到下雨天就疼,就是那时候刚生完孩子,没有好好养着。"舅舅出生在 6 月底,正是早稻收割好、晚稻插秧的时候。插秧时节,前一天会有生产队的队长告知明日必须完成的农活。外公第二天会趁着太阳还没有升起,脱下鞋子放在田埂上,挽起袖子和裤脚,头上绑着毛巾,深一脚浅一脚地踩在泥浆里。等到天快亮的时候,外婆就身上背着舅舅,也到秧田里和外公一起拔秧。之后是插秧——把水稻秧苗从秧田移植到稻田里。连续插秧好几天,一块稻田已经插上了绿油油的秧苗,外祖父母每次回来都弓着腰用手敲着自己的背。

晚上气候转寒,一家老小就围在灶炉旁相互倚着睡觉。就靠外祖父母在田间起早贪黑地耕种维持一个家。

外祖父母把三个孩子拉扯长大了,最小的舅舅也 11 岁了。国家迎来了改革开放的年代,老钱家不仅分到了自己的土地,还承包村头的池塘开始养鱼。"他一点点地摸索,先选择鱼塘的经济鱼苗:鲤鱼、草鱼、白鲢、鲫鱼,然后向隔壁村会养鱼的田老头请教给鱼苗投喂什么。草鱼吃草,鲤鱼吃草鱼的排泄物,鲫鱼是杂食性的而且吃鲤鱼的排泄物,白鲢有清污作用。"

第一年收网捕鱼,村里来了很多人赶着凑热闹。外公早早地把池塘堵水口打开了,留下了一部分水,他请了村里青年人和他一起下水撒网,自四角和中间把网一拉,塘里的鱼就都抓好了。大鱼放在待卖的水箱里,小鱼重新放回池塘。大概过了两年,外公的腰包比之前鼓了,但是造新房的钱还是差了点,只能再等一两年。舅舅虽小却有经商头脑,给外祖父提议可以卖菜。妈妈和舅舅,他们姐弟俩,凌晨 4 点后踏着三轮车,骑到城里的农贸市场采购,然后满载而归把一车蔬菜水果带到黄甲山村的村头,村里的人就陆陆续续来买菜,妈妈扯开嗓子喊着:"卖菜啦……"大概一个上午菜都会卖完。妈妈洪亮的叫卖声和舅舅自学的车技成为附近村内最出名的卖菜组合,他们成为老钱家的又一个支柱。

老钱家的积蓄多了,有了造新房的实力。三个孩子帮外祖父母打下手,搬砖、煮饭、卖菜各司其职，三层楼的新房终于造好了，全家搬到了新家。三层新房面积大，老钱家又有新的点子，开了碾坊，负责把稻子在机器里去壳或者是把米磨成粉，还做卖豆腐的生意。

老钱家的三个孩子长大了，阿姨、妈妈的户口从村里迁了出去，只有舅舅的名字还在那本户口本上。舅舅喜欢捯饬东西，他外出闯荡到萧山卤味师傅那学手艺去了。他学会了做烤鸭却没学着师傅开个卤味店，而是去了瓷器厂里做透明的瓷盘。舅舅也有了自己的家庭，他得扛起整个老钱家。

舅舅算是有头脑的人，打算和他当学徒时认识的好友合作创业，做袜子出口生意。外行看不懂内行，袜子看着简单，只要招工人把缝合的手艺教会他们，打包出口就行。但是袜子生产的关键点并不是简单的缝合和袜子产品本身的质量问题，还需要考虑袜子染色的问题以及产生废水处理污染问题是否可以通过有关环保部门的审核，最终他这个外行人在首次创业中失败了。

舅舅选择进入一家企业成为打工人，每月有着稳定的收入来维持着老钱家的生活支出。舅舅想给表弟提供更好的学习环境和外祖父母更好的养老环境，他选择了漂泊国外工作。相比较而言，国外的薪资待遇会比待在国内的薪资要高，但是和妻儿、父母的见面机会也相对减少。

时代在不断发展，原来普通的黄甲山村因为村里的孟姜古塔带来的特殊文化，得了新的村名——孟姜村。孟姜塔周围的田地被征用，进行了合理的规划，老钱家恰巧有这么一块地被规划在内。现在的老钱家地少了一块，但是家周围的环境有了儒雅的文化气息。现在两位老人已经年过花甲，每月都会有社会养老金补贴生活。老钱家的经济支柱主要来自舅舅，精神支柱也是如此。

现在老钱家的成员不再是三兄妹，又有新成员的加入，孙子也都长大了。老钱家的支柱也在一代代更替传承……夜深了，外祖父母说："老钱家现在好！"

Quzhou
Cheng Shuqi (Class 202, Majoring in Journalism)

The "Pillars" of the Qians

"Well, if I knew they would become treasures, I would also bury some in the soil," my grandparents commented when watching the documentary *National Treasure*, "How could we possibly know this at that time?" As they spoke, time seemed to date back to the times of their age.

The father of my grandmother was the master of Wu family in Xishan Village, Yunxi Town, Qujiang District, Quzhou. It was a large local family. He enjoyed collecting antiques, calligraphy, paintings and ink treasures at leisure time. After the Qing Dynasty, the imperial system was abolished and people cut their braids. The founding of the People's Republic of China announced a brand-new era, and my great grandfather got a share of his land. All the antiques, calligraphy and paintings of his collection were thrown away, and the gate of the Wu's mansion were also sealed.

My grandmother was the third child in her family. When she was old enough for marriage, she followed her parents' instruction and married my grandfather, son of the Qians who lived next door. Since then, the new couple lived in the marriage room in Huangjia mountain village in Yunxi. The house was built with stones and yellow mud by grandfather, inside of which there was some new furniture, including a bed, two wooden cases and a wardrobe.

Later, they were assigned into the same production team. The production team allocated a lot of work. They had to get up early at dawn every single day. It was usually late at night when they got home with the food allocated. With two daughters and one son, they got much pressure in making a living. They often drank thin rice porridge and left the steamed rice to the children. The children were also very sensible. When they came home late at night, there would often be small chairs beside the stove and food in the stove. Just as an old saying goes, "Children of the poor always grow mature early." More often than not, the family ran out of food. Without any rice or vegetables, my grandparents had to dig sweet potatoes and wild vegetables on hills, so that they could make some sweet potato porridge and wild vegetable soup. If they could see wood for the stove on the road, they would always be thankful, "We're lucky today." Then he would leave his hoe, look for the withered grass to make straw ropes, pile the wood together, and carry it all home. He was afraid others might take the wood away if he hesitated.

According to my grandmother, my uncle happened to be born at a transplanting period, which made the hardest time of her life. As she often recalled, "My leg hurts on rainy days. I suppose it was because I didn't take enough rest after giving birth to him." My uncle was born at the end of June, when the early rice was harvested and the late rice was to be transplanted. During the transplanting season, the leader of the production team would urge everyone to finish their work next day. Next morning before the sunrise, he'd take off his shoes and put them on the ridge of the field, roll up his sleeves and trouser legs, tie a towel on his head and step on the mud. When it was almost dawn, grandma would join him to pull the seedlings with my uncle on her back. Then they had to transplant rice seedlings from the seeding beds to the fields. Within a couple of days, a rice field would be filled with green seedlings. Every time my grandparents came back, they needed to bow and knock on their back with their hands.

At night when the weather got colder, the whole family always slept around the stove. It was my grandparents' hard work in the field that supported the whole family.

As time went by, my grandparents brought up all the three children. When the youngest kid was 11 years old, China ushered in the era of reform and opening-up. They not only got land of their own, but also contracted the pond at the entrance of the village and began to raise fish. "He learnt by himself step by step. First, he chose the economic species, such as carps, grass carps, silver carps and crucian carps. He also asked Mr. Tian who knew how to raise fish for advice. Grass carps eat grass; carps eat grass carp excreta; crucian carps are omnivorous and eat carp excreta, and silver carps can clean the pond up."

In the first year, many people came to witness the fish harvest.

Grandfather opened the water outlet of the pond early, leaving some water inside. He invited the young people in the village to cast the net. Once the net was pulled at the four corners and in the middle, all the fish in the pond were caught. He put big fish in a water tank for sale, and the small ones back into the pond. About two years later, my grandfather earned a lot of money from his pond, but it was not enough for a new house. So he had to wait for another year or two. Although my uncle was little, he was smart in business and suggested to sell vegetables. His suggestion was adopted. Since then, my mom and uncle started to purchase product in the market downtown by tricycle as early as 4:00 a. m. , and returned with a full load of vegetables and fruits. People in the village came to buy vegetables one after another. Mom promoted, "Vegetables! Fresh vegetables!" The fruits and vegetables would usually sell out in the morning. Mom's loud promotion and uncle's driving skills had made them the most famous vegetable-selling group in the nearby village, and they have become another pillar of the Qians.

As they had more savings, they could afford building a new house. The three kids help to move bricks, cook and sell vegetables respectively. Finally, a three-story new house was well-constructed, and the whole family moved into it. The new house was so big that the whole family sparkled another new idea of opening a mill, which shells rice in machines and grinds rice into powder. They also sold tofu.

The three children gradually grew up. Only uncle's name remained in the household registration booklet. Both my mom and my aunt moved out of the village. My uncle likes to learn a skill. Later, he learnt his craft in Xiaoshan to make sauced meat, but then he didn't open a shop after knowing how to make roast duck. Instead, he went to a porcelain factory to make transparent porcelain plates. Soon after, he had a family of his own and needed to support the family on his own.

My uncle is a wise man. He planned to start a sock export business with his apprentice friends. However, the layman couldn't understand what exactly was going on. Making socks looked simple, which might only need workers to sew and pack them for export. But the key point of sock production was not simply stitching and the quality. A businessman also has to consider dyeing and wastewater treatment as required by relevant environmental protection departments. In the end, my uncle, the layman failed in his first venture in the foreign trade industry.

Then, he entered an enterprise as an employer. With a stable monthly income, he could support the living expenses of his family. In order to provide a better learning environment for his son and a better living environment for my grandparents, he then went abroad to seek a fortune. The salary abroad was indeed higher than that at home, but the opportunities to meet with his wife, children and parents were also relatively reduced.

With rapid development, the ordinary village has been given a new name-Mengjiang village, because of the culture by the ancient pagoda of Mengjiang. The land around Mengjiang tower was expropriated and reasonably planned out. The Qians' land happened to be included into such a piece of land. Now, they don't have the piece of land any more, but the environment around is full of refined culture. My grandparents over 60 years old can enjoy a social pension from the government to subsidize their lives every month. My uncle has become both the economic and spiritual pillar of the whole family.

Now, the Qians is no longer limited to the family of three brothers and sisters. It becomes a larger family as their grandchildren all grow up. The pillars of the Qians have been passed on from generation to generation. Late at night, my grandparents said, "How wonderful our life is now!"

“岛”的隐喻

刘建民

“岛”是一个地理概念，指四面环水并在涨潮时高于水面的自然形成的陆地区域，且能维持人类居住或本身的经济生活。中国面积在500平方米以上的岛屿有7372个，其中有人居住的岛屿为450个，《离岛、归岛》作者的家，舟山嵊泗县一座名叫黄龙岛的小岛就是其中的一个，在占了中国岛屿总数的60%的东海之上。

说实话，看到作者的父亲出海、母亲上山挑石下海担沙，我都忍不住为这个东海石村的历史流下心酸的眼泪。当然，当我看到这个母亲为了孩子的学习离岛打拼，再因为海岛旅游又回到岛上开起饭店的结局，又抑制不住地兴奋。这个故事，这个“岛”也为我们带来一些隐喻。

原岛的"认知隐喻"里，孤独的石村或许藏着一个精神的“石化”过程，岛民不安的梦，被海洋禁闭的身体，渐渐变成石头“牢房”的一部分才是曾经的现实；离岛的“行为隐喻”可以理解为对困境的反抗有很多种路径，子女教育的逼迫使大部分岛民选择离乡为天然已任，愿意依赖群体化获得安全感；而加强海岛生态保护，推进生态岛礁、和美海岛建设背景下返岛的“治理机制隐喻”，也给我们的思考留下一些切口。

故事的重新讲述过程也是一种隐喻。鲁迅认为文化本身就是铁屋子，打破黑暗的力量来自于人的觉醒。“岛”的隐喻最终要在海洋文明的潜流中寻求新生。

千百年来似镶嵌在东海洋面上的一颗颗珍珠，孕天地之精气，怀万物之萃华，山岛绰约，港湾绵延，成为多元文化的交汇点。或许未来隅居一岛，却浴风耕海，吐故纳新，将敢立潮头、海纳百川的海洋精神诠释得奇妙无比，那将是一个更光明的隐喻。

（浙大宁波理工学院传媒与法学院，高级编辑）

故事

舟山

王永明(新闻学专业202专班)

离岛,归岛

“我当时和你爸结婚的时候,两个人口袋空空,跟你奶奶借了五六万元在村子的一条小路边盖了一套俩人的新房子。”妈妈在我小时候,常常给我讲她过去生活的故事。过去的生活很艰难,她说:“1996年,我和你爸结婚,你奶奶就给我们几只新碗、5斤米、5斤油,外加一只新锅,我们的新生活就开始了。”

我家的生活环境有点特别,居住在舟山嵊泗县一座名叫黄龙岛的小岛上。岛上的房子大多都是用石头堆砌起来,那时候只有有钱人家才会选用水泥盖房子,我们的岛也因此被称作“东海石村”。

我家岛上的房子坐落在小路旁,是石头和水泥的混合品,两层楼高,简陋的屋子后边还有自家小小的一块田。据我妈回忆,当初盖这套房子可是个大工程。上世纪90年代的时候,岛上物资短缺,交通也十分不方便,没有过多的物资可以及时输送过来,盖房子的材料全部来自从山上去打的一块块石头。我爸是个渔民,不能时时刻刻都呆在家里,他出海捕鱼的时候,就由妈妈来负责。为了节约人力成本,妈妈每天都一个人背着一条扁担、两只箩筐上山去捡小石子。有时候水泥不够用,自己一个人还得去沙滩挑一袋重重的沙子。冬日里的海风刺骨,一个身高只有一米五几的女人每天都得上山下山,去挑一筐又一筐的小石子,原本白皙的脸庞上慢慢长出了淡淡的皱纹。为了省钱,妈妈舍不得给自己买昂贵的护肤品。

“半个月后,你爸爸出海回来,看到地基上堆满了一堆盖房子要用的材料,一下子震惊了,迟迟没有说话。后来,你爸为了心疼我,雇了四五个工人。”妈妈说完这段话的时候,眼里闪着泪光。从那以后,爸爸只要一出海回来,就全程接管。他和工人们一起上山去打石头、挑石头,一路抬到盖房子的地方,难得停歇。在爸妈和四五个工人们的共同努力下,石屋房渐渐有了雏形。从1995年2月至10月,历时9个月,岛上的房子诞生了,这也是属于我们的第一个家,石屋房凝聚了爸妈的汗水和深厚的感情。

1998年夏天,我出生了。妈妈说生我的时候,拿着外婆给的嫁妆勉强凑够了生产的费用。90年代的小岛还很落后，再加上爸妈都不是知识分子，想找一份工作非常困难。为了生计，爸爸出海捕鱼，妈妈在岛上找了份织网的活。她常常会跟我说："那时候你才1岁，你爸出海的时候，我就出去织网。白天要照顾你，晚上等你睡着的时候才能动工，有时候熬到12点，有时候凌晨一两点，每天都要挤出一点时间来去赚外快。织网的活跟别的活不一样，一针不来，一针不去，只要一针织不上，网的长度就上不去。那段时间每天都是这样熬过来的，肩椎炎就这样落下了。"

爸妈平时都非常节俭，为了挣钱，牺牲了很多业余时间，石屋房里的每一天都在为了生计忙忙碌碌。

步入21世纪，爸爸渔船的生意越来越好，挣的钱也开始慢慢多起来，之前盖房子背的债基本都还清了。我5岁的时候，家里开始有了积蓄，日子也慢慢好起来。

2005年，我开始上小学一年级。第二年，妈妈为了我能受到更好的教育，决定把我送到菜园镇上的小学去念书。从小岛到镇上要坐渡船，不能随时回家，这也意味着我妈和我要过上租房的日子了。

初到镇上上学的第一年，是2006年的冬天。租房对我们娘俩来说，是一件陌生的事情。通过别人的介绍，我们租了一间七八平方米的房子，母子俩的吃喝拉撒全在一个房间里面解决，连呼吸都是一种奢侈。在这间窄小的出租屋里生活了大概半年，实在受不了这密闭的环境，我们决定搬家。第二次租的房子是在学校的对面，从家里到教室上课只要5分钟。这次租的房子就大了许多，吃饭和睡觉的地方能够单独分隔出来了。

镇上的日子暂时稳定下来，妈妈也想着为这个家贡献出一点自己的力量，开始去市面上寻找各种招聘信息，通过每天的留心观察，最后在服装店找到了一份导购的工作。我白天出去上学，妈妈出去工作，远在汪洋大海上的爸爸在奋力捕鱼，一家三口都在为将来能够住上更好的房子努力着。

2008年，我上小学四年级，为了我能够拥有一个更好的学习环境，我家搬到了一个高档商品房里，这是我们在镇上的第三次搬家。100多平方米的毛坯房里住了我家和另外一户人家，这也是我们第一次体验合租生活。

日子还是和往常一样忙忙碌碌，爸妈为了更好的生活品质，没有停下奋斗的脚步。

2010年年初，妈妈有了在镇上买房的想法。为了看房，她跑遍了镇上的所有中介，一家一家地问，一个房子一个房子地看。最后，等到一家新的楼盘开张，妈妈顺利地摇到了新房子的号码。

2010年5月的某一天，爸妈在购房合同上签下了名字，交了首付，那一瞬间，一家人漂泊的心好像有了归宿。

“想想那段日子，真是辛酸，老妈我每天都不敢给自己多花一分钱，更别说一件好看的衣服了，1 块 10 块地节省下来。”这是妈妈多年后回忆起那段日子的感慨。交完首付后，妈妈开始打双份工，早上和晚上在眼镜店上班，下午去机关单位打扫卫生。有时候帮我做好饭，自己就在包里塞两个馒头，连吃口饭的时间都没有，骑着辆破破的蓝色自行车，前往下一个工作地。这种日子维持了一年多，这一年多里，妈妈整整瘦了 10 斤，她的肩椎炎也复发了。

买房后，爸爸挣钱更加卖力了。暑假禁渔期，他都会去外面继续接活干，赚点外快，有时候晚上十一二点才回家。那段时间爸妈都很累，为了房子，为了一个温暖的家，拼尽了全力。

2011 年 5 月，我们家终于结束了租房的日子，拎着大包小包，搬进了刚装修好的商品房。新房子的环境很好，有保安管理，绿化优美。住惯了简朴的出租房，一下子住进这 80 多平方米大装修过的房子里，好像眼前的这一切那么远，又那么近。

这段镇上的租房漂泊生活就此画上了圆满的句号，我们一家也开始过上了稳定的生活。

2017 年，岛上的旅游业不断发展。我们家迎来了一个赚钱的好机会——办渔家乐。爸妈重新装修了岛上的石屋房，开了一家名叫“龙泉湾”的饭店，寓意着生意能像蛟龙一样，慢慢起色。我妈说：“生活真奇妙啊，想不到有一天，以前不怎么值钱的老房子，现在也有它的价值了。”饭店的生意一直都不错，妈妈也有了稳定的收入，我们家的生活离小康又进了一步。

Zhoushan
Wang Yongming (Class 202, Majoring in Journalism)

Leave and Return to the Island

“Penniless when we got married, your dad and I built up a new house by a path in the village with nearly sixty thousand yuan we borrowed from your paternal grandma.” My mom often told me about the past when I was a kid. Life was hard then. She recalled, “Several new bowls, 2.5kg rice, 2.5kg oil and a new pot were all we got from your paternal grandma when we got married back in 1996. That was how our marriage life began."

My family live on a small island called Huanglong in Shengsi County, Zhoushan—a very special living environment. Years ago, most houses on the island were built of stones and only rich islanders would use cement. The island was thus known as the "Stone Village on the East China Sea".

My home, a humble two-story house made of stones and cement and with a small backyard for farming, was located by the roadside. It was by no means an easy task to build it, according to my mom. Back in the 1990s, every stone used for house building needed to be cut from mountains because of scarce materials and the poor transportation infrastructure on the island. My father was a fisherman, and whenever he was out fishing, it was up to my mom to cut stones. To save labor costs, my mom would collect small stones on mountains and put them into two bamboo baskets hung on a shoulder pole. She even had to carry sacks of sand from the beach when cement couldn't meet the construction needs. My mom, less than five feet tall, had to carry baskets of stones up and down mountains while braving the biting wind in winter. Consequently, her previously fair skin began to wrinkle, but she still begrudged spending money on expensive skin care products.

"Your father, coming back half a month later, was too shocked to say anything when he saw stacks of building materials piled up on the house base. He then hired several workers to spare me all the harsh work," said my mom, with tears in her eyes. Ever since, my father would take over the whole thing once he returned from fishing. He and workers would cut stones on mountains and carry them back home without any rest. The stone house gradually took shape with the joint efforts of my parents and several workers, and was finally built up after nine months hard work from February to October of 1995. The house, our first home, embodied my parent's perspiration and affection.

I was born in the summer of 1998. My mom said when she gave birth to me, she barely managed to pay for the birth with the dowry my grandmother had given her. Back in the 1990s, it was by no means easy to find a job on this backward island, and even harder for my parents who received little education. In order to make ends meet, my father went fishing and my mother found a net weaving job. "I wove nets when your father was out fishing. You were only one year old. Since I needed to take care of you by day, I could start weaving only when you were asleep at night. Sometimes I stayed up until midnight or even later just to make some extra money. This job was quite different for even a missing stitch would ruin a whole fishing net. My shoulder spondylitis is exactly the result of that harsh period of time."

My thrifty parents, busy making a living, had sacrificed much leisure time in order to earn more money.

Ever since 2000, my father had seen an increase in his salaries as the fishing business was getting better, and my parents were almost clear of their debts from house building. When I was five years old, my parents even had some money to spare. Life finally became better.

I went to elementary school in 2005. The second year, my mom decided to send me to another one in Caiyuan Town so that I could receive better education. That meant I was no longer able to return home as frequently since I had to take a ferry to get to the town. As a result, my mom and I had to rent a house near the new school.

The winter of 2006 witnessed the start of my new life in the town. My mom and I knew nothing about how to rent a house. Through a referral, we rented a room of seven or eight square meters, where my mom and I ate, drank and defecated all in one room, and even breathing was like a luxury. Such a life continued for around half a year. Unable to bear such confined space, we decided to move to another house opposite the school. Only five minutes' walk from the school, our new dwelling was big enough to have a dining room and bedrooms.

After we settled down, my mom, determined to make her due contribution to our family, started searching for a job. She eventually found one as a shop assistant in a clothing store. Ever since, my family had been striving to move to a better house: I studied diligently in the school, my mother worked industriously in the store, and my father buried himself in fishing at sea.

We moved to another deluxe residential house after my mom decided to give me a better learning environment when I was in the fourth grade back in 2008. That had been our third move ever since we arrived in the town. My family shared an undecorated house covering an area of 100 square meters with another family. This was our first flat-sharing experience.

My parents, busy as usual, never stopped their steps towards a better life.

My mom, planning to buy a house in the town, frequented housing agencies and saw a lot of houses from early 2010. Eventually my mom won the house lottery for a house newly circulated in the market.

My parents signed the house purchase contract and paid the down payment one day in May, 2010. That moment we felt we finally settled down, just like a ship which eventually lay at anchor after years of wandering.

"It's so bitter when you think about those days. I didn't even dare to spend a penny on myself every day, let alone a nice dress. I saved every penny I could." This was the sentiment of my mom when she recalled those days years later. She, having paid the down payment, started undertaking two gig jobs, working at the optician's every morning and evening while as a cleaner in a government agency every afternoon. Sometimes after having prepared my meal, she would stuff two buns in her bag, not even having the time to sit down and eat, and ride a battered blue bike to her next place of work. Life like this continued for an entire year, during which time she lost five kilograms and relapsed into her shoulder spondylitis.

My father worked even harder after buying the new house, doing part-time jobs every summer when fishing was prohibited. Sometimes he didn't even get back until midnight. My parents, both exhausted at that time, went all out for the new house and a warm home.

In May, 2011, we finally moved out of the rented apartment and moved into the newly decorated house with all of our belongings. The new house enjoyed a good enviroment. There were security staff and greenery. Having been used to the simplicity of a rented house, suddenly living in this large renovated house of more than 80 square meters seemed like a dream far away and yet so close.

Years of wandering finally came to an end, and a new tranquil and stable life began.

In 2017, the island tourism industry was booming, giving our family an excellent opportunity to make money. My parents turned our stone house on the island into a restaurant called Longquanwan, which symbolized flourishing business. My mom said, "Life is full of magic. Who would have known that a worthless old house could one day show its value." The business has been quite good, and my mom now has a stable income. We are one step closer to a moderately prosperous life.

细心、细致、细腻、细微之处见时代

孟志强

勤劳智慧的爷爷，百折不挠的爸爸，两代人共筑起了这个美好的家，这就是钟周宏阳《两代人垒筑一个家》给我们讲述的家的故事和这个时代的变迁。

作者用生动的语言给我们展现了一幅爷孙对话的有趣场面。现在的爷爷衣食无忧，逍遥自在，但一谈起过去，却是充满了痛苦和艰辛以及深深的感叹——十几亩地要去耕作，要换着法子种更多的作物，都是为了两个嗷嗷待哺的孩子。没有时间照顾孩子，只能把他放在木桶里；没有保暖的衣物，孩子冻得嗷嗷在哭。我们仿佛回到了那个辛酸的年代。但是爷爷是智慧的，多出的粮食和作物拿到集市上去卖或者置换，卖不了，就给人家当力工拉货，他用尽了自己所有的力气和有限的资源，抓住每一个可以利用的机会，为这个家积攒着每一分钱，度过了那个缺衣少粮的年代。

爸爸没有读书，但也没有去务农，赶上了商品经济的时代，凑钱买车搞运输，一车一车挣着自己的辛苦钱。市场需求旺盛的时候，挣了一笔好钱。因为没有知识和文化，看不清未来市场的变化，二次投资遭受了惨重的失败，负债累累，压得自己喘不过气来。虽然从车老板变成了打工者，但是爸爸并没有就此沉沦，而是咬紧牙关拼命还债，漆黑的夜晚，吃泡面，喝开水，风吹日晒，体力透支，为了这个家，为了还清债，爸爸苦苦熬了十几年。

而如今，一家三代，不愁吃不愁穿，家庭经营了民宿，爷爷安度晚年，爸爸不用再操劳，而他们的孩子也就是作者也上了大学。作者没有刻意地去把时代的变迁和家庭的变化连在一起，用生硬的描述和严谨的逻辑去说明，而是用细心的观察、细致的情节、细腻的手法，讲述了一个两代人共同筑起一个美好家庭的平凡故事，但是我们读完之后能够感受到一个道理，即便是每个家庭成员都非常勤奋努力，但如果我们处在一个不好的时代，也不会有一个美好的生活。

人是时代的产物，家庭也如此。爷爷处在一个计划经济的年代，即便自己勤劳智慧也只能勉强养家糊口；爸爸处在一个商品经济的年代，即便自己百折不挠也不能保证在市场浪潮中不翻船。作者的家庭之所以有美好的今天，得益于社会主义新农村的建设，得益于人民物质生活水平得到提高、乡村旅游业得到发展。放下锄头去开车，放下车辆做民宿，不仅仅是一个家庭的生态变化，也是这个时代给这个家庭带来的命运的改变。

在城乡二元结构尚未完全破除之前，流动依然是当代中国人的常态。

（北京时代兴邦咨询公司董事长）

故事

丽水

钟周宏阳（新闻学专业 192 班）

两代人垒筑一个家

我的家在松阳县象溪镇雅溪口村。

“唉……”一声长叹，刚吃完饭的爷爷径直坐在古朴精致的实木椅上，随手拿起一根香烟，缓缓地抽了起来，眼盯窗外，思绪不知飞往何处。我问爷爷：“在想什么呢？这么入神。”爷爷张了张嘴，又停了停，说了句：“现在的生活真是过去比不上的，好太多太多。”“好在现在的生活，不愁吃喝穿，不愁屋漏雨”，不知何时坐在爷爷身旁喝着茶的奶奶说道：“这一切却是用双手和一把锄头干出来的。但以前的日子可真是苦啊，苦到……”

“我跟你爷爷便扛着锄头早出晚归，也只会扛锄头，想着每天尽量多做点，多做点”，奶奶平静地说着，“田里的事都已经让我们头疼，家里还有两个要照顾，咋办？”

“你爸那时还小得很，你姑也没法带他，所以直接把他放进木桶当中，一起担着放到田间，陪着我们一起干。寒冷冬天也不例外，现在的冬天比以前暖和多了，你爸爸在桶里穿着薄破的棉衣冻得哇哇直哭”，爷爷直直地看着我讲。

日子就这样没日没夜熬过去了好些年，虽比以前好了不少，但也还是经常吃不到米饭啊，穿不了好棉衣啊。“爷爷，我也吃过玉米糊，还不错唉”，我有些窃喜地说道。爷爷却突然大声叫唤着：“玉米糊啊，这东西，难吃得紧，全家也就你把它当宝，一听，就没过过苦日子。要是你从小吃到大，还会觉得好吃？”

实行家庭联产承包责任制那个时候，我们家就包了有十几亩田。

“真的？十几亩田，只有两个可用劳动力，都种稻谷吗？这怎么种得出头啊？也没什么利润。”我瞪大眼睛，挤着眉头问道。“傻瓜，怎么可能，十几亩田肯定不会只种水稻，种了很多很多其他的，比如玉米、大豆、黄豆、辣椒、豇豆、板栗、梨树、蚕豆……都种过”，奶奶说，“还得垦荒，撒种，施肥，翻土，浇水，除草。”

每家每户基本上都是这么种，忙得自己都顾不过来，哪里还有空理别人。不过自己干不过来，也得干；白天干不完，晚上接着干；风霜雨露，也得撑着。因为种得越多，收得越多，剩余的越多，留给自己就越多，自己家的生活水平也慢慢提高了。产量大，吃不完怎么办？那自是出售，所以我和你爷爷也就做起拉手推车的买卖，赚起了另一份收入。

在没有农活时或是有人需要时抑或是整收粮食谷物之后，我们便会推着木制的两轮间夹着木板的手推车，噶嘎噶嘎，在铺满碎石的路上走上十二三里地，到板桥去卖货、送货。要么是将自己剩余的谷物出售给其他人，赚粮食钱；要么就是给那里的人带些柴米油盐，赚些差价；要么就是帮别人运些货物，赚些路费。

就这样，慢慢攒着，积存的钱越来越多，家里缺胳膊少腿的家具被新木具取代，生活处境越来越好。心想：人还得靠自己一步一步做出来。

都说男儿志在四方，不展风云志，空负八尺躯。爸爸又何尝不是？但爸爸不喜学习，便去学了开车这技术，开启了车闯的征程。所以在2000年，我两岁的时候，爸爸将自己的积蓄拿了出来，向爷爷、奶奶、姑姑以及其他亲戚朋友借钱，终于凑够了买运输车的钱。

为了能更好地接活，爸爸还特意搬家到县城姑姑家租住。一开始，爸爸既是老板也是员工，开着这辆载着水泥、煤料、统料的运输车在各个地方不断地来回穿梭，赚着辛苦运费。这段时间，货物量大，市场需求高，运输人员少，便赚了不少钱。爸爸说：“照这个情形下去，自己都觉得自己快要发达了，所以爸爸就将盈利的钱买了第二辆运输车。那会儿就连平常关系不好的亲戚朋友都频频串门。”

天有不测风云，人有悲欢离合。好景不长，由于爸爸的学历不高，不懂如何经营；学识少使得格局眼界不够，捕捉不了市场的瞬息万变；再加上发生了安全事故，赔偿费用庞大，爸爸的第二辆车经营便开始由盈转亏，但父亲并没有就这样放弃，即使每天吃着泡面，穿着破衣，住在车上，也捉襟见肘地经营着。但最后的最后，第一辆车也被牵连，爸爸欠债累累。

欠债也没钱继续租住，便身无分文，爸爸灰溜溜搬回了原家。我还就记得当时我问了爸爸一句：“爸爸，这是哪？我们来这干嘛？”记得爸爸闭着眼，抿抿嘴，回答道：“乖，我们以后就住这里了。”

这一句话似乎用尽了父亲全身的力气，爸爸也明白这条路算是走到头了。路是走到头，债却没还完，压得万斤重，喘不过气来。

2006 年，爸爸便将两辆运输车都抵押给了县城长运公司，但仍是还不了债，也没人肯借钱给我们。

俗话说，“置之死地而后生”。没有一个人一生是一帆风顺，总有跌倒的时候，命运把人抛入低谷，却是给人转折的最好机会。在后有债主追债，在前有孩子嗷嗷待哺，在上有诚信家规压着。在这种境遇下，爸爸没有也不能绝望，他必须往前走。

爸爸重新找了一份开运输车的活计，帮他人打工，他比那里的人都要努力、踏实。自那时起，爸爸便开始了没日没夜的工作，家也慢慢步入正轨。有一次我和爸爸一起，那是一个漆黑的夜晚，随着车子时不时的摇晃，我的眼皮也在不停地一睁一合。我看向爸爸，爸爸的眼睛却一直瞪着，高度集中注意力，等我睡一觉醒来发现爸爸还在开着车，眼睛一下就酸了。饭点也只是吃一碗泡面，喝一杯水，原来爸爸就是这样在外工作还债，养活全家的。

慢慢地，十几年过去了，爸爸不分昼夜地开长途运输车也已经十几年了，爸爸终于将债务全部还清，供得起全家人生活的基本要求和发展要求，也有了自己的存款，吃得好，穿得好，用得好，一家人也过上了好日子。但爸爸的身体早已受不住早年高强度的工作量。

2013 年，我上初一时，爸爸买了第一辆四轮汽车，我们再也不用怕在雨天被淋湿，在雪天被风冻，在炎日下被晒伤。

2019 年下半年，我的家进行大修缮，建改民宿，烟囱被油烟机替代，电风扇被空调代替，竹床被四柱床替代，白炽灯被古朴吊灯替代，天然气浴室供水被太阳能热水器代替……整个家焕然一新。

Lishui
Zhong Zhouhongyang (Class 192, Majoring in Journalism)

A Home Built with Two Generations' Efforts

I live in Xikou Village, Xiangxi Town, Songyang County.

"Alas..." With a long sigh, my grandfather who had just finished his meal sat down on a plain and delicate wood chair. He picked up a cigarette casually and began to smoke slowly. Staring out of the window, he sank into deep thoughts. "What are you thinking about? You are so enthralled by it that you have been lost in thought," I asked him. My grandfather opened his mouth, paused for a while, then said: "Today's life is incomparable and much better than life in the past." "Fortunately, nowadays we needn't worry about eating and drinking, clothing and housing". My grandmother sat beside my grandfather quietly, drinking tea and said, "all these were accomplished with hands and a hoe, and the life in the past was really, really hard."

"Your grandpa and I went out early and came back late with hoes. That was all what we could do, so we tried our best to do more every day," my grandma said peacefully. "Everything in the farmland was worrisome, and we had two children to take care of at home. What could we do?"

"Your father was very young at that time, and your aunt could not take care of him, so we had no option but to put him into a bucket and took him along to the field with us. There was no exception even in cold winter. The winter in the past was much colder than the winter nowadays, so your father, wearing thin cotton clothes in the bucket, cried loudly because of coldness," my grandpa looked straight at me and said.

We endured those days and nights for many years. Although it got much better than before, rice and warm cotton clothes were hard to get. "Grandpa, I have tried corn paste once, and I didn't think it tasted bad," I said with a chuckle. Grandpa suddenly lifted his voice and said loudly, "the corn paste tastes bad. You are the only one in our family who considers it honey, and it is certainly because you haven't gone through those hard times. If you grew up eating it, would it still be tasty to you?"

When the household contract responsibility system was implemented, our family contracted more than ten mus of land (Mu is a Chinese unit of area).

"Really? More than ten mu of land with only two labores force? Rice was the only thing you grew? How could this work? Is there any profit?" I asked, staring and frowning. "Oh, you fool. How was it possible that we only grew rice on that ten mu of land. Many other plants were grown there as well, such as corns, soybeans, chilis, cowpeas, chestnuts, pears, broad beans and so on," said my grandma, "and we had to cultivate the land, sow, fertilize, turn over the soil, water and weed."

Almost every family did it in this way, and they were too busy to take time to take notice of others. Even if there was too much to be done on your own, you still had to finish it. If the work couldn't be finished in the daytime, then we had to continue working in the evening. No matter it was windy or rainy, we had to hold on finishing it. It's because the more you planted, the more you would harvest, and the more you had left over, the more you could keep for yourself, so the living standard of the family improved gradually. What if the output of production was too much to be consumed? Of course it could be sold, so your grandpa and I got another source of income by selling food with carts.

When there was no farm work, or when there was a need, or when there was a harvest of grain, we would trundle the wooden cart which had wooden boards between two wheels, walked twelve or thirteen miles on the gravel road to Banqiao street so as to sell and deliver goods. We earned money by selling the surplus grain to other people, or by bringing some daily necessities to people there so as to benefit from the price difference, or by helping others to deliver some goods so as to demand some traveling expenses.

In this way, more and more money was accumulated gradually. The broken furniture in our home was replaced by new wooden ones and the living situation became better and better, so I thought people could only achieve their goals by themselves step by step.

It was said that men should have great ambitions, and it was wasteful for them to have a strong body if their ambitions didn't realize. My father was exactly a man like this, but he didn't like learning, so he chose to learn how to drive, and started his journey with cars. In 2000, when I was two years old, my father took out his own savings, and borrowed some money from my grandparents, my aunt, other relatives and his friends. Finally he scraped together enough money to buy a truck.

In order to get work more easily, my father deliberately moved to my aunt's home in the county. At the beginning, my father was the boss and employee, driving this truck carrying cement, coal and material to and fro in various places so as to earn transportation fees laboriously. This was a period that there was a large quantity of goods, and market demand was great but lacked staff of transportation. Hence, he earned a lot of money. My father said, "If things kept going on like that, I myself felt that I would come rich soon. Therefore I bought a second truck with the money I had earned. Distant relatives and friends who used to be unfriendly came to pay visits frequently."

There are ups and downs in life, and everyone has joys and sorrows. Good luck didn't last for a long time. Because of little education, he didn't know how to run the business. The lack of knowledge narrowed his horizon and made it difficult to capture the rapid changes of the market. In addition, a safety accident occurred, and the compensation was huge. My father came to lose money instead of earning money from his second car. However, my father did not give up. Even though he ate instant noodles, wore ragged clothes and lived in the car every day, even though he ran out of his money, he kept the business running. But in the end, his first car went into the same situation, and he was heavily in debt.

Without the money to continue renting a house, my father was penniless and moved back to the previous home frustratingly. I still remembered at that time I asked my father: "Dad, where is this? What are we doing here?" I remembered my father closed his eyes, twisted his lips and answered: "My good daughter, we will live here from now on."

These words seemed to use all his strength, and he knew that the road was coming to an end. The road might come to the end, but the debt had not been paid off. The debt was so heavy that my father was under great pressure.

In 2006, my father mortgaged both trucks to a long-distance transportation company in the county. However, the debt still couldn't be repaid completely, and no one would like to lend us any money.

As an old saying goes, "Only when people face death can they learn how to survive." No one's life is completely smooth and there are times that people may fall down. The fate throws people into the valley of life, but it also gives them the best chance to make a change. My father not only had to face the creditors who kept asking him to pay the debt, but also had the child to be fed; besides, he bore in mind that the family rule of integrity should never be violated. Under such circumstances, my father didn't and shouldn't despair. He had to move on.

My father found a job to make a living by driving a truck again. He worked for others, and he worked much harder and more down-to-earth than other people there. Since then, my father began to work day and night, and the family was slowly back on the right track. Once I was with my dad on a dark night, and my eyelids kept opening and closing as the car swayed. When I looked at my father, he focused on looking ahead. Tears came to my eyes when I woke up and found that my father was still driving the car. What he had for meals was only a bowl of instant noodles and a glass of water. That was how my father worked to pay off the debts and to support our family.

More than a decade had passed. It had been more than ten years since my father drove long distance day and night. He paid off all the debt at last, and was able to cover household expenses. Also, money could be saved and was enough for us to eat, wear and live well. The whole family lived a good life as well, but my father was unable to bear the heavy workload of his early years.

In 2013, when I was a junior student in the middle school, my father bought the first four-wheel car. We were no longer afraid of getting wet on rainy days, feeling cold by wind on snowy days or getting sunburned on hot days.

In the second half of 2019, my house was renovated into a homestay. The chimney was replaced by a kitchen hood; the electric fan was replaced by an air conditioner; the bamboo bed was replaced by a four-post bed; the incandescent was replaced by ceiling lamp which was of primitive simplicity; hot water supply by the natural gas in the bathroom was replaced by a solar water heater. The whole house was brand new.

039

观察

一栋房子，一种乡愁

刘云珠

对于大多数中国人而言，房子不仅是每个人的栖身之所，也是终其一生安放心灵的港湾。不同的房子里窖藏着不同的故事，岁月有心，悄悄地将它们装成坛、酿成酒，让它成为只属于我们自己的乡愁。

《漏雨的日子不再来》的作者是一位年轻的大学生，她向我们讲述了家中三栋房子的故事。

解放前，爷爷靠打零工挣来的血汗钱买下一栋漏雨的木头房子。虽然日子过得清苦，可是一家人得以繁衍生息。20 世纪 80 年代，通过移民安置，他们家盖起了灰色的水泥房。这是作者出生的地方，也是盛满了她儿时美好记忆的百草园。第三栋房子是爸爸妈妈创业成功后，在老宅院内新建的一栋贴着黄色瓷砖的漂亮房子。只不过，此时作者已外出求学，不在家中常住了。

这篇文章之所以触动我，是因为我在年轻时也经历过苦日子，也住过漏雨的房子。每到雨天，母亲一边在屋里用盆接水，一边喊我上房窜瓦。可那几片瓦无论怎么摆弄，总是逢雨必漏。我为此害了心病，常常在梦里梦到屋子漏雨。既便后来条件好了，住进了楼房，也常有此梦。家国相连。在贫穷落后的年代里，有谁不是从苦水里泡大的？又有谁的家里没漏过雨呢？我想，有着类似经历的人不在少数吧。

房子是一个家庭重要的幸福指数。“安得广厦千万间，大庇天下寒士俱欢颜?”古人的梦想历经千年，如今终成现实。草房，瓦房，楼房……从有其屋到优其屋，随着开革开放的成果不断惠及民生，中国普通百姓的住房条件日益改善。文中这个农民家庭的居住史，正是千千万万个中国家庭从贫穷苦难迈向小康生活的缩影。

（辽宁省盘锦日报社副总编辑）

故事

台州

阮箭芬(新闻学专业 201 专升本班)

漏雨的日子不再来

“以前啊,你爷爷和你爸爸可是很苦的。”聊起爷爷奶奶那时的生活,奶奶留下一句话,起身向厨房走去。

眼前的爷爷已是坐在轮椅上。2019 年夏天的一个早晨,爷爷准备起身,眼前一黑。自此,他就没能自己站起来走路。以前的他,精神矍铄,走过的路可多哩。

用木头做的房子——

爷爷是一个农民,1928 年出生在台州市黄岩区的小村庄——杨恩村,曾祖父也是个普通的农民。爷爷小时候念过书,念到小学便不再继续读,在家干农活。成年后便离家工作,那是爷爷第一次出远门赚钱。步行 5 天的路程,到了宁波的另一个村庄——燕子巢村。之后的三年里,他在一户养牛的人家放牛谋生。成年之前在家放牛、砍柴,做些杂活,这样的经验使他能够胜任这份工作。那时候的工资是用谷物结的,卖掉谷物来换“大洋”。三年的时间,存了些钱,又是一次徒步“旅行”。可是这一次,爷爷走到临海时遭遇了抢劫,我的脑海里突然就出现了电视里那些五大三粗的强盗在抢劫的画面,爷爷身上所有的钱被抢走,在路上买的一些布也都被抢走。回到家之后,爷爷便另寻生活,帮别人割稻子赚钱。就这样爷爷用攒下的大洋买下了第一个房子。房子是用木头做的两层楼,上面盖着一层瓦片,风大的时候时常会漏雨,爸爸便经常要爬上屋顶去整理瓦片。门前有两棵板栗树,还有很多柏树,后门有个水井,当时没有自来水,只能挖水井,用桶去井里打水喝。当时的生活条件,一般都只能吃番薯、土豆、芋头……没有条件经常吃上米饭。熬油时会加很多盐,咸菜里也有很多盐,爸爸皱着眉头对我吐槽:“咸得很,感觉下不了口。”也有要借食物吃的时候,爷爷就去比较富有的人家借“番薯丝”来当作一家人的粮食,之后需要用米去还,借了 100 斤的番薯丝,之后就要用 100 斤的米偿还。

那以后爷爷就没有再出远门赚钱,只是在家干农活,和当地的很多人一样,爷爷在合适的年纪遇到了心仪的对象,和奶奶结了婚,有了自己的家庭。爷爷有

4个女儿、2个儿子，我的爸爸就是大儿子。后来有了集体小队，几户人家分到地一起种，生活条件在慢慢变好。再后来就有了自己的地种，能吃上饭的日子也越来越多。

灰色的水泥房——

1989年，因为移民，要搬家了，本来可以到相较于这个村庄更大的地方去，但是爷爷没有选择去那儿，他留在这里，迁到了距离老家500米的山脚下。他说家里还有些地，还有些种的东西在这儿，不想走。1999年我出生了，在这个房子里长大。房子是二层楼的四间房，外面没有贴瓷砖，只是灰色的。爸爸和叔叔一人两间，爷爷和奶奶则住在后院的一间小房子里。房子都是水泥房了，下雨天的心情大概有所不同罢。即使是漏雨，也是四五个小地方，把水桶正对着漏雨的点接着滴下来的水。那时候，我在家时候喜欢做的事情之一，就是帮奶奶做手工艺品，下雨天在楼下和奶奶促膝坐着的日子里，总是伴随着滴答滴答的声音。我最喜欢的另一件事就是去后院爷爷奶奶住处旁的池塘，一汪幽幽的山泉水，一池淡淡的水草，还有好些爸爸钓的鱼儿。我常顽皮，去那儿大多是探索，总希望发现一些“新鲜玩意儿”，比如：青蛙生下的卵、只有一两厘米长的游得很快的小鱼、能在水上爬的奇特物种……不久，爷爷便有了“危机感”，生怕我带着其他孩子来危险区域探险，干脆把池塘填了。填了这一块偌大的后院用来做什么呢？爷爷想得奇妙，买了几株丹桂种上。不过多久，家里的另两边空地也都被栽满水果蔬菜，近处有樱桃树、金桔树、枇杷树、梨树、柿子树……再远一点儿就是各类蔬菜：小青菜、土豆、番薯、四季豆、姜、蒜……俨然是一个百宝园。我觉得爷爷种过所有能种的东西。爷爷又是个特别温柔的人，爸爸对我说过：爷爷从来不曾打骂过他们。

贴着黄色瓷砖的房子——

爸爸原本是个木工，可是爸爸应该也是个有志青年吧。1989年，18岁的他坐了十几个小时的客车去上海工作，在高桥、南汇、川沙这三个地方拉黄包车，我眼前不禁浮现出看过的繁华的上海滩，并伴随着《夜上海》那首歌的配乐。爸爸说就和电视里放的一样。不过在那儿赚的钱都花完了，也没有什么积蓄，一年后就回家继续做他的木匠，帮别人盖房子或者做家具。几年后就遇见了妈妈，和她组建了家庭。妈妈在一个离家很近的眼镜厂上班。2010年，姑姑和姑父做的生意有了起色，和我爸妈商议一起做生意去，爸爸妈妈决定和姑父学习经验，自己卖东西。在爸妈的7年努力拼搏下，经商存了些钱。2017年，我家决定建新房子。挖土机把园子毁掉了，我最喜欢的几株樱桃树没有了，只剩下三棵桂花树。宽敞又沉重的房子建在以前的园子上，外面贴着好看精致的瓷砖。我住在里面，刮台风都不会漏雨，安静的下雨天里也听不见水桶接雨滴的声音了。生活条件日益好起来，但爷爷的园子一直在我心中。

我想：当我能在家常住时，我会重新栽下爷爷栽过的树、种过的菜。爷爷种地的日子已经过去，漏雨的日子也不再来。

Taizhou
Ruan Jianfen (Class 201, Majoring in Journalism)

No Leaking Roofs Any More

"Your grandfather and father used to live a tough life." Talking about their life at that time, grandma left a word, got up and walked to the kitchen.

Now, my grandfather has already been in a wheelchair. On a summer morning of 2019, he passed out when he was ready to get up. Since then, grandpa has never been able to stand up and walk on his own any more. But he used to be a hale man who passed by many roads.

House Made of Wood

My grandfather is a farmer born in an ordinary farmers' family in Yangen village, a small village in Huangyan District, Taizhou of Zhejiang Province in 1928. During childhood, he learnt something as a student until his primary school, and then took on farming at home. After growing into an adult, he left home to seek fortune. It was the first time that he went outside of the small village to make a living. After a five-day walk, he arrived at Yan Zichao Village in Ningbo. In the next three years, grandfather made a living by herding cattle in a family. His childhood experience to herd cattle, cut firewood and do chores at home qualified him for the new job. Wages were paid with grain in exchange for "Da Yang(silver dollar)" back then. The three-year salary supported him to go further away on his own. Unluckily, he was robbed in Linhai County this time. A picture of fierce burglars robbing a man that I'd seen on TV comes to my mind. All of his cash was snatched away, and even some of the cloth he bought along the way. He soon came back home and had to make a living in another way by helping others cut rice. As time passed by, he saved enough silver dollars for his first house. The house was a wooden one with two floors, with the roofs covered by a layer of tiles. When there was a strong wind, tiles would be always in a mess, so my father had to climb up to tidy up. In front of the front door were two chestnut trees and many cypress trees, and at the back door was a well. At that time, there was no running water, so we had to dig a well and drew water with buckets from it. The living conditions then only permitted sweet potatoes, potatoes and taros, and even rice. We used to put much salt into boiled oil and pickles, but my father always frowned at me and complained: "They're too salty to eat." Sometimes, when the food ran out, we had to borrow food from others. My grandfather borrowed "sweet potato shreds" to support our family, but he had to pay back with rice, which meant that 50 kilograms of sweet potato shreds required the equal amount of rice for the repayment.

My grandfather never went outside to seek a fortune any more. Like most of the locals, he took on farming, fell in love, got married and set up a family with my grandmother at a proper age. My father is the elder brother of the family's two sons, and my grandfather also has four sisters. Later, farmers started to work in groups with allocated lands, so the living standard was gradually improved. Soon, he got his own land to take care of and life had also totally changed.

Grey Cement House

In 1989, my family had to move due to the migration policy. They could have moved to a larger village, but my grandfather refused to go there. Instead, he stayed in the same village and moved to the foot of a mountain 500 meters away from the old house. Grandfather said that there was still some land and the crops remaining there, so he felt reluctant to leave. In 1999, I was born in this house. It was a grey house of two floors and four rooms with no tiles outside. Each two of the rooms separately belonged to my father and my uncle, while my grandparents lived in a small house in the backyard. In the cement houses, we had different moods, especially on rainy days. Even the raindrops were not so annoying. There were only some small drips on the roof, so all we had to do was to put a bucket under each of the drips. One of my favorite things to do was to help grandma with her handicrafts. On such rainy days, I enjoyed sitting downstairs close to her, accompanied by the tick-tock of water. Another thing I enjoyed most was to go to the pond next to my grandparents' residence in the backyard, where there was a mountain spring, a pool of water plants, and a lot of fish that Dad caught. I was naughty enough to go there for exploration, hoping to find something "interesting", such as: eggs born by frogs, two-centimeter-long fish that swam fast, strange species that could climb above the water. Soon, grandpa felt a sense of "crisis". For fear that I would take other children to explore dangerous areas, he simply filled the pond up. With a large area of extra land, how could he make full use of it? My brilliant grandfather bought a few Osmanthus fragrans and planted them there. Soon after, the other two sides of open spaces were also planted with fruits and vegetables, including cherry trees, kumquat trees, loquat trees, pear trees, persimmon trees. Further were the pak choi, potatoes, sweet potatoes, string beans, ginger, garlic. The backyard became a treasure garden! As far as I'm concerned, my grandfather must have planted everything he could plant. Besides, he's a gentle father. Just as Dad once told me, he never beat or scolded the kids.

A House with Yellow Tiles

Dad was a carpenter, but he was also a young man with ambitions. In 1989, at the age of 18, he took a bus for more than ten hours to work in Shanghai. He drove rickshaws in Gaoqiao, Nanhui and Chuansha. I couldn't help thinking of the bustling Old Shanghai I'd seen before, along with the background music "Shanghai Nights". According to Dad, Shanghai was the same as it was on TV. However, he spent all the money he earned. Without any savings, he decided to return home one year later and continued his career as a carpenter, building houses and furniture. After a few years, he met Mom and started a family with her. My mother worked in a glass factory close to home. In 2010, as the business of my aunt and uncle started to thrive, my parents made up their minds to work with them. They learnt a lot from my uncle and sold products by themselves. Seven year's hard work finally paid off. They started to build a new house with the money they earned in the year of 2017. The garden was destroyed by an excavator, with none of my favorite cherry trees and only three of the Osmanthus trees left. A spacious and solid house was built on the former garden, with beautiful and exquisite tiles attached to its outside. It would never leak even if there's a typhoon. The house became quiet on rainy days without any sound of the raindrops' drippling. While our living conditions get better day by day, my grandfather's garden has always been in my heart.

I wondered: When I can settle down in the house, I will replant the same trees and vegetables as my grandfather did. The days of my grandfather's farming are all gone, and there's no leaking roofs any more.

异乡即故乡

邱子桐

谭静怡同学在《落地生根》中并没有表达出对父母亲的故乡——吉林舒兰和甘肃白银有太多的依恋;对出生于浙江嘉兴的她来说,嘉兴便是她落地生根的故乡。她笔下的家,是在嘉兴不断奋斗且相互扶持的父母亲。1990 年父母双双来到浙江经济高等专科学校读书,随后就展开了开挂的人生:顺利就业、工作、结婚、买房、生娃、买车。父亲的事业越做越大,后因身体原因投身教育行业开设国学培训,母亲也在金融业内越做越好,从柜员到网点经理最后做到行长。他们一家从原来的一无所有到如今拥有良好环境。

有趣的是,上世纪 90 年代中国开启了改革开放的新节点:作为"劳务"移民的千万农民工奔赴中国的东部沿海发达城市,形成巨大的人口流动。而与很多"农民工"漂流的故事不一样的是,谭静怡的父母是 90 年代的大学生,在那个时代属于"高材生",甚至可说是国内"教育移民"的早期样本。他们有一般移民的拼搏精神,同时他们保持着持续的再学习和专业提升,在异乡选择主动生根成长。

（浙大宁波理工学院传媒与法学院副教授,博士）

故事

嘉兴

谭静怡(新闻学专业 202 专班)

落地生根

我的父亲来自吉林舒兰,我的母亲来自甘肃白银,我出生于浙江嘉兴。我家的故事，要从曾经的两个大学生背井离乡来到嘉兴上大学说起。

我的父亲出生于吉林省舒兰县的一个小村庄，他在家中排行老二，有一个姐姐和一个妹妹。父亲的家境并不好，爷爷是普通的农民，身体不好，家里的重担一直压在每一位家庭成员的肩膀上。我的父亲从小就承担起了家里的农活，但也从来没有停止过学习的脚步，他想凭借自己的力量走出农村。我的父亲经历过两次高考失利，也同样经历过两次痛苦的复读。家里有成堆成堆的麦谷要收，还有成群成群的猪要喂养。父亲边处理着家里的农活边读书，想要去往更大世界的决心让他坚持了下来，直到拿到录取通知书。父亲说从拿到录取通知书那天起他的人生真正开启了新的征途，那个名为嘉兴的目的地，距离吉林千万里远的地方，成为他的第二个家。

我的母亲是县长的女儿，全县人都这么叫她，说她是县长最疼爱的小女儿。我的母亲在家里排行老四，有三个哥哥，哥哥的年纪都比她年长许多。我母亲出生后不久，大舅就投入工作了。我的姥爷那个时候月月都有国家给的工资拿，因此我的母亲小时候没有怎么吃过苦，物质条件和同龄人相比好很多，没有养家负担的她一直努力读书，考上了当时白银最好的高中。之后参加高考，如愿以偿地成为一名大学生。我问她怎么选择了嘉兴，母亲笑着说："那个时候和同学对着中国地图扔飞镖玩，飞镖扔中了嘉兴，就记住了。"

1990年，我的父亲和母亲拿着录取通知书报到于浙江经济高等专科学校，后来他们相爱了。

1994年，父亲和母亲毕业了。父亲选择留在嘉兴发展，母亲也因此放弃了家里人安排好的工作留在了嘉兴。父亲在一家贸易公司做会计，母亲则就职于中国建设银行成为一名小柜员。工作后，在嘉兴这片陌生又孤独的土地上，两人成为彼此唯一的依靠。1996年10月1日，父亲和母亲结婚了。同年，我们家买了第一套房子。这一套75平方米的小平房承载着父亲和母亲对生活的憧憬，以及对未来的向往。父亲获得了更好的工作机会，开始从事贸易工作，随着收入的提高，我们家的生活也越来越好。1998年，母亲怀孕了。怀孕期间母亲也没有闲下来，上班的同时上着函授的夜校，还在自学会计师职称考试科目。那时的母亲一个人搬了张桌子在底楼的车库里学习，寒来暑往，母亲从未停下学习的脚步，以致每每到老房子的车库，我都仿佛能看见年轻的母亲正在伏案写字。

1999年8月，我出生了。父亲和母亲又多了一份责任，这份责任推着他们更加努力地前行。2000年母亲考出了会计师职称，父亲也因工作需要离开嘉兴，去往天津，在之后的8年时光里，我们一家过着聚少离多的日子。父亲每每提起这段时光总是会很愧疚，母亲的工作本就很忙，还让她一个人拉扯尚在襁褓中的我长大。对于我8岁之前父爱的缺失，父亲从天津回来后也一直在尽他所能补偿。但其实我一直觉得，我们一家人能够在一起就是最好。

父亲在天津跟着公司开疆拓土，事业越来越红火，有些业务甚至从国内发展到了国外，父亲也因为这些越来越广泛的业务赚了更多的钱。然而最让我骄傲的是父亲在这期间成为一名光荣的共产党员。另一边母亲也在嘉兴努力奋斗，母亲在百忙之中考出了会计主管资格证书，从小柜员晋升成了网点营业经理，不论是在工作上还是在家庭上，都承担着比以往更大的责任。

2008年悄然到来，这一年对于我家来说是充满变化的一年。父亲由于身体不好，选择离开天津回到嘉兴，之后父亲找了份安稳的贸易工作，承担起了抚育我的责任。同年，我们家买了第二套房子，139平方米，很大，大到能装下全家的梦想。之后母亲升职成为建行网点行长，更加忙碌了，除了工作日的早出晚归，周末也经常会加班。于是我和父亲的相处时间渐渐大于和母亲的相处时间，我开始慢慢了解父亲，渐渐填补了之前父亲在我人生中的空缺。2010年，父亲买了第一辆汽车，他会开车带着我和母亲出行，也会开车接送母亲上下班，还会送我去离家很远的英语辅导班上课。这一辆车承载着我们一家的许多美好回忆，年轻的父母和年少的我在这辆车上度过了一个又一个美好的日子。

我的父亲其实是个不甘平凡的人，他从东北一步步走出来就注定着他心中始终燃烧着一团火焰。回到嘉兴后，平静的生活让他开始琢磨是不是能做点别的什么，虽然这个阶段在父亲的描述里叫"路多阻碍"，但是那时敢想敢做的他毅然决然投身了教育行业。2012年，他开了家培训机构。这家培训机构不讲数学也不讲英语，只讲语文，或者说叫国学。从天津回到嘉兴成为清闲散人的他对国学萌发出了极其强烈的兴趣。于是父亲开始钻研国学，认识了一些对国学颇有研究的老师，也教了一些学生，但机构始终不怎么赚钱，毕竟在成绩更重要的当代，这个培训机构的业务并不吃香，也少有家长买国学这门课的账。但父亲其实还挺开心，觉得自己在做有意思的事。

这边父亲的培训机构不咸不淡地开着班，另一边母亲离开工作了十几年的中国建设银行，去到了广发银行做了副行长，这对母亲而言并不是一个容易做的决定，但是母亲最终还是迈出了这一步，为自己，也是为我，更是为我们一家。2014年母亲买了属于她的第一辆汽车，母亲开始开着她的汽车雷厉风行地穿行在嘉兴这座小城，创造着属于她的辉煌。于是一直到今天，我家都共存着两个极端性格，母亲的风风火火和父亲的平静淡然。

父亲的身体一直不是很好，2017年做了一场大手术，我们一家也因为这场手术经受了非常痛苦的煎熬，但是好在所有的事都守得云开见月明。在父亲康复的同时我意识到，对于我而言，我从来不希望我家有多大富大贵，只要一家人长长久久在一起，就是全世界最幸福的一家。

我的父亲和母亲来自不同的地方，最终却在嘉兴这座小城落地生根，从当初来到陌生地方的一无所有，到如今所拥有的一切，无一不是父亲和母亲努力奋斗的结果。我无比感激父母给我创造的良好环境，也期待着不久以后接过他们手中的接力棒，续写我家的故事。

Jiaxing
Tan Jingyi (Class 202, Majoring in Journalism)

Settle Down

My father comes from Shulan, Jilin Province, and my mother Baiyin, Gansu Province. As for me, I was born in Jiaxing, Zhejiang Province. The story of my family started with two college students leaving their hometowns to study in Jiaxing.

My father, born in a small village in Shulan County, Jilin Province, was the second child in a poor family; he has one elder sister and one younger sister. My grandfather was an ordinary farmer. Since he was in poor health, the heavy life burden was on every family member. My father took on the farm work from a very young age, yet he never stopped learning, for he wanted to step out of the village on his own. My father failed twice in the college entrance examination, which meant he had to go through painstaking preparations for the tests two more times. While he was studying, stacks of grain waited to be harvested and a herd of pigs to be fed. Later, he attended to studies and farm work at the same time, and it was the determination to go to the bigger world that kept him going till the day he received the admission letter from a university. My father said that was the day when he embarked on a brand-new journey, and Jiaxing, thousands of miles away from Jilin, became his second home.

My mother, daughter of the county mayor, was said to be the apple of her father's eye. My mother is the little sister to her three elder brothers, who are much older than her. Her eldest brother started working shortly after she was born. Her father was paid by the government every month at that time, so she barely endured any hardship when young. With much better living conditions and without family burdens, my mom studied diligently and went to the best high school in Baiyin. She later duly became a college student after the college entrance examination. She replied with a smile when I asked her why she chose Jiaxing, "My classmates and I were throwing darts after class, and I kept this name in mind after my dart thudded into this place."

My father and mother reported to then Zhejiang Economic College in 1990. Later, they fell in love with each other.

After they graduated from the college back in 1994, my father chose to stay, and consequently my mother gave up the job her family had arranged for her back in the hometown and stayed in Jiaxing. My father became an accountant in a trading company while my mother a clerk of China Construction Bank. They only had each other to rely on in this strange land. They got married on October 1st, 1996, and bought their first house the same year. This bungalow, which covered an area of 75 square meters, carried my parents' aspiration for a better life and a brighter future. Later, my father, getting a better-paid job, was engaged in trading business and life got better along with his increased salaries. My mother, getting pregnant in 1998, didn't slacken off. She took correspondence courses in a night school while working by day, and independently prepared for title tests for accountants. She moved a desk to the garage on the ground floor, and learned diligently there, having never stopped be it in hot summer or cold winter. I would have the illusion of seeing my mother engulfed in reading whenever I pass by the old garage.

More responsibilities were put over my parents' shoulders along with my birth, which pushed them to forge ahead. My mom got her accountant certificate and my father left Jiaxing for Tianjin as required by his work. In the next eight years, the whole family seldom got together. My father felt sorry whenever he thought of the past days because he owed a lot to my mom who, while busy working, raised me up all on her own. He has tried every means possible since he returned from Tianjin to make up for the paternal company and love absent in the past eight years. But for me, there is nothing better than a reunited family.

My father, blazing a trail for business in Tianjin and even overseas, made a lot of money from his flourishing career. Yet the thing I was most proud of about my father was that he joined the Communist Party of China. As for my mother, she managed to obtain the certificate for director accountants and was promoted to executive manager for the sub-branch she was working in, shouldering much greater responsibilities than ever both in work and family.

The year 2008 was full of twists and turns for my family. My father chose to return to Jiaxing considering his poor health and landed a stable job relating to trading business. He then started taking care of me himself. We had our second dwelling with an area of 139 square meters, big enough to house all of our dreams. My mother got busier after being promoted to the sub-branch governor, working extra hours on weekends besides the already busy weekdays. From then on, I got to know my father better since I spent more time with him. The absent paternal love was finally made up. He bought our first car in 2010, with which he would take my mom and me out for travelling, take my mom to and from work and send me to attend English tutorials far away from home. The car, carrying wonderful memories, recorded every beautiful day that my parents and I spent in it in the early days.

My father is an enthusiastic and ambitious man. After he returned to Jiaxing, my father, unrelunctant to live in an ordinary life, wondered if there was anything special he could do. Resolute in action, he immediately buried himself into education section though he described it a bumpy course. He then started up a training agency in 2012, which only offered classes of Chinese classics instead of math or English. He lived an idle life returning Jiaxing from Tianjina, and he showed great interests in Chinese classics. Therefore, he began to study Chinese classics, and made acquaintances with some accomplished teachers and taught some students. However, the school barely made a profit. Chinese classics were not a popular subject since grades were of the utmost importance. Therefore, few parents would pay for this course. Despite all these, my dad was delightful because he thought he was doing something meaningful.

While my dad's business was slack, my mom became the deputy governor of China Guangfa Bank after leaving China Construction Bank where she worked for over ten years. It was by no means an easy decision to make, yet she still made up her mind, for herself, for me, and above all, for the whole family. She bought her first car in 2014, and ever since she has streaked through Jiaxing while charting her own glory. Two personalities at different ends of the spectrum—my brisk and hurried mom and my calm and serene dad—exist in my family today.

My father, in poor health, underwent a major operation in 2017. It was an agonizing period of time for the whole family. Luckily, there is always light at the end of the tunnel. While my father was recovering from his illness, it dawned on me that the only thing I always wished for my family was never material affluence but lasting reunion and happiness.

My parents, coming from two different places, have been rooted in the small city of Jiaxing. They started from scratch and earned everything we own now with their bare hands. I greatly appreciate the sound conditions they have created for me, and look forward to the day when I take the baton that they pass on to me and continue the story of my family.

“老杭漂”图鉴

邱子桐

杭州作为“新一线”城市，在过去的几年间依托规模化与行业化的网红经济迅速崛起。2019年，杭州超越深圳，净流入人口55.4万，在全国人口净流入的榜单中排名第一；同时，整个浙江省在2017—1018年连续两年人口净流入位列全国第二，在2019年成为全国第一，达到了113万（参见郎友兴《人口净迁入对浙江意味着什么》，载《浙江经济》2020年5月20日）。在网络媒体和社交平台中，新一代杭漂人的“漂流”经验高度可见。

而在徐莹的《妈妈的杭漂史》中，我们看见了“老杭漂”的“漂流”人生。徐莹的“70后”母亲，从一开始在印刷厂做“厂妹”，到在小餐馆做帮工，再到在大饭店当服务员，到在西湖时代广场做销售，再到简短的一段“全职母亲”的工作，最后到铝合金拉弯厂做会计至今。忙碌的工作节奏中，徐莹的母亲——就像现在众多职场母亲一样——仍然担当起了照顾家庭的大部分责任：早上她要在老公出门前就烧好早饭，早期要将女儿送到幼儿园；下班后开始高速运转，接娃、买菜、做饭、搞卫生，参与家庭的买房决策。文章勾勒出了一位从“杭漂”到“新杭州人”的母亲的画像：一位不断兼顾工作与家庭的职场母亲。而正是过去几十年千千万万的“杭漂”职场母亲——在浙江各种各样的厂子里、店里、公司里——的奋斗和坚持，才持续铸就了浙江兴盛的民营经济与发达的专业市场，助力了近年来以杭州为代表的浙江区域经济转型升级，才让如今随处可见的媒体“新杭漂”故事成为可能。

（浙大宁波理工学院传媒与法学院副教授，博士）

故事

杭州

徐莹(新闻学专业202专升本班)

妈妈的杭漂史

1973年5月25日,浙江诸暨吕家村一个女娃呱呱坠地,伴随着哭泣声,女孩的一生由此开始。

1990年,17岁的妈妈在小姐妹带领下怀揣着对大城市生活的美好向往与同乡的人一起来到杭州务工,然而杭州的生活并不像同伴口中的那样美好。老乡给妈妈介绍的工作是在清河坊的一个印刷厂里折书本。“一个厂子里的女工住在一个寝室里,上下铺的。天天吃海带,晚上还要点煤油灯呢,电太贵了……”然后没多久她就跑回了家。

第一次杭漂失败后,妈妈在村子里一家餐馆里帮忙炒菜洗碗。餐馆位于一个高速路口旁,每天来来往往许多大卡车司机在餐馆里吃饭休息。“我哪里会炒菜啊,都是随便煮熟就好了的,又没人教我而且还要洗碗嘞。包吃包住的,一天才10块钱。”餐馆的工作并没有比印刷厂的工作轻松多少,显然这也不是妈妈心目中的好工作好生活。

再去杭州的机会来得很突然,一个休假回乡的小姐妹告诉妈妈她在杭州找到了新工作,在河海饭店里当服务员,那可是个大饭店呢!并跟妈妈承诺可以把她也介绍进去干活。妈妈再一次心动了。“我又不比别人差,别人能做我也可以!”她撇下餐馆工作,跟随小姐妹再次回到杭州一起去河海饭店工作。这一去,她就彻底在杭州扎下了根。

在河海饭店里妈妈从叠被子、铺床单的服务员干起,慢慢地成了前台,甚至最后还当上了值班经理。同时也是在这家饭店,妈妈认识了当时还在工地上做铝材的爸爸。1997年,在二次杭漂4年后的妈妈选择在这里与同样杭漂的爸爸组成家庭,次年,他们的女儿——我就出生了。结婚生子后的妈妈,依然在河海饭店工作,她每天认真核对入住人员信息,结算当天业绩。但新的挑战接踵而至。

“那时候啊,我们住在(杭州)东站,我每天要骑着脚踏车先送你去幼儿园,再骑一个小时去西湖边上班,你都不记得啦?”

因为河海饭店内部进行了体制改革，妈妈的工作待遇大不如前，加之搬家、我渐渐长大要上幼儿园等原因，妈妈一狠心就辞去了饭店的工作。经过舅妈介绍她在西湖时代广场的大厦里做起了售货员，卖的是杯子。妈妈说，那时最累的不是站一天的班，而是每天忙得像打仗一样的上班和下班。早上她要在爸爸出门前就烧好早饭，要在上课前送我到幼儿园。“你有时还不听话，不肯上幼儿园，还要哄还要骗。”一顿哭闹之后，早上的时间被压缩得更紧了。送完孩子，再吭哧吭哧地骑一个小时的自行车去上班，一天才刚开始，妈妈就已精疲力竭。

傍晚又是新一轮的战斗，妈妈从下班起就开始高速运转，接娃、买菜、做饭、搞卫生一样都不能少。有时妈妈还会轮值晚班，早上的时间是充裕了，傍晚却也没法接孩子了。我成了幼儿园里最后一个被家长接走的孩子。为了节约交通时间，家里斥“巨资”给妈妈换了一台电瓶车，可还没有骑几天，连车带电瓶就都被小偷给顺了去。“你妈哭得可伤心了呢。”

爸爸为了安慰妈妈，又出资买了一辆新的电瓶车，这一次妈妈可谨慎了，轮胎要锁，把手也要锁，最好还要锁在粗电线杆或树旁边。但电瓶车如果耗光了电，就成了一辆负重的自行车，好几次妈妈都踩着没电的电瓶车在马路上艰难前行。“这样子好多年，一直到你上了小学才结束的。”妈妈对于这段过往，有太多的感慨。

升入小学后，爸爸妈妈的工作更忙了。一次放学是爸爸来接我的，他带我去了一栋我从没去过的楼房。他把我领上楼梯：“我们搬家了。你就一直往上走，走到5楼就好了，妈妈在家的。”说完爸爸就下楼梯走了。我好像听懂了，又好像没听懂，等反应过来下楼去追爸爸时，已经没有影了，我也不记得该往哪里走了。大约几个小时后，爸爸回到家没有看到我，爸妈才发现我走丢了。妈妈哭着埋怨爸爸，爸爸眉头紧锁一声不吭，他们在附近几条街里寻找我的踪影，好久之后才在一个街头角落里找到了满脸泪痕的我。

这事以后，妈妈决定辞去工作，专心照顾我，照顾这个家。

五年级时我们又搬家了，我还转学到了家附近的学校，可以自己上下学了。妈妈又开始上班，在爸爸介绍的一家铝合金拉弯厂里当会计，负责记账、做单子。妈妈虽然没有干过这类活，但她心细，人缘又好，很快就将这份工作做得得心应手。原本在家时，妈妈总会感到身上莫名的疼痛，胸闷气短，上班后，非但人不难受了还变得开朗起来。也就是在这一年，爸爸妈妈拿出所有积蓄在余杭乔司买下来一套78平方米的房子，至此我们家算是真正在杭州扎下了根。

“要不是我点子准，这套房就买不了了呢！”

2016年，G20峰会使杭州一下成为世界瞩目的焦点。而就在这之前一年，妈妈在小区门口的房屋销售牌上看到了一条顶楼大套房屋的转让消息。妈妈是个心思缜密的人，她早就想到之后女儿成家立业，家里人变多了，小房子是不够住的。她产生了换房的想法。在得到中介的那条房屋转让消息后，妈妈当晚就和爸爸商量，隔天两人就去看了房子。没过多久我们家就办了贷款，将这套高层套房收入囊中。次年，杭州房价因 G20 峰会的召开而飙升，这套房在妈妈手里赚了不少。2018 年的冬天，我们一家人搬入了新装修好的房子。

但新房子还没有住多久，我们一家三口就要面临三地分居的情况。我是要去嘉兴平湖上学，而妈妈因为厂子搬迁的原因要去径山上班，周末才能回家，只有爸爸一个人守在家里了。他开始向妈妈抱怨："老都老了，还要分居。"妈妈也想过要辞职，到家附近再找份工作。但妈妈舍不得做了十几年的工作，舍不得厂子每年给她交的养老保险，"还有两年就满十五年了，现在放弃，太可惜了吧"。除此之外，妈妈又在厂子里兼职了另一份工作。因为厂子搬迁，手头上的文案活变少了，装卸铝材的活变多了，妈妈开始在大卡车下帮着工人一起卸货，多赚一份工资。"你干嘛去卸货啊，累么累死，我们家又不缺这份工资……"每次我和爸爸劝她要爱惜自己的身体，不要再"要钱不要命"时，她总是回答道："现在待在厂里又没事，我不做点活儿，你让我干嘛去啊！我就在车下面帮他们搭把手，我自己有数的，再说了，又不是每天都有货要卸。"妈妈总有一大堆说辞等着我们，就是闲不下来。

现在我们一家都成了新杭州人，妈妈的杭漂史也到此为止了，但她的奋斗还在继续。

Hangzhou
Xu Ying (Class 202, Majoring in Journalism)

My Mom's Story as a Hangzhou Drifter

A baby girl was born on May 25, 1973 in Lvjia Village, Zhuji City in Zhejiang Province, and embarked on her life journey with a cry. That baby girl is my mom.

In 1990, my 17-year-old mom, yearning for the colorful urban life, tried her luck in Hangzhou with her fellow villagers. Yet the life in Hangzhou was not as wonderful as described by her friends. The job her fellow villager introduced to her was to fold books in a printing factory in Qinghefang, an ancient street in Hangzhou. "All female workers were living in one dormitory with many bunk beds. We ate seaweed every day and had to use kerosene lamps at night for we couldn't afford electricity bills." Before long, she rushed back home.

My mom later helped cook and wash dishes in a restaurant after her first failed attempt to settle in Hangzhou. Located next to a highway exit, the restaurant was quite busy serving many truck drivers. "I didn't know anything about cooking, and all I did was to make sure that food was edible. Nobody was there to teach me, and I also didn't have time to learn since I needed to wash loads of dishes. Accommodation was covered, and I only earned 10 yuan each day." Clearly no better than the previous book-folding job, the restaurant work was by no means ideal for my mom.

The second chance to go to Hangzhou came out of the blue when a friend of my mom's returned home on leave. She told my mom that she was working as a waitress in the prestigious Hehai Hotel and also promised my mom a job there, too. Once again, my mother was motivated. She thought: "I am not worse than others. I can do it just like them!" She then left the restaurant job behind and headed for Hangzhou. And this time, she settled down there.

In Hehai Hotel, my mom moved up the career ladder, starting from a waitress whose job was to make the bed, to a receptionist and even a manager on duty. It was also in this hotel that my mom met my dad, who was then making aluminum products in construction sites. In 1997, four years after my mom set foot in Hangzhou again, she married my dad, who was also a Hangzhou drifter. One year later, I was born. My mom still worked in the hotel, checking guest information and balancing the books. But new challenges flooded in.

"We lived near Hangzhou East Railway Station at that time. I had to send you to the kindergarten by bike every morning and then biked to my work place by West Lake after one hour's riding. Don't you remember?"

My mom later resigned from Hehai Hotel partly because the remuneration was greatly reduced after its administrative reform and partly because the hotel was far away from our new home and my kindergarten. Thanks to her sister-in-law's help, my mom later worked as a shop assistant in a cup store in West

Lake Times Square. She said the most excruciating part of life was not standing all day long to sell cups, but how busy she was on the way of going to work and leaving work. She needed to prepare breakfast for my dad and had to send me to the kindergarten before the class began. "Sometimes you were so disobedient that I had to cheat you into going to the kindergarten." My crying made the morning time even shorter. After rushing me to the kindergarten, she biked one hour to work. She thus felt almost exhausted even though the day just began.

She threw herself into another similar battle at dusk, picking me up in the kindergarten, buying food for dinner, cooking and cleaning. I became the last child to be picked up from the kindergarten when my mom was on night shifts when the moring time was enough but it was impossible to pick me up at dusk. My parents later bought an electromobile with a huge amount of money so as to reduce the commuting time, but it was soon stolen along with the battery. "Your mom cried her eyes out."

My dad bought another electromobile in order to console my mom. This time, she was so careful and vigilant, locking everything from wheels to the handlebar and even chaining it to a wire pole or a big tree. My mom had to ride the vehicle by herself when the battery went out. "This kind of life didn't come to an end until you entered the elementary school," said my mom emotionally while recalling that harsh period of time.

My parents were even busier after I entered the elementary school. One day, my dad picked me up and took me to a house I had never seen before. He asked me to go upstairs, "This is our new home, and it's on the fifth floor. You just walk upstairs and your mom is at home waiting for you." Before I could even figure out what he meant by saying those words, he already left. I rushed downstairs, only to find he was already gone and that I didn't remember which floor I was supposed to go to. It was not until several hours later when my dad didn't see me upon arriving at home that they noticed I was missing. My mother cried and complained about my father while he frowned and said nothing. They searched the immediate neighborhood, and finally found me at a street corner, with tears all over my face.

After this incident, my mom decided to quit her job to take good care of me and the whole family.

We moved again when I was in the fifth grade and I transferred to a nearby elementary school, so I could get to and leave school on my own. My mom resumed work again. She worked as an accountant in an aluminum alloy stretch bending factory, a job introduced by my father. There she was responsible for bookkeeping and making orders. Though a total green hand, my meticulous and popular mom soon got pretty good at the work. My mom, feeling unutterable pain all over her body, tightness in her chest and shortness in her breath, felt quite well after resuming work. It was exactly in the same year that my parents bought a house covering 78 square meters in Qiaosi, Yuhang District with all their savings. That was when our family truly settled down in Hangzhou.

"Such a good timing. Otherwise, we couldn't have been able to buy this house."

In 2016, Hangzhou was under the spotlight after it was announced that G20 summit was to be held here. My far-sighted mom, well before 2016, had already decided to buy a more spacious house because she believed the current one was not big enough for so many people to live in once I got married and had children in the future. Naturally, when she learned in 2015 from a real estate agency that a top-floor room was for sale, she immediately went to see the house with my dad after family discussions. Before long, we bought that top-floor room with loans. The very next year, house price in Hangzhou surged with the convening of the G20 summit, and that house thus appreciated a lot. In the winter of 2018, our family finally moved into the newly-decorated home.

However, the three of us had to live separately shortly afterwards. I went to a school in Pinghu, Jiaxing City, while my mom had to work near Jingshan after the factory moved there and could only be back on weekends, leaving my dad at home alone. He complained to my mom, "It's unbelievable that we have to live far away from each other even at this age." Hearing my father's complaint, my mom once thought of resigning and finding a new job nearby, but finally banished the thought, for she was unwilling to quit the job she worked for over ten years and give up the endowment insurance. "Two more years and the factory will have been providing the endowment insurance for 15 years. It would be a shame if I give up now." My mom started making some extra money by helping workers unload aluminum products when paperwork decreased after they moved to the new site. "Why do you do the unload job? It is so tiring and tough! I know you want to support the family, but you could have found an easier job." Whenever my dad and I tried to talk her out of this part-time job and asked her to pay attention to health instead of money, she would reply, "I have nothing to do in the factory. What else can I do if I don't get myself some work? I just help them unload the goods beside the truck. Don't worry about me. I can take good care of myself. And by the way, there are not so many goods that need to be unloaded every day." My mom prepared loads of excuses; she just couldn't stand having nothing to do.

My mom's story as a Hangzhou drifter has come to an end since we three have all become permanent Hangzhou residents. However, her story of constantly forging ahead will continue.

家庭团聚:艰辛生活里的动力与幸福

文　娟

与资源有效配置的市场经济发展需求相呼应,流动成为现代社会生活和社会关系的重要表征。中国改革开放丰硕果实的获取,在很大程度上便依赖于人、财、物在960万平方公里土地上的自由流动。尤其是人口的自由流动,为中国工业社会的形成、夯实以及转型和升级换代提供了源源不断的劳动力支撑,同时也促发了中国国民生产总值的不断攀升,极大地改善和提升了广大人民的物质生活水平,为全面小康社会的到来打下了坚实的物质基础。只是,这份由流动促成的富足背后,还充盈着数以亿计农民工背井离乡的劳累心酸、托付儿童的悲伤思念以及年迈老人的重压和伤痛。这也是当下我们国家在加速推进城镇化进程之时,不遗余力地施行乡村振兴战略的重要原因。毕竟,于民众而言,真正的富足和美好,是有居有食有进步希望的家人团聚和共享天伦。

雨欣的这篇《买房记》,看似在记叙父母为了买房而一路奔波的艰辛生活,实则是父母异地打拼的心酸精神史。妻女绕膝的爸爸为了全家生计,不得不离家打拼;为了孩子的教育基金,父母不得不携带幼子、托付女儿于外公外婆,流动到离家几千里的大同讨生活。打工生活的忙碌、繁重、枯燥,水土不服,尤其是儿女教育的无暇顾及等成为他们生命中的难以承受之重。所以,他们用十多年的艰辛打拼,买一套房,结束流动务工,与儿女团聚相守。

事实上,不管是别家离子的流动务工还是回归故土的多样化谋生,父母能够抵御生活艰辛的动力都源于家庭团聚的愿望。齐整的四口之家,让他们体味着摸得着的幸福和看得见的美好未来。相信在乡村振兴战略的稳步推进下,未来还有更多的家庭结束别离,尽享团聚的幸福和美好。

(浙大宁波理工学院传媒与法学院讲师,博士)

故事

温州

黄雨欣(新闻学专业192班)

买房记

9年时间,我家从浙江省温州市龙港市一个叫做薛家桥的小农村搬到了龙港市的一个套房。父母用经年打拼将一室昏暗变成了开阔明净。

爸妈都是龙港人。1995年,叔父带着19岁的爸爸去瑞安做皮鞋,一做就是11年。19岁的妈妈来到了爸爸的村子帮别人家织毛毯。龙港和瑞安离得不远,爸爸隔一两个月回来一次,待个一两天再走,期间便认识了在隔壁织毛毯的妈妈。一来二去,两人情投意合,爸爸每次从瑞安回来都要看看妈妈,感情培养了差不多一年,很快就到了谈婚论嫁的阶段。婚后第一年便有了我。爸爸在家帮忙照顾了几个月便出去继续工作,妈妈为了照顾我只能在家做零工。随着我一天天长大,爸爸在皮鞋厂的收入只能勉强支撑基本生活,考虑到上学的问题,便打算去外地谋生路。

正愁不知到哪里谋生计,恰巧在山西大同的姑姑一家提出让我爸妈去帮忙。2008年,爸妈带着三个月大的弟弟去了大同,把我交托给住在龙港镇上的外公外婆来照顾。刚开始的时候妈妈放心不下在老家的我,听爸爸说她总是因为想我而在夜里偷偷流眼泪,待了没三个月便急着回来。在家照顾了我半年,又因为爸爸那边忙不过来,没法只得又去了大同和爸爸一起。自此我就一直跟着外公外婆,从小学二年级到高中二年级,9年的时间在我对父母的思念中缓缓流过。

在外打工的日子很难熬,光是水土不服就让爸爸妈妈吃了不少苦头。即便是天气过关了,口味却是一时难更改。爸爸依旧有一个沿海人的胃和嗜螃蟹如命的心,大同作为一个内陆城市,菜场里几乎见不到新鲜的海产,就算偶尔见到价格也让人望而却步。无论住多久,这一点始终难以习惯。为此,外公外婆会从菜场买来可以长久存放的虾皮和鱼干寄过去,也算告慰乡愁。

姑姑一家做的是批发衬衣的买卖,当时正缺送货的人手,所以爸妈每天都需要从离商场很远的库房里面调货配货,捧着一摞摞比人高的衬衣盒在商场里来回穿梭。库房建在地下室,温度很低,就算到了夏天,在里面呆久了也让人浑身发抖。生意好的时候,爸爸妈妈一整天都要在库房里工作,重复着把厚重的衬衣盒从货架上抽出再放进纸板箱最后用胶带纸封起来的动作。纸箱打包好后要放到小推车上，有时候货多，一车放个五六箱，走路就摇摇晃晃也看不清前面的人。“有一次货配过来，经过商场门帘的时候，因为门帘太厚了一个人没法推开，有个人帮忙推了一下，我连忙说谢谢。结果转身手机没了，以为是好人，结果是小偷，真的气死了。”问起工作时最累的一刻，爸爸叹了口气，“那就是生意太好，最忙的时候，有句成语叫什么来着，忙得不可开交。这里刚刚配货，那边又打电话过来催送货，我有时候急了把整个箱子都扔出去了。就发泄一下，扔完了还要自己去捡回来”。

由于爸妈工作太忙碌，弟弟不到两周岁就被送去幼儿园，又因为饮食和天气各方面不适应，头一个月基本上都在诊所度过。那会儿正值老商场要搬迁，处理旧货成了一大难题，妈妈便每天一大早站在店门口叫卖，很晚才结束工作。而商场离幼儿园又有一段很长的距离，走路至少要半小时。“每天早上六点多就要起来做饭，送弟弟上学再去商场。有一次雪下得很大，零下二十几度，我一只手抱着你弟弟，还有一只手拿着饭桶，摔倒了，饭桶扔了孩子还抱着。”那段时间成了妈妈最艰难的日子。

起早贪黑，积年劳累，爸爸落下了腰疼的毛病，妈妈的胳膊肘也经常因为脱力而抬不起来。

大同和温州相隔甚远，来回的路费加起来最少要2000多元，为了省钱，爸爸妈妈只在过年的时候才回来。到了年关，爸妈就把我从外婆家接到村里的老房子住一个月。老房子由于经年空着，每每回去里面都充满着一股难以驱散的霉味和潮湿感。习惯了北方冬天暖气的爸妈也开始对南方的阴冷感到不适。村里还有两三户人养鸡鸭，门前屋后总能见到新鲜的粪便，只要一会儿没看住，它们就直接跑进房子里撒野。再者村里和镇上相隔很远，交通也不方便。而我跟着外婆在小镇上住，早已习惯了干干净净的房间，习惯一出门就能吃到各种小吃，习惯走几步路就能去街上逛逛。农村的环境对于在别处生活了一段时间的我们来说都很不适应。一间干净敞亮的新房子成了我们一家共同的期许。

有了买房子的愿景，爸爸妈妈工作辛苦程度自不必说。但需求强烈，生意却难做。随着网购的普及，电商飞速发展，实体店的生存空间越发狭窄。往后的生意再没有头三年那么火爆，一天零售两三万的盛景都只是过去的泡影。就这样过了9年，我即将迎来高考，成绩却一路下滑，妈妈放心不下，一心只想回家照料我。刚好亲戚手里有套房，离我就读的高中很近，价格地段也算不错，权衡一番爸妈便收拾行囊从大同回家，买下了房子开始装修。

几个月后，我们一家住进了窗明几净的房子里，然而生计却是摆在面前的难题。一套房子花光了爸妈9年的积蓄，老家就业机会少，爸爸妈妈一回家就面临失业危机。爸爸文化水平不高，应聘送快递这样的体力活处处碰壁，后来又跟着我姑父去广州批发貂皮大衣，每天忍着腰疼灰头土脸地搬运货物，晚上龟缩在一个小厂房里。6月的广州，潮湿闷热无比，厂房没有空调，蚊子又多，爸爸和我们视频的时候总说待不下去了，想回家，但还是咬牙坚持着。干了半年，生意毫无起色，身体却吃不消了。无奈，爸爸只得在家休息了一年。妈妈经人介绍去了离家不远的包装厂工作，从早上6点到晚上11点，我们全家靠着妈妈微薄的收入勉强支撑。高强度的工作给妈妈带来的是肉眼可见的消瘦，深夜回家时常常没说两句话就已经累得闭上了眼睛。

再后来，就是现在，爸爸借了点钱买了辆小面包车给人家送货，妈妈也不再工作到深夜。尽管现在的生活仅仅是勉强维持，爸爸也还是常常因为焦虑而一根接一根地抽烟，但我相信家永远是幸福的港湾，我们一家四口整整齐齐，未来的生活一定会更好。

Wenzhou
Huang Yuxin (Class 192, Majoring in Journalism)

A Story About Buying a House

The past nine years has witnessed my family's moving from Xuejiaqiao which was in the countryside to a suite in Longgang City. After years of striving, my parents have turned our tiny, shabby house into a spacious and bright one.

My parents are both native people in Longgang. In the year of 1995, my father, led by his uncle, went to Rui'an to make leather shoes where he had been working for 11 years. My mother happened to knit blankets in the village where my father worked. It was not far away from Longgang to Rui'an. They acquainted with each other when my father went back on his day off, usually one or two days per month. Through frequent communication, they fell in love. Every time my father came back from Rui'an, he would pay my mother a visit. After a year or so, they got married. I came to the world at the first year they married. After taking care of me several months, my father went out to work for our family. To look after me, my mother could only do some odd jobs at home. As time went by, my father's income in leather factory hardly met the end. Considering that more money would be needed when I attended school, he intended to seek a livelihood in another province.

When my parents worried about where to find a job, my aunt whose family was in Datong of Shanxi Province asked my parents to help. Therefore, my parents went there with my younger brother in 2008, leaving me with my grandparents in Longgang. My mother felt worried about me in the beginning, and my father told me that she always cried on the sly at night for missing me so much, so she came back home anxiously to take care of me for half a year. However, when my father had got too much work to do, she had no choice but go to Datong to help my father. Since then, I lived with my grandparents for the next nine years. It was a time when I studied from Grade Two of primary school to Grade Two of high school. Those nine years passed with my deep yearning for my parents.

Years of working outside was tough. My parents suffered from not being acclimatized. Even if they got used to the climate, they found it difficult to change their taste in food. As a person growing up in coastal areas, my father had a liking for seafood, especially crabs. However, Datong was an inland city, and fresh seafood as rare to be found in the market. Even if there was some seafood, the price was extremely high so that people would hesitate to buy it. No matter how long they had been living there, it was hard for them to change their habit and liking. Hence, my grandparents would send dried small shrimp and dried fish which could be preserved for a long time from the market to satisfy their craving for seafood.

My aunt's family did shirt wholesale business, and they needed a delivery man at that time. My parents should transfer and distribute goods from a warehouse far away from the shopping mall, weaving their way through the crowds with piles of shirt boxes higher than themselves. The warehouse was built in the basement, and the temperature was quite low even in summer. Staying in it for a long time would be cold enough to make them shudder. When business was good, my parents had to work in the warehouse all day, repeating the routine of pulling heavy shirt boxes off the shelves, putting them in cardboard boxes, and then sealing them with tape. When the cardboard boxes were packed, they had to be put on the trolley. Sometimes goods were so many that five or six cardboard boxes would be put in each trolley. It would be hard to see the people in the front. "Once, I was passing by the door curtain of the shopping mall when distributing goods. The curtain was too heavy for me to pull, then someone helped me pull it. I expressed my gratitude to him immediately. I had thought he was a good guy, but it turned out to be a thief, because I found my mobile phone was stolen. It's really annoying." When I asked my father when was the moment he felt exhausted, he said with a sigh, "The busiest moment was when the business was good. We would be terribly busy. When we just finished goods distribution and delivery, an urgent call was made for more goods delivery. Sometimes I would throw the box down when I felt anxious. I just gave vent to my anxiety in this way, so I needed to pick it up by myself."

Since my parents were busy with their work, my younger brother was sent to the kindergarten when he was only two years old. He did not get used to the food and climate, so he spent a lot of time in the clinic in the first month. It was the time when the old shopping mall was to relocate, so how to deal with the stock was a hard nut to crack. Then my mother peddled loudly in front of the store till late every day. It was a long way from the shopping mall to kindergarten, and it usually took half an hour at least on foot. My mother said, "at that time I had to get up at 6 a.m. to cook breakfast. After I sent your brother to the kindergarten, I went to the shopping mall. Once it was snowing heavily, and it was below twenty centigrade degrees outside. Holding your younger brother in one hand, I took a lunchbox in another hand. Then I fell down and the lunchbox had been thrown away, but I held your brother tightly in my arm." That was a tough time for her.

After years of hard work from dawn to night, my father had a backache and my mother could not raise her elbow because of overwork.

Datong was far away from Wenzhou, so return tickets would cost us at least more than 2000 yuan. To save money, my parents did not come back until the Spring Festival approached. My parents would take me to the old house from grandma's family and lived there for a month at the end of a year. That old house had been empty for years, so it smelled of mildew and damp, which was hard to dispelled. Getting used to the heating in the northern

China, my parents felt uncomfortable with the chill in the south. There were also two or three families that raised chickens and ducks in the village, so there would always be fresh feces on the front door and the back door. As long as people didn't keep an eye on them, they would run directly into the house and made trouble. Moreover, the village was far away from the town, and the transportation was inconvenient. I lived in a small town with my grandmother, so I had been used to having a clean room, having a variety of snacks whenever I walked out of the door, and having access to stroll down the street after several minute's walk. The rural environment was not suitable to all of us who had lived elsewhere for some time. A clean, bright new house became our common aspiration.

With the prospect of buying a house, my father and mother worked harder than before. However, the stronger the demand was, the harder it was to do business. With the popularity of online shopping and the rapid development of e-commerce, the brick-and-mortar stores were declining. The business was not as good as that in the first three years, and a retail sale of 20,000 to 30,000 yuan a day had gone. We had spent nine years in this way. I was about to take the college entrance examination, but my grades declined greatly. My mother was concerned about me and all she wanted was to go back home and take care of me. My relatives happened to have a suite close to the high school I attended, and the price and location was also quite good. After careful consideration, my parents packed up and came back from Datong. They bought the house and began to decorate.

A few months later, we moved into a clean and spacious house, but the difficulty we faced was to make ends meet. Nine years of my parents' savings were used up on this house, and there were few job opportunities in my hometown. My parents were faced with an unemployment crisis as soon as they returned home. My father was not well-educated, so he had always been turned down when applying for manual jobs like delivery. Then he followed my uncle to Guangzhou and did mink-coat wholesale. He endured the backache to carry goods with dusty face, and slept in a small workshop at night. At Guangzhou in June, it was very humid and sultry. There were no air conditioners in the factory and there were many mosquitoes. When my father had a video call with us, he always said that he couldn't bear staying any longer and wanted to go home, but he still kept his chin up. After working for half a year, the business didn't turn better, and he had worn himself out. My father had to rest at home for a year. My mother was introduced to work in a package factory which was not far from home. She worked there from 6 a. m. to 11 p. m.. Our whole family scaped a living by my mother's meager income. She grew thin visibly because of high-intensity work. When she came home at night, she often was too tired to say a word and fell asleep.

Nowadays, my father borrowed some money to buy a minivan to deliver goods. My mother needn't work late at night. Although we barely made ends meet and my father chain-smoked because of anxiety, I still believe that home will always be a happy harbor for us. Our family of four being together, the future is sure to get better.

素朴之心记家史

邱 闳

“每个人的人生都是一部独特的书”，这是人生丰盈、或曲折或多彩的一种常见比喻，至少，这比喻对有些人而言足可成立。当然，一部书的内容也可以压缩成一篇文章，比如韦红同学这篇2000余字《漫漫岁月起高楼》的家庭叙事。

这篇文章的主角是作者的父母，他们虽然是大时代下的小人物，也无有惊心动魄的传奇故事，却也有着足够的信息量。文章介绍了父母至今的人生履历，有基本的时间线，也有某些人生关键的细节描述，读后令人生发出颇多思量和颇多感慨。

有意思的是，韦红同学对其父母经历的叙述不急不躁，平静又不乏深情。作者的母亲，无疑是一个经历坎坷又坚强的女性，无论情路历程还是生活历程，曲折而丰盈。母亲是村长的女儿，但上世纪70年代的村长，似乎并不拥有过多的经济特权和身份优势，所以，作为村长女儿的母亲，从小便辍学而选择打工谋生，但也因为这样的选择，使得母亲有着更强的求存欲望和拼搏努力，走出山村，去大城市寻求更适合或更美好的境遇。在城市里，她也算如愿找到了自己的爱情和工作，回家结婚生子，为人妻，为人母，日子按照预设的轨迹运行，却不幸遭遇了一场失败的婚姻。这使得她再次走出乡村，走向城市，也找到了第二次婚姻。尽管夫妻恩爱，但物质生活依然捉襟见肘。由此，作为一个时代剧变中的女性，她毅然选择工作上的自主独立。通过多年的坚持和打拼，小有斩获。而韦红的父亲，同样努力经营事业，屡败屡战，与命运对赌，依靠不懈努力改变现状。

对于平凡的小人物而言，这样的经历和努力，无疑也充满了跌宕起伏的剧情，也正是由这样千千万万种不同又相似的剧情，才荟集成改革开放时代的鸿篇巨制。

尤其令我欣赏的是，作者对父母婚史或者说情史的叙述传达，是如此平和本真。比如，母亲年轻时生活的艰苦和颠沛，曾经遭遇到的情变，母亲离异的经历，以及相差14岁的父母年龄，这于某些世俗观念，都是一种不愿启齿的不堪甚至“家丑”，但在韦红的笔下，却是如此坦然，如此诚挚，难能可贵。

虽然，这篇短文并不属于文采斐然的文学性作品，在语言上也不具有多大的吸引力，但我以为，记叙类文章，内容为王，有“故事”的内容就是值得咀嚼的意涵。记录历史，最有价值的是不带有多少情绪和艺术渲染的陈述。也许作者并没意识到这样的“技巧”，但相由心生，文由情生，一颗质朴的心，便能暗合了这样的技巧法则。

或许，也恰是因为作者平静而素朴的叙事笔调，读来尤显生的沉重，也复得活的释然。

（策划人、媒体人、诗人，居宁波）

故事

杭州

韦红（新闻学专业 192 班）

漫漫岁月起高楼

1972 年，伴随着一声响亮的婴儿啼哭，安徽省黄山市歙县杞梓里镇车田村村长的女儿出生了。而这位被村长小心翼翼地抱在怀里的女婴，就是我的母亲。

妈妈 13 岁读完小学后就在家帮忙干农活，一直到 21 岁，她的姐妹提出来杭州打工，外婆不同意，因为当时出来打工的大多是男生，但是妈妈坚持出来，外婆拗不过倔强的母亲，最终还是同意了。

而在母亲出生的 14 年前，杭州市上城区小营巷的一位木工家庭里，我的父亲出生了。爸爸初中毕业于杭州第十中学，毕业后在杭州罐头食品厂打零工，当时的工资是 8 毛钱一天。爸爸在 21 岁的时候进入了杭州市上城区第二建筑工程公司工作。

妈妈 21 岁从安徽来到杭州，在饭店里打工时认识了她的第一任丈夫，他是一位厨师长，两人相识相恋，最后回到男方老家千岛湖结婚并生下了她的第一第二个孩子。

在母亲 26 岁的时候，千岛湖涨了大水，淹没了家里的房子，政府补贴了 1 万元造房子，房子造完后她的第一任丈夫提出要去外面工作，而妈妈就留在了千岛湖。结果过了一年外出打工的丈夫竟然杳无音信，后来妈妈才知道他在外面找了个女人，并且生下了一个私生子，妈妈得知此事后愤怒、绝望却又无可奈何，最终起诉离婚。母亲把姐姐带回安徽老家交给外婆抚养，自己带着离婚得到的赔偿金回到杭州打工。

而我的爸爸21岁进入杭州市上城区第二建筑工程公司工作后，单位推荐他进修建筑工程预决算，爸爸欣然接受，认真学习了两年后开始跟着师傅跑工地进行实地学习。

1988年爸爸又进入了华日冰箱厂，在基本建设科任副科长。做了一年副科长后爸爸觉得差不多已经积累了一定的技术知识与管理经验，他打算开始自己创业。

于是1989年爸爸办理了离职手续，和朋友一起开始研究市场需求、原料价格、商业结构等等，最终爸爸拿着之前工作存下来的钱创办了一个公司，名叫意达工贸公司，并且有了自己的核心商业团队。爷爷奶奶也给了爸爸一笔钱表示支持，爸爸就用这笔钱买入了各种仪器设备，开始生产并销售各种玩具。当时爸爸销售的玩具正好迎合了市场的需求，产品的销量持续走高，爸爸的事业蒸蒸日上，同时公司的楼层也越来越高。

与此同时，妈妈不甘心没文化，于是拿着补偿金的一部分钱报名读了成人学校，开始学习文化知识。妈妈在学校认识了去那儿找好朋友的我爸，巧的是，妈妈的老师就是爸爸的好朋友；更巧的是，爸爸对妈妈一见钟情，开始了对妈妈热烈的追求。妈妈在相处的过程中也被爸爸打动，虽然两人相差了14岁，但是爱情战胜了一切。外公外婆一开始也因为爸爸的年纪十分反对，但是还是被爸爸的诚意打动了。最后爸爸妈妈结婚并生下了我。

婚后妈妈在家带了我一段时间，但是不习惯不工作的日子，于是又进入了一家电线厂工作，工资是月结的，多劳多得，所以妈妈拿过高薪，也拿过低薪。但是好景不长，没过几年厂子倒闭了，妈妈和姐妹们又辗转找到了一家医药公司上班，但是待遇就没有电线厂那么好了。据妈妈回忆，这个公司天天加班，更过分的是加班的时间越来越晚，从五点到六点，又从六点到七点……最后妈妈为了照顾我还是决定辞职换一个工作。

在妈妈辞职后，爸爸的公司也出现了危机。从台湾进口的IBS塑料原材料由于国际因素价格大幅度上涨，从一开始的1万元左右一吨猛地翻了倍，成本过高，且市场趋于饱和，供过于求，造成产品大量滞销，亏损越来越多。最终在2006年，爸爸与合作伙伴商量，决定结清工人们的工资后关闭公司。

家里一下子陷入了经济问题的漩涡之中。

爸爸的公司关闭之后，各方面压力都一下子气势汹汹地扑来。首先是奶奶生病住院了，每个月都要支出一笔巨大的医药费；其次是我的教育费用，这时的我已经要步入小学，还报了一堆价格昂贵的兴趣班；除此之外家里还有各种开销，每笔钱都足够让父母皱眉头。

妈妈靠着做一些手艺，比如做花、刺绣等勉强维持着日常开销，但是爸妈却出现了观念上的矛盾，外公因病去世了，爸爸家里人也不是很喜欢妈妈，各种问题都累积到了一起，从没见过妈妈哭的我在看到她和爸爸吵完架后第一次见到她抱着我哭了。

后来爸爸权衡之下还是决定拿出做生意赚来的钱又投资了朋友的网吧，妈妈也考取了美容师资格证，拿着自己多年存下来的钱开了一家化妆品店。开店的同时，妈妈又自学考上了成人大学，还考出了高级茶艺师的证书和保险销售从业人员资格证，妈妈靠着这些证书还能一边开店一边做别的业务。

2016年，父母觉得我已经长大了，就和我沟通他们想要离婚的事，我虽然一开始很难过，但也表示理解。最终，两人在2016年协议离婚。

两人离婚后爸爸继续做投资，妈妈又开了一家旅游店，旅游行业需要经常用到电脑录入信息，而妈妈又是刚转行，为了快速掌握电脑知识，妈妈常常一坐就是一下午。

妈妈的人缘不错，很多在妈妈那里买过化妆品的客人也愿意再来妈妈这里报名参加旅游项目，她们来过的人觉得不错，又介绍朋友也来，于是妈妈旅游店的生意也一直在变好。

最近因为疫情的原因，旅游业遭受冲击，妈妈的旅游店生意有一定的损失，好在万达广场免了一个月的租金，多多少少还是起到一些补偿作用。也多亏了疫情，忙碌了好久的妈妈终于可以停下工作好好休息一下了。

爸爸妈妈的事业都蒸蒸日上，我相信一切都在向好的方向发展。

我的妈妈也靠着自己的努力买了辆车，并且计划再开几家分店，未来几年再在杭州买套房子。

漫漫岁月起高楼。作为大时代里的小人物，我们幸福并感激着。

Hangzhou
Wei Hong (Class 192, Majoring in Journalism)

One's Good Life Comes from His Striving

Chetian village was located in Qizili Town, She County, Huangshan City, Anhui Province. In 1972, with a loud baby crying, the daughter of the village head was born. She was cradled by the village head in his arms with great care. This baby girl was my mother.

When my mother was thirteen and graduated from primary school, she began to help with agricultural work at home till she was twenty-one. Her elder sister proposed to work in Hangzhou, but my grandmother disagreed because most of the people who went out to work were boys at that time. However, my mother insisted on going out for a job. My grandmother was unable to talk her out of it, so finally she had no choice but let her go.

14 years before my mother's birth, my father was born in a carpenter's family in Xiaoying Lane, Shangcheng District, Hangzhou. He graduated from Hangzhou No. 10 Middle school, and worked as an odd-job man in Hangzhou Cannery factory. At that time, his salary was eighty cents a day. He joined The Second Construction Engineering Company in Shangcheng District at the age of 21.

My mother came to Hangzhou from Anhui at the age of 21. When she worked in a restaurant she met her first husband, who was a chef. They fell in love with each other and returned to his hometown, Qiandao Lake. They got married and my mom gave birth to her first and second child.

When my mother was 26, the water in Qiandao Lake rose greatly and flooded their house, so the government subsidized them 10,000 yuan to build a new house. After the house was built, her first husband said that he wanted to work away from home, so my mother stayed at home. Unexpectedly, no news had been received from her husband for a whole year. Later, my mom found that he had an affair with another woman and gave birth to an illegitimate child. She was furious and desperate. However, she had no alternative but to sue for divorce finally. She took my sister back to her hometown in Anhui and asked my grandmother to raise my sister. She returned to Hangzhou to work with the compensation she had received from the divorce.

As for my father, after he worked in the Second Construction Engineering Company in Shangcheng District, Hangzhou, at the age of 21, he was recommended to study the financial budget and final accounts of the construction project by the company. He accepted it gladly and began to follow "shifu" (the most popular form of address among workers) for field study in the construction site after two years' learning.

In 1988, my dad entered Huari Refrigerator Factory, and worked as a deputy section chief in the construction department. One year later, he felt that he had accumulated enough technical knowledge and management experience, and he planned to start his own business.

In 1989, he processed the resignation procedures and began to research things like the market demand, raw material price, and business structure with his friends. After that, he started his own company, which was named Yida Industry Company, with the money he had saved from his previous salary. He also had his own core business team. My grandparents also gave a sum of money as their support to him. He used it to buy various instruments and devices to produce and sell all kinds of toys. At that time, his toys happened to cater to the market demand. As a result, the sales continued to rise and his career was booming. Meanwhile, the building of the company was higher and higher.

At the same time, my mom was unwilling to be illiterate, so she signed up for an adult school with a part of the compensation and began to study. It was in that school that my mother met my father who went there to find his good friend who happened to be my mom's teacher. Coincidentally, my father fell in love with my mother at first sight and began to pursue her with great enthusiasm. My mother was moved by him when they got alone with each other. Although the age gap between them was as large as fourteen years, love overwhelmed everything. My grandparents disagreed at the beginning because of my dad's age, but they were moved by his sincerity. Finally, my parents got married and gave birth to me.

After marriage, my mom took care of me at home for a period of time. However, she felt that she did not get used to the days without work, so she went to work in a wire factory. The salary there was paid monthly, and the more she worked, the more she earned. Therefore, sometimes she got a high salary and sometimes a low salary. However, good times didn't last long. The factory went bankrupt after a few years, so my mom and her sisters tried hard and found a new job in a pharmaceutical company, but the salary there was not as high as before. According to my mom, they were asked to work overtime everyday in that company. What couldn't be borne was that the time they got off work was getting later and later, which was put off from five o'clock to six o'clock, and then from six o'clock to seven o'clock. Finally, my mom decided to resign and looked for another job in order to take care of me.

However, my dad's company went into crisis after my mom had resigned. The price of IBS plastic raw materials imported from Taiwan had soared due to international factors. The original price of 10, 000 yuan per ton at the beginning had been doubled suddenly, which resulted in high cost. Meanwhile, the market had become saturated and the supply exceeded the demand, so a large number of unsaleable goods caused more and more losses. Finally, in 2006, my father decided to settle the worker's wages and closed down the company after the negotiation with his partners.

Our family was suddenly trapped in a whirlpool of economic problems.

My father was overwhelmed by all kinds of pressure suddenly after his company closed down. To begin with, my grandma fell ill and was hospitalized, so a large amount of medical fees should be paid every month. Then it was my educational fee. It was time that I should go to primary school and had signed up many expensive extracurricular classes. In addition, there were various expenses in the family, each of which cost enough to make my parents worried.

My mom made do with our daily expenses by making some crafts, such as making flowers and embroideries. But some conceptual contradictions had occurred between my parents. My grandparents passed away because of illness. Also, members from my dad's family didn't like my mother very much. All kinds of problems had accumulated together. It was my first time to see my mother cry. She hugged me crying after she had a quarrel with my dad.

After considering the pros and cons, my dad decided to take out the money earned from the business to invest his friend's Internet cafe. My mom obtained the Beautician Qualification Certificate and opened a cosmetics shop with the money she had saved over the years. At the same time, she was admitted into college of continuing studies through self-learning and also got the Certificate of Senior Tea Sommelier and the Qualification Certificate of Insurance Salesman. With these certificates, my mom could manage the store as well as doing other business.

In 2016, my parents thought that I had already grown up, so they talked to me about their divorce. I felt sad at first, but I could understand them. They divorced by agreement that year.

After the divorce, my dad continued to invest while my mom opened a travel agency. Since information needed to be recorded by computers in the tourism industry and my mom just changed to this different profession, she often sat there for the whole afternoon in order to master computer knowledge quickly.

My mom was a people person. Many customers who had bought cosmetics before were willing to join tour in my mom's travel agency, and they would also introduce their friends to come after having a good experience. Therefore, my mom's business in travel agency has been better and better.

Recently, due to the COVID-19, the tourism industry was disrupted and my mother's tourist business also suffered a certain loss. Fortunately, the rent in Wanda square was exempted for a month, which was more or less compensated for the loss. Because of the COVID-19, my mother could have a good rest from busy work.

My parents' career has been on the up, and I believe that everything is developing in a good way.

My mother also bought a car through her hard work. She is planning to open more branches, and buy a house in Hangzhou in the near future.

One's good life comes from his striving. As common people in the great era, we are happy and grateful.

幸福感的累积

王　蔚

正如司徒青同学的妈妈所言,"我们现在的幸福生活,都是你爷爷、爸爸,祖祖辈辈慢慢累积起来的"。幸福从来就不会自己来敲门,它伴随着家国奋斗的历程,也因时代而变迁。

经济学的边际效用递减规律提醒我们,幸福感并不总是随绝对收入的增加而提高,"幸福悖论"常常存在。马斯洛需求层次理论认为,当人们对基本需求满足之后,人类对精神领域的需求就会显现。人民群众日益增长的美好生活需要随着时代发展而变化,人民群众的需要范围在扩大,质量在提升,人民的需要从"有没有"的温饱问题到"好不好"的发展问题。在困难时期,苦难和幸福是矛盾的辩证体,吃得苦中苦,方为人上人,生活的苦难可以磨练出幸福感。在发展年代,幸福感又如何体现?同时,相对剥夺感和社会比较理论也认为,有时候幸福是一种相对幸福,是相较于参照群体而言的,即通过与别人的比较产生愉悦感和快乐感。那么,在新时期如何通过彰显和践行公平、正义,守护社会正气也是幸福感累积所值得深思的问题。

不忘初心,方得始终。我认为司徒青同学的爷爷,那位有着 58 年党龄的老共产党员,在平凡的岗位上兢兢业业、勤勤勉勉的爷爷是幸福的。对美好生活的向往和全面小康的梦想是指引我们创造幸福、累积幸福的初心和光亮。

(浙大宁波理工学院传媒与法学院讲师,博士)

故事

宁波

司徒青(网络与新媒体专业 182 班)

慢慢累积的幸福

我的爷爷今年 87 岁,是一名有着 58 年党龄的老共产党员,曾是奉化区江口街道徒家村村民委员会副主任。在这个平凡的岗位上,爷爷一干就是 20 余年。他既是旧社会饥寒交迫的经历者,也是在党的领导下迈向幸福生活的受益者。

爷爷参加工作前在村里插秧、割稻、捡茶籽,每天的工分也就一毛五分钱,只能买一瓶橘子汽水喝。为了调动群众的积极性,生产大队长就鼓舞社员们开展劳动竞赛,大家干劲十足。生产队集体资产从无到有,给村里添置了新农具和耕牛,实实在在发展了农业生产。最令爷爷印象深刻的还是三年自然灾害时期,粮食最紧张的时候吃不饱饭,也睡不好觉,有一些年长体虚患上浮肿病的,因为得不到及时治疗抱病而去,但多数人都坚持下来了。

那时候闹饥荒,条件差,但爷爷仍以满腔的赤诚之心选择入党。发展党员要接受层层把关,不但要积极参加村党支部学习教育,还要日常表现积极,只有政治理论过硬、干事踏实、群众认可,才能成为一名党员。“广场上,十多个人排齐了在一起宣誓,那一刻很难忘的。”

上个世纪的 70 年代,爷爷所在的徒家村还没有便通的道路,村里决定征地造路,刚开始村民们的顾虑很多,都不愿意签字,给建设带来了很大的困难。爷爷和村主任认为在关键时刻要首先发挥带头作用。于是,他们召集家人开会,做通了家人的思想工作,带头先签字,不分昼夜地在田间地头给群众做工作。尽管遭到了不少白眼和冷漠,但在他的带动下,村民还是意识到建设道路的重要性。如今,道路越拓越宽,爷爷家就在道路的一侧,离村口不到 50 米的距离。爷爷会经常拿着把扫帚去村口的道路上清清尘,这么一干又是几十年。

1964 年,爷爷和奶奶结婚,之后有了 3 个儿子和 1 个闺女,爸爸排行老二。爷爷奶奶的收入所得养活家里 6 口人月月不够用,把家里的柴米油盐补齐,除去伙食上的开支,这样就已经所剩无几了,其他的开支只能量力而行。爷爷家背面的晒场上,总有一些卖菜卖肉的商贩每天清晨赶趟儿,家里为了改善伙食,有时也会备着点油腥儿,猪肉熬出猪油,用来拌饭或者再做成猪油渣,那是父辈小时候最喜欢的吃食。

从上世纪 50 年代一直到 90 年代之前，因为物资紧张，购买布料需要有布票，购买粮食需要用粮票，老百姓的穿衣吃饭所需的生活必需品都被计划着。直到 1982 年，实行了农村土地承包责任制，家里每个人都能分到一亩地。爷爷辞去村委会工作，开始从事农活。爷爷奶奶每天劳碌在地里，除了种些口粮，还种些油菜、甘蔗、香椿，养些蚕，不分昼夜地，“那时候村里根据每户人家的收成，到了年底就会有计划地分红，哪里还顾得上吃饭，只好没日没夜地在田里干活”。

后来孩子们渐渐长大，家里就支持着大伯上了大学。爸爸在初中就辍学了，跟着爷爷在生产大队勤恳工作了两年。

1983 年，爸爸 17 岁，奶奶认为爸爸需要学一门手艺，便让他跟着村里有经验的师傅学做零件生产。当学徒的日子是没有工资的，爸爸在师傅家的后院从一点一点学起，那时候师傅带着的 10 余个徒弟，16 岁到 25 岁不等，都是男孩。半年后，师傅带着爸爸进了工厂，奶奶每天拿一件不太体面的衣服给爸爸干活去，生怕他穿出几个洞回来。我的叔叔去开了货车帮人拉货，姑姑也早早去隔壁村的服装作坊里上班。

爸爸挣了些钱，加上爷爷奶奶的支持，花了 4000 元左右买了一辆摩托车，从镇里骑回来一路都是威风。但是后来因为事故，爸爸对摩托车产生了畏惧，再也不敢碰了。

1989 年，爸爸 23 岁，他用 7 年攒下的积蓄，从租房、置办设备开始，和当时一起的伙伴成立了一个小机械加工厂。考虑资金的投入和所需工人的数量，那时候选择机床就前前后后花了一个半月的时间。“前期几乎没有什么订单，我们也没有多余资金雇更多的工人，找了三个朋友来帮忙，只能先停掉一些机床的运转。”后来通过朋友的介绍，做了一个铝合金结构件套组大单，收入不少，随后订单也越来越多，工厂的规模越来越大。这中间确实吃了不少亏，所幸的是日子渐渐有了出路。

同年，爸妈经人介绍相识，妈妈那年 24 岁。

妈妈小学辍学。“那时候家里孩子多，没条件供养那么多孩子上学，女孩子就早早放弃读书了。”母亲从 16 岁开始就跟着外婆在服装厂工作。为了维持生计，她带着外婆亲手缝制的护身符，独自一人奔走在温州、上海等地寻找适合自己的工作。那时候家里的女性都是偏好服装这样细心的工作，妈妈在外打工期间，干的都是服装厂桌板工的活儿。妈妈说，在温州正式上班后，厂里面总共有 69 条厂规：上班时间不准迟到、不准旷工、不准睡等这一大串规矩。进入工厂车间里，只看到工人们都是拼命地埋头苦干，并没有稍微抬起头来看新人们一眼，仿佛都忙于手头的工作，以至于无暇顾及外面发生什么。

1987年，因为外公外婆身体不好，需要人照顾，妈妈只能辞去工作，回到老家，去了离家不远的服装厂上班。经人介绍，她和爸爸相识、相爱。

1990年，爸妈结婚。1992年，我的姐姐出生。1999年，我出生了。

2000年，爸爸觉得我们应该走出去。为了方便我们上学，也为了我们受到更好的教育，他决定从农村搬到城里，就在我1岁的时候，带着我们全家来到了奉化的锦屏街道。我家在学区里买了80多平方米的套房，妈妈做了家庭主妇，爸爸一个人承担起了养活全家的重担。

这些年里，爸爸稳步加购着在奉化区江口街道的工厂的新设备，厂房也在不断翻新。家里买了车，搬了新房，姐姐嫁了人。

妈妈说："我们现在的幸福生活，都是你爷爷、爸爸，祖祖辈辈慢慢累积来的。"

Ningbo
Situ Qing (Class 182, Majoring in Network and New Media)

Accumulative Happiness

My grandpa is eighty-seven years old. He is a Communist Party member for 58 years and was a deputy director of the village committee in Tujia Village, Jiangkou Street, Fenghua District. My grandpa had been working for more than 20 years in this ordinary post. He not only experienced hunger and cold in the old society, but also was a beneficiary of the happy life under the leadership of the Communist Party of China.

My grandpa transplanted rice seedlings, harvested rice and picked up tea seed before he began to work. Daily workpoints was fifteen fen which could only buy a bottle of orange soda. In order to arouse the enthusiasm of the masses, the production captain encouraged the commune members to carry out labor competitions and they worked energetically. Collective assets of the production team grew out of nothing, which enabled the village to buy new farm tools and cattle and truly promoted the agricultural production. What impressed my grandpa most was the three-year natural disaster period. During the time that food was far from enough, people went hungry and sleep badly. Some of the old and the weak suffered from edema disease and died without receiving timely treatment. Fortunately, most people survived.

Despite of famine and poor conditions at that time, my grandpa still chose to join the party with full sincerity. To be a recruiting party member, my grandfather needed to undertake tests at all levels. He should not only participate in the education of village party branch, but also perform actively every day. Only when he well mastered the political theories, worked earnestly and was accepted by the masses could he be recruited as a CPC party member. "On the square, it was very unforgettable that more than ten people lined up to take the vow together."

In the 1970s, there was no access to Tujia village where my grandpa had lived. The village decided to requisition the land and build roads. At first, the villagers had a lot of worries and were unwilling to sign their names, which brought great difficulties to the construction. My grandpa and the village director believed that party members should play a leading role at the critical moment, so they called a meeting of their families to communicate with them and got family members' agreement, so that their family members took the lead to sign their name first. They also tried their best to persuade the masses day and night in the fields. Although he suffered people's contempt and indifference, villagers finally realized the importance of building roads under his influence. Now, the road is wider and wider. My grandpa's house is on one side of the road and less than 50 meters away from the village entrance. He always took a broom to clean the road, which he kept doing for dozens of years.

In 1964, my grandparents got married, and they had three sons and a daughter afterwards. My father was the second child in the family. It was difficult to support the family of six every month with their income. It was almost used up after buying all daily necessities and food expenses, so they had to think twice before they bought other stuff. On the back of Grandpa's house was a threshing ground. There were always some traders who sold vegetables and meat every morning. To improve the family's food, they sometimes prepared some lard boiled from pork to mix rice or made cracklings, which were my father's favorite food when he was a child.

From the 1950s to the 1990s, because of material constraints, the purchase of cloth needed to have cloth coupons and the purchase of food needed food coupons. The necessities of daily life for the common people were planned. Until 1982, the rural land contract responsibility system was implemented and everyone in the family could be given a land of 666 square meters. My grandpa resigned from the village committee and began to engage in agricultural work. My grandparents worked in the field every day. Apart from planting some grain, they also planted some oilseed rape, sugarcane, cedrela sinensis and raised silkworm day and night. "At that time, according to the harvest of each family, the village would have a planned dividend by the end of the year, so everyone was too busy to think of meals and worked in the fields day and night."

Later, the children grew up and the family supported my uncle to go to college. My father dropped out of middle school. He worked hard with my grandpa in the production team for two years.

In 1983, when my father was 17 years old, my grandma thought that he needed to learn a skill, so she asked my father to follow an experienced master in the village to learn how to produce parts. The days of apprenticeship were unpaid, and my father learned little by little in the master's backyard. At that time, the master had more than a dozen apprentices who were boys aged 16 to 25. Half a year later, the master took my father into the factory. My grandma took a suit of clothes that was not so decent, for fear that he would come back with a few holes on his clothes. My uncle went to drive a truck to help people pull goods and aunt also went to work early in the next village clothing workshop.

My father earned some money and with the support of grandparents, he spent about 4000 yuan to buy a motorcycle, riding back from the town disposedly. However, because of the accident, my father was afraid of motorcycles and did not ride it again.

When father was 23 years old in 1989, he used the savings of 7 years to rent a house and buy equipment. Then together with partners, he set up a small machinery processing plant, considered money invested and the number of workers needed. It took them a month and a half to choose the machine tools. "There were few orders in the early days, and we didn't have any extra money to hire more workers. We just found three friends to help, and stopped some machine tools." Later through the introduction of some friends, they finished a big order to made an aluminum alloy structural parts set from which they made a lot of money. Then they began to get more and more orders, and the size of the factory was getting larger and larger. They did suffer a lot in the middle, fortunately, life was getting better and better.

In the same year, my parents were introduced to get to know each other, and my mother was 24 years old that year.

My mother dropped out of primary school. "At that time, there were so many children in the family that they couldn't afford all of us to school, so girls had to give up studying early." My mother had been working with her mother's in the garment factory since she was sixteen. In order to make a living, with her mother's hand-made amulet, she went to Wenzhou, Shanghai and other places alone to find a suitable work. Women in her family preferred working in the clothing industry, which needs meticulousness. Therefore, all the jobs that my mother had done was inspection in a clothing factory. My mother said that after she officially worked in Wenzhou, there were a total 69 factory rules: don't be late, don't be absent, don't sleep and so on. Entering the factory workshop, the workers were working so hard that they didn't take a look at the new workers. They seemed to be so busy with their work that they had no time to pay attention to what happened outside.

In 1987, my mother had to resign from her job and came back to her hometown to work in a clothing factory not far from home because her parents were in poor health and needed care. Introduced by others, she met my father and fell in love with him.

In 1990, they got married. In 1992, my sister was born. In 1999, I was born.

In 2000, my father thought we should go out of the countryside. For the sake of our convenience to go to school so as to get better education, he decided to move out of the countryside into the city. When I was one year old, he took our whole family to Jinping Street, Fenghua. He purchased an entire suite which had more than 80 square meters in the school district. My mother was a housewife and my father took the burden of the whole family on his own.

Over these years, my father continually bought new equipment for the factory in the Jiangkou Street, Fenghua District. The factory has been constantly renovated. In addition, we bought a car and moved to a new house. My sister got married.

My mother said: "the happy life we are now living is slowly accumulated by your grandfather and your father, and it has been accumulated for generations."

好时代不会亏待每一个努力生活的人

郭雪飞

社会转型的大时代，剧烈的变动很容易给人以不确定感。对于普通人来说，一方面是不知道也不清楚时代会对个人命运产生什么样的影响，另一方面是我们必须要做点什么，尤其是要通过个人的努力来对冲快速变化的时代所带来的各种不确定性，因为这时候我们的努力恰是我们所能够抓住的东西，它像主心骨一样让我们感到心安。

吴梦婧同学的叙说，为我们展现了她的父母在年轻时代的努力和拼搏。尽管年代有差异，但是他们还是像极了《平凡的世界》里的孙少安孙少平兄弟，经过改革开放的洗礼，他们对新生活充满了年轻人所特有的热情与渴望。但是要看到，在上个世纪 90 年代初，中国改革正经历一个特殊的阶段，困惑与希望交织在一起，不管是在城市还是在农村，都面临何去何从的问题，这些问题，正有待于一位老人以他的南方之行去燃旺改革开放的热情和火焰。

但作为基层单位的乡村，对于承接这次改革浪潮显然准备还不足，即便是在杭州附近——这个在今天看来已属中国最为发达的地区。彼时，距离杭州不远处邻省的苏南和苏北，关于发展模式的差异和争论正渐渐地开始冒头，不久之后，这一轮改革在中央的全力推动下，将彻底改变中国的面貌。

吴梦婧同学所提到的“纺织热潮”发生在上世纪 90 年代中后期，改革开放总设计师邓小平南方谈话之后，中央开始布局，强力推动新一轮改革，江浙一带作为重点地区率先兴起家庭工厂。吴梦婧的父母也成为这只弄潮大军中的一员。如果没有意外，他们的辛苦和努力必然会使这个家庭成为这一轮突飞猛进运动中的受益者。从文字中，我们无从得知作者舅舅的意外去世与其父母 20 万外债之间的关系，但毫无疑问，这一次意外打击对这个刚见起色的家庭影响是致命的。

从文中看得出作者是个很敏感很懂事的孩子，她亲证了父母在大时代下的命运轨迹，既能体谅他们的不易，同时心怀希望。其实这正是一个好的时代所应有的状态——尽管没有让每个人都成为命运的宠儿，但是也没有抛弃每一个人，依然有能力让每个努力奋斗的人过上安定的小康生活。

（吉林省长春市媒体人）

故事

杭州

吴梦婧(网络与新媒体专业182班)

没有迈不过去的坎儿

我的爸爸1967年出生于杭州市萧山区义桥镇的一个小村庄——河西村，他不是独生子，爷爷奶奶膝下还有一个儿子，也就是我的小伯父。

爸爸很喜欢读书写字，现在空闲时间也会在家里练字。爸爸作为家里的长子，7岁就开始搬着小板凳爬上土灶做饭炒菜，接送小伯父上下学，放学和周末做完作业就帮着爷爷奶奶去地里浇菜施肥。爸爸干完活以后，每天唯一的学习时间只有晚上8点到10点，因为那时候村子穷，都是在10点实行统一断电的。断电后，幸运的话能碰到家里刚过完节的情况，爸爸可以点燃祭祖用剩的小半截蜡烛继续学习一小段时间。

1992年，1967年出生的爸爸和同样也是1967年出生的妈妈在经过5年的同窗情谊和两年的恋爱之后修成正果，喜结连理。因为他们两个都属羊，所以我们老吴家还有个不成文的规定：不吃羊肉。

爸妈刚结婚的时候，爷爷奶奶造了一间占地面积仅50平方米的三层小平房，准确地来说，是为爸爸和小伯父一起造的房子。虽然是有了一间新房，与此同时也留下了3万元的债务，而且当时我姐姐也刚出生，家里开销大，“那是挺困难的一段日子了，但是我们至少有一个自己的小家呀，而且你姐姐的出生让我们第一次尝到做父母的滋味，也还挺幸福的。”妈妈戴着老花镜，一针一线地缝着我小外甥的毛袜，笑着回忆道。

2005年，也就是在我出生后的第5个年头，我刚上幼儿园，姐姐刚上初中，妈妈正好有了时间可以干活。那几年正值“纺织热潮”，于是爸爸妈妈在刚还完当年造新房的债务没多久时，咬咬牙问亲戚朋友借了2万元买了两台纺织机，在家前面的平地上建起了一个小厂房，开启了他们的纺织创业。这次创业还算顺利,两年来陆陆续续还完债务也存了点小钱准备用来盖新房子。

世事难料,2007年由于大舅舅的意外离世,我们刚有点起色的经济状况又一落千丈,爸爸妈妈又背负了20万元的债务。无奈之下,造新房子的计划只能推迟,为了尽快还清债务,爸爸妈妈用前两年存的仅有的积蓄又买了四台纺织机,并且扩建了原先的厂房。但是二次创业并没有想象中的那么顺利,由于后来出现了一种可以电脑操作的纺织机,我们厂房的这些老式人工操作的纺织机已经落伍了,原先为我们提供货物单的大厂渐渐地给的单子少了很多,而将大部分单子都给了有新型纺织机的厂家。以前每天晚上都伴着机器运作的声音入睡,我还总在餐桌上抱怨,现在因为没有单子所以只有两三台机器在运作。我隐隐约约知道,爸爸妈妈好像正在经历一段困难的时光。

2012年,爸爸妈妈选择卖掉小厂房里的6台纺织机,当年前前后后花了近10万元买的机器最后却在"纺织低潮"期间以不到2万元的价格被回收。那之后,爸爸妈妈在家的日子就很少了,他们奔波着去各种工厂面试,由于年纪大的缘故,只能在工厂干搬运货布、管理机器、清洗布料的辛苦活。那时我刚上初一,每天早上出门前只能看到餐桌上妈妈留的早饭。用一个淘米的不锈钢漏筛罩住,上面贴着小纸条提醒我吃早饭。有时候大概是妈妈太累了起晚了,就会留几张零钱让我去学校门口买点早饭。晚上放学后我都是在学校外买张饼或者买个糯米饭吃完后再回家。因为当我做完作业上楼睡觉的时候爸爸妈妈还没回家。我在睡前会学着爸爸妈妈的样子,在米缸舀两罐大米,放在漏筛里这么揉搓几下,倒入电饭煲,像妈妈一样用食指试试水,因为不会做菜,就打个鸡蛋加点水蒸在电饭煲内架上,然后在纸条上写下:"爸爸妈妈,电饭煲里有饭记得趁热吃,你们辛苦啦。"那时候住的还是老房子,家里没有多余的房间,我和姐姐住一屋,爸爸和妈妈住一屋,我们的房间是连在一起的,爸爸妈妈进房间会路过我们住的屋。有几晚睡眠浅,在半夜迷迷糊糊能听到开房门的声音,然后感觉有人在帮我盖被子,摸了摸我的头发,然后轻手轻脚地进了里屋。

2015年,用前几年生产布料存的积蓄,加上这几年爸爸妈妈早出晚归打工赚的钱,再问亲戚朋友借了一笔钱,我们终于盖起了新房子。盖房子那段日子,爸爸每天白天去基地帮着提砖、砌墙,因为爸爸年轻的时候干过水泥工,而且爸爸自己帮着干,可以少付一个工头的工资。傍晚等工头们下班,爸爸就扛着水枪爬上去,从最高一层开始,一层一层地给墙面冲水,防止第二天太阳暴晒使墙面出现裂缝。有一次我牵着家里的狗狗去新家玩的时候,看到爸爸站在窗边,两眼无神地望着窗外,嘴里叼着一根烟,手上拿着他那个沾满茶渍的杯子,地上一地的烟头。见我来了,忙掐掉嘴里的烟,若无其事地把烟头踢到角落里,抿一口茶水笑着对我说:"你来啦,来,我带你去你的房间看看。"说着便把我推搡着出了房间。经过大半年的建造和装修,我们一家终于在年底举办完简单的乔迁酒席之后搬进了新房子。那天晚上,我们 4 个人坐在二楼的平台上,吹着冷风,喝着热茶,一起说笑着。奇怪的是,明明是寒冬腊月冰冷刺骨的节气,我们一点都没感觉到冷意,反而觉得很暖很安逸,大概是因为那壶热茶?

现在已经是 2020 年了,虽然我们家发生了很多事,但都是过去式了。爸爸妈妈背负的债务也还得差不多了,2016 年家里还进行了二次装修,举办了姐姐结婚的喜宴。在今年的 5 月中旬,姐姐经过十月怀胎生下了一个可爱的小外甥,为我们的全家福新添了一个新成员。2017 年家里买了车,我去上学也不用挤公交了,并且在今年摇到号以后又换了一辆新车。家里的生活条件越来越好,我再也不用像小时候那样,在超市看到喜欢的零食不敢驻足,爸爸妈妈赚钱太辛苦了,我常告诫自己不能乱花钱。现在可以经常去超市买喜欢的零食,去商场买好看的衣服,餐桌上也多了很多以前舍不得买的昂贵的食材。一切都在往好的方向发展,就像爸爸常说的并且也一直在践行着的那样,“只要笑一笑,没什么大不了”。微笑不仅是一种表情,更是对生活的一种态度。微笑着面对生活中的困难,全家人风雨同舟,就没什么过不去的坎。

Hangzhou
Wu Mengjing (Class 182, Majoring in Network and New Media)

There Is No Insurmountable Obstacle

My father was born in a small village called Hexi in Yiqiao Town, Xiaoshan District, Hangzhou City in 1967. He is not the only child of my grandparents; he also has a younger brother.

My father liked reading and calligraphy. He often practiced his calligraphy whenever he had leisure time. As the eldest son in the family, he learned to cook standing on a stool, picked up his younger brother from the school, and helped his parents to water and fertilize vegetables after classes were over or finishing homework on weekends. After a day's toiling, my father could only study between 8 to 10pm; in this poor village, power was cut off after 10pm. After ancestor worship ceremonies during traditional holidays or festivals, there were some left-over stumps of candles, with which my father could keep on learning for a while.

My parents, both born in 1967 (the Year of Sheep), used to be classmates for five years and finally got married after being in a relationship for two years. My family even observed an unofficial rule of not eating mutton because they were of the same zodiac sign of sheep.

When my parents just got married, my paternal grandparents built a three-story house covering an area of 50 square meters for them, or to be more specific, for my father and my uncle. The newly built house left my family a debt of 30,000 yuan and the daily expenditure increased along with my elder sister's birth. "Although it was a difficult period of time, at least we had a family of our own. And along with your sister's birth, we have tasted the happiness of being parents," recalled my mom while sewing socks for my little nephew with her presbyopic glasses on.

In 2005, or five years after my birth, I went to kindergarten and my sister became a middle school student. My mom finally got some spare time to earn money. Since there was a "textile rush" back at that time, my parents bought two looms with 20,000 yuan borrowed from relatives and friends and started up their textile business shortly after they paid off all their debts for building the house. The small factory was located in front of our home. This attempt was smooth and we finally managed to clear debts and even saved some money for building a new house.

Yet you can never tell what is waiting for you. In 2007, my mom's eldest brother passed away unexpectedly. His death left us a debt of 200,000 yuan, which hit our life hard financially. We had no alternative but to postpone our plan to build a new house. To pay off the debt as quickly as possible, they bought four more looms and extended the factory with some extra money they had saved over the past several years. But the second attempt wasn't as smooth as expected because our obsolete manual looms were gradually taken place by computerized ones. Our former major clients withdrew most of their orders and turned to those factories using more advanced machines. In the past, I would always complain at table about how the roaring machines had influenced my sleep. But later because of a lack of orders, only two or three looms were in operation. I vaguely knew that my parents seemed to go through a hard period of time.

In 2012, my parents chose to sell six looms at less than 20,000 yuan during the low ebb of the textile trend. They originally cost us nearly 100,000 yuan. After that, my parents barely stayed home because they had job interviews in different factories. They ended up doing laborious work like carrying cloth, cleaning cloth and managing machines since they were too old for other jobs. When I was in the seventh grade, every morning I could only see the breakfast left by my mom on the table covered by a stainless-steel colander and a notice reminding me to eat breakfast on time. My mom sometimes left me some change to buy breakfast when she slept in after a day's hard work. I would buy a pancake or glutinous rice outside the school for dinner because they probably hadn't returned home when I went to bed. I would rinse two bowls of rice in the colander and measure the water level using my index finger after pouring the rice into the rice cooker. I didn't know how to cook, so I would put a bowl of egg with water in it on the top of the rice cooker to make steamed egg custard. I would leave a message saying "Daddy and mommy, don't forget to eat it when it's still hot. Many thanks to your hard work." Back at that time, my sister and I shared one room and the other bedroom belonged to my parents. They needed to pass our room before them entered theirs since the two bedrooms were next to each other. Sometimes I was in a light sleep, and I could hear them enter our room, tuck us in, touch our hair and then tiptoe out of the room.

In 2015, we finally managed to build a new house with savings from manufacturing cloths, salaries my parents made by working in factories and some money they borrowed from relatives and friends. My father was a plasterer when young, so he carried bricks and built walls during the construction process, which could also reduce the labor cost. Every day after builders finished their work, my father would flush walls with water from the top floor to the house base so as to avoid cracks from sun exposure the next day. I once took our pet dog to visit our new house, and found my father, holding a stained tea cup and smoking, looking out of the window blankly. Cigarette ends were all over the ground. Having seen me, he immediately stubbed out the cigarette and kicked the end into the corner, acting like nothing had happened. He sipped tea water and said to me with a smile,

"There you are. Let me show you your room." I was then bundled out. The building and decoration lasted for half a year, and we finally moved into the new house after a simple housewarming banquet at the end of the year. That night, we, braving the cold wind and drinking hot tea on the balcony of the second floor, talked gaily and it was strange that we didn't feel cold at all on that freezing winter day. Probably it was for that kettle of hot tea.

Time flies and it is the year 2020 now. We have gone through a bunch of things but they are what have happened in the past. My parents debt has been paid off, and we renovated our home once again and celebrated my sister's wedding ceremony in 2016. My sister gave birth to an adorable baby boy in mid-May this year, adding a new member to this family. We bought a car in 2017, thanks to which I no longer needed to take a bus to school, and we bought another car after winning the license lottery. A better-off life means I now have the luxury of buying my favorite snacks in the supermarket, a thing I never did when I was a kid because I knew my parents' money was hard-earned and would consequently restrain myself from binge spending. Besides, I can now buy beautiful clothes and eat nutritious yet expensive dishes. Every aspect of life is improving, just as my father's motto goes, "There is nothing so serious once you smile," a principle my father has always followed and practiced. Smile is not just a facial expression, but a life attitude. There is nothing insurmountable as long as the whole family go through ups and downs with one heart and with a big smile.

生活之树常青 奋斗之人不息

贠馨怡

生活最大的魅力来自于源源不断的生命力，尽管时间不断地流逝，时代不断地变化，我们也难免面临物是人非的伤感，但在每一次的变化中都蕴藏着巨大的生命力，为我们带来全新的生机与活力，也更好地激发着我们的斗志。

《习近平谈治国理政》（第3卷）中提到："生活之树常青。"这棵郁郁葱葱的常青树背后，是一个又一个奋斗不息的普通人。

从努力工作买上村里第一台电视机的爷爷奶奶，到开拓进取创建第一间商铺成功创业的叔叔婶婶，再到团队协作完成人生中第一支广告的"我"，钟齐淇同学笔下的家庭故事，让我们切实感受到，在过去近百年的历史进程中，这个浙江家庭中三代人身上所焕发出的"生命不息奋斗不止"的伟大精神。

第一次无疑是美好的，在生活中很多人面临第一次的挑战时，都会抱着满腔的雄心壮志，自信满满，拼尽全力。困难的，不是对第一次抱有满腔的热情，而是对后面的每一次都满怀希望，并且不遗余力。人生的魅力不在于生活本身有多么精彩，而在于我们对生活倾注了多大的热情。相信我们激情满满地去拥抱每一天的太阳，面对生活中的每一件小事，永不停歇自己前进的脚步，生活也会随着变得更加迷人和灿烂。

生活的脚步不断向前，每一天都焕发出新的美好，可爱的人们，请不要停下自己的脚步，用奋斗的双手去迎接更美好的明天吧！

（浙大宁波理工学院传媒与法学院网络与新媒体专业2018级学生）

故事

杭州

钟齐淇(网络与新媒体专业182班)

每一个第一次都是非凡

外公和外婆都在桐庐县新合乡的一个小村庄里长大。如果说要用一个词语来形容他们的爱情,那一定是:日久生情。

年轻的时候,小外公小外婆在外屋生活,外公外婆就在里屋生活。到后来,外公外婆自己存钱在村子里造房子,房子的结构大都保留到了现在,里面的陈设随着时代的进步却有了翻天覆地的变化。以前的水泥地被大理石覆盖了,木制的楼梯被重新建造得焕然一新,房间里的老式木板床也早就变成具有现代化风格的席梦思大床。

外公小学毕业后就选择去大队开拖拉机,帮助村子运输一些柴火、石头。运一车石头有两块钱的工资,而当时的肉价是在几分钱。除了钱之外,有时候运一车石头出去,拖拉机带回来的也有可能是一车的甘蔗、橘子。外婆是在高中毕业后去到了乡里的水电站工作。水电站的建造与工作使用,外婆都参与其中。一直到水电站被私人老板买走后,年过半百的外婆才离开。

我们家有一台老式黑白电视机,静静地躺在杂物间的角落里。经常听外婆提起:"我们家是村子里第一个买电视机的,当年买电视是因为桐庐县城里有一个活动政策。可以分期支付,每个月交25元钱,交满12个月便可以购买一台电视机。"这第一台电视机是一台12吋的黑白电视,虽然经过几十年的更新换代,电视机越换越薄,屏幕越换越大。但是这个老家伙一直安安静静地呆在我们家中。当时买一台电视机算得上是整个村子的大事了。外公外婆将电视机放在家门口,只要《霍元甲》的开头曲一响起来,屋里屋外的半个村子的人就会一下子安静下来。

在我小的时候,爸爸妈妈忙于工作,我有很长一段时间是和叔叔婶婶住在一起的。叔叔大学毕业之后,选择到坐落于杭州萧山的圣奥公司工作。在自身不断的努力与积累之下,他成为圣奥的财务总监,在21世纪初期,年薪就高达几十万。这是一个在外人看起来十分光鲜并且舒适安逸的工作。然而对于叔叔而言:"想到之后几十年一直在同一个工作环境做着类似的工作,不禁觉得生活有些枯燥。”在他的认知中，“生活是需要去闯一闯的”。

婶婶在读完大学之后，兜兜转转也进入了圣奥公司工作，在市场部历练了几年之后，积攒了一些创业基金与工作经验。在兴趣的支持下，婶婶走上了与家具“相爱相杀”的道路。第一间商铺是在杭州的和平广场，选择了她自己相对了解的板式家具。在婶婶创业不久后，叔叔选择辞掉高薪的工作，与其共同奋斗。除了板式家具，两人的专业范畴也渐渐开始涉及欧式、轻奢等家具。除了学习家具知识，也不放过室内设计部分。两个人共同协作，在杭城的数十年，家居事业做得也还算是顺利。

然而在众人眼中创业顺利的他们，并没有将人生挑战止步于此。他们将那一句“生活是需要去闯一闯的”做得淋漓尽致。在杭州从事家具行业近10年后，叔叔和婶婶又做出了一个不一样的选择，他们选择回到叔叔的家乡——金华浦江。2018年，他们在浦江的和平南路创建出一家属于自己并且符合自己心目中所想的家居馆。浦江因浦阳江而美，杭璞家居因浦江而生。杭璞国际家居的营业面积达2500多平方米，不仅经营美国舒达、唯煌、羽珀等数十家中高端家具品牌，而且具备有专业的软装、全案装饰设计师，可以为顾客提供专业的服务。自杭璞家居落地的那天起，叔叔和婶婶便又多了一项需要他们悉心呵护、经营的事业。

婶婶也曾很多次问过叔叔：如果有机会可以重来，你还会选择卖掉在杭州的三套房子，去浦江投资创业吗？叔叔的回答让我记忆深刻：可能还是一样会犹豫，但最后应该还是会选择卖房去投资创业，钱在自己手中固然安稳，但一想到后面的生活可能就是这样平平淡淡的，就会觉得生活缺点意思。生活还是需要闯荡的，可能对我来说，有波澜的人生才有意义吧。

有时候安逸会成为前进的障碍，而我们需要做的就是拒绝安逸，敢于挑战。

我出生于2000年。生长在浙江杭州无疑是一件很幸运的事情：从小到大，我不需要担心衣食住行。比起外公外婆他们需要自己攒钱读书，我考虑更多的是：妈妈今天能不能带我去买新衣服？爸爸有没有给我买芭比娃娃？在我的生活中没有为生存奔波的压力，如果一定要说有压力，可能学习是那为数不多会对我的生活造成压力的事情。

今年我参加了大广赛，由于爸爸妈妈十几年来对我的保护，使我对自己有莫名的自信。最开始我信心满满，认为只要我肯努力，没有什么问题是解决不了的。但是大广赛就好比一场马拉松，当还没跑到一半的时候，我就因为创意不断被否决而担心，创意所遇到的瓶颈也让我整个人感到焦虑。曾经我以为的团队精神都是存在于文字中，这一次却让我感触最深。我们进行了无数次发散思维训练，在这些思维网络中寻找灵感，在拍摄制作中进行反复修改。我们在困难面前，凝聚力量共同面对。在最绝望的时候站在一起，互相安慰。

这是我第一次正式拍摄的一个广告，中间有过许多操作性困难、时间调节困难，我有过很多抱怨，也生过很多闷气，但是当我看到最终剪辑出来的成片时，这些想起来有些痛苦的回忆好像都不算什么了。当我经历过由几次通宵拍摄、无数次头脑风暴、小组成员互相依靠、互相鼓励后，我发现结果真的不重要了。因为这个作品是我们用心去完成的，我第一次体会到"过程大于结果"。

人生就是由无数个第一次组成的，因为有了第一次，后面才会有那么多丰富多彩的故事。每个第一次都需要不凡的勇气。

第一台黑白电视机承载着外公外婆对过去的回忆，第一间商铺是叔叔和婶婶创业梦想的启航，而我现在所要做的，就是勇敢地迈出第一步。

Hangzhou
Zhong Qiqi (Class 182, Majoring in Network and New Media)

Every Endeavour Is Extraordinary for the First Time

My grandparents grew up in a small village in Xinhe Village, Tonglu County. If one sentence should be used for describing their love story, that is, love grows over time.

When they were young, my grandparents lived in the outer room while their grandparents in the inner room. Afterwards, my grandparents saved money to build a house in the village. The structure of the house had been largely preserved till today, and the furnishings have seen profound changes as time advanced. The former concrete floor was covered with marble; the wooden staircase had been rebuilt and the ancient plank bed in the room had long been replaced by a modern Simmons bed.

After graduating from primary school, my grandfather chose to drive a tractor to help the village deliver some firewood and stones. He could get an income of two yuan for a load of stones, and the price of meat was roughly a few fen. In addition to money, sometimes a load of stones was carried out, and a load of sugar cane and orange might be brought back. After graduating from high school, my grandmother went to work at a hydropower station in the village. She was involved in the construction and operation of the hydropower station. It was not until this place was bought by a private owner that my grandma left when she was over 50.

We had an old black-and-white TV in the corner of the utility room. I often heard my grandmother say, "our family was the first in the village to buy a TV set because of a preferential policy in Tonglu County. They could pay in installments with 25 yuan per month, and if the installments had been paid for 12 consecutive months, then they could buy a TV set. The first TV set was a 12-inch black-and-white one. Though the TV set had been replaced by the thinner one and the bigger one over the decades, it had been kept all the time in our house. It was a major event to buy a television in the village at that time. My grandparents put the television in the doorway, and as soon as the theme song of TV series "Huo Yuanjia" rang, half of the villagers inside and outside would quiet down.

When I was young, my parents were busy with work, so I lived with my aunt and my uncle for a long time. After graduating from the university, my uncle chose to work for Sunon Group Co. Ltd., located in Xiaoshan District, Hangzhou City. With his own continuous efforts and accumulation, he became the financial director of Sunon Group. In the early 21st century, his salaries were as high as over hundreds of thousands of yuan per year. It was a glamorous and comfortable job for the outsiders. For my uncle, however, "life was a little dull considering that he spent the several decades doing the similar jobs in the same workplace." In his mind, "life was about tempering oneself in the world."

After graduating from university, my aunt also went to work for Sunon Group. She had accumulated some venture fund and working experience in the marketing department within a few years. Because of her personal interest, she hit the road of doing furniture business. The first shop was in Hangzhou's Peace Square and the business scope was the panel furniture that she had known well. Soon after my aunt started her own business, my uncle chose to quit his well-paid job and worked with her. In addition to the panel furniture, their professional categories also gradually began to touch the European-style, light luxury and other types of furniture. They not only learned the furniture knowledge, but also interior design. They cooperated with each other and these decades have witnessed a relatively smooth development of their household furnishing business.

Successful as they were in the eyes of the public, they did not stop their life challenge. They gave a vivid and luscious performance of the saying that "life is about tempering oneself in the world." After nearly 10 years in the furniture industry in Hangzhou, they made a unique choice. They chose to return to their uncle's home—Pujiang County, Jinhua City. In 2018, they set up a household furnishing on Heping South Road in Pujiang, which was their own and in line with their vision. As Pujiang was beautiful for the Puyang River, so Hangpu Home was named after Pujiang. With the business area of more than 2500 square meters, Hangpu Home not only held dozens of medium and high-end furniture such as Serta in the US, Weihuang and Yupo in China, but also boasts specialized designers in soft-loading and full-case decoration, thus providing superior service for customers. From the day that Hangpu Home settled down, my uncle and aunt had a new business to run with their utmost care.

My aunt had also asked her husband many times that if he had the chance to do it all over again, would he still choose to sell the three houses in Hangzhou and go to Pujiang County to invest and start a business? My uncle's reply left a deep impression on me. Hesitation may linger, but I would choose to sell my houses to invest and start a business finally. Indeed, money was safe in my hands, but when thinking of the life behind me might be so insipid, I would feel that it lacked something special. After all, life was about tempering oneself in the world, perhaps for me, cleaving waves would make life meaningful.

Sometimes comfort could be a barrier to progress, and what we needed to do was step out of the comfort zone and boldly go ahead for challenge.

I was born in 2000, in Hangzhou, Zhejiang, which was undoubtedly a very lucky thing. Since my childhood, I did not need to worry about the basic life necessities like food, clothing, shelter and means of travelling. Instead of my grandparents having to save up for school, I was more concerned about whether my mother would take me shopping for new clothes today and whether my father would buy me a Barbie doll. In my life, there was no pressure for survival; if it did exist, study might be one of the few things causing pressure in my life.

This year, I participated in the national advertising art design competition for college students. I felt strangely confident because of the care and protection from my parents over ten years. At first, I was full of confidence that as long as I worked hard, all problems could be solved. But this competition was like a marathon. When I hadn't been halfway through the competition, I was worried about the situation that my creativity kept getting rejected, and I felt anxious when my creativity hit a bottleneck. The team spirit I had believed was in the words, which left me the deepest impression this time. We had done countless divergent thinking training so as to find inspiration in these idea networks and we repeatedly revised when shooting the advertisement. In the face of difficulties, we gathered our strength to tackle them, and we comforted each other in lines to go through our darkest times.

This was the first time I had shot an advertisement, and I had encountered a lot of difficulties, including operation and time adjustment. I had complained and I had been angry a lot about it. However, when I saw the final cut of the advertisement, all these painful memories seemed to be nothing at all. After a few all-night shoots, a lot of brainstorming, much support and encouragement from my team members, I realized that the result really didn't matter. Because this advertisement was made with our dedication, this was the first time that I realized the fact that the process was more important than the result.

Life is made up of countless first-times. Thanks to the first-time, there comes so many colorful stories in the following. Every endeavor takes extraordinary courage for the first time.

The first black-and-white TV set carried my grandparents' memories of the past. The first shop set the sail for my uncle and my aunt's entrepreneurial dream. Now what I should do is take the first step bravely.

浪潮之巅,“地球村”外

王天娇

最近30年,全球化大潮几乎席卷了世界上每一个国家。空间、时间的边界都在迅速压缩,形成了所谓的“地球村”。

中国在改革开放的同时,搭上了全球化的快车,将种类繁多的中国制造输送到亚、非、拉、美、欧等各大洲。第一次让世界全面见识了中国制造的高效快捷与质优价廉。同时,越来越多中国人的生活也嵌入到世界大循环中——网络连通了一个个陌生的面孔,地域的边界正在消失。

作为全球化的主要受益国,中国凭借人口红利,在相当长的时间里,保持了经济的高速增长。这改变了很多人的生活。从旧有的城乡二元结构到迅速铺开的城市化进程。9000多万人从村镇走入城市。他们被裹挟在全球化浪潮中,见识了花花世界,也第一次体会到互联互通的网络技术、巨形城市之间的全球物流、以知识为基础的信息经济给生活带来的全面改变。

裹挟在快速的变革中,我们常常忘记那些被排斥在“地球村”外的人。他们依旧靠着简单、原始的手艺糊口;他们留在原地,过着与祖辈差不多的生活;他们只在政策性的变革迫降生活时,才被浪潮之巅的风暴边缘扫过,看一眼门缝里的“地球村”,说一句:哦,生活在变呢。

他们并非不想乘风破浪,只是他们看不见外面的翻天覆地。有人说,把他们关在“地球村”外的是贫穷,其实,贫穷的根源是教育。在这个信息就是资本、知识就是力量的时代,教育程度带来的信息沟、知识沟,不断扩大着不同受教育群体在信息接触、知识积累方面的差距。越有识者越能快速掌握新的信息传播技术,加快知识资本的变现;越有知识的阶层越能以较快的速度吸纳新的资讯,成为浪潮中的“弄潮儿”。

全球化、地球村、知识经济——所有这些热闹,都只属于一部分人。在浪潮之巅,“地球村”外,请不要忘记那些被折叠起来的、看不见的生活。

(广东外语外贸大学新闻与传播学院讲师,博士)

故事

金华市
余沁怡(网络与新媒体专业193班)

摸爬滚打半辈子

我很少与爸爸妈妈交流,我对他们前30多年的生活知之甚少,只能偶尔从他们口中听到:我们之前多苦啊,哪像你们现在这样幸福,还不知足。当我慢慢了解他们的人生轨迹时,我才能真正理解他们是怎么一步一步摸爬滚打给了我今天的生活的。

妈妈出生在浙江省金华市的一个小村庄——鞋塘,她是家里的老大,有一个弟弟。妈妈小时候家里比较穷,靠着大自然的馈赠吃饭。那个时候的孩子总是被迫成熟,需要承担家里的家务,还要帮爸爸妈妈赚钱,他们从小就承担了生活的重任。

初中毕业后,妈妈就没有再读书了,她去了金华市里的一个纺织厂上班,一个月工资两三百块钱,住在厂里的宿舍,经常要上夜班熬到很晚。那是家里最困难的一段时间,外公外婆赚不到什么钱,妈妈上班赚来的工资几乎全部都要拿回家,吃的是蒸的毛芋或茄子加酱油拌饭,过得很艰苦。之后妈妈用自己赚的钱买了一辆100多块的自行车,她很开心,这辆自行车也是她唯一能往返于工厂和家的交通工具。

在纺织厂干了4年之后,妈妈回了家,在离家比较近的一个饲料厂当了仓管员,但一年不到饲料厂就倒闭了,妈妈也因此丢了工作。外婆年轻时学过理发,妈妈也想去学,那也算是一门赚钱的手艺。于是她去了市里学了理发,学了一年多之后回到镇上租了一间房,和外婆一起开了一家小小的理发店。妈妈开理发店时,外公也在自家的田里种了葡萄,妈妈一家的生活从这时开始逐渐好了起来。

爸爸出生在金华的另外一个小村庄——胡塘,他是家里的老二,有一个姐姐和一个妹妹。爸爸小时候条件并不差,爷爷很会干农活,那时是种菜专业户,还上过报纸。爷爷有七八亩田,种四季豆、小青菜等,每天摘菜要摘二十几筐。在那个普遍一个家庭一年只能赚一两千的年代,爸爸家是村里的万元户。爷爷靠种菜养活了一家5口人,也靠种菜在省道旁边造了一幢150平方米的四层楼,在那之前,爸爸一家5口住在一个两层楼的用木板分隔一二层的老房子里。

12岁起，爸爸就骑自行车去乡镇上卖菜，初中读了半个学期就辍学回家了。他每天跟着爷爷种菜卖菜，起早贪黑，骑着自行车到90公里外的地方卖秧苗，路是砂石路，并不平整。爸爸喜欢炒菜，小时候想当厨师，跑去培训班交了钱，被爷爷抓了回来，因为家里种菜太忙了，不让去。就这样，他一直种菜，种到31岁，种了19年。

爸爸和妈妈很早就认识。两个村庄隔着不远，爸爸在镇上卖菜，妈妈在镇上理发，后来经亲戚介绍，两个人就在一起了，然后结婚，再然后有了我。结婚时，爸爸26岁，妈妈27岁。结婚之后，妈妈把理发店开到了省道旁边的房子里，爸爸继续种菜，日子过得虽然并不富裕，但也算不上差。

5年之后，田地被开发，爷爷的七八亩田全没了，爸爸结束了自己的种菜生涯，有了人生中的第一个大转折。因为征收田地，我们一家分到了十来万块钱，爸爸买了第一台汽车，五菱汽车，用来跑出租，帮别人拉货。就是指把货装在车厢里，然后他开车运到目的地，这个生意有风险，会被交警抓，爸爸曾经被抓到罚了一万多，一万多在当时已经是很大的一笔钱了。

葡萄上市时爸爸就到镇上收葡萄，拉到义乌农贸市场批发。那时我已经有一点点记忆了，卖葡萄时爸爸妈妈经常不在家。我小时候特别黏人，不想让爸爸妈妈走，他们就会答应给我带点东西回来补偿，我就会特别开心。他们一般傍晚的时候走，把葡萄从车上搬下来忙到地上，然后在地上摆一张凉席自己坐。我跟着他们去过一次，很快就在凉席上睡着了，他们却忙到了深夜。凌晨时我醒来，发现他们一晚没睡。

因为葡萄上市只有一个季节，而拉货也赚不到什么钱，爸爸和大姑姑在省道边的房子里开了一个饭店，大姑姑负责炒菜，爸爸负责打点，妈妈在另一间理发，生活也还过得去。饭店开了两三年，生意渐渐冷清，爸爸就把饭店关了，开了一个小便利店，在门口的空地上放了两张台球桌。我记得开业那天特别热闹，村子里很多人来了，还有我的小伙伴，爸爸还送了他们一点小礼物。小店不忙，爸爸有空时会教我打桌球，会去隔壁帮妈妈的客人洗头，爸妈晚上还会出去走走。因为利润低，爸爸做起了批发饮料生意，经常要装车出去送货，回来时总是很累，也渐渐没有了陪我们的时间。

2013年是我们家很紧张的一年，我还在读小学，某个星期五我放学回家，发现妈妈不在，我问爸爸妈妈在哪儿，爸爸说妈妈在医院里。幸运的是妈妈的肿瘤是良性的，我已经忘了那次我到底有没有跟爸爸去医院，只记得后来几次去看望妈妈时，她很虚弱，我说不出什么安慰的话，却很心疼，也很害怕。妈妈的手术很顺利，因为身体原因她出院后把理发店关了，和爸爸一起经营批发部。

爸爸的生意越做越大，雇了小工，也添置了货车用来运货，可他跟妈妈越来越忙，起早贪黑，每天都累得筋疲力尽。几年后爸爸在离家不远的地方租了一个七八百平方米的一楼厂房开了超市。为了照看超市，他们逐渐把家搬到了超市的一个小房间里，修了一个小小的厕所和厨房。爸爸又租了一个很大的仓库放货，一直努力地奋斗着事业，直到现在。这几年我们家的条件在逐渐变好，但我看着爸爸妈妈的白头发越来越多，越来越疲惫，我意识到他们为我，为弟弟，为这个家付出了很多，我却不能帮他们分担。

爸爸小时候家庭条件还算好，所以他会在有条件的情况下去追求自己想要的东西，他会开半个小时的车只为了吃一碗好吃的面，会偶尔出去旅游放松自己，而妈妈因为小时候家里很拮据，她经常会想的是怎么节约，怎么省钱，不会要求生活品质。我很想告诉他们，对自己好一点，多去享受享受生活，去做自己想做的事情。

爸爸说，下半年要把老房子拆了重新造，做三个卧室，我们一家人住进去，开始我们的新生活。

Jinhua
Yu Qinyi (Class 193, Majoring in Network and New Media)

Struggling for Half a Lifetime

I know very little about the life my parents led thirty years ago for I seldom talked about it with them. Occasionally I would hear them say, "What a hard and miserable life we used to lead. It was nothing like the happy life you are having now. But your generation just takes it for granted." It was not until I came to know their previous life experiences that I truly understand how they underwent trials and tribulations to offer me current life conditions.

Born in a small village called Xietang which was located in Jinhua City, my mom had a younger brother. Since her poor family lived at the mercy of nature, she, like other kids at that time, was forced to grow up and bear the heavy life burden prematurely, such as doing chores and making money.

My mom discontinued her study after graduating from the junior middle school and she found a job in a textile mill where she earned a monthly salary of 200-300 yuan. Living in the dormitory, she had to stay up because of night shifts. Life was extremely hard during that period of time. Sending back almost all the salaries in order to support the family for my grandparents barely made any money then, my mom lived on steamed taros or eggplants with soy sauce. She was happy when she was finally able to buy a 100-yuan bicycle, the only vehicle she could use to get to and from her home back at that time.

After working in the textile mill for four years, she resigned and became a warehouse keeper in a feed mill near home. Unfortunately, she lost the job less than one year later when the mill was out of business. She, knowing that my grandma learned hairdressing skills when young, decided to earn her living as a hairdresser, too. She later opened a small hair salon with my grandma after receiving training in town for over a year. My grandpa also started growing grapes at that time, and that was when life gradually improved.

My father, born at another village called Hutang in the same city, was the middle child between two sisters. Actually, my father lived in a much better condition than my mother since his father was good at farm work, especially growing vegetables, so good that his name even appeared in newspaper articles. My grandpa's eight-mu land could produce vegetables like French beans and pakchoi cabbages enough to fill a score of baskets every day, earning them an annual income of tens of thousands of yuan while an average household then could earn only several thousand yuan. By growing vegetables, my grandpa fed a family of five and built up a four-story house covering an area of 150 square meters next to the provincial highway. Previously they lived in a two-story old house separated by wooden planks.

My father biked to the town to sell home-grown vegetables since 12, and dropped out of the junior middle school after half a semester. Ever since, he bent his efforts to grow and sell vegetables, toiling from dawn to night. Sometimes they had to sell rice seedlings after biking 90 kilometers on rough gravel paths. My father, interested in cooking, once paid fees to a vocational school when young in order to realize his dream of being a chef, but was asked back by my grandpa in the end because my grandpa was up to his neck with all the vegetable business and couldn't do without my father's help. Consequently, he continued growing vegetables until 31, spending 19 years in the field.

My parents, living in two nearby villages, had known each other for a long time before they got married. They both worked in the town—one as a vegetable vendor and the other hairdresser. They became a loving couple after being introduced by a relative. My dad and mom got married at 26 and 27 respectively and finally had me. My mom later moved her hair salon to that four-story house next to the provincial highway, while my dad continued his vegetable business. We were not rich, but life was not so bad then.

Their first turning point of life came five years later as my father ended his farm life after my grandpa's eight-mu land was requisitioned for city development. With land compensation of over 100,000 yuan, my father bought his first Wuling (a Chinese household auto brand) to do car hailing and freight businesses. He would send goods loaded in the car to the destination. It was actually risky and he was once fined 10,000 yuan, a load of money back at that time, after being caught by a traffic policeman.

When it was grape season, my father would buy grapes in huge quantities from growers and then sell them wholesale in farmer's markets in Yiwu. I was old enough then to remember they were seldom at home because they were so busy selling grapes in markets. As a clingy child, I didn't want my parents to leave, so they would mollify me by promising me some nice gifts as a compensation. They usually left at dusk, and unloaded grapes onto the ground when they arrived at the market, after which they sat on a mat put nearby and started waiting for buyers. I joined them once and I quickly fell asleep while they continued into night. I woke up in the small hours of the next day, only to find they didn't sleep at all.

My father and his elder sister started the restaurant business in the house next to the provincial highway for a living since my father didn't make much money by selling grapes or delivering goods. My aunt cooked while my father was in charge of logistics. With money my mom made by running a hair salon, we made a modest living. The restaurant didn't last long—it was closed a couple of years later for not making many profits. It was soon replaced by a convenience store with two billiard tables in front of the door. I still remember it was busy and lively on the first day of business, with so many villagers coming to send their congratulations. My friends also came and my father gave them some small gifts. When it was not busy, my father would teach me billiards and help with hair washing in my mom's salon next door. They would also go for a walk after dinner. My father later started the wholesale business of soft drinks for low profits in running the convenience store. He had to deliver goods on a regular basis and always returned home tired. Gradually he even didn't have time to accompany us.

2013 was a difficult year for my family. One Friday I returned home from the elementary school, only to find my mom was not at home. My father told me that she was in hospital when asked where she was. Luckily the tumor was benign. My memory failed me as to whether I went to the hospital with my father that day; I only remember when I visited her later, I felt sad seeing her so frail-looking and also very scared even though I didn't say anything to comfort them. The operation to remove the tumor was successful. Out of the concern for her health, my mom closed the hair salon after leaving hospital and started helping my father with the wholesale business.

The business grew so rapidly that my father later hired helpers and bought a truck for goods delivery. They got busier, and consequently exhausted from working day and night without much rest. A couple of years later, my father turned a rented factory with an area of 700-800 square meters into a supermarket. In order to keep an eye on the supermarket, they moved into a small room there and even built a bathroom and kitchen. They later rented a huge warehouse for goods storage and kept on their business until now. Life has been improving in recent years at the expense of my parents' gray hair and poorer health. Though clearly aware of the sacrifice my parents have made for me, for my brother and for the whole family, I am unable to share the burden.

My father, having a relatively decent life when young, will pursue whatever he wants dearly when the conditions allow. For example, he will drive for half an hour to enjoy a delicious bowl of noodles or have a relaxing trip. On the contrary, my mom, getting used to a poor and hard life ever since she was a child, will take frugality instead of life quality or enjoyment as her life motto. I really want to tell them that they deserve to treat themselves, to enjoy colorful lives and to do whatever they want.

My father once said in the second half of this year he would demolish the old house and build a new one with three bedrooms, where we could start a new life.

财富密码的代际传承

孙长夫

如果研究代际传承，温州人是最好的样本。

温州人经商是父传子、兄带妹，老乡带老乡。每一个个体的努力，积蕴成集体的意识，并将这意识写进温州人的DNA当中。

林同学写这《摸爬滚打生意经》时，他在追忆母亲艰难跋涉的经商人生，而我看到的是他通过这追忆完成了财富密码的代际传承。

这密码写的是什么？就是他所描述的父辈的坚持、追索、承受、开拓。

他叙述的口吻充满了骄傲与自豪，证明代际传承的完整。

我们所能观察到的，完整的代际传承促进人群进步，推动地域发展。

而代际传承断裂之处，也会造成落后与失望，在现在的某些落后地区，首先是代际传承的断裂，儿女不以父辈为荣，人群暮气沉沉，生命的存在显得没有意义，也就意味着精神与经验都没有良好的传承。

时间的绵延传承了生命的意义，在生命存在意义的追问中，我们可以看到不在场的未来人和在场的现代人的关系。一代人生命的过程成为下一代人的追忆，这追忆就是一连串密码，开启DNA中储存的生命信息，踏上进化的阶梯。

（吉林省长春市媒体人）

故事
绍兴
林温铋(新闻学专业192班)

摸爬滚打生意经

永嘉县位于瓯江下游,濒临东海,与温州市区隔江相望。我的母亲出生于千石村的一户普通温饱的家庭,在这片取其“水长而美”之意为名的土地上长大。

“以前哪有这么好啊,你们这代人就是太幸福了,所以身在福中不知福。”母亲望着桌上的饭菜出了神。

小时候母亲眼看家中贫困,外公需要四处借钱供她们上学,心思便不在读书了,觉得出门赚钱更能减轻家里的负担,所以没有继续上高中,这也是她辍学打工的直接原因。“那时候只觉得赚钱很有意思,不知道读书也等于赚钱,想想也蛮可惜的。”她说,她也早已习惯了做一个生活庸碌、夜以继日,生意一不好就会有危机感的小老板。

“那几年不知道打过多少份工,什么都干过,重活也全是我干。印象最深的就是打烊时要把一块块的门板推上去关好,那是我的身体完全无法承受的重量。其他人的个子都比我要高,不知比我要轻松多少。但是我不敢说啊,只能硬撑。”母亲说,每推一块板,都要用尽全身的力量,这对于一米五五个子的她来说,已经是极限了。

确切地说,母亲是从1992年订婚后开始创业的。这年,她20岁,和父亲相识,转而开了间服装店,父亲则在爷爷的投资下和大伯继续经营拉链厂。

母亲说,每到进货的时候,就要去到温州市区的批发市场,途中花费两个小时。期间除了骑自行车,还乘渡轮,回来的时候要带着很重的货物,都是自己一批一批搬运的。“有次在路上还被小偷偷了1200多块钱,那时候的1200块多值钱啊,买一间小平房都绰绰有余了!心里又气又急,可是又没什么办法。哎,太无助了!一路哭着回到家,整个人都是懵的。”为了不影响生意,母亲都是早上四五点就起床,急着进完货赶回来看店。那几年,她也都是只身一人坚守着门店。

两年后,相爱多年的母亲和父亲终于修成了正果。母亲也转行开了影碟带出租店,希望能够安心地过段衣食无忧的日子。但好景不长,拉链厂最终还是亏损,欠下了整整40万元的债,影碟带出租店也相继关了门。

做了妈妈的母亲才顿悟家庭走入了困境，必须要承担起养家的责任。“本来是没有概念的，觉得女人只要养活自己就可以了，而且你爸爸当时的家庭算是比较好的，就想着爸爸办了拉链厂也可以养我，谁知道拉链厂亏了，还欠了一屁股债。后来因为成了家，有了责任感，才知道要继续赚钱。”

2003年，父亲又在爷爷的安排下，去意大利帮三爷爷打理服装生意，母亲则在家帮衬，国内发柜。

次年，母亲再次选择了外出。虽然心中极其不舍，但她还是忍痛丢下了年幼的我，独自提着一个行李袋，顶着凛冽的寒风，只身一人来到了绍兴柯桥的轻纺城市场。还是当初的卖布生意，阿姨的父母真是母亲的贵人。

从此，我们一家人分隔三地，各居一方。

在帮忙打理门市的过程中，母亲非常努力地学习，很快便上了手，成为店里的股东。“刚来柯桥的时候的确什么也不会，一切都需要从零开始，但是一心就想着要好好学。每天都要不停地打电话，把样品送给各个服装厂打样，把新产品送到服装市场推销。虽然有时候会看到他人的黑脸，但还是会不厌其烦地给他们说产品的优点。结果连股东爷爷奶奶也没想到，我能一个星期就把所有的事情都掌握，他们对我的出色表现非常认可。”母亲若有所思地说着，似是对当时的苦日子还回味无穷，我捕捉到她眼中闪过的一丝自豪。

“那时的条件还很艰苦，没有装空调，夏天住在6层顶楼的小房间睡觉的时候，半夜都要起来冲澡，实在是太热了。”最终，母亲还是坚持下来了，她的努力打动了几个大厂的老总，其中几个一直到现在还与我们保持着合作关系，是我们的稳定客源。客户对母亲的评价是：讲信誉、重品质，像男人一样，说一不二。

那年，父亲在国外赚到的工资加上母亲在柯桥赚来的分红，整整花了两年的时间，才把债连本带利地一一还清。这曲折坎坷的年头总算是跌跌撞撞地过去了。

为了不让我吃苦，来柯桥的第二年，母亲顶着爷爷奶奶反对的压力，坚决把我从老家接来身边上小学。

最初，母亲只有20%的股份。但慢慢地，母亲通过自己的努力，凭借自己善良忠实、吃苦耐劳的精神赢得了爷爷奶奶的信任，依靠自己出色的工作能力，获得了爷爷奶奶的赏识。

合伙6年后，爷爷奶奶最终将整个店面全权托付给了母亲——也就是2010年，妈妈终于有了属于自己的门店。每每回想起来到柯桥的这些年，母亲常会跟我说：“十几年前，拿着一个行李包，孤军奋战地创业，一步步地摸索、请教，再一点点靠自己的双手，用自己的勤劳和智慧，得到了现在的一切和一个小有成就的公司，现在想来还历历在目呢。”这一路筚路蓝缕，可算是苦尽甘来了。

2008年，母亲买了车，又在2013年买了房。而前不久，我们买下了第二辆车、第二套房。这一切，全是她靠着自己的双手，一天一天、一点一点打拼出来的。

10年过去，在2020年的今天，父亲和母亲依然一起经营着自己的小公司，我们的生活过得有滋有味，算得上是安居乐业了。在辛劳之余，我们也慢慢在奔着小康生活而去。

母亲在创业的路上遇到过很多困难，却总是迎难而上、艰苦奋战，她一直是一个敢拼敢闯、吃苦耐劳、又有主见的人。从一无所有，到有车有房，这拼搏奋斗的一生，她自己动手，丰衣足食，撑起了这个家，着实让人佩服。她的故事不算特别，尝起来像一碗淡汤，但却有着自己独一无二的味道。

Shaoxing
Lin Wenbi (Class 192, Majoring in Journalism)

A Struggling Journey of Business

Yongjia County is located in the lower reaches of Oujiang River, and bordered on the East China Sea, facing the urban area of Wenzhou across the river. My mother was born in a moderate family in Qianshi Village and brought up on the island whose name implied the meaning of long and beautiful river.

"Our generation didn't have such a good life in the past. Your generation just doesn't know what a good life you are living." My mother, staring at the meals on the table, was lost in thought.

When she was a child, her family was so poor that my grandpa had to borrow money all around for the tuition fee of the children. On seeing this, my mother was in no mood for studying at school. She thought she could reduce the family burden by working early, so she quit from senior high school later, which was also the direct reason for her drop-out to work. "At that time, I found making money was interesting. Unfortunately, I had no idea that studying was one way of making money," said my mom. She had already got used to being a self-employed laborer who was busy day and night and had the sense of crisis when business went poorly.

My mother said, "I couldn't remember how many jobs I had done in those previous years because I almost did jobs of all kinds, even the muscular labor. What impressed me most was the slab doors should be put in the right place when it came to the closing hour, because I couldn't bear such weight of the slab door. I was shorter than other people, so it was much harder for me. But I didn't dare to tell them that I couldn't make it but hold on to place them." Therefore, my mother, 1.55 meters in height, placed each door slab with all her strength, which had already reached her utmost limit.

In fact, my mother began to start up her own business after the engagement in 1992. She made acquaintance with my father at the age of 20. After that, she ran a clothing shop, and my father continued his business in zipper factory with my uncle, which was invested by my grandpa.

My mother said that it cost her two hours each time to reach the wholesale market in the urban area of Wenzhou to buy clothes. She went there by bike and then ferry. Moreover, she had to carry those heavy goods back by herself. "There was a time that my 1200 yuan was stolen on the way. At that time, 1,200 yuan was valuable enough to buy a small bungalow! I could do nothing but got angry and anxious. I was so helpless that I cried all the way home and was totally at a loss." In order not to affect the business, my mother woke up at four or five clock in the morning and returned back hurriedly to run the shop after replenishing her stock. In those few years, she was the only one who ran the shop.

Two years later, she married my father and opened a DVD rental store instead, hoping that they could live a life with nothing to worry about. But good days didn't last long, the zipper factory was at a loss of 400,000 yuan and the DVD rental store also collapsed after that.

After being a mother, she suddenly realized that it was necessary to assume the responsibility when the family was in trouble. "I had thought that all women should do was support themselves, and your father's family was relatively good, so he could support me by running the zipper factory. Nobody could have known that the zipper factory would be at a loss and in debt. It was after I got married that I raised my sense of responsibility. Then I knew that I must continue to earn money."

In 2003, under the arrangement of my grandfather, my father went to Italy to help my granduncle to run the clothing business, while my mother helped at home to deliver goods from China.

In the second year, my mother chose to go out again. Despite all her reluctance to leave, she bore her sadness and left me, who was a small child. In a day with freezing wind, she went to the China Textile City Market in Keqiao, Shaoxing alone with only a duffel bag. She sold cloth there, and my aunt's parents were such good helpers to my mother.

Since then, our family had been forced to live in three different places.

When helping to run the business, my mother studied very hard, so she could deal with it soon and became a shareholder in the store. "When I first came to Keqiao, I really didn't know anything. Everything needed to be started from scratch, but I wanted to master the way of doing business. I made phone calls again and again, sending samples to various garment factories for proofing and sending new products to the clothing market for sale every day. Although sometimes some people might be unfriendly to me, I was never tired of talking to them about the advantages of the product. As a result, even your grandparents did not expect that I could master everything in one week. They recognized my outstanding performance very much." My mother said as if she was deep in thought, lingering on the memory of those hard days. I caught a glimmer of pride in her eyes.

"The conditions at that time were very difficult. There was no air conditioner. When sleeping in a small room on the 6th floor in summer, I had to get up in the middle of the night and take a shower because it was too hot to fall asleep." In the end, my mother stuck with it. Her efforts touched the bosses of several big factories, some of whom have maintained cooperative relations with us until now. They are our regular customers. Their evaluation of the mother was a person of credibility, quality, integrity and a person of her word.

It took two years to pay off the debts one by one with the wages my father earned abroad plus the dividends my mother earned in Keqiao. These twisting and bumpy years finally had been stumbled through.

In order to keep me away from hardship, my mother brought me over from home to study in the primary school in Keqiao, though my grandparent's strongly disagreed on it.

At first, my mother only had 20% of the shares. But gradually, through her own efforts, she won the trust of my grandparents with her kindness, honesty, hardiness, and patience, she won my grandparent's trust. With her excellent ability in work, she gained my grandparent's recognition.

After 6 years of partnership, my grandparent's finally entrusted the entire store to my mother in 2010, so it was in this year that my mother had her own store. Every time she thought of the years in Keqiao, my mother would often say to me: "a decade ago, I started a business alone with only a duffel bag in hand. I groped and asked for advice step by step; I got everything we have now and run a successful company by my own hands through hard work and wisdom. Every time I think about it, it leaps before my eyes." It was hard but rewarding.

My mother bought a car in 2008 and a house in 2013. Before long, we bought our second car and second house. All these were earned by herself little by little.

Ten years has passed since my parents ran their small company together. Up till now in 2020, our life is very enjoyable, and we live and work in peace and contentment. Despite hard work, we are gradually heading for a well-off life.

My mother had encountered many difficulties on the road to start a business, but she always faced them and worked hard to settle them. She has always been a person who dares to fight, endures hardships and works hard, and she has a mind of her own. She started from nothing to having a car and a house, and she worked on her own to obtain ample food and clothing so as to support this family. I really admire her for her painstaking striving in life. Her story is not special. Although it tastes like a bowl of thin soup, it is unique.

049

观察

艰难方显勇毅，磨砺始得玉成

胡鹿鸣

站在“两个一百年”的历史交汇点，看倪淼丽奶奶跨越两个世纪的人生历程，“原味鱼”“童养媳”“文盲”等词的概念之于现代的孩子，也许只能去小说或课本中寻找答案了。“开拖拉机、务农、黑白电视、烟囱、蜂窝煤……冬储大白菜、炉子烤白薯、生火取暖……”这些或许也只能留在笔者的回忆里。习近平总书记在2021年的新年贺词中自豪地向全国人民及全世界宣告，中国的“十三五”圆满收官，“十四五”全面擘画。我国在世界主要经济体中率先实现正增长，预计2020年国内生产总值迈上百万亿元新台阶。粮食生产喜获“十七连丰”。“天问一号”“嫦娥五号”“奋斗者”号等科学探测实现重大突破。我们还抵御了严重洪涝灾害，广大军民不畏艰险，同心协力抗洪救灾，努力把损失降到了最低。2020年，全面建成小康社会取得伟大历史性成就，决战脱贫攻坚取得决定性胜利。历经8年，现行标准下近1亿农村贫困人口全部脱贫，832个贫困县全部摘帽。这些伟大的历史成就，现代人民的幸福生活，对比于老人上世纪前半段的艰苦生活，真的是发生了翻天覆地、不敢想象的巨大变化。习总书记说得好，“艰难方显勇毅，磨砺始得玉成”。我们在忆苦思甜中，更珍惜当前幸福生活的来之不易，青年学子们更要努力成长为社会主义现代化国家的建设者，一代人接着一代人，勇往直前，继续奋斗！

（浙大宁波理工学院传媒与法学院党委副书记、纪委书记）

故事

湖州

倪森丽(网络与新媒体专业193班)

奶奶走过的艰辛岁月

我的奶奶今年86岁,经历了抗日战争、解放战争、新中国成立、改革开放,到2020年全面建成小康社会,可以说是见证了近百年历史。但是每每听她讲起她的故事和人生我总会鼻头一酸,奶奶总说我们这代人真的是太身在福中不知福了,在她的故事里我难以想象那些艰苦的岁月她们是怎么熬过来的。

奶奶1935年出生于湖州市长兴县吕山乡许家村,那时候家里很穷,她3岁时妈妈便去做奶妈。奶奶几乎就是她的奶奶养大的。奶奶家就住在河边,经常去河里捉鱼吃,有了长期吃"原味鱼"的经历,奶奶至今都不爱吃鱼,也经常开玩笑似地说自己小时候吃够了鱼。

奶奶有好几个兄弟姐妹,但是家里已经难以抚养这么多孩子。那时候"重男轻女"的思想还是根深蒂固。为了让男孩子可以上学读书,在她7岁的时候奶奶的父母把她给了别人家去做女儿,可是没多久那人家生了个孩子,奶奶竟逐渐变成了佣人。8岁开始割草,一直割到13岁,她一个人要养活13只羊和1头黄牛。奶奶是个文盲,她根本没有机会去读书,有时候割草经过学校听到读书声真的很羡慕,她说经常会趴在窗户边上偷看,所以啊她也经常告诫我有这么好的机会和条件就更应该好好读书好好珍惜。

有一天把一只羊放丢了,谁曾想回到家后养父母用那种桑树枝干鞭打她后,把她锁在放柴的屋里什么都不给她吃,让她饿了一天一夜。实在受不了这样的生活,奶奶在13岁时逃回家里。

奈何家里实在没有能力抚养她,所以她爸爸又把她做"童养媳"送给另一户人家,去之后也还是没日没夜地干活。放羊,割草,洗衣烧饭,大大小小里里外外的活都是她干。后来因为长期泡在水里干活,有一只腿发病肿胀又没钱去看病,最后整个小腿连着脚全部肿胀着直到现在。现在爸爸姑姑总说带她去看看,她怎么也不愿意,就说反正这么大岁数了也不痛没什么大碍没必要再去看了。

也就因为肿胀的腿,那户人家就嫌弃不要了。18岁的奶奶又回到了娘家,可没过多久她又被送去一户新的人家当"童养媳",听到这些我真的眼泪止不住,本应该是花季少女的年纪，却被百般嫌弃当作物品一样送来送去，内心该有多么坚强才能撑过来。奶奶依稀记得四五岁时每当日本兵进村时他们便在荷塘边挖个大洞躲在里面，尤其是黄花大闺女一定要藏好不然就会被抓走。

20岁来到了同一个乡的龙溪村爷爷家，可奶奶还是没有过上好日子。爷爷一家本也是靠田为生。奈何来的那一年1954年正好遭遇百年一见的大洪水，长江中下游出现了近100年间最大的洪水，造成了严重的洪涝灾害。只有一层的泥土房早已被水包围，好多东西都给泡烂了。这样的洪水对庄稼是致命的打击。田没有收成，荷塘也没有藕，大家每天过着有上顿不知下顿的生活。

爷爷很老实，但是脾气很好，对奶奶很好。我的太奶奶也就是爷爷的妈妈在他7岁的时候就不在了，所以婆媳矛盾那种事情奶奶没经历，所以她说能嫁给爷爷还是件幸运又幸福的事情。虽说没有享大福，但是生儿育女，平平淡淡安安稳稳地过日子便是幸福。

奶奶有5个子女，我爸爸是最小的一个。爷爷奶奶本来是不打算生我爸爸的，但是在那个需要劳动力吃饭的年代，只有一个男丁的奶奶爷爷实在是太需要多个劳动力养家糊口。那时“重男轻女”的思想还是挺牢固的。爸爸有机会去上学，但是初中都没有毕业就不愿意读书了，任凭爷爷追着打追着骂都没用。听奶奶说，有一天傍晚爸爸逃学被爷爷知道了，气得他拿着扫把就出去了，满村地找却怎么也没找到。池塘边看见个人影很像爸爸，但一溜烟工夫又没了，大晚上的农村里不会有什么灯也看不分明。后来也不知怎么爸爸偷偷回来了，让奶奶帮他圆谎，最终逃过了爷爷的魔棍。小姑姑学习成绩很好也很愿意读书，但是由于家里供不起没读大学，而大姑姑就像是奶奶年轻时候的翻版，任劳任怨，割草放羊、洗衣做饭，小小年纪的她早已熟练地做这些而且放弃了学习的机会。直到现在大家都说大姑姑真的和奶奶很像。

1978年改革开放后，家里慢慢地攒了些钱，1990年盖起来小楼房，也正好为爸爸娶新娘子做准备，开始置办起来小彩电和一些家具。

娶了妈妈没多久，爸爸在33岁时有了我。爸爸没读什么书所以只能干一些糙活重活。当时爷爷奶奶给爸爸买了一个拖拉机，他去矿山里面拉货，妈妈在纺织工厂里面做零工。爷爷奶奶在家务农，种菜拿到街上去卖。家庭的生活逐渐好转起来。但是在我两岁时出了意外，爷爷本打算给我洗个澡，先在澡盆里放了刚烧好的滚烫热水，我当时又小又调皮，将一只手臂不慎放进去，整个右手严重烫伤，当时把所有人都吓得不轻，爷爷也非常自责。意外和危险总是在不经意间来临，在我5岁的时候，爸爸也出了意外，在开拖拉机运货的时候出了交通事故，拖拉机整个翻倒，爸爸的右手大拇指当场断裂，直到现在手指上面一截都没有了。所以他现在是个左撇子，写字吃饭都是用的左手。

幸好，在这两次意外之后，家里人没再出过什么事情，都很平安。爸爸妈妈做过很多事，承包鱼塘、工地上班、工厂工作、承包芦笋基地等等。整个家庭说不上富裕，但也很幸福。爷爷自小就很宠我，偷偷给我买零食，偷偷塞零花钱给我，为此经常被奶奶骂。可是在我 12 岁时，他便因为脑溢血离开了我。

家是心灵的港湾，而房子是家的栖息地。一个“大杂院”承载了几辈人的时代记忆，“黑白电视、烟囱、蜂窝煤……冬储大白菜、炉子烤白薯、生火取暖……”而就在前不久，新农村建设规划下，大家统一规划建造房屋。见着生活了近 20 年的房子一瞬间倒塌，心里还是有些不舍，毕竟那是我的童年回忆。但这也意味着我们的生活条件在不断地改善。

回想从前，老一辈似乎有诉不完的苦；着眼当下，他们脸上洋溢着幸福的笑容。

Huzhou
Ni Miaoli (Class 193, Majoring in Network and New Media)

The Difficult Years My Grandmother Has Gone Through

My grandmother is 86 years old this year. She has experienced the War of Resistance against Japan, the War of Liberation, the founding of New China, the Reform and Opening Up, and the period of building a well-off society in an all-round way by the year of 2020. She can be said to be a witness of a history of nearly a hundred years. However, every time I hear her tell me about her life stories, I will feel a lump in my throat. She always says that your generation takes for granted the happy life you live nowadays. It is hard for me to imagine how they survived those hard times that she told me in her stories.

My grandmother was born in 1935 in Xujia Village, Lyushan Township, Changxing County, Huzhou City. At that time, the family was extremely poor. Her mother went to be a wet nurse when she was 3 years old. She was practically raised by her grandmother. My grandma's house was by the river, so she often went to the river to catch fish. Having eaten so much fresh fish, she dislikes eating fish nowadays. She often joked that she had eaten enough fish when she was a child.

My grandmother has several brothers and sisters, but it was difficult to raise so many children for her family. The idea of son preference over a daughter was still deep-rooted back then. In order to support sons to go to school, her parents sent her to another family to be a daughter when she was seven years old. However, it was not long before that family had their own child, so they treated her as a servant. She began to mow the grass at the age of eight, and to feed 13 sheep and a cow on her own. She was illiterate, because she didn't have any chance to study in school. Sometimes she passed the school when she mowed the grass, she heard the sound of reading and she was really envious. She told me that she often secretly peeked at them through the window, so she often asked me to cherish the good opportunities and conditions to study hard.

One day, she lost a sheep. Her adoptive parents whipped her with a mulberry branch and locked her in the firewood room. They gave her nothing to eat, leaving her hungry for the whole day and night. They even didn't give her a drop of water. She couldn't endure such a life any more, so she fled back home at the age of 13.

However, her family couldn't afford raising her, so her father sent her to another family as a child bride. After she entered that family, she still had to work day and night. She did a lot of work, such as herding sheep, mowing grass washing clothes, and cooking meals. Later, one of her legs became swollen, because of prolonged immersion in the water when she worked. And she did not have money to see a doctor, so her whole calf and the foot were all badly swollen until now. Now my father and my aunt wanted to take her to see a doctor, but she always refused and said that she was old and the leg was not painful any longer, so there was no need to seek medical attention.

Just because of the swollen leg, that family disliked my grandmother and didn't want her to be their daughter-in-law any more. The 18-year-old grandmother returned to her family, but it was not long before she was sent to a new family to become a child bride. When I heard this, I could not help crying. She should have enjoyed her life as an adolescent girl; instead, she was abandoned and sent to several families as an object in disgust. She must have had a strong will to get it through. She vaguely remembered that when she was four or five years old, villagers dug a big hole in the lotus pond and hid in it every time the Japanese soldiers came. Unmarried young women must hide well or they would be caught.

At the age of 20, my grandmother became a member of my grandfather's family, but still, she was unable to live a better life. My grandfather's family made a living on farmlands. Unfortunately, when my grandmother came to my grandfather's family in 1954, there occurred the biggest flood rarely seen in nearly 100 years in the middle and lower reaches of the Yangtze River, which caused a serious flood disaster. The mud house with one floor only was surrounded by water, so many things had been soaked by the flood. Such a flood was a deadly blow to the crops, and the harvest was impossible. There was no lotus root in the pond. Therefore, they always had to worry about how to get their next meal.

My grandfather was honest and good to my grandmother, and he was a mild-tempered man. My great-grandmother passed away when my grandfather was seven years old, which spared my grandmother the trouble of having conflicts with her mother-in-law. Thus, my grandmother said that she was lucky and happy to marry my grandpa though she didn't live in ease and comfort; however, living a simple and peaceful life was happiness.

My grandmother had five children and my father was the youngest one. Originally she had intended not to have the fifth kid. But in those days when people needed workforce, they really needed more sons to support their families. The idea of son preference was still deeply rooted. Although my father had the opportunity to go to school, he was unwilling to study before graduating from middle school despite my grandfather cudgeling and scolding him. My grandmother told me that when my grandfather learned that my father skipped school, he was so angry that he grabbed a broom and went out to find my father, but he couldn't find my father in the village. He had seen a figure that looked like my father by a pond, but it disappeared suddenly again. There was no lights in the countryside at night. I did not know how my father secretly sneaked back later and persuaded my grandmother to help him tell a lie. In the end, he escaped being punished by my grandfather. On the contrary, my younger aunt did well in school and liked to study very much, but she never went to college because the family could not afford it. My elder aunt was a carbon copy of my grandmother in her youth. She was working hard, mowing grass, herding sheep, washing, and cooking. Small as she was, she had already been very adept at that work and gave up the opportunity of school. Until now, everyone says she is really my grandmother's double.

After the reform and opening up in 1978, they saved some money gradually. In 1990, the family built a small building, which was also a preparation for my father's marriage. They also began to buy a small color TV set and some furniture.

Not long after he married my mother, I was born when my father was at the age of 33. He didn't receive much education so he could only do some heavy work. At that time, and my grandparents bought him a tractor to deliver coals from the mine, and my mother did odd jobs in a textile factory. My grandparents farmed at home and grew vegetables which could be sold on the streets. The life and economy of the family were gradually getting better. However, when I was two years old, I had an accident when my grandfather wanted to bathe me. As soon as he put some boiling hot water in the bathtub, I, as a small and naughty girl, put one of my arms into it. Consequently, the whole right arm was badly scalded. At that time, everyone was terribly scared and my grandfather blamed himself very much. Accidents and dangers always come inadvertently. When I was five years old, my father had an accident. When he was driving a tractor to deliver goods, a traffic accident happened, and the tractor rolled over and the thumb of his right hand was broken immediately. He lost the upper part of his thumb till today, so he changed into a left-hander, writing and eating by his left hand.

Fortunately, nothing bad happened to our family and everyone was safe after these two accidents. My parents had also done many businesses such as contracting fish ponds, working on construction sites, working in the factories and contracting asparagus bases. The family is not rich but happy. My grandfather spoiled me a lot since I was a child, secretly buying me snacks and stuffing me with pocket money. He was often scolded by my grandmother. However, he died of a cerebral hemorrhage and left me when I was 12.

Home is the harbor of the soul, and the house is the habitat of the home. The compound that we live in carries the memories of several generations, such as black-and-white televisions, chimneys, honeycomb-shaped briquet, Chinese cabbages preserved in winter, roasting sweet potatoes within a stove, making a fire to keep warm and so on. And not long ago, the construction of new countryside was carried out under a call from the government. Villages made their planning and built according to the design of the government at the same time. I was a little reluctant to see the house I lived in for nearly 20 years demolished in a flash. After all, it was a memory of my childhood, but it was also a reflection that our living conditions are constantly improving.

Thinking back on the past, the older generation seems to have endless bitterness to tell. Looking at the present, their faces brim with happy smiles.

70后的爱情,烙上时代的红章

徐　静

70后一代也是当代中国急剧变化的见证人,流动和变迁是时代的核心特征。即便是非常私人化的恋爱、婚育也会被时代所裹挟,出现前所未有的新气象。小季同学的父母完成美丽的邂逅,“日久生情”,千里姻缘一线牵,是时代制造的幸福。

我经常跟同学们说,我的政治偶像是“老邓”邓小平,音乐偶像是“小邓”邓丽君。20世纪80年代流行一个说法:“白天听‘老邓’,晚上听‘小邓’。”1979年,邓小平在南海边“画了一个圈”,1992年又在南海边“写下诗篇”,中国走进了春天,中国人开启了幸福生活。历史书告诉我们宏大的历史,而家庭的柴米油盐酱醋茶则给了我们小百姓品味美好生活的机会。

习主席提出“追求美好生活是永远的进行时”。我想,改革开放除了让一部分人先富起来,先富带动后富,整个社会创造了巨量财富之外,对于普通人而言,更大的意义,就是破除了枷锁,解放了人性。恋爱对任何人来说都是一件大事,能够自由选择爱的人,想必也是一种解放。于我们70后而言,是一种常情,也是一种国家赋能,一种福报。“生活是生活,岁月是岁月”,岁月静好,只因有国。

(宁波工程学院副教授,博士)

故事

金华

季燕婷(新闻学专升本 201 班)

你在义乌,我在鹰潭

1974 年,妈妈出生在江西鹰潭的郑家村。一年后,比妈妈小一岁的爸爸出生在浙江义乌的喻宅村。虽然相隔 300 多公里,但是在那个年代的农村,却是一样的经济困难。

妈妈是家里最小的孩子,有四个姐姐和一个哥哥,家里孩子多,都等着吃饭,每天最大的问题就是想着怎么填饱家人的肚子,怎么早点交上孩子们欠下的学费。

外公外婆都是农民,种田是唯一的营生,每日起早贪黑,面朝黄土背朝天,在田垄里种植蔬菜和稻谷,只盼着风调雨顺,稻谷能有一个好收成,多卖些钱。孩子们只要一放学,第一件事不是写作业,而是扔下书包卷起袖子,上山砍柴、灶头烧火、猪圈喂猪。春要插秧秋要收谷,老师也会特意给学生放农忙假。吃完晚饭,孩子们才有空挤在一张桌子上埋头写作业。

当时小学一学期的学费只要 5 块,上了初中也才 108 块。那时候的钱比现在耐用,1 块钱可以买很多东西,圆珠笔芯才 1 毛一根,但是文具盒里的笔,也不会超过 3 支。穿的衣服都是哥哥姐姐穿不下了,弟弟妹妹接着穿,真是“新三年,旧三年,缝缝补补又三年”。

上学路上几乎看不到公交车,更别说校车。妈妈读小学时,就已经习惯每天徒步三四公里从家里出发到学校。上了初中,用外婆亲手缝制的碎花书包,背上一星期吃的米、两罐外婆炒的咸菜,还得走上十几公里的山路。

初中的寝室,一间间就像教室那么大,全是一排排的上下铺,十五六张床几乎睡下整个班的女生。

妈妈初二时,舅舅要成家,外公外婆拿不出钱,只能卖了家里的牛。妈妈年纪最小却也最懂事,自己主动和外婆说不读书了,干脆外出打工贴补家用。外婆没说话,只能点点头,但是每次看到村里读书的孩子放学归来,外婆还是会觉得愧疚而红了眼。

爸爸也是老幺,一个姐姐一个哥哥,爷爷奶奶日夜忙着种庄稼。

爷爷总是戴着一顶稻草杆子编制的草帽，帽顶被手指常年捏出了倒三角，雨天就再披上蓑衣，扁担筐里一头放肥料，一头放镰刀，一挑上肩膀，就晃晃悠悠出门下地了。

院子是奶奶的工作场，十几口大缸堆满了院子。将门口成堆码放着的雪里蕻和萝卜放进缸清洗，接着放进下一个缸里腌制。腌咸菜的缸子又深又大，眼见着菜就到了缸口，便交叉放了竹条再压上大石头，得要咸水盖过了菜才好。天一出太阳，奶奶便在缸口放上大案板，把腌好的咸菜整颗用手抓得紧紧的，一下一下细细地切着，扫净院子摊开旧席子，就开始晒咸菜。

晒干的咸菜装袋密封，放得越久，颜色越深，味道越香。那一口热腾腾香喷喷的梅干菜扣肉，永远是爸爸的最爱。

爸爸童年里也有一个月亮下的故事，是月色下，坐在爷爷肩头，去田埂里散步，回来时坐着木制的独轮推车，被爷爷逗笑着推回家。不是什么特别的经历，只是因为在那早晚忙碌劳作的日子里，这样悠闲惬意的时刻就显得弥足珍贵。

爸爸上学时，白色铝制饭盒里每餐都是红薯，却好歹初中毕业了。十五六岁的肩膀还嫩着呢，就跟着村里卖瓜子的大人晒瓜子，用木耙子一遍遍地拨动着晒谷场上的瓜子，再装袋捆扎。每日只得25块工钱，爸爸只留几块饭钱，其余全部上交给奶奶。

没有晒多久的瓜子，爸爸便换了一个地方工作，在一个小工厂里做小商品加工员，吃住也在单位里。

辍学后的妈妈跟着村里先前在外打工的小姐妹，一起坐着绿皮火车，辗转5个多小时，第一次离开外公外婆，出了远门，来到了浙江义乌打工。

妈妈刚好在爸爸的单位里做手工，认识了爸爸。爸爸那时还是一个毛头小子，刚刚离家工作，煮饭洗衣都不太会，妈妈热心肠，常过去给爸爸帮忙。渐渐地，爸爸就对妈妈日久生情，决定要和妈妈结婚。

妈妈一通电话，告诉了远在江西那一头的外公外婆，外公外婆一听，立马就急了，马上坐了火车过来。爷爷奶奶家穷得啥也没有，一对一样的枕套也凑不齐，急急忙忙向邻居家借了电视机摆在家里，终于和亲家见了面。

妈妈用爸爸的老实本分，说服了外公外婆。

终于，爸爸妈妈领了证，组成了自己的一个小家。成家后，爷爷奶奶没有什么给爸爸的，爸爸也没什么积蓄。

爸爸后来跟着一位老师傅学了木工手艺，在建筑工地上支、拆混凝土模板。工作很辛苦，不管是酷暑还是严冬都要出工。嘴含铁钉手敲榔头，上衣的汗可以直接手拧。

木工的工资比以前做半成品多一点。每月末包工头来家里结算工资的时候，爸爸都会仔细翻着账本核算工资，再留包工头一起吃顿饭。

妈妈在加工厂里做手工，每天在桌前一坐就是一整天，包装假发、制作日历、手帕纸印花，这些妈妈都做过。那时我还小，就坐在妈妈手工桌下自己玩，身下垫着纸箱，等妈妈下班再一起回家。

一点点积攒有了些积蓄后，爸爸给妈妈补齐了三大件：手表、自行车、缝纫机，还有收音机，合成了“三转一响”。

一对手表是牡丹牌的，银色搭扣，爸妈每晚睡前都仔细取下，软布擦净再放到抽屉里。

自行车是上海永久牌的，车架有一条高高的单杠，爸爸常常会骑着它带着我们出去转悠，车后坐着妈妈，单杠坐着小小的我。车轮一圈圈地转，我们的日子一天天地过。

缝纫机是西湖牌的，比我还大两岁，在 1996 年花了 300 多元买下。

妈妈偶尔也会到厂里接活在家做，帮厂里加工衣服、帽子，按件计薪，一件普通的布衣服加工费七八毛，好一点的皮衣之类三毛一件，一天最多做十一二件，补贴家用。

一直到现在，这台缝纫机也还在我们家里，虽然经过多次的故障和维修，但仍然还能使用。偶尔爸爸的裤脚要裁剪，我的校服开了线，妈妈都会坐在缝纫机前，娴熟地用缝纫机的压脚压住衣裤，用手拨动着转轴，双脚踩着踏板，麻利地在衣服上踩上细细的针脚。

就这样在岁月一圈圈的年轮下，全靠爸爸妈妈两个人的辛勤工作和相互扶持，才让家里的日子越过越好。我们不必再为温饱担忧，住上了新房，也有了小汽车。

正是因为有了爱，才让我觉得生活是生活，岁月是岁月。

Jinhua
Ji Yanting (Class 201, Majoring in Journalism)

Dad in Yiwu and Mom in Yingtan

My mom was born in Zhengjia Village, Yingtan City, Jiangxi Province in 1974. One year later, my dad was born in Yuzhai Village, Yiwu City,

Zhejiang Province. 300 kilometers away from each other, the two villages saw no difference in their poverty.

My mom, having four elder sisters and one elder brother, was the youngest child in the family. With so many kids, my maternal grandparents struggled every day to feed the family and pay for their children's overdue tuition fees.

My grandparents, making a living solely on growing vegetables and grains, worked from dawn to dusk in the field. The only things they wished for were fair weather and consequent good harvest, which would mean more income to them. Once classes were over, kids soon left their homework behind. They dropped the schoolbag and rushed to the hill firewood, or burnt the fire at the stove, or perhaps fed the pigs in the pigsty. Students also had farming holidays in spring when they had to plant rice and in autumn, the harvest season. It was only after dinner that children were free to huddle at a table and start doing their homework.

The tuition fee was merely five yuan for one semester in elementary school, and 108 in junior middle school. At that time, people could buy a lot of things with one yuan. A refill for a ball-point pen only cost 0.1 yuan, and there were no more than 3 pens in the stationery box. Once the elder in the family had outgrown their clothes, those clothes then belonged to younger kids and were worn for a longer time even with patches.

There were barely any buses on the way to school, let alone a school bus. When she was in elementary school, my mom got used to walking three or four kilometers every day to and from the school. When my mother went to junior high school, she loaded the schoolbag, a bag with cotton prints made by my grandmother, with rice that could be consumed for a week and two jars of home fried pickles. With that heavy bag, she still had to walk on the mountainous road for more than ten kilometers.

The dormitory at the junior high school was as big as a classroom, with 15—16 bunk beds side by side. It could accommodate almost all the girls of the whole class.

My uncle was to get married when my mom was in the eighth grade. Unable to come up with such a large amount of money, my grandparents had no choice but to sell cows. Being the youngest yet the most sensible child in the family, my mom offered to drop out and start working. My grandma nodded without saying anything, but her eyes would turn red out of guilt every time she saw other kids return home from school.

My dad, having an elder sister and elder brother, was also the youngest child in the family. My paternal grandparents were busy farming day and night.

My grandpa always wore a straw hat made of stalks, the top of which was pinched out by fingers for years with inverted triangles. He often put on a straw rain cape on rainy days and shouldered fertilizer in one end of the wooden basket and a sickle in the other as he wandered out into the farmland.

My grandma usually worked in the yard, in which a dozen large jars spread out. She would put the brassica juncea and radish, piled at the door, into a jar before washing them and putting them into another jar to start pickling. The jar was so deep and big, and the salted vegetables almost filled the jar to the brim, so two bamboo strips and a large stone were placed on the top of the jar, and it would be better if the water overflowed the pickles. When it was sunny, my grandma would put a big chopping board on the mouth of the jar. Then with the whole pickled vegetable holding tightly in one hand, she carefully chopped it bit by bit with the other hand. The yard was then cleaned and the old mat spread—pickles could bask in the sunshine on it.

Dried pickled vegetables were then sealed in plastic bags. They got more aromatic as time went by. The steaming and delicious braised pork with preserved vegetables in soy sauce was my father's favorite dish.

There was also a story happening under the moon during my father's childhood. At that time, he was sitting on my grandfather's shoulder, going for a walk in the moonlit fields. On the way back, he took a wooden one-wheeled cart, being pushed by my grandfather, who amused him from time to time. It was not a special experience, but indeed quite precious during those busy days, when they worked days and nights on the land, with less time to relax themselves.

When my dad went to school, his white aluminum lunch box was always filled with sweet potatoes, but at least he managed to graduate from junior high school. At the age of 15 or 16, my father was too young to bear heavy loads, so he learned to dry the melon seeds just as the adults selling melon seeds in the village did. He used a wooden rake to poke the melon seeds on the sunbed again and again, and then packaged them in bags. By doing so, he could earn 25 yuan per day, but he only kept a few bucks to get something to eat, and gave the rest to grandma.

Shortly after that, my father changed his job and began to work in a small factory with accommodation included, where he served as a small item processor.

My mom, after dropping out of school, went to Yiwu to try her luck and got aboard green trains together with her friends who previously worked away from home. It took her five hours to finally arrive at the destination. For the very first time, she left my grandparents and started living in a strange place on her own.

She happened to do manual work in the same factory where my dad worked and naturally made the acquaintance of my dad, who just left home and didn't know how to cook or do laundry. My warm-hearted mom often gave him a helping hand. And gradually my dad fell in love with my mom and decided to marry her.

After my mom told them about my dad's proposal over the phone, my maternal grandparents took the train to visit my father's family immediately. My paternal grandparents were so poor that they couldn't even have a pair of pillowcases with the same pattern. They hastily borrowed a TV from a neighbor and set it up at home. Finally, four of them met with each other.

My mom eventually talked her parents into assenting to this marriage with my dad's honesty and integrity.

They finally got married and formed a family of their own. My paternal grandparents were too poor to pass down anything to my dad who barely had any savings.

He, later apprenticed to an experienced carpenter, started putting up and dismantling concrete forms on construction sites. It was by no means an easy job since he needed to work in the scorching hot summer and freezing cold winter. With nails in the mouth and a hammer in the hand, he would be soaked in sweat after a day's work.

He earned a little bit more from carpentry than from making semi-finished products.. At the end of each month, when the contractor came to the house to settle the wages, my father would carefully go through the account book to check the wages and then invited the contractor for dinner.

My mom, doing manual work in a processing factory, spent the whole day before her workbench packing wigs, making calendars and printing patterns on tissues. I would play with myself sitting on the flattened cardboard boxes under my mom's workbench, while waiting for her to finish her work.

After my father had savings, he bought my mother a watch, a bicycle, a sewing machine and a radio, four typical items in the traditional betrothal gifts.

The pair of Peony watches with silver buckles were taken down very carefully and then put in the drawer after being cleaned with a soft cloth.

The Forever bicycle had a crossbar over the frame. My dad often carried my mom and me for a jaunt by bike. Days just went by like rolling wheels.

The West Lake sewing machine, two years older than me, cost my dad 300 yuan back in 1996.

My mother sometimes went to the factory to get some work back, such as making clothes and hats. The wage for processing a piece of ordinary clothes was 0.7—0.8 yuan, and for better leather clothes, she earned 0.3 yuan for each. She could work on up to eleven or twelve pieces of clothes each day, in an attempt to support the family.

The sewing machine is kept in our house until now and it can still work despite many breakdowns and repairs. Sometimes when my father's trouser legs had to be cut or my school uniform came unsewn, my mother would sit in front of the sewing machine to skillfully press down on the garment with the presser foot of the machine, pluck at the spindle with her hands and step on the pedal with both feet, leaving fine stitches on the clothes.

Time goes by and life gets better thanks to my parents' hard work and their mutual support. We don't have to worry about having no adequate food and clothing anymore and have our new house and new car.

It is because of love that I feel life and time are worth it.

051

观察

此处安心是吾家

包静昇

周国平在散文《家》中写道:如果把人生比作一种漂流——它确实是的,对于有些人来说是漂过许多地方,对于所有人来说是漂过岁月之河——那么,家是什么呢？家是一只船,在漂流中有了亲爱。

有人说,以船比喻家,那不是太动荡了吗？每当在靠海的小岛上,总能看见以船为家的渔民们,孩子们在船上打闹,妻子们在洗洗涮涮,到饭点时船上飘出阵阵饭菜香,这一片温馨祥和岂不就是家吗？而家,也确实太平凡了,再温馨也会有小吵小闹,就像白炳益写的关于自己的家:“老爸和老妈在相互拌嘴和各种小插曲中仍然不断相互支持着前进。”

家文化经过中华上下几千年的文明不断孕育,慢慢形成了中华民族独有的文化体系,形成了新时代培养社会主义核心价值观的文化载体。在古代有《礼记·大学》的“物格而后知至,知至而后意诚,意诚而后心正,心正而后身修,身修而后家齐,家齐而后国治,国治而后天下平”,现在有“家是最小国,国是千万家”的论述,都是家国情怀的时代呈现。习近平总书记也对家国情怀作出了“爱国情怀是实现中国梦的重要力量”的重要论述。

“万里归来年愈少,微笑,时时犹带岭梅香。试问岭南应不好？却道:此心安处是吾乡。”改革开放40余年以来,不论是“小家”还是“大家”都在飞速地发展,不论我们身处何地,有家在,就心安。

(浙大宁波理工学院商学院团委书记,硕士)

故事
温州
白炳益(网络与新媒体专业181班)

瓯南小镇里的家

我家在浙江省温州市平阳县的一个不起眼的小镇。“山川毓秀,腾蛟起凤。”腾蛟,正是它的名字。说它不起眼,是因为它坐落在众多浙南丘陵之间,被小丘陵环抱,但它却是数学家苏步青和象棋棋王谢侠逊的故里,是一处至今仍有部分古迹保留的文化古镇,也是一个与现代文明接轨的工业小镇。

每一个全新的家庭,都是从父母的相识开始。大约1990年,我的老爸和老妈经人介绍认识,简单地说就是相亲吧。现在看来可以算作早婚,他们结婚的时候只有20出头。

老爸老妈和我说,他们结婚前甚至只是见了几面,放现在,熟悉的朋友都算不上。但是,快要30年了,老爸和老妈之间虽然多有拌嘴和丰富生活味道的小插曲,但在老妈对家里“绝对掌权”和老爸的“绝对拥护”条件之下,老爸和老妈确是相互爱护、相互支持地让我们的家从无到有,从匮乏到富足。老爸和老妈始终在追求“安安稳稳往前行,平平淡淡才是真”。这也正是我所看到的,老爸和老妈之间无需言表的朴素浪漫。

我家老房是一间半木结构老房,是小镇的传统民居,在现在赤岩山景区内的一个半山腰,那时的交通较为不利,所以我家其实不能算作真正意义上的“镇上居民”。老房的隔壁是一所面积很小的乡村小学,不过在我家搬离老房不久,这所小学就已经被拆分合并到小镇经济和交通比较发达的街道区的两所小学。

如今的老房已经破旧不堪,但是老爸总是会带着一家人常常回到老房子看看,因为老房才是老爸出生长大和老妈相识的地方,是家开始的地方。

老爸最早是在镇上干一些零活,再靠一些农事补贴家用。老爸还爱好中式乐器,那是曾祖父教给老爸的,他有时跟着中乐队演奏,也有一些收入。老爸有几年还曾经外出去省外打工,老爸说那是第一次出远门,回想那段经历,老爸总会用一口不标准的普通话学唱那年火车上播放的歌曲,慢慢地就开始感叹自己的青春岁月。

我问老爸,为啥后来又不出去打工了,老爸说,一个是因为小镇的工业后来开始迅速发展了，来我们镇上打工的工人都开始慢慢变多，用不着外出打工了。另外就是因为老妈担心他的安全，老爸孤身在外打工，老妈总说她会很担心。

那时候的老妈则是包揽全部的家务，同时又在家里开了一个小零食铺子，做起了属于自己的小生意，靠向在附近学校的学生售卖零食和学习用品赚取一些家中的零用钱。

老爸和老妈这些零零碎碎的收入虽然不能让家里非常富足，可是几年下来，老爸和老妈总算让家里从一穷二白变成家有所余。家里开始拥有了电视、电风扇和双筒洗衣机这样的大件电器。

在上个世纪末，也就是老爸和老妈在老房共同生活了几年以后，小镇开始了比较大规模的工业化，镇上的印刷业和皮革业开始大力发展了，经济开始了飞速的增长。原本比较闭塞的小镇，开始了比较大规模的对外经济文化等多方面的交流，而老房周边，也开始了一波“搬家潮”。许多邻居们开始在街道区买房和租房，因为住在不便的半山，实在不合时宜。

于是，决定着家里财政大权并且又高瞻远瞩的老妈决定拿出全部积蓄，再借一些钱买新房，而后来的事实也证明，老妈的决定很是正确。因为之后的房价始终在涨，借钱买房无疑是最为机智的决定。说起这段往事，老妈会翻出来当年按照家乡传统习惯用毛笔字撰写的购房交易书，而我在饶有趣味地看交易书的时候，总能听见老妈在夸奖当年自己的行事果断和细致盘算。

我们一家终于住进了高大敞亮的楼房，这座落地式楼房正是我长大的家。老爸和老妈还常常说笑着谈起刚买新房时的兴奋，他们说，刚买房时新房里虽然空荡荡的，整个房子里也没有几个像样的大件儿，但是他们总是每天打扫，每天都会把地板拖一遍，那时候家里的地面总是被打扫得锃光瓦亮。

买了新房以后，给家里带来的最大改变，是家里的谋生方式改变了。新房不再受制于交通，门前门后都是路，老爸和老妈开始从事工业范畴内的工作，成为小镇特色工业的从业者。新房子一楼的前半间，用来作为工作的地方最是合适，而相对自由的工作时间，也方便老爸老妈照看我们几个孩子。最重要的是，这为我们家带来了越来越高的收入。

老爸和老妈日日夜夜辛苦地工作，使得家里的经济慢慢变得宽裕，家里开始添许多的大件儿，空荡的新房慢慢被很多东西填满，新房不再只是新房，填满奋斗和温暖气息的新房终于成了新家。除开老爸买的第一部手机，冰箱算是新房里真正意义上的第一个高科技大件儿，也是让我印象最深刻的大件儿之一。虽然家里拥有的第一台冰箱不像现在的新冰箱那么大，我却永远记得第一次把一箱冰棍装进冷冻室时的兴奋。当然，后来家里又陆陆续续添了空调、电脑、新的洗衣机等很多大件儿。近几年家里甚至还添置了许多像电子钢琴这样的非生活必需的大件。此外，老爸当然还会为自己添几件上好的中式乐器来自娱自乐。而添这些大件，添的不仅仅是一份生活的富足，添的还是一份生活的方便和趣味，是一份家里生活的气息。

我站在房间的阳台上远眺，又环顾这个我生长的小镇。余晖下，对面的新楼房仿佛与远山一样高，楼下的柏油马路是全新的，上面来来往往的车辆，它们各有自己的目的地，但是我知道它们有一个共同的方向，那就是搭载着小镇驶向全新的明天。

反过身背靠阳台，再看自己的小家，忽然感觉熟悉又陌生。因为小家是我生活了无数个日日夜夜的地方，它的气息我不能更熟悉了，而小家跟随着小镇发展的步伐，在老爸和老妈的日夜拼搏努力中，小家也每时每刻都在发生着变化，时时刻刻都有着微小的新鲜感。小家续行不止，因为我们这一家对更加美好的幸福生活的向往不会停止。

Wenzhou
Bai Bingyi (Class 181, Majoring in Network and New Media)

My Home in a Town in the South of Wenzhou

My home is in an unremarkable small town in Pingyang County, Wenzhou City, Zhejiang Province. Tengjiao is my hometown's name, and it is named after a saying that "mountains and rivers are extraordinarily beautiful, and talents are raised here." It is not eye-catching because of its remote location. It is surrounded by small hills in southern Zhejiang. However, it is also the hometown of mathematician Su Buqing, and Chess King, Xie Xiaxun. My hometown is an ancient cultural town with some historical sites still preserved, and it is also an industrial town in line with modern civilization.

Every brand new family starts from the acquaintance of parents. Around 1990, my parents met on a blind date. They got married at the age of twenty, which is counted as early marriage nowadays.

My parents told me that before they got married, they met only a few times. They were not exactly familiar friends in the eyes of people today.

However, for nearly 30 years, although there were many quarrels and many small episodes in life between them, my mother got the "absolute power" at home and my father provided the "absolute support" to her. They loved mutually and supported each other to change our home from being poor to being well-off. My parents are always in the pursuit of safe progress and simple happiness. And the simple romance beyond words between my parents was exactly what I see.

My previous home was an old house made of a half timbered structure, which was a traditional dwelling in the town. It was on a hillside in the scenic spot of Chiyan Mountain. At that time, the traffic was rather bad, so my families could not be counted as true "townsmen". Next door to the old house was a small village primary school, but soon after we moved out of the old house, the school was split up and merged into two primary schools in a block with relatively developed economy and transportation.

Though the old house couldn't be more dilapidated now, my father still always took our family back to the old house. Because here was the place where my father was born, grew up and met my mother. It was the beginning of our family.

My father did some odd jobs in the town at first, and then depended on some farm work to support our family. He also loved Chinese musical instruments, which were taught by my great-grandfather. Sometimes, he played with Chinese bands to earn some money. My father had gone out to work outside the province once for a few years. He said that it was the first time that he went so far away from home. Every time when recalling that experience, he would learn to sing the songs played on the train that year with his non-standard Mandarin, and slowly began to sigh his youth years.

I asked my father why he didn't go out to work again later. He said that one reason was that the industry in our town began to grow rapidly afterwards, and more workers came to work in our town, so there was no need to work outside. The other reason is that my mother was worried about his safety. When my father worked alone outside, she said that she always worried about him.

At that time, my mother took on all the housework. At the same time, she opened a snack shop at home, then she started her own small business. By selling snacks and school supplies to some students in the nearby school, she could earn some pocket money needed at home.

Although these bits and pieces of my parents' income didn't make the family very rich, but after a few years, they finally turned our home from having nothing to having something. Big appliances such as televisions, electric fans and two-cylinder washing machines began to appear in our home.

At the end of the last century, when my parents had lived in the old house for a few years. The town began to industrialize on a relatively large scale. The printing and leather industries began to flourish in the town, and the economy began to soar. The previous relatively isolated small town started to carry out large-scale foreign economic and cultural exchanges and also some communication in other aspects. A wave of moving out started surrounding the old house. Many neighbors started to buy and rent houses in the block because living in the middle of the hill was inconvenient.

Therefore, my forward-looking mother who got the fiscal firepower of the family, decided to take out all the savings and borrow some more money to buy a new house, which turned out to be the right decision later. Because the house prices have been rising ever since, borrowing money to buy a house was surely the wisest decision. Whenever speaking of this past, my mother always took out the purchase transaction book written in Chinese calligraphy, which was the traditional habits of my hometown in those days. Every time I read the transaction book enjoyably, I could always hear her praising her decisive act and careful calculation at that time.

Our family finally lived in a tall, spacious building and this floor-to-ceiling building was the house where I grew up. My parents often talked about the excitement of buying this new house. They said that though the new house was empty and didn't have much big furniture at first, they cleaned the house every day. Every day the floor was mopped so that the floor was always clean and bright.

After we bought a new house, the biggest change in our family was our way of making a living. Living in the new home, we were no longer restricted by inconvenient traffic and there were roads whenever you opened the door. My parents began to engage in work related to industry, and became the practitioners of the characteristic industry of the town. The front half of the first floor of our new house was the most suitable place for work, and the relatively free working hours were good for them to look after us. Most importantly, this brought more income to our family.

My parents worked hard day and night to make our family slowly well-off. We began to buy a lot of big furniture into our house, so this empty new house was slowly filled with a lot of things. It was no longer just a new house. Filled with striving and warm breath, the new house finally became a new home. Except the first mobile phone of my father, the refrigerator was the first high-tech electrical appliance in our new house in the true sense, which was also one of the big appliances that impressed me most. Although the first refrigerator isn't as big as the new refrigerator we use now, I always remember the thrill of putting a box of popsicles into it for the first time. Of course, we bought air-conditioners, computers, new washing machines and many other big items into our house gradually then. In recent years, our family even added a lot of extra non-essential furniture such as an electronic piano. What's more, my father also bought some great Chinese instruments to amuse himself. Having these big items was actually not only a reflection of our well-to-do life, but also the convenience and delight of life. It was a flavour of our life.

Standing on the balcony of my room, I looked out into the distance, and then looked around the town where I grew up. In the afterglow, the new building on the opposite side of my home seemed to be as high as the distant mountain. The asphalt road downstairs was brand new and cars coming and going. Each car had its own destination, but I knew they had the same direction, that is, they were all driving the town to a brand new tomorrow.

Turning around against the balcony, I looked at my small house, and I felt familiar and strange suddenly. The small house is the place that I have lived countless days and nights, so I can't get more familiar with its smell. However, keeping up with the pace of the town's development, my home is also changing all the time through the day and night struggle of my parents. Every moment, it has some slight senses of novelty. Our home is constantly changing and developing, because our family will not stop yearning for a better and happier life.

幸福感的源泉

王　蔚

幸福感源自哪里?

幸福感是现实而具体的。幸福感的影响因素包含经济收入、社会支持、文化消费等诸多变量。例如,有学者认为家用汽车的拥有水平可以显著提升居民幸福感。还有科研人员发现,新鲜的、多样化的经历较多的人,幸福感更高,因为这种探索周围环境所体验到的新奇和多样,有助于提高幸福感。幸福的生活源自于个体的事业发展(学手艺、办工厂、添设备)和家庭建设(结婚、生子);幸福的生活是钱袋子鼓了、房子越住越大、车子越开越好的物质表现,也是人际和谐、心情舒畅的精神表现。

同时,中国人的幸福感也是家国相连的。让人民群众有更多的获得感、幸福感、安全感是我们党始终不渝的追求目标。习近平总书记在深圳经济特区建立40周年庆祝大会上强调,“生活过得好不好,人民群众最有发言权”,要“努力让人民群众的获得感成色更足、幸福感更持续、安全感更有保障”。悠悠万事,民生为大,将国家的宏观政策润物无声地融进人民柴米油盐的平凡生活中,在政府实施积极的就业政策,倡导更公平的教育,推进住房保障和供应体系建设,深化医疗卫生体制改革等各项事业的发展过程中,也是每位浙江儿女勇立潮头,勤劳拼搏,为家庭奋斗,创造幸福生活的缩影。中国人的幸福感是一种源自家国情怀的深沉的力量!

(浙大宁波理工学院传媒与法学院讲师,博士)

故事

嘉兴

朱艺(新闻学专业 191 班)

平凡的幸福

“其实我们家这几十年来一直过得都平平淡淡的,也没有什么惊天动地的大事情,就跟普通人家一样,柴米油盐、粗茶淡饭。出生长大都是在农村,在桐乡这片土地上扎了几十年的根,一切都是靠自己,通过自己的努力去改善生活环境。”父亲弹了弹手中的烟头,对我平静地说道。父亲出生于 1974 年的冬天,是家里的第二个孩子,家中还有一个大他三岁的姐姐,也就是我的姑姑。

我家位于浙江省嘉兴市桐乡市石门镇部墩村中节里组,是户地地道道的乡下人家。我生于桐乡、长于桐乡,足足待了有 18 年之久,当然,“桐乡”二字,不仅仅于我,更是我们一家人的羁绊。

孩童时候的父亲,会趁大人不注意偷吃,也会在上学路上逃课和朋友结伴去游泳。以前父亲跟我说过,一到夏天的时候,他们在河里玩起来都会忘了去学校上课。那个时候的男孩子都很单纯,有可能也是因为条件不好,游泳对他们来说已经很满足了。“那个时候家里条件挺苦的,四个人挤在一间小房子里,我们又没有固定的工作收入,我白天在家就织织布干干农活什么的,你爷爷后来去了砖瓦厂工作,我们家也算有了一点固定收入。”在洗碗的奶奶听到我们在聊之前的故事,也插了几句话进来。

姑姑读完小学六年级就辍学了,去了皮鞋厂务工赚钱,毕竟家里经济条件不好,还要供父亲上初中,家里把所有的期望都寄托在了父亲的身上。据父亲回忆,他初中的时候成绩还行,据说语文课上老师还让他当着全班同学的面读优秀作文,其实我也不知道他是不是在跟我吹牛,但后来父亲没有去考高中。1989 年,父亲初中毕业后,和当时大多数人一样,去了皮鞋厂打工。这一去,父亲认识了同样在皮鞋厂打工的母亲,爸爸妈妈也因此跟皮鞋行业打了 30 多年的交道。

上世纪 90 年代初,爷爷给家里盖了一间新房子,虽然只有一个侧面,不过家里都很开心。在皮鞋厂干了几年活的父亲被老板派去上海还有无锡做销售。据父亲回忆,那是一段很开心的日子,一个农村的孩子突然来到了大城市,说不兴奋那肯定是假的。也正是那一段时间,父亲真正领略到了大城市的风采,第一次看到了外面的世界，上海外滩、无锡影视城……很多地方都留下了父亲的足迹。“好像是1995年左右吧，我从无锡回到了桐乡，回到了熟悉的工作岗位，没过多久就和你妈妈订婚了。后来，家里拿出积蓄在原来房子的基础上又造了一个侧面，为我和你妈妈做了婚房。”

世纪之交的那两天，爸爸妈妈举行了婚礼，长大后我还跟他们开玩笑地说道，你们这个结婚的日子过于隆重，而母亲只是低头一笑，说那时候只是想挑个大家放假的时间而已。或许，父母亲也是认真考虑过才选的那两天，谁不想拥有一个终身难忘的婚礼呢，只是他们把自己的小心思隐藏起来罢了。2001年夏天的尾巴，我呱呱坠地，为小家增添了不一样的色彩，从此，我们一家五口开启了全新的生活。

“2009年的夏天吧，家里东拼西凑地拿出积蓄盖了一间新房子，现在想想，那个时候真的是苦啊。因为要造新房子，村委会要求让我们把老房子拆了，那个时候我和你妈妈去镇上租了一间小房子，房子很小很小，而且特别阴暗潮湿，真的就只能摆一张床。你和爷爷奶奶就到村上的亲戚家里去住了一段时间，当时也没多想啊，也就只是找了个临时的落脚点而已。”父亲又点了一支烟，向我说道。

我是一个记事比较早的孩子，4岁之后的事情我基本上就都记得了。那一年我9岁，因为舍不得贴在老房子墙上的奖状就这么没了，自己一个人跑去那里，结果遭遇了右脚被卡进电瓶车轮胎的意外。也经历过没有电而吃不上饭的尴尬，更体验过一日三餐都只有一碗红烧萝卜的生活。更有，奶奶告诉我，她当时崩溃的时候，会趁我不在，一个人偷偷地跑到新房的地基上大哭。“后来，我们自己的新房子造了一点点，因为不想打扰到别人的生活，我们就搬去了新房那里，虽然环境真的很简陋，但那里才是我们真正的家啊。你爷爷搭了一个床给我们俩睡觉，自己却在房子后面守夜。你知道吗，那张床就搭在了泥地上，一到下雨天我们就只能在上面铺一个那种大的塑料袋，有时候真的半夜睡着睡着就有感觉自己被淋到雨了。那一年真的很苦，但是咬咬牙也就这么过来了。”将近10年过后，奶奶聊起这件事更为云淡风轻了。

“造完房子的第二年，我们就把家里给装修了，当时在外面也欠了好多债，后来还了好一段时间，还好你没有去城里读初中，不然我哪拿得出这么多钱啊”，父亲开玩笑地说道，“虽然也快过去八九年了，我现在有时候和你妈聊起来真的觉得当时我们太勇敢了，造完新房装修完我们马上就办了上梁酒，第二年又贷款买了辆车，你说真的，我们当年哪来的钱啊。不过当时也没多想，生活还在继续，我们一家都在变得越来越好，这才是最重要的啊。”父亲换了个更舒适的位置，继续向我讲道，“后来的那几年，日子虽偶尔有摩擦，我们过上了安稳的生活，每个人都在忙碌,却又不失平淡幸福,这大概就是向往的生活吧。也有可能是咱们家这边的人比较顾家,我们这一辈的人很少有去外面闯荡的,大家都喜欢过踏实的生活。你是独生子女,爸爸妈妈陪着你长大,度过懵懂的童年和叛逆的青春期,虽然工作都挺忙的,经常加班到半夜,但每天回家掩开房门看见你睡得很好,就很幸福。"

说着说着,父亲笑了。

Jiaxing
Zhu Yi (Class 191, Majoring in Journalism)

The Ordinary Happiness

"In fact, our family has been living in an ordinary life over the past few decades, and there are no earth-shattering changes. Just like other families, we need daily necessities like fuel, rice, cooking oil, salt, tea and rice. Born and raised in the countryside of Tongxiang city, we have been rooted in this land for decades. We depend on ourselves, trying to make every effort to improve the quality of life,"my father, flicking the cigarette butt in his hand, said to me peacefully. He was born as the second child in the family in the winter of 1974. He is three years younger than his elder sister whom I call aunt.

My home is located in Zhongjieli Group, Gaodun Village, Shimen Town, Tongxiang City, Jiaxing City, Zhejiang Province. It is an authentic rural family. I was born and grew up in Tongxiang, so I have stayed there for 18 years. Therefore, the word "Tongxiang" is a bond and care not only for me, but also for my family.

When my father was a child, he would sneak food when adults didn't notice. He would also skip classes on his way to school and went swimming with friends. My father told me that when summer day came, they were so indulged in playing in the river that they forgot to go to school. At that time, the boys were very innocent. Maybe because of poor living conditions, swimming was already very satisfying for them. Probably because the living conditions were not good, the boys who were innocent at that time, had been very satisfied with swimming. "At that time, it was not easy to make a living for our family, because four people were packed together in a small house and we had no fixed income. I weaved cloth or did farm work in the daytime. Your grandfather worked in a brick and tile factory. That was the slim income we lived on," said my grandma. She heard us talking about the past when she washed the dishes.

My aunt dropped out of school after finishing the sixth-grade study in elementary school. Then she began to work in a leather shoe factory to earn money, because the family was very poor, and everyone tried to support my father's study in middle school. The whole family placed their expectations on my father. In my father's memory, he was good at his study. It was said that the Chinese teacher asked him to read an excellent composition which was written by him to all the students in the classroom. Actually, I didn't know if he made a brag on it, because he didn't take the high school examination. In 1989, after graduating from middle school, my father, like most people at the time, went to work in a leather shoe factory. This was the time when my father met my mother who also worked in a leather shoe factory. As a result, my parents worked in the leather shoe industry for more than 30 years.

In the early 1990s, my grandfather built a new room on one side of the old house. Even though it was just a room, the whole family were very happy. My father, who had worked in a shoe factory for several years, was promoted to be a salesman by the boss to Shanghai and Wuxi. My father said that it was a happy time when a countryside boy freshly came to a big city, he couldn't be more excited. It was also during that period that my father truly experienced the elegance of a big city, and it was the first time he saw the outside world. He left his footprints in such places as Shanghai Bund, and Wuxi Film and Television City. "I think it was around 1995. I returned to Tongxiang from Wuxi and worked on the previous job. It wasn't long before I got engaged to your mother. Later, the family took out the savings and built another room for my wedding on the basis of the original house."

On the first two days at the turn of the century, my parents held their wedding. When I grew up, I joked to them that the day they married was such a big day. My mother just bowed her head and smiled, saying that she just wanted to pick a time that everyone was on vacation. Perhaps my parents chose those two days after full consideration. I suppose that everyone wants to have a memorable wedding in his life, and my parents just keep their real thought as a secret. I was born at the end of summer in 2001, giving this small family difference and more joy. Since then, our family of five started a new life.

"In the summer of 2009, my family pieced together their savings to build a new house. Now when thinking about it, I found that it was an extremely tough time. Because we were going to build a new house, the village committee asked us to tear down the old house. At that time, your mother and I had to rent a small house in town. That house was really small, dark and humid, and we could only put one bed in it. Your grandparents went to live with the relatives in the village for a period of time. They didn't think much about it. They just wanted a temporary place to stay at." My father lit another cigarette.

I began to remember things when I was a little child. I basically understood most of the things after the age of 4. When I was nine years old, I ran to the old house alone for the certificates on the wall which might be gone during the house demolition. Unfortunately, my right foot was stuck in the tire of a electric bicycle. I experienced the embarrassment that there was nothing to eat because of power outage. I also experienced the life of only having a bowl of braised radish each time for three meals a day. What's more, my grandmother told me that when she collapsed at the time, she would secretly rush to the base of the new house and cry. "Later, when our new house was not fully built, we moved to the new house for we didn't want to disturb others. Although the environment was bad, it was our real home. Your grandfather made a bed for both of us, while he stayed at the back of the house to keep watch. You know, that bed was built on the muddy land. When it rained, we had to put a large plastic bag above the bed. There were times that we felt that we got wet in the rain when we fell asleep in the middle of the night. It was a hard year, but we got through it." Nearly 10 years later, my grandma talked about it peacefully.

"In the second year after the house was built, we decorated our house, so we owed a lot of debts outside, and it took us a long time to repay the debts.

Fortunately, you didn't go to middle school in the city. Otherwise, I couldn't offer such a large sum of money," my father joked, "although eight or nine years has passed, when I talked to your mother at times, I always thought we were so brave. After the decoration of our new house, we immediately started to serve Shangliang wine, which was a Chinese tradition to celebrate the completion of the house by putting the last beam on the roof. We borrowed money to buy a car in the following year. We didn't have much money, however, we didn't think much about it at the time. The most important thing is our family life is moving on and getting better and better." My father changed to a more comfortable position and continued to talk to me, "In the years that followed, although there were occasional conflicts in life, we lived a stable life. Everyone was busy but happy. This is probably the life we have always been yearning for. Probably because our family are family centered, people of our generation seldom make a living away from home. We all like to live a down-to-earth life. You are the only child. Your mother and I get older with you and accompany you to grow up, to go through the ignorant childhood and teenage rebellion. Although we are very busy at work and often work overtime till midnight, but when we open the door, seeing you sleeping well, we feel happy."

My father talked with a smile on his face.

平平淡淡总是真

孟志强

四套房，三代人，两条线，这就是肖妍萱为我们讲述的《平凡日子里的四套房子》故事的情感脉络。

故事的主人公是作者的外公，一位与新中国同一年代出生的普普通通的农民，他出生的房子是一个破旧的小屋，承载着他艰辛的童年；他和外婆搭起了二层简易小房，哺育了三个儿女；土地置换后建起的四层独院小楼，为这个家撑起了一片快乐的蓝天；而如今，高层大房是三代人共享天伦之乐的幸福空间。四套房子，四段经历，呈现出了一个家族生生不息，追求美好生活的历史印记，同时记录了新中国从贫穷走向温饱，再走向富裕的伟大历程。

童年时代就在农田辛勤劳作的外公，是新中国贫困年代顽强生存的一代人，赶上了国家征用土地，换取了一份正式的职业。外公和外婆勤俭持家，养儿育女，供阿姨和舅舅上了大学，外公又把自己的职业转给了舅舅，后来又转给了妈妈，为他们的小家筑起了生活的港湾。而如今，这个家庭又培养出了作者，这位新一代的大学生，在美丽的校园快乐地学习，探索科学与生命的意义。40后、70后、00后，三代人，三个人生主题，生存、生活、生命，预示着我们这个伟大民族从站起来、富起来到强起来的历史必然。

整篇故事贯穿了两条情感线，一条是作者对亲人的挚爱，一条是对这个国家的感怀，正所谓家国情怀。作者用细腻的语言穿越历史，讲述家族生生不息的内在精神。妈妈一宿没睡，紧紧抓住被大风吹起的尼龙纸，因为那个小屋没有玻璃窗户；外公外婆含辛茹苦供养出了两个大学生，并把自己的正式工作传给了舅舅和妈妈；舅舅又亲情回馈，出钱相助，为这个家庭圆了高层大房的梦……我们与作者一起共同感受到这个普通家庭成员之间深深的爱。正是因为有了土地征用，外公有了正式工作；正是因为有了高考制度，两代人上了大学；正是因为有了土地置换，才住上了楼房；正是有了国家改革开放和利民政策，才有了这个家今天的小康。

没有华丽的词藻，没有反转的情节，没有勉强的升华，整篇文章平铺直叙但真情流淌，讲述着家族平凡的日子，但记录着伟大时代带给我们的沧桑巨变。

（北京时代兴邦咨询公司董事长）

故事

温州

肖妍萱（网络与新媒体专业193班）

平凡岁月中的四套房子

我的外公出生在1949年，也就是新中国成立的那一年；我的母亲，出生于1974年，在她4岁的时候，中国迎来了改革开放；而我，出生于2001年，这个科技腾飞、生活加速现代化的千禧时代。我们这三代人各自的成长记忆，可谓印证了新中国成立以来几个重要转折点发生前后普通老百姓的生活状态。与此同时，外公、母亲和我的生活现状的改变与进步恰巧体现在了外公的四套房子里。

外公居住的第一套房子，装载的是外公小时候和刚结婚时的回忆与生活状况。外公在1949年出生，1973年结婚，1974年有了第一个孩子，也就是我的母亲。后来在1976年有了第二个孩子，我的阿姨，在1978年有了第三个孩子，也就是我的舅舅。

外公刚结婚，住的是一层的一个小房间，到后来有了三个孩子，才又自己砌了一个小房间给孩子住。外公现在能够笑称那时的房子跟猪圈一样，因为当时养猪、养鹅、养鸭、养鸡，一进家门就可以看到成群飞舞着的苍蝇蚊子。

外公回忆说，很小很小的时候过得很苦，后来稍微大一点就可以在生产大队做事儿了，日子也就稍微好过一些。外公八九岁的时候就开始在生产队里帮忙，赶牛、割草，一直延续到了十几岁。这个阶段没有什么饭吃，只能吃番薯和番薯干。再后来20岁往后的日子，直到农田被征用、提前退休，生活年复一年、日复一日地被各种各样的农活塞满，农田里仿佛有忙不完的事儿。

外婆说，我妈妈刚生下来的时候，也是他们干农活干得最苦的时候，每天早上四五点就出门了，直到晚上8点多才结束回家，非常的忙碌。在我的母亲两岁时，外公开始到外贸单位上班，为了上班方便，还借钱买了一辆70元的二八自行车，那也是家里的第一辆自行车。

后来，在我母亲五六岁的时候，家里四处借钱，在亲戚朋友的帮助下搭建了一幢两层楼的新房子，也就是外公居住的第二套房。那时一个月的工资有十几块钱都已经称得上有余了，家里在负债几百元后，日子纵然艰辛，还是奋力过了下去。说是二层高的房子，也只是一栋比毛坯房好不了多少的框架，连窗户上该有的玻璃都是用尼龙纸代替的，二层更是空空如也，说是家徒四壁也不为过。

妈妈说："那二楼的地板都是你外公自己铺的，是木地板，先铺的前面，后来再铺的后面一半，墙上的油漆也是外公自己刷的。"外婆说："有一天刮台风，家里窗户上的尼龙纸破了，风大得太吓人了，我拉着窗帘坐了一夜。"

外婆刚开始和外公一样，也是在家里忙农活。后来到了舅舅四五岁的时候，外婆开始到纺织厂工作，有了稳定的工资。借着在纺织厂工作的便利，外婆可以拿到一些工厂里剩余的布料和棉花等填充物，母亲姐弟三人在过年时也有了暖和的崭新的棉大衣穿。我还记得，就连我小时候上幼儿园时的夏天的睡衣也是外婆亲手做的。

这时候家里的农田一直种植着水稻。

一直到我母亲读初中前，家里只有唯一的"大件"——自行车。在我母亲读初中的过程中，因为姐弟三人到他们的同学家看电视，舅舅不小心从楼梯上摔了下来，外公外婆就决定借钱买一台黑白电视机放在家里二楼。至此以后，家里拥有了第一台电视机。

与此同时，在我母亲读初一的时候，村里的土地被国家征用了。家里的农忙生活也从此画上了一个句号，而我们家也因此被补偿了一个工作岗位。本来这个名额是外公弟弟的，是外公花钱从他那里买了过来放在了舅舅的名下。我母亲初中毕业后，因为能力有限没能继续读高中，外公就又把这个名额转给了我母亲。我母亲至此就到客运中心的售票处做了临时工，做了几年后，转成了正式员工，一直干到现在。而我的舅舅和阿姨都读到了大学毕业。舅舅算是"继承"了外公的"衣钵"，外公在54岁提前退休，把工作岗位给了舅舅，舅舅也在这个外贸公司做到现在，还升了职。家里的孩子都有了固定的工作和稳定的收入，生活也就愈发蒸蒸日上。

在我母亲二十四五岁的时候，也就是20世纪90年代末，外公有了第三套房子。这套房子是完全请师傅建的一幢四层楼高、带院子的房子，也是我从小居住成长的地方。在搬家的时候，家具几乎全部都换了新，还换了一个新的彩色电视机。

这栋房子是我启蒙成长的起点，有我无忧无虑的童年记忆。在我的童年记忆里，这栋房子的前院种着一列树木：两棵桂花树、两棵铁树以及两棵玉兰树。我们一大家子在夏天会在院子里吃晚饭，感受着夏日傍晚的凉风，消解一天的暑气。每当夏季的暴雨过后，院子里的空气中掺杂了树木和泥土的清香，闻起来尤为清甜，深得我心。我还记得，院子里用石头做的灰色的洗衣台，在夏日夜晚摸起来很是凉爽。

到了2015年，外公家所在的这一片区域被划分为拆迁的区域，舅舅就补了一些钱，换到了现在居住的高楼里——温州鹿城区的鸿豪锦园。这也是外公居住的第四套房子。这套房子是完完全全的现代化装修，外公外婆和舅舅一家住在这里。这套现代化的高层楼房更能象征着我们迈向小康之家的起点。外公外婆的退休工资在不断地上涨，舅舅舅妈在工作上也颇有能力，工资水平十分不错，外公家里的生活条件已完全“小康”，外公外婆也算是怡然自得地安享晚年了。

旧屋虽拆，旧事已去，但，明日会如约而至。

Wenzhou
Xiao Yanxuan (Class 193, Majoring in Network and New Media)

Four Houses in Simple Days

My grandfather was born in 1949 when the People's Republic of China was founded. My mother was born in 1974. When she was four years old, China opened itself up to the world. In 2001, I was born in this fast-developing world full of technological advances. Each one of our three generations witnessed many turning points of this country and their influence on people's livelihoods. At the same time, the life story of my grandfather, my mother and I were well shown through four houses of my grandfather.

The first house of my grandfather was filled with memories of his childhood and wedding. Born in 1949, my grandpa married in 1973 and had his first child, my mother, in 1974. In 1976, my aunt was born into this world and two years later, in 1978, arrived his third child, my uncle.

My grandfather lived in a single-story house when he just got married. Later on he built a small room with bricks to accommodate his three children. He always joked that he had lived inside a pigsty. Back then, my grandparents raised pigs, geese, ducks and hens, so swarms of flies and mosquitoes were seen hovering there every time he entered the gate of that house.

According to my grandfather, he had lived a harsh life when he was a child. As he got older, he began to work for the production brigade so the family could make ends meet. At the age of eight or nine, my grandpa began to herd cattle and cut grass, which went on till his teens. Food was scarce at that time, and the only thing he could eat was sweet potatoes and dried sweet potatoes. My grandpa had been busy with all kinds of farm work ever since his 20s. He never stopped working until he was retired early and his land was expropriated.

My grandmother said they were in the busiest time with farm work when my mother was just born. They needed to leave their home at four or five in the morning and they didn't come back until around eight in the evening. When my mother was two years old, my grandpa started to work for a foreign-trade organization. To get to work faster, he borrowed money from his friends, and spent 70 yuan to buy a "two eight" bicycle which was the first bicycle that the family bought ("two eight" bicycle was named because the diameter of its wheel was 28 inches).

Then when my mom was five or six years old, my grandfather borrowed money from friends and neighbors to build a two-story house, which was his second property. A salary of more than ten yuan could provide a well-off life at that time. Despite the hardship, they managed to live with several hundred yuan in debt. Their two-story house was just a framework, no better than a roughcast house. Instead of glass, the family used nylon papers to cover the windows; the second floor was empty; it was not too much to say that we used to live in a house that had nothing but four bare walls.

My mom said, "it was your grandfather who put down the wooden floor on his own. He put down the first half, then the second half. He also painted the wall by himself." Then my grandmother said, "one day, the nylon paper on the window broke because of the typhoon. The wind was so big that I sat by the window to drag the curtains all night".

My grandparents did some farm work at home in the beginning. When my uncle was four or five, she began to work in the textile mill, so she was able to have stable salary. Taking advantage of working in the textile mill, she could get some fabric and cotton padding which was left over from the factory. And from then on, her children had some warm and new cotton coats to wear during Chinese New Year. I still remembered that my grandmother made summer pajamas for me when I was a kid in kindergarten.

At that time, they had kept planting rice in the farmland.

Before my mother went to the middle school, the only valuable piece at home was a bicycle. My mother and his brothers would often visit her classmates to watch television. One day, my uncle fell from the stairs in his classmate's house, and that was when my grandparents decided to buy a black and white television which was put on the second floor. Since then, they had the first TV at home.

The land in the village was requisitioned by the government when my mom was in her first year in middle school. Therefore, they no longer needed to work on farmland and they were compensated with a job. My grandfather bought the job for my uncle for it was supposed to be his brother's. However, my mother got the job at last for she was unable to enter high school. Since then, my mother worked in the ticket office of the passenger transportation center as a temporary worker. After several years, she became a regular employee and has been working there until now. Meanwhile, my uncle and my aunt graduated from universities. My uncle took on the mantle of my grandfather, who was retired in advance to give him the opportunity. He worked in the foreign trade company till now and got a promotion. Children's permanent jobs and regular salaries contributed to the improvement of the family's economy and life conditions.

In the late 1990s when my mother was 24 or 25, my grandfather had his third house built. This was a four-story house with a garden. I spent the majority of my childhood there. All furniture was new, and they even bought a colour TV.

This house was the symbol of my early growth and my carefree childhood. I remembered that there were two cinnamon trees, sago cycas, and magnolia trees planted in the front courtyard of the house. My whole family would have meals in the courtyard, feeling the cool breeze in scorching summer days. What impressed me most was the pleasant smell which mixed the aroma of trees and soil after a summer storm. I still remembered the grey laundry table made of stone, which felt pleasantly cool when touched in summer evenings.

In 2015, the area where my grandfather had lived was designated a demolition area. My uncle paid extra money to get a new apartment where he has been living with my grandparents until now. This was the fourth house that my grandfather lived in, which is completely modern-furnished. My grandparents and my uncle's family live here together. This modernized high-rise apartment is the symbol of the beginning of our family towards a well-off family. My grandparents' retirement salary is constantly rising. My uncle and my aunt are so competent that they get high salary. Their family has reached a well-off standard of living, so my grandparents can enjoy their well-funded golden years.

The old house has been demolished, and our past has already gone forever. However, a better tomorrow will come to us as promised.

创业之帆乘风破浪

赵 红

作者父亲的创业经历读来让人心潮澎湃，生病的经历看着揪心，所幸现在一切和顺。作者父亲的创业之路也是杨汛桥的城镇化之路，这个近两年的“全国综合实力千强镇”，紧紧抓住时代的机遇，在这片开遍紫薇的土地上也开出了经济腾飞之花，而作者父亲凭借敏锐的商业头脑和无惧困难敢想敢做的毅力闯出了一片天。改革开放40余年间，中国经济增长的动力从“工业化”转型为“城市化”，早期的杨汛桥抓住了工业化的第一波浪潮，当时社会对于快速流动、节约时间成本的欲望增加，作者父亲抓住人们对于“行”的需求，做起“招手车”“大集团驾驶员”工作，立业成家，日子平稳。随着工业化的长足发展，越来越多的农村人口涌入城镇，对于在城镇中“食”“衣”“住”的需求不断增长，作者父亲抓住商机，相继开了超市、服装卖场、旅馆，并开发本土化销路，创业风生水起，这是作者父亲本人的魄力所在，他也是城市化进程的受益者。2013年，中国经济增长出现拐点，标志着经济增长模式从工业驱动转为城市驱动，而作者父亲在城市化浪潮袭来之前就打下知名度，做了第一个吃螃蟹的人，充分尝到了创业的甜头。其中过程尽管艰辛坎坷，但收获的是阅尽千帆后的从容以及给子女的榜样教育。

（浙大宁波理工学院思政讲师，硕士）

故事

绍兴

夏今阳(网络与新媒体专业182班)

千帆过尽自从容

杨汛桥是我父亲的出生地与打拼地,位于浙江绍兴的西北部,这里开遍了紫薇花。上世纪80年代,“星星之火”点燃了杨汛桥人的创业激情,杨汛桥的第一批开拓者凭借独特的“永不平庸、永不放弃、永不满足”的杨汛桥精神,开启了杨汛桥人的第一次创业——“农村工业化”。

我的父亲出生于一个穷苦家庭,读完初中便没有继续上学,满18周岁就选择了入伍。1993年退伍归来,他做过很多工作,去菜市场运货,在亲戚的厂里打工,还学了一阵子的木工。

后来他去考了驾驶证,用到处打工攒下来的钱买了一辆二手车,开始了第一次“创业”——做“招手车”生意。当了一年半的招手车司机,我的父亲萌生了去大集团锻炼的念头。

在集团的第一份工作也是当驾驶员,一年后由于表现出色,外加是退伍兵,体格健壮,性格比较适合管理别人,被老板提拔成了保卫科长,这一干就是7年。

在这7年间,他经同事介绍,认识了同在集团工作的我的母亲,两个人相恋继而结婚,日子过得平淡安稳。随着乡镇企业蓬勃发展,杨汛桥镇迎来了越来越多的外来打工者,老百姓的消费需求增长,这些变化我的父亲都看在眼里,他本就不安现状的心开始蠢蠢欲动。

城市中已经出现了连锁超市,但在镇子里还没有一家大型的综合超市,商店里卖的货物品种都相对单一,已经不符合老百姓的消费需求了。老百姓需要更多样化的选择,于是在杨汛桥镇开一家超市成为他的创业目标。经过摸索找寻,他看上了镇中的一幢废弃办公楼,为了拿下这幢办公楼,他到处托人打听谈判。

一幢三层高的办公楼租金显然不会便宜,一年40万的租金对当时的父亲来讲可以算得上天价,那时口袋里只有5万块钱的他东拼西凑,到处借钱,最后凑了120万元左右,拿下了这个店面。资金还是紧张,他就把那辆招手车也卖了。“那是我人生中买的第一辆车,桑塔纳牌子的,当时买进是12.8万元,以7.5万元的价格卖掉,也都投入到超市里面去了。”尽管过了将近20年,父亲还是能清晰地想起这些数字。这些数字的背后是父亲豁出去的决心、孤注一掷的勇气。

店面搞定以后，我的父亲找到了上海联华超市总部，和他们沟通洽谈，达成了加盟协议。在上海总部老师们的指导下，进行装潢策划，内部规划布置，经过3个月的装修之后，联华超市正式开业了。

开业之后，销售额却没有达到我父亲的预期。预期中超市一天的营业额可以达到3万元，结果平常的日子只能做到1.3万元左右。经过仔细观察，他找到了原因。由于加盟的是上海的超市，很多货都是由上海总部配送的，不符合杨汛桥镇当地百姓的购买习惯。他马上进行了调整，把原来80%的上海品牌换成了浙江本土品牌为主。自己买了辆面包车去各地进货。真正了解了当地老百姓的需求，他又进行了一系列的营销活动，让利给顾客，通过在方圆5公里的各个村庄人工分发宣传单，扩大了知名度，营业额大大提升。

父亲讲到这里的时候，他的讲述和我的记忆逐渐重合了起来。稍微小一点的时候，我也曾经跟着超市里的叔叔阿姨一起去市场之类热闹的地方派发传单。三四个人在一辆面包车里，每人一沓传单，到一个地方就下去分发介绍，发完了再回到车上去往下一个地点。我就在旁边跟着做，也不知道就是这一张张的传单带来了更多的顾客。

在开业时，父亲把所有的租金成本都押在一楼，只开发了一楼作为超市，二三楼都是空置的。他第一个想法就是把二三楼租出去，把成本摊低。由于租地的旁边是一条“断头路”，是一块田地，还没有被开发，人流不是很大，每次和租主谈到租金成本的时候，很多想租的人考虑后都选择了放弃。没有人愿意租，那就只能自己来做。经过深思熟虑，他决定把二楼打造成服装卖场。父亲卖服装的时候，每天早上3点多就要起床去杭州进货，甚至还出过车祸，他的车翻入了田地，两个门牙都砸掉了，幸好被围墙挡住才没有翻进河里。

服装市场靠着薄利多销在小镇中一炮打响。原本以为服装卖场一天只能有1万元的收入，结果连续30天，每天都超过了4万元的营业额，连带着一楼超市的生意也变得更好了。超市，盘活了。

一二楼都获得了成功，我的父亲决定趁热打铁，把空置的三楼也利用起来。他大胆地追加投资，开起了旅馆，用星级酒店的模式装修，以旅馆的价钱经营。一共30个房间，天天爆满，不过大半年就收回了成本。

经过几年的发展，我的父亲已经拥有了丰富的经营经验和完整的管理体系，他不满足于一个超市的成功，有了更大的目标。他在周边城镇考察，寻找机会，开起了第二家、第三家。

2013年，我的弟弟出生，我即将上高中，到目前为止仿佛一切都还算顺风顺水，但父亲突如其来的癌症差点压垮了我们这个家。父亲前往上海治疗，高昂的医疗费让他不得不放弃一些生意，将超市转让出租，原本打算过几年就搬进去的房子也卖了。

“生病前总想着我的年纪正是奋斗的年纪，还能拼，要把生意做大，再去哪里哪里开几家分店，房子也换个更好的。到鬼门关走了一遭之后，那种拼的劲儿就没有了。”讲述这些话时父亲的语气和之前讲创业之旅时的语气已经大不一样，经历过沧桑，有点看破红尘、看淡人生的样子。

我也能想起那时放暑假去上海陪父亲的样子，上海医院旁边的小区，地方不大租金却十分昂贵，我在旁边写作业，父亲躺在床上插着雾化器的管子。炎热的夏天，潮湿而漫长。一切仿佛还发生在昨天。

如今，癌症给我们家庭带来的影响慢慢减弱，爸爸恢复了工作，继续管理超市，但已经没有精力和欲望扩大商业版图了。债务全部还清，老家也盖了新房。弟弟健康成长，我好好念书，家庭和睦，也没有什么不满足的了。

父亲的创业之路，艰难颇多，坎坷颇多，但他深刻贯彻了“永不平庸、永不放弃、永不满足”的杨汛桥精神，善于抓住机会，大胆尝试，遇到困难也毫不畏惧，努力突破。初中毕业，毫无创业经验，对于超市经营一窍不通的父亲却敢做镇里第一个吃螃蟹的人。他的这些宝贵精神通过言传身教，教育着我和弟弟。

Shaoxing
Xia Jinyang (Class 182, Majoring in Network and New Media)

The Abundant Life Experiences Bring Peace of Mind

Yangxunqiao is where my father was born and fought for life. It is located in the northwest of Shaoxing, Zhejiang Province, where crape myrtle bloom everywhere. In the 1980s, the single spark ignited the entrepreneurial passion of the people in Yangxunqiao. The first pioneers of Yangxunqiao relied on the unique spirit of "never being mediocre, never giving up, never being satisfied" and started their first entrepreneurship——the rural industrialization.

My father was born in a poor family and did not go to school after middle school. When he was eighteen he chose to join the army and did a lot of jobs after discharge from the army. He delivered goods to the vegetable market; he worked in a relative's factory, and also learned carpentry for a while.

He obtained his driving license later, so he bought a used car with the money he had saved from his hard work, then he started his first business as a taxi driver. After one and a half years as a taxi driver, my father had the idea of going to a big company for self-training.

His first job in the company was also a driver. However, after a year, he was promoted to be the chief of the security section by the boss due to his excellent performance. The other reason was he was a retired soldier with a strong physique, and his personality was suitable for the post of management. He worked on this job for seven years.

During the seven years, he was introduced by colleagues to my mother, who worked in the same company. They fell in love and then got married, leading an insipid and stable life. With the booming development of township enterprises, Yangxunqiao town ushered in more and more migrant workers, and people's demand of consumption increased. These changes opened my father's eyes to opportunities, and he wanted to do something for he was always uneasy with the status quo.

While supermarket chains had appeared in the city, there was still no general supermarket in the town. The variety of goods sold in the shops relatively lacked diversity, which no longer met the consumption needs of ordinary people. People needed more diversified choices, so opening a supermarket in Yangxunqiao became my father's business goal. After groping around, he targeted an abandoned office building in the town. In order to rent the office building, he inquired about the negotiations everywhere.

Obviously, the rent of a three-storey office building was not cheap. The annual rent of 400,000 yuan was a sky-high price for my father at that time. With only 50,000 yuan in his pocket, he went around borrowing money from others and scraped together 1.2 million yuan or so to rent the office. However, he still had fund shortage, so he sold the car he had used to serve as a taxi. "It was the first car I bought in my life, a Santana. I bought it at 128,000 yuan, but sold it at 75,000 yuan, which was also put into the supermarket business." Nearly 20 years later, my father could still remember the numbers clearly. Behind these figures were my father's determination to start his first business and his courage to bear all-for-nothing risk.

After the storefront was settled, my father found the headquarters of Shanghai Lianhua Supermarket and negotiated with them. They reached the franchise agreement. Under the guidance of staff in Shanghai headquarters, the decoration planning and internal planning were carried out. After three months' decoration, the first Lianhua supermarket in our town officially opened.

After opening, sales fell short of my father's expectations. Originally, it was expected that the daily turnover of the supermarket could reach 30,000 yuan, but it could only make a profit of 13,000 every day. After careful observation, he found the reason. As the supermarket was franchised to the Shanghai supermarket, most of the goods were distributed by the Shanghai headquarters, not in line with the buying habits of local people in Yangxunqiao Town. He immediately made a change, replacing 80 percent of Shanghai brands with Zhejiang brands. My father bought a van and went to different places to get some supplies. Having truly understood the needs of local people, he carried out a series of marketing activities to make discounts for customers. By manually distributing leaflets in every village within five kilometers, he expanded his popularity and greatly increased the turnover.

Little by little what my father told me overlapped with my memory. When I was younger, I used to go with the staff in supermarkets to hand out leaflets in busy places like markets. Three or four people were in a van, each with a stack of leaflets. They handed out the leaflets of our supermarket when arriving in a certain place. Then they returned to the car for the next destination. I followed along without realizing that the leaflets would bring more customers to the supermarket.

When the supermarket opened, my father put all his rent costs on the first floor, which was developed as the supermarket. The second and third floors were left unused. His first idea was to rent out the second and third floors to lower the costs. Because next to the leased land was a "dead end way", which was a piece of farmland that had not been developed yet, and few people travelled here. Every time when talking about the rent cost with the landlord, many people who wanted to rent gave up after consideration. No one wanted to rent it, so we had to make good use of it ourselves. After careful consideration, he decided to turn the second floor into a clothing store. When my father sold clothes, he had to get up at 3 o'clock every morning to buy some goods in Hangzhou. There was even an accident in which his car overturned in a field. He lost two of his front teeth; fortunately, he was blocked by the wall so that he was prevented from falling into the river.

With the advantage of small profits and large sales, the clothing store quickly became famous in the town. Originally, we thought the clothing store could only have a daily income of 10,000 yuan. However, the daily turnover exceeded 40,000 yuan for 30 consecutive days, and the business of the first floor supermarket also became better. Our supermarket has been vitalized.

After he made the success of business on the first and second floors, my father decided to immediately put the vacant third floor into use. He boldly added investment to decorate the third floor into a hotel, which applied the star hotel's model and ran at the price of common hotel. The hotel had 30 rooms in total, and was booked out every day, so it just took my father half a year to recover his costs.

After several years of development, my father had rich operating experience and established a complete management system. He was not satisfied with the success of a supermarket and had a bigger goal. He explored the surrounding towns, looking for opportunities. Then he opened a second and a third one.

In 2013, my younger brother was born and I was about to start high school. So far, everything seemed to be going well, but my father got cancer suddenly, which almost overwhelmed our family. When my father went to Shanghai for medical treatment, the high medical expenses forced him to give up some businesses. He leased out the supermarket and sold the house that he planned to move into in a few years.

"Before I fell ill, I always thought that my age was the age for struggle, that I could still work hard and I wanted to expand my business, to open a few branches and to get a better house. When I was saved from the jaws of death, the spirit has gone away." When telling these words, my father's tone was quite different from the tone he had talked about his entrepreneurial journey before. After experiencing the vicissitudes of life, he seems to be disillusioned with the mortal world and the life.

I could also recall the memory when I went to accompany my father in

Shanghai during the summer holiday. In the small community near Shanghai Hospital, the house was not big but its rent was very expensive. I was doing my homework beside my father while he was lying on the bed with the atomizer pipe on his body. It was a hot summer day, which was damp and long. Everything seemed to have just happened yesterday.

Now that the impact of my father's cancer on our family slowly faded away, my father returned to work and continued to run the supermarket, but he had no energy or desire to expand his business. The family's debts had been paid off and a new house was built in our hometown. My brother grew up healthily while I studied hard, my family lived in harmony, and we were satisfied with everything.

My father's entrepreneurial road was quite difficult and bumpy, but he deeply carried out the Yangxunqiao spirit of "never being mediocre, never giving up, never being satisfied". He was good at seizing opportunities, making bold attempts, and striving to break through difficulties without fear. My father, a man of little education and no entrepreneurial experience, knew nothing about supermarket management, but he dared to be the first person to start market business in the town. He set an example for my younger brother and me through his precious spirit.

三代人的三种生活折射中国社会伟大变革

崔　雨

许费凡同学的《三代人的三种生活》展现了三代人的三种生活图景：爷爷带着贫困烙印的粗放生活；父亲告别贫困的温饱生活；作者染着小康色彩的品质生活。这启发我思考：100年来，在中国共产党的领导下，中国社会发生着怎样的变革，中国人民命运发生着怎样的变化？

爷爷的粗放生活。新中国成立之初，由于卫生工作的进步和人民生活条件的改善，人的寿命延长。但是，人口增长过快，导致全国人民在吃饭、穿衣、住房、交通、教育、卫生就业等方面都遇到困难。1971年，我国把控制人口增长的指标首次纳入国民经济发展计划。1982年，党的十二大把计划生育确定为基本国策。爷爷的生活是粗放的——“那时候哪来的计划生育？”结果是缺衣少食。

父亲的温饱生活。实行计划生育后，人口数量得到控制、质量大幅提升，人们过上了温饱生活。更重要的是，文明程度越来越高，人们对教育越来越重视。姑姑由于学习成绩好，奶奶表示“就算是把家里的东西卖了，也要让她读下去”。姑姑最终考取浙江师范大学，毕业后当中学老师。作者回忆：“爸爸妈妈不用再为能不能吃饱饭而担忧，而且可以接受一定的文化教育，过着基本满足的生活。”

作者的品质生活。2001年，作者出生。跨入新世纪、迈向新时代，我国进入全面建设小康社会、加快推进社会主义现代化的发展新阶段。作者出生前两年，爸爸辞掉厂里的工作做起批发水产的生意，妈妈转到了村里的丝厂工作。2012年11月，党的十八召开，开启了共创中国人民和中华民族更加幸福美好未来的崭新征程。这一年，家里买了小别墅。两年后，爸爸承包鱼塘做起了养殖生意。作者说：“我出生在最好的年代，不用为生活担忧。”

（宁波卫生职业技术学院，副研究员）

故事

湖州

许费凡(新闻学专业 192 班)

三代人的三种生活

爷爷说:“那时候哪来的计划生育,所有人都想多生。那时候,生得多就是厉害。但是人多就没衣服穿,过年的时候,就把稍微好一点的旧衣服补一下当新衣服穿。穿不着的衣服就会留下来给你姑婆他们长大了穿,我穿的就是你大爷爷穿不着剩下来的。”我爷爷有六个兄弟姐妹,他排行第三;我奶奶也有六个兄弟姐妹,也是排行第三。

爷爷没有上过学,在十一二岁的时候就和大人下地干活了。“你们那时候都去地里干什么?”我问爷爷。

“十几岁的时候,就只能在田里挑泥,一次就是几十斤,想想看你十一二岁的时候,你现在都不一定行。所以有人说那时候的人长得矮就是因为小时候每天挑泥压得骨头长不起来。等到十五六岁的时候就和大人划船去别的地方割喂鱼吃的草。养春蚕和秋蚕的时候,就要和村里的小队出去摘桑叶。养蚕的时候,半夜一两点要起床去喂蚕。那时候,大人和小队出去干一天活基本是 10 个工分,女人是 8 个工分,小孩子是 5 个工分,一个工分大概是三四分钱左右。我记得我十几岁的时候,一天家里就 30 多个工分,家里有 10 个人,你想想看那时候有多苦。”

“我记得有一年冬天要把鱼塘里的鱼捞出来卖,我要去把鱼塘里的水用水泵抽到河里,在河边装管子的时候踩空掉进水里,冬天穿着棉袄,吸了水很重,根本游不起来,要不是有人刚好划船经过看见,我差点就没命了。还有啊,那时候夏天连电风扇都没有,干了一天活回来,躺在床上扇蒲扇,扇着扇着累了就睡着了,半夜热醒了就继续扇。你山里的姑婆,夏天热得床都躺不下去了,就在通风的弄堂里放个养蚕用的匾,躺在匾里睡觉。”爷爷这一辈子是个地地道道的农民,只会种田养鱼这些农活,一直呆在村里,去市区的次数都屈指可数。问起他最骄傲的事,就是 1997 年和村里的人一起去北京做生意,去毛主席纪念堂瞻仰了毛主席的遗体。

我妈妈初中毕业就去参加工作了,那时她只有 16 岁。“你为什么不继续读呢？就算考不上高中，上个中专也好啊。”

“因为家里没钱。我初中的时候成绩不好，也不喜欢读书，而你姑姑读书厉害，成绩好，还经常参加比赛拿奖，所以就准备让她初中毕业继续读，后来你姑姑考上了菱湖中学的高师预科班。高师预科班就是你高中毕业后，如果不考大学，就可以直接去做小学老师。你姑姑高师预科班毕业的时候，村里的人都劝你奶奶，让你姑姑别考大学，去当个小学老师算了，要是没考上大学，就白读了。你奶奶说：‘她要是想考大学，继续读，就算是把家里的东西卖了，我们过得苦一点，也要让她读下去，要不然她和我们都会后悔一辈子的。’在农村，读书是唯一的出路，后来你姑姑考上了浙江师范大学，毕业后就在菱湖中学当老师。”

“那你怪爷爷奶奶不让你继续读吗？”

“刚毕业的时候还开心，终于不用读书了。后来工作了几年，嫌工作累了，就有点怪你爷爷奶奶。长大了就想通了，只能怪自己读书不用心，要是当时我读书成绩好，你爷爷奶奶就算再苦也会想办法让我继续读的。”

“那你最开始的工作是什么呀？”

“我初中毕业那年只有16岁，要自己骑自行车去菱湖镇上的丝厂上班。村里会有人一起去上班。那时候是三班制，早上6点到下午2点半是第一班，下午2点半到晚上11点是第二班，晚上11点到第二天6点是第三班。要是上第一班，凌晨三四点就要起床了，从家里去上班骑自行车都要半个多小时，而且那时候都是小路，边上都是桑叶地和鱼塘。有时候两辆自行车交叉过，稍微让一下，一不小心就会掉到鱼塘里去，我都不知道掉了多少次了。要是上第二班，有伴就会晚上一起回家睡觉，要是没有人，就睡在厂里，第二天早上回家，然后吃完中饭又要骑车出来上班，那时候也是傻，回家干嘛，刚到家，吃个饭又要回去上班，而且大夏天，去上第二班、第三班的时候，太阳正大，到厂里的时候整个人都是汗，衣服都湿光了，厂里会发免费的盐水棒冰，我的胃就是那时候吃坏的。”

1999年，我妈和我爸结婚，她就转到了村里的丝厂上班。

“你是怎么认识我妈的啊？”我问我爸。

“那说来就话长了，当时我和你妈是在同一个丝厂里工作认识的。我因为初中成绩差，初三毕业就去干活了，和你外公一起养了几个鱼塘，就这样干了三年，有了些积蓄，造了四间楼房，就是现在还在的那四间。当时在村里，楼房是算好的，所以还很风光。造好房子，我就和你外公去嘉善那边承包鱼塘养鱼，就这样，和你外公养了两年鱼没有赚到钱，就回家了。你外公托关系让我进了菱湖的溪西丝厂，做结头工，两年后认识了也在丝厂上班的你妈。那年我25岁，你妈22岁。1999年我就和你妈结婚了。”

我爸爸妈妈和爷爷奶奶那个年代相比，不用再为能不能吃饱饭而担忧，而且可以接受一定的文化教育，但是因为受到经济条件、文化水平的限制，仍然没有走出农村，每日辛苦工作，过着基本满足的生活。

2001年，我来到了这个家里，自我出生以来，家里的大人经常告诉我，我出生的时间非常幸运。1999年，刚结婚的爸爸妈妈想为将来出生的我提供一个更好的生活条件，我爸辞掉了厂里的工作，做起批发水产的生意，我妈转到了村里的丝厂继续工作。

“虽然那时候赚的钱更多，但是也更辛苦。特别是冬天的时候，大家养的鱼都是这个时候捞起来卖，凌晨两三点就要起床，天刚亮的时候就要把刚捞起来的鱼运到杭州、余杭、萧山、嘉兴，还有苏州去卖。2004年的时候，村里的丝厂关了，你妈就去锦山上班。2010年的时候，村里有人新开了一家丝厂，你妈就又回到村里来上班了。2012年，因为你长大了，我和你妈结婚的时候造的新房又显得太小，我们就在村里买了一套小别墅，也就是我们现在住的这套。”

2014年，爸爸经过十几年的在外奔波，决定不再继续做批发生意，就承包了几十亩的鱼塘，雇了几个人，做起了养殖生意。

所以说，我是很幸运的，出生在最好的年代，不用为自己的生活担忧，更不用考虑能不能吃饱饭。纵观三种生活，几代人的奋斗，如今的小康生活正是由长辈的不懈努力得来的。

Huzhou
Xu Feifan (Class 192, Majoring in Journalism)

Three Lives of Three Generations

My grandpa said, “At that time, everyone wanted to have more kids, having no idea about family planning. From their point of view, the more children, the better. As a result, many people had no clothes to wear. During the Spring Festival, we put on the ‘new’ dresses, which actually were the old ones that were mended. The clothes that were too small for us to wear would be passed down to our sisters when they grew up. What I wore was the clothes that my elder brother had worn before.” My grandfather, having six siblings, was the third of seven children in the family; the same was the case with my grandmother.

My grandpa was illiterate, and he began to do farm work with his parents when he was eleven or twelve years old. "What did you do in the farmland at that time?" I asked my grandpa.

"When I was a teenager, I could only carry loads of mud to and from the farmland, dozens of jin at a time (Jin is a Chinese unit of weight). You could imagine whether you could do that or not when you were 11 or 12 years old. You even might not be able to do it now. So it's said that people at that time were short due to the fact that the bones couldn't develop well because the bones were pressed every day when they carried the heavy mud. When I was around sixteen, I would go boating with the adult to other places for cutting grass to feed fish. When rearing silkworms in spring and autumn, I had to go out with the village group to pick mulberry leaves. When feeding silkworms, I must drag myself out of the bed to feed them around the wee hours. At that time, adults and small groups earned approximately 10 workpoints when working for a day, while women earned 8 workpoints, and children earned 5 workpoints. One workpoint was equivalent to 3 or 4 fen (fen is a Chinese unit of money). I remembered when I was a teenager, our family had ten persons, but we could only gain around 30 workpoints in a day. What a hard period."

"I remembered that I needed to scoop the fish out of the fishpond to sell in winter. Therefore, I had to pump the water from the fishpond into the river. But I fell into the river when I tried installing the pipe on the riverside. The padded jacket that I wore became heavy after soaking in water, so I couldn't swim. I would have died if no one had happened to row on the river and saw me drowning. What's more, there was no electric fan in summer. I just lay on the bed after a day of work, fanned myself till falling asleep. If the heat woke me up in the night, I would continue to fan. It was so hot that your aunt who lived in the mountains couldn't even lie down in bed in summer, so she put a basket used for raising silkworm in the airy lane and slept in it." My grandpa was a typical farmer all his life who only knew how to farm and fish. He stayed in the village all the time, and went to the city only a few times. When I asked him about the most proud thing in his life, he would say that he viewed Chairman Mao's body with reverence in the Chairman Mao Memorial Hall when he had a business trip with people in the village group to Beijing in 1997.

My mother dropped out of junior high school. When she began to work, she was only sixteen. "Why didn't you continue to study? If you couldn't be admitted by the high school, you should try entering a technical secondary school."

"Because my family was poor. When I was in junior high school, I was bad in my study and disliked learning. On the contrary, your aunt was good at study and got high scores. She won lots of prizes in many competitions, so she wanted to go on with her studies. Fortunately, your aunt was admitted to preparatory class for normal school in Linghu Middle School. Entering this class meant if she didn't want to go to the university after graduation, she could also be a primary school teacher. The villagers all advised your grandma to dissuade your aunt from taking the national entrance examination of the university, and asked my aunt to be a primary school teacher. If she wasn't admitted to the university, all she had done would be in vain. Your grandmother told those people that if your aunt wanted to go to college and continue her studies, she would definitely let her continue to study even if she had to sell all the furniture at home and live a harder life. Otherwise, she believed that they would regret it for the rest of their lives. In the countryside, studying was the only way to succeed. Afterwards, your aunt was accepted by Zhejiang Normal University and then became a teacher at Linghu Middle School after graduation."

"Do you blame my grandparents for not allowing you to continue studying?"

"At that time, I was happy when I just graduated, because I didn't need to study. However, after several years of work, I felt tired of working, so I blamed your grandparents a little bit. When I grew up, I could only blame myself for not studying diligently. If I had been good at school, your grandparents would have tried to support my study, no matter how hard it was."

"So what was your first job?"

"I was only 16 when I graduated from junior high school. I had to ride my bike to work in a silk factory in Linghu town. People from the village would go to work together. At that time, there were three shifts. The first shift was from 6 a.m. to 2:30 p.m.; the second shift was from 2:30 p.m. to 11

p. m. , and the third shift was from 11 p. m. to 6 a. m. on the next day. If I took the first shift, I had to get up at 3 or 4 o'clock in the morning, and it took me more than half an hour to go to work by bike. Moreover, it was a narrow road with mulberry fields and fish ponds on each side of the road. Sometimes when two bicycles went in the opposite directions, we would probably fall into the fish pond by accident if we gave a little way to each other. I couldn't remember how many times I had fallen into the pond. If I worked on the second shift, I would go home to sleep when I was accompanied. If there was nobody accompanying me, I would sleep in the factory and then go back home in the morning. After lunch, I would ride to work again. Thinking of that time, I was such a fool to waste time on going back. It wasted time to go back home. I came home just to have a meal, then I had to go back to the factory to work. And in the hot summer, the sun was scorching when I worked the second or the third shift. I was drenched in sweat, and my clothes were wet completely. The factory would offer a free saltwater Popsicle to every worker. That's how I got my stomachache."

In 1999, when my mother married my father, she changed to work for the silk factory in the village.

"How did you meet my mom?" I asked my dad.

"That's a long story. I met your mother when she and I worked in the same silk factory. Because of my poor grades in junior high school, I went to work when I graduated. I rented several fish ponds for rearing fish with your grandfather and worked in this way for three years. With some savings, I built four bungalows that have remained there till now. At that time, my house was the best among the village, so we were quite proud of ourselves. After all bungalows were completed, I went to Jiashan with your grandfather to contract for fish ponds. After raising fish with your grandfather for two years without making any money, we went back home. Your grandfather pulled a few strings to get me into Xixi silk factory in Linghu. Two years later, I met your mother. She also worked in a silk factory. I was 25 and your mother was 22 that year, and we got married later in 1999."

Compared with my grandparents in that period, my parents no longer had to worry about clothes and food. They had the chance to receive some education. However, due to the poor economic conditions and educational level, they still couldn't go out of the countryside and worked hard every day. They could just satisfy their basic needs in life.

I was born in 2001. The adults often told me that I was born in a very lucky time. My parents just got married in 1999. In order to provide better living conditions for me who would be born in the near future, my father quit his job in the factory and started his business in the wholesale aquatic products. My mother changed to a new job, to work in village silk factory.

"We made more money at the time, but it was also harder during that period. Especially in winter when people scooped up fish to sell, people got up at 2 or 3 o'clock and carried the fish to Yuhang, Xiaoshan, Jiaxing and Suzhou as soon as the fish were trawled from the fish pond at dawn. In 2004, when the silk factory in the village closed, your mother went to work in Jinshan. In 2010, someone in the village opened another silk factory, so your mother came back to work. In 2012, since you had grown up, the house I built when we got married was too small to live in, so we brought a villa in the village. It is the house we are living in now.

In 2014, after more than ten years of doing business far away from his hometown, my father decided not to continue to do wholesale business. Instead, he contracted for a fish pond of several mu and hired some people to start the fish-breeding business.

Generally speaking, I was lucky enough to be born in the best of times. I don't have to worry about my life and food. Taking a look on the three kinds of life that several generations strove for, we find that the well-off life today comes from the unremitting efforts of the elders.

方寸票证　巨变中国

聂迎娉

票证是什么？它既是一个凭证，也是岁月的印记。三张票子一本书，小小的四纸票证，是一个典型家庭的缩影，见证了中国从计划经济向市场经济的转型，见证了中国高考制度的变迁，也见证了一个小家脱贫奔小康的历程。

马克思指出，人们会在自己生活的社会生产中，产生“同他们的物质生产力的一定阶段相适合的生产关系”，物质生活的生产方式制约着整个社会生活、政治生活和精神生活的过程。成长于信息化时代的青年学生，每天面对的是琳琅满目的商品，是可即时满足需求的各类服务。但在父辈祖辈心中，一纸粮票便替他们守住了整个票证时代的记忆。那时国家还处于计划经济时代，物资贫乏，所以生活物资只能凭票供应，所以有粮票、布票、油票……有新闻媒体统计，上个世纪 50 年代到改革开放前，全国共发行了 500 多种票证，几乎所有的物资都曾发放计划票，甚至可以说无票“寸步难行”。直到 1993 年，经济社会迅速发展，物资逐渐丰盈，票证正式退出历史舞台。

票证时代的结束受益于改革开放，生产力的解放与发展，计划经济转向市场经济。但改革并不仅局限于经济的发展。电影，作为一种艺术表现形式，承载的是人们对社会生活的理解、情感和愿望等，是社会意识丰富的缩影；交通工具，承载着一个家庭努力奋斗奔小康的希望，是科学技术走进人们日常生活的缩影；高等教育，承载的是一个国家培养未来人才的重任，是促进人全面发展的重要手段。这一张张小纸片，串联起的是从站起来到富起来再到强起来的中国变化。

（浙大宁波理工学院马克思主义学院副教授，博士）

故事
绍兴
应凯丽(新闻学专业 201 专升本班)

三张票子一纸书

粮票——

父亲生于 20 世纪 70 年代初的绍兴嵊州市贵门乡上坞山村。父亲说他小时候吃饭要用粮票兑换粮食,而粮票则是按照集体分配的。集体分配就会面临一系列的问题。劳动力少的家庭难免会有吃了上顿没下顿的局面,父亲是比较幸运的,祖上不算大富之家,但也小有积蓄,算是介于富农和贫农之间的家庭。父亲没怎么过过缺衣短食的日子,但是童年终究还是辛苦了些。很小的时候,父亲就得跟着祖父去地里干农活,靠劳动力换取粮票。粮票是极其珍贵的物件,找不到粮票就没有粮食,除了粮食,布匹、农药、食油等物件也需要用票证来兑换,这一张张珍贵的历史产物也见证了一个特殊的票证经济时代。

十一届三中全会以后,改革开放的春风徐徐吹遍大江南北,那个时候父亲刚上小学。经济复苏,物资不再短缺,严格的票证制度逐渐松动起来,部分产品不再需要票证兑换。从那时起教育开始普及,各个村子都已经有了小学,只是条件艰苦,教学环境差。父亲在家门口的嵊县贵门乡上坞山完小里读了五年学。没过两年,改革开放进了农村,集体经营也转换成了个体独立,粮票就不复存在了。也是在那之后,父亲几乎不再为吃的发愁,家里的条件也渐渐好转了。

父亲反复提到了票,那大概是他童年最深的记忆了。父亲说当时除了买肉不需要票,因为基本没有,其他几乎都要用票,粮票只是最常见的,还有肥料票等等。而对于当时的农民,肉是过年也吃不上的奢侈品。而票证经济落幕后,购买粮食物品也方便了许多。农民的日子也开始好过了起来。

电影票——

父亲成绩不错,一路上了高中,本来可以跨进大学的校门,但遗憾的是,人生总是充满戏剧性。父亲高考那年,迷上了看电影,耽误了学业,加上那时大学本就是难以企及的梦,父亲梦碎了。

本想着复读再考一年,结果命运总是捉弄他。高考改革不分文理的消息一路传来,彻底粉碎了父亲作为文科生的大学梦。父亲放弃了复读,走上了代课老师的路，在嵊县贵门乡上坞山完小、贵门乡柏春坑村校、贵门乡梓溪完小等多个小学辗转代课，结果代课大半年后又传来高考不改革的消息。父亲已经来不及准备高考了，这成了父亲一生的遗憾。命运总是捉弄人。

父亲成为代课老师时，政策是教满 3 年就能转正，但是父亲将要转正之际，改革又开始了，代课老师都需要自考才能转正，而自考很难，希望渺茫，父亲便放弃了。结果又传来了所有参与自考的代课老师都能转正的消息。不得不说，父亲的人生充满着戏剧性，但也是他自己错失了机遇，就像那张张无辜的电影票，葬送了他初次高考的希望，也改变了他一生的际遇。往事不可追，世上也没有后悔药，即便没有最初的电影票，怕也会有其他的票。

车票——

父亲辞去教师一职后，转而在上坞山村里卖了两年豆腐，靠着卖豆腐的钱，在上坞山村里盖了一幢楼房。时至今日，我们家还会在年末的时候自制豆腐，还能喝上热气腾腾的豆浆。卖了几年豆腐，父亲也老大不小，到了适婚的年纪。在爷爷的介绍下，父亲结识了我的母亲，第二年就有了我。

卖豆腐难以支撑一整个家庭更好的生活，为了一家的生计，父亲带着一张车票去了嘉兴打工，学了水电手艺，成了一名在工地里风吹日晒的水电工人，这份手艺也伴随了他的后半生，撑起了一个家庭的希望。

父亲的工地宿舍里都是大包小包带着行囊的外来务工者，一个工程结束又赶紧辗转于另外的工地，漂泊无依。父亲除了专事水电还会做一些搬砖之类的体力活，以此赚取更多的工资。每次发工资了，他都会打电话给母亲。长年累月，父亲的双手早已皲裂，而我们的家庭条件也越来越好了。

我的童年乃至少年时期，父亲不断辗转于嘉兴、杭州、宁波、绍兴等地，而我也成了留守儿童，不断地期待着那一张车票能将远方的父亲送回到我身边。没有父爱的童年成了我一生无法弥补的遗憾，那一张张斑驳的车票带走了我的父亲，也带走了我的童年。但是多年之后，也带来了一个家庭经济的复兴。

2008 年的时候，我迎来了我的弟弟。2011 年，我们一家团圆，举家来到嵊州市市区打工。

我老家绍兴市嵊州市贵门乡上坞山村，以茶叶生意闻名全市。祖祖辈辈都种茶。父亲外出务工的日子，全靠祖父一人采茶。父亲在回到嵊州市打工后，也每每在采茶旺季就停工回乡采茶，再将茶叶销售到市里，父亲的同学也常常照顾我家，将茶叶销售到上海北京等地，我们家的经济条件在上半年采茶、下半年务工中蒸蒸日上。2017 年的时候，我们顺利地在市区买下了属于自己的房子，结束了反复搬迁的租房生活。

录取通知书——

父亲一生的遗憾就是没能考上大学，因此我成了全家的希望，12年寒窗苦读赢得了一张大学录取的圆梦书，这不仅是我的圆梦书，也是父亲对多年前错失的命运的慰藉信。我记得录取结果出来的时候，父亲十分高兴，我们家里终究还是出了一位大学生，虽然晚了些年，但是终究还是来了。父亲一直视我为骄傲，而我同样觉得父亲也是我这一生最崇拜的人。

父亲一生错失了太多的机遇，同样我也在不断努力，最终抓回断线的风筝。

父亲50岁了，50年的变迁，无论是国还是家都有了翻天覆地的变化，从当年泥土房里破旧的粮票，到后来学堂里飞出的梦想，再到通往远方的车票，及至下一代实现梦想的录取通知书，万事万物不断变迁，生活终将越来越好。

Shaoxing
Ying Kaili (Class 201, Majoring in Journalism)

Three Tickets and One Letter

Food Tickets (Coupons)—

My father was born in Shangwushan Village, Guimen Township, Shenghzhou, Shaoxing City in the early 1970s. My father recalled that when he was still a child, people needed to exchange food coupons for food. Since coupons were collectively distributed by the government, problems naturally occurred. Households with a small workforce would live in the state that they didn't know where the next meal came from. My father was lucky; his family, though not rich, had some savings, and he was thus spared from hunger and cold. Even though, his childhood was by no means an easy and happy one. He had to labor and toil in the farm land in order to exchange for valuable food coupons, without which people were unable to have food, clothes, farm chemicals or cooking oil. These coupons which are currently an antique in the museum once witnessed that special coupon-based time period.

My father was in the elementary school when the reform and opening up policy was implemented nationwide after the convening of the third plenary session of the 11th Party Congress. As the economy gradually recovered, there was an abundant supply of materials and relaxation of the coupon-based system, which meant food coupons were no longer needed to buy certain goods. With the educational popularization, elementary schools, though poorly equipped, were set up in every village. My father studied in a local elementary school for five years. Two years later, as the reform and opening up policy was introduced to rural areas, food coupons no longer existed as the collective economy was replaced by the self-employed economy. Ever since, my father hardly worried about food, and living conditions gradually improved.

Movie Tickets—

My father, with good academic performance, could have entered university after graduating from the senior high school. Unfortunately, in a dramatic turn of events, my father got so addicted to watching films that he fell behind in his schooling. The already slim chances of being admitted to a university became even remoter, and his college dream shattered.

Fate liked to play tricks on him. My father, who had planned to give it another try, finally gave up his dream of being a college student of liberal arts after the news came from the central government that all college candidates would take uniform college entrance tests, instead of taking separate tests based on liberal arts or science. He later became a substitute teacher in a number of local elementary schools for much of the next year, only to hear the news that the college entrance examination reform was abolished. This led to the biggest regret in my father's entire life for there was not enough time for him to prepare for the upcoming national tests.

Policies had it that every substitute teacher could automatically be a full-time employee of the school after three years of teaching. But when that day was finally coming, another institutional reform took effect, which stipulated that one needed to pass College Examinations for the Self-taught in order to become a full-time employee. My father gave it up because the examination was difficult. Shortly after he quit, news came that all substitute teachers who attended the examinations could be full-time teachers. My father's life was indeed full of twists and turns, but he had nobody else to blame but himself because those opportunities were missed out exactly by himself. Every turn of events, just like the movie tickets which shattered his dream of being a college student in the first place, changed his entire life. But the past cannot be traced back, and there is no magic drug which can reverse time. Even without the original movie tickets, there would have been other disruptions or unexpected events.

Coach Tickets—

My father became a tofu vendor in the village for a couple of years after he resigned from the elementary school, and built a house there with the money he made by selling tofu. Even today, we would make tofu and steaming soy bean milk by ourselves at the end of the year. My father was later introduced to my mom by my paternal grandpa. They got married and the next year I was born.

Since he was unable to make ends meet by selling tofu alone, my father went to Jiaxing City by coach where he became a migrant electrician and plumber in construction sites after mastering the skills there. The skills were kept for the rest of his life and helped him provide for the whole family.

My father lived in the dormitory with other migrant workers who carried huge packs with them. They flitted between different construction sites and barely settled. He also did labor work like carrying bricks to make more money. He would call my mom on payday. My father's hands, after years of hard work, chapped, but at the same time, our life got better.

My father flitted between different cities like Jiaxing, Ningbo, Hangzhou and Shaoxing, and I thus became a left-behind child. I was waiting for a coach ticket which could one day send my wandering father back to my side. A childhood without my father's company could never be made up for. Torn tickets took my father and my happy childhood away from me, but also brought a better-off life for our family.

I had one little brother in 2008 and three years later, my whole family moved to the downtown areas to work. It was since then that our family had finally got together.

My hometown is famous for its tea business, which has been continued for generations. Previously, my paternal grandpa picked tea leaves to feed the whole family when my father was out working. After we moved to the downtown areas, my father would return to the village to pick tea leaves during the peak season. He would then sell tea leaves back in the downtown areas. Some of his old classmates would help us sell tea in larger cities like

Shanghai and Beijing. Thus, our financial conditions gradually improved. In 2017, we bought a house of our own in the downtown areas, and no longer needed to move between rented houses.

Admission Letter—

My father's only regret was the failure to be a college student, and I consequently became the hope of the whole family. After 12 years of diligent study, I finally received the admission letter and realized my dream. More importantly, it brought comfort to my father. I still remember when I got my test results my father was elated—finally, the whole family produced a college student. My father has always regarded me as the pride of the family. Actually, the feeling is mutual; I have always been proud of him.

I am unremittingly forging ahead, trying to make up for numerous opportunities my father missed out in his entire life.

My father is 50 years old now. The past five decades has witnessed earthshaking changes to the family and the country as well. From torn food coupons in the clay house and the academic dream coming out of schools, to coach tickets which link the outside world and the admission letter which helps realize the dream of the next generation—things keep on changing and life is getting even better.

生存与满怀希望的延续

李义杰

《生存之路，请多关照》这个标题起得很有意思，当然故事也很让人触动。生存是人不得不面向的根本问题，也是最本质的真实，无论从生物层面还是社会层面，生存或许是推动生命延续和组织发展的最原始驱动力。“生存之路，请多关照”是在充满乐观和希望地打招呼还是在表露生存之艰辛和无奈的请求？或许都有吧！但又会是向谁打招呼？向谁请求或祈求呢？

故事作者占龙的父亲出生于江西一个小乡村，初二辍学到烟厂工作，不满现状，到东阳服装厂打工，与母亲结识、成家，经历上司单飞后的失败，打算经商，先后在工地开小饭店，办服装厂。服装厂势头正好时，因借车事故和客户等原因倒闭，后又经历多次辗转不同地方办厂，终因赔偿等纠纷关闭，于是另谋生存之路，父亲现在经营一家门店，母亲去一个服装厂工作。家庭幸福平静。

可以看出，作者之所以发出“生存”的呼喊，与其父亲或家庭事业多变和失败有关，作者深刻体验到了生活的不易、生存的艰难。每次的变故下，父母都必须再寻找生存之路。为了让家庭过得更好，他们虽然“微小如尘，却活得认真”，仍然是充满了坚强和希望。这种精神在作者这里更得到了延续：“属于我们新一代的时代已经到来了。现在从这里出发，开始书写新的故事。生活，请多关照。”至此，或许我们能体会到“生存之路，请多关照”的意味，它有艰辛、有无奈，甚至是痛苦，但更有乐观、有希望，它可能是向生活、向这个时代、向所有奋斗者、向老天爷……在诉说、呼喊，但更可能是向着自己。

但无论怎样，在这个伟大的时代，小人物也有自己的时代，或者说小人物才有了自己的时代，而不会出现老舍、鲁迅笔下那些没有自我、被压榨、辛劳一生却最终卑微而去的人物，并且我们从来相信人民的力量，认可群众对历史的创造。作为千千万万的普通群众、小人物，或许我们从来不显，但在大时代中，我们从未缺席，我们拥有自己的时代。

（浙大宁波理工学院传媒与法学院副教授，博士）

故事
金华
占龙(网络与新媒体专业181班)

生存之路,请多关照

我的父亲出生在江西的一个小乡村。他家境贫寒,在初二的时候就辍学了,为了分担家庭的压力,与自己的哥哥去做了水泥工,但是这并不是长久之计,后来他又与自己的同学去了县里的卷烟厂工作。卷烟厂的工作环境非常糟糕,睡的床就是简单的木板,被子里也时常会掺有沙子。一个十六七岁的少年,在那样的夜晚翻来覆去地睡不着。

父亲觉得自己的生活不该如此,想改变生活的现状,他决定出发了。父亲有个儿时的玩伴,先两年出省打拼,这次回乡,便问父亲要不要与他一起出省去浙江东阳,换个地方工作。父亲了解了情况,便二话不说辞掉了在卷烟厂里的工作,和好友来到了浙江,开始了他90年代的新旅途。

“来东阳的时候是坐火车来的,实在是太挤了。当时就是把行李往人群里一扔,谁都不愿意头上顶着个行李,他们就陆陆续续地把行李往前送。那时候我个子比较小嘛,你两个伯父就把我也抬起来,就这样在人群上追着自己的行李。车开了十几分钟,我都没有碰到地面,太挤了。”父亲说的时候笑了,这是他年轻时候的记忆,现在想起来还是颇觉有趣。

来到东阳,父亲便去好友所在的服装厂上班,生活的艰苦让父亲忘却了初来时的热情,一心只为求得生存。“我记得当时我还生了一场大病,几天都吃不下饭,特别想回家。”父亲说道。几经波折,父亲来来回回换了好几个工作的地方,不过都是在服装厂上班。两年的奋斗让他觉得自己可以靠手艺吃饭了。

在服装厂工作的时候,父亲认识了我的母亲。我的母亲是一个坚强开朗的人,我从小就觉得母亲实在是太过伟大,父亲所做的一切都有母亲在背后默默支持着。他们两个人一起度过了最艰难的岁月。

父亲和母亲一起来到了另一个服装厂。这个服装厂有点特殊,是半年发一次工资的,当时父亲和母亲过得也是勉勉强强,但是这特殊的工资制度却为夫妻俩存下了一笔小钱。原本父亲是打算在这个服装厂呆上一段时间的,但是父亲的上司与老板闹不和,想出去单干,他便拉上父亲等一些人出去自己办服装厂。

但是计划总赶不上变化，单飞出去的服装厂没过多久就破产了。父亲想到时机也算成熟了，自己也不想一直打工下去，便开始想着经商。

他最先想到的是开饭店。他和妈妈从服装厂出来之后，观察到就近有一片工地正在施工，附近也没有开设餐馆，他们就商量着如果在这里开一个小饭店应该会很不错。于是父亲就这么做了，这个时候是2003年。开饭店的劳累和焦虑都让父亲胖了好多。

父亲在服装厂上班的时候就心里想过，自己做了这么多年的服装，去了这么多家服装厂上过班，也懂了其中的一点门道，想办一个属于自己的服装厂。于是父亲租了一栋楼作为服装厂，然后购买了好多做服装用的机车。在我印象中，那楼不大也不小，我小时候经常会在附近玩耍。服装厂后来越办越大了，人数也有百来号。我记得当时自己偶尔也会跑到车间去玩。

服装厂小有成色，父亲正想扩大规模，但是命运的安排总是可笑的。

4年后，父亲的服装厂倒下了，"我其实运气很不好，就像刚从地里探出头的芽一样，一脚就被人踩了回去"。父亲点了一支烟。

命运的拐点是在办厂的一年后，父亲的员工向他借摩托车用，父亲觉得借给他应该没什么问题，谁知道这一借就借出了事端，他的员工开车把人撞死了。这是多么大的一个打击，员工没有能力偿还法院判下的赔款清单，对方就要求法院也判车主代偿。这次事件，把父亲的思绪搅乱了，心情也变得一团糟，人不是自己撞的，借车也借的是有驾驶证的人，自己为什么要承担这样大的代价。被判的员工没有偿还赔款，逃回了自己的家乡，而在本地办厂的父亲就成了法院和受害一方骚扰的对象。父亲顶着压力继续开办着自己的小服装厂，但是随着法院和受害人方的侵扰，父亲不得不缩小规模。

2008年，父亲谈了一个比较大的项目，但是甲方的家庭出了一些矛盾，夫妻意见不合离异了，他们都想与父亲进行合作，但是他们觉得两个人如果都和父亲合作有可能会泄露自己的机密，最后这个单子落了空。刚好又赶上经济危机，父亲再次缩小了厂的规模，换了一个地方继续自己的事业。小归小，但是办得也还算不错。可是当之前车祸的受害人和法院再次找上门来，向父亲要赔偿费用，甚至还看上了家里的房子的时候，父亲顶不住压力，关闭了自己的服装厂。他履行了法律的清单，让这个事情结束了，但是也因此丢了这么多年努力的成果。

父亲和母亲所经营起来的厂没有了，只能另求生存之路。母亲选择了去一家大的服装厂工作，这一呆就是10年，母亲在服装厂当了一个小厂长。我的妈妈真的非常坚强，她与父亲一起经历了开饭店的起早贪黑和经营服装厂的灯火通明，面对困难时候也想着只要解决了就好。父亲与母亲真的是分不开的，我看见过他们吵架的样子，但是我知道这就是生活。父亲经营了一家门店，还是像往常一样做生意，后来家里生活一直都很平静。

父母亲的一半人生，活得虽认真，却微小如尘。属于我们新一代的时代已经到来了。现在从这里出发，开始书写新的故事。生活，请多关照。

Jinhua
Zhan Long (Class 181, Majoring in Network and New Media)

Life, Please Don't Push Hard

My father was born in a small village in Jiangxi Province. During the second year in the middle school, he had to drop out because of the financial difficulties in the family. To share the pressure of his family, he and his brother went to do cement work. However, this was not a long-term solution, so he went to work in a cigarette factory in the county with his classmates. The working conditions in the cigarette factory were very terrible. The beds were made of simple wooden boards and the quilts were often mixed with sand. A young boy of 16 tossed and turned on those nights, unable to sleep.

My father felt that his life should not be like this, and he wanted to change the status quo, so he set off. My father had a childhood friend who had left the province two years ago for work; when he returned to his hometown, he asked my father if he wanted to leave the province with him to go to Dongyang, Zhejiang, for a change of environment. After knowing the situation, my father quit his job in the cigarette factory immediately and set off with his best friend to Zhejiang, starting his new journey in the 1990s.

"When I came to Dongyang by train, it was just too crowded. At that time, we just threw our luggage into the crowd because no one wanted to carry it on their heads, so the crowd carried it forward one after another. At that time, I was quite small, so your two uncles lifted me up and it appeared that I chased my luggage through the crowd. For over ten minutes, I did not even land on the ground. It was too crowded." My father laughed as he spoke. It was a memory from his youth and it is still quite amusing to think about it now.

When he arrived in Dongyang, my father went to work in the garment factory where his best friend worked. The hardships of life made him forget the enthusiasm he had when he first arrived, and he was determined to survive. "I remembered I was very sick, and I couldn't eat for a few days. I wanted to go home so badly," my father said. After a few twists and turns, my father changed jobs back and forth, but all of them were related to garment factories. Two years of struggle made him feel he could make a living by virtue of his skills.

While working for the garment factory, my father met my mother. My mother was a strong and cheerful person and I grew up thinking that my mother was great. She supported my father and the two of them got through the toughest years together.

My father and mother went to another garment factory together. This garment factory was a bit special in that employees got paid every 6 months. At that time my father and mother were barely able to make ends meet, but the special wage system did save the couple a small amount of money. Originally my father intended to stay in the garment factory for a bit longer, but my father's supervisor fell out with his boss so he quit his job and started a new garment factory with my father; however, the new garment factory only lasted for a short time. It was not long before that the factory was closed because of bankruptcy. This was when my father believed his time had come. He no longer wanted to work for others, so he started to think about doing business on his own.

The first thing that came to his mind was to open a restaurant. After my parents got out of the garment factory, there was a construction site nearby and there were no restaurants to serve the workers, so they discussed together and thought that it would be good if they opened a small restaurant there. The restaurant opened in 2003, but the stress and anxiety of running a business made my father gain a lot of weight.

When my father worked in a garment factory, he had thought to himself that he had been making garments for so many years and had worked in so many garment factories that he knew well about them and wanted to set up his own garment factory. At that time, my father rented a building for the garment factory and bought a lot of machinery for garment making. The garment factory later grew bigger and bigger and employed hundreds of people. I remembered that I would occasionally run to the workshop to play.

The garment factory had made a small success and my father was thinking about expanding the factory, but fate's arrangement was always ridiculous.

Four years later, my father's garment factory collapsed. "I had very bad luck. It felt like getting kicked back to where you came from." My father lit a cigarette.

A year after he started the factory, his father's employee borrowed a motorbike from him. My father thought it would be alright, but who knew there would be an accident after that. The employee did not have the means to repay the list of damages ordered by the court, and the victim asked the court to order the bike owner to pay for the damages as well. Such an incident messed up my father's mind and his mood. He did not personally cause the accident and had lent the car to someone who had a driving licence, so he was confused why he should have to bear such a huge cost. The convicted employee did not pay back the compensation and fled to his home town. My father, who ran the factory locally, became the subject of harassment by the court and the victim. My father continued to run his small garment factory under pressure, but with the harassment from the court and the injured party, he had to downsize the factory.

In 2008, my father negotiated a relatively large project, but there was some conflict in the family of the client. The divorced couple both wanted to work with my father, but they were also worried that the other party might leak the business secrets. In the end, the order fell through because of their family issues. Just in time for the economic crisis, my father once again downsized the factory. He continued his business in a different location, which was small, but not bad. But when the motobike accident victim and the courts came to the door again and demanded repayment from my father, he couldn't withstand the pressure and closed his garment factory. He fulfilled his legal liabilities and got this thing over with, but all those years of his hard work came to nothing.

Without the factory, my parents had to find an alternative way to live. My mother chose to work in a large garment factory where she stayed for 10 years, and then she became a factory manager. My mother was really strong. Together with my father, they had run restaurants and factories from dawn to night. Her only thought when facing the difficulties was to solve problems. My father and my mother were really inseparable. I had seen them fighting, but I knew that was life. My father ran a shop and did business as usual. The family life later was very peaceful.

My parents lived half of their lives peacefully and diligently. The time has come for our generation. From now on, a new chapter begins. Life, please don't push hard on us.

创新创业的中国家庭样本

崔　雨

“惟改革者进，惟创新者强，惟改革创新者胜。”2013年，习近平总书记在欧美同学会成立一百周年庆祝大会上如此强调。党的十八大以来，在习近平总书记的公开讲话和报道中，“创新”一词出现超过上千次。

2014年夏季达沃斯论坛上，李克强总理提出，要在960万平方公里土地上掀起“大众创业”“草根创业”的新浪潮，形成“万众创新”“人人创新”的新势态。此后，他在首届世界互联网大会、2015年《政府工作报告》中频频阐释“大众创业，万众创新”，希望激发民族的创业精神和创新基因。

邵怡娜同学的《失败，再出发》向我们讲述了自己家庭创业的真实故事：1993年，爸爸中专毕业进入乡镇企业；一年后，不满足微薄的工资停薪留职，进入某有限公司，从车间干起晋升到了主任……

有人说，“双创”需要专业人才。我认为，这些专业人才不是天生的，而是在市场历练中成长发展的。比如阿里巴巴等世界级互联网企业，都是从草根起家，不断坚持创新创业才成功的。“双创”有机遇更有挑战，有丰收更伴随着风险。创业不言败；失败，再出发。正如刘欢所唱“看成败人生豪迈，只不过是从头再来”。

2004年，爸爸开始创业，最终倒闭，亏损了30万元。后来，爸爸进入柳桥集团、大立建设集团。2010年左右，家里建乡村小屋；2013年左右，家里建新房买新车。

“双创”可以促使众人的奇思妙想变为现实，有助于社会最终实现共同富裕。当前，“双创”的理念日益深入人心，有效激发了社会活力，释放了巨大创造力，成为经济发展的一大亮点。

“创新是一个民族进步的灵魂，是一个国家兴旺发达的不竭动力”，习近平总书记曾这样指出。盼望更多人搭上“双创”幸福列车，驶向美好的明天。

（宁波卫生职业技术学院，副研究员）

故事

杭州

邵怡娜(新闻学专业191班)

失败,再出发

爸爸出生在浙江省杭州市萧山区义桥镇的一个小村庄里,爷爷只是一个普通的建筑小工,爷爷和奶奶文化水平都不高,干的都是一些苦力活,收入很低,也因此爸爸小时候的生活很艰苦。听爸爸说他小时候是一大家子人住在一起的。说起在老宅院里的故事,爸爸就起了兴,那种兴奋感是由内而外散发的,很久很久都没有看到过爸爸这个样子:“那时候虽然穷,但是大家都是差不多,能吃饱穿暖就行,哪里有现在这样的生活。衣服补补还能再穿,猪肉一年只能吃几次,有的时候没人找你爷爷帮工,家里就可能吃不上饭,要靠姨婆们帮衬着。那个时候是苦的啊!”奶奶常说:“穷有穷的过法。”在我理解便是,苦日子也能过出别样的甜味。

岁月流逝,宅院里的住户都渐渐搬走自立门户。爷爷也在村里找了一块地盘建造了一间属于自己的普通的小屋。一个毛坯房就花光了家里所有积蓄,他们甚至还问亲戚朋友借了一些钱,这令生活更加艰苦。说起爷爷,爸爸充满愧疚,“你爷爷这一辈子都很不容易,当小工挣的钱很少,还要被人看不起,得养活我们一家人。那个时候为了造房子到处揽活,眼睛被钢筋崩了,人变成了独眼龙。老来又走得早也没享受几年好日子,苦了一辈子。”在我印象中,爷爷是一个面容慈善的老人,小时候我还老是模仿爷爷独眼龙的样子,5岁的记忆并不深刻,只是听到爸爸感慨,我心中也不是滋味。

房子的建造使得那时的生活格外艰苦,为了偿还债务,爸爸也早早出来工作,寻路。1993年中,爸爸中专毕业,家里经济条件不好,加上他也不爱学习,便进入了乡镇企业,成为杭州雪峰链条有限公司技术部的车间工人。那时工作一天只有28元人民币,在车间的平均工资加起来每月有350元左右,年轻气盛的爸爸不满足于这微薄的工资,在工作一年之后放弃了停薪留职,出去另寻工作。大概由于专业技术过硬,父亲辞职后不久便进入了山洪羽毛有限公司,从车间干起,业绩越来越好,慢慢地晋升到了主任。爸爸陆陆续续当了几年的车间主任,家里生活也越来越好,有了一些积蓄,用攒下的钱还清了之前爷爷造房子时欠下的债务，同时也将之前的毛坯房简单地装修了一下。日子开始有了盼头。

爸爸在山洪羽毛厂工作期间认识了那时在车间工作的妈妈，他们的故事就这么开始了……

2004年弟弟出生，爸爸在公司任职学习一些关于全自动麻将机的知识，全面了解了全自动麻将机这个行业之后决定自己创业。主要是想给我和弟弟更好的生活条件，但是这个举动却成为一个个困境的开端。创办了全自动麻将机零件厂后，爸爸每天都出去跑业务联系客户，加上他有专业知识，开始行情是不错的，妈妈一直负责爸爸工厂的后勤工作，厂子开始有了盈利。但是毕竟市场在变化，全自动麻将机这一领域越来越不景气，爸爸的稳定客户也纷纷不再从事这一行，加上经营不善，这个厂最终倒闭了，把机器之类的物件卖掉也亏损了不少钱，据爸爸所说大概是在30万元左右，几乎亏光了爸爸妈妈的积蓄。

创业失败对爸爸打击巨大，爷爷查出癌症更是雪上加霜。那段时间简直是爸爸人生中最灰暗的时光，“本来办厂就亏了那么多钱，积蓄差不多都没了，结果你爷爷又被查出来癌症，我能怎么办啊，总得治病啊。”爸爸说这些话的时候十分的无助，事业失败和亲人罹患绝症的双重打击，令爸爸深感无力。他在医院里守夜，整宿不睡觉。那时奶奶的精神状态也很差，他作为大儿子当然得表现得坚强一点，白天还得安慰着奶奶。爷爷动手术需要大笔的钱，住院以及后续治疗所需要的金钱对于刚刚创业失败的爸爸来说可以说是天文数字了，叔叔出了大部分钱。尽管如此爷爷还是在不久后离开了我们。一切又回到起点。

都说成功的男人背后都有一个伟大的女人，我觉得失败的男人背后也有一个坚强的女人，而我的妈妈就是这样一个女人。爷爷去世、积蓄散尽的打击让爸爸萎靡了很久，创业失败意味着爸爸又得从零开始，在三十几岁出头成了无业游民，找工作的压力巨大。这时的妈妈在做了几年全职主妇之后又开始从事服装产业，并且鼓励爸爸重新出去找工作。要说争吵那肯定也是有的，妈妈对爸爸的消沉不满，他们感情也出现了问题，好几次吵着要离婚。转折是一次争吵完后，妈妈哭着诉说，劝爸爸重拾希望，要有男人担当。“你妈都这样了，那时候你和你弟也都还小，我要是不出去赚钱养家，你们怎么办?”

在朋友的介绍下，爸爸进入了柳桥集团，成为一名普通的项目经理，开启了平平淡淡的企业职工生活。收入虽说不高但也还算可以，加上妈妈也在工作，几年过后家里存下了一点积蓄。2010年左右，爸爸妈妈觉得是时候购置新房了。妈妈的想法是去市区买一套商品房，差点连首付都交了，但是受到奶奶和外公外婆的影响，老人都说自己造的房子宽敞舒服，最终爸爸还是决定在村里盘下一块位置比较好的地，造一栋属于我们一家四口的乡村小屋。

2013年左右，爸爸进入了大立建设集团工作，生活也越来越稳定，造了新房也买了新车，日子又开始有了希望。虽说不是大富大贵，但是像这样的安安稳稳的日子也正是我们所希望的。1993年到现在，经历过失败又重新出发，平平淡淡地在企业工作，稳步向前，买了车也造了新房，重要的不是结果，而是我们一起经历过。

爸爸的人生也许算不上是很完美，有起有落，有过机遇也有挫折，失败过也谈不上成功，平平淡淡的人生，儿女双全，人生足矣。

Hangzhou
Shao Yina (Class 191, Majoring in Journalism)

Failure and Restart

My father was born in a small village in Yiqiao Town, Xiaoshan District, Hangzhou City, Zhejiang Province. My grandpa was an ordinary construction worker. As my grandparents were illiterate, they usually worked as coolies with low income. Hence, my father lived a tough life when he was a child. My father had told me that his family lived in a large house which was like a courtyard house where many families could live together when he was a child. Every time my father talked about what happened in this house, he would be talkative and felt excited from inside out. I hadn't seen my father so excited like this for a long time. My father said, "Although we were poor at that time, all we wanted was to keep ourselves well-fed and clothed. I didn't expect to have a life like what we have today. "We mended the clothes and wore them again. Pork could only be served in a few occasions within a year. Nobody hired your grandpa to work for them, his family would have nothing to eat. Luckily, your grandaunts would come to help us. At that time life was tough!" My grandma always said, "Even if we were poor, life had to go on." In my opinion, what she meant was that they tried to look for happiness from the tough life.

As time goes by, people living in this large house were gradually moving away and they set up their own family. My grandpa also found a plot of land in the village to build our own house. The house was rough, but this roughcast house had already cost the entire savings of their family. My grandpa also brought some money from his relatives and friends. Life was tougher than before. Speaking of my grandpa, my father was laden with guilt. He said, "Your grandpa's life was uneasy. Working as a labor worker to feed the whole family, your grandpa earned little and was looked down on by others. In order to earn enough money to build the house, he did a lot of work. His eye was cracked by the steel bars. From then on, he became a one-eyed person. Your grandpa was unable to enjoy the good days because he died early. He lived toughly all his life." In my impression, he possesses a benevolent countenance. When I was a child, I always imitated his one-eyed appearance. Although I could hardly remember what he look liked because I was five years old, I also felt upset when hearing my father's words.

The construction of the house made life extremely difficult at that time. My father also had to work when he was young to pay the debts and to find the goal of his life. In mid-1993, my father graduated from the technical secondary school. Since the family was poor and he disliked studying, he entered a township enterprise and became a workshop worker in the technical department of Hangzhou Xuefeng Chain Co., Ltd. At that period, my father only earned 28 yuan per day and the average salary in the workshop totaled about 350 yuan per month. My father was young and ambitious, so he was not satisfied with this meager salary. After working for a year, he refused the unpaid leave the company offered and decided to seek another job. Probably because of his professional skills, he joined Shanhong Feather Co., Ltd. soon after resigning from the previous company. My father started as a worker in the workshop. His achievement was getting better and better. Gradually he was promoted as a director of the workshop. After he had been the director for several years, life in our family was getting better and better, so my father was able to save money. With a down-to-earth attitude, he used the money he had saved to pay off the debts my grandpa owed when building the house. In the same time he decorated the previous roughcast house in a simple way. There was hope then.

While working in Shanhong Feather Co., Ltd., he met my mom who also worked at that workshop. Their stories began.

My brother was born in 2004. In the same year, my father learned something about the automatic mahjong machines in the company. After knowing all the facts about this industry, he decided to start his own business to give my brother and me a better life, but it brought about many difficulties. After setting up the Automatic Mahjong Machine Parts Factory, my father went out for business to meet clients every day. With my father's professional knowledge, the market was going well at the beginning. My mom was in charge of the logistic work in the factory. The factory started profitable. However, the market kept changing. The automatic mahjong machine industry was in a slump. My father's regular clients were no longer engaged in this field. In addition to the poor management, the factory eventually closed down. My father still had a big loss although he had sold articles like machines. According to my father, it was losses of about 30 thousand, which hit our family as a bolt from the blue. My parents' savings had all gone.

The failure of the business was a huge shock to my father. What made things worse was that my grandpa was diagnosed with cancer. It was the most gloomy period in my father's life. "Almost all the savings had gone with the close-down of the factory. Then your grandpa was diagnosed with cancer. I felt hopeless, and your grandpa was waiting to be treated," my father said helplessly. The failure that my father suffered in business and my grandpa's cancer was a double blow to my father. There was not much he could do but spend all night taking care of my grandpa. My grandma was not in good health, either. As the eldest son in the family, my father had to behave as a tough man to encourage my grandma in the daytime. Lots of money was needed for my grandpa's surgery, hospitalization and follow-up treatment, which was astronomical to my father who just failed in business. My uncle paid most of the money. However, my grandpa passed away shortly afterwards. Everything was back to the beginning.

It is said that there is a great woman behind every successful man. In my view, my mom is a woman of this kind. It took a long time for my father to come out of the depression that my grandpa died and all the family's savings were gone. The failure of the business meant that he had to start from scratch again. In his early thirties, he became a person who was unemployed and facing tremendous pressure in finding another job. As a full-time housewife for a few years, my mom returned to the clothing industry again and encouraged my father to look for a new job. Quarrels were unavoidable between my parents. My mom was dissatisfied with my father' s depression, and conflicts appeared, so they talked about divorce several times. Once after a quarrel, my mom cried, persuading father to regain hope and shoulder a man ' s responsibility. "I was moved by your mom's remarks. Also considering that you and your brother were still young, I had to go out to be the breadwinner. If I didn't do it, how would you survive?" said my father.

One of my father's friends introduced him to join the Liuqiao Group and he became a project manager to begin his peaceful life in the enterprise. His salary was not high but sufficient. My mom also got a salary from her job. After several years, they had some savings. Around 2010, my parents thought it was time to buy a new house. My mom tended to buy a downtown commodity house and she wanted to pay the down payment, but my grandparents all believed that the house built by ourselves was bigger and more comfortable. My father was influenced by their opinion, so he decided to rent a plot of land with good location to build a house for us, a family of four.

In the year of 2013, my father joined the Dali Construction Group. Life was becoming more and more stable. He built a new house and bought a new car. Our life was full of hope again. Although we were not rich and famous, this kind of peaceful life was what we expected to have. From 1993 until now, we've experienced failures and restarts. My father worked in a company in an ordinary way, steadily moving forward. Finally, he bought a new car and a new house. What counts most is what we have gone through together rather than what we have gained.

Perhaps my father's life was not perfect. There are ups and downs; there are opportunities and setbacks. He failed and he was not much of a successful man. However, it is enough for him to have a peaceful life with a daughter and a son.

奋斗改变命运

董亚钊

古往今来，中国人对于科举、高考有着特殊的情结，直到今天，“高考”依然是很多青年学子打破阶层壁垒的必由之路。“高考”成为考生生命历程的组成部分，成为个人奋斗和拼搏的写照，它就像是一个富有文化象征意义的符号，至今还在不断延续！何流在《守寒窗，跃农门》一文中通过对父母辈个人奋斗经历的刻画和描述，记录和追忆了他们参加高考以及对人生的改变历程。

1977年中国正式恢复高考制度，这不仅成为一代人的集体记忆，也给很多寒门学子改变命运带来了希望！正如何流在文中所写的那样，“1977年底，高考恢复正常，一年后的炎炎夏日，舅舅和无数农村学子一样，怀揣着忐忑与兴奋，踏入了高考考场，考完后平复了心情，依然回到生产队干活”。这种记忆的深刻性和历久弥新不仅是对那些经历过那个特殊时代高考的学子而言的，而且成为中国历史上具有特殊意义的“非常时刻”。

《守寒窗，跃农门》一文的作者以一个旁观者的身份，重新审视了高考的意义，以及社会变革带给个人的影响。公允地看，对于多数人来说，今天的高考，依然是改变命运的主流方式，而且这种主流方式的角色定位，在很长时间内都不会改变！

（浙大宁波理工学院传媒与法学院讲师，硕士）

故事
杭州
何流(新闻学专业193班)

守寒窗,跃农门

在我眼里,外公外婆是伟大的人,外公只有小学的学历,外婆目不识丁,他们却教导出了4个大学生,培养出了4个老师。

妈妈是家里最小的,她有一个大哥和两个姐姐。一家人都是老师,妈妈是函授本科,她的哥哥姐姐都是大学毕业的师范生。

1977年底,高考恢复,一年后的炎炎夏日,舅舅和无数农村学子一样,怀揣着忐忑与兴奋,踏入了高考考场,考完后平复了心情,依然回到生产队干活。一个月过去了,舅舅每天都会紧赶慢赶到公社看看邮递员有没有带来录取通知书,可得到的却是每天的失望。舅舅没有选择放弃,在干活维持家用的同时,每天也都在学习,捧着课本,一看就看到月亮爬上树梢,繁星缀满黑夜。1979年1月,舅舅突然收到了杭州师范大学的一封信,打开一看,工整的油墨字大气地铺开——录取通知书,仿佛还带着特有的香味儿,薄薄的纸上没有多余的装饰,十足的书卷气,简单明了的几个字明晃晃地印在舅舅的眼眸里。

考上了啊。

原来是因为杭师大在9月招生时还未创办生物系,所以学校只好一边招生再一边扩展新的专业学科,直到来年1月份,舅舅才等来心心念念的录取通知书。他也是当年村里唯一考上大学的学生。

舅舅高考那年,大阿姨正读高一。3年后,她也迎来了人生中最重要的一次考验,可是这一次,大阿姨没有如愿以偿,她落榜了。阿姨不想停止继续求学的步伐,开始了一年的自学复习。1982年再次走进考场,她多添了一份从容,终于在9月如愿以偿地走进了杭师大的校园,就读中文系。大阿姨也是当年村里唯一的大学本科生。

我曾经问过阿姨,为什么一家人都能考上大学,当时的大学录取率并不高,高考的选拔可谓百里挑一。大阿姨说了两个对家庭影响最大的人,一个是外公,一个是舅舅,外公培养了良好的家风,舅舅树立了优秀的榜样。

外公小学毕业后就没有再读书了,之后担任了民兵连长,20岁那年当上了青江村村支书，一当就是19年。外公酷爱看书，虽然只有小学的学历却有着极高的口才。在子女的记忆中，他总是一手捧着一本书，一手拿着一个青绿色的瓷茶杯，坐在不怎么宽敞的几案前仔细地翻阅品读书籍。那时候外公时常要奔波各处做宣讲、开大会，但是外公从不需要写稿，光是站在台上一股脑地说，一说就是3个小时不带重复，且思路清晰明了，内容条理严谨，毫不生涩难懂，老百姓听了都纷纷点头。他那口若悬河、滔滔不绝之势是别人照本宣读没法具备的，村民也乐意听。大家都很爱戴外公。他们相信他，因为外公是一个待人真诚、做事认真的人，总是把村里的事摆在第一位。哪家哪户有点儿事都爱往外公这里跑，外公也是来者不拒，不管多大的事，他一去就必须给解决了，不然不回家吃饭。这股劲儿一直支撑着外公，令他被杭州市评为社会主义建设先进分子，成为方圆百里的标杆形象。

外公一心为公，把工作摆在第一位，每天都很忙，家里的事也就都压在了外婆的身上。里里外外上上下下，外婆打理着家中的一切，管好几个儿女，种菜喂鸡，洗衣做饭……外婆不认识字，但也总给自己的儿女讲道理。外婆是很有原则的人，现在回到老家去探望她，她也时常爱跟我说道说道，什么勤奋读书才是唯一的出路，要做对国家有用的人，要相信共产党、相信国家等。有时候也不知道她是在对我说，还是嘴里念念有词地说给自己听。一些简单的道理，反而是很多人容易忽略的，外婆一直重复着拿来教育孩子以及她孩子的孩子。

1967年是家庭变动的一年。这一年，外公被抓走了，被游斗，在批斗大会上经历过两次假枪毙，之后便一直在坐牢。外公被抓走后，外婆和舅舅成为家里的顶梁柱，家里人被当作反革命分子家属，日子一天比一天难过。舅舅阿姨没有了玩乐的时间，放学后都会去地里采猪草，尽己所能地分担家里的农活，外婆起早贪黑拉扯3个孩子，3个孩子也争气，没有因此怨天尤人自暴自弃，该认真学习就认真学，该干农活就好好干，如同父亲言传身教的那般，一心扑在一件事上，做了就要认真做好。

1972年外公获得平反回到村里，在坐了6年牢之后，他重新当上了青江村村支书。但狱中的6年也给他的身体带来了不可挽回的损害，肺部的疾病使得外公时常咳嗽不止。

1981年家庭联产承包责任制在村里落实的时候，家里的条件开始改善了。外公规划着村子的事，实现了田地整改，村里的粮食产量涨了又涨，同时青江村也成为富阳第一个拉上电线杆的村子，外地的村支书都来学习。虽说都是村支书，但外公和他们有一点是不一样的，外公的满腹诗书，使得他拥有了更为广阔的视野和更合理的思路。之后外公在场口创办了天线厂，直接对接杭州的电视制造厂，自己也成为工办副主任。虽然外公“身居要职”，在工农兵大学生名额推荐上有较大的发言权,但舅舅阿姨们都是凭自己的实力考上的大学。

舅舅大学毕业后到了场口中学担任科学老师,并用工资供大阿姨上大学。大阿姨毕业后于1986年进入了场口中学当语文老师,她每个月的10块钱师范生活补助和工资,帮助了1986年考上杭师院本科政治系的二阿姨读完了大学。

2020年的现在,舅舅已经从场口中学退休了。大阿姨在场口中学当了10年语文老师后于1997年1月调入党校任教,现在已经任教23年了。二阿姨在郁达夫中学任政治和历史教师。妈妈在受降幼儿园任总务主任。兄弟姐妹4人终于跃出了农门。

2007年,外公因为肺病去世了,送行的那一天,鹅毛般的大雪铺天盖地飞舞,厚厚的白雪重重覆盖着这个世界,我想,这也许是上天对外公普通又传奇的一生所唱诵的最后的挽歌吧。

直到现在,外婆偶尔也会一个人看看外公的照片,念念有词地说着什么,或是怀念,或是感叹,怀念的是他们和子女一起走过的寒窗,感叹的是他们的子女跃出的农门。

Hangzhou
He Liu (Class 193, Majoring in Journalism)

Study Hard to Change One's Destiny of Being a Farmer

In my eyes, my grandparents are great people. My grandfather graduated from primary school, and my grandmother was illiterate, but those four children that they raised all entered the university and became four teachers afterwards.

My mother was the youngest in the family. She had an elder brother and two elder sisters. They were all teachers. My mother was an undergraduate graduated from a correspondence college, and her siblings all graduated from normal university.

At the end of 1977, the college entrance examination was resumed. One year later in the hot summer, my uncle, like many rural students, went into the examination room with anxiety and excitement. After the examination, he calmed down and returned to work in the production team. A month passed, my uncle would hurry to the commune to see if the postman brought the letter of admission, but all he got was disappointment every day. Instead of giving up, my uncle studied every day while he worked to support the family. He did not stop studying every day. With textbook in his hands he often studied till the moon appeared high above the treetops and the stars studded the sky. In January of 1979, my uncle received a letter from Hangzhou Normal University. When opening it, he found the "Letter of Admission" was solemnly printed in neat ink style, which seemed to have a special flavor. There was no extra decoration on the thin paper, but it was full of the elegance of being knowledgeable. These few simple words shone brightly in my uncle's eyes.

He was admitted to the university.

It was because the Department of Biology had not been established when Hangzhou Normal University enrolled students in September, so the university had to recruit students and establish the new professional disciplines at the same time. It wasn't until the next January that my uncle received the admission notice he had been longing for. He was also the only student in the village who was admitted to university.

In the year of my uncle taking the college entrance examination, my elder aunt was a freshman in high school. Three years later, she also ushered in the most important test of her life. However this time, my aunt did not get what she wanted. She failed the college entrance examination, but she did not want to stop the pace of continuing to study, so she began a year of self-study. In 1982, she walked into the examination room again with an air of calm. Finally in September, she got her wish and was admitted by the Department of Chinese Language and Literature in Hangzhou Normal University. She was also the only undergraduate student in the village that year.

I once asked my elder aunt about why they were able to be admitted to the university since the university enrollment rate was low then and one student who passed the college entrance examination was chosen in a million. She told me that there were two people who had the greatest influence on the family. One was my grandfather, and the other was my uncle. My grandfather had cultivated a good family customs, and my uncle had set an excellent example.

After graduating from primary school, my grandfather did not go to school any more. He became a militia company commander later. When he was 20 years old, he became the party secretary of Qingjiang Village, which he worked for the next 19 years. Grandpa loved reading very much. Although he graduated from primary school, he was proficient in literature. In the memory of his children, he always sat in front of a small table reading books earnestly, holding a book in one hand and a turquoise China tea cup in the other. In those days, my grandpa always delivered speeches and held big meetings everywhere, but my grandpa didn't need a speech draft before making speech. Standing on the stage, he could speak for three hours without repetition. His thought was clear; the content was rigorous and easy to understand. He was such a fluent speaker that those who read a script couldn't compete. In addition, the villagers loved to listen to his speech. Everyone respected my grandpa. They believed in him because my grandpa was a sincere and earnest man who always put the affairs of the village first. Every family liked to come to my grandpa to ask for help. My grandpa never turned them down. No matter how big the matter was, he must solve it once he went, or he wouldn't go home for dinner. He was sustained by this spirit, which earned him the title of "Excellent Individual for Socialist Construction" by Hangzhou City. He became a good example for many people.

My grandpa was very dedicated to his job. He put his work first and was very busy every day, so my grandmother took over everything in the family. My grandma took care of everything in the house, including raising children, planting vegetables, feeding chickens, cooking and doing laundry. My grandma could not read, but she always reasoned with her children. My grandmother was a very principled person. When I went back to my hometown to visit her, she often told me that studying hard was the only way to change your destiny, you should be a useful person for the country and you should believe in the Communist Party and believe in the country. Sometimes I didn't know whether she said it to me or said it to herself. Some simple truths were easy to be ignored by many people. My grandmother kept repeating those words to teach her grandchildren.

1967 was a year of family change. In this year, my grandfather was arrested and criticized in a parade. He was threatened with being shot twice at the criticism meeting. After that, he was put into prison. After my grandfather was taken away, my grandmother and my uncle became the backbone of the family. The family members were treated as the relatives of counter-revolutionaries, and life became more and more difficult day by day. My uncle and my aunts had no time to play, because they had to go to the field to pick pigweed after school, trying their best to share the farm work in the family. My grandmother worked from dawn to dusk, raising the three children. Her three children also lived up to her expectation. Instead of complaining and giving up on themselves, they studied hard and did the farm work well. As their father taught them by words and deeds, once they start to do something, they should do it well by all their heart.

In 1972, my grandfather was rehabilitated and returned to the village. After six years in prison, he became the party secretary of Qingjiang village again. However, six years' life in prison also brought irreparable damage to his body. His lung disease made him cough constantly.

In 1981, when the household contract responsibility system was implemented in the village, the conditions of the family began to improve. My grandfather made a plan for the village and achieved the reform of the fields. The grain output in the village increased again and again. At the same time, Qingjiang was the first village to have the telegraph poles in Fuyang, so other village party secretaries came to study. Although all of them were village party secretaries, there was one thing that my grandpa was different from them. My grandpa was knowledgeable, which allowed him to have a broader vision and more reasonable ideas. Later, my grandfather set up an antenna factory in Changkou, which was directly connected to the TV manufacturer in Hangzhou. My grandfather also became the deputy director of the executive's office. Although my grandpa occupied an important position, and he had an important right to recommend workers, farmers and soldiers to go to the university, my uncle and my aunts were admitted to the university through their own strength.

After my uncle graduated from university, he worked as a science teacher in Changkou Middle School and provided his salary for my aunt to go to university. After graduation, my aunt joined Changkou Middle School as a

Chinese teacher in 1986. With her living allowance of 10 yuan in the normal university and salary per month, she helped my second aunt who was admitted to the Political Science department of Hangzhou Normal University in 1986 to finish her university education.

My uncle had retired from Changkou Middle School in 2020, and my aunt was transferred to the Party school to teach in January 1997 after 10 years as a Chinese teacher in Changkou Middle School. Now she has been teaching for 23 years. My second aunt was a politics and history teacher in Yudafu Middle School; my mother was director of general affairs in Shoujiang kindergarten. All of them finally changed the destiny of being a farmer.

In 2007, my grandpa died of lung disease. On the day of the funeral, the snowflakes fluttered and thick snow tightly squeezed the world. I thought, this might be the last elegy given by god to my grandpa's ordinary and legendary life.

Until now, sometimes my grandmother would look at my grandfather's photos alone, murmuring to herself. It might be the recall or sigh. What she thought about was the tough years that they had gone through with their children, and what she sighed was that their children had changed the destiny of being a farmer.

默默耕耘,梦想自会开花

贠馨怡

树高叶茂,系于深根。

植物的生长依托于深埋的根系,而梦想的实现依赖于不懈的耕耘。正如陈梦洁同学在《叔叔的店》一文中所写到的,那样两次失败让叔叔无缘实现自己的大学梦,只好按照家里的意愿学了手艺,并开了一家打银店,在某种意义上实现了爷爷奶奶对叔叔的期待——饿不着自己就好。随着不断的努力,叔叔结识了婶婶,成了家;店里的生意也越做越好,店面不断扩大并拓宽业务,成功立了业。家里生意越做越大的同时,叔叔的儿子也一年一年茁壮成长,顺利收到了大学录取通知书。

诚然,儿子的录取通知书并不意味着满足了叔叔内心深处的大学梦,但不失为实现梦想的又一方法和路径。

任何梦想的实现,都离不开辛勤浇灌的土壤,对于叔叔而言,亦是如此。尽管没能通过自己的努力考上大学,甚至以后也没有机会徜徉大学校园学习文化知识,但好在叔叔没有放弃奋斗,将自己努力拼搏的精气神从读书转移到学手艺和开店上,并一路经营了打银店、米店,将生意做到学校食堂,让家里的日子越过越好。

默默耕耘,梦想自会开花,叔叔通过自己的努力改善了家庭的条件,为儿子能够有好的学习环境并最终考上大学奠定了基础。孩子学业有成所带来的喜悦,应该仅次于圆了自己的大学梦吧。在今天的社会上,读书是每一个人追求梦想的必由之路,但是,一个人的成功绝不是一个人的功劳,这往往是一个家庭共同努力的结果。或许,叔叔的努力并没有让大学圆梦的花朵开在自己的青年时代,但是不用着急,只要继续努力,成功的花儿就在路上。

(浙大宁波理工学院传媒与法学院网络与新媒体专业 2018 级学生)

故事

衢州

陈梦洁(新闻学专业201专升本班)

叔叔的店

1989年,我叔在衢州二中读高三。高考结束后,我叔落榜了。1990年,复读一年后,叔叔再次参加高考,又落榜了。494分,跟大学的分数线就差一分。

这一年,我叔的爸爸妈妈,也就是我的爷爷和奶奶老来得子,给我叔生了个妹妹。爷爷对我叔说:“你年纪也不小了,不是我不让你上学,这大学也考了两次了,你也该死心了。还是去学门手艺吧,饿不着自己就好。”

我叔听了这些话,就知道这大学肯定是没法上了。叔叔说:“那天天特别热,心里闷得慌。”虽然打心眼里不情愿,但还是听了爷爷的话,在爷爷远房表哥的介绍下去江山市赖师傅那儿学了两年打银,吃住都在赖师傅家。

22岁那年,从江山回来后,爷爷奶奶出了一些钱,叔叔在石梁镇的镇尾营盘路上租了个15平方米的店面,一年租金500元。这是叔叔的第一家店。

他照着江山赖师傅的那家打银店,给自己的这个小店也取了个名字。“店面虽然不如我师傅家的一半大,自己却越看越顺眼,像那么回事儿了。”叔叔笑着,眉毛和额头上的肉皱在了一块。

他从家里的灶台边挑了两块黑炭,在店门口的墙上竖着写上“傅氏金银加工”几个大字,字不算漂亮,但是起码端端正正,店名写好了,店的排面就有了。

靠近店门口就可以看到一个大小适中的玻璃柜台,里面放着打银的首饰和模型,玻璃台面上放着几本模型书。紧挨着玻璃台的是叔叔的工作台,上面摆放着一些日常用的工具以及一台淬火设备和一台挤压机,还有一个专门给他照明用的台灯。这些也都是照着赖师傅家的样子摆的,就是那个玻璃柜台不如师傅家的大,台灯由于是新买的,着实要比师傅家的亮一些。

一开始店里的生意没那么好,来店里的头几个客人,是隔壁几个村的表叔表婶。这是爷爷在背后偷偷帮的忙。

如果走在石梁镇尾的营盘路上,你就总是能听到这个小作坊里传出来叮叮咚咚的打银声。叔叔说:“生意不好手也不能停,手不能生了。”“还有嘛……就是这样叮叮咚咚的才好把人家吸引过来啊。”

1994年，当时金子的价格是75块钱1克。店里的客人来来往往，用叔叔的话来说："不算热闹，但倒也算是有人气。"有来打结婚戒指的一对准新人，有孩子满月来打一对银手镯的奶奶，这两种情况都算是大喜事，来的人通常会塞一把染着红颜料的花生给叔叔。还有赶时髦的已婚妇女，把自己的嫁妆手镯熔了，打成项链。叔叔说最赚钱的活来自那些赶时髦的年轻人，她们要漂亮的有花样的款式，他就去市场上买模具，带回来给她们打，这种定制的款式，可以多收点加工费。

25岁那年，李家村的张姐把自己家的侄女介绍给了叔叔。在这之前，叔叔打了一对对的镯子和戒指，心里也盼望着什么时候能给自己和对象打一对结婚戒指。叔叔和这个女孩见了几次面，感觉挺不错。听说她很能干，饭做得也好吃，叔叔想着，竟笑了起来。

我叔26岁时，这个女孩就变成了我的婶婶，叔叔和婶婶住在爷爷奶奶家的泥房子里，白天婶婶在家做饭。叔叔忙的时候，婶婶会把饭盒给叔叔送到店里去。

2001年，傅氏金银加工店的生意越来越红火，叔叔的儿子也到了上幼儿园的年纪。叔叔在靠近石梁镇中间的位置租了个30左右平方米的房子，900块一年。这是叔叔的第二家店，足足比之前的大一倍。为此，叔叔还专门找加工师傅做了一块不锈钢的新招牌横挂在店门口。

同时，叔叔和婶婶为了生活方便一些，就从爷爷奶奶那儿搬了出来，自己用木头板子隔出了一个10平方米的小房间出来住。房间外面就是打银店，布置得和原来店里一样，唯一不同的就是那个进门的玻璃柜子换成了稍大一点的。

"老婆孩子都可以一起在店里摆个桌子吃饭了。"叔叔回忆着说。"那年生意好，我还把自行车给卖了，换了辆三轮摩托车，是蓝色的，你哥哥喜欢蓝色。"

儿子上小学那一年，叔叔手头已经存起一笔钱。听说朋友的一家米店要转让，叔叔便盘算着拿出那笔积蓄盘下米店。米店位于石梁镇的镇中心，比营盘路热闹，店门口来来往往的人和车都多了。和原先两个小平房不一样，米店有三层楼。一楼是店铺，二楼有两个房间可以住人，三楼可以堆放一些杂物。叔叔便带着老婆和孩子搬进米店，一家3口住在二楼。叔叔回忆说："刚租下它的那一年，房租是3000块一年，等儿子上了初中，房租也涨到7000块了。"

新店开张前，叔叔给米店取了个新名字。婶婶叫江月花，所以就给米店取名为"江月花粮油经营部"。

在粮油经营部的后面，叔叔花了10万块买了一个200多平方米的大平房，准备作为米店的仓库。叔叔说这个仓库也是自己捡了个大便宜，前几年一场大火把仓库烧着了。搁置了好几年都没人搭理它，他盘算着就买了下来，自己找人重新整理了一番。

这家米店原先共有两个门面，现在叔叔依然保留着它原来的格局，只是一边拿来开米店，一边继续做金银加工。婶婶平时看米店，叔叔在隔壁打银。

过了一年，叔叔为了方便送货买了一辆皮卡车。“当时儿子很开心，躲在驾驶室里，下大雨了也不怕。”叔叔笑着说。

儿子初一时，叔叔把原先买下的大仓库重新装修了。仓库共有7个房间，叔叔带着婶婶和儿子住进了其中两个房间。但米店生意越做越好的同时，叔叔打银店的生意却渐渐暗淡了。结婚也好，小孩满月也好，大家似乎都更喜欢去衢州城里那些有牌子的金店买首饰了，很少有人再愿意来光顾这个无名银匠的小作坊。除了几个年纪大的老客户，大抵也是看在以往的交情上吧。

叔叔只好先放下打银店，一心和婶婶经营米店，不只是等着人家来买米，还把米生意做到了学校的食堂里。那一年，叔叔拿下了衢州一中食堂一楼的大米配送权。第三年重新招标时，叔叔一次性拿下了衢州七家学校食堂的大米配送权。那段时间，叔叔每天就开着皮卡把大米一袋袋往食堂送。

周围人都说叔叔家的大米挺实惠的，口口相传，来叔叔家买米的人便越来越多，一时间，江月花粮油经营部就成了当时石梁镇最大、出货量最高的米店。忙不过来时，叔叔还特意请了两个小工替他送米。

眼看着米店生意这么忙活，叔叔就想着把打银店面也装修成米店。“就老老实实当小老板呗。”叔叔笑着说。

2014年，三层楼房的合同到期了。叔叔的生意范围开始扩大，可以直接去和经销商合作，自己定米的价格，手里有了余钱，还装修了之前买的仓库，一半自己住，一半出租。

儿子高中毕业时，叔叔开始承包衢州一中、衢州广播电视大学等学校食堂的供应链，正式成为多家学校食堂大米的供货商。同年暑假，也是一个大热天，儿子收到了江西师范大学的录取通知书。

米店在一点点扩大，儿子在一年年长大。当年我叔虽然没能上大学，现如今他自己培养出一个大学生，别提有多高兴了。送米的时候碰到街坊邻居和学校食堂的老板，逢人就说：“我儿子考上大学了，9月份就要去江西上师范大学。”

Quzhou
Chen Mengjie (Class 201, Majoring in Journalism)

My Uncle's Shops

It was 1989 when my uncle who studied in Quzhou No. 2 High School failed in the entrance exam for university for the first time. The next year he failed again. But this time he scored 494, only one point away from university.

It was also in 1990 when his parents gave birth to his little sister. His father therefore said to my uncle, "You're a grown-up now. I don't mean that I don't approve of you to continue study, but you've tried twice already, it's time to give up. Learn a trade, that'll help you make a living."

Upon hearing that, my uncle knew that he was not going to university. He told me that it was a very hot and muggy day when his father had that conversation with him. Although he did not want to give up at all, he did as his father said. With the help of a relative on his father's side, he became an apprentice to a silversmith called Master Lai in Jiangshan city.

At the age of 22, my uncle came home from Jiangshan and rented a 15-square-meter space for 500 yuan per year with the money his parents gave him. The space was on Yingpan Road in the corner of the Shiliang town. That was his first shop.

My uncle named his shop the same name as Master Lai's. "It was not as big as half of my master's, but I gradually grew to like it," he said to me, smiling, wrinkles creeping on his forehead.

He wrote the name of his shop, "Fu's Gold & Silver Smith", on the wall at the door with some black charcoal he picked up from the hearth in his house. The characters were not beautifully written, but at least legible. Once he wrote down the name of a shop, it was ready to open.

In the shop, there was a medium-sized glass showcase placed near the door with silver works in it. On the showcase there were some book models. My uncle's worktable was next to the counter, with some tools, a quenching machine, an extruder and a lamp on it. Everything was placed the same way as in Master Lai's shop, only the showcase was not as big, and the lamp was a new one and was therefore brighter than the one Master Lai had.

The business in the shop did not start off well. The first few customers my uncle had were some of his relatives, who were there because of his father.

You could always hear my uncle hammering in that little shop if you walked down Yingpan Road. He told me that he did not stop working even when he had no customers because he wanted to keep his skills sharp. Moreover, the banging sounds could also attract potential customers to his shop.

Then it was 1994. The price of gold was 75 yuan per gram. The business of my uncle's shop went well that year, or in his words, "It was popular but not crowded". Sometimes there would be a couple who came to get a pair of wedding rings, or an old woman who came to get a silver bracelet for her grandchild as the first-month birthday gift, which were big events. People who came for events like those would always bring a handful of peanuts which were painted red. There were also fashionable married women who came to have their dowry bracelets turned into necklaces. My uncle said the most profitable jobs were crafting for fashionable youngsters. He had to go to the market to buy special molds for those works, so he could charge extra money.

When he was 25, Mrs Zhang in Lijia Village introduced him to her niece. By that time, my uncle had already made many bracelets and wedding rings for his customers. He was hoping that he could make one for himself someday. He met with that girl a few of times, and both had good feelings for each other. My uncle smiled when he heard that the girl was not only smart but also cooked well.

They got married the next year, and lived in the mud house with my grandparents. My aunt would bring meals from home to my uncle when he was too busy in the shop.

In 2001, the business of my uncle's little shop went even better, and his son was going to kindergarten. My uncle rented a 30-square-meter house around the town center for 900 yuan per year. There he opened his second shop. The second shop was twice as big as the first one. My uncle ordered a new stainless steel sign for the shop which was hung over the door.

In the same year, my uncle moved out from my grandparents' house with his wife and child. They separated out one third of the space in the new shop to sleep in. The rest of the shop was placed the same way as the first one, only the showcase was bigger.

"The place was big enough for me to put a table in it to dine with my wife and son," my uncle said, "The business was pretty good that year. I sold my bicycle and bought a new motor tricycle. It was blue, my son's favorite color."

The year when his son went to primary school, he took over a rice shop from one of his friends with his savings. The rice shop was in the town center, a busier place than Yingpan Road with more people and cars passing by. The rice shop was a three-story house, with the shop on the first floor, two bedrooms on the second, and a storeroom on the third. They moved into the rice shop. As my uncle recalled, the rent of the rice shop was 3,000 yuan per year when they moved in. The year when his son went to middle school, it went up to 7,000 per year.

My uncle named the shop after his wife, Jiang Yuehua, as "Jiang Yuehua Grain & Oil Shop".

My uncle bought a 200-square-meter bungalow behind the shop for 100,000 yuan, and turned it into a warehouse. It was a huge bargain. The bungalow was abandoned for years after a fire before my uncle found it, so he bought it for a very cheap price and renovated.

There were two shop spaces in the rice shop, so my uncle opened his silversmith shop in one of the spaces and my aunt opened the rice shop in the other. My aunt attended to the rice shop while my uncle crafted silver works next door.

The next year, my uncle bought a pick-up truck for delivery. "My son was so excited for he no longer had to worry about the rain since he could hide in the cab," my uncle said.

When his son went to middle school, my uncle renovated the warehouse. The warehouse had seven rooms among which they lived in two. While the business of the rice shop kept getting better, my uncle's silversmith business went down since people preferred big brands rather than little workshops for their wedding rings and one-month birthday gifts. Only a few old customers would visit my uncle's shop for friendship's sake.

My uncle thus had to close his silversmith shop. After closing his shop, he started to help his wife with the rice business. The rice shop did not only sell rice to individual customers, but also had deals with school canteens. They had their first deal with one of the canteens in Quzhou No. 1 High School that same year. Two years later, they were selling rice to seven school canteens. My uncle was busy delivering rice to schools everyday at that time.

Since many agreed that the rice price was fair in my uncle's shop, more and more people bought rice from their shop. Jiang Yuehua Grain & Oil Shop became the biggest rice shop that sold the most rice at that time. Sometimes the shop was so busy that my uncle hired workers to deliver rice for him.

Since the business in the rice shop went so well, my uncle decided to turn the silversmith shop to a rice shop as well. "I just wanted to be a shop owner after all," my uncle said and smiled.

In 2014, the lease on the rice shop was due. My uncle's business had expanded, and he was able to do business with distributors directly and set the rice price himself. With more money in hand, he renovated the warehouse again. His family lived in half of the house, the other half was for rent.

When his son graduated from high school, my uncle was already doing business with many schools and universities. That summer, also on a very hot day, his son was admitted into Jiangxi Normal University.

As the business of the rice shop continued to grow, my uncle's son grew up as well. Although my uncle did not go to the university himself, he raised a son who became a university student. He was so happy that summer that every time he met our neighbors and the bosses of school canteens when delivering rice, he would tell them, again and again, that his son was going to Jiangxi Normal University that September.

幸福地理学：四海为家创业路

郭小春

时空是我们理解社会结构和历史变迁的关键要素。安东尼·吉登斯认为现代社会活动和社会关系超越具体地方的局限而实现更加广泛的联合，所谓“时空分离”是也。项婷同学的父母从家乡浙江温州乐清到西安，再艰辛辗转，到浙江台州黄岩、山东、云南，“四海为家”谋生创业，是中国社会发展的缩微景观。我国每年数以亿计的农民工走出家乡，在中西部和东部沿海、工厂和田间、城市和乡村之间流动，改变了社会和经济发展中地区之间的关系，也为中国改革开放提供了不竭动力。

千千万万东奔西走的人口流动为改革的中国全面建设小康社会打下了坚实的物质基础，推动了中国社会关系和社会秩序的重组。流动的人口延展了自己的生活空间，也压缩了社会空间——经历、甚至融合了不同地方的文化，形成了愈加进取、愈加奋发的社会文化空间。这种地理尺度的跃升和文化界限的模糊，既是改革开放的硕果，又成为进一步改革开放的动因。在此过程中，技术更迭在小家奔幸福、社会奔小康的路上不断为个体赋能、为社会助力。交通工具、通信方式、家用电器随着劳动收入的提高而改善，家庭劳动结构也相应发生改变。

性格坚韧、勤劳奋进的中国人历来信奉幸福都是奋斗出来的。南下北上创业路，历尽苦难痴心在。把没有门窗的房子建设成“一家人齐聚，不再东奔西跑”稳定温暖的家。地理学家说，都城、家乡和工作地是中国人心中最基本的被认同的地方，尤其是家乡，“它是中国人的根，具有恒久价值，也是大地上最有人情味的地方”。[①] 腾挪周折的创业之路虽然艰辛，却展现了中国人民以劳动追求幸福的价值观和中国社会积极、乐观、进取的文化生态。

（宁波工程学院副教授，博士）

① 唐晓峰：《文化地理学讲义》，北京：学苑出版社，2012年，第191页。

故事

温州

项婷(新闻学专业191班)

四海为家

我家位于浙江省温州市乐清市的一个小镇。

每次我在饭桌上挑食,爸爸就会感叹:“以前我们哪有现在这样的条件啊,一年才能吃上一次肉,有时候一年都吃不上。每天就吃吃山里挖来的野菜,米饭配酱油也是常常吃的。哪敢像你们一样挑剔啊,我们不想吃就只能饿死,哪像你们还有那么多选择。”每次听完这些话,我都非常非常愧疚,物质生活的保障确实让我们挑剔了不少,即便生活变好,我们也应该珍惜粮食。

妈妈的童年也是非常艰苦的。外婆在已经拥有3个女儿的情况下,还是和外公一起逃计划生育到外地去生下了舅舅。所以妈妈和两个阿姨打小就开始自己做饭,自己洗衣服,还要喂养家里的鸡鸭。才上小学的她们根本够不到灶台,每次做饭都是搬一张凳子站上去。没有大人在身边就没有经济来源,所以白米饭只能配着酱油吃。那时候的冰棍只有五分钱一根,即便这样,妈妈和阿姨们还是买不起。每次看到别的小朋友吃冰棍,他们都羡慕不已,有时候别家的小孩会把他们吃过的冰棍给妈妈舔一口,听到这我疑惑地问妈妈:“吃过的吗?而且就给你舔一口?”妈妈说:“对啊,能舔一口已经很高兴了,还管什么吃过的没吃过的。”那时候也没有电视,全村只有一户人家有那种带天线的黑白电视,他们家的电视一开机,所有的小孩都围过去一起看。有时候信号不好,还要轮流出去调整天线。

因为不爱学习且贪玩,爸爸上完小学就没有继续上学了。而妈妈因为成绩太差,也早早地在初中就放弃了学业。

1995年,16岁的妈妈迎来了她人生的第一份工作,是和外公一起在乐清市虹桥灯泡厂工作,基本工作时间是8:00—17:00,但工厂常常加班到21:00,有时候甚至直接加班到第二天早上。高强度的工作给未成年的妈妈一记重击,她的身体吃不消,常常流鼻血。工厂的住宿环境也很不好,十几个人挤在一间小屋子里睡大通铺,有的稍微大点的房子还要挤下二十几个人。

1997年,妈妈跟着外公来到西安,在一个小破商场露天摆摊卖布料。西安的冬天非常冷，室外摆摊没有墙壁去阻挡寒风，妈妈的手上和脸上都长满了冻疮。因为是外地来的，在那里多少会遭受点歧视。有次一个路人经过妈妈的铺子时，自己的东西不小心掉下来滚到铺子下，那个人一口咬定是妈妈偷了他的东西，然后二话不说抢走了妈妈铺子上的一大卷布料转身就跑。当时一个商场都是老乡，他们看到这种情景发生就都追了出去，于是一群人发生了肢体冲突，甚至有人还拿了刀。最后闹到了派出所。因为妈妈刚成年，又是在外地，所以即使是自己有理有据，也不敢再继续追究。

也是在这个小破商场，妈妈认识了同样外出打工的爸爸。

认识妈妈以后，爸爸花费大约1200元买了人生中第一台BB机，是摩托罗拉牌的。小破商场拆迁后，爸爸妈妈分别转到附近的两个小商场卖衣服。

2001年，妈妈在西安生下我之后，跟爸爸回了家。那时候爸爸还没有自己独立的房子，只建造了后面一部分，因为前边有高压电，所以造房子的事情一直耽搁，爸爸妈妈一起在那个连门都没有的房子里生活了一年左右。

在我1岁多点时，爸妈把我托付给奶奶照顾，他们出发去了台州黄岩的一个摩托车零部件加工厂工作。每天打卡上班，两元多一个小时。因为租房和工作的地方有一定距离，爸爸买了一辆凤凰牌自行车，每天载着妈妈去上班，这也是他们艰苦日子里的唯一浪漫。为了联系方便，爸爸还买了人生中第一部手机，是波导牌的翻盖手机，BB机从此退场。有了手机后，爸爸妈妈不用再每次花费2元去小店打电话，而是随时想打就可以打。

黄岩工作结束后，他们先后去了乐清白石和陕西龙岭。在陕西龙岭，他们开了一家属于自己的服装店。和以前不同的是，这次他们可以自由支配自己的工作时间，独立的个体店铺也比以前省了很多麻烦。本来稳定平凡的日子却被一个意外打破——2010年12月25日，我在学校因为意外摔伤。爸爸妈妈接到消息后关店回家陪我进行治疗。住院加上出院后陪我休养的时间，让原来店铺的囤货也不了了之，爸爸妈妈只能另寻工作。

2011年，他们来到山东的一个杀鸡厂工作，这是一个流水线工厂，爸爸负责称重，妈妈负责包装。因为日子过于无聊，爸爸用许久的积蓄买了一台电脑，工作之余和我妈一起用电脑看剧。那时候的治安还不是很好，有天下午爸爸在自己的房间里放音乐，由于声音开得太大，引起了附近盗贼的注意。当天晚上，盗贼趁爸爸熟睡，撬开门锁，偷走了爸爸刚买的电脑。爸爸妈妈立刻就去报了警，只是在科技不那么发达的年代，想追究也无从下手，爸爸的第一台电脑就这样没有了。

2012年，爸爸和妈妈在云南和其他合伙人一起开了一家生活超市。逢年过节的时候，生意都比较好。超市雇的员工也都愿意勤勤恳恳地工作，超市的运行也一直很稳定。由于离家有一定距离，爸爸赚来的钱除了供他们生活，还拿出一部分交给我叔叔，让他帮忙监督家里房子的建造和装修。超市的其中一个合伙人总是好吃懒做，对仓库的东西也是照拿不讳，导致爸爸对账的时候总是对不上。合伙人的不敬业是一向认真做事的爸爸无法忍受的，因此，爸爸主动退出了与他们的合作，带着妈妈回到了自己的家。

2014年，我第一次真正住进了自己家，和爸爸妈妈还有妹妹一起。由于要照顾我和妹妹，妈妈决定留在家做一个家庭主妇。爸爸从此一个人在外工作，慢慢地为家里添置洗衣机、空调、数字电视等。为了减轻爸爸的负担，妈妈在照顾我们之余，在家附近为自己找了份工作。生活从此变得稳定起来，一家人齐聚，不再东奔西跑，"四海为家"。

Wenzhou
Xiang Ting (Class 191, Majoring in Journalism)

Leading a Wandering Life

Our home is in a small town of Yueqing, Wenzhou City, Zhejiang Province.

Every time when I was picky about food at the dinner table, my father would say with a sigh, "Life in the past was harder than that nowadays. We could only eat meat once in a year, and sometimes we had no meat to eat for a whole year. What we had were just wild vegetables dug from mountains, and rice served with soy sauce was also frequent for meals. How dare we complain in the way you do? Poorly fed like us, there were few options for our generation. Unlike you guys, we had to accept every humble meal in order not to be starving." A lingering sense of guilt would overcome me every time I heard these words. The improvement of material life made us much pickier than we used to be. Even if our lives are getting better, food should be cherished.

The childhood of my mother was also quite tough and hard. Although there had been three daughters in my mother's family, my grandparents were determined to have a son despite the Family Planning Policy. In order to avoid being punished, my grandparents ran away from their hometown so as to give birth to my uncle. Thus my mother and her sisters had to cook for themselves, to wash clothes, and to feed the chickens and ducks that were raised by the family from a very young age. As children in the primary school, they could hardly reach the stove. Every time they needed to cook, they had to stand on a stool in order to reach the stove. With no parents around and no financial support, my mother and her sisters had to eat white rice without any dishes but soy sauce. At that time, a popsicle only cost five cents. Even so, my mother and my aunts could not afford it. When they saw their friends enjoying popsicles, they always looked enviously. Sometimes other children would ask my mother to have a taste of their popsicles. On hearing that, I asked my mother in confusion, "Had the popsicle ever been eaten before? And they offered you only one lick?" My mom replied, "Yes, I was quite satisfied to have a lick, so how would I care whether it was eaten or not." There was no TV at my mother's home at that time, and only one family in the village had that kind of black-and-white TV with antenna. Whenever the only TV was turned on, all the children in the village would gather around to watch it. Once the signal was bad, children would have to take turns to adjust the antenna.

As for my father, since he wasn't interested in learning and was quite playful, my father quit school after he finished his study in primary school. And my mother also gave up her studies after middle school because of her poor grades.

In 1995 when she was 16, my mother, together with my grandfather, got her first job as a factory worker in the Hongqiao Bulb Factory in Yueqing City. The working hours should have been from 8 to 17; however, they often worked overtime till 21:00, and sometimes even till the next morning. The intense work gave a heavy blow to my mom who was only under 18. She couldn't bear the heavy workload and always got a nosebleed. What's worse, the accommodation in the factory was bad. A dozen people squeezed on a shared bed in a tiny room. If the room was big, more than 20 people would be arranged to live inside.

In 1997, my mother moved to Xi'an together with her father. They sold cloth at an open-air stall in a small shabby mall. It was cold in Xi'an when the winter came. With no walls to prevent the freezing wind, severe frostbite grew over my mother's face and hands. Regarded as strangers there, they would somewhat encounter prejudices against them. Once there was a passerby who passed my mother's stall, and his belongings accidentally dropped and rolled to my mother's stall. He insisted that his belongings were stolen by my mom. He snatched a large roll of cloth from her stall without a word and turned around to run away. Thanks to the fellow townsmen who worked in the shop, they ran out to chase that man at the sight of what had happened. Fierce conflicts took place and some even took a knife as a weapon. Finally, they went to the police station. Because she was only 18 at that time and she was an out-of-towner, my mom daren't ask for the punishment to the man though she had firm evidence.

It was also in this small shabby mall that my mother met my father who also worked away from his hometown to earn his bread.

After getting to know my mom, my dad spent about 1,200 yuan on his first beeper whose brand was Motorola. After the demolition of the mall, my parents moved to two small malls nearby to sell clothes respectively.

In 2001, after giving birth to me in Xi'an, my mother went back home with my father. At that time, my father didn't have his own house. The house wasn't finished yet and only a back part of a house was built. The construction of the house had been delayed because of high-voltage electricity in the front. My parents lived in this doorless house for about a year.

When I was one year old or so, my parents left me in my grandmother's care. They set off to work in a motorcycle parts processing plant in Huangyan, Taizhou. They had to clock in every day and were paid two yuan an hour in return. In consideration of the distance between their rented house and working place, my father bought a Phoenix bicycle and took my mom to work every day. That was the only romance in their hard days. To keep in contact with us, my dad also bought the first mobile phone in his life, which was a BIRD flip phone. The beeper was no longer used in his life afterwards. With this mobile phone, they could make phone calls whenever they wanted, and they needn't spend 2 yuan making a telephone call in the grocery store any more.

When finishing the work in Huangyan, they went to Baishi in Yueqing and then Longling in Shanxi. In Longling, Shanxi, they started to run a clothing store of their own. What's different from before was that working hours was at their disposal this time, and having a store owned by themselves saved a lot of trouble they met before. The peaceful days were interrupted by an accident. On December 25, 2010, I was injured unexpectedly at school. On hearing the news, my parents closed the store and went back to accompany me during the treatment. I needed to be hospitalized and recuperated after being discharged from the hospital, so the stocks in the store had to be left aside, and my parents had to seek for new jobs.

In 2011, they worked in a poultry processing plant in Shandong. This plant adopted assembly line production. My dad was responsible for weighing and my mom packaging. In order to get rid of the boredom in their spare time, my father bought a computer with the money that he had saved for a long time. He would watch TV series with my mother on the computer after work. At that time, the public security was bad. One afternoon, my dad played music in his room so loudly that a thief noticed. When my dad slept soundly in the evening, the thief forced open the door and stole the computer that my dad had just bought. My parents immediately reported to the police, but in the age when technology wasn't so advanced, it was impossible to catch the thief. Hence, my dad's computer was stolen and never found.

In 2012, they opened a supermarket in Yunnan with several partners. The business of the supermarket during holidays was always better than that on other days. Staff members that were employed there always worked diligently, and the operation of the supermarket was quite good. Because of the distance from the supermarket to their home, apart from the daily expense, my dad had to offer a part of his income to my uncle who helped them to oversee the construction and decoration of our house. A partner of the supermarket was gluttonous and lazy, and he always took away goods to meet his own needs, which caused my father plenty of trouble when he verified the accounting record. The lack of dedication of that partner was indeed unbearable for my father who had always been serious and particular. Therefore, my father voluntarily withdrew from the partnership of the supermarket and went back home with my mom.

It was in 2014 that I first moved into a house that belonged to ourselves, with the company of my parents and younger sister. To take care of my sister and me, my mother made the decision to be a housewife. From then on, my father worked to support our family, and bought household appliances like washing machine, air conditioner, and digital TV into our home gradually. In order to reduce the burden my father shouldered, my mother made use of the leisure time after taking care of us, and found herself a job nearby. We finally settled down and reunited as a family. We don't lead a wandering life any more.

家的变迁营造出浙江的地方感

郭小春

尽管岁月在流逝，一代人变成了四代人同居一个屋檐下，在作者的心目中老家依然是一个难以忘怀的地方，成为地理学意义上的地方，即一个意义单元，表明客观世界和主体的关联性。从爷爷(实质上是外公)、爸爸先后入赘沈家，就和现在的家产生了联系，形成新的家文化，形成了空间形象和时间形象融合为一体的四世同堂景象，地方感在这个家里就变成了具体可感的对家的情愫。

"家门口的电线杆、杆下的枇杷林、林中的池塘和塘里的蝌蚪"早已被高楼大厦所取代，但是几代人对家园变化的记忆塑造了作者的自我意识和身份意识。这是经历着翻天覆地社会经济变迁而迈向小康生活的浙江人、中国人的集体记忆之缩影。

四世同堂揭示的时间意识塑造了一家人的空间意识(对家的感知)。作者在这里"唤起地方感和过去感的努力"①，其内在动因不仅是感怀，更是对于前辈奋斗的理解和认可，更在于长江后浪推前浪的文化延续。地方感串联起了一家人和家在情感上的联系，家在时间流转中凝结了一家人温暖的依恋感。千户奋斗、万家灯火，终于织造出浙江大地温润的地方感来。此间最具传播力的是作者由衷的胸臆直抒："我们这一大家子人现在过着还算不错的生活，是每一代人的奋斗造就了今天，对于家人，我唯一的希望，就是他们都能健健康康快快乐乐的，这四世同堂的故事，就交给我们来续写吧！"

(宁波工程学院副教授，博士)

① Yi-Fu Tuan. Space and Place: the Perspective of Experience [D]. Minneapolis, Minnesota: The University of Minnesota, 1977: 198.

故事

杭州

沈晨娇(新闻学专业192班)

四世同堂

杭州市余杭区临平街道南公河社区5组柴家河18号，这是我的老家。老房子早已被高楼大厦替代，即使现在故地重游，也找不到那栋三层小楼的位置了。但记忆中家门口的电线杆、杆下的枇杷林、林中的池塘和塘里的蝌蚪都记录着家的位置，也见证着四代人一路走来的风风雨雨，纵然时过境迁，但每一代人奋斗的历程仍然历历在目……

我的阿太，也就是我奶奶的母亲，出生于1929年，那是一个与我而言非常陌生的年代，我像翻看一本古籍一般，走进了阿太的半生……

“我们小的时候是没有拖鞋穿的，当时就是用两块木板拼起来作鞋穿。”阿太玩笑似地说道。19世纪三四十年代，只有条件非常好的地主官员人家子弟才能拥有上学念书的机会。阿太生在一个普通人家，或者说比普通人家的条件还差点。当时的人们主要就是下地干农活，白天弄麦秸，晚上提着蜡烛种麦子，还要上交公粮，要是碰上贪污的干部，是要吃不少苦头的。

“我们都是光着脚下到田里的呀，夏天田里的水烫得脚根本踩不下去。”阿太说着摸了一把自己的脚，皱起眉头摇了摇头。1946年，阿太17岁，那年阿太迎来了人生中的一个转折点。阿太去茅山的舅舅家做客，舅舅告诉她，你要不要学织麻布。当时村里并没有人接触这项技艺，也不知道要怎么做，做来怎么赚钱，我的阿太就成为当时村里“第一个吃螃蟹的人”。

“我虽然条件一般，但做过的活可不比他们男人少。”阿太自豪地说。于是，17岁的阿太在舅舅那里学习怎么处理络麻，怎么晾晒加工，怎么编织成麻布。后来阿太去小林置办了原材料和设备，开始在家里织起了麻布。一张麻布要织2到3天左右，阿太常常一次进12张麻布的原材料，边种地边织布，用完这些原材料大概要两个月左右的时间，一张麻布大约可以卖一块多，当时的一块多已经是非常可观的收入了。

“当时第一次拿了六张麻布去卖，一张可以卖一块多，太开心了，然后就用这些钱去买了两件大衣当作嫁妆，这才体面了一点。”

“解放军来的时候带来了一些药水，那年种出来的谷子没有一颗是瘪的。后来还普及了砖头的做法，大家就开始烧砖，之前的房子都是用水泥造的，用木板隔开做墙，用木头堆成屋顶，放上瓦片房子就造好了，有了砖头后就可以造楼了。”一说到解放军，阿太就开始滔滔不绝起来。

1958年开始，村里以小队为单位在公共的地里干活，每到下地时间广播就响起来，定时按照工作的量算工分发钱。当时的大食堂是设在我家的，一到吃饭时间，大家伙儿就聚到一起吃饭，当时的阿太在下地干活之余，还在坚持织麻布，攒下一些钱供家里造房子，就这么干着干着，奶奶长大了，开始了下一辈的奋斗故事……

1953年奶奶出生了，取名为沈金娣；1953年，爷爷出生，取名为柴应龙；1970年，爷爷入赘我家。爷爷奶奶结婚的第二年有了第一个孩子就是我的妈妈。在我妈妈出生后，爷爷奶奶主要是烧窑做砖，奶奶将泥和成砖头的形状，爷爷拿去窑子里烧，当时砖头是自己家用来造平房的，这是我家第一栋用砖头造的房子，只有一层。在烧窑的同时，爷爷奶奶也在家织麻布，下地种田，并通过卖麻布、农作物和多余的砖头获得收益。一块砖头只能卖2～5分，平均下来奶奶一天能赚个三五毛，爷爷能赚一块左右，零零总总算下来，家庭一年的收入也就在三五千元的样子，这些钱是攒下来造楼用的。

1984年，我家造楼了。

当时推行家庭联产承包责任制，实施包产到户，家里分到了10亩地，开始种植菜籽、甘蔗、枇杷等农作物，做菜籽油、养蚕宝宝、养猪养羊，再拿去卖。加上之前的积蓄，我们造了属于我们家的第一幢两层的小楼房。造房子只用了两个月，花了一万元左右。过了三年，爷爷奶奶开始去厂里上班了，奶奶在纺织厂织布，工资从三四十到两三百元一个月，就这样做了有十年之久。而爷爷去了麻绳厂做了业务员，头年工资也就一百多元一个月。爷爷奶奶刚工作不久，看邻里乡亲都造起了三层的房子，碍于面子，就匆匆忙忙借钱造起了三层的楼。这次造房花费了两万八千元左右。为了还清债务，爷爷开始去各种地方跑业务，然后在1989年做了厂长。

1992年化工产业特别兴盛，于是爷爷辞去了麻绳厂的工作，去了小林东风化工厂做销售，主要是卖盐酸给电镀厂。当时的基础工资只有120元一个月，厂里会给你基础业务，卖得多的部分可以拿一般的提成，虽然基础工资少，爷爷凭借自身超强的业务能力，每个月可以再得两千元左右的提成，在这个厂里做了13年，还清了家里的债务，日子也好了起来。2007年，爷爷去了我姑父的镀层厂烧煤，2007—2015年这八年，日夜颠倒的生活、化工染料的侵蚀给爷爷的身体加重了负担。在家人的劝说下，爷爷辞去了工作，在家调理身体。其实爷爷奶奶一早就可以放下担子了，也许是出于惯性，他们在女儿独立后还是奋斗了很久，其实很早便已经切换到我妈妈奋斗的故事了……

冬天，我坐在电瓶车的后座，抱住前面妈妈的腰，一身的疲惫、寒冷与饥饿。我只是来饭店里帮了一天的忙，就已经累得说话的力气都没了，可妈妈对着一切似乎都习以为常。一件倒穿的大衣，一辆"敞篷"的电瓶车，就这样熬过一个冬天的奔波；一台吊风的油烟机，一瓶捂热了的矿泉水，就这样挨过一个夏天的闷热。

妈妈16岁初中毕业后就开始工作了，最开始是跟着我干奶奶去杭州红太阳小商品市场摆地摊，那会儿是离家住在那里的。妈妈17岁回家进了我奶奶工作的那家纺织厂工作，后来转到在家里接活帮人家织布，收入大概在3万元一年。她24岁那年，爸爸入赘我们家，他们结婚的后一年，我的姐姐就出生了。又过了5年，我出生了。意识到他们两人现在的收入是不足以抚养两个孩子的，我妈妈决定去开饭店。

每次到过年是全家出动的时候，服务员放假回老家了，生意又好，妈妈一个人忙不过来，所以除了阿太因年纪太大待在家里，爷爷、奶奶、我和姐姐都会去店里当服务员，每次去都是忙得不可开交，店里手忙脚乱跟打架一样，一天下来，一身油烟味不说，二手烟都吸得头晕。我简直不敢想象，这15年，妈妈是怎么熬过来的，她为这个家真的付出了太多太多……

我们这一大家子人现在过着还算不错的生活，是每一代人的奋斗造就了今天，对于家人，我唯一的希望，就是他们都能健健康康快快乐乐的，这四世同堂的故事，就交给我们来续写吧！

Hangzhou
Shen Chenjiao (Class 192, Majoring in Journalism)

Four Generations under One Roof

My hometown is in No. 18 Chaijiahe, Group 5 Nangonghe Community, Linping Street, Yuhang District, Hangzhou. The old house has already been replaced by tall buildings. Even if I came back to the old place, I could not find the location of our three-story building. But the telegraph pole in front of my home, the loquat trees next to the pole, the pond in the grove and the tadpoles in the pond have all witnessed the location of my home in my memory, which also witnessed the ups and downs experienced by the four generations. Circumstances change with the passage of time, but the struggle of each generation appears vividly before the eyes.

My great grandmother was born in 1929. It is an age that I know little about. Just like reading an ancient book, I get to know about the former half of my great grandmother's life.

"We didn't have slippers to wear when we were children. We made a pair shoes out of two boards," my great grandmother said jokingly. In the 1930s and 1940s, only children of wealthy landlords and officials had the opportunity to go to school. My great grandmother was born into an ordinary family, or we could say that its condition was worse than that of other ordinary families. At that time, people mainly did farm work, bundling up the wheat straws during the day and holding candles to plant wheat at night. We should turn over the "Gong Liang"① or public grain to government. If there were corrupt cadres, farmers would suffer a lot.

"We all went to the farmland barefoot in summer, and the water there was so hot that it was impossible for us to step into it," said my great grandmother, who then touched her feet, frowned and shook her head. In 1946, my great grandmother ushered in a turning point in her life when she was 17 years old. She paid a visit to her uncle who lived in Maoshan. Her uncle asked her whether she wanted to learn how to weave linen or not. At that time, none of villagers learned about this skill, nor did they know how to do and how to make money from it. My great grandma became the "first mover" in the village at that time.

"I did more work than men though I was just a common girl," she said proudly. My great grandmother, who was 17 years old, learned from her uncle how to deal with jute, how to dry and process it and how to weave it into linen. She went to Xiaolin to purchase raw materials and equipment, and began

① "Gong Liang" is also known as agriculture tax. Since 1958, Chinese farmers and organization that engaged in farming are required to turn over a portion of grain according to "Regulations for the Agricultural Tax of the People's Republic of China". This agriculture tax was abolished in 2006, which emancipated the productive forces in rural areas.

to weave linen at home later. It took her about 2 to 3 days to weave a linen cloth, so she would purchase raw materials enough for 12 pieces of linen at a time and started weaving linen while doing farm work. It took about two months to use up these raw materials. A linen cloth could be sold for more than one yuan and it was a very considerable income at that time.

"I took six linen cloths to sell the first time. I was so happy because each one could be sold for more than one yuan. Then I used the money to buy two coats as a dowry that made me a bit decent."

"When the PLA came, they brought some agricultural chemicals, so none of the millet planted that year was shriveled. The method to make bricks was popularized afterwards and everyone began to bake bricks. The previous houses were made of cement, and boards were used as walls to separate rooms. After lots of wood was piled up to make roofs, tiles were placed on the wood, then a house was well-built. With bricks we could make a building." When referring to the PLA, my great grandmother talked volubly.

Since 1958, villagers worked in public farmlands in separate teams. When it was the time for the farmlands, the broadcast would be on. Money was distributed according to the amount of people's work. At that time, my house was requisitioned as the canteen. At mealtimes everybody would gather here to eat. At that time, my great grandmother worked on the farmland. Meanwhile, she kept weaving linen cloth to save some money so as to build a house. As time went by, my great grandmother grew up and the fighting story of the next generation began.

My grandma was born in 1953, and she was named Shen Jindi; my grandpa was born in the same year, and he was named Chai Yinglong. In 1970, Grandpa married into and lived with my grandma's family. My grandparents had their first child who was my mother in the second year of their marriage. After my mother was born, my grandparents mainly burned bricks in kilns. My grandma shaped mud into bricks, then my grandpa took them to the kiln to burn them. At that time, bricks were used to build our own bungalow. This was the first brick house of my family, which only had one floor. Apart from baking bricks, my grandparents also weaved linen at home, farmed and gained income through selling linen, crops and surplus bricks. A brick can only be sold for 2 to 5 cents. My grandmother could earn 30 to 50 cents a day on average, while my grandpa could earn about one yuan. The family's annual income was 3,000 to 5,000 in total, which was saved to build a house.

In 1984, we built a house.

At that time, the household contract responsibility system was carried out, so work and production were contracted to households. My family was given ten mu of land (around 1.65 acres). We began to grow rapeseed, sugar cane, loquat and other crops, and we also made vegetable oil, raised silkworms, pigs and sheep, and then sold them. With our savings, we built our first two-story building. It took only two months to build the house, which cost about ten thousand yuan. After three years, my grandparents began to work in the factory. My grandmother weaved at the mill, with wages raised from 30-40 to 200-300 a month. This situation lasted for ten years. My grandpa worked as a salesman in the hemp rope factory. His salary in the first year was more than 100 yuan per month. Seeing that the villagers had already built a three-story house when they just began to work, my grandparents borrowed money to build a three-story house in a hurry for saving their dignity. The building cost about 28,000 yuan. In order to pay off their debts, my grandpa began to run business in various places. He became the head of a factory in 1989.

The chemical industry was particularly prosperous in 1992, so grandpa quit his job at the hemp rope factory and worked in Xiaolin Dongfeng Chemical Plant as a salesman, mainly selling hydrochloric acid to electroplating plants. At that time, the basic salary was only 120 yuan a month. The factory would give him some clients. If he could develop more clients, then he would get half the extra revenues he generated. Although the basic salary was low, my grandpa still could get a commission of 2,000 yuan a month with his own strong sales ability. He worked in this factory for 13 years and paid off the family debt. The living condition became better. In 2007, my grandpa went to my uncle-in-law's coating factory to burn coal. During the eight years from 2007 to 2015, irregular life routines and damage caused by chemical dyes burdened his body. Persuaded by family members, my grandpa quit his job, recuperated at home. Actually, my grandparents could have put down the burden early. Perhaps it was because of habit for years, after their daughter lived independently, they still struggled for a long time. Now, I'd like to talk about a story of my mother's struggle...

I sat in the back of the scooter in winter, hugging my mother's waist in front of me with tiredness, cold and hunger. Although I just came to the restaurant to help for a day, I was too tired to say a word. However, my mother seemed to be used to everything. A back-to-front coat and a "roofless" scooter were all she had to make it through the hard work in winter; a soot hood for extracting smoke and a bottle of hot mineral water were all she had to get over the scorching heat in summer.

My mother began to work after graduation from junior high school at age 16. At first, she ran a street stall with her godmother in Red Sun Small Commodity Market in Hangzhou. At that time she was away from home and lived close to the market. At the age of 17, She went back home to work in the textile mill where my grandmother worked, and then weaved cloth for other people at home. The income was about thirty thousand yuan a year. At the age of 24, my father married my mother, and lived in my mother's house. One year after they got married, my sister was born. Five years later, I was born. Realizing that their income was not enough to raise two children, my mother decided to open a restaurant.

When the Chinese New Year came, it was time for the whole family to work together. The waiters all went back to their home for vacation, however, the business during the Chinese New Year was so good that my mother could not manage it alone. Therefore, my grandparents, my sister and I would go to the restaurant as waiters except my great grandmother who had to stay at home because of her age. Every time we went there, it was terribly busy, and we always had our hands full. When we finished work, greasy cooking odors were all over our body and we felt dizzy because of second-hand smoke. I couldn't imagine how my mother endured during these 15 years. She really devoted too much to this family...

Now we are living a pretty good life. It is the struggle of all generations that makes today's life possible. My only hope for my family is that they are healthy and happy. As for the following story of four generations, let my generation be the next writer!

063

观察

多变中的不变

刘高烽

世界上最值得赞赏的生活态度，就是明知道生活充满了艰辛和坎坷，仍然义无反顾地热爱并追寻着属于未来的美好。尹飞宇记录的妈妈及其家庭的创业故事，既彰显了这样的生活态度，又将多变中的不变这属于哲学体系中的大问题，以生活小视角完美诠释出来。

高中毕业的尹飞宇妈妈，从冲床厂工人、打火机厂工人做到餐馆服务员，又从开理发店创业，做小商品赚钱，自办卖菜摊床，做到了鞋厂老板。今年刚刚54岁的女性，既结婚生子，又做了七份工作来实现拥有美好生活的愿望，这需要的不仅仅是坚忍不拔的毅力，还有坚不可摧的强大内心。

从尹飞宇的白描式讲述中，我们依然能够感受到，这个中年女人盘桓在内心深处的不变的追求。“让日子越过越好”，这几乎是所有人的愿望，却并不是所有人的收获，如同这个世界上无时无刻不在发生的变化，难以改变的其实是月圆月缺的规律，有的人在这个规律中感受着痛苦和无奈，有的人在这个规律中，把日子过成了诗。变化的是世界，不变的其实是内心对世界变化的感知。感知的变化越大，内心却越是坚定。

这份坚定，或许就是初心，也或许是精神世界的追求，也或许就是最朴素的不放弃的人性。人性是静的，永恒不变，而环境与时代却是动的，绵延不绝地变化着的。在这一动一静之间，并不是每个人都能找到变与不变的真谛。有的人在寻找过程中迷失了；而有的人，却无论生活给予怎样的风雨和坎坷，她依然坚定。尹飞宇妈妈就是后者。

想到了仓央嘉措。变与不变，她对生活的热爱都在那里，难与不难，她对自我的坚守都不曾改变。风雨抹不去的是骨子里的奋斗精神，失败打不垮的，是奔向美好的勇气。浙江的女人们如此，这样的女人教育出来的孩子们，依然如此。

（吉林省长春市媒体人）

故事
台州
尹飞宇(网络与新媒体专业 184 班)

踏平坎坷成大道

我的母亲生于 1967 年的春夏之交,在浙江台州的农村,家里以种田养猪作为生计,她和另外 3 个兄弟姐妹一起长大。1985 年高中毕业以后,18 岁的母亲没能考上大学,就只身前往温州打工。

母亲的第一份工作是在冲床厂里上班。由于在冲床厂里男性偏多,女性不受待见,母亲就辞职了。

母亲的第二份工作是在一家打火机制造厂上班。主要就是制造打火机的零配件,但是由于这家打火机制造厂的工资太低,母亲选择另谋一份工作。

母亲的第三份工作是在一家餐馆当服务员,主要是端盘子洗盘子等。由于那时来餐馆吃饭的人都是一些工地上的人,他们总是会在吃饭的时候为难母亲,对母亲说一些难听的话,她接受不了,就向老板娘提出了辞职。

在一次次受挫之后,母亲决定学一门手艺,自己开一家店。母亲选择的是学习理发,她向理发师傅学习了三四个月之后,就决定开店了。由于母亲的手艺不是很娴熟,许多顾客对母亲的手艺并不是很满意,因此母亲的理发店也就坚持不下去了。

渐渐地母亲也到了谈婚论嫁的年龄。母亲与父亲是通过介绍认识的,父亲比母亲大了 5 岁,父亲性格比较腼腆,母亲则比较开朗,很快他们便成婚了,没有经历什么波折。

在结婚之后,父亲和母亲就一起前往郑州打工了。因为有熟人在那边,所以他们也决定一起去试试。他们做的是小商品,但是由于人生地不熟的,也没有什么门道,没有什么经验,很快就遇到困难而亏了本。母亲提出回到浙江去发展。

回到浙江之后,母亲决定去椒江菜场卖菜。母亲为在菜场卖菜做足了准备:摊位的选择、供应商的寻找、住宿地方的寻找等等。由于在郑州做生意的亏本,父母身上所剩的钱已经不足以在菜场卖菜了。母亲说,“借!”母亲向我的三叔借了 8000 块钱,准备开张。母亲很会找机会,因为菜场摊位刚开张,并没有什么生意,她就去外面的餐馆,一家家询问是否需要菜的供应,愿意以最低价供应,最终拉到了好几家大餐馆的生意。母亲说，目前价格什么的不是最关键的，最关键的是先留住顾客。后来，菜场的生意总算是有了起色，慢慢变好了，向三叔借来的钱也都还上了。

其实卖菜这门行业是很辛苦的。父亲需要在第二天开店以前就把菜进好，因此他时常要凌晨一两点起来开着三轮车去进货，早上五六点回来把菜给母亲，母亲也就是在五六点的时候起床，把菜拉到菜场的摊位去摆好，然后就会有人陆陆续续来买菜了，因为在早晨的时候菜是最新鲜的。卖菜是一门辛苦的行当，起早贪黑的，特别辛苦。虽然在卖菜的时候赚到了一点钱，母亲还是决定再换一份工作。

母亲先来到台州温岭，张罗着准备开一家鞋厂。去到温岭开鞋厂是因为有很多老乡都在那边开鞋厂，听说行情比较好，并且有不懂的老乡之间也可以有个照应，母亲就带着年幼的我前往了。打探了一番之后，忙前忙后找到合适的店面，注册许可证，雇佣工人，一切都准备就绪。其实鞋子样板的设计、鞋子该用什么样的布料、如何处理和加工、怎样装运等，母亲一开始什么也不懂，但是她凭着一己之力，渐渐地搞清楚了这个复杂的过程。

在初期，鞋厂面向商店直接销售。母亲说第一笔生意让她印象很深刻，她刚设计好的两双鞋子放在门口的柜台上，然后有两个顾客前来询问关于价格面料之类的事宜，谁知这两个顾客一上来竟然就预定了整整30件货，要知道，一件货里面有40双鞋子，30件货对于刚开始这个生意的母亲来说简直是一个天大的惊喜。母亲说当时和两个老板说话都是带了一点结巴的，拿鞋子的那双手也是颤抖的，不仅仅是因为第一次接生意时的紧张，还包含了对这笔大单子的期待。就这样，在又紧张又激动的心情下开始了第一单生意。

刚开始设计出来的鞋子就很受市场欢迎，父亲和母亲时常做到夜里12点多都还做不完。我还记得我那时候特别害怕一个人上楼睡觉，但是父母要工作无暇顾及我，我就常常自己坐在楼下的靠椅上睡觉。2000年初的时候还没那么先进，给鞋子定型、烘干什么的都是要用煤球的，母亲常常四五点钟就起来，顶着浓浓的睡意去烧煤球，为早上的工作做准备。

让母亲记忆深刻的还有一件事情。那时候我还读一年级，那天早上是我的转学考试，本来准备出发了，但是我的叔叔开电锯的时候没拿稳，不小心把自己手背的筋给锯到了，鲜血直流，滴在地上。我当时吓坏了，母亲着急忙慌地找了人陪我叔叔去了医院，随后就带我去考试了。但考试的结果并不理想，我因为考得太差，没法成功转学。由于都已经快要开学了，找别的学校已经来不及，母亲就去学校找到了一个教导主任，教导主任人也很好，他去各个教室转了一圈，说有一个老生没来，就同意我去读了。这件事情解决了之后，母亲又去医院看望我叔叔,那时我父亲还没有来到温岭,还在菜场处理剩下的一些事,只能由我母亲去照顾。

母亲说,做鞋这门生意,风险其实很大,生意好的时候是很好,但是一亏空就会亏得厉害。我们厂家都是先供货再收钱的,这就会承受很大的风险。比如说有一次,我们先向顾客供应了大量的货,但是这个顾客突然生病去世,平常母亲只与这个人联系,并没他亲朋好友的联系方式,这就直接导致我们鞋厂损失了一大笔钱。还有一次,有个顾客已经收到货了,但却拖欠着迟迟不交钱,母亲也催过很多次,那个顾客自己过得风生水起的,但就是不给我们那笔欠款,最后拖着拖着就没了,又损失了一大笔。

家里的鞋厂一开就是十几年,我们生活渐渐地好了起来,从两层楼的农村小土屋变成了套间,从自行车变成了汽车。家是靠双手一点一滴地打拼出来的,奋斗才是幸福的基础。

最后用母亲说的一句话结尾:人的一生啊,会有很多坎坷,平平淡淡的岁月才是真,家人安康,生活美满,便足矣。

Taizhou
Yin Feiyu (Class 184, Majoring in Network and New Media)

Trodding the Bumpy Road to Greate a Smooth One

My mother was born at the end of spring and the beginning of summer in 1967 in rural Taizhou, Zhejiang Province. Her family farmed and raised pigs for a living and she grew up with three other siblings. After graduating from high school in 1985 at the age of 18, she failed to get into a university and went to work in Wenzhou by herself.

My mother's first job was to work in a punch factory. As there were more men than women in the factory, and female workers were not favored there, she quit her job.

My mother's second job was to work in a lighter manufacturer. Her main responsibility was to make lighter parts, but the low wage forced my mother to seek another job.

My mother's third job was to be a waitress in a restaurant, serving plates, washing dishes and so on. The people who came to the restaurant at that time were workers from the construction sites, and they always embarrassed my mother with nasty remarks. She could not endure it anymore, so she tendered her resignation to the boss's wife.

After one setback after another, my mother decided to learn a trade and open a shop of her own. My mother chose the trade of hairdressing, and after three or four months of learning from a hairdresser, she decided to open her own shop. As she was not very skillful, many customers were not very happy with her work and so her shop did not last long.

Gradually, my mother reached marriageable age. She met my father, who was five years older than her, through a matchmaker. He was shy while she was outgoing. Soon they got married, without experiencing much difficulty.

After they got married, they left for Zhengzhou together to work. As they had acquaintances there, they decided to try it out there. They worked in the small commodity market, but as they were unfamiliar with the area and had no contacts and little experience, they soon ran into difficulties and lost money. My mother proposed to go back to Zhejiang Province.

After returning to Zhejiang, my mother decided to sell vegetables in a market in Jiaojiang. She made all the preparations for selling vegetables in the market: choosing a stall, finding a supplier, finding a place to live, etc. Due to the loss of money from the business in Zhengzhou, the money left with my parents was not enough to sell vegetables in the market. My mother decided to borrow money. She borrowed 8,000 yuan from my third uncle to prepare for the opening of her business. She was very good at finding opportunities; as the vegetable market stall just opened and not much business was done, she went to the restaurants outside and asked one by one if they needed a supply of vegetables at the lowest price. Eventually, she succeeded in getting business from several large restaurants. She said that the most important thing was not making profits but keeping the customers. Later on, their business finally got better, and the money borrowed from my third uncle was paid back.

In fact, selling vegetables was very laborious. My father often got up at 1 or 2 o'clock in the morning to get the stock ready; he returned on his tricycle full of vegetables at 5 or 6 o'clock, and my mother, who also got up at 5 or 6, took the vegetables to her stall for sale. Soon vegetable shoppers would come one after another because vegetables were fresh in the morning. This was a hard job, and it was extremely difficult to get up so early every morning and come home late in the evening. Though she made some money by selling vegetables, she decided to change her line of work once again.

She first went to Wenling, Taizhou, to start a shoe factory. She went to Wenling because many fellow townsmen opened shoe businesses there. It was said that the market was good and one could seek help from fellow townsmen when there were things he or she didn't know how to deal with, so my mother took me there with her. After some inquiry, she was busy with finding a suitable place, registering the license and hiring workers. Everything was ready. At first, my mother knew nothing about shoe patterns, what kind of fabric to use, how to process, how to ship and so on, but she gradually figured out the complicated process on her own.

In the early days, the shoe factory sold shoes directly to shops. My mother said that the first deal was very impressive. She had just designed two pairs of shoes and placed them on the counter at the door; then, two customers came to ask about prices and fabrics. She never expected that they would place 30 orders, with 40 pairs of shoes for each order. This was really a big surprise to my mother, who was a beginner in this field. My mother told me that she even stammered when talking to the two bosses, and her hands were trembling, not only because she was nervous about her first business negotiation, but also because she was looking forward to this significant deal. And so it was with a mixed feeling of nervousness and excitement that she made the first deal.

The shoes they designed were very popular and too often my parents were unable to finish their work even when they worked past midnight. I remembered I was too afraid to go upstairs and sleep alone, but my parents had to work and could not be there to accompany me, so I used to sleep on the cushioned chair downstairs on my own. In early 2000, when technology was not that advanced, briquettes were used for shaping and drying, and my mother used to get up at four or five o'clock to burn briquettes with heavy eyelids so as to prepare for the morning work.

There was another incident that impressed my mother a lot. I was in

Grade One at that time, and one morning I was supposed to sit my school transfer exam. I was ready to go, but my uncle didn't have a steady hold on the chainsaw and accidentally cut the tendon in the back of his hand. His hand was bloody, and the blood kept dripping onto the floor. I was terrified and my mother rushed to find someone to accompany my uncle to the hospital and then took me to take the exam. The exam results didn't turn out well, so I couldn't transfer to that school. It was too late to find another school as the school year was about to start, so my mother went to the school and found the head teacher who was very nice. He checked every class and agreed to let me take the place of another student who had given up on his seat. After this matter was settled, my mother went to the hospital to visit my uncle. My father had not yet come to Wenling and was still at the vegetable stall dealing with the rest of the stuff, so my mother had to take care of my uncle on her own.

My mother said that the shoe business was actually very risky. Though they could earn a lot when the business was good, any mishap would create big loss. Manufacturers like us needed to supply goods before getting the money, which would lead to great risks. For example, once, we supplied a large amount of goods to a customer, who suddenly became ill and passed away. Since my mother only contacted with him and didn't have any contact information of his friends and family, our factory suffered great loss. On another occasion, a customer had received the goods but was late in paying, and my mother had urged him to do so many times. The customer was living a good life, but he refused to pay us the money on time. In the end, we suffered our second great loss.

The family's shoe factory has been running for more than ten years, and gradually our life is getting better. The small two-storey rural hut has been changed to a suite, and the bicycle to a car. Our home is built by hands, and striving is the basis of happiness.

Finally, I would like to end the story with a quote from my mother: there are many ups and downs in one's life, but the only true thing is to have a simple day, a happy life and a healthy family.

幸福是一种感知

王　蔚

幸福是什么？从积极心理学的视角来看，幸福是人类生活得更加丰富充实，能追求生命本身的快乐和意义。随着社会经济的发展和居民物质财富的增加，社会各界开始以幸福指数作为民生改善的衡量指标，而不仅仅以GDP指数作为衡量标准。

幸福是一种感知。塞里格曼教授认为，可以用五个维度来定义幸福感，由此提出了著名的PERMA模型，分别是积极情绪（Positive emotion）、沉浸（Engagement）、关系（Relation）、意义（Meaning）、成就（Accomplishment）。可见，愉悦开心的正向情绪体验，做事时的投入度和沉浸感，良性的社会支持，发现生活的意义，以及日常的收获感和小确幸都是对幸福的体验和感知。

每个个体对幸福的感知是不同的。不同人群的幸福感，以及每个人在不同人生阶段的幸福感知亦存在差异。翻看同学们的家庭叙事，可以看出爷爷辈的幸福可能是在困难时期还能如愿入党，完成自己的政治信仰；父亲辈的幸福是做时代的弄潮儿，跟随大时代步伐，奋起拼搏，扛起家庭的重任；妈妈们的幸福可能是在某个瞬间，选择在世纪之交和心上人结婚；而同学们印象深刻的童年幸福却是舍不得一次喝完的娃哈哈AD钙奶。

经历时代洪流是幸福，平平淡淡的柴米油盐也是一种幸福。此时，阳光透过窗户，享受冬日里难得的一米阳光和一丝暖意是一种幸福，坐在书桌前翻阅和感受学生们鲜活的幸福家庭故事，也让我个人的幸福感得到加持。

（浙大宁波理工学院传媒与法学院讲师，博士）

故事

绍兴

谢子弘(网络与新媒体专业182班)

踏上幸福的路

光透进来,恼人的蝉不知疲倦地叫嚣,我站在窗口,想起小时候坐在田间看到的天空。那是乡下在奶奶家的日子,大片的田,澄澈的湖,就我一个人在山头当大王,在茶树丛间撒野奔跑。

以前,奶奶家在嵊州三界的小山里,有村落的地方山头都种满了茶树,从奶奶家走到镇上要花半个小时,奶奶家的小平房虽然破旧,可在我眼里却是豪宅,因为好像住在那里,无论是旁边的羊圈,石子小路尽头的池塘,还是房子背后连绵的茶山,都是小平房的附属品。我从小住在奶奶家,后来到了城里读小学,从课本上知道了四合院,我心想,奶奶家就是四合院,一排屋子围起来,屋前还有好大一片空地,而且奶奶家的房子和村子里其他人住的房子不一样。别人家养的顶多是鸭子,而奶奶家养了好几头羊,这一定是所谓的"大户"人家。后来因为城市开发,奶奶家要拆迁了,我才知道原来爷爷和奶奶一直是租住在这里的,童年回忆里的小平房,已经变成了别墅区,我掌管的山头也夷为了平地。

爸爸是在山东长大的,因为太公那时候是当兵的,要把农村户口转成居民户口,分配来了嵊州,然后定居在三界。以前的户口有粮票、布票可以分,到1997年以后,农村户口和城市户口就没多大差别了。爸爸搬到嵊州来的时候已经14岁了。那时候的房子只有小小的两间,冬天冷得像个冰窖,有时还会漏雨。早年上学不正规,那时候就只有两本课本,那时候的课本两三毛钱一本,那时候没有课桌,就自己背着一个大凳子和一个小凳子。那时候人多,一家有三四个兄弟姐妹都是很平常的,每个村镇都是有小学的,可是很少有人读初中,到了读初中的年纪就一般不读书,回家帮忙种田去了。在农村里最好的出路就是当兵。那时候小孩多就靠布票和粮票过日子,老大穿过给老二穿,老二穿过给老三穿,每件衣服上都很多补丁,袖子和裤脚都是一截接一截。爸爸有三个兄弟姐妹,一个哥哥一个姐姐和一个妹妹。爸爸穿的衣服都是哥哥穿过的,缝缝补补又三年。那时候根本没有什么新衣服穿,所有的衣服也都是自己做的。到后来1982年计划生育之后,小孩变少了,家里才会在过年的时候给小孩买新衣服穿。爸爸小时候在学校不小心打碎了一扇窗户，他担惊受怕了好几天，不敢跟家里说，他的姐姐偷偷给了他5毛钱去赔偿玻璃。因为那时候真的很穷，这样一件小事他也记了很久。

爸爸说他在十三四岁的时候有了一辆自行车，在这之前完全是靠双腿走路，去稍微远一点的地方要走好久，走好几公里路那是常有的事。村子里有些年纪大的人，连县城都没到过。再后面就有了拖拉机，再过了五六年就有了三卡。后来城市发展得越来越快，就算是相隔千里的城市也可以很快地到达。

我记得读小学的时候，爸爸有时候会开着三轮摩托车来接我放学，那是爸爸厂里的车，坐上去可威风了，就像民国时候的探长要出门办案的样子。夹杂着发动机的噪声，风呼呼地从耳边刮过，我从来不知道三个轮子可以比两个轮子快那么多。

妈妈小的时候住在南京浦口，那时候家里穷，一家5个人住在老房子里，因为是农村户口，粮食都是生产大队里分配的，家里粮食不够吃，会种一些香瓜和西瓜去卖钱。外婆外公去生产队干活，每天也只有2毛钱，后来提高到了6毛钱。妈妈在很小的时候就去看田，防着别人来偷，就在田里看着，晚上看，白天也看。但是因为年纪太小了，看到有大人偷田里的西瓜也不敢上前去理论。后来大一点了，放学就要回家烧饭，然后去割草喂猪。稻子成熟的季节差不多凌晨3点就起床去割稻，中午顶着大太阳也不休息。那时候还养了很多蚕，晚上每两个小时就要起床去喂蚕，蚕茧卖了之后才有钱交学费。要是没有卖出去，就要向别人借钱才能读书。妈妈读书的时候，总是没有菜吃，就会炒芝麻加点盐拿到学校里当菜吃，有时候还会用酱油汤来下饭。

夏天的时候，总有人会在自行车后面装个箱子盖一床被子卖白糖棒冰，因为舍不得花钱，家里也不会去买。有一次有个亲戚来做客，给小孩买了棒冰吃，妈妈尝到了棒冰，开心了好久。

爸爸妈妈同在县城的热力发电厂工作，相识相知，到后来就决定相守白头。那时候一桌酒席要将近一千块，爸爸妈妈的工资不高，所以结婚的时候租借了酒店的场地，自己备好了酒席要上的菜，让酒店帮忙做。婚礼办了八桌酒，来了很多朋友。房子是单位里集资建的，买房子和装修花了不少钱，也欠了一点钱，那段时候算是比较艰难的。

我小的时候在夏天很容易长痱子，妈妈看着我惨不忍睹的背，就一咬牙拿出家里的全部积蓄去买了一台空调。有了一台空调之后，每个夏天的晚上，我们一家人都窝在同一个房间里。我长大了一些之后，为了省电费，一家人还是窝在一间房里，我跟爸爸轮换着打地铺。久而久之这就成了年年夏天的惯例。现在我们家多了好几台空调，每间房都装了一台，也不再会为了省电费而挤在一间房里了。

2012 年，弟弟出生了，那时候我正在读小学 6 年级，我们家从此多了一个人。因为弟弟需要喂奶，我们搬到了离妈妈公司很近的地方去住，在那里呆了将近两个月，后来妈妈辞职了，在家带弟弟。条件也比我出生的时候好了很多。在我小的时候，爸爸会买 5 毛钱的茶叶蛋给我吃，哄我开心。娃哈哈几乎是童年的标配，那个时候我也是把它当成难得的奖品，常常舍不得喝，一条 AD 钙奶可以喝很久。

随着时间的变迁，家里的电器已经更新了一轮又一轮，保暖已不是穿衣的首选标准。餐桌上的菜色也越来越丰富，十几年前舍不得买的水果零食，也变成了"居家必备"。煮饭用的是电饭煲，炒菜用的是天然气。现在的房子既宽敞又明亮，小区的停车位也越来越紧张，傍晚的时候总是满满当当。

Shaoxing
Xie Zihong (Class 182, Majoring in Network and New Media)

On the Way Towards Happiness

The light came in, and the annoying cicadas screamed tirelessly. Standing by the window, I recalled the sky I saw sitting in the field when I was a child. It was my grandmother's home in the countryside, with large fields and clear lakes. I was the king of the hills, running wildly among the tea bushes.

In the past, my grandmother's house was in the hills of Sanjie Town, Shengzhou. There were villages where the hills were full of tea trees. It took half an hour to walk from grandmother's home to the town. Although grandmother's small bungalow was dilapidated, it was a mansion in my eyes, because when living there, I felt that the nearby sheepfold, the pond at the end of the gravel path and the continuous tea mountain behind the house were all accessories of the small bungalow. I grew up living in my grandma's house, and then I went to the city to study in primary school. I learned about the Siheyuan, or quadrangle courtyard, from textbooks. I thought to myself that my grandma's house was exactly a quadrangle courtyard. It was built by connecting the rows of houses in all directions together, and then a large open space was surrounded in the middle by the houses. Besides, her house was different from the houses where other people live in the village. My grandma raised several sheep while others could only raise ducks. This must be the so-called "big family". Later, due to urban development, my grandmother's house was to be demolished. It was until that time that I realized that the house was rented by my grandparents. The small bungalows in my childhood memories have become villas, and the hills I had been in charge of have been razed to the ground.

My father grew up in Shandong Province, because my great grandfather was a soldier at that time, and he wanted to change his rural household registration to an urban one. Therefore, he wasn't assigned to Shengzhou, and then settled in Sanjie Town. In the past, food coupons and clothing coupons would be distributed to each urban resident. After 1997, there was no significant difference between rural household registration and urban household registration. My father was 14 years old when he moved to Shengzhou. There were only two small rooms in their house at that time. The house was as cold as an ice cellar in winter, and sometimes the rain leaked into the house. In the early years, school was not so formal. At that time, there were only two textbooks, and each textbook only cost 0.2 or 0.3 yuan. Students had to carry one large stool and one small stool on their back to school, because there was no desk or chair in the classroom. There were a lot of people in a family at that time, so it was common for a family to have three or four children. Every village and town had a primary school, but few people went to middle school. When they reached the age to study in middle school, they would give up studying and went home to help farming. The best way out in the countryside was to be a soldier. At that time, if there were many children in a family, they would depend on cloth coupons and food coupons. The clothes that were worn by the eldest child were left for the second child, and then were left for the third child. There were many patches on each piece of clothing, and the sleeves and the bottom end of trousers were extended by sewing up new cloth. My father had three siblings. They are his elder brother, elder sister and younger sister. The clothes my father wore were those worn by his elder brother, and they were stitched and mended so as to be worn for another three years. At that time, there were no new clothes to wear, and all the clothes were all self-made. It wasn't until the year of 1982 when the family planning was carried out and there were fewer children that people would buy new clothes for children during the Spring Festival. When my father was a child, he accidentally broke a window at school. He was terrified for several days and daren't tell his family. Later, his sister secretly gave him 0. 5 yuan to pay for the glass. Because he was really poor at that time, he remembered such a trifle for such a long time.

My father said that he had a bicycle when he was thirteen or fourteen. Before that, he travelled completely on foot. It took a long time to go a little farther, and it was common for people to walk several kilometers. Some older people in the village hadn't even been to the county all their lives. Then there came the tractors, and then trucks after five or six years. Later, the city developed faster and faster, and even cities that thousands of miles away could be reached quickly.

I remembered when I was in primary school, my father sometimes drove a three-wheeled motorcycle to pick me up from school. That vehicle belonged to my father's factory. It was awesome cool to ride on it, just like the detective in the Republic of China who was going out to handle a case. Mixed with the noise of the engine, the wind blew through my ears. I never knew that a motorcycle with three wheels could be faster than that with two wheels.

When my mother was a child, she lived in Pukou, Nanjing City. At that time, her family was poor, and the family of five lived in an old house. Because they were rural residents, the food was distributed by the production brigade. There was not enough food at home, so they would grow melons and watermelons to sell for money. My grandparents went to work in the production team, and they only earned 0. 2 yuan a day, which was increased to 0. 6 yuan a day later. When my mother was just a little child, she went to guard the fields to prevent others from stealing. She watched in the fields day and night. However she was too young to argue bravely with the adults who stole watermelons from the field. Later, when she got older, she would go home to cook after school, and then cut grass to feed pigs. When the rice was ripe, she would get up at about 3 o'clock to harvest rice, and she never rested even under the scorching sun at noon. At that time, she also raised a lot of silkworms, so she had to get up every two hours at night to feed the silkworms. Only after the cocoons were sold did she have money to pay the tuition. If not, she would have to borrow money from others so as to continue her study. When my mother was a student, she always had no dishes to eat. She would fry sesame seeds and add some salt. Then she took it to school as a dish, and sometimes she would use soy sauce soup to serve meals.

In summer, there were always people who put a box covered with a quilt on the back of the bicycle to sell sugar lollipops. Because she didn't want to spend money, she never bought one. Once a relative paid a visit to her family and bought popsicles for the kids, so my mom got the chance to taste the popsicle, and she was happy for a long time.

Working at the same thermal power plant in the county, my parents got to know each other and later decided to stay together. At that time, the wedding-feast would cost nearly 1,000 yuan per table. Their wages were not high, so when they got married, they rented the hotel venue but prepared the ingredients by themselves, and then asked the hotel to look. They arranged eight tables in the wedding feast and many friends came. The house was provided by the plant, which was built by raising funds from individuals. It took a lot of money to buy and decorate the house, and they also owed a little money. At that time, life was relatively tough.

When I was a child, it was easy for me to get prickly heat in summer. Looking at my terrible back, my mother made up her mind and took out all the savings to buy an air conditioner. With the air conditioner, our family stayed in the same room every summer night. After I grew up a little bit, in order to save electricity, our family still stayed in the same room, and my father and I took it in turns to sleep on the floor. Over time, it became a routine every summer. Now we have several more air conditioners in our house, one for each room, and we no longer squeeze in one room to save electricity.

In 2012, my brother was born. At that time, I was in the sixth grade of primary school, and we had one more member in our family. Because my brother needed to drink breast milk, we moved to live in a place close to my mother's company. We stayed there for nearly two months. Later, my mother resigned and took care of my brother at home. Conditions got much better than when I was born. When I was young, my father would buy me eggs stewed in tea that cost 0.5 yuan each to make me happy. Wahaha AD Calcium Rich Milk was a typical drink in childhood. At that time, I also regarded it as a rare prize. I often cherished it so much that I didn't want to drink it, so a pack of milk could be kept for a long time.

With the time going by, our household appliances renewed again and again. Keeping warm is no longer the first criterion for dressing. The dishes on the table are becoming more and more abundant, and the fruit and the snacks that were luxuries more than ten years ago have also become a must in our family. Rice cookers are used for cooking rice and natural gas is used for preparing dishes. The house is now spacious and bright. There are fewer parking spaces in the community, and there is almost no empty space at nightfall.

在“顽童”外公的背后

丁良飞

台州是浙江“七山一水两分田”的缩影，是山、海、水和谐的生态福地。“台州地阔海溟溟，云水长和岛屿青”，杜甫短短两语将浙江台州的美丽与辽阔描绘得淋漓尽致，引得历代世人对这片土地满怀憧憬和向往。

2005年，时任浙江省委书记习近平在考察时首次提出“绿水青山就是金山银山”理念。2019年，习近平总书记作出重要批示：“浙江‘千村示范、万村整治’工程起步早、方向准、成效好，不仅对全国有示范作用，在国际上也得到认可。要深入总结经验，指导督促各地朝着既定目标，持续发力，久久为功，不断谱写美丽中国建设的新篇章。”

从改革开放到新时代中国特色社会主义思想在浙江的萌发，今天的浙江，站在了更高的新起点，生活在秀美山水之间的浙江人，不仅具有诗意的情怀，他们勇于创新、勤于创业，敢做新时代的弄潮儿，更有着爱国爱党的光荣传统，有着敢为人先的奋斗基因，有着干在实处的优秀品格。台州温岭就是浙江“高水平推进省域治理现代化”的典型样本。

“顽童”外公几乎和新中国同岁，他当过兵、吃过苦，经历过改革开放带来的变化，在面对新型冠状病毒时能撸起袖子走在前面，面对互联网发展的浪潮，能积极探索，在群众中起到良好的示范作用，这是人民对党的信任、对国家的信任的体现，也是浙江实现习近平总书记提出的“高水平全面建成小康社会、高水平推进社会主义现代化建设，继续发挥先行和示范作用”的生动样本。

在绿水青山的背后，是温岭在经济建设、政治建设、文化建设、社会建设、生态文明建设各方面“五位一体”均衡发展，成为中国县域治理的模范生和全面小康示范县。在“顽童”外公的背后，揭示的是国家治理体系和治理能力现代化水平明显提高，凸显的是中国共产党人践行初心使命，永远把人民对美好生活的向往作为奋斗目标的庄重承诺。

（宁波海和森食品有限公司总经理）

故事

台州

莫海勇(网络与新媒体专业 193 班)

外公是个老顽童

我的外公，出生在浙江温岭新河村。他几乎和新中国同岁，是看着阿中哥哥长大的老顽童。

外公外婆是在土地上撒野、在农村扎根的一代人，从小就受到各种传统思想的熏陶。他们的婚姻自然也是“父母之命、媒妁之言”的产物，但好在俩人性格契合、相处融洽，能安稳过日子。

外公说，在传统的封建观念中，女子一直处于家庭地位链的底端。外婆一心想怀“龙胎”，执意要个堂堂正正跟父姓的男孩。可事与愿违，在这个家庭里先后诞生了两姐妹。外婆外公好面子，受不了邻居的白眼，想生个男娃。功夫不负有心人，他来了。老人家乐坏了，好的补的都送到男孩嘴边，是真的含在嘴里怕化，捧在手心又怕掉。但男孩突如其来的病给了好不容易“快活”起来的一家子一个晴天霹雳，不过数月男孩走了。此后外公外婆更是抬不起头，每天夜里烧香，只为求个男孩子。但结果并不如意，后来断断续续生了三个，都是女孩子，但她们乖巧懂事，也在各自的成长之路上做出了成绩。老人家渐渐接受了现实。一家七口人，六个女汉子也能撑起大半边天。

如今外公再谈起几个女儿，嘴角总藏不住开心和甜蜜。都说女儿是父亲的棉袄，外公也这么说。外公现在子孙满堂，逢年过节大家都聚在一起其乐融融，他也常常调侃说：“生女孩多好，还知道常回家看看……”

一点儿也不夸张，共产主义是外公毕生的信仰。外公是中国共产党的坚决拥护者，据外公回忆，他年轻时过了兵检，在部队呆过一阵，也上过战场。他一直把毛泽东视为自己的偶像，直到现在老人家的寒舍里还挂着主席的画像。他说穿军装、摸枪杆的滋味别提多自豪了，我要是对他的衷心表示出一点点的质疑，他就教训我没有责任和担当。在他的观念里，军人是神圣而庄重的，而中国共产党的领导就像是指路明灯，让一个个迷途而不知所措的孩子找到了归宿。

后来退伍回家，外公继续经营自家小农户的农耕生活，但还是时常和外婆、女儿提起在军队的辉煌时刻，妈妈回忆说他那段光荣的历史前前后后说了不下一百次。新中国成立后，中国社会保障制度逐步确立，让外公尝到了不少甜头。其中优抚安置是指政府对军属、烈属、复员转业军人、残废军人予以优待抚恤的制度。优抚安置的内容，主要包括提供抚恤金、优待金、补助金，举办军人疗养院、光荣院，安置复员退伍军人等。外公每每拿到补贴，都会操着一口不大清晰的普通话说："还是共产党好，为人民服务的共产党好！"

2020年初，新型冠状病毒蔓延。严峻的疫情让本是合家团圆的日子变得非同寻常。外公每天都会询问感染数据，关心家人身体情况，他甚至早起到大队部报名参加疫情防控小组，他说即便是在村口帮忙测量体温也好。后来封城封村，百姓"足不出户"，在各方力量的统筹配合下，全国人民战胜了疫情。外公说这次战"疫"，让他回忆起了那段满腔热血、慷慨激昂的岁月。

外公总开玩笑说要活到百岁，想把科技进步、社会发展带来的甜头尝个遍。记得手机、互联网和平板电脑等新媒体兴起没多久，外公就嚷嚷着要试一试，他那长满茧子、粗糙的手掌在滑溜的屏幕、先进的科技面前有几分返老还童的模样。他吃力地学了很多天，终于弄懂了微信，添加了好友，还时不时弹个视频给女儿问候身体情况，甚至在朋友圈转发年轻人热衷的推送。他一边说着"活到老学到老"，又一边嫉妒着年轻一辈"身在福中不知福"。

外公有严重的膝骨性关节炎，去趟菜场买米、到街坊搓顿麻将、去村部交个公费都有可能发作，他说这病疼起来要命，甚至会牵动自己的神经，有时说话都困难。女儿们常年在外地经商，老人家怕给她们添麻烦永远报喜不报忧，对老寒腿的事情总是闭口不提。但2018年，外公的病情恶化，连走路都成了难题。大女儿家庭责任感强，联络好四个姐妹第二天就赶到了杭州，三女儿人脉广，联系杭州有名的医生。没几天，外公就顺利完成了手术。住院期间，他感动女儿们有心、感激科技进步、感叹社会发展，他说："如果老伴晚个十几年再走该多好，现在的医学水平够用了！"

记得当封路封村、统一使用健康码的时候，老一辈都坚决反对，抱怨程序繁琐复杂。而外公不但帮助社区工作人员宣传疫情防控知识、普及医用口罩佩戴方法，还强烈支持健康码的使用，他认为通过这种小程序完成用户定位、了解用户身体状况对于疫情防控举足轻重，只有重视并且严格把关每个环节，才能打赢抗疫之战。如今病毒势力大减，外公依然提倡出行使用健康码，他说："这么一项大发明，浪费了多可惜。"

无论是互联网的兴起、医疗水平的进步抑或是健康码小程序的应用，在外公眼里都是科技发展带来的福音。如今我国已实现全面小康，外公说这一系列成就离不开党和国家的领导，我想说也离不开像外公一样渺小却心系国家、有大我精神的芸芸众生啊！

这就是我的外公，一个几乎和新中国同岁，敢于突破封建思想、破除陈规，坚决拥护党的领导，又品尝着科技进步、社会发展蜜果的老人！

Taizhou
Mo Haiyong (Class 193, Majoring in Network and New Media)

Grandpa Is a Kidult

My maternal grandpa, born in Xinhe Village, Wenlin, southeastern China's Zhejiang Province, is of almost the same age as New China. He is just like a kidult who sees his elder brother—China—grow up.

My maternal grandparents, playing without restraint in the fields and deeply rooted in the ground just like trees, were edified by traditional ideas. Their marriage was naturally arranged by their familiese and the match maker. Luckily, they have led a stable life since they are compatible with each other in personality and get along just fine together.

My grandpa mentioned that females were at the bottom of every family according to feudalistic ideas. My grandma always wanted to have a son. But things do not happen as one wishes. My grandma gave birth to two daughters, a disgrace to her and her husband who didn't want to lose face or to be looked down upon by neighbors. Their efforts finally paid off—they had a baby boy! Naturally he became the apple of my grandparents' eye. Quality and nutritious food was all there for him to eat. There was finally "joy" in this family. Unfortunately, the baby boy's sudden illness dealt a huge blow to the family, and several months later, he died prematurely. Ever since then, they had buried themselves in deeper shame, and had been burning incense and begging for another son day and night. Things didn't turn out as wished. They had three more daughters. But fortunately, their daughters are all sensible and adorable, and are quite successful in their own lives. My grandparents gradually came to terms with reality. In the family of seven, six women could also hold up more than half the sky.

When my grandpa talks about his daughters today, he couldn't hide the happiness and sweetness in the corners of his mouth. Others say that a daughter is her father's warm padded jacket, and so does he. He now has many children and grandchildren, and on New Year's Day and other festivals, the whole family would all get together and have a good time. He would often joke, "It's good to have daughters, for they know they should come back home often!"

Without any exaggeration, communism has been my grandpa's lifelong belief, and he is its staunch supporter. My grandpa recalled that he joined the army for a while after passing the physical examination and even fought on the battleground. A portrait of Chairman Mao still hangs in his humble house for he has always regarded Chairman Mao as his icon. He said he felt proud to wear military uniform and carry guns with him. If I dared to question even a tiny bit of his loyalty, he would scold me for lacking a sense of responsibility. In his view soldiers are sacred and serious, and the Communist Party of China is akin to a beacon, leading stray and confused children home safe and sound.

My grandpa continued his life as a farmer after being demobilized, and would often mention his glorious days in the military to his wife and daughters. According to my mom, she heard about those stories at least 100 times. My grandpa benefited a lot from the social security system which was established after the founding of the new China. Among the social security package plans are preferential treatment and resettlement, which refer to pensions, subsidies, the establishment of military sanatoria and glory hospitals, and resettling of demobilized veterans. The preferential treatment is offered to military dependents, martyrs' dependents, demobilized soldiers and disabled soldiers. Every time he receives the subsidies, my grandpa would say in his nonstandard mandarin, "What a good deed done by the Communist Party of China! Such service to the Chinese people!"

In early 2020, the widespread and severe novel coronavirus pandemic changed the Spring Festival, a period of time for family reunion in China. My grandfather asked about the infection data every day and cared about the health of every family member. He even got up early and offered to help with the epidemic prevention and control efforts in the village committee. He said even simple things like taking temperature at the entrance to the village would be helpful to contain the virus. Later, a nationwide lockdown was imposed to fight the disease with chinese people staying at home, and to our relief, the whole nation finally defeated the pandemic with synergized efforts of all sectors of society. My grandfather said that the war against the epidemic reminded him of his impassioned military life.

My grandfather always joked that he wanted to be a happy centenarian, and that he wanted to taste all the benefits brought about by scientific, technological and social development. I remember that whenever new media such as mobile phones, the Internet and tablet computers emerged, my grandfather would try them out. He seemed to return to his youth when his callous and rough palm slid across the smooth screen while trying to figure out all the advanced technology. After studying hard for many days, he was finally able to use Wechat. He added new friends, started a video call from time to time to his daughters to send greetings, and even forwarded messages popular among young people in his Wechat Moments. While saying "it is never too old to learn", he was at the same time jealous of the younger generation, who, according to him, "live in happiness but take it for granted".

My grandfather suffered from severe knee osteoarthritis, which might attack anytime when he bought rice in the market, played mahjong with his neighbors, or went to pay the union fee in the village committee. He complained that the pain was killing him. In the worst case scenario, he even had difficulty speaking because the disease attacked his nerves. His daughters were engaged in business in other places all year round. Unwilling to cause his daughters any trouble or distract them from their business, my grandpa never mentioned his pain to his six daughters. But in 2018, grandpa's health deteriorated, and it was difficult for him to even walk. His eldest daughter, out of a strong sense of family responsibility, immediately summoned four of her five siblings to come back to Hangzhou the very next day. The third daughter, having a wide range of contacts, found him prestigious doctors in Hangzhou. In a few days, my grandfather underwent a successful operation. During his stay in hospital, he was greatly touched by his daughters' filial piety and amazed by scientific, technological and social progresses. He said, "My wife would have been cured by the incredible modern medicine if she could hold on for a dozen years."

I remember that when most of the elderly opposed closing roads and complained about the complicated health code system, it was my grandpa who helped the community staff to publicize the knowledge of epidemic prevention and control and popularize how to properly and correctly wear medical masks. He also strongly supported the use of the health code which he believed was very important for epidemic prevention and control because it was able to position health code holders and collect their health data. Only by paying attention to and strictly following every rule could we win the fight against the epidemic. Today, when the virus is less contagious, my grandfather still advocates the use of the health code, saying, "It's a pity that such a great invention should be wasted."

To my grandpa, the emergence of the Internet, the improvement of medical care and the application of the health code system are a boon brought about by scientific and technological progress. Now, we are more than halfway through 2020, and China has built a moderately prosperous society in all aspects, an achievement which, in my grandpa's opinion, couldn't have been realized without the Party and the country. Actually, I want to add that it couldn't have been achieved without ordinary yet selfless people who always care about the country just like my grandpa!

So that is my grandfather, who is almost the same age as the new China. He dares to break feudalistic ideas and stereotypes, firmly supports the leadership of the Party, and has tasted the fruits of scientific, technological and social development!

心气儿在，方万能

刘亚娟

时间来到2021年，我们生活在一个便捷的网络社会，缺了什么，打开手机，一键下单，送上门来，只有想不到，没有买不到。就连房子都不用一砖一瓦建了，据说现在的3D打印3天就能建一套别墅。

但是，钻研精神、手工技艺不能“网购”。

在朱智凤同学《万能“师傅”》的文章里，我们看到，改革开放前，人们自己动手，小到刷碗的炊帚，大到房子都要亲自上阵。这其中首要原因当然是时间比钱富裕；但另一个重要原因大概就在一股心气儿了。在一个笃信勤劳致富的时代，付出体力动手去做，付出头脑用心去钻研，总能找到生活下去的方向和动力；这种信仰、信念、信心能够帮助人们在遇到困难时愈挫愈勇，能够在物质相对不富裕的时代自给自足，走过寒冬迎来春暖花开。

在文章里，我们同样看到，随着时代变化，这一家人的生活轨迹在变化，父亲的职业从体力活到监管机器，背后正体现了从改革开放前自己动手创造生活中延续而来的那股心气儿，面对新环境、新问题，去学习、适应、做出改变。这种信仰、信念、信心能够得到传承和焕发，更能帮助人们在物质相对丰富的时代懂得珍惜与自省。

师傅也好，师父也罢，焕发在中国人身上的关于信仰、信念、信心的“心气儿”，就是创造美好生活的一把钥匙，也是一把能够传承的火焰。

（浙大宁波理工学院传媒与法学院讲师，博士）

故事

湖州

朱智凤(新闻学专业192班)

万能“师傅”

它不同于现在市面上的锅铲,它是铁匠用厚重的铁打磨成的。它的年龄比我还大,已经30多岁,拿在手中,沉甸甸的,给人安稳感。

妈妈说,它是最好用的锅铲,是我们家的传家宝。

时光穿梭回20世纪70年代,湖州市吴兴区织里镇李家坝村,村口桥下的那条河流清澈见底,鱼儿在水中游,十几岁的父亲和几个好兄弟一起下水捉鱼。岸旁的芦苇飘荡,小穗低垂,他会想着去寻找一种叫白草的野草,这种野草可以用来做炊帚,那是当时农村常见的刷锅洗碗的工具。

爸爸用木棍炒菜,用野草制成的炊帚刷锅洗碗。“那个时候什么也没有,用的东西都是自己做的。”爸爸说。

“这个炊帚做起来很简单的,把白草的根放到一起,再把一个粗一点的木棍放到中间,然后用绳子或铁丝捆起来,晒晒干,就可以用了。”

“阿爸,那你为什么不做个像炊帚一样酷的锅铲?”在我心中,爸爸好像成为一个手工艺术家。

“那我又不会打铁,拿个木棍随便搞搞就用了。”爸爸摇了勺汤,看了看勺子,补充了一句“那个时候连个像样的勺子也没有”。

我似乎隐隐开始明白为什么如今我们家已经走向小康,已经不用为衣食住行而担忧,但他却还是热衷于做一位生活中的“维修师傅”。那种从小时候起就开始培养的动手能力,让他不论面临怎么样的生活困境都能自食其力。而在动手中培养的工匠精神,也为我们家越来越好提供了源源不断的动力。

“阿爸,1978年改革开放以后,发生了什么你还记得吗?”

1978年,爸爸学会了做泥砖。烈日下,他推着小车来到泥沙旁,脚用力踩锹,再将铁锹用力往上翘,将铁锹中的泥沙倒入小车中,一套动作行云流水。一个鲜活的“水泥师傅”的形象出现在了我的脑海中。

“那时候一块砖一分钱,我就拿着卖砖头得来的钱,去邻村买些枕套,然后我再去杭州之类的大城市将这些枕套卖掉,一天可以赚三四块。这在当时已经很不错了!”爸爸有些自豪地说着。爸爸将生意越做越大。他换上了白衬衫,衬衫的口袋里插着一支笔,一副文化人的模样。带着少年人的英气、傲气,他走过了中国的许多地方。

在武汉,他遇见了妈妈。

“你爸爸当时到武汉来做生意,卖香皂,当时宾馆的老板娘跟我关系挺不错,于是就介绍我和他认识,我就帮他卖东西了。”妈妈说道。

“爸爸还会做香皂?! 我怎么不知道?”我惊讶之意丝毫没有掩饰住。

后来我问爸爸,爸爸说:“哎呀,做香皂不是很简单的嘛,我当时买了块香皂,然后看了看,就知道怎么做了。”于是爸爸开始兴致勃勃地跟我讲述他做香皂的过程,“把香料化开,然后放到一个铁盒里……”从爸爸的口述中,我意识到了其实并没有那么简单,如果让我来进行香料的提取和香皂的冷凝,我一定会借助网络,然后购置许多“装备”,可是爸爸却用有限的工具自己研究了出来。

“我做的香皂大家可喜欢了,你叔叔他们都来我这里买。”

一个“香皂师傅”的形象出现在了我的脑海中。

之后,爸爸和妈妈一起从武汉回到了浙江。妈妈刚来时什么也不会,知道爸爸做枕头生意,于是她去做枕套的人家当学徒,很快学会了做枕套。在我儿时的记忆中,织布机的声音伴我入眠,妈妈总是工作至深夜,听到机杼声就像是妈妈在一旁轻声细语。在我看来,我的妈妈是“万能的纺织师”。

妈妈的纺织技艺越来越好,于是她借了钱,买了几台纺织机,请她的朋友来家中一起做枕套。

有一天,妈妈去一起工作的一个阿姨家吃饭,被一把铸铁的锅铲吸引了。过了几天,阿姨又请制作锅铲的阿康叔叔做了一把新的送给妈妈。木质手柄牢牢地和铁制的锅铲柄连在一起,椭圆的手柄形状,握起来十分舒适,沉甸甸的,用起来很得心应手,妈妈拿在手上喜欢得不得了。

同年,姐姐出生了。这是改革开放后的第一个 10 年,1988 年。这让这把锅铲多了一层意义。妈妈说:“你姐姐多大了,这把锅铲就跟了我们多久了。”

2014 年,我家的楼房造起来了。那时我已经 14 岁,奔跑在乡间,悠闲自在。造楼房的那段日子,每天都能吃上很多好吃的菜,妈妈会用那把手工铁铸的锅铲做很多佳肴。在我眼里,我的妈妈俨然是一位厨艺了得的“大厨师”!

爸爸那段时间得空就会加入建筑工人之列,拿起砖头、铅锤,有模有样地造起房子来,休息时,他会和阿叔们一起喝口茶,看着亲手搭建起来的房屋,喜滋滋地笑着,对未来的生活充满了无限的遐想。那个时候,他已经不仅是位水泥师傅,还是一位新晋的“建筑师傅”。

后来家中经商失败,父亲到了一家工厂工作。父亲又拿起了他的铁锹,脚用力踩锹，再将铁锹用力往上翘，将铁锹中的煤炭倒入小车中，运到锅炉旁，一套动作行云流水。虽然不像16岁时那般意气风发，但他仍然十分有力，对生活充满着希望，努力地生活着。

如今，父亲已经在工厂中工作许多年，从煤炭到天然气，从体力活到监管机器，他在他身处的行业领域，已经成为一位老师傅，一位在背后为人们提供动力的"燃气师傅"!

我的妈妈，她选择了在一家服装公司工作。"因为很多事情我都会做，所以老板很器重我，我一个人可以顶好几个人。"妈妈说。我想，勤劳能干的妈妈已经成为他们眼中的"万能师傅"，她什么事情都能够做好，有她在就会安心。

记得儿时很想拥有一台广告里的豆浆机，于是爸爸做了一个磨豆浆的机器。"当时家里没有多少钱，豆浆机又贵，但是又想让你喝上自己做的豆浆，所以想了那么一个法子。"爸爸笑着说道。

"虽然现在有了智能豆浆机，但我更想要那个手磨的。"

我想，爸爸是我生活中的启蒙师，是我的"师傅"。我多想学会他身上一半的本领。

当我从父母几十年的故事中游历穿梭回来，再看这把锅铲时，它仿佛带着父亲和母亲面对生活坚韧不拔的毅力，带着越磨越锋利的光芒。

Huzhou
Zhu Zhifeng (Class 192, Majoring in Journalism)

An Omnipotent Master

It was nothing like the spatula on the market today. Made of heavy iron, it was hammered and polished by a blacksmith. It was made 30 years ago, so it was older than me. It gave people a sense of security when you took it in hand and felt its weight.

My mother said that it was the best spatula and it was an heirloom of our family.

The story happened in Lijiaba Village, Zhili Town, Wuxing District, Huzhou City in the 1970s. The river behind the bridge at the entrance to the village was so clear that the bottom of the river could be seen and fish were swimming in the water. My father, who was a teenager at that time, went into the water to catch fish with several of his good brothers. Reeds fluttered and spikelet dropped low along the shore. He wanted to look for a kind of weed called white grass, which could be used to make cooking brooms. It was a common tool for washing pots and dishes in countryside at that time.

My father made the dishes with wooden sticks and washed the dishes with a kitchen broom made of wild grass. "At that time, there was nothing. Everything was made by ourselves," said my father.

"This broom was very simple to make. We put the roots of white grass together with a thicker stick in the middle; then we tied it up with ropes or wires, dried it in the sun, and it could be used after that."

"Daddy, why don't you make a spatula as good as a kitchen broom?" In my heart, he seemed to have been a craftsman.

"I don't know how to strike the iron, so I just made do with a wooden stick." He bailed out the soup, looked at the spoon and added, "There wasn't even a decent spoon at that time."

I seem to understand why he is still keen on being a "maintenance man" in his life though our family has become well-off now and we needn't worry about food, clothing, housing, transportation. This kind of hands-on ability, which he began to cultivate from a young age, enabled him to stand on his own feet no matter what life difficulties he faced. Also, the craftsmanship cultivated in the hands-on operation also provided a continuous source of the drive for our family to get better and better.

"Daddy, do you remember what happened after the reform and opening up in 1978?"

In 1978, my dad learned how to make clay bricks. Under the scorching sun, he pushed the wheelbarrow next to the sand, and stepped hard on the shovel with his foot, pushed the shovel upward, and poured the sand into the wheelbarrow with a set of natural and smooth movements. A vivid image of "cement master" appeared in my mind.

"At that time, every brick was worth a cent, then I took the money from selling bricks to buy some pillowcases in the neighboring village. Then I sold these pillowcases in big cities like Hangzhou. I could earn three or four yuan a day. That was pretty good at the time." My father said with pride, and his business grew bigger and bigger. He put on a white shirt with a pen in his pocket, looking like an intellectual. With the heroic spirit and pride of a young man, he had been to many places in China.

In Wuhan, he met my mother.

"Your father came to Wuhan to sell soap. At that time, the wife of the owner of the hotel had a good relationship with me, so she introduced me to your father, and I helped him sell goods," said my mother.

"Dad can make soap? How come I know nothing about it?" My surprise was not concealed in the least.

Later, I asked my father about this. He said, "Oh, making soap is a piece of cake. I bought a piece of soap at that time, and I knew how to make it after I observed it for a while." Then my father began to tell me about his soap making process with great interest, "Melt the spices and put them in an iron box..." From my father's words, I realized that it was actually not so easy. If I was asked to extract spices and condense a soap, I would certainly search the Internet and purchase a lot of equipment, but my father used simple tools to figure it out by himself.

"Everyone liked the soap I made. Your uncles all came to buy it from me."

The image of a "soap master" appeared in my mind.

After that, my father returned to Zhejiang Province from Wuhan City with my mother. When my mother first came, she could do nothing. She knew that my father was running the pillow business, so she worked as an apprentice in a family which made pillowcases, and soon she learned how to make pillowcases. In my childhood memory, the sound of the loom accompanied me to sleep. My mother always worked late into midnight. Hearing the loom sound was just like mom whispering by the side. In my opinion, my mother is the "omnipotent weaver".

My mother's textile skills got better and better, so she borrowed money and bought several textile machines. Then she asked her friends to make pillowcases in our home.

One day, my mother had a meal in an aunts whom she worked with, and she was attracted to an iron spatula. After a few days, the aunt asked Uncle

Kang, who made the spatula, to make a new one for my mother. The wooden handle was firmly connected with the iron spatula handle. The oval-shaped handle was very comfortable to hold. Although it was heavy, it was very handy to use. My mother liked it very much.

In the same year, my elder sister was born. That year was 1988, the first tenth anniversary of the decade after reform and opening up. This made the spatula more meaningful. My mother said, "Your sister's age shows how long this spatula has been with us."

In 2014, our house was built. I was 14 years old, running in the countryside and living a leisurely and free life. In those days when the house was being built, I could eat a lot of delicious dishes every day. My mother would make many delicious dishes with the handmade iron spatula. In my eyes, my mother looked like a good "chef"!

My father would join the construction workers in his spare time. He took up bricks, the plumb, and built the house in a certain way. When he had a rest, he would have a cup of tea with workers. He looked at the house that was built by himself with a happy smile. He was full of infinite reverie about his future life. At that time, he was not only a cement master, but also a new "construction master".

Later, my family failed in business, and my father went to work in a factory. He picked up his shovel again, put his foot hard on it, pushed the spade upward again, and poured the coal from the shovel into the wheelbarrow and transported it to the boiler with a set of natural and smooth movements. Although not as high spirited as what he was like at the age of 16, he was still very powerful, full of hope for life and working hard.

Now, my father has been working in the factory for many years from coal to natural gas, from manual work to supervising machines—in the industry he is engaged in, he has become an experienced master, a "gas master" who provides power for people!

My mother chose to work in a clothing company. "Because I could do a lot of things, the boss thought highly of me. I could replace several people," she said. I think my industrious mother has become the omnipotent master in their eyes. She could do everything so well that everyone felt relieved to have her around.

I remembered that when I was a child, I wanted to have a soybean milk machine in the advertisement, so my father made me a soybean milk grinding machine. "At that time, there was not much money at home, and the soybean milk machine was expensive, but I wanted you to drink self-made soybean milk, so I came up with such a solution," he said with a smile.

"Though now there is an intelligent soybean milk machine, I prefer the one used by hand."

I think my father is my enlightenment teacher and master in my life. How I wish I could learn half of his skills.

When I came back from my parents' decade—long stories and when I looked at this spatula again, it seemed to be with the perseverance that my parents demonstrated when facing difficulties in their life and with the glare that becomes brighter after each sharpening.

乡土社会变迁的最直观体现

柳　五

中国人安土重迁，在众多怀旧文字中，从来不乏对各种老房子的记忆。也因此，我们能够从房子的变化来观察乡土社会的变迁。

从作者住过的四个房子，我们不难看到：在上个世纪八九十年代，改革开放的财富效应开始显现，在满足了基本的温饱之后，农民首先想到的就是改善住房。稍早一些时候，由于还不是特别富裕，很多人拆掉土坯房后，建起了“砖挂面”——也就是外面是一层立砖，里面是土坯等，晚一些时候钱更充裕一些，才开始盖上全部砖瓦的房子。随着时间的推移，砖瓦房也由碎石地基开始用上钢筋混凝土，房子越建越结实。

房子是家的外在呈现。居住条件的改善与家庭生活的殷实程度很多时候互为表里，对房子而言，除了体现居住的舒适程度，还是一个家庭外在形象的综合体现和宣示。我们习惯称有地位或者富裕的家庭是高门(深宅)大院，一般人家叫小门小户。好的家庭条件反映了主人的社会关系和能力，表现良好的家庭体现了主人集纳社会资源实现自我发展的潜力。在特定时间段内，房子越建越好，越来越舒适，表明财富状况和社会地位的提升。

但是随着改革开放不断深入，社会持续发展，家庭收入水平普遍提高，农村的房子占家庭投入比例越来越小，最终会在一定程度上弱化甚至丧失房子所体现出来的政治意味，在变得越来越不值钱的同时，就会发生转移，所以我们会看到，农村的房子越来越便宜，但是土地则不断增值。尤其是在发达地区，工业化和城镇化的进展也推动和加快了乡村建设的现代化进程，政府对乡村的规划能力越来越强。

与此同时，家庭又是社会的基层单位，承载着宏观政策作用于微观时的效应，同时反映着宏观政策成败。在这一背景下，我们可以看到，以改革开放为特征的持续多年的发展主义策略，深刻改变了基层面貌，除了物质层面(以房子为代表)的变化外，人们的精神状态也发生了巨大的改观，变得更加自信和开放。在城市化与乡村振兴的大背景下，城市和乡村先是人口流动越来越大越来越自由，伴随着的是城乡二元结构在逐渐被打破，进而给人以无限想象的空间。

（吉林日报评论员）

故事

金华

楼康婷（新闻学专业 201 专升本班）

我曾生活过的四个房子

时间无形，却时刻催促我们长大，成长既漫长也迅速，那些美好瞬间来不及回味就在记忆章节里被时间悄悄抹去。好在有些物件包裹着记忆存在，通过他们能回望过去。于我而言，这能储存记忆的宝藏就是我曾生活过的四个房子。

第一个房子

1974 年，爸爸出生在浙江金华的一个五口之家里，是家中的第三个儿子。“那个年代生活物质虽然一般，但日子过得还挺快乐自在。”这是爸爸对过去生活的总结。当我问到爸爸心中最具代表性的能证明生活在进步的东西时，爸爸脱口而出：“那最明显的就是房子了呀，住的房子越来越好，生活那不就是越来越好了嘛。”话语中带着骄傲和藏不住的开心。“生活总是艰苦的，只要不断努力，日子一定会越过越好。”这是爸爸一直以来的生活信条，激励着他向前，也影响着我。

“那就说说房子吧。”第一个房子是爸爸从 1974 年出生开始住的房子，位于金华浦江的一个小村庄，房子的年头有些久远，大小总共两层，墙体是用泥巴建造而成的。现在看来是个破旧的老房子，但在 20 世纪 80 年代前在当地还是一种建筑特色，周围的每个村庄几乎都采用了类似的构造。房子虽破旧，却寄存了老爸全部的美好童年记忆。“当年的房子都是一排排贴着建的，邻里之间一堵墙之隔，关系都很好，家家孩子的年龄也都相仿，最不缺的就是玩伴，我们会成群结队在家门口、弄堂里玩撞拐子，到田间小河中练憋气扎猛子，也会在田野间相互追逐比赛。”爸爸说这些的时候，语气生动，仿佛那些日子近在眼前，然而在话题结束时的一声感叹也表明他接受了那些时光属于过去。房子再老再旧，在爸爸心里都是宝藏，到现在每逢过年，爸爸还是会留一张红纸贴在老房子的墙上。房子本身不大，刚开始一家5口住起来也还不觉得挤，但随着三个孩子的长大，全家对房子的不满足越来越明显，房子太小，没有单独的房间，少了保护自己隐私的空间，住着多少有些不便利了。终于在1990年，爷爷向全家道出了要再建一个房子的计划，全员欣然赞同。

第二个房子

1990年，爸爸16岁。在那时这个年纪也不算小，上学的继续上学，不想读书直接去工作，也是普遍现象。大伯比爸爸年长许多，早早就离家去了安徽宁国的红砖厂工作，二伯则正离家求学。作为家里的老幺，承担起了自己的一份责任，造房子时帮爷爷打下手。爷爷会看图纸，身边也有一帮朋友帮衬着，所以第二个房子的建造大都是爷爷亲力亲为。“当时年纪小不懂事，玩心太重，心思没有放在学习上，放学后倒是会野，但是向爷爷学和水泥、垒砖墙也没有落下。”爸爸淡淡地说：“造房子的本事就是那会儿跟爷爷学起来的。”当我问爸爸建房子是否很辛苦时，还沉浸在回忆中的他轻笑一声：“造新房子高兴呀，有新房子住，高兴都来不及还会觉得辛苦吗?”房子建得很快，一年左右时间就完成了。房子总共有三层，青砖瓦墙，每层都有三个房间，住进刚建成的新房全家的喜悦不用多说。

1995年，爸爸21岁，青春正好。少年总按捺不住那颗躁动的心想出去看看，在经过爷爷的同意后他带着妈妈一起去了云南，在那边做起了衣服饰品的小生意。从一开始的流动摊位到后来拥有自己的一家固定小店，离家走这一遭也算没有白费。“不趁年轻去外面看一看，怎么能知道自己是喜欢漂泊还是安定呢?”1999年，我出生了。小小的孩子给一个家庭带去活力的同时也给爸爸妈妈更多的责任。小小的我一直需要爸爸妈妈无微不至的照顾，逐渐地，老爸心里想要一个安定的家的念头越来越强，最终和妈妈商量后达成一致，在2002年回了金华。我和房子的故事由此展开。

这座跨世纪的房子最让我印象深刻，在我4岁有记忆的时候进入这个房子，吃的饭是用一个大家伙——土灶烧出来的，客厅放着老式缝纫机，偶尔会看到奶奶拿出来踩一踩，家里那会儿唯一的交通公具是凤凰牌老式二八自行车，爷爷会骑着它抱我坐在车架上送我上幼儿园。悄悄地土灶被便捷的煤气灶取代，自行车和老式缝纫机也被堆到了杂物房的一角。房子一直是那个房子，只是被更新的家具、更现代的电器装满，它无声地见证着时代的发展，记录着我家生活的进步。

第三个房子

第二个房子，一直住到我8岁。2007年，全家搬进了第三个完全现代的房子里。第三个房子整体都是爸爸一手操持。问爸爸是什么时候开始计划的，爸爸想了想："是在回到金华的第二年就开始打算的，多了你和妈妈，再加上爷爷奶奶年纪也大了，总是想让全家都住得舒服些，于是就有这个念头了，再加上当时有块地空着，就跟你爷爷说了这个想法，爷爷同意，就这么建了。"爸爸说得很轻描淡写，但从中能感受到爸爸对这个家付出的努力和他自己心中把握着的责任。在我的记忆里，爸爸一手建起的小家真的很舒服，第一次让我拥有了自己的小房间以及认识了一群年龄相仿的朋友。我心无旁骛地长大，生活有条不紊地继续。

第四个房子

新农村建设的大环境下建造了第四个房子。2012 年，爸爸最开始收到拆迁消息的时候，心里五味杂陈。"这个房子才建了没几年，都没住热乎，就要拆了，当然舍不得。"但经过多番思考，最终决定跟随大步伐。"旧的不去，新的不来嘛。"整个村子发展的势头还是猛的，很快爸爸就收到了村里重建的规划图景。在看到图上呈现的大致全貌时，父亲心里到底还是高兴的。整个村庄不再杂乱无章，房子的位置被安排得整整齐齐，户型、外观都做了统一，村中有绿化、篮球场，周围还会有广场。看到这里，爸爸心里的石头落了地。有过之前造房子的经验，爸爸知道造房子不是一件轻松的事情，便早早做好了打算，从打地基开始，就时常泡在工地上，对于造房子要用的钢筋、泥沙，也是细细交代。那段时间爸爸脸上的疲态现在也能回忆起来，是真的辛苦。房子总共五层半，历时差不多一年的样子。2014 年的暑假，我们正式搬进了这个新家。在这个房子里，我经历了阶段性的长大，从初中升入高中，最后步入大学。

未来的日子很长，房子与我家还会有更多更精彩的故事继续。

Jinhua
Lou Kangting (Class 201, Majoring in Journalism)

Four Houses I Have Lived in

Time is invisible, but always urges us to grow up. Growth is both fast and slow. Those beautiful moments in the memory, not having been savored yet, are quietly erased by time. The good news is that some objects carry memories with them, through which one can look back. For me, the treasure troves of memories are the four houses I have lived in.

First House

In 1974, Dad was born in Jinhua City, Zhejiang Province. He was the third son of a family of five. "In those days, life was quite happy and comfortable despite the modest living conditions," Dad recalled his past life. When I asked about the most representative thing in his heart that could prove that life was progressing, Dad blurted out, "That must be the house obviously. The house you live in is getting better and better, and life must be getting better and better as well." The words were filled with pride and joy that could not be concealed. "Life is always hard. As long as you keep trying, the day will be better and better." This is the creed of his life, which has inspired him to move forward and also has encouraged me.

"Let's talk about the house then." The first house, which was located in a small village in Pujiang County, Jinhua City, was the one my father had lived in since he was born in 1974, Jinhua City. It was an old two-story house with walls made of mud. The house looks decrepit and old now, but it has revealed the local architectural features before the 1980s. Almost every village in the neighborhood adopted a similar structure. Shabby as it was, the house carried all of Dad's happy childhood memories. "The houses back then were built in rows. Neighbors were separated only by a wall with good relationships. All the children were of about the same age. Playmates were never lacked. On our doorsteps and in the lane, we would gang up and play a game called zhuang-guai-zi, which meant you stood on one foot and hit each other with the curved knee. In the river, we would also practice holding breath underwater and zha-meng-zi, which was putting the head down to the river rapidly. In the fields we chased each other." Dad told this in a vivid tone as if those days were close at hand. But a sigh at the end of the conversation suggested that he had accepted those days were in the past. No matter how old the house is, it is a treasure in Dad's heart. Even now, Dad will leave a piece of red paper and stick it on its wall every Chinese New Year. The house itself was not big, and the family of five didn't feel crowded at first. As the three children grew up, the family were more and more dissatisfied with the house. It was too small for five and there was no separate room. It was somewhat inconvenient to live without your own private space. Finally, in 1990, Grandpa told the whole family his plan to build another house, and all the members readily agreed.

Second House

In 1990, Dad was 16 years old. This age was considered not so young at that time. Some peers stayed in school while many others dropped out of school and went to work. My eldest uncle was much older than Dad and left home early to work in the red brick factory in Ningguo City, Anhui Province. My second uncle was studying away from home. As the youngest child of the family, Dad took on his own responsibility to help Grandpa build the house. Grandpa could read the drawings and had a group of friends around to help him, so the second house was mostly built by Grandpa himself. "I was young, ignorant and too playful then. I never concentrated on studying. I was unstrained after school but never forgot to learn mixing concrete with water and building brick walls from your Grandpa." Dad said lightly, "The skill of building a house was just learned from your Grandpa at that time." When I asked him whether it was hard, Dad chuckled, still immersed in the memory, "We are happy. We cannot be happier to live in a new house and how would we feel hard?" The house was built very quickly and was finished in a year or so. It had three floors in total and three rooms on each floor. Walls were made of grey bricks and tiles. It was needless to say the whole family were extremely happy to live in the newly built house.

In 1995, Dad was 21 years old and he was at the best time of his youth. The young man couldn't suppress his restless heart to go out for a look. With the consent of Grandpa, he took Mom to Yunnan Province and started a small business selling clothes and accessories. From the mobile booth at first to a fixed store later, it was worth it to leave home. "If you don't take a look outside when you are young, how can you know whether you like to drift or settle down?" In 1999, I was born. A small child brought vitality to a family and more responsibilities to take for my parents at the same time. I always needed their meticulous care. Gradually, the thought of settling down became stronger and stronger in Dad's mind. Finally, he reached an agreement with Mom after discussion. We returned to Jinhua in 2002. And the story between me and the second house unfolded.

This cross-century house impressed me the most. I first entered it when I was 4 years old, the age old enough for me to remember things. The meal was cooked by a big tool, an earthen stove. Occasionally Grandma would take out the old-fashioned sewing machine in the living room for use. The only means of transportation in the family was an old-fashioned Phoenix 28 bicycle (whose wheel diameter was 28 inches). Grandpa would ride it to send me to kindergarten with me seated on the frame. Gradually the earthen stove was replaced by a convenient gas stove. The bicycle and the old-fashioned sewing machine were left in a corner of the storage room. The house has always been the same one, just filled with more novel furniture and modern electric appliances. It silently witnesses the development of the times and records the progress of our life.

Third House

We lived in the second house until I was 8 years old. In 2007, our family moved into the third house, which was completely modern. The entire house was built by Dad. When asked about the time he started planning, Dad thought for a while, "I started planning in the second year after returning to Jinhua. You and your Mom joined our family. Grandma and Grandpa were getting older. The idea occurred when I always wanted the whole family to live more comfortably. In addition, a piece of land was just vacant then. I told your Grandpa this idea. Grandpa agreed, so it was built." Dad said lightly, from which I could feel his commitment to the family and the responsibility in his heart. In my memory, the little home Dad built was really comfortable. For the first time, I had my own room and met a group of friends of a similar age. I grew up without distraction, and our life continued in an orderly way.

Fourth House

The fourth house was built in the context of the new rural construction. When Dad first received the news that the house would be demolished and that we would be relocated in 2012, there were mixed feelings. "The last house had only been built and lived in for a few years. Naturally I couldn't bear seeing it being demolished." But after reconsideration, he finally decided to follow the pace of our country. "The new should replace the old." The development momentum of the whole village was strong, and soon Dad received a plan for the reconstruction of the village. Seeing the overall picture, he was happy after all. The whole village was no longer in a muddle. The layout of the houses was arranged neatly and the house type and appearance were uniform. There would be green space and a basketball court inside the village, with a square around. Seeing this, Dad was fully relieved. With his past experience in building, Dad knew that it was not an easy thing, so he made plans early. Starting from laying the foundation, he would often stay on the construction site. He would even explain the rebar and sand used in building in detail. Even now I can recall the fatigue on Dad's face at that time. It was really hard work. The house has a total of five and a half floors, which was finished almost a year later. In the summer vacation of 2014, the whole family finally moved into this new home. In this house, I went through some stages of growing up, from junior high school to senior high school, and finally to college.

The days to come will be long, and there will be more and more exciting stories about the house and my family.

时代是出卷人，我们是答卷人

陈雪军

《我的军人父亲》一文行云流水，讲述了出身农村家庭的父亲通过当兵，一路改变自身命运的故事，向我们展现了在过去的岁月里，通过一代人的努力改变两代人乃至三代人家庭生活的奋斗图景。

正如文中所说，在董琨同学父亲的那个年代里，想要实现社会阶层的转变，当兵是为数不多的可行方案之一。尽管从军之路一波三折，经历了祖辈的阻挠和部队铁一般的纪律磨练，父亲也还是靠着自己的打拼，一步步成为军中的骨干，并从排长一路晋升为副团长，并在副团长的位置上转业回乡。

一直以来，通过自身努力实现社会阶级的跨越，从而改变自身和家庭的命运，是一代又一代国人不懈的追求。从董琨同学的祖辈，到军人父亲，再到身为新时代大学生的董琨同学自己，不断变化着的是外部环境和人们所选择的身份，不变的是一脉相承的奋斗精神。

习近平总书记在《习近平谈治国理政》第三卷中写到：时代是出卷人，我们是答卷人，人民是阅卷人。对于一个小家的奋斗而言，又何尝不是如此？变化着的是时代的命题，而每一个个体都在选择适合自己的方式，交出自己心中最满意的答案。军人父亲将自己的青春和生命献给了20多年的军旅生涯，书写了属于父亲的奋斗人生，而作为新时代青年的董琨同学，正如初升的太阳，朝气蓬勃，也将面临属于自己的时代命题，书写自己的奋斗篇章，为自己的人生作答。

时代是出卷人，我们是答卷人。每一个小我都是推动社会不断向前发展的力量之源，每一个家庭的奋斗历史都是时代不断进步的缩影，这揭示出最朴实的道理——幸福是奋斗出来的！

（浙大宁波理工学院传媒与法学院教授，博士）

故事

湖州

董琨(网络与新媒体专业 184 班)

我的军人父亲

父亲当兵,说实话是一段意外又曲折的经历。

1970 年 9 月出生的他从小生活在湖州长兴一个农村家庭,家中共有三个兄弟姐妹。虽然家境贫寒,生活艰辛,但这样的环境不但没能将父亲打倒,反而激发了他对外面世界的向往。

1988 年的夏日,父亲读完了高中,但因为家境原因没能继续上学。按照那时的社会规则,农村家的孩子的出路并不是特别多,种田、打工是绝大多数人的选择。而要想实现社会阶层的转变,能走的路更是寥寥无几,当兵便是其中一条。可是"可怜天下父母心"啊,我的奶奶,我父亲的母亲,心中并不愿意让父亲去当兵,去吃苦。于是在高中念完的那个暑假,也就是每年夏季征兵的开始,奶奶为了不让父亲去当兵,刻意隐瞒了当兵体检的时间。而"傻乎乎"的父亲则在家中等待体检消息。

命运总是爱捉弄人,当百无聊赖的父亲坐在自家门口时,好巧不巧地遇到了刚刚体检完的好友"阿三",询问一番过后才知道今天县里正在进行征兵体检,恍然大悟的父亲匆匆和奶奶说了一句,甚至来不及过多地埋怨奶奶便与同村的其他两人一起踏上了征兵体检的道路。

"当我看见与他同行的两个人回来而他没来时,我就知道他要去当兵了。"这是过世的奶奶曾对我说过的话。也正是如此,在这个 1988 年的夏天,父亲开启了他长达 21 年的军旅生涯。

体检成功后的父亲被分配到了福建省厦门市杏林区的高炮团中,那年父亲正好 18 岁,而 18 岁的少年正是血气方刚,心气盛旺,极易与领导发生冲突的年纪。

"我当新兵那会,经常不服从部队规章管理,脾气暴,爱吵架,做事从不循规蹈矩,时间久了,别人就给我起了个外号'土匪'!"每当讲起这些故事时父亲总会点起一根中华牌的香烟,翘起二郎腿,面带笑容地看着我。"那时候部队有规定不准在节假日外的日子里喝酒,不然要严惩不贷,可是我偏偏不信这个邪,大半夜怂恿上三四个战友，偷偷跑到集训旁的树林中去喝酒。没想到正好撞见了巡逻值夜班的班长，本来那班长想借此训斥我一顿，结果那时他竟然拿我没办法，愣是请了连长和指导员来轮流给我做思想工作，才让我服软写了几千字的检讨。”

因为身体素质、军事素养实在是太好，在部队大大小小的比赛里总是能拿第一名，因此父亲被推选为保送军校的培养人才之一。1991年至1994年，父亲先是在河南郑州进行军校的训练，在那里毕业后，又转到江苏镇江军校去学习军事理论知识。在军校的那段日子给了父亲极其深刻的印象，“拥有专业素养的人才到底是不一样的”，父亲如是说道。也正是这种别样的见识，让父亲开拓了眼界。

军校一毕业，父亲就回到了原来的高炮团，当上了排长，那年是1994年，父亲的本命年。随后的日子里父亲靠着自己的打拼一步步成为军中的骨干——1994年排长、1995年副连长、1997年连长、1999年副营长、2001年营长、2005年副团长。

随着职位的一步步提升，父亲也深感自己的肩上责任重大。从原来的新兵蛋子变为了军队骨干，放荡不羁的浪子也逐渐学会了谦卑。

2008年的奥运会是个举国欢庆的日子，对于我们家也是，只不过不同的是这年也是父亲事业的转折年，团长的选拔事关重大，父亲对待此事也是愈发的认真。

可惜人外有人，父亲落选，第二年便转业回到了家乡。那年是2009年，也是中华人民共和国成立60周年。那年的10月1日国庆节，父亲躺在床上和我们一起看着国庆阅兵仪式，当看见自己的战友坐在熟悉的高射炮前从天安门缓缓经过的那一刻，父亲平静的脸上绽放出了久违的笑容。

政府妥善安排了父亲的工作，让他回到家乡，做了当地县政府的政法委负责人，主要管理当地治安和防治邪教的工作，也算是“专业对口”吧。此后10年父亲便在这一领域一直工作着。

当父亲转业回乡，许多变故让其焦头烂额，生活条件和生活方式也发生了改变。在部队中我和母亲的身份是军人家属，住的地方自然是统一的家属房，虽然不算精美但也是宽敞和干净的，至于伙食，那自然是吃着部队大锅饭长大的，父亲作为团职干部每月5000元的收入不用在饮食起居上大费操劳。可是转业一回来，事情就变了。柴米油盐酱醋茶，生活的方方面面都要考虑进去，工资没涨多少，花销却成倍增长。更何况，当时家中并没有多少储蓄，因此也没能在家乡购置一套房子，所以从小学到初中毕业，也就是2009年到2015年这6年我们一直借住在外婆家中。这一切对于一个中年男人是一个巨大的冲击。

此外部队里的生活习惯显然与这里的人们有着一些区别，在部队5点起床

9 点熄灯，有时半夜紧急集合那是常态，因此对于人员素质的要求也是以雷厉风行的作风和绝对服从为主。生活节奏一下子变慢让父亲全身上下都不自在，好在军队中锻炼出的顽强毅力让他扛过了这一切。2015 年我们搬进了新家，不久又有了新车。日子也在一天天地变好。

随着时间的流逝，家里的液晶电视也增添了两台，实用保暖也已不是穿衣的首选标准，饮食的标准也从“吃饱”变为了“吃好”。从前父母结婚，父亲提的 2 万元彩礼都是分三次交给母亲的，所谓的婚车也仅仅只有 3 辆，但纵使条件艰苦，父母也并没有相互嫌弃对方。幸福总是突然的，母亲婚后没多久就怀上了我，一家人其乐融融地庆祝着新生命的诞生。可是幸福却又是短暂的，父亲请假回家的时间即将截止，部队休假的时间规定又不能违反，没办法父亲只能放下怀孕的母亲赶回部队进行训练。所幸，当母亲临产时，父亲得到批准有了 20 多天的产假，守在母亲身边迎接了我的到来。

我的父亲，20 多年的军旅生涯，他将自己的青春和生命都奉献给了军营。

Huzhou
Dong Kun (Class 184, Majoring in Network and New Media)

Father Is a Soldier

My father's experience as a soldier, to be frank, was full of accidents and twists and turns.

He was born into a rural family in Changxing, Huzhou City, in southeastern China's Zhejiang Province back in September, 1970, and he has two siblings. A poor and hard life didn't knock out my father; the very opposite, the humble background aroused his longing for the outside world.

My father finished senior high school in the summer of 1988, but didn't further his study for a lack of money. Restricted by social norms at that time, children from a rural family usually ended up as a farmer or a migrant worker. There were few options for them to change their congenital social classes, and joining the army was one of them. But no parents in this world want to see their children suffer. So did my grandma, who hated it that my father should go through such hardship in the army. To keep my father from joining the army, my grandma purposefully concealed the time for applicants to have the physical examination when the annual army conscription began in the summer when he finished high school. My father, completely in the dark, was waiting for the message at home.

In a remarkable turn of events, my father, waiting idly for the news at his doorstep, came across his friend A' san who just finished the physical examination. Knowing that the physical examination was going on in the county, my father told my grandma that he would go and then rushed to the county with two fellow villagers, not even having time to blame his mother for deliberately concealing the truth.

"The moment I saw the other two villagers come back without him, I knew that he would be a soldier," my late grandma said so to me. It was exactly in the summer of 1988 that my father embarked on a military journey which lasted for 21 years.

My father, having passed the physical examination, was assigned to the anti-aircraft artillery corps in Xinlin District, Xiamen City, southern China's Fujian Province. That year, my 18-year-old father was rebellious and ambitious, often going into conflicts with army officers.

"When I was a recruit, I disobeyed orders and disciplines, easily lost my temper, was spoiling for a fight and never followed rules. I was thus nicknamed 'Bandit'." Every time my father recalled the past, he would sit cross-legged with a Chunghwa cigarette between his fingers. He looked at me with a smile and continued, "We were forbidden to go for a drink except for during holidays and weekends at that time. If we broke the rule, we would be severely punished. But I was so rebellious that I would persuade three or four recruits to have a drink secretly in the woods next to the place where we got trained. I didn't expect to be caught by our squad leader who was on the night patrol. He thought he could have given me a rap on the knuckles, but he ended up asking the company commander and the instructor to give me a lecture, who finally talked me into writing thousands of words for introspection."

My father always snatched up the top prize in various competitions in the army due to his physical agility and military skills, and was soon recommended to the military school. He then got trained in Zhengzhou City in central

China's Henan Province from 1991 to 1994, after which he was sent to learn military theories in another military school in Zhenjiang in southeastern China's Jiangsu Province. "There are indeed huge gaps between professionals and non-professionals," said my father, who was deeply impressed by those days in military schools. Those extraordinary experiences greatly broadened his horizon.

My father was sent back to the anti-aircraft artillery corps once he graduated from the military school and became the platoon leader in 1994, his year of fate according to the Chinese horoscope. In the following years, with his hard work, my father gradually became the backbone of the army—platoon leader in 1994, deputy company commander in 1995, company commander in 1997, deputy battalion commander in 1999, battalion commander in 2001 and deputy regimental commander in 2005.

My father felt the increasingly heavy responsibility over his shoulders as he climbed up his military ladder. From a naughty recruit to the backbone of the army, my father, once uninhibited, learned to be humble and modest.

Soon it was 2008. Beijing Olympics were celebrated nationwide. My family was no exception. But 2008 was special for us also because it was a turning point for my father's career. My father was then a candidate for the position of regimental commander, and he took it seriously.

Yet there is always someone out there who is better than you. My father failed in his attempt to be the regimental commander, and consequently transferred to civil work in his hometown the next year. It was in 2009, the 60th anniversary of the establishment of New China. On the National Day that year, my father watched the National Day Military Parade with us while lying on the bed, and finally smiled when he saw his comrades passing Tian'anmen Square in anti-aircraft guns he was so familiar with.

The government properly arranged my father's job, assigning him to be in charge of local security and the prevention and control of evil cults in the political and law committee of the county government, a job somewhat relevant to his professional skills. My father continued the job in the following one decade.

After my father returned to his hometown, many mishaps left him in a mess, and greatly changed our living condition and lifestyles. In the past, my mom and I, as military relatives, lived in the military dormitory which was, though not well-decorated, spacious and clean, and ate"food prepared in a big pot". My father spent very little of his monthly salary of 5,000 yuan on accommodation at that time. But things changed when he left the military. Salary didn't increase much but expenses soared because my father needed to pay for daily necessities. To make things even worse, my parents couldn't afford a residential house in the hometown for they didn't save much and as a result, we had to live in my maternal parents' home for six years from 2009 to 2015, a huge blow to a middle-aged man.

Besides, life habits my father formed in the army were obviously different from those of people here. My father used to get up at five and go to bed at nine. Resolution and unconditional obedience were required of military personnel for it was commonplace to muster soldiers at midnight. The slowing down of the life rhythm distressed my father, but he managed to handle this with the perseverance and endurance he developed as a soldier. We moved into a new house in 2015 and before long we bought a new car. It seemed that life was getting better.

As time went by, we bought two LCD television sets and we wanted quality clothes instead of just warm ones, nutritious food instead of just enough food. When my parents got married, dowries to my mom's family were given in three installments, and there were only three wedding cars on their wedding day. But despite all the difficulty, my parents never gave each other a cold shoulder. Happiness was always around the corner and before long, my mom got pregnant. Everyone in the family was waiting for my birth. But happiness was also transient, for my father had to return to the army when his short leave was over. Having to obey rules, my father had no choice but to hurry back for training. Luckily, my father was given paternity leave of over 20 days when my mom was about to undergo the labor and he was able to personally welcome me to this world.

My father, a soldier for two decades, has dedicated his youth and life to the army.

大时代与小人物

周茂江

今年是中华人民共和国成立72周年，与共和国几乎同龄的中国人正在逐渐老去。他们的经历正好与共和国发展轨迹同步。本文作者的外公外婆出生于新中国成立初期，由于家庭经济条件的差异，外公不如外婆幸运，与教育失之交臂。外公17岁穿上军装保家卫国，而外婆则读完高中走上工作岗位。外公复员后经友介绍与外婆相识相知相爱，组建家庭，孕育子女。

随着上世纪80年代改革开放的春风吹遍神州大地，外公下海经商，得益于国家形势政策的利好，成为人生赢家。为了支撑整个家庭，外公年事渐高仍继续走南闯北开拓事业，谱写出大时代下小人物的勇气与担当。按照中国传统男主外女主内的风俗，外婆勤俭持家、抚育儿孙，成为外公在外打拼的坚不可摧的大后方，也为后辈营造出温馨宜人的家庭环境。时至晚年外公才放弃事业，回家与外婆及儿孙共度美好时光，聚少离多的日子得以结束。

“家是最小国，国是千万家”，中华儿女总是以实际行动为家国情怀做出生动注脚。外公外婆虽然没有因为国家的需要而牺牲自我，但在国家经济发展、政治稳定、文化昌盛的时代背景下，他们在尽力做好小人物的本分的同时，何尝不是推动社会澎湃前进的动力。也印证了那句话：国好才能家好，国泰才能民安！

（浙大宁波理工学院马克思主义学院讲师，博士）

故事

温州

郑含潞(网络与新媒体专业 191 班)

我的外公外婆

“你爷爷啊,家里这么多孩子最喜欢的就是你啦。你两个月大他就一只手抱着你一只手开车,所以你长这么大从来没有晕过车……”同样的话,从小到大我听了无数遍,外婆也不厌其烦地每次都会提起。外公在我心中一直是高大挺拔,是我随时能够撒娇耍赖,能够保护我的依靠,可渐渐看到他白发越来越多,时常腰疼膝盖疼,我越发意识到生命衰老的不可抗性,而现在我能做的只有尽可能多地陪伴。

上个世纪 50 年代初,外公就出生在温州市乐清一户普普通通的人家里。那时候的经济条件很差,家里孩子也很多,外公小小年纪就要帮家里干一些农活。因为家里很穷,对教育也没有那么重视,他连小学都没上完就辍学去放牛放羊了。这也成为后来他一直耿耿于怀的事情,他不止一次对我说:“爷爷就是吃了没文化的亏,走了好多弯路,你一定一定要好好读书啊。”相比之下,外婆是家里最大的孩子,下面还有六个弟弟妹妹,但也许是太婆婆认为知识重要,所以让外婆一直读到了高中。要知道那个年代,我们县城也只有一所初高中,能读到高中是多么不容易的事。

17 岁的时候,外公服了兵役,成为一名海军通信员,在军队里开始了长达两年的军营生活,那里的日子对他后来的经历也有很大的影响。他说军队生活教会了他要有坚忍不拔的精神,要不怕困难、苦难,要保护自己想保护的人。他也曾自豪地说自己也是开过枪的人呐。在那里他结识了很多好战友,至今都时常往来。因为当过兵,外公一直是精神挺拔的样子,送我上学时还有同学以为他是我爸爸。我上大学那天一家人都送我去了学校,领了军训服之后,外公看着我头上的帽子笑着说他们以前的帽子和这个很像,拉着我穿好军训服和他合照。我看出了他眼里的怀念。

外婆高中后就进入工厂工作,她说有时工作到太晚,回家看到桌上有太爷爷放凉等第二天当早饭的稀粥,会忍不住饿偷偷喝掉。为此也受了不少太爷爷的抱怨。外婆左手食指的指甲是没有的,只有一个在别人看来有些难看的伤疤。

她说那是以前在工厂用机器的时候,一不留神把手指卷进去了。还好反应及时只削掉了半块肉,不然可能手指都不保。可是就是这样一双手养育了两代人,在外公和爸爸都出差工作时,和妈妈一起撑起了我们的家。我到十来岁因为怕黑还是和外婆一起睡觉的,小时候有段时间家里只有我们两个人,我记得每天门口信箱里的热牛奶,记得幼儿园门口来接我的身影,也记得夕阳下一起坐在家门口吃的番茄饭。

退役后,外公回到了乐清,也被分配到了当地的工厂里工作。工作不久,就被人介绍和外婆认识,没过多久他们便结婚了。到现在,每次外公出差后,给我打电话,都会说你一定要多陪陪外婆,不要让她太孤单了。

外公结婚后就分了家,那个有些小的老房子就是妈妈和舅舅长大的地方。因为外公外婆工作太忙,妈妈和舅舅小时候也常常待在太婆的家里,因为太婆家人太多,妈妈有时不得不睡在姨婆的脚下。但她说那段时光也最最快乐,有石榴树、葡萄树、桔子树等,院子里也养了一些小鸡,夏天门口下水道里还有从河里跳出来的小青蛙。

80 年代,经商的热潮开始兴起,外公也决定试一试。他去过江苏也去过上海做电器,所幸也干出了一点名堂来。妈妈说那时候我们家是全村里最早安电话和买电视的人,一到傍晚下课了,就呼朋唤友叫自己的小伙伴带着小板凳,到自家的院子里来看电视,这对妈妈来说是特别自豪的事情。

后来外公和朋友在乐清合作的公司步入了正轨,为了发展业务,开始了频繁出差,同时也积攒了一些财力,在 1996 年用了 20 万元在市区里盖了一幢五层楼的房子。这幢房子一直住到了现在,有我童年所有的回忆。妈妈在北京读完书回来在银行做了会计,后来在外公公司里遇到了年轻的爸爸,就结了婚,有了我,还有了弟弟。因为时常会去上海出差谈合作,外公便在上海也买了小房子,这样也方便。也没有想到,后来我出生后,因为从小体弱常常生病,总是在上海杭州奔波看病,上海的房子倒也派上了用场,我还记得在那里养过很多只可爱的小鸡。待我长大了点,不再常常生病,外公公司的业务也不再留在上海,就把房子卖掉了。

再后来,机缘巧合下,外公和爸爸找了人去湖南合开了矿业公司,于是爸爸便常驻在了湖南,隔几个月才会回来看看,每次待不了几天就又要走。因此,我和弟弟从小就是在妈妈和外婆身边长大的。外公继续待在乐清处理这边的事情,到了要退休的年龄,便从公司里退了休。但外公想啊,还有我还有弟弟妹妹,等我们长大需要很多东西,他还得再拼几年命。不顾家人的劝阻,这一拼,就去了遥远的新疆。那么远的地方,我们谁也没去过,谁也不知道是什么样的状况,可他还是义无反顾地去了。一去就是近十年,偶尔外婆也坐飞机去那边照顾他。

好在现在，他终于放掉了新疆那边的事情，回到了家乡，开始了晚年的生活。

外公是个闲不住的人，动不动就去杭州、湖州探望老朋友，带着外婆去好多有山有水的地方小小地旅游一下。2020年疫情的四个多月，他们俩在家最大的活动就是打麻将，两个人打四个人的麻将，可以打一整天。即使外婆总是抱怨外公输了就要赖，可还是依然乐此不疲地陪他继续玩下去。看着晚饭后躺在沙发上的两人，外公偶尔会摸摸外婆的小卷发，我也体会到了平凡的幸福就是这样的。

外公休息了下来，而爸爸还在湖南继续为了我们的生活奋斗着。爸爸说想着老了以后回乐清开个小店，和妈妈过上安安稳稳的老年生活。

"阿婆都快要70岁啦，也不知道还能陪你们多久，算算也就十几年了吧……"外婆前几天晚上突然对我说到，我心里一紧，但也没有表现出来。谁都会面对这样的事情，只是希望晚一点再晚一点，每次想到都会觉得喉咙哽住。

Wenzhou
Zheng Hanlu (Class 191, Majoring in Network and New Media)

My Grandparents

"Speaking of your grandpa, you were his favorite child in the family. When you were two months old, he held you in one hand and drove with the other hand, so you have never got carsick till now." Since I was a child, I had listened to it hundreds of times, and my grandma was never tired of mentioning it. My grandpa had always been tall and ramrod straight in my mind. He was the man that I could act up around and protected me at any time. Gradually, I saw him have more and more gray hairs, frequent backaches and knee pains. I got to realize the irreversible nature of aging. All I could do now was to accompany him as much as possible.

In the early 1950s, my grandpa was born into an ordinary family in Yueqing, Wenzhou. At that time, the economic conditions were very bad, and there were many children in the family. He had to help with farming at a very young age. His family was very poor at that time and did't pay much attention to education, so he dropped out of school to tend cattle and sheep before finishing elementary school. It became one thing that rankled him afterwards. Again and again, he said to me, "A lack of education put your grandpa at a disadvantage, and I suffered a lot. You must study hard." On the contrary, my grandma was the eldest child in the family and had six younger siblings. However, perhaps my great-grandmother knew the importance of knowledge, so my grandma was able to study in high school. You know, at that time, there was only one middle and high school in our county, so it was not easy to go to high school.

At the age of 17, my grandfather served in the military and became a naval correspondent. He had been in the army for two years. The days there also played a big role in his later experience. He said that life in the army taught him to persevere, not to be afraid of difficulties, and to protect those he wanted to protect. He was proud to say that he was the one who had fired a gun. He also met a lot of friends and army comrades there, and they still keep in touch nowadays. Having been a soldier was the reason why my grandfather was always energetic and ramrod straight. Therefore, when he sent me to school, some of my classmates would mistake him for my father. On the day I went to college, the whole family sent me to school. After receiving the military uniform, my grandfather looked at the hat on my head. He told me with a smile that their previous hats were very similar to this one. He asked me to put on the military uniform and then took a photo with me. I saw the nostalgia in his eyes.

My grandma found a job in the factory after high school. She told me that sometimes she came home from work late. When she saw the porridge that my great-grandfather cooled on the table, she was unable to stand the hunger and ate the porridge secretly which my great-grandfather had planned to eat the next morning. Thus, she was often blamed by my great-grandfather. My grandma's left index finger had no nails but a scar that looked ugly to others. She told me that when she was operating a machine, her finger was caught into the machine accidentally. Fortunately, she acted quickly so that only some flesh was cut, otherwise she would have lost the whole finger. Actually, it was with such two hands that she had raised two generations of people. When my grandfather and my father were on business trips, my grandmother, together with my mother, supported our family. When I was about ten years old, I still slept with my grandmother because I was afraid of the dark. When I was young, there were only two of us at home for some time. I remembered the hot milk in the mailbox at the door every day, the person who picked me up at the gate of the kindergarten, and the tomato rice we ate at the door in the late afternoon sun.

After retiring from the army, my grandpa returned to Yueqing and was also assigned to a local factory. Shortly after he got a job, he was introduced to my grandmother and it was not long before they got married. Up to now, every time my grandfather was away on business, he would make a phone call to ask me to spend more time accompanying my grandma and never make her feel lonely.

After my grandfather got married, he lived apart from his parents and set up his own family. It was in a small old house that my mother and my uncle grew up. Because my grandparents were extremely busy with work, my mother and my uncle often stayed at my great-grandma's house when they were young. There were so many people in my great-grandma's family that my mother sometimes had to sleep at the feet of her great-aunt. But she said that was the happiest time. Besides pomegranate trees, grape vines and orange trees, there were also some chicks in the yard. In summer, small frogs that jumped out of the river would appear in the drains near the door.

In the 1980s, the business boom was emerging, so my grandpa decided to give it a try. He had been to Jiangsu and Shanghai to sell electric appliances. Fortunately, he made some achievement. My mother said that at that time our family was the first to have a telephone and television in the village. When the class was over in the evening, she called friends to bring a small stool to watch TV in the yard. My mother felt so proud of this.

Afterwards, the company that my grandfather and his friends cooperated in Yueqing was back on track. In order to develop the new business, they started frequent business trips and also accumulated some financial resources. In 1996, they spent 200,000 yuan building a five-story house in the city. We have been living in this house till now, and it has all the memories of my childhood. My mother worked as an accountant in a bank after graduating from a school in Beijing. She met my young father later in my grandpa's company.

Then they got married. She gave birth to me and my younger brother. My grandfather often went to Shanghai to discuss business cooperation, so he bought a small house in Shanghai for convenience. Against all expecations, I was weak since I was young. I often got ill, so I always rushed about in Shanghai and Hangzhou to see a doctor. The house in Shanghai came in handy. I remembered that I had raised a lot of cute chicks there. When I got older, I was seldom ill. My grandpa's company wasn't engaged in business in Shanghai anymore, so he sold the house.

Later on, my grandpa and my father were serendipitous enough to find someone to open a mining company in Hunan Province, so my father stayed permanently in Hunan Province. My father lived in Hunan, and he would come back home every few months, but he usually stayed home no more that several days. Therefore, my younger brother and I grew up with my grandmother and mother. My grandpa continued to stay in Yueqing to deal with matters and when he reached the age of retirement, he retired from the company. But my grandpa thought that when I and my younger siblings grew up, a lot of things would be needed, so he had to work hard for a few more years. Regardless of the family's dissuasion, he went to the remote Xinjiang Uygur Autonomous Region. None of us had been to such a distant place, so no one knew what the situation was, but he still went there without hesitation. He stayed there for nearly ten years, and occasionally my grandmother would fly there to take care of him. Fortunately, now, he finally let go of things in Xinjiang, returned to his hometown, and began his later life.

My grandfather is a person who can't stay idle, so he often goes to Hangzhou and Huzhou to visit old friends, and he will take my grandma to many places with mountains and rivers for a trip. During the four-month period of COVID-19 in 2020, their main activity at home was playing mahjong. Two of them played Mahjong which should be played by four people, and they could play it for a whole day. Even though my grandmother always complained that my grandpa refused to admit his failure when he lost the game, but she would still continue to play with him happily. When I looked at the two people lying on the sofa after dinner, and my grandpa occasionally touching my grandma's curly hair, I realized that was the ordinary happiness.

Although my grandpa stopped doing business, my father continued to strive for our life in Hunan. My father said he wanted to open a small shop in Yueqing when he was old, and live a stable life with my mother for the rest of their life.

"I am about to be 70 years old, and I don't know how long I can stay with you. Maybe I only have ten years or so." My grandma suddenly said to me the other night. I felt sad suddenly, but I did not show it. No one will escape from facing it one day. What I wish is that day should not come so early. Every time I think about it, I will feel a lump in my throat.

“贴近式”采访，方显“化人”传播魅力

陈征北

“贴近式”采访，是马克思主义新闻观的“贴近生活”“贴近实际”“贴近群众”新闻工作三个贴近的最基本的观点和原则。

俞安琦同学《我的爷爷奶奶》一稿，以第一人称，记叙的是我最亲近的人——爷爷奶奶，贴近生活，通过采访爷爷奶奶，真实记录了60多年的历史跨度所发生的变化，用事实告诉受众我和我的爷爷奶奶所亲历的巨变，而这个巨变恰恰发生在中国共产党成立100年的历史长河之中……

2021年是中国共产党成立100周年，浙大宁波理工学院《行走的新闻》2021年度观察结集为《浙里是我家 ·纪念中国共产党诞辰100周年100个中国家庭故事》，新闻学院的学生用“贴近式”采访的方式，采访“我”的家庭，讲述“我”家的故事，报道接地气，亲切，真实，让读者自然而然地就融入其中……

达到新闻采访的四境界：真实、真相、真理、真情，“贴近式”采访是最好的手段。在新闻专业的本科教育阶段让学生们掌握“贴近式”采访的基本技能，加强训练，写出脚底粘泥，带着露珠，冒着热气，有真情实感的新闻作品，为日后参加工作打下坚实基础，无疑是有百利而无一害的。

新闻报道不是自娱自乐，是要感化人，感染人，是要成风化人……

新闻报道何以“成风”？又怎样“化人”？这始终是主流媒体所追求的最高境界。从“贴近式”采访入手，培养学生，浙大宁波理工学院10多年来持之以恒坚持“行走的新闻”，走出了一条新闻专业大学本科教育的新路，这也是实践性很强的新闻专业教育的必由之路，也符合党中央对新闻工作强化“脚力”的要求。

小荷才露尖尖角，尽管我们的学生的习作还略显稚嫩、青涩，但是，我觉得在以实践为重的新闻本科教育理念指引下，一定能办出一流的新闻本科教育，培养出一流的实用新闻本科人才。万丈高楼平地起，培养新闻人才从“贴近式”采访抓起，坚持下去，必将功德无量！

（浙大宁波理工学院传媒与法学院，主任记者）

故事

嘉兴

俞安琦(新闻学专业 191 班)

我的爷爷奶奶

我的爷爷奶奶住在海宁市的一个小镇上。

爷爷奶奶出生于 20 世纪 40 年代,可以说是和新中国共同成长起来的一代人。新中国成立的初期,大部分的孩子还是很难有学上的,人们普遍的教育水平都不太高,家里如果有一个上大学的孩子那可以被吹捧好久。当时,家里人得知奶奶考上了海宁师范的时候,晚餐特地多做了一份红烧肉来为她庆祝,这是她们家两个月来第一次见到新鲜的肉。

1960 年,大学毕业后没多久,爷爷就被分配去了袁花镇第二中学教珠心算,奶奶则在袁花镇花宾小学任语文及数学老师。当时的教学环境不好,工作条件也是非常艰苦。奶奶回忆起这段经历的时候是这样说的:"我在 1960 年参加工作,当时工作条件是非常艰苦的,现在的人想都不敢想。教室都是平房,而且非常矮小,学校里的人也很少。我记得那个时候我们学校一共才三个老师,只是教教最基础的语文课、数学课。一个年级只有五六个学生,条件不足就只能坐在同一间教室上课,不像现在的教学楼都是五层楼起步,条件好的还配备电梯。我们学校门前都没有操场,要上体育课只有到农田里面去找空地。我们那时候真的很苦。记得我和另外一个老师结伴从家里走到镇上的学校用了两个小时,晚上才有时间在微弱的灯光下备课。"

因为上班路途遥远,学校想办法给老师们配备了宿舍。当初刚工作的时候,爷爷任教学校的条件只够给出两间房间,分配下来是三个老师住在一间,而且一间房只有大概 13 平方米,放了床和生活用品以后已经是挤到挪不动脚步的地步了。即使是这样,放在那个时候,这种居住的条件也算是比较好了,毕竟自己家里也只有 20 平方米,还要和父亲母亲、弟弟妹妹们挤在同一个房间里睡,根本没有活动的空间。

改革开放以后,国家越发重视教育事业的发展。教育法律法规不断完善,像我爷爷奶奶这一教师群体的生活水平和地位也有了提升,最能直接体现的就是工资待遇。爷爷奶奶参加工作的时候,一个月的工资只有 25 元,第二年才上调到了27元。而这27元一个月的工资，他们整整拿了10年。当时又要养老人，还要养两个小孩，一家5口人只能挤在一个房间里。1990年以后，国家增加了教育资金的投入，爷爷奶奶的工资也慢慢地增加到了三十几元，他们的生活水平比以前有所好转。爷爷奶奶在他们工作的第30年重新分配到了一套新房。虽然仍是在教师公寓里，但是已经具备了两室一厅的条件，可以和孩子们分开住了，同时还附带一个露天的小阳台，奶奶在那里种满了花花草草，闲暇时刻可以叫朋友们小聚。家离学校只隔一条马路，大大方便了他们的上班和起居。

60年代是爷爷奶奶工作的前几年，社会普遍存在这样一个现象，大家对老师的态度不够尊重。有时老师们走过路过，学生们看见了，竟没有一个人和他们打招呼，甚至有的人会唾弃、辱骂老师。因为那个时候很多家庭都没有条件供孩子去上学，大多数人都缺乏受教育观念。每一家几乎都有四五口人，吃穿都成问题，所以很多人选择了放弃学习的机会，初中高中毕业就出去工作了，反而会认为老师们是在浪费他们赚钱养家的时间。而后来慢慢地，人们的生活条件好起来了，教育观也随之改变，人们对老师也越来越尊重，许多学生高考填报志愿都是想要做老师。

工资待遇变好了，为人们所尊重了，带来的一个非常现实的变化就是生活上变得宽裕了，爷爷奶奶的人脉变多，也带来生活上很多方便。如今已经退休的他们还能享受到各种国家给予的优质的待遇，包括经济方面和娱乐方面，比如一年两次的退休教师协会组织的小旅游。

我的奶奶一直是一个公认的尽职尽责的人，不论是作为老师还是作为母亲。在她任教期间，学生们对她的印象就是严厉。那个时候有的男同学天性顽皮，经常上课不认真听讲，甚至逃课出去打篮球，都是奶奶去把他们抓回来敦促学习，最严格的时候是罚他们抄课文100遍。直到现在，这些学生回想起来都感到有些后怕。

1988年，浙江省人民政府为了表彰人民教师的辛勤劳动，首次设置了“春蚕奖”这一奖项。这对浙江省的中小学教师来说是极高的荣誉。就在1989年，我的奶奶获得了浙江省第二届“春蚕奖”。1988年以后的5年，是奶奶教育生涯的巅峰时期。她不仅获得了嘉兴市“小学高级教师”“先进工作者”等荣誉，还将复式教育的经验带给了更多中小学的老师。

Jiaxing
Yu Anqi (Class 191, Majoring in Journalism)

My Grandparents

My grandparents live in a small town in Haining City.

My grandparents, born in the 1940s, can be said to be a generation growing up with New China. In the early days of New China, it was difficult for most children to go to school. People were generally not very well educated. If there was a university student in a family, people would boast about it for a long time. When my family learned that my grandmother had been enrolled by Haining Normal College, they made pork braised in soy sauce as a special dish for dinner to celebrate. It was the first time the family ate fresh meat in two months.

In 1960, shortly after graduating from college, my grandfather was assigned to teach Abacus Mental Calculation in No. 2 Middle School in Yuanhua Town, while my grandmother taught Chinese and Mathematics at Huabin Primary School in Yuanhua Town. The teaching environment and the working conditions were bad at that time. When recalling this experience, she said, "I started working in 1960. The working conditions were so hard that people could not imagine nowadays. The classrooms were small bungalows, and there were few people in the school. At that time, there were only three teachers in our school who only taught basic courses like Chinese and math. Unlike the current teaching buildings which have five floors or more and are equipped with elevators, there were only five or six students in a grade, so students of all grades had to learn in the same classroom when there were not enough classrooms available. There was no playground in front of our school, so we had to go to the farm to find an open space for PE classes. We suffered a lot at that time. I remembered that it took me two hours to walk from my home to the school in town with another teacher, and only when it was at night that I had time to prepare lessons under the dim light."

Because of the long distance, the school tried and finally provided dormitories for teachers. At the beginning, the school where my grandfather taught could only offer two rooms. Three teachers were assigned to live in a room whose area was only about 13 square meters. After putting in the bed and household items, the room was too crowded for people to move their feet. Even so, such living conditions could be regarded as fairly good. After all, their own house, only 20 square meters, was packed with their father, mother, younger brothers and sisters. There was no room for recreational activities.

After the reform and opening up, China attached great importance to the development of education. As the educational laws and regulations improved continually, the living standard and status of teachers like my grandparents also got elevated. Salary was the best embodiment. When my grandparents began their teaching, their monthly salary was only 25 yuan. It was raised to 27 yuan in the second year, which lasted for 10 years. With the elderly and two young children to support, the family of five had to crowd into the same room. After 1990, the government increased the investment in education funds, my grandparents' wages also increased to more than 30 yuan. Their living standard got better than before. My grandparents were offered a new house in their thirtieth year of work. Although it was still in the teachers' apartment, it had two bedrooms and one living room, so they and their children could have their own room. Meanwhile, it also had a small open-air balcony. My grandma planted flowers and grass there, and invited her friends to get together in her spare time. Their home was across the road from the school, which brought much convenience to their work and living.

In the 1960s, in the first few years of their work, there was a widespread phenomenon that people were not respectful enough towards their teachers. No students would greet their teachers when they saw their teachers pass by. Some people would disdain and abuse their teachers. Because at that time, many families were too poor to afford to send their children to school, most people didn't think it was necessary to get educated. There were four or five members in each family, and they lacked food and clothing. Therefore, many people chose to give up the opportunity to study and went out to work after graduating from middle school or high school. Consequently, they thought that the time to earn money and support their family was wasted by teachers. Gradually, people's living conditions improved, and people's views on education changed accordingly. People showed more respect to their teachers. Many students wanted to be a teacher when they filled in the application form for college admission after the national university entrance exam.

The increase of their wages and others' respect brought about a comfortable life. My grandparents made more acquaintances, which gave more convenience in life. After retirement, they could even enjoy various benefits provided by our country, including financial and recreational benefits, such as the travel organized by the Retired Teachers' Association, which they could join twice a year.

My grandmother, whether being a teacher or a mother, has always been recognized as a conscientious person. When she taught, her students had the impression that she was strict. At that time, some boys were very naughty, and often didn't study carefully in class, or even skipped class to play basketball. My grandmother always got them back and urged them to study. The most strict punishment she imposed was asking them to copy the text 100 times. Up till now, these students still feel afraid when recalling those days.

In 1988, the People's Government of Zhejiang Province set up the "Spring Silkworm Prize" for the first time in order to commend the hard work of teachers. This was the greatest honor for primary and secondary school teachers in Zhejiang. It was in 1989 that my grandma won the second "Spring Silkworm Prize of Zhejiang Province". The five years after 1988 were the peak of my grandma's educational career. She not only won honors like "Senior Primary School Teacher" and "Advanced Worker" in Jiaxing, but also brought the experience of combined instruction to more primary and secondary school teachers.

一位新时代独立女性的画像

王军伟

我非常钦佩吴思柳在《我的与众不同的妈妈》一文中所呈现的母亲形象，爱美、顾家、经济独立，乐观，甚至还有些强大。“70后”的母亲还是学生时就帮父母采茶叶；初中毕业后就开启了打工之路，从在老家的镇上当洗碗工到上杭州的四季青服装批发市场做导购员，之后就去亲戚家开的文具店当店主。店主的经历让她认识了当时开出租车的父亲并结了婚，在婚后不久生下了吴同学。在吴同学矫正眼睛的八年中，母亲给予了全部的爱：“妈妈抱着睡熟的我在凌晨三四点的寒风中等那一班开往杭州的公交车[……]妈妈为了挂到专家号，在医院门口打地铺彻夜排队”，也许是这段求医的经历使得父母感情出现了裂痕，在吴同学初二的时候两人便离婚了。在吴同学身体恢复后，母亲就决定自己独立开店开始了艰辛的创业之路。从字里行间，我们能够体会到社会与生活对离异女性的不友善，但是母亲坚韧、乐观、独立，在经历各种挫折之后依旧把生活过得有滋有味。

我认为吴同学文字中的母亲形象并不像很多电视剧中的苦难离异母亲的形象，甚至可以说是一种反媒体的离异女性呈现。吴同学也并不像很多媒介研究中的父母离异的青少年形象，文中描述母亲的文字中充满了轻松调侃的语气，同时也表达了一种正直的，以人为本的性别观念：“我不会催促她赶紧找个好男人，托付下半辈子，只愿她以后都为自己而活，做一辈子爱美的少女。”这样的母亲，可以说是新时代独立女性的一个标准画像。

（浙大宁波理工学院传媒与法学院副院长、副教授，博士）

故事
杭州
吴思柳(新闻学专业 201 专升本班)

我的与众不同的妈妈

我的妈妈出生于 1976 年,是家中长女,她还有一个小她一岁的妹妹,也就是我的阿姨。在我妈 3 岁以前,他们一家 4 口住在杭州市建德市乾潭镇罗村。

1983 年初,农村家庭联产承包责任制在全国范围内全面推广,外公外婆家也被分到了一块茶山。因此,妈妈放学后又多了一项任务——采茶叶。

1993 年妈妈在初中毕业之后就进入了社会,开始了艰苦的打工之路。起初,妈妈在小镇里一家名叫"粮油饭店"的餐厅当洗碗工,没什么技术含量,一个月 60 元,包吃住,将将够用。过了大半年,妈妈辞去了这份工作去往杭州。经历磕磕绊绊的求职之路后,在四季青一个服装店做起了导购员。看着试穿漂亮衣服的客人,妈妈的爱美之心开始萌芽。来到杭州后,工资涨到了 500 元一个月,却多了许多看不见的消费,更别提还得租房子住了。1996 年,外公告诉妈妈,在新安江有个还不错的工作,每月 300 元,并且可以住在姑姑家,这样可以省去租房子的钱,也不用早出晚归了。听到这消息,妈妈就屁颠屁颠跑了回来。两年的导购员生活已经让妈妈像个"时髦的城里人",每月发工资的第一件事,就是花它个 100 多元买最喜欢的服饰,然后剩下的 30 天,每天吃包子度日。可妈妈却乐此不疲。

又过了一年半,才 21 岁的妈妈因为贪玩又辞职回家了,在家呆了一个半月后,被外公外婆赶到了亲戚家开的家具店当店主。也就是这个时候,她认识了我当时开出租车的爸爸。车是爸爸贷款 12 万元买的二手车,在不工作时就是普通的私家车。半年之后,我妈和我的爸爸步入了婚姻的殿堂。

婚后不久,妈妈便怀了我,辞去了工作,在家安心养胎。高昂的车贷占去了爸爸绝大部分的工资。几个月后,我出生了,全家人都欢天喜地的,妈妈第一次把我抱在手上,她慈爱地看着我的眼睛,隐隐感觉有些不大对劲。大约在我一周岁时,妈妈又重新回到了家具店上班,而我也被托付给爷爷奶奶抚养。

在此期间,妈妈和爸爸会时不时来爷爷奶奶家看看我。一天妈妈看着我稚嫩的双眼,笑容却僵硬在脸上。她发现我的一个眼睛的瞳孔好似是斜的。当她把这个困惑告诉奶奶时，换来的却是责骂。直到我 4 岁上幼儿园时，老师跟我奶奶反映，我连坐到第一排的位置都看不到黑板上的字，奶奶这才着急了起来，火急火燎地告诉了我妈妈。妈妈听后，毅然决然把我带到了浙二眼科。

就这样，我开始了长达 8 年的矫正眼睛之路。我记得我戴着半包眼睛被叫“独眼侠”的日子，记得不管走到哪里都要背着矫正器的日子，记得吃热腾腾的面时，眼镜唰地一下起了雾被同学嘲笑的日子，却不记得妈妈抱着睡熟的我在凌晨三四点的寒风中等那一班开往杭州的公交车的日子，不记得妈妈为了挂到专家号，在医院门口打地铺彻夜排队的日子，也不记得妈妈因为种种压力落下晶莹的泪花却又一把袖子抹干净的日子，更不记得那时的她也不过是 26 岁的姑娘而已。

也就是那时，爸爸妈妈的感情开始逐渐破裂。

慢慢地，我长大了，身体开始变好。终于，我要上一年级了，可以由老师看管了。这时她做了一个决定——自己开店。可是开什么类型的店呢？她找爸爸商量，换来的是爸爸的反对。但我知道，妈妈一直都和很多传统的女人不一样，她是我们小镇上第一个去割双眼皮的女人，在其他人都想做而又有所顾虑时。她从来都敢于尝试新鲜事物，不怕失败。说做就做，妈妈随即开始向各种朋友打听我们小镇的大头产业以及经济形势，最终确定了开一间辅料店，向各个家纺厂供应原料。

说起最初开店的这段经历，妈妈似乎有些不愿意回忆，她皱着眉头说道：“什么都得从头开始学，什么都得自己费心。那么多线的色号、手枪针的型号、拉链的长度、剪刀的类型等等，我都得一个个熟悉直到了如指掌。还有什么搞营业执照、消防证这些都不说了。最难的还是和义乌的供货商协商。我那时候哪里懂怎么和老板谈价格啊，每次给的价格我都不满意，却又不知道怎么开口，他们可都是老手，哪里说得过他们啊！之后就是搬货了，可是交通不发达啊，我就坐那个大巴车运货，坐了一趟又一趟，才勉勉强强把这个店开起来。”说到这儿，妈妈停顿了一会儿，眉头皱得更深了：“因为没有像我这样的店的缘故，前半年生意还算不错的，大概赚了三四万吧。但这个钱是没有到手的，因为大部分的厂拿货都是先欠着，过年的时候再结清。第一次去厂里讨账的时候，我以为是坐着喝喝茶聊聊天等别人把钱拿过来，可现实却是听到了这辈子没听过的难听的脏话，且是对着我说的。真的是硬生生被骂哭了。”

“可是再委屈有什么用，怕他们第二年会不来我这里进货了，这些辱骂我也只能忍了，钱能要到就好。当然，后面遇得多了我也就有点习惯了。到现在为止大概遇到了十几个厂老板跑路了吧……哈哈哈哈。”我不懂为什么妈妈突然笑了起来，幸好她坚持下去了。在我四年级的时候，这个店终于真真正正属于她自己了。又过了两年，她偷偷在外面买了一套房产证上只有她一个人名字的排屋。

但我甚至连爸妈离婚了也不知道，还是初二的时候翻东西翻到他们的离婚证我才被迫知晓，那时的惊慌和心跳还记忆犹新。我只知道初二之后我跟妈妈搬进了新的房子，过上了没有爸爸的日子。“我们离婚了。”这句话他们至今也没有和我说过。

人生就像一杯茶，不会苦一辈子，但会苦一阵子。而我妈妈的这“一阵子”真的有些长了。一个我们小镇上有名的混混，大概是听到我妈妈恢复了单身，又长得好看会打扮，便时不时地来店里骚扰她，随之换来的只有妈妈的冷眼和不留情面的驱逐。于是恼羞成怒的混混，在无人的夜里，砸碎了店里的窗户，倒上汽油，一把火烧了妈妈辛辛苦苦经营的店。大火在破晓时被扑灭，她站在废墟前，看着自己的心血一点一点随着浓烟飘散……

妈妈从来不是一个活在过去的人，她扛着我们的“需要”又一步一步地把店重新开了起来。因为长期郁结于心，她的肺里发现了肿瘤，不过好在是良性的。生活也慢慢开始眷顾她了。术后，妈妈对事情看开了很多，不再总把眉头紧皱。如今她44岁了，我也在外面上大学，我以为偌大的房子只剩她一人，多少会有些孤单。事实是我想多了，她的单身小日子过得有滋有味，在店里和朋友聊聊天，喜欢的衣服想买便买，偶尔去美个容，出去旅个游。我不会催促她赶紧找个好男人托付下半辈子，只愿她以后都为自己而活，做一辈子爱美的少女。

Hangzhou
Wu Siliu (Class 201, Majoring in Journalism)

My Unusual Mom

Born in 1976, Mom is the eldest daughter of the family. She has a sister one year younger than her, that is, my aunt. Before my mother was 3 years old, the family of four lived in Luo Village, Qiantan Town, Jiande City, Hangzhou City.

At the beginning of 1983, the rural household contract responsibility system was promoted nationwide. A tea hill was assigned to my grandparents. Thus, Mom had one more task after school, tea picking.

After graduating from junior high school in 1993, Mom entered society and started the arduous working life. In the beginning, she worked as a dishwasher at a restaurant called "Oil and Foodstuffs Restaurant" in town. This work required no skills and provided free food and accommodation. My mom earned a monthly salary of 60 yuan, which was just enough for her to make ends meet. After more than half a year, she quit and went to Hangzhou. She met a lot of difficulties when applying for a job, and finally became a shopping guide at a clothing store in the wholesale market called Sijiqing. While looking at customers trying on beautiful clothes, Mom's love for beauty began to sprout. After she went to Hangzhou, her salary was increased to 500 yuan a month. But there were more hidden expenses, let alone the house rent. In 1996, my grandfather told her there was a good job in Xin'anjiang with a monthly salary of 300 yuan. And she could live in her aunt's house, which would not only save the house rent, but also spare her the trouble of going out early and coming back late. Mom came back happily on hearing the information. Two years of life as a shopping guide had made her a "fashionable city dweller". Once she got her salary every month, the first thing was to spend more than 100 yuan on her favorite clothes. Then she had to survive on steamed stuffed buns every day for the whole month. But she could always find pleasure in it.

After another year and a half, Mom was only 21 years old and was a good-time girl, so she quit again and went home. One month and a half later, she was the forced to work as the shopkeeper of a furniture store owned by our relatives at the request of my grandparents. It was then that she met my father who was a taxi driver. The taxi was a second-hand car bought by my dad with a loan of 120,000 yuan, which was also used as a private car when he was off work. Half a year later, my parents got married.

Soon after, Mom was pregnant and quit to nourish the fetus at home. High car loans cost most of Dad's salary. A few months later, I was born, which sent the whole family into raptures. For the first time, Mom held me in her hands and looked lovingly into my eyes, vaguely feeling something was wrong. When I was about one year old, she restarted the work in the furniture store, and I was left with my paternal grandparents.

My parents would come to visit me from time to time. One day Mom looked at my tender eyes and suddenly the smile froze on her face. She found one of my pupils seemed to squint. She told my grandmother the doubt but only got scolded in return. I started kindergarten at 4. It was when the teacher told her that I couldn't see the words on the blackboard even in the first row that she got worried. She told Mom in a hurry. At the news, Mom resolutely took me to the Department of Ophthalmology in the Second Affiliated Hospital of Zhejiang University School of Medicine.

I started the 8-year journey of vision correction. I remember the days when I was called "One-Eyed Man" with one of my eyes covered, the days when I had to carry orthotics wherever I went, and the moment when my classmates laughed because my glasses fogged up when I was eating hot noodles. But I don't remember the days when Mom held me in her arms waiting for the bus to Hangzhou in the icy wind at three or four o'clock in the morning, the days when Mom lined up all night for me to see the specialist and even slept on the floor in front of the hospital, or the days when tears were shining in her eyes for pressure but were wiped right away. Moreover, I almost forget that she was just a 26-year-old girl then.

It was then that my parents gradually broke up.

Slowly, I grew up and began to get better. Finally, I was about to begin my primary school under the care of teachers. At this time, she made a decision to open her own shop. But what kind of shop should she open? She discussed with Dad, but only received his refusal. I know that my Mom has always been different from many traditional women. She was the first woman in our town to do double eyelid operation. She has always dared to try new things with no fear of failure when others wait and see with hesitation. No sooner said than done, Mom started asking friends about the main industries and economic situation in our town. Finally, she decided to open a shop to supply raw materials to home textile factories.

Speaking of the first experience of opening the shop, Mom seemed a little unwilling to recall. She frowned and said, "You have to learn everything from scratch, and worry about everything by yourself. I had to be familiar with all the things, such as thread colors, pistol needle models, the length of zippers, the type of scissors and so on until I knew them like the back of my hand. Besides a business license and fire safety certificate, the most difficult part was to negotiate with suppliers in Yiwu. I knew nothing about how to bargain with the bosses then. And I was in a puzzle every time I wasn't satisfied with the price. I couldn't succeed because they were all past masters. The next problem was the delivery of goods. I had to take one trip after another by bus to deliver goods because of the inconvenient transportation. This was how this shop was barely opened." She paused here for a while and her frown became deeper, "Because there were few similar shops, the business in the first half of the year was pretty good with a profit of 30,000 or 40,000 yuan. But the money was not in the hand. Most of the factories took the goods first and settled the bill during the Chinese New Year. The first time I went to collect overdue payment, I had thought I was just sitting and chatting over a cup of tea and someone would bring the money. But the reality was that I heard some harsh swearwords that I had never heard in my life. And it was said to me! I was totally scolded to cry."

"But there was no use of feeling wronged. I had to bear these insults lest they wouldn't purchase my goods the next year. It was all right as long as I could get the money. Of course, I was more used to this later. So far, I have probably met a dozen factory owners who ran away. Hahaha..." I could't understand why Mom suddenly laughed. Fortunately, she kept going. When I was in the fourth grade, the shop finally really belonged to her. Two years later, she secretly bought a townhouse with her own name on the property ownership certificate.

But I didn't even know that they were divorced until I rummaged around in the house and happened to see their divorce certificate in my second year of junior high school. The panic and heartbeat then still remain fresh in my memory. All I know is that Mom and I moved into a new house and lived without Dad after that. "We're divorced." They haven't said that to me yet.

Life is like a cup of tea. It will not taste bitter for a lifetime, but it will taste bitter for a while. But "the while" for Mom is really a bit longer. A notorious rascal in our small town probably heard that Mom, who was such a beauty and knew how to dress up, was single again. He came to our shop to harass her from time to time. But all he got was her indifference and straight driving away. Ashamed into anger, he smashed the window, poured gasoline and burned the shop she had been devoted to running. The fire was put out at the break of dawn. Mom stood in front of the ruins, watching her efforts drift away with the smoke...

Mom is never the person who lives in the past. She reopened the shop step by step shouldering the family burden. Because of long-term frustration, a lung tumor was found in her body but fortunately it was benign. Life began to favor her. After the operation, she began to let go of many things and no longer frowned. Now she is 44 years old, and I am also in college away from home. I thought she would feel somewhat lonely to live alone in the huge house. The fact is just the opposite. Her single life is very enjoyable. She chats with her friends in the store, buys whatever clothes she likes, and occasionally goes to the beauty salon or goes for a trip. I will not urge her to find a good man and trust the rest of her life with him. All I hope is that she can live for herself in the future and be a girl that pursues beauty for a lifetime.

“红船精神”让日子越过越好

王军伟

提到嘉兴，很多人会想到“轻烟拂渚，微风欲来”的江南名湖之一的南湖和那艘标记了共产党最为重要时刻的游船。一方面，江南水乡嘉兴似乎承载了百年现代中国浓厚的“红色精神”。另一方面，嘉兴作为长江三角洲持续经济一体化的前沿城市之一，伴随沪苏嘉同城一体化急速发展，嘉兴城市的经济持续蓬勃发展。而这两方面在张晓宇同学《我与TA的关系》一文中体现出来。

一方面，红色精神在文中被强调和聚焦。张同学的外公年少时参加抗美援朝，家里最重要的物件之一，就是外公在抗美援朝回来后拍摄的一张照片，照片中，外公手举着一把枪，佩戴两枚勋章，英姿飒爽。而外公也成为他们家族的骄傲。张同学自己也回想每一次观望“红船”时候的激动和敬畏的心情。另一方面，张同学勾勒出三代人的变化。共产党诞生前后生人的外公外婆经历了烽火连天的抗日战争年代，贫苦的生活使得他们特别勤俭节约的习惯延续至今。而贫困同样是张同学的爷爷奶奶的生活境况。因为穷困爷爷家里的人只能带着他“去地里挖草根、割榆树皮、偷无花头（嘉兴方言）”吃；因为穷困，爷爷未能完成高中学业便辍学，因为穷困，“60”后的父亲和姑姑甚至也读不起书。而这一切在20世纪80年代，伴随着国家改革开放而渐渐改观。父母和爷爷一起做运输船的生意，慢慢地改变了家里的状况，造好了自家的房子；姑父姑姑家办起了植绒厂，生活变得越来越好。

（浙大宁波理工学院传媒与法学院副院长、副教授，博士）

故事

嘉兴

张晓宇(新闻学专业 192 班)

我与 TA 的关系

那张照片还放在桌上，因为我告诉了母亲，我写给外公的作文得到了老师的表扬，她很高兴。

照片上的男子英姿飒爽，手举着一把枪，胸前有两枚勋章，和电视里阅兵仪式上最前面的几辆车里坐着的老兵佩戴的一样。

这位年轻男子便是我的外公，照片拍摄于他抗美援朝回来后。

这张照片上其实有两位男子，我开始并没有认出我的外公。母亲 16 岁时他便去世了，就连母亲都知之甚少。在本来照片就稀有的年代，我从没有见过一张外公老年的照片，所以，他在我的印象里并不是一位和蔼可亲的老人，而是意气风发的战斗青年，而我也可以单单通过一张照片，就穿越到那个烽火连天的时代。

很多年之后的 2016 年，91 岁高龄的外婆走了，就连墓碑上的照片，也是青年时期的外公和老年时期的外婆放在一起。我的外婆应该是这个时代变化里最好的见证者吧。

外公和外婆分别出生在 1919 年和 1925 年的浙江嘉兴，正是 1921 年中国共产党诞生的一前一后。

那些日子，外公外婆到底是怎么过的，母亲不清楚。只记得外婆以前说过当时日军来了，许多人就跑到东南面的河坝那里的一处躲藏点，所有人都害怕得不得了，弯着背，低着头，蜷缩着躲在一起。

等到日军的警报过了，还是继续在地里干活，头顶上经常有飞机“轰隆隆”地飞过。

那段真实、贫苦的日子外婆从未好好提起，我却在每次去外婆家时都可以看到，不愿意装空调的房间、破旧却不舍扔掉的碗、简单的有些没营养的饭菜，还有灶台前永远在忙碌的身影。

她从来都是最后一个吃饭，等到我们都吃完了，才端出一碗隔夜菜。

母亲经常扮演坏女儿，把她的剩菜剩饭都倒掉，然后总是争执不休。外婆觉得母亲过分，然后生气地哭，母亲进退两难，坐在一边，两个人都像是做了错事的孩子，一言不发。

可是我们都知道，我们只能这么做，以希望外婆健康的名义。

这是一场上世纪中叶的习惯和21世纪舒适、富足的生活之间的争执，年轻的母亲一定会赢，可是外婆的"坏"习惯好像也没有错。从前的日子里，每个人都是这么过的，只是外婆的朋友们早她一步去了，只剩她一人孤独地生活在这一大家子人里，"偷偷摸摸"地观察这个世界巨大的变化，她跟不上了，但还可以好好看看。

那天接奶奶去城里看病，拿着奶奶的身份证，我才第一次确切地知道奶奶生于1948年7月30日，出生在新中国诞生的前夕。爷爷比奶奶大4岁，1944年生。

奶奶向我娓娓讲述了她听爷爷说起的从前事。

在爷爷的妈妈27岁时，爷爷的爸爸就走了，那个时候爷爷1岁。家里真的穷得没东西吃了，姐姐带着弟弟去地里挖草根、割榆树皮、偷无花头(嘉兴方言)，这些东西晒一晒，磨成粉都可以糊着一点点饭吃。

苦于没钱，爷爷高中未读完就辍学了。

1960年，16岁的爷爷只能跟着大人去挖泥，做瓦。可是一直在读书的爷爷怎么会精通农活呢，老是被人欺负，也没人愿意带着他。

1965年17岁的奶奶就嫁过来了，想来前几年辍学的遗憾，爷爷一定时常跟奶奶提起。

可是读不起书的窘境还是发生在姑姑和爸爸身上。

其实家里的情况，在奶奶嫁过来之后有了一点点改善。爷爷脾气好，在大队里总被人欺负，很多好的活轮不上，就没有工分，更没有收入。奶奶的暴脾气是忍不了的，和那些欺负我们的人吵架是经常的事，就这样，慢慢地没人敢欺负我们了，队里发下来的活也多了一点。

1967年姑姑出生，1969年爸爸出生，家里的负担又重了很多。

奶奶说她愿意嫁过来，其实是看到爷爷提着一篮子番薯。只是一篮子番薯，在当时就已经是稀罕物了。当时奶奶和爷爷的定情礼是一块新手帕，里面裹了3个大饼。

其实奶奶还略带嘲笑地跟我说了一件事，她结婚前几天，爷爷的几个表兄弟凑了钱给奶奶做了一件20块钱的毛呢大衣送了过去，爷爷听说这件事气得晕了过去，在床上躺了好几天。作为家里最大男丁的爷爷，看到家里的米缸，再看看几十块钱的衣服，当然生气，毕竟自己的婚服不过是一身找邻居借来的中山装。

到了80年代，我家倒是先盖起了砖制的水泥房，只是4400元的建房子花销又让家庭经济陷入低迷。那天运砖石，奶奶和爸爸各在一艘租来的机船上，一直开到杭州，去山上的烧砖厂运回来。那些造房子的钱是爷爷奶奶每天一点点省吃俭用辛辛苦苦攒下来的。

过了没几年，队里开始包产到户了，我家 2 亩多一点的地，每年要交 1000 斤稻谷，烧瓦也没有停下来。爷爷奶奶拼命地忙农活、做生产队的工作，总算把房子的债还上，还有一点钱，留给爸爸结婚用。家里的条件是在 80 年代承包制实行之后有了很好的改善。

妈妈嫁过来是 1991 年，爸爸和爷爷已经在开船了。没过多久，妈妈也上了船，帮爸爸一起做运送废铁的生意。历经十多年的勤勤恳恳，爸爸妈妈攒下了不少的钱，房子又造了更高更大的。

本世纪初，我出生的时候，虽然刚造好房子，爷爷又正在生病，但家里好歹有了些钱，也造了好的房子。姑父姑姑家办起了植绒厂，一家人的生活状况有了很好的改善。比起我的外公、外婆和爷爷、奶奶，我长大的道路上再没有经历过这些，也从来没见过草根、树皮这些爷爷小时候拼命寻找的吃食。

可我又怎么会和那个时代没有一点关系呢。中国共产党的青年时期，也是外公外婆的青年；新中国的青年是爷爷奶奶的青年；爸爸妈妈的青年，正逢改革开放、家庭联产承包责任制的初期阶段，党的百年历程伴随着每一代千千万万普通百姓的成长。

是外公外婆和爷爷奶奶的那个时代、那些经历成就了现在的我们，给了我们不断向前的动力。

我站在我高中教学楼的 2 楼，透过树的间隙，望向这艘百年前的船——南湖红船。它当年不过是一艘普普通通的游船，我曾经也不过是一个普普通通的考生。

高三时去楼梯那儿站一会儿，望一望静静的湖面和船，有时守一守落日，压力也可以减小一点点。或许我已经知道为何虽是黄昏却满眼尽是希望了。我脚下踩的，是我的长辈们不敢企及的高中时代，正走向我憧憬的大学；放眼望去的，是中华民族的信仰，诞生于嘉兴南湖的中国共产党正带着她的人民走向辉煌的未来。

我们都充满希望。

Jiaxing
Zhang Xiaoyu (Class 192, Majoring in Journalism)

My Relationship with Them

That photograph was still on the table because I told my mother that the composition I wrote to my maternal grandfather had been highly praised by my teacher and she was very pleased.

The man in the photograph, holding a gun in his hand and wearing two medals on his chest, looked valiant and heroic. His medals were the same as those worn by the veterans who sat in the first several vehicles in the military parade on television.

This young man is my maternal grandfather. The picture was taken after he triumphantly returned from the War to Resist U. S. Aggression and Aid Korea.

Actually, there are two men in this picture. I did not recognize my maternal grandfather at my first glance. He passed away when my mother was 16, so my mother knew little about him. I had never seen a picture of him in old age during those days when photographs were very rare. Therefore, in my impression, my maternal grandfather was an energetic soldier rather than an amiable old man. Furthermore, I can also travel through this single photo back to that era when the flames of war raged everywhere.

After many years, in 2016, my maternal grandmother also passed away in peace at the age of 91. On the gravestone were my grandpa's photo in his youth and my grandma's in her old age. My maternal grandmother must be one of the best witnesses to this changing era.

My maternal grandparents were born in Jiaxing in 1919 and 1925 respectively, and the birth year of the Communist Party of China, which was 1921, was just in between.

My mother has no clue as to how my grandparents pulled through those old days. All she has remembered is that my maternal grandmother once said when the Japanese troops came into the village, many villagers ran to a hiding place in the river dam in the southeast of the village. Everyone was too frightened to raise their heads or stand up; they just hunched over and huddled together.

However, once the alert for Japanese troops was over, those villagers would continue their farm work, often with aircrafts rumbling overhead.

My maternal grandmother never mentioned much about the poor and bitter life, but I was able to see through during each visit to her home. Because she was unwilling to install an air conditioner in her room; she was reluctant to throw away those old and broken bowls; she ate those foods that are too simple to be nutritious; she was always busy in front of the stove.

She was always the last person to eat. She waited until every one of us finished our dishes and then took out a bowl of leftovers from yesterday to eat.

My mother often played the part of a bad daughter and dumped all her leftovers, triggering constant arguments. My grandmother thought what my mother had done was too much and burst into tears out of anger while my mother sat aside in a dilemma. They sat without a word, acting like two kids who had done something wrong.

We all knew, however, that we had no choice but to do it in this way for her health.

That was a battle between habits from the middle of the last century and a comfortable and abundant life in the 21st century. We knew that my young mother was bound to win, but it seemed that my grandmother's "bad" habits were reasonable. Everyone coming from those old days lived their lives in that way. The only problem is that her bosom friends have all gone away a step earlier than her, leaving her alone to live in this big family and to "furtively" take a glimpse at those great changes in the world. She may be too old to keep up but was still able to have a good look at this world.

One day, I picked up my paternal grandmother to see a doctor downtown. Holding her ID card, I just knew for the first time that she was born on July 30th, 1948, shortly after the birth of New China. Born in 1944, my paternal grandfather was four years older than her.

She told to me the old story she had heard from my grandfather.

My grandfather's father died when his mother was only 27 years old but my grandfather was only one year old. At that time, the family was really too poor to have anything to eat. The elder sister took her little brother to dig out grassroots in the field, to cut elm bark and to steal the "wu hua tou" (the seedpod of the lotus in Jiaxing dialect). They exposed these things to the sunlight and ground into powder to eat.

My grandfather did not finish his high school. He dropped out of school due to the lack of money.

In 1960, my grandfather, a 16-year-old boy, had no choice but to dig dirt and make tiles with adults. The problem was that he had always been in school before and was not proficient in farm work then, so he was always bullied by others and no one wanted to teach him skills.

In 1965, my grandmother married him at the age of 18. I think he must have often mentioned to her his regret of dropping out a few years ago.

However, the dilemma of being unable to afford to go to school happened to my aunt and my father once again.

Frankly speaking, situations in the family had improved a little bit since my grandparents got married. My grandfather was good-tempered, so he always got bullied in the brigade. There was no chance for him to get good jobs, so it was impossible to earn work points, let alone the income. On the contrary, my grandmother was bad-tempered and could not stand it. Therefore, it was quite common that my grandmother quarreled with those who bullied us. Gradually, no one dared to bully us, and we could get more work from the brigade too.

With my aunt's birth in 1967 and then my father's in 1969, the burden on the family grew much heavier.

My grandmother told me the reason why she was willing to marry my grandfather was that she saw him carrying a basket of sweet potatoes. Although it was just a basket of sweet potatoes, those things were quite rare then. At that time, my grandfather gave my grandmother a new handkerchief as their love token, in which three big pancakes were wrapped up.

In fact, she also told me a story teasingly. A few days before her wedding, several cousins of my grandpa all scraped together enough money to make her a woolen coat which cost 20 yuan and then sent it to her. Upon hearing about this "big issue", my grandpa fainted away with anger, and lay in bed for days. As the oldest male laborer in the family, my grandfather had good reason to be angry after checking the rice jar and looking at the clothes that was worth dozens of yuan. His own wedding outfit was a Chinese tunic suit borrowed from a neighbor, after all.

By the 1980s, my family had become one of the first in the village to build a brick and cement house, but a building expenditure of 4,400 yuan once again plunged the family economy into a slump. On the day of transporting bricks and stones, my grandmother and my father each took a chartered motor vessel to Hangzhou for the bricks and stones at a brick factory on a mountain. The money for building the house was saved penny by penny by my grandparents every day.

After a few years, the production brigade began to contract output quotas to households. My family had a little more than 2 mu (about 1333 square meters) of land and we needed to hand in 1000 jin (500 kilograms) of rice each year from the land, but they did not stop making tiles. They worked hard on farming and the affairs in the brigade, and finally paid off the debt we owed on the house. There was a little money left for my father's marriage. It was in the 1980s when the household contract responsibility system was carried out that the situation in my family was greatly improved.

My father and my grandfather had already been sailing the boat when my mother married into this family in 1991. My mother also got on the boat before long and helped my father to run the business of transporting the scrap iron. After over a dozen years of hard work, my parents saved plenty of money to build a taller and bigger house.

At the beginning of this century when I was born, although my family had just a new house and my grandfather was ill, we had some savings and a nice house. My aunt and her husband also established their flocking factory, and the living conditions of my whole family were improved significantly. Compared with my paternal grandparents and maternal grandparents, I have never experienced those hardships when I was growing up, nor have I ever seen such foods as grass roots and bark that my grandfather desperately sought for in his childhood.

However, how is it possible that I'm not involved with that era? The youth of the Communist Party of China witnessed the youth of my maternal grandparents; the youth of New China witnessed the youth of my grandparents; the youth of my parents was in the early stage of the reform and opening up and the household contract responsibility system; the Communist Party of China's century-old course has been accompanied by the growth of millions of ordinary people in each generation.

It is the times and experiences of my paternal and maternal grandparents that make us who we are now and motivate us to move forward.

Standing on the second floor of my high school building, I was looking through those trees at this century-old boat, Nanhu Red Boat. It was just an ordinary cruise boat that year, and I was just an ordinary student, too.

When I was in the twelfth grade, I would go and stand for a while on the stairs. I looked at that quiet lake and the boat; sometimes, I would also watch the sunset so that I could get relief from the stress for a little bit. Maybe I already figured out why my eyes were full of hope although it was dusk then. I was studying in a high school which none of my elders had dared to dream of, and I was heading for my dream university. I was looking at the faith of the Chinese nation. The Communist Party of China born in the South Lake of Jiaxing is always guiding her people towards their glorious future.

We are full of hope.

新的传奇将如何续写?

孙祥生

习近平总书记在2018年新年贺词中有一句话,“幸福都是奋斗出来的”。改革开放40年,中国发生了翻天覆地的变化,取得了举世瞩目的成就,一跃成为世界第二大经济体。这一奇迹的背后,是亿万中国人共同奋斗的结果,是每一个勤劳、智慧、坚韧的中国人在追求幸福生活的过程中用自己的双手一点一点创造出来的。对于中国社会40年的巨大变迁,无论是当代中国史还是马克思主义政治教育,更多是通过宏大历史叙事,讲述国家重大事件与发展成就,这些内容对于00后这一代,较多停留在书本层面,还缺乏切身的体会与感受。

衢州的张淼《我住过的五个家》通过住房讲述家的变迁,展示了老一辈人用自己的汗水与奋斗创造幸福生活的艰辛历程,这何尝不是一部传奇?“100个中国家庭故事”活动是一堂生动的爱国主义教育课,让新生代的年轻人知道现在的一切来之不易,备加珍惜今天美好的生活,不负韶华,在中华民族伟大复兴的道路上勇敢担负起他们这一代人的使命与责任。正如作者所言,“40年间经济发展水平的提高,给我们这样一个平凡的家庭带来的变化是显而易见的,我住过的五间房子就是最好的证明。”每一个新生代年轻人应当和他们先辈一样,用汗水和热血铸就中华民族伟大复兴新的篇章,去书写新的平凡传奇。

(浙大宁波理工学院传媒与法学院副教授,博士)

故事

衢州

张森(网络与新媒体专业 193 班)

我住过的五个家

我的妈妈于 1978 年出生于浙江省衢州市龙游县的一个小乡村。

外婆外公家的房子是砂石房,一直陪伴外公外婆一家人走过了风雨飘摇的 40 年,因为实在是太久了,被鉴定为危房,2020 年 4 月才决定拆掉建一栋新的房子。

1995 年,妈妈读完初中后不再上学,开始了外出打工的生活。1996 年,妈妈到镇上的供销社当营业员,当时一个月的工资是一百多块。在供销社工作了两年之后,妈妈想去城市找一份更好的工作。于是在 1998 年,妈妈只身一人去到上海,找了一份餐厅服务员的工作。但在大城市,没有知识文凭是绝对找不到好工作的,加上妈妈年纪轻轻,一个人离家太远外婆并不放心。妈妈在上海工作了一年后就回到原来的县城,选择从事了就业门槛相对较低的服务行业。

就在妈妈单身独自打拼的时光里,她与爸爸相遇并且相恋。爸爸也是本地人,不是很有文化,家境也不算特别富裕,爷爷是一名教师,奶奶则在家里务农。1999 年,他们结婚了。结婚时,爸爸也是用汽车把穿着婚纱的妈妈从娘家接到婆家,并且办了酒席。当时爸爸家里给的彩礼是最经典的“家电套装”和“三金”,即彩电、冰箱、洗衣机、影碟机和金项链、金手镯、金戒指。这些嫁妆在当时算是很标准的嫁妆了。在那之后,妈妈与爸爸一同在城里打拼,虽然漂泊,但起码妈妈不是一个人无依无靠了。

2001 年 7 月,我出生了。2002 年 4 月,爸爸妈妈外出打工,年仅 9 个月的我开始跟随外婆生活,爸爸妈妈则去了建德新安江的工地里工作。

第一个家——2004 年,在乡下上了一段时间的幼儿园后,妈妈坚持要送我去县里上幼儿园,于是费了很大的劲把我送进了县里的一个公办幼儿园。同年,妈妈找到了一份在化妆品店里的工作,爸爸则凭借出色的厨艺,在饭馆里当上了厨师,两个人都找到了稳定的工作。在我上幼儿园前,他们在一个小区租了一间房子,那个房子不大,两室一厅一卫一厨。那是我在县城的第一个家,不算很大,但很温馨。但好景不长,2006 年时,爸爸妈妈感情破裂,两个人离了婚。当时的我还太小，并不知道这件事，爸爸妈妈打算先瞒着我，等我上了小学稳定了再说。2007年，我就读了小区旁边的一所公办小学，因为农村户籍，当时还交了一笔“赞助费”。上了小学后，爸爸搬了出去，妈妈开始一个人抚养我。

第二个家——2007年年末，我们搬家了。妈妈为了让我上学方便，没有选择离学校远的房子，而是租了一个车库，说白了那其实就是一个地下室。只有一个很小的窗户，很黑，也有很多蟑螂，没有一件家具，卧室就是隔出来的一个小空间，我们搬进去的东西只有一张床、一张桌子和一台妈妈结婚时的电视机。但那是我和妈妈的家，妈妈在化妆品店一个月的收入只有七八百元，不仅要生活，还要抚养我，我们的日子过得很拮据。但是我还是记得，妈妈会和我一起做盐水泡鸡蛋的实验，会给我准备圣诞礼物，没有吃不饱穿不暖，我并没有觉得我们过得多不好。2009年，为了让我过上更好的生活，妈妈离开化妆品店，去了商场里当销售员，工资稍微多了一些，一个月能有2000多元。妈妈不再愿意让我住在阴暗的地下室，我们又搬家了。

第三个家——妈妈在之前的小区租了一室一厅的房子，那是我的第三个家。在我的小学期间，我都是自己走路上下学，从不要妈妈接送，但我其实很黏妈妈，要是上晚班，我就会去商场里找她。没多久，妈妈认识了从四川到浙江工作的叔叔，也就是我现在的爸爸。当时爸爸的工作也不是非常的稳定，但每个月的工资能有1万元左右，这对于我们家来说，无疑是雪中送炭。2012年，爸爸买了一辆奇瑞汽车，我们日常的出行不再是问题。2013年，妈妈决定了与爸爸结婚，组建一个新的家庭。同年，我从小学毕业，我们也再一次选择搬家。

第四个家——我们搬到了一个靠近县中心的老小区，两室一厅一卫，进入青春期的我也第一次拥有了属于自己的房间。妈妈在商场里工作一段时间后，商场的就业氛围让妈妈很有压力，爸爸就不再让妈妈去工作，从此，妈妈就再也没有工作过了。好在爸爸从原来的公司跳槽去了上海的公司，作为浙江省的销售经理，爸爸每月的工资比原来多了一倍，那时的生活过得比较宽裕，家里也有了一些小积蓄。

2015年，爸爸把奇瑞卖掉买了一辆奇亚越野车，同年，家里买了第一件奢侈的数码产品iPad Air 2。初中入学时我的学习成绩并不算很好，因为就读的初中并不是最好的，是那种名声很差的学校。后来觉得自己不能再堕落下去，想到妈妈之前一个人带我非常的辛苦，决心要好好念书，不辜负妈妈的期望。初二升初三，我的成绩有了巨大的进步。在校期间我全身心投入到学习中，成绩也已经稳定在年级前20名，我的目标是考上县里最好的重点高中。

第五个家——2015年底，妈妈怀上了妹妹，考虑到我要毕业和妹妹要出生，妈妈开始物色，准备买房子。那时候外婆把她打零工的积蓄拿出一部分资助我们，妈妈看了我们现在的家之后，就决定要买下这套房子，小区离我想去的高中也很近，当天妈妈就付了首付，在这个小县城我们终于有了自己的一栋房子。

2016 年 3 月，妹妹出生了。家里虽然多了一大笔开销，但是多了一个小宝贝也多了一份幸福。2016 年 6 月，我正常发挥顺利地考上了县里的重点高中，妈妈说那是“双喜临门”。

2016 年到现在，我们家虽然说不上富裕，但也达到了小康的水平。五次搬家，五间房子，家里的生活条件也慢慢变好。我们家除了生活必需品也出现了一些高档奢侈品，爸爸妈妈对妹妹也是有求必应，我们还经常出远门去拜访在四川的爷爷奶奶。外公外婆在乡下的老房子现在也拆了，正在建一栋新的楼房。40 年间经济发展水平的提高，给我们这样一个平凡的家庭带来的变化是显而易见的，我住过的五间房子就是最好的证明。

Quzhou

Zhang Miao (Class 193, Majoring in Network and New Media)

Five Houses I've Lived in

My mother was born in 1978 in a small village in Longyou County, Quzhou City, Zhejiang Province.

The house of my maternal grandparents, which was made of sandstone, had accompanied the whole family through the turbulent 40 years. It was condemned as unfit to live in any more, because it was too old. It was not until April of 2020 that the decision was made to tear it down to build a new house.

In 1995, after finishing middle school, my mother quit school and began to work outside. In 1996, she worked as a salesgirl at a supply and marketing cooperative in the town, earning more than 100 yuan a month. After working there for two years, my mother wanted to go to the city to find a better job. Therefore, in 1998, she went to Shanghai alone and worked there as a waitress. However, in such a big city, a person without knowledge and a diploma was absolutely unable to find a good job. In addition, my mother was young, so my maternal grandmother was worried about her living far away from home alone. She returned to the county after working in Shanghai for a year, and then found a job in the service industry which had relatively low requirements for employees.

When my mother was single and struggled while a living alone, she met and fell in love with my father. My father was also a local. He received little education, and his family wasn't rich. My paternal grandpa was a teacher, and my paternal grandma was a farmer. My parents got married in 1999. On their wedding day, my father picked up my mother dressed in her wedding gown from her home in a car to his home, and my father held a wedding banquet. At that time, the dowries that my father gave to my mother's family were the so-called typical "household electrical appliance set" and "three pieces gold of jewelry"—a color TV, a refrigerator, a washing machine, a DVD player, a gold necklace, gold bracelet and a gold ring. These were standard dowries at that time. After getting married, my parents worked together in the city. Although drifting around in the city, my mother was no longer alone and helpless.

I was born in July 2001. In April 2002, my parents went out to work. They found a job at a construction site in Xin'anjiang, Jiande City, so I began to live with my maternal grandmother when I was only 9 months old.

The first house—In 2004, after spending some time in a rural kindergarten, my mother insisted on sending me to a county kindergarten, so with great difficulty I was sent to a county kindergarten. In the same year, my mother got a job in a cosmetics store, and my father became a cook in a restaurant because of his excellent cooking skills. Both of them found a stable job. Before I went to the kindergarten, they rented a house in a community, which was small with two bedrooms, one living room, one bathroom and one kitchen. Not big but quite cozy, it was my first home in the county. However, good things didn't last long. In 2006, my parents broke up and divorced. At that time, I was too young to know this, and they planned to hide the truth from me until I was in primary school when everything settled down. In 2007, I went to a public primary school next to my community. My parents paid a "sponsorship fee" due to my rural resident status. After that, my father moved out and my mother began to raise me alone.

The second house—Late 2007, we moved house. To make it convenient for me to go to school, my mother did not choose a house far away from the school; instead, she rented a garage, which was actually a basement. It was very dark there. There was not a single piece of furniture but one small window. Lots of cockroaches could be seen everywhere, and the bedroom was actually little space created by partitioning the basement. The only things we moved into the basement were a bed, a table and a TV set which was my mother's dowry before. But that was the home of my mother and me. My mother's salary in the cosmetics shop was only about 700 or 800 yuan a month, which she used not only for living, but also bringing me up, so we really lived on the breadline. However, I remembered that she would do the experiment with me during which we soaked eggs in salt water, and she would prepare Christmas presents for me. There was no lack of food and clothes, and I didn't think we had a bad life. In 2009, in order to create a better life, my mother left the cosmetics store and worked as a saleswoman in a shopping mall. Her salary, more than 2,000 yuan a month, was slightly higher. She didn't want to see me living in the dark basement any more, so we moved again.

The third house—My mom rented a house with a bedroom and a living room in the community we had lived before and that was our third home. When I was in primary school, I walked to and from school on my own, never asking my mother to pick me up, but actually I was very clingy to her. So every time she worked on night shift, I would go to the mall to stay with her. Before long, my mother met a man who came from Sichuan and worked in Zhejiang. He became my stepfather afterwards. At that time, his job was not very stable, however, the monthly salary could reach about 10,000 yuan, which was undoubtedly a timely help to our family. In 2012, he bought a Chery car, so our daily traveling was no longer a problem. In 2013, my mother decided to marry him and start a new family. The same year I graduated from primary school, and we moved again.

The fourth house—We moved to an apartment in an old neighborhood near the center of the county. It had two bedrooms, a living room and a bathroom. This is the first time that I had my own room when I was in my early adolescence. My mother worked in the mall for a period of time. She felt pressed when working in the competitive atmosphere, so my father didn't let her work any more. From then on, my mother stopped working outside. Fortunately, my father switched to another company in Shanghai from the previous company. As the sales manager in Zhejiang Province, my father's monthly salary was twice as much as before. Therefore, we lived a relatively comfortable life and had some savings.

In 2015, my father sold the Chery and bought a Kia SUV. In the same year, we owned our first luxury digital product —an iPad Air 2. When I entered middle school, I was a poor performer at school. That was because the school I attended was not the best, but that kind of school with a bad reputation. Later I realized that I should not be like this anymore. Thinking of the hardship that my mother experienced to raise me in the past on her own, I was determined to study hard so as to live up to her expectations. Thus, my grades in Grade Eight and Grade Nine went up. I devoted myself to my study in school, and I was always among the top 20 in my grade. I set a goal that I must be admitted to the best key high school in the county.

The fifth house—At the end of 2015, my mother was pregnant with my sister. Considering that I was going to graduate and my sister was about to be born, my mother decided to buy a new house, so she began to look for a house. At that time, my maternal grandmother took out part of her savings she gained from part-time jobs to support us. After seeing the house which we are living in now, my mother made the decision to buy it. The community where the new house was located was also close to the high school I wanted to go to. And she paid the down payment on that day immediately, and we finally had a house of our own in this small county.

In March 2016, my younger sister was born. Although her birth meant more expense to our family, but having a lovely baby also brought a lot of happiness. In June 2016, I was successfully admitted to a key high school in the county. My mother said it was a "double blessing".

From 2016 to now, our family, though by no means rich, has achieved a well-off level. We moved five times, and lived in five different houses. The living conditions of the family are gradually getting better. In addition to the daily necessities of life, our family also have some high-end luxuries. My parents also grant whatever is requested by my little sister. And we often go to visit my paternal grandparents in Sichuan Province. What's more, my maternal grandparents' old house in the country has been torn down and a new building is being built. The economic development of the past 40 years has made a significant difference to our ordinary family, and the five houses I have lived in are the best proof.

“流动”与“悬浮”中的心灵处所

徐　静

在城乡二元结构尚未完全破除之前，流动依然是当代中国人的常态。“老刘”一家是一种典型的样本，从吉安的乡村到都市杭州，再从杭州返乡创业，抛妻别子、辗转反侧，以及颠沛流离。流动是为了家人更好地生活，流动也难免造成亲情的缺憾与伤痛。但这就是一个实在的充满悖论的框架，成为一条试图突破身份、认同、阶层桎梏的引线，也是另一种枷锁。牛津大学人类学家项飙提出了“悬浮”的概念。所谓“悬浮”，指的就是“所有人都在追求一个更好的明天，更好的明天具体是什么样的，他们并不清楚，但可以肯定的是，今天的生活是不太值得过的，所以要对现在进行否定，因此无法真正介入到现实中去。”项飙的观点略带悲观色彩，但“悬浮”心态也的确是当下中国大多数群体所面临的困境，是来自人类学一种充满悲悯情怀的真切观照。或者也可以理解为一种挣扎。

但是，人又是有能动性的个体。人一直没有放弃对自我的追问，对人性解放的追求以及对终极幸福、生命体验的追索。即使社会性的身体被约束，也要让心灵去旅行。“小刘”关于父亲创业史的白描充满天然的对父辈的崇拜，父亲不仅是传统意义上的“顶梁柱”，更是少年入世的精神导师。而对个人生活史的刻画以及两个“家乡”的描摹，则是一个热切的青年观察者孜孜探索自我的生动写照。我们终其一生，都在尝试去认同环境，认同群体，最终实现自我认同。“家乡”作为空间实体，早已不再是传统观念中“落叶归根”的那个乌托邦载体。父亲、母亲、家人以及自我才是心灵值得托付的“家乡”。

“流动”是常态，是实然。“悬浮”是异化，是反噬。前者是个体被时代裹挟的表征，是逃不脱的网。后者是造成我们焦虑、苦痛甚至苦难的渊薮。那么，“应然”是什么？以及在“流动”和“悬浮”双重夹击之下，如何找到“应然”？特别是大众自媒体众声喧哗、杂乱纷扰不堪的时代，我们如何找回自己？对我来说，开出“药方”实在是一件困难的事情，因为我也深处漩涡之中，也是一个“流动者”“悬浮人”。如果非得给出一些“土方子”，我则认为，阅读、书写与旅行大约是可能有效的“非处方药”。

我也算是看着“行走的新闻”长大的，历经十余载，引导数千理工学子一直行走在新闻理想的大道上，走在既仰望星空又俯视大地的田野上。这是极其有益的、有机的、生态的、生命的教学体验。尽管身在“他乡”，我依然能感受诗人老剑的痴情、热情、激情。“侣行”、行摄、诗唱……他不曾停留的体验方式是我生活的导师。他就是一个摆脱“悬浮”，走向生活本真的榜样。

（宁波工程学院副教授，博士）

故事

杭州

刘玫（新闻学专业202专升本班）

吾心安处是家乡

家是出生起就携带的辣的味道。

时间追溯回1999年，小刘出生了，在江西南部的农村——吉安市吉水县上。不久后，她就被老刘带到了杭州。小刘待在老家的时间屈指可数，但不论多远，都没有忘记故乡。

很多时间我觉得我已经习惯了在杭州的生活，酸甜的食物、养生的凉茶已经成为我的日常，外婆家、奶茶店，休息的时候和朋友约个下午茶，也都早就刻印进我的生活里。可是，哪怕它们贯穿着我生活中的点滴，骨子里的家乡是不会忘记的。

在吉安的街上顺着风飘来的是泥土的味道，空气中是剁辣椒的酸味和酒酿的甜味。在街边小巷里，孩童、瓜果、虫蝇和犬吠，足以撑起一个夏天的记忆。到了饭点，是家家户户起锅烧油的菜籽油烟味和辣椒味……

90年代的江西农村，家家户户都是个体承包土地，以解决温饱问题。我父亲是80年代的大学生，他知道只有走出去，才能见识更广阔的世界。于是，老刘决定去那个繁华而又经济快速发展的地方：浙江杭州。

那个时候的杭州工厂制衣生意很兴旺。父亲拿出多年的积蓄，办了一家制衣后道加工厂。父亲至今仍能清楚地记得那段时间的辛苦与劳碌。当时大功率设备只有6台，工人也大多是同村的村民，彻夜加工是再寻常不过的事。再加上照顾刚出世的小刘，恨不得一天掰成 48 个小时用。

“苦日子总是能熬出头。”

每年春节过后的三四月份，都是招工旺季。满大街都是招工牌，街道上人流攒动。2000 年时我家在杭州的定海村，说来也是巧，我父亲名为水清，“定海”这个村名似乎寓意着让父亲在此安家立业。

这里聚集了大大小小的制衣厂，形成了杭州 20 年来成衣制造与后道加工的缩影。父亲确定了自己的主营方向，用真诚细心的态度积累客户，同时还要留住工人和提升机器设备，每一项决策，都要做好不赚钱的打算。经营意识、管理组织、生产管理，每一次适应也是在创新。平稳运转的制衣加工厂背后，凝聚着父亲的辛勤付出。

在村里的人纷纷效仿我父亲时，在后道加工厂势头正好时，他却毅然决定去帮朋友的忙：回江西老家管理一家工厂。那时我家在杭州已有车有房，我也将从小学毕业。

一切似乎都走在了正轨上，但父亲作为火车头，却转向另一条轨迹。

6 月对中国的孩子是特殊的，中考、高考、毕业，成年前的所有转折点都发生在夏天。对我来说，6 月还象征着离别。无处可藏的炙热意味着过往的终结和新生活的开启，逼迫着对成熟毫无心理准备的我往前走。

2011 年 6 月，父亲母亲把刚工作不久的哥哥和我留在了杭州，他们又踏上了征程。

在我的成长过程中，长兄如父是对我最好的诠释。他长我 10 岁，我敬兄长，我怕兄长，我也爱兄长。跌跌撞撞地，我初中毕业了。

这个时候，父亲还是像以前一样忙碌，一周和我通一次电话。寒暑假是我唯一能和父母团聚的日子。在这珍贵的两个月里，我总是跟在他们身后走走转转，父亲主外，母亲主内。在父亲的身影背后，这个工厂终于在我的眼里有了雏形。

这个工厂主要是制砖。每天会有无数的大卡车载着煤驶进，卸下煤后，又载着一车砖驶出。2011 年，吉安市大部分人家过上了小康之家的生活，家家户户拿出积蓄来盖房子，要盖房子，就要有砖，这就导致了市场供不应求。砖厂的原料以及工艺注定砖厂厂址只能选在偏僻的地方。于是父亲每天 6 点半就要起床，7 点去上班。而与此同时，厂里已经运行了几个小时，这就意味着工人们至少 4 点就要起床开始工作。

“这算什么辛苦，一开始才是最辛苦的。”父亲看着我说，“人生哪有顺风顺水的。”他严格规范建厂，落实好各项环保措施，同时还要将工厂分为几块管理，其中最重要的是砖机生产和销售及日常管理。进机必须做好安全措施，进出的卡车进行严格管控，安装在线监测设备，等到天气不好还需要错峰生产或者干脆停机一天。

时光是一条大河，不管你有没有准备好，都裹挟着我们朝前走。我刚合上六年级的书本，下一瞬，翻开的是高三的课本。这一年，2017。

也正是2017年，江西省政府的环境保护文件下来了，父亲身为党员，积极响应政府号召，关闭了工厂，至今也没开过。除了环境保护文件，一同下达的，还有村庄建设文件，江西开始建设村庄规划编制试点工作。父亲又动了心，他也确实这么做了。又一次，父亲踏上新的征程，直到现在，他也在建设我们家乡的村庄。

今年年初，我时隔多年回了这个故地。村子通了公路，家家户户装了网络，各式复楼、小洋房平地而起，不仅如此，田野的一部分改成了大型停车场，许多年轻人也回来了，老人脸上终于有了笑容。

这3年，我一直在外上学，这期间父亲对村庄付出的辛苦不言而喻。我无从提问也无从下笔，无论以什么语言都无法写出这份不为人知的辛酸经历。

对我来说，江西的吉安，不仅是家乡的意思，还是父母在的地方，是我的避风港。它没有杭州的一块地那么值钱，但却是我心脏跳动的动力。街上的车都是赣D，有天虹、星巴克、海底捞，这里不是很繁华，但是我的牵挂都在这里。

我从小就很崇拜我父亲，相隔两地让我在这份崇拜中又多了几分敬畏。父亲总是脚步匆匆，电话响个不停，他忙着浇灌事业的饥渴。他让自己像是敞开的桶子，随时准备装入更多、更多。他总是觉得时间太短。父亲的脑子里总是有许多想法，日积月累，他拥有了更广阔的视野、更深邃的思想。身处这样一个浮躁的时代，能坚持自己的想法、做自己的事的人，更显可贵。

Hangzhou
Liu Mei (Class 202, Majoring in Journalism)

Home, Where My Heart Feels at Ease

There has been a spicy aroma in my home ever since I was born.

Turn the clock back to 1999, and that was when I was born in Jishui County, Ji'an City—a village in the south of southeastern China's Jiangxi Province. Shortly afterwards, I was taken by my father to Hangzhou, capital city of southeast China's Zhejiang Province. Seldom have I lived in my hometown, yet I have never forgotten it no matter how far I am away from it.

Too often I have an illusion that I have already been accustomed to the life style in Hangzhou, with sour and sweet food and herbal tea already being part of my daily routine. I also frequently go to restaurants offering Hangzhou-style cuisine, buy a cup of bubble milk tea or enjoy desserts with my friends during the teatime. However, even though those elements have occupied much of my life, I will never forget my hometown because the memory of it is engraved in my DNA.

You can smell soil, sour and spicy chopped pepper and sweet fermented glutinous rice when you walk on the streets of Ji'an. Lively kids, aromatic melons, buzzing flies and barking dogs in alleys fill up one's memory of summer days. Smells of rapeseed oil and pepper come out of every household's chimney as villagers start preparing meals.

Back in the 1990s, every household in villages of Jiangxi made a living by contracting land independently. Aware that one could see the bigger world only after stepping out of his or her hometown, my father, a college student in the 1980s, decided to head for Hangzhou, a prosperous and bustling city in Zhejiang Province.

Seeing the thriving clothing business in Hangzhou, my father set up a factory for the back end of line processing with his savings. He still remembers the toil and hardship he went through at that period of time. Workers were mainly fellow villagers. It was commonplace for them to work overnight since there were only six high-power machines. Additionally, I was just born, and my father wished that there could be 48 hours in a day.

"There is always light at the end of the tunnel."

Every March and April after the Spring Festival, it was the recruitment season. Job recruitment notices were put up all over streets, luring numerous applicants. It was a coincidence that my father's given name "Shuiqing" meant "clear water" while the village where we lived back in 2000 was called Dinghai, which meant "calm sea". "Water" ends up in "sea", which implied my father was destined to settle down here.

With clothing factories of various sizes converging here, this village was a perfect epitome of Hangzhou's clothing production and back end of line processing industries in the past 20 years. My father, having decided upon the business scope of his factory, won a lot of loyal customers with his sincere and meticulous attitude and tried every means possible to retain workers and upgrade equipment. Whenever he made a decision, he needed to be fully aware that he might not make any money from it. Business consciousness, organizational management, and production management—every adaption meant innovation. Behind the smooth operation of the factory was my father's hard work.

When fellow villagers tried to follow my father's business model, he decided to stop the factory exactly in the prime time of the back end of line processing industry and offered to give a helping hand to his friend: to manage a factory back in the hometown in Jiangxi. Back at that time, we already had a roof to live under and a car to drive in Hangzhou and I was about to finish my elementary school.

When everything seemed to be on the right track, my father, as the locomotive, turned in another direction.

Every June is special to children in China, for it's when important turning points before adult life like the high school entrance examination, college entrance examination and graduation take place. It also symbolizes separation to me. June, with its pervasive heat, means the past comes to an end and that the new life just begins, and it pushes me constantly forward even when I'm not psychologically prepared to be nature.

My parent, leaving behind my elder brother who just started working and me in Hangzhou, embarked on a new journey in June, 2011.

I could totally relate to the Chinese saying that the elder brother is like father. My brother, ten years older than me, is someone I respect, fear and love at the same time. Finally, tottering and tumbling, I graduated from my junior middle school.

At that time, my father was just as busy and called us once every week. Winter and summer vacations were the only time that I got to get together with my parents. My father took care of the business while my mother took care of the family. I always followed them around just like a tail in those two precious months. The factory gradually unfolded itself before my eyes as I frequently visited it following my father.

This brick-making factory would witness numerous trucks carrying in coals and out with bricks. Back in 2011, as most households in Ji'an were leading a moderately prosperous life and wanted to build houses with their savings, there was a shortage of brick supply, an important material for house building. Considering raw materials and production techniques, brick factories had be set up in remote areas, which meant that my father needed to get up at 6:30 a.m. and start working half an hour later. The operation started even earlier, which meant workers needed to get up at 4:00 a.m..

"It was no hardship at all. The most difficult part lay in the beginning," said my dad, looking directly into my eyes. "Life isn't all plain sailing." He strictly followed rules and regulations, carried out environmental-protection measures and divided the factory into different departments for better management, with special attention paid to production and sale of brick machines and daily management. He saw to it that safety measures were taken when brick machines were brought in, trucks were under strict control and real-time monitoring equipment was installed. In case of bad weather, staggered production hours should be observed or production be stopped altogether.

Time, like a river, carries us forward no matter whether we are prepared or not. I just closed the sixth-grade textbooks, and the very next moment, I opened the twelfth-grade ones—I was in the final year of the senior high school in 2017.

It was in exactly the same year that the provincial government's environmental protection documents were issued. My father, a loyal party member answering the official call, shut the factory down; it remains closed until today. Documents concerning village development were also promulgated. Village planning pilot projects started in Jiangxi. The vision was tempting and my father took action. My father, determined to build his hometown, once again, embarked on a new journey which he continues until now.

When I returned to my hometown early this year, I saw broad roads, ubiquitous Internet connections, beautiful maisonettes and western-style houses, and farm land-turned parking lots. Young people started to come back and the elderly were delightful.

My father must have dedicated a lot to this village during the past three years when I studied at another city. I don't know how to depict his experiences; it seems that no language is vivid enough to show the trials and tribulations my father has gone through.

To me, Ji'an, a city in Jiangxi Province, is not only my birthplace, but also where my parents are living. It means a haven to me. It's not as valuable as a piece of land in Hangzhou, but it's what has kept my heart beating. The street is full of cars with license plate labelled Gan D (representing Ji'an City), with Rainbow Shopping Mall, Starbucks and Haidilao (a hot pot restaurant chain). It's not really a very flourishing place, but it's where my ties are.

I have admired my father ever since I was a child, and the distance between us has added some respect to this admiration. Always in a hurry, he is busy answering phone calls and developing his career. Feeling there is always not enough time, he is ready to take in as much knowledge as possible just like a bucket without a cover. He has a lot of ideas, which have transformed into broader horizons and more profound thoughts. It's quite valuable to have someone who can actually stick to his or her own ideas and carry them out in this fast-paced world.

学会讲故事

陈征北

学会讲故事,新闻专业学生必须擦亮的武器。

讲好中国故事,是习近平总书记对新闻工作者的要求。作为新闻专业的本科学生,在大学期间就应该学会“讲故事”。

漫漫长河一百年,“我”家的故事万万千,从哪里讲起?讲什么才能感人?怎样才能成为经典永久流传?刘诗婷同学《细流成河老一辈》巧妙地选取了自己的爷爷奶奶外公外婆作为故事的主人翁,讲述他/她们的人生故事……拉家常式地娓娓道来,从解放前到三年自然灾害,从改革开放到建成小康……历史上重要的节点,都有爷爷、奶奶、外公、外婆的故事……

肯尼斯·伯克说:故事是人生必需的设备。一个能把好故事讲好的人,才是传播的高手。从瞬间到永恒,从方寸到寰宇,每个人物的生命故事都提供了百科全书般的可能性。大师的标志就是仅仅从中挑选出几个瞬间,却能向我们展示其整个人生。

要学会讲故事,首先要学会观察生活,从观察身边的人和事开始。刘诗婷同学选择观察自己的爷爷、奶奶、外公、外婆,无疑是个聪明的选择。当然,除了观察身边的人和事,还要深入到社会生活的方方面面,才能观察到更多的闪光点,积累故事素材。

其次是善于捕捉典型细节。穆青在采写长篇通讯《县委书记的好榜样——焦裕禄》时捕捉到了这样一个细节:焦裕禄患肝癌仍然坚持工作,肝痛剧烈,他就用茶缸盖一头顶在肝部,一头顶在藤椅上,时间长了,藤椅被顶出了一个洞……这样的典型细节,胜过千言万语,焦裕禄崇高的精神境界跃然纸上。

再次是让主人翁“说话”。《天使日记》是中央广播电视总台中国之声推出的特别策划节目。邀请抗疫一线医护人员以语音自述方式向广大受众讲述发生在战“疫”最前线的故事。2020年1月29日到3月22日,节目播出。54期节目,共有343位医护人员,从重症监护室、普通病房、方舱医院发来349篇声音日记,汇聚成战“疫”一线最真实也最动人的“声音故事”,那些南腔北调的语音自述会带您身临其境，催人泪下……

新闻专业本科四年，学生个个都能会讲故事，个个都能讲好故事，这不是一个梦想，应该而且必须是新闻本科学历教育评价的“硬性”标准。

（浙大宁波理工学院传媒与法学院，主任记者）

故事

丽水

刘施婷（新闻学专业 191 班）

细流成河

我的爷爷奶奶、外公外婆都在一个村里——丽水市遂昌县云峰街道龙口村。

我的爷爷刘关进出生于 1936 年，从小失去了父亲，他作为家中的长子，承担了家中的重担。爷爷上初中那会儿，有一天，家里安了盏小小的电灯。那电灯如同萤火虫般发出来十分微弱的光。尽管如此，爷爷还是兴奋了好几天，似乎家里镶嵌了颗海底明珠，到处炫耀，走街串巷，忙得不亦乐乎。爷爷的学历不高，因为要为太婆分担家中的事务，初中还没有毕业就开始帮着太婆干活，照顾家里唯一的妹妹。如今爷爷经常和我念叨读书有多么重要，他很惋惜那时候因为条件的限制没有多认识几个字，所以现在很多事情都需要别人来帮忙。

1963 年，爷爷与奶奶相识并结婚。爷爷与奶奶有 7 个孩子，但我的大姑姑是爷爷奶奶在村子里面捡来的孩子，我有 5 个姑姑和 1 个伯伯，我的爸爸在他的兄弟姐妹中位列倒数第二。别人家都是一家五口，而我爷爷那时候是一家九口人，可想而知，生活该过得多么艰辛。一家人挤在小小的土坯房里，任由风吹雨打，偶尔天逢连夜雨，家中会漏水，搞得异常潮湿。因为年少时没有念过书，再考虑到家中有这么多的小孩，爷爷不得不放弃让每个孩子都去念书的想法，让我的小姑姑还有我父亲去读了书。但因为我父亲不爱读书，所以就开启了他的放牛童年生涯。

经党中央、国务院批准，民政部、财政部在《关于调整部分优抚对象等人员抚恤和生活补助标准的通知》中规定，从 2006 年 1 月 1 日起，对新中国成立前入党的农村老党员和未享受离退休待遇的城镇老党员发放生活补贴。现如今，爷爷说他可以享受国家的补助养老，再加上姑姑伯伯现在有一定的经济能力，每个月有时间就会来看爷爷奶奶并给予生活费。

在没有知道这些事情之前，我对爷爷的印象就是脾气温和的一个老人。但爷爷回忆往事时眼角挂着的泪珠让我重新认识了年轻时候的他。1978年改革开放，到现在已经42年了。古人说："四十而不惑。"如果说从改革开放起，中国是一次涅槃重生，那么今年的中国已是不惑。而如今的我们普通的家庭，也步入了新生活。

我的外公小时候每天都和几个同龄的小孩子结伴一起去山坡上放羊。羊儿总是美美地享受着嫩嫩的绿草儿，他和其他孩子们则在一旁玩耍，嘴里还时不时地哼几句小山歌。

1959—1961年我国经历了"三年经济困难"时期。那时候的人们，最大的苦恼就是今天怎么办，今天的食物解决了，明天怎么办，明天也能够过了，那以后怎么办。外公当时的家庭状况还算正常，没到那种连饭都吃不上的地步。外公是长子，加上最小的弟弟，家里一共有6个孩子。那么多人啊，真心不容易啊！我心想。只是外公还算幸运，当时的他正好在读书，学校是住宿制的，生活待遇不错，压根就不用愁吃的。

1978年，改革开放初期，外公外婆都会去田里打稻谷，但一天下来好像赚的钱并不是很多。但1982年农村家庭联产承包责任制的推行让外公一家忙活了起来，个人付出与收入挂钩，使生产的积极性大增，解放了农村生产力。

80年代以后，随着生产力的改变，农村实行包干到户，粮食连年丰收，就从那个时候，我的家乡人人都能吃上白面馒头了。这时候，我就问外公：是不是就天天过年了？外公说：比过年都要好了。但让外公生活有明显好转的还是他在1988年买下的那片地。外公买下那片田地之后建了个简易的面粉厂，帮村里的人碾米。再后来到了90年代，在政府的引导下，我的老家种上了大棚蔬菜，一年四季都能吃上新鲜的蔬菜。面粉厂后面的空地有两百多平方米，外公把这块地分成了两个区，前面种菜，后面养殖。菜地上，外公把它弄成了三层，请人来帮忙运土、填土，挑了很多种子来播种。后来，外公觉得只养鸡和鸭太空旷了，便又去张罗买了几头猪来。现在那猪棚还留在面粉厂旁边呢。

外公一家的生活水平逐步提高，成为村子里第一个盖起了小洋房和拥有两辆摩托车的人。正因为外公是个善良的人，村子里很多人会问外公借钱，我妈妈和小姨、舅舅都劝他不要借给别人那么大的金额，自己辛苦挣的钱不舍得花，却借给别人，那些人还不还。确实，在我眼里，外公其实不愁钱，但他却还是省吃俭用，不舍得乱花钱。我想这是老一辈的人留下来的习惯吧。

外公的面粉厂现在还在帮邻里碾米粉之类的，只不过还多了一样，制作年糕。我记得小时候,我经常会去面粉厂蹭刚做好的年糕吃,很是幸福。外公用劳苦汗水与岁月眼泪,在那么久的奋斗生活中,让一家人的生活水平提高,提升了幸福感,同时我也希望外公可以多出去旅旅游,让自己后半辈子多享点福气。

老一辈的人因身处在这个快速变化的时代而感受到了翻天覆地的变化,他们见证了过去几十年的变化,而我们这一代人,将是未来的见证者。当历史大潮冲过新时代的门槛,我们站到了一个新的起点上,新的传奇将如何续写?

Lishuì
Liu Shiting (Class 191, Majoring in Journalism)

Every Single Drop Contributes to a River

My paternal and maternal grandparents all live in the same village—Longkou Village, Yunfeng Street, Suichang County, Lishui City.

My paternal grandfather Liu Guanjin was born in 1936. He was the eldest son of the family, and he lost his father at an early age. All the family burdens were placed on him. When my grandpa was in middle school, a small electric lamp was installed in the house. The dim light that the electric lamp gave out was like that of a firefly. Even so, my grandpa was still excited for several days, as if there was a pearl from the bottom of the sea at home. He went round the streets, and was busy showing off this small dim lamp everywhere. My grandpa didn't receive much education, because he had to help my great-grandmother with housework. He had already started to help my great-grandmother and take care of his only younger sister before graduating from middle school. Nowadays, my grandfather often told me about how important study was. He regretted that he hadn't learned more words at that time due to poor conditions, resulting in the fact that he would need others' help on many things.

In 1963, my paternal grandparents met and married. They had seven children, but my eldest aunt was an abandoned child who was picked up by my grandparents in the village. I have five aunts and one uncle. My father is the sixth child. Other families usually had five members, but there were nine people in my grandfather's family. It's not difficult to imagine how hard their life would be. The whole family squeezed in to a small mud house, which was exposed to wind and rain. When it rained all day, the house would leak and became extremely damp. My grandpa didn't have the chance to study when he was young. In addition, considering that there were so many children in the family, my grandpa had no way but to give up the idea of allowing every child to go to school. He let my youngest aunt and my father go to school. However, my father didn't like studying, so he started to pasture cattle for the family.

According to the "Notice on Adjusting the Standards of Compensation and Living Subsidies for Some Entitled Persons" which was approved by the CPC and the State Council, the Ministry of Civil Affairs and the Ministry of Finance stipulate that starting from January 1st of 2006, the government will offer living subsidies to old party members living in rural areas who joined the Party before the founding of the People's Republic of China and those old party members living in the city who haven't enjoyed retirement welfare. Nowadays, my grandpa says that he is entitled to the subsidy given by the government to enjoy the rest of his life. Besides, my aunts and my uncle now have good financial conditions, and they visit my grandparents when they have free time and give them living expenses every month.

Before I knew about these things, my grandfather impressed me as an old man of good temper. When my grandfather recalled the past, the teardrops on the corners of his eyes made me realize what he was like when he was young. Since the reform and opening up in 1978, it has been 42 years. The ancients said, "One has no doubts at forty." If the beginning of reform and opening-up is a rebirth for China, China is no longer confused this year. Ordinary families like ours today have also started a new life.

When my maternal grandfather was a child, he went to herd sheep on the hillside with several children of the same age every day. Sheep always enjoyed tender green grass, while he and other children played nearby and sang a few lines of folk songs.

From 1959 to 1961, China experienced three years of economic difficulties. The problem of food was solved. At that time, the biggest distress to think about was what to eat today. When making it through today, people would worry about what to eat tomorrow; after tomorrow, people would worry about what to eat afterward. At that time, my grandfather's family was fine, and needn't worry about what to eat. My grandfather was the eldest son. Counting his youngest brother in, there were six children in his family. With so many people in a family, it was not easy to live, I thought. But my grandfather was lucky. During that period, he happened to study at a boarding school. He led a good life there and he didn't need to worry about hunger at all.

In 1978, when the reform and opening up just started, my grandparents would go to farmlands to thresh rice. However, they didn't seem to make much money at the end of the day. However, in 1982, the implementation of the rural household contract responsibility system made my grandfather's family busy. Personal contribution was related to the income, which greatly increased the enthusiasm for production and liberated the rural productivity.

After the 1980s, with the change of productivity, work was contracted to every household in rural areas, so farmers had a good harvest year after year. From then on, everyone in my hometown could eat steamed bread made from white flour. Then I asked my grandpa, "Does that mean we could celebrate the New Year every day?" My grandpa said, "It is better than the New Year." But it was the land he bought in 1988 that made my grandpa's life significantly better. After my grandfather bought this land, he built a flour mill to help the villagers grind rice. Then in the 1990s, under the guidance of the government, he established vegetable greenhouses in our hometown, and people could eat fresh vegetables all year round. The open space behind the flour mill was more than 200 square meters. My grandpa divided the land into two areas. They planted vegetables in the front and bred poultries in the back.

My grandfather turned the vegetable plot into three layers. He asked others to help deliver the soil, fill the land, and picked a lot of seeds to sow. My grandfather felt that it was too big to just breed chickens and ducks, so he bought some pigs. Now the pig barn is still there next to the flour mill.

The living standards of my grandfather's family gradually improved and he became the first person in the village to build a small villa and owned two motorcycles. My grandfather was a kind person, so many people in the village would borrow money from him. My mother, my aunt and my uncle tried to persuade him out of lending such a large sum of money to others. He didn't want to spend his hard-earned money, but he would lend it to others. Sometimes some people did not pay it back. Indeed, in my eyes, my grandfather needn't worry about money, but he was still frugal and wouldn't like to spend money on unnecessary things. I think this is a habit formed by the older generation.

My grandpa's mill is still helping the neighbors to grind rice, and now there is one more task: making rice cakes. I remember when I was young, I often went to the mill to eat the freshly-made rice cake, and I was very happy. In such a long life of struggle, my grandpa improved the living standard and brought more happiness with his hard work, perspiration and tears. At the same time, I also hope that my grandpa can travel more and live in ease and comfort for the rest of his life.

The older generation have experienced earth-shaking changes due to this rapidly changing era. They have witnessed the changes in the past few decades, and our generation will be the witnesses of the future. After the tide of history crosses the threshold of the new era, we are now standing on a new starting point. How will the new legend be continued?

年轻人的眼光

储召生

在00后作者的眼里，这只是硖石镇一个普通的人家：从爷爷辈开始就住在这里，住房条件从筒子楼到居民区200平方米的大房子，经济状况从清贫到小有积蓄；作者也亲历了20年来这座古镇的变迁，“小城的故事便是我家的故事”。

因为年轻，作者的眼睛是平视的。爷爷是海宁广播电视局局长，奶奶是海宁造船厂厂长兼任财务总管，或许在作者看来，也不过是一个科级小官而已。爸爸参军后上了大学，1980年毕业回到硖石镇当了公务员，在作者看来似乎也是司空见惯。硖石镇上曾经出过徐志摩、张宗祥等名人，和他们比起来，自己家里这些人也太普通了。

因为年轻，作者的情感是平稳的。几十年来家族里的改变，作者不无幽默地平铺直叙，娓娓道来。你只能从只言片语中感受人生百态：比如爷爷的英年早逝，比如父亲的短暂婚史，比如母亲的闯荡江湖。或许在作者看来，这不过是大千世界的普通一面，鸡零狗碎，不足为外人道也。

这正是00后这一代人的优点。他们不再纠结于父辈的往事，不局限于过往的辛酸，而把眼光更多地投向未来。他们亲眼看到了国家的富强，看到了普通百姓家庭实实在在的改变，也对自己的未来充满了期待。

这或许也是这一代人的局限。他们见惯了太平盛世，因为缺少对上一辈人的深入了解，甚至缺乏对周围底层社会的细致考察，他们不能深刻体会过往，也难说把握将来。如果能在某一个观察点上直切下去，我相信作者能看到五彩斑斓的横截面，行文会深刻得多。

硖石镇里故事多，放到改革开放40年的大背景下，我越发觉得，这并非只是一个普通人家。

（中国教育报副总编辑）

故事

嘉兴

高恺悦(网络与新媒体专业181班)

硖石镇上的普通人家

硖石地方凭水依山，依的山是东西二山，凭的水有洛塘河和市河；旧有十二景，自紫微春晓至东岳霁雪缘此绕匝，这座古城孕育了徐志摩、张宗祥等文人，实乃风水清灵之宝地。父辈们开垦，子孙辈乘荫蔽，而我家所有的故事也都在这片土地上被讲述。

爷爷幼时，祖国刚解放，家里人知道读书要紧，便让他读镇上的私塾，那时候的学费还不是"人民币"，而是靠的爷爷的父母每个月给私塾塞一斗米。一月一斗米，便也允许他在学堂识字了。爷爷自己争气，最后读得小有名头，坐到了海宁县广播站站长的位置；奶奶是大家闺秀，位及海宁县造船厂厂长兼任财务总管。他们结婚时没有计划生育，于是就有了三个儿子，其中，我爸是长子。

我爸是1958年出生的，正是大跃进开始那一年，我爷爷为了响应号召，在他的名字里也带上了跃字。我爸爸出生在县广播站，长大也是在硖石镇。他戏称自己小时候是海宁街头的小霸王，成天打些小男孩的架，周围学校的人遇到他都要喊一声霸王，结果被爷爷碰上了，抄起椅子就是一顿打。

聊到这里，我爸笑着回忆说，因为他是长子，爷爷经常揍他。两个弟弟管得不好要揍他，读书读得不好要揍他，被别人家父母告了状也要揍他，他就是被揍大的。但他也说，爷爷其实是每天都很乐呵的一个老好人，嗓门亮，说话妙语连珠，不摆官架子，因此他也总是积极乐观的。我想，这种乐观积极的精神也有许多顺着血脉继承到了我身上吧。

我爸就这样在硖石读完了小初高，高中毕业时，我爸听毛主席的话，做知青下乡去了。

我爸18岁下乡到袁花夹山大队，呆了两年零三个月后，我爷爷让他去参加中国人民解放军，他从小听话，于是就去了。大连冰雪连天，那时候我爸也就和我现在一个年纪，他去到大连空军地勤某部队，整整三年，靠自己的勤奋和努力成为一名中共预备党员，遂再次回到海宁，就读了大学。

我爸读书毕业后，1980年进了海宁市行政管理局，工作至退休，退休时单位改名为海宁市市场监督管理局。我爷爷年轻时经历了文革，当时是被重点批斗的知识分子，身体不甚好，50多岁便高血压病发辞世，那时候他已经是海宁市广播电视局局长。

我妈妈出生得晚些，1971年她在海宁市硖石人民医院落地时的海宁已经有了规规矩矩的医院。绕不开的硖石镇将我们一家串在一起。

妈妈在南关厢社区跟着外婆长大，我外婆在南关厢纽扣厂工作，外公是煤矿工人。不用我妈补充，我都记得我外公也算是知识分子，化学元素周期表倒背如流，很是厉害。我妈虽然对数理化一窍不通，耳濡目染下也会背方言版的化学周期表，以至于我幼儿园的时候最喜欢的事就是躺在床上缠着我妈教我那一个一个神奇的音节。

我妈幼时辗转动荡，4岁的时候被送到宁波的奶奶处，我爸爸调侃她是“宁波麦穗田边捡麦穗长大的小姑娘”。她8岁再回到我外公身边，去上了三年小学。到了四年级，又随着外公工作变动转学到了硖石三小，一直读到海宁一中初中毕业，考取了职高。但是她对学习没兴趣，就直接出来就业了，做过服务员、营业员等工作，认识我爸时，也自学了一些事务，以至于能留在医药公司做文书工作。

我父母都出生在海宁县，相识时海宁已然从县转市。那时候我父亲有过一段婚姻，不过我妈勇敢，不在意过往。他们在海宁一条名叫长埭的路上结了婚，这条路上栽满了梧桐，也栽满了我的整个童年。那时候家里住的还是广播电视局分配的宿舍，三室一厅一厨一卫一阳台，住着我们一家三口和奶奶，生了我之后母亲就辞职在家照顾小孩。

2000年2月份，家里有了我，在此之前，家里一直过着平淡又顺遂的日子，父亲领着公务员的稳定工资，养着一家四张嘴，日子不算难，但也一直不甚宽裕。赶着时代的潮流，我们家也添了电脑，我小时候最鲜明的记忆就是看到父母坐在电脑前练习五笔输入、做驾照的模拟考题。

在我读大班的时候，母亲觉得现在的家里太小了，我将要上小学，应该有自己的房间，这套旧居不合适再住下去。于是父母一合计，拿出点存款付了首付，又去银行贷了些款，买了一套200平方米的房子。后来这套房子我一住就是14年。

我家的日子真正宽裕起来，要从我上初中时母亲去做皮革生意开始。大家都知道海宁皮革城的名声，我家正是乘上了这阵风头。

一直到我读初中，母亲都是待业在家的，但这也没磨灭她作为一名女性独立自主的盼头。父亲靠自己以及爷爷那代祖祖辈辈积攒在海宁镇上的人脉，帮母亲摸清了一些门道，两人一起做货源筹备、店铺装修、宣传等工作，甚至我年幼自学的一点 photoshop 三脚猫功夫都被他们征用去做宣传海报。

除了在海宁市皮革城做了一些生意，接下来的几年里，我妈也独自碾转湖北、山东、江苏等地经营，有一阵是做皮革，有一阵是做衣服，总之步履不曾停过。父亲因为有公务员的工作在身，而我还在读初中，所以呆在海宁，一家人常年分居两地。那几年，我被送到隔壁的老师家，在他们家度过了小学的五六年级和整个初中。那段时间，我常年没有父母在身边，偶尔想家，就回家和爸爸一起住。那一段的记忆总是很模糊，我似乎是在几个不同选址的厂房间混着混着混大的，也似乎是一直在老师家的阁楼房间里听着风声长大的。

对于生意人来说，越是节假日越不得空闲。新年时分是做这个生意的好时间，年初那几天许多人都喜欢去皮革商场购物。因此，母亲做生意那几年，我们都不曾享受过什么在家放松过年的生活，我脑海里也少有春节走亲访友的记忆。往往一次大考完，我就先坐上长途巴士去找妈妈，路上父亲总会找一个人照料我。到了山东或者湖北的车站，妈妈就站在站台下等我，接到我之后就跟她去她的住处。再过几天，爸爸休假了，也来到妈妈的地方，一家人简简单单烧一顿年夜饭，吃完了早早睡觉，第二天妈妈照常去工作。

回望40余年来，父母们一致认为他们的生活之变化是“翻天覆地”的。从前的经济水平和现在的经济水平会产生如此巨大的差别，归根到底还是国家的富强所致。

时运并济，硖石镇的日渐繁华中也倒映着我家的变迁。从筒子楼到居民区，从清贫到小有积蓄，这座小城的故事便是我家的故事，我家的故事也是这座小城的故事。

Jiaxing
Gao Kaiyue (Class 181, Majoring in Network and New Media)

An Ordinary Family in Xiashi Town

Xiashi Town is located at the foot of East and West Mountains and by the rivers of Luotang and Shihe. There were 12 scenic spots in the old days. East and West Mountains surround this place. The time-honored town, cradle of intellectuals like Xu Zhimo and Zhang Zongxiang, is a treasure land where ancestors blaze the trail while posterity enjoys the fruits. It is on this land that the stories of my family are unfolding.

My paternal grandfather was at a young age when New China was established. He was sent to an old-style private school for learning by his parents who were well aware of the importance of receiving education. The tuition fees, back at that time, were paid in the form of grain instead of cash. It was thanks to the monthly 6.25 kilograms of rice that my grandpa was allowed to study in the private school. He learned so diligently and his efforts finally paid off; he became the head of a radio station in Haining County. My grandmother, who was born and raised up in a respectable family, climbed up the career ladder all the way to the head and financial director of the shipyard in Haining County. Since the family planning policy hadn't been implemented when they got married, my grandparents had three sons, the eldest being my father.

Born in 1958 when the Great Leap Forward Movement (1958-1960) began, my father was thus given a name containing "Yue", which means "leap" in Chinese, to show my grandpa's support for the national policy. He was born at the county radio station, and was raised up at Xiashi Town. Fighting with other boys fiercely earned him the nickname of Bully in the Town, but unfortunately and students from nearby schools alway called him by this name. He was once caught by my grandpa fighting with others. Of course, he was beaten hard by my grandpa with a chair.

My father, wearing a smile on his face, recalled that he was often beaten simply because he was the eldest son. He was the one who got beaten hard when his two younger brothers behaved badly, when he got bad grades in the school or were told on by other parents. In that way, he grew up. Despite all the beatings, my father knew that my grandpa, a witty speaker with a sonorous voice, always had an up-lifting spirit and never put on airs. My father inherited this optimism, which, I believe, was more or less passed down to me.

My father, having finished his studies in elementary, middle and high schools in Xiashi, volunteered to help with the rural development as an educated youth answering the call of Chairman Mao after graduating from high school.

After staying in Jiashan Village, Yuanhua Town for 27 months since he arrived there at the age of 18, he joined the People's Liberation Army as asked by my grandpa—he was always obedient from childhood. At exactly my age, my father, braving the frigid weather in Dalian, a city in northeastern China's Liaoning Province, became a soldier in Division 78 of a unit of the Air Force Ground Service there for entirely three years. He became a probationary CPC member with his diligence and hard work and then returned to Haining, his hometown, for college.

My father then landed a job in the municipal administrative bureau after graduation and worked there until retirement when its name was changed to Haining Administration for Market Regulation. My grandpa experienced the Cltural Revolution (1966-1976) when he was young. He was in poor health because of harsh punishment targeted at intellectuals like him at that time, so he died prematurely in his fifties when hypertension struck. He was then the head of Haining Radio and Television Administration.

As for my mother, she was born much later than my father. She was born in Haining Xiashi People's Hospital back in 1971, Where Hainng already had decent and standardized hospitals at that time. Xiashi Town connected my family.

My mother grew up in Nanguanxiang Community. My grandma worked in Nanguanxiang Button Factory and my grandpa a coal mining factory. No need to be reminded by my mother—I remember that my grandpa could be called an intellectual because was able to fluently recite the periodic table of chemical elements. My mother, as his daughter, though knowing nothing about math, physics or chemistry, was unknowingly able to recite the periodic table in her dialect. As for me, the thing I liked to do the most when I was in the kindergarten was to pester my mother to teach me those magic chemical elements.

My mom, flitting between different places, had a tumultuous childhood. She was sent to her grandma's side at four, so my father would banter with her, saying she was a girl growing up in Ningbo while picking up wheat ears in paddy fields. She was sent back to her father at eight and studied in elementary school there for three years. She then transferred to No. 3 Elementary School one year later because of changes in her father's job. She was admitted to a vocational high school after graduating from Haining No. 1 Junior High School, but gave up the chance to further her study for she had no interest in learning at all. She tried jobs like being a waitress and a shop assistant, and when she got to know my father, she had already learned by herself some administrative affairs, which helped her find a job as a secretary in a pharmaceutic company.

My parents were both born in Haining County, which was later upgraded to a city when they were acquainted with each other. My mother, a brave woman, didn't care much about my father's previous marriage. They later got married on Changdai Street, a street full of Chinese parasol trees where I spent my entire childhood. When I was young, we lived in a dormitory assigned by Haining Radio and Television Administration, which, with three bedrooms, one living room, one kitchen, one bathroom and one balcony, accommodated my paternal grandma, my parents and me. My mother resigned after giving birth to me and took care of me whole-heartedly.

I was born in February, 2000, breaking the quiet and smooth life pattern of the whole family. Ever since then, my father had to provide for a family of four members with his stable salary as a civil servant. We started a modest living. Keeping up with the trend, we later bought a computer. I still remember vividly that my parents practiced five-stroke typing or took mock tests for driver's license sitting before the computer screen.

When I was in the final year of kindergarten, my mom believed the current house was too small to accommodate us since I, who was about to enter elementary school, needed a room of my own. Therefore, after family discussions, my parents bought a house covering an area of 200 square meters using their savings as the down payment and borrowing money from the bank. We lived in that house for 14 years.

It was not until my mom started the leather business when I was in middle school that we finally got rich. You must have heard of the reputation of Haining Leather City. We took advantage of the booming leather business.

My mom, a housewife until I was in middle school, never had her dream as an independent woman erased from her mind. After my dad helped my mom figure out the business rules using social connections he and his ancestors accumulated over the years, they started searching for goods suppliers, decorating the store and advertising. Even I, who scratched the surface of photoshop which I taught myself when I was a child, was asked to make posters for them.

Besides the leather business in Haining Leather City, my mom was also engaged in leather, clothes or other businesses in provinces like Hubei, Shandong and Jiangsu. Never had she stopped. During that period of time, my family seldom got reunited because my dad had to stay in the hometown as a civil servant and I was then studying in middle school in Haining. Actually, I was fostered by my teacher who lived next to my home during my last two years of elementary school and the entire middle school. Without my parents' company, I would go back home and live with my dad whenever I was homesick. The memory of that period of time is not clear. I vaguely remember that I muddled along between different factories, and grew up hearing winds blowing windows of the attic of my teacher's home.

Business people never even got one day off during festivals and holidays. The Spring Festival was a perfect time to do business since many people liked to go shopping in the leather markets in the first several days of the lunar new year. My mom was no exception. As a result, seldom did we have a relaxing Spring Festival or visit relatives. I was sent to my mom's side on a coach after the final examinations were over and my dad always asked someone to take care of me on the way. After I arrived at the coach station in Shandong or Hubei, my mom, who had been waiting for me at the platform, would take me to her place. My dad would come several days later when he was off from the work. We would have a very simple family reunion dinner on the lunar New Year's Eve and went to bed early. The very next day, my mom would go to work, as usual.

Looking back upon the past 40 years, my parents both agree that the changes in their lives are earth-shaking. In the final analysis, great strides we have made in economic development are attributed to the national prosperity.

We have gone through ups and downs, and so has this town. The flourishing Xiashi Town also reflects the changes of my family all the way from living in a dormitory to a residential community, from being poor to moderately prosperous. The story of this small town witnesses the story of my family, while the story of my family is an epitome of the story of this small town.

改革开放中的社会变迁

陈　伟

社会的变迁伴随时代的急流，始终处于流变之中，改革开放后的中国是社会变迁速度最快的国家之一。从学理的角度而言，我们可以在宏观层面探究这个过程中家庭结构、城市结构、组织结构、社会阶层结构等社会结构的变迁，而《向上的楼梯》则是从一个微观的个体生活史的视角入手，描述改革开放以来社会变迁给我们的日常生活带来的变化。

温州龙港，在上个世纪80年代可谓轰动全国，这是中国第一座由农民自费建起来的城市，也是改革开放的产物。自1984年建镇起，实现了从小渔村到农民城、到产业城、再到新兴城市的跨越。伴随着城镇化发展，逐渐加速的经济社会转型，推动作者的家庭组织形式从大家族的聚居逐渐转为分散的核心小家庭，于是“一整栋楼住着我们一大家子人”变成“我一个人的地盘”。改革开放让草根经济如野草逢春，百业兴盛使得作者父母那一代人的奋斗获得了丰厚的回报，从做搬运工为生到开店收租，在当时算是最普通不过的生活模式，反映的确是龙港地区社会阶层的整体跃升。城市的变迁带动了城市附近村庄集体经济的发展，村里的安置房就是城镇化发展过程中带来的红利，于是有了“母亲一直想开的花店”和“家里添置的一辆私家轿车”。在笔者看来，作者关于“三套房子”的叙事使我们能够更加完整地理解、把握那些社会变迁现实，关注到改革开放以来社会变迁带来的巨大影响。

（浙大宁波理工学院马克思主义学院讲师，博士）

故事

温州

高婷婷(网络与新媒体专业193班)

向上的"楼梯"

我家住在浙江省温州市龙港镇。原来的龙港是一个小渔村,后来慢慢发展富裕起来,农民们集资建镇,成为中国"农民第一城"。

在1983年,爷爷靠着十几年的积蓄,一咬牙一跺脚,用几千块在村里盖了一栋水泥房,也是我们家的第一栋房子。

我父亲初中毕业就直接工作贴补家里。父亲的第一份工作是经人介绍进入龙华大酒店做服务员,而我的母亲则和朋友一起经营一家裁缝店,父母都是那种平平凡凡过日子的普通人。随后两人相亲认识,结婚,于2001年生下我,正式开启了一家三口的日子。

2001年,我还没有开始记事,那时候家里还是木头做的楼梯,人踩在上面就会吱呀作响。那时候一整栋楼住着我们一大家子人,有爷爷奶奶,大伯大伯母,叔叔和婶婶,还有父亲母亲和我。每一层一个小家庭,4层构成了我们一个大家庭,虽然很小,但也有种说不清的温馨感。楼上楼下有什么需要呼喝一声就可以了。料酒没了,"咚咚咚"下楼梯,随时可以拿奶奶家自酿的酒补上。柴米油盐没了,"噔噔噔"爬上楼,去叔叔伯伯家借借也可以先凑合上一顿。夏天最好的待遇就是电风扇、冰西瓜和凉竹席。等我长大了,家里先后有了以前老式的那种四四方方的彩色电视和台式电脑,两个后面都拖着笨重的"脑袋",屏幕就A4笔记本大小,但在当时也足够我们一家3口看得津津有味。

2006年,爷爷奶奶他们都搬进公寓房,我父亲则花钱买下这一栋老房子。因此这四层木楼梯也自然而然变成我一个人的地盘,每天好长一段时间都是我在"噔噔噔""咚咚咚"上下楼跑动玩闹。这段木头楼梯可以说是我童年印象最深刻的回忆了。

在我还没出生之前,我父亲是做搬运工的。生下我之后,夫妻俩就包下一楼的前间,经营起一家零售小店,向街坊邻里售卖油米酱醋、零食饮料。楼上的空余房间就租给别家人居住,也能收收房租增补家用。靠四五层的民房开店收租在当时算是最普通不过的生活模式。

2010年前后，我们家靠着辛苦挣钱和节俭积攒下来的全部存款在公寓里买下一间套房。是那种一整栋都用石泥砌成，全部做套房，一层两间，每间两室一厅一厨，算是当时常见的房子样式。新的东西总是好的，我们一家也就这样高高兴兴地搬了进去。

新家的生活质量比以前好上了几倍，门口有连通一栋楼各家的门铃，主人只需摁着按键，通过声音辨认来客的身份，安全性与老房子相比提升不少。进门之后，就是记忆里最深刻的长长的石楼梯和"高耸"的楼层。上下楼隔着一层长长的石阶梯，走上个三四层都得喘上一会儿，更别提走到6楼的家有多累人，我要抬脚迈上一层又一层的台阶，心里默默倒数已经走过的楼层数，只盼能快点结束这段"征程"。

父母还是经营原来那家小店面，不过爸爸开始去工厂上班。经常是白天母亲煮好早餐，我们一家人吃完早点，父亲送我上学然后赶去上班，母亲则直接去开店。然后下午放学后我自己走回店里，待着直到关店拉下铁卷帘门，再和母亲或父亲一起准备回家。天早就暗下来，夜空漆黑一片没有星星点缀，我就一手拉着父亲、一手拉着母亲慢慢走在归家的路上。小孩子大抵都能随时随刻开心，所以与辛苦一天疲惫不已的父母不同，我经常兴奋地跳上楼梯，拽着父母让他们快走，想着："爬过这层石楼梯就能到家啦，回家就能躺着咯！"

2014年，村子的发展势头更是突飞猛进。河底高村召开代表大会，表决通过了村集体股改实施方案。河底高村经济合作社资产股权量化分配制度改革后，新的经济组织为"苍南县龙港镇河底高村股份经济合作社"。这样的改革推动了村集体经济的发展。除此之外村里还向我们承诺村民的福利会越来越好。也就是在初三那年，我们每家村民都分到一套安置房，只要等大厦建好就能入住。

这项福利大大改善了家里状况，父母亲决定将小店转手，不仅筹备起母亲一直想开的花店，还贷款给家里添置了一辆私家轿车。从此，家里的生活开始蒸蒸日上。

2017年左右，私家车司机开始流行，我父亲也趁空闲去赚个几趟钱。但是花店生意越来越繁忙，光送花收花的活就应接不暇了，当司机的事也只得搁置。而我恰逢高二，学校换到新的校区之后改成全寄宿制，我回家也少了。

"开花店也很辛苦，生意都是一阵一阵的。旺季的时候，我和你爸爸整天起早摸黑工作，早晨6点多就要去店里选花包花，经常一天十几份订单，歇脚的时间也没有，做完腰酸背痛，回家还得爬6层的楼梯，特别不方便，走到家的时候都要站不住了。可淡季时，又清闲得要命，没什么钱赚，真是艰难啊。"这些也是后来从母亲口中得知的事情。

在我高二升高三前的最后一个学期，繁重的工作压垮了母亲的身体，母亲走路不稳，摔到腰受了伤，还动了手术。等母亲出院也只能躺在家里静养，花店做不下去，家里全是靠父亲一人的肩膀撑起，忙得昏天黑地，回家倒头就睡。

2018 年我升入高三，进入了最紧张的备考阶段。母亲的病已然养好，却也经不起劳累，所以留在家做做家务。父亲则开私家车挣钱。生活总算渐渐有了起色。

2019 年，龙港因为发展趋势向好，正式宣布撤镇批市，商业圈附近的楼房更是加紧盖好。我们家就把原来的套间卖掉，全家搬进新建好的安置房。上楼终于不再需要费力走 6 层的楼梯，只需乘几秒的电梯就轻松到家。小区位于龙港最繁华的商业区附近，超市小店林立，交通方便，生活非常便利。加上我又顺利考上大学，家里的生活也逐渐稳定下来。母亲对此感到十分满足："没有什么比生活富裕、家庭美满更让人开心。"

我们家先后经历三套房子，从木楼梯到石楼梯再到电梯，每一次都是向前进的，向上走的。我们每踏上一阶，我们家也更上一层楼，朝小康的目标越来越近。

就像时代不会停下脚步，我们的身边也分分秒秒都在变化，相信我们的城镇也好，我们的家也好，全都在进步着。

Wenzhou
Gao Tingting (Class 193, Majoring in Network and New Media)

Upward "Stairs"

My family lives in Longgang, a town in Wenzhou City, Zhejiang Province. Originally a small fishing village, Longgang gradually developed and became rich. Local farmers pooled their money for the town's development, and now, Longgang is China's "first city of farmers".

In 1983, with more than 10 years of savings, my grandfather made up his mind and built a concrete house in the village with several thousand yuan, and that was the first house of our family.

My father joined the workforce to support his family after graduating from middle school. He managed to work as a waiter at Longhua Hotel with others' help. My mother ran a tailor's shop with her friend. Both of them were ordinary people who lived an ordinary life. Later, they met each other through a matchmaker and fell in love and finally got married. I was born in 2001 as the third member to this sweet family.

In 2001, I hadn't started to remember things clearly. There was a wooden staircase in my house; it would make a squeaking sound every time you stepped on it. The entire extended family lived in the same building: my paternal grandparents, uncles, aunts, my parents and me. Four families each living on one floor, formed a big extended family. Small as it was, the house gave us inexplicable warmth. Whatever we needed, we could borrow from other families. When the cooking wine was used up, we could go and fetch some home-made cooking wine from my grandparents' home downstairs; when we needed other daily necessities, we could borrow some from my two uncle's homes upstairs. The best ways to spend a long summer were electric fan, ice watermelon and cool bamboo mat. By the time I grew up, my family had an old-fashioned color TV and a desktop computer, both of them having a boxy and heavy "head". They had a screen as big as an A4 notebook, but the three of us could not watch it enough.

In 2006, my grandparents moved into an apartment and my father purchased the old house. The wooden staircase that connected four floors, subsequently, came under my reign. Every day, I would spend a lot of time clattering up and down stairs. That was the sweetest memory in my childhood!

My father worked as a porter before I was born. After my birth, my parents occupied the front room of the ground floor and started a small retail shop selling daily necessities like edible oil, rice, soy sauce, snacks and drinks. The spare rooms upstairs were rented to other families, which added more income to the household. Back then, it was common to run a store in a four or five-story building and collect rent.

Around 2010, our family bought an apartment suite with every penny we had saved through hard work over the years. The building was made of stone and cement and was separated into suites. There were two suites on each floor, and each one had a living room and a kitchen, which was a typical style of that time. New things are always good, so our family moved in happily.

The life quality in the new home was much better than before. There was an intercom connecting each suite at the entrance to the building. The owner only needed to press a button and identify the visitor through his/her voice. Security improved a lot compared with the old houses. After entering the door, a long stone staircase and "towering" floors were quite impressive. There was a long stone staircase between floors; you would easily lose your breath just walking to the third or fourth floor, not to mention how tiring it was to walk all the way to the sixth floor. I had to labor my way through the stairs one after another while counting the floors that I had passed, wanting this agony to end as soon as possible.

My parents still attended that small shop, but my dad started his new job at a factory. Our daily routine usually began with breakfast, which my mother prepared. After that, my father would accompany me to school before heading straight to work; my mother would go to the store. Then in the afternoon, I would walk back to the store by myself after school, and I would stay there until they pulled down the rolling door. Then my parents and I would return home together. The sky had already been dark without any sight of stars. I, holding my parents' hands, walked slowly on the way home. Children could be happy at any time. Unlike my parents who were exhausted after a day's hard work. I would often jump up the stairs excitedly, tugging my parents' clothes to hurry them along. I thought that I would get home after climbing this stone staircase, and the bed was awaiting me!

In 2014, our village gained stronger momentum in development. Hedigao Village held a general meeting of household representatives during which villagers voted on and approved the implementation plan of village collective share-holding system reform. After the reform of the quantitative distribution of stock rights of Economic Cooperative of Hedigao Village, Joint Stock Economic Cooperative of Hedigao Village, Longgang Town, Cangnan County was established. Such a measure boosted the collective economy of our village. In addition, the village promised better welfare for villagers. In my third year of middle school, every household was offered a settlement house, and they would move in as long as the mansion was built.

The welfare greatly improved the family's financial situation. My parents decided to sell the store and open a florist's as wished by my mother. They also took a loan from the bank and purchased a new car. Since then, life started booming.

In 2017, ride-sharing became popular, and my father spent his spare time earning extra bucks for the family. But the business in the florist's was getting busier. Since he was too busy delivering flowers to customers, my father had to put his side job on hold. I could not go home so frequently as my high school adopted the boarding system after moving to a new location when I was in the second grade of high school.

"It's hard to manage a florist's. There were peak and off seasons. During the peak season, your father and I got up early and worked till night every day. We had to go to the store to pick and wrap flowers at about 6 o'clock in the morning. We often had a dozen orders in a day, and there was no time to rest. We felt great pain all over the body. We had to climb six floors when we got back home; sometimes, we couldn't even stand still after a day's hard work. But in the off season, there were no customers and no income. It was really hard." These are the things that I learned from my mother later.

During the last semester of my second year in high school, the heavy workload exhausted my mother. She tripped and hurt her waist and had to be sent to a hospital for surgery. Even after discharge, my mother could do nothing but lying on the bed and rest. We lost the flower shop. My father became the only person to support our family. He was so tired that he would fall asleep as soon as his head touched the pillow every night.

In 2018, I entered the third year of high school, which was the highly-tense preparation stage. My mother had recovered, but she could no longer bear any overwork. Therefore, she stayed at home to do light housework while my father earned money from car-hailing. Life was getting better.

In 2019, because of the strong economic development, Longgang upgraded its title from a town to a city; more buildings emerged in the central business district. Our family sold the original suite and moved into the newly built settlement house. Finally, we no longer had to endure the 6-storey stairs. Taking the elevator, it only takes us several seconds to get home with ease. The community was located near the most prosperous business district in Longgang, where we could find numerous supermarkets and shops. The transportation and life were convenient. In addition, I was successfully admitted to a university, and we gradually settled down. My mother was very satisfied with this, "Nothing is more pleasing than a life of abundance and a happy family."

Our family experienced three houses, from wooden stairs to stone stairs and then to elevators. Every time, it moved forward and upward. Every time we climbed up a step, we were one step closer to moderate prosperity.

Times never stop changing, nor does everything that is around us. I believe that both our towns and cities and our homes are making progress.

从守护到开拓:法治推动实现中国梦

韩小梅

《浙里是我家》展示了100个区域性样本,即100个浙江家庭二三代人在新中国成立后、改革开放后开拓进取、生活逐步改善和走向富裕的过程。在这一历史进程中,法治在其中的保障和推动作用值得关注。

《向未来砥砺前行》等若干个故事中,都郑重地提到了20世纪80年代初在浙江各地开始实行家庭联产承包责任制。以此为起点,人们的生活都得到了显著改善。从电视机、自行车到商品房、小汽车,到教育、旅游,人们的消费水平和生活品质都得到了极大提升。而家庭联产承包责任制这个奔向美好生活的起点不曾被忘记。

1980年,邓小平在一次重要谈话中公开肯定小岗村“大包干”的做法。1982年1月,中共中央批转《全国农村工作会议纪要》指出,农村实行的各种责任制都是社会主义集体经济的生产责任制。为保障农民的土地经营权,1982年《宪法》、1986年6月《土地管理法》在规定农村土地集体所有的同时,把土地的所有权、经营权分开,打破了束缚,极大调动了农民的积极性。而2020年新《土地管理法》允许集体经营性建设用地直接入市,土地所有权人可以通过出让、出租等方式交由单位或者个人使用,改变了过去农村的土地必须征为国有才能进入市场的问题,能够为农民直接增加财产性的收入。

在积极立法的当下,法治对于社会改革发展的作用体现出从守护到开拓的风格转变。我们有理由相信,未来的中国会更加充满活力,法治也将在实现中国梦的航程中继续发挥无可替代的积极作用!

(浙大宁波理工学院传媒与法学院讲师,博士)

故事

绍兴

李东腾(网络与新媒体专业 193 班)

向未来砥砺前行

我出生于浙江绍兴的一个小县城——新昌。从我有记忆开始,便听着长辈们讲述着他们那时候的故事。

外公出生于 1933 年,9 岁时便不幸丧父,随之而来的是母亲改嫁的沉重打击,外公与其姊妹相依为命,居无定所,下雨时甚至只能在别人的屋檐下或者借把伞来躲雨。"吃顿饱饭"更是一种奢望。伴随着新中国的成立,外公在村子里凭着吃苦肯干的精神给村里乡亲们留下了良好的印象,在村里人的帮助下,外公终于建起了自己的房子——一间砂石堆砌的屋子。外公回忆道:"那时候想着,终于有个自己的家了。"

1981 年,家庭联产承包责任制在澄潭镇大枫树村开始实行,分田包产到户。外公一家这时总算是守得云开见月明。依靠辛勤的劳动,两层楼的新房子也开始建起。1985 年,外公买了全村第一台黑白电视机。母亲在述说全村人围在外公家的院子里看电视的时候,那种飞扬的神情所透露出的自豪是无法掩饰的。我想,这大概是对辛劳大半辈子的外公外婆最好的嘉奖。

如果说外公一家的故事是随着时代前进的奋斗史,那爷爷一家的故事便映现出我心中共产党员的样子。1961 年,爷爷是回山镇李间村的党支部书记,奶奶是妇女主任。在 90 岁高龄的奶奶口中,村子里的水电站便是她与爷爷心血的结晶。水电站的建设完全由爷爷奶奶以及一些村里的共产党员来承担。几年中日复一日,挑着沙石走几里路去建造这个从无到有的水电站。几个馒头配咸菜便是一天的伙食。在自己家人的温饱都不能保证的情况下,爷爷还要去接济一些村子里的困难户。1985 年,水电站建设完成,爷爷也卸任了,陪着奶奶一起种田。这时候爷爷才算是重新重视起自己的小家。当然,村民们有困难,第一时间想到的还是寻求我爷爷奶奶的帮助,爷爷虽然已从岗位上卸任,但对于他人的求助都是尽心竭力。为了大家忙碌了大半辈子的爷爷,最终也是归于小家,与奶奶厮守一生。提起那段日子,两位老人除了感叹过程不易,更多的是脸上那神采奕奕的光芒,似乎又回到了那风华正茂、意气风发的青春岁月。

我的母亲在我眼中是一阵风，做事果断，积极上进。母亲出生于1972年，初中毕业时，由于家里经济条件无力支持她继续上学，16岁便从村子里进城打工。她清楚地记得在城里校办胶囊厂中第一月的工资为37元。除去花销，存了将近20元。在夏季，因为天气原因，白天胶囊无法正常生产。母亲与工友们往往从凌晨两三点干到早晨7点。为了多省点钱，母亲每天的伙食就是家里带去的梅干菜泡水就饭吃。2年中，母亲用自己存下的钱买了一辆凤凰牌自行车，在那个年代，这无疑是十分时髦的一件事，也是母亲现在津津乐道的辉煌故事。

由于胶囊厂的工资微薄，1996年母亲进入了国邦兽药公司，成为一名销售。在我不太清晰的记忆中，母亲似乎大部分时间都在出差。当时的交通不便，所有的货物都要亲自送上门，挑着货物走几公里路才能到达乡镇的公司。

如果说母亲是风，那么我的父亲便是树，深深扎根在新昌。父亲于1988年中专电工专业毕业后便在县里的一个风机厂当电工。收入不多，但也算稳定。1995年，父亲四处借钱买下了县政府对面的一套房子，从乡下搬到了县里。房子大概100平方米左右，四室一厅，这也是我成长的地方。后在母亲同事的介绍下，1998年父亲与我母亲结婚，彩礼中有经典的家电套装（彩电，冰箱，影碟机，洗衣机），也有奶奶给母亲的银镯子等。家中买了第一辆雅马哈摩托车。一家子的生活向着美好的未来稳步前行。

2000年2月，我出生了。那个恣肆飞扬、骑着凤凰牌自行车在街上肆无忌惮欢笑的女孩也终为人母。她的满腔热血化为对我无尽的爱，最终羁留在这片故里。为了照顾我，把乡下的爷爷奶奶接到县里，母亲继续出差工作，父亲也辞去了电工的工作，在朋友创办的一家机械厂做起了销售。为了让我接受更好的教育，父母不惜花费更多的钱让我去县里的私立学校上学。从小学开始我便开始有了住校的生活经历。为了记录下我的成长过程，母亲还专门买了当时可算是奢侈品的相机给我拍照。2006年家中买了第一台车，是东风日产的骐达。至今，我仍记得第一次见到自己家车子时的兴奋之情。2008年，母亲辞去了国邦的工作，开始经营起自己的个体兽药生意，父亲也被公司调回了县里，有了更多陪伴我的时间。

然而要强的风终究无法被随遇而安的树所羁绊。父亲母亲因为性格上的不合最终离婚了。而我由于还在小学，懵懵懂懂并没有什么概念，也无力去劝和。万幸的是，风仍会为她的孩子拭去眼角的泪，树也永远为孩子撑起一片天地。之后的日子里，我随父亲生活在县政府对面的房子里，偶尔也会到母亲的家中住几天。慢慢地，父亲母亲有了新的家庭，但对我的爱却未曾减少丝毫，母亲时刻关心着我的生活与学习，一有时间便带我出去游玩，小心翼翼地保护着我幼小的心灵。母亲说："妈妈想让你知道，你和别的孩子没什么区别，爸爸妈妈还是像从前一样爱着你的。"叔叔阿姨也对我视如己出，我未曾以自己来自离异家庭而自卑，我明白，我与一般家庭的孩子并无两样，甚至还多出一些特殊的爱。

2017 年，由于县里基础建设的需要，县府对面那间充满我美好回忆的房子不得不拆迁，心中虽十分不舍，但也无可奈何。现在，用政府给的拆迁款，我们买了新的房子，面积比之前的大了，小区的美化也做得很好。而我也考上了大学，带着父母们的期望走出了这座小县城，正如他们当年从村子里来到县城那样，我也向着崭新的未来砥砺前行。但新昌这片故里承载的是一家人美好的回忆，也是对未来的憧憬与向往。

我想记录下来的，就是浙江一个平凡家庭随着祖国发展而向着美好生活前行的故事。

Shaoxing
Li Dongteng (Class 193, Majoring in Network and New Media)

Forging Ahead into the Future

I was born in Xinchang, a small town in Shaoxing, Zhejiang Province. I grew up with the stories of the past told by the elders.

My maternal grandfather was born in 1933. When he was nine years old, he lost his father, which was followed by the heavy blow of his mother's remarriage. He and his sisters depended on each other for survival and had no fixed abode. They even had to shelter under other people's eaves or borrow an umbrella when it rained. Filling their belly was a kind of wild wish for them. With the founding of the People's Republic of China, my maternal grandpa left a good impression on the villagers with his hard-working spirit. With the help of the villagers, he finally built his own house which was made of sand and gravel. My grandfather recalled, "I though I had a home at last."

In 1981, the household contract responsibility system was put into effect in Dafengshu Village, Chengtan Town, which was to contract output to each household. Every cloud has a silver lining. With hard work, a two-story house was built. In 1985, my maternal grandpa became the first one in the village who bought a black and white TV set. As my mother recounted the scene in which the whole village gathered in their family's yard for watching TV, her fluttering expression of pride was hard to conceal. This was probably the best reward for my maternal grandparents who have labored most of their lives.

If the story of my maternal grandpa's family was the history of stuggle with the advance of the times, then the story of my paternal grandpa's family reflected the communist party members in my mind. In 1961, my paternal grandfather was the Party branch secretary in Lijian Village, Huishan Town. Meanwhile, my paternal grandmother was the director of women's affairs. According to my 90-year-old paternal grandmother, the village hydropower station was the crystallization of her painstaking effort with her husband. The construction of the hydropower station was entirely undertaken by my grandparents and some communist party members in the village. Day in and day out for years, they carried sand and gravel for miles to build this hydroelectric station from scratch. A few steamed buns and pickles made a day's meal. Even when his own family didn't have enough food and clothing, my paternal grandpa would help out those poor families in the village. In 1985, when the construction of the hydropower station was completed, my paternal grandfather resigned and farmed in the fields with my grandmother. It was then that he began to attach importance to his little house again. Of course, when the villagers had difficulties, their first thought was to seek help from my paternal grandpa. Although he had retired from his post, he would strain every nerve to help them. He had spent most of his life helping the villagers, and finally came back to his small family to be together with my grandmother. Mentioning that period of time, the two old people said with a sigh that the process was not easy, but their faces were mostly illuminated by the bright light, as if they had been back to the prime of their youth when they were high-spirited.

In my impression, my mother was a decisive, positive and progressive person, just like a gust of wind. My mother was born in 1972. Due to the financial difficulties of her family, she could not continue her education. When she graduated from middle school, she left the village to work in the city at the age of 16. She vividly remembered the first month's salary at the school-run capsule factory in the city was 37 yuan.

Minus daily expenses, she saved nearly 20 yuan. In summer, because of the weather, they could not carry out normal production of the capsule during the daytime. My mother and her workmates often worked from 2 or 3 a. m. to 7 a. m. To save more money, she soaked dried prunes brought from home in water and ate them with rice. During these two years, she used her savings to buy a Phoenix bicycle. It was certainly in vogue at the time, and was a glorious story my mother took delight in talking about.

Due to the meager salary of the capsule factory, my mother applied for a job in Guobang Veterinary Medicine Company in 1996 and became a saleswoman. I vaguely remembered that my mother seemed to be away on business trips a lot. The transportation was not convenient and there was no logistics at that time, so all the goods had to be delivered to the customer's home in person. She had to carry the goods for several kilometers to reach the company in the town.

If my mother was like the wind, then my father was like a tree deeply rooted in Xinchang. My father graduated from a technical secondary school in 1988 and worked as an electrician in a ventilator factory in the county. His income was not so much, but it was stable. In 1995, my father borrowed money and bought a house which was across from the county government and moved from the countryside to the county. The house was about 100 square meters big and had four bedrooms and a living room. It was the place where I grew up. Later, my parents got married in 1998 after being introduced by a colleague of my mother's to each other. The betrothal gifts included a typical set of household appliances (a color TV set, a refrigerator, a DVD player, a washing machine) as well as silver bracelets from my paternal grandmother. They bought their first Yamaha motorcycle. Their life was moving steadily toward a bright future.

In February 2000, I was born. That girl who had lived a carefree life and laughed freely riding a Phoenix brand bicycle in the street finally became a mother. Her passion turned into an endless love and stayed in her hometown for me. In order to take care of me, my paternal grandparents who lived in the countryside were taken to the county. My mother continued to travel on business trips while my father quit his job as an electrician and worked as a salesman in a machinery factory founded by his friend. To let me receive a better education, my parents spared no money to send me to a private school in the county. Therefore, I began my boarding life since primary school. In order to record my growth, my mother bought a camera, which was a luxury at that time, to take pictures of me. The family's first car, a Nissan TIIDA, was purchased in 2006. I still remembered the excitement I felt when I first saw the car. In 2008, my mother quit her job in Guobang to start her own business on veterinary drug and my father was transferred back to the county by the company, which gave him more time to accompany me.

A strong wind can never be tied up by a tree that grows comfortably wherever it's rooted. My parents divorced because of personality clashes. As I was still in primary school, I had no idea about that and I was unable to talk them out of it. Fortunately, the wind would still wipe the tears from her child's eyes, and the tree would always hold up a space for the child. Later, I lived with my father in the house across from the county government and occasionally stayed with my mother for a few days. Gradually, my parents had their own new family, but their love for me did not diminish. My mother often cared about my life and study and took me out to play in her free time. She carefully protected me from being hurt. She said, "Mom wants you to know that you are no different from other children and that Mom and Dad love you just as before." My stepfather and my stepmother also treated me as their own child. I did not feel inferior just because I was from a divorced family. I knew that I was no different from other children. By contrast, I even had more special love.

In 2017, due to the need of infrastructure construction in the county, the house across from the county government had to be demolished though it was full of my happy memories. Although I was very reluctant to leave, there was nothing I could do. Now, with the demolition compensation given by the government, we bought a new house with a larger area than the previous one, and the living environment of the community was great. Later on, I was admitted to college and walked out of this small town with my parents' expectations. Just as how they come like when they came to the county from the village that year, I'm forging ahead into a new future. Xinchang, our hometown, carries not only our family's wonderful memories, but also our longing for the future.

What I want to write down is a story of an ordinary family in Zhejiang which is forging ahead towards a happy life with the development of our motherland.

人是社会变迁中最为活跃的因素

柳　五

人是社会变迁中最为活跃的因素。人的活跃程度,取决于人基于自身特质的应变应激能力,以及外部环境的促进和影响。二者之间如果能够形成良性互动,则会推动社会快速发展,如果只有其中的一个因素起作用,而另一个因素不活跃,或者活跃度不够,则会制约社会的快速发展。

从金煜同学的《小家变迁史》中,我们能够看到,他的爷爷是一个性格积极乐观、头脑灵活的人。他能够在任何环境条件下保持向上努力进取的姿态,这使得他总能够在同等情况下,比别人获得更好的生存境遇,这说明他的个人应变应激能力比较强,能够更好地适应社会。

但是在一个相对封闭、规制过多而又严格的社会环境下,个人活力释放度是不够的,这使他的创造力会受到影响,改善自身生存条件的努力所取得的效果有限。

作者的父亲明显继承了来自爷爷比较活跃的性格,而且在他的父亲成长的时代,这个国家变得越来越开放,以前不敢想、不能做的事情,在作者父亲的时代,尽可以放开手脚去尝试。他的勇敢给了他机会,为他在这个国家改革开放的拓荒年代获得了丰厚的回报,取得了比作者祖父更大的成绩。可见,个人的创造活力必须要与大时代合拍,这样才能够敏锐地把握住时代赋予的机会。

事实上,中国的改革开放就是通过持续放权来改善发展环境,从而不断地释放人们改善自我与发展自我的能动性。在这个过程中,不管是环境还是社会个体,在变化的限度上,都没有一个清晰而明确的"度",需要以探索的方式来寻找最佳的结合点,所以当个体的创造性脱离了其所能够承受的度,也就是作者所说的"贪婪是恶魔",加上专业知识不足,导致了父亲在股市上的失败,不得不另起炉灶,而且环境与个人之间也在不断地相互塑造,开放的环境提升了人的自由度,人的自由程度又推动了环境的更加宽容和开放。大势既成,历史便在既定的轨道上展现出迷人的面貌和魅力。

(吉林日报评论员)

故事
金华
金煜盛(网络与新媒体专业 192 班)

小家变迁史

我爷爷出生于 1940 年,在那战火纷飞的岁月里,爷爷一家人颠沛流离。爷爷有一个哥哥,年幼时不小心被火烧伤,最终不治而终。太爷爷在爷爷很小的时候也去世了。爷爷只能与太婆母子两人相依为命。

新中国成立以后,20 岁的爷爷应征入伍。在爷爷的记忆里,那是一段无比美好、难忘的时光,在他至今 80 多年的岁月长河中,熠熠生辉。

爷爷很上进,为期三个月的新兵集训时期,别的新兵每天只完成连队规定的训练项目,而我爷爷总是要比别人多做一点。三个月后的新兵考核中,爷爷总成绩拿了全团第一,还破了武装泅渡项目的纪录,他被各连队争着抢着要,还有首长点名要爷爷做他的警卫。

除了身体方面的强化训练,思想上的武装爷爷也不曾落下。爷爷的日记本扉页,能够看到这样一句话:文明其精神,野蛮其体魄——毛泽东。

复员之后,爷爷经历了三年自然灾害时期,也经历了太婆因疾辞世。后来,爷爷在镇上办的小学当教员,一个月的工资有 60 多元。也是在那个时候,爷爷经人介绍,认识了在工厂做活的奶奶,直到如今,他们携手走过了无数程的山河,共度了一甲子的岁月。

奶奶生了三个孩子,都是男丁,我父亲排行第二。爷爷在农村造了一栋小屋子,上下两层,有百来平方米,他与奶奶住楼下,三个儿子住楼上。一家人相依为命。

爷爷开始另谋出路。爷爷有枪,夏天,他常常在夜里骑几十里的自行车,载着一只狗,到永康的大山里打猎,他打过鹿和野猪等。归家之后,将动物处理好,分类出售,以此补贴家用。小学时我常常和爷爷一起住,那时候最爱听的就是他打猎的故事。冬天,爷爷会带着大伯去网鱼网鳖。

就这样,日子变得越来越好,奶奶总是很骄傲地跟我们孙辈说,"咱家是当时好几个村里第一个买上放映机的,那时候,好几里外的后生小伙都赶过来看,屋里坐满了人。你爷爷就站在机器后面摇啊摇,给大家放《济公传》哩。"那时候的爷爷也算是有商业头脑，在家门口卖起了瓜子和凉茶，一毛钱一份，一个月下来，能给家里额外增添很多钱。

父亲丧失了去全县最好的高中念书的机会，只能在金华东阳市南马镇上的高中就读，一来是免学费，二来是可以照应家里。据父亲说，他在高中的成绩几乎门门年级第一，但是越来越没了学习的兴趣，他想去更辽阔更遥远的世界。

1987年，父亲揣着准备高三用一年的钱，坐上了南下的绿皮车，去了广州，一个人。爷爷起初很是反对，认为父亲最少也应该先考上大学再去闯荡社会。父亲却说，他已经受够了小地方，他绝不愿意再多呆一天，他答应爷爷，准时回来参加高考。

父亲初至广州，因为未满18岁，很少有单位肯用他。后来他在邮局谎报了年龄，获得了一份可以解决一天三个馒头的差事。当时，他几乎天天睡在医院的过道。半个月后，他顺利进入一家油漆厂，当起了油漆工人。父亲学习能力很强，不到一个月，工作效率已然接近老员工。当时油漆工的工资很高，父亲又省吃俭用，原始资本在疯狂积累。

那一年，桑塔纳重拳出击，开启中国汽车消费潮。从未涉足汽车行业的父亲开始努力往这方面发展，他认为，这是红利期，这是商机。父亲白天做着油漆厂的工作，晚上则潜心学习有关汽车方面的知识，不出一个月，他摇身一变，成了汽车销售员，工装服变成了西装，解放靴变成了皮鞋，工资也翻了数倍。

一年后，父亲骑着摩托车，带着五颜六色的回乡货回家时，爷爷给了他一巴掌，责问他为什么不回来高考？父亲回答："高考是为了赚钱，可是我现在已经很赚钱了。"爷爷怒极，又踹了父亲一脚。

1990年，我国A股开市，激发了全民热情，父亲就是那个时候进军股市的。他和绝大多数的人一样，并没有专业知识，更没有相关经验。他只是在开市的日子里，每天坐车几十公里，去义乌看趋势，那时候的电子显示屏上，绿色是稀有的，一年半内，指数从两位数蹿到近一千五。如此牛市大背景下，闭着眼睛盲选都是大概率赚钱的。

父亲在头一年半的时间里，赚了一笔又一笔，他拿着这些钱，在街边批了地基，还在镇上和朋友一起办了服装厂，风头一时尽出。然而，贪婪是恶魔。父亲在股票大跌之前，押上了所有的现金，在那短短的时间里，跌幅超70%。

我一向认为，没有经验与专业知识的股票交易，无异于赌博，而我父亲，正是一位狂热的赌徒。他不相信自己的本钱会赔光，他想要东山再起，于是转让了服装厂，还卖掉了如今价值疯涨的地基，在股市里七进七出。

从概率上说，如果一个人赢不收手、输不止损，那么结果必定是血本无归，父亲的经历印证了这个道理。好在他明白了一个点，获取财富的方式固然重要，但踏踏实实的工作绝不至于走向绝路。沉寂之后，他开始了新的生活，将目光转向了木雕。他从学徒开始，一步一个脚印，到最后招了几名师傅开了个小作坊。

父亲与我母亲相识，是在1996年的夏天，他们从相遇到相识，从相知到相爱，再到我的出生，用了三年多的时间。在这三年多的时间里，他们造了一小栋房子，那可是正儿八经拿砖头垒起来的，在当时并不是一件容易的事。

1999年的圣诞，我出生在这个平凡的家庭，童年最大的乐趣是一台索佳的影碟机，插入碟片，连上手柄与电视，就可以玩游戏，玩累了就换上麦克风咿呀唱歌。如此，一晃又是十年。十年里，我国加入了世贸，举办了奥运会，全国经济飞速发展。接下来的十年，我们共同走进了小康社会。

Jinhua
Jin Yusheng (Class 192, Majoring in Network and New Media)

Changes in a Small Family

My grandfather was born in 1940. During those war-ridden years, my grandpa's family suffered a total dislocation of their lives. He had an elder brother who was accidentally burned at an early age. Later on he died because of it. My great grandfather passed away when my grandfather was very young, so my grandpa and his mother could only depended on each other for survival.

After the founding of the People's Republic of China, the 20-year-old grandpa enlisted in the army. In his memory, it was an extremely beautiful and unforgettable period of time, shining brightly through his 80 years of life.

My grandpa was very aspirant. In the three-month new recruit training, other new recruits only completed the training items prescribed by the company every day, but my grandpa always did a little bit more than others. During the new recruit assessment three months later, he took the first place in the regiment and even broke the army's record in the armed swim-cross. He was popular among various companies, and a senior military officer personally appointed my grandfather to be his guard.

In addition to the intensive physical training, my grandpa had never forgotten to equip himself ideologically. On the front page of his diary, there was a sentence by Mao Zedong: To civilize one's spirit, one should firm himself up.

After the demobilisation, my grandfather went through the hard days of the great famine (1959—1961); afterwards, his mother died of illness. Later on my grandpa worked as a teacher in the elementary school run by the town, and his salary was more than 60 yuan a month. It was also at that time that he got to know my grandmother, a factory worker, through other people. Until now, they have gone through countless obstacles hand in hand and spent a total of sixty years together.

My grandma gave birth to three children. All of them were boys, and my father was the second. My grandpa built a small house in the countryside with two floors, which was approximately a hundred square meters big. My grandparents lived downstairs while three children lived upstairs. The family depended on each other.

My grandfather decided to find a way out. He had a gun. During the summer, he would ride his bicycle, travel dozens of miles with his dog and hunt animals in the mountains of YongKang. He had shot deer and wild boars. After returning home, the animals were cleaned, sorted out and sold to subsidize the family. When I was in primary school, I used to live with my grandpa. At that time, my favorite thing was listening to his hunting stories. In winter, he would take the fishing net to catch fish and turtles with my eldest uncle.

In this way, life got better and better. My grandma would always tell her grandchildren with pride, "Our family was the first in the village to buy a projector. At that time, young boys rushed here from several miles away. The house was full of people. Standing behind the machine to crank the handle, your grandfather would play The Tale of Jigong for everyone!" With all these people coming and going, my business-savvy grandfather started to sell sunflower seeds and herbal tea on the doorstep. He charged 0.01 yuan for each serve. He earned a lot of money for the family every month.

My father didn't get the chance to go to the best high school in the county. Instead, he chose a school in Nanma Town, Dongyang, Jinhua City, because it was tuition-free; besides, he could take care of the family.

According to my father, almost all of his grades in school were the highest, so he gradually lost interest in studying, and he wanted to leave home and see a bigger world, a distant world.

In 1987, my father took the money that was supposed to pay for his third year in the senior high school and left for the southern city of Guangzhou on a green-coated train alone. My grandpa opposed this idea, believing that a college education was a must before trying his luck in society. But my father insisted that he was tired of the small town and he in no way would stay here for one more day. However, he promised my grandpa that he would come back for the college entrance examination.

When my father first arrived in Guangzhou, few companies were willing to employ my father because he was under 18 years old. Later on he lied about his age at the post office and got an errand which could cover meal cost. At that time, he slept in the hospital aisle almost every day. Half a month later, he successfully entered a paint factory and became a painter. My father was a great learner. In less than a month, he was able to work as efficiently as senior employees. Meanwhile, a painter's salary was considerable, and my father led a simple life, so the original capital was accumulated rapidly.

That year, the introduction of Volkswagen Santana to the Chinese market set off a wave of automobile purchasing in the country. My father, who had never been involved in the automobile industry, began to dabble in this area. He believed that the automobile industry was the next bonus creator and was full of business opportunities. He worked in the paint factory during the day, and he devoted himself to learning about automobiles at night. Within a month, he became a car salesman. His factory uniform was changed into a business suit and his boots into leather shoes. His salary was multiplied several times.

One year later, my father returned home on his new motorcycle and with fancy goods. My grandpa slapped him and asked him why he didn't come back for the college entrance examination. My father replied, "People go to college so as to make money, but I have already earned money!" Hearing this, my grandpa was so furious that he kicked my father.

In 1990 came China's own stock market: A-Share. Investors were in frenzy. That was when my father entered the stock market. Like most people, he had no professional knowledge or relevant experience. He would travel dozens of kilometres to Yiwu just to see how the market was developing on trading days. Few stocks would fall at that time, and indices surged from double digits all the way to nearly 1500. In a bull market like this, chances were that one could pick a stock with his eyes closed and still make a fortune.

In the first year and a half, my father made one fortune after another. He took the money and bought land on a street; he also started a clothing factory in the town with his friends, which made him a well-known figure in the neighbourhood. However, greed is the devil. My father bet all his cash in the stock market, but the market plummeted by over 70%.

I always believed that investing in the stock market without experience or proper training was a form of gambling, and my father was exactly an avid gambler. He didn't believe that all his capital would be lost. He wanted to stage a comeback, so he sold the clothing industry and his land which is now soaring in value, just hoping to try his luck in the stock market.

The rule of probability tells us that a person is bound to lose if he doesn't know when to stop. My father was the living embodiment of this rule. Fortunately, he came to the realisation that there were many ways to make a fortune, and making money through sweat and tears was the safest one. After all of his ventures, he started a new life as a wood-carving apprentice. He did it one step at a time, and in the end, he opened a small workshop together with his fellow craftsmen.

My father and my mother met in the summer of 1996. It took them more than three years to know each other, to fall in love and to give birth to me. During these sweet years, they built a small brick house, which was not easy at that time.

On the Christmas of 1999, I was born into this ordinary family. The greatest joy of my childhood came from a Sokkia DVD player. I inserted the disc, connected the console with television, and I would be able to play games. When I was tired, I would change the console to a microphone and sing. In the next ten years, China joined the WTO and hosted the Olympic Games. The national economy developed rapidly. In the next ten years, let's embrace a well-off society together!

梦想如影随形

陈　恩

《礼记·大学》有言:“古之欲明明德于天下者,先治其国;欲治其国者,先齐其家;欲齐其家者,先修其身;欲齐其身者,先正其心;……心正而后身修,身修而后家齐,家齐而后国治,国治而后天下平。”这样的论述简而概之即可为“修身、齐家、治国、平天下”,与“一屋不扫,何以扫天下”一样,均论证的是有家才有国。

“家是最小的国,国是千万家。”习近平总书记曾说:一个国家,一个民族,只有找到适合自己条件的道路,才能实现自己的发展目标。在探索中国道路的过程中,家庭作为构成社会的最小单元,是最具有中国特性的本源性传统,是国家发展、民族进步、社会和谐的重要基点。

40余年波澜壮阔,40余年沧桑巨变,衢州县城北端的小溪边村一户人家的生活奋斗史,从面朝黄土背朝天到拜师学艺,从城里打工到有房有车。看似平淡如水的故事,却是道出了一代人不凡的家庭变迁,反映出改革开放40余年大背景下农村和城市的发展。海阔凭鱼跃,天高任鸟飞。改革开放,给无数人带来选择的机会,可以见识更广阔的天地,成就更丰富的人生,拥抱更美好的未来。中国梦从未像今天这样真切可期,改革和梦想也从未像今天这样如影随形。多少中国人的梦想,因改革破土重生,因改革自由飞翔。

(浙大宁波理工学院党委宣传部)

故事

衢州

余月祥(新闻学专业192班)

心之所向　素履以往

清明的时候,父亲带我来到了村头镇镇上,在给他作古两个月的师父烧香点炮之后,望着寥寥数字的石碑,这个素来寡言严肃的男人的眼里竟然泛红了。

父亲曾不止一次地跟我说过师父对他的好,然而因为这场疫情,父亲也没能在师父弥留之际去送送他。

1985年,没考上初中的父亲被祖父领着去了镇上学手艺,师父是个木匠,也算祖父的族内兄弟。尽管将要长期寄人篱下,但对于父亲来说,这只不过是换个地方吃饭罢了,而头也不回的祖父步伐显得轻松了许多。

衢州市开化县位于浙江省最西部,这里九山半水半分田,尽管有着优美的生态环境,但由于偏僻闭塞,长期以来这里的经济发展和生活水平在全省一直靠后。父亲的家在县城北端的一个小山村——小溪边村,在这片群山绵延的土地上,我的祖祖辈辈们生老病死于此,面朝黄土背朝天于此。

父亲的学习成绩并不好。在村小上了五年学之后的父亲没能考上初中,在那时自然就不能再上学了。父亲于是在大队里的矿洞挑砂石,直到突然有一天祖父带他去了镇上学木工。

"师父和你爷爷差不多大,他没有子女,老婆在早年害疯病死了。"父亲说,"他是整个镇最好的木匠。"

"我当学徒的第一年,是帮师父做杂活,扫地、挑水、拉锯、磨刨……他教我的几年从来没有像其他的师父那样动辄打骂,即使我做错了他也都只是说'可惜了这块木头了,下次注意噢'。师父去东家家做事总会带上学徒,吃饭时师父和东家坐在八仙桌上席,徒弟坐两侧。按照规矩,师傅先动筷,徒弟才能吃。师父吃完了,徒弟一定得把碗放下,不许再吃。所以很多徒弟都是只吃得半饱。但是我师父每次出去做事吃饭时都往我这儿看,他总是慢慢地吃,等他看到我吃得差不多了才开始加快速度吃饭。睡东家家里时,虽然只有一张床,但是师父从来都是让我跟他挤一挤。师父从来不扣我的工钱,别人有活找他他还向别人推荐我去做。他更像是我的父亲,教会了我技术,也教会了我做人。"在这曾经给予他数不尽温情的地方回首往事，父亲的话越发动情。

父亲跟着师父学了4年，出师之后的父亲用他的所学在乡里给人家做家具、修犁具。父亲干活娴熟能吃苦，很快就闻名乡里。

“后来我时常会听到镇里有谁在城里打工‘阔了’的消息。我年轻躁动，也想去干一番事业。”在几乎没有犹豫的情况下，父亲带上了几年来积攒的钱，搭上了大队里开往县城的拖拉机，又辗转来到了市里，最后在警察同志的帮助下赶上了开往上海的火车。这一年是1990年，父亲20岁。在这一年的4月18日，国务院正式宣布开发开放浦东。

在天桥下蹲了半个多月、一直睡广场的父亲终于被一个施工队录用了，父亲的工作是给浦东的一个大酒店装潢。相对之前高许多的工资使父亲第一次尝到了闯荡的甜头。

“下工之后我喜欢穿着衬衫牛仔裤去南京路转转，啃着烧饼，吸着老酸奶，走到外滩，看着对面一幢幢楼房飞快长高，那感觉太震撼了。”父亲边开着电瓶车边和我回忆。

1995年，独自闯荡了5年的父亲回到家乡，和母亲结了婚，婚后的两人一起在上海打拼，租住在金山区的镇上。父亲给饭店旅馆装潢，母亲在灯泡厂做组装。之后几年在父母的辛勤劳动下，我们家陆续增添了一些新玩意儿，永久自行车、西湖缝纫机、康佳彩电、金正影碟机……但是父母又要面临这么一个难题：有了两个孩子以后是继续留在上海还是回到老家。将孩子带在身边固然好，但是会耽误父母务工；将孩子放到老家估计祖父母照顾不好我们。思前想后，他们决定由母亲在老家抚养我们，父亲独自在外打工。

2001年，母亲带着长我5岁的姐姐和襁褓中的我坐上了回乡的列车，我们家的故事翻开了新的一页。2006年，父母犹豫再三，做了一个艰难的决定：造房子。其实这些年来家中的积蓄还不足以造上一座新的洋房，尽管父亲的足迹踏遍了大半个中国，但由于工作的不稳定性，收入并不可观。可是老房子实在是破败不堪，随时都有坍塌风险。就这样，父母白天买材料搭架子，晚上拿着电筒找熟人借钱。很快一座三层楼房就搭建好了，但它只是一个毛坯，没有任何装饰。我们把家具搬到了新房子，就这样住下了。时至今日，当父亲回想起那番场景时，心中仍然十分不甘与愧疚。

2008年，通过在县城当老师的亲戚的帮助，我和姐姐分别进了县城里的小学和初中读书。父亲继续在外靠装潢赚钱，母亲在县城带我们俩顺便打打零工。我们在县城的住所是一个废弃的啤酒厂，薄薄的三合板拼出来5个逼仄的房间，每间住着一户人家，共用厕所和厨房，没有热水。同住的邻居换了一批又一批，而因为两百元的房租，我们在这里住了8年，直到我初中毕业了这一片被国家征收我们才搬出。

母亲前前后后不知道做了多少零工，在饭店端菜，做来料加工，在学校打杂，给人家做保姆带小孩。在那有雄心且敏感的年龄里，父母憔悴的面容、糟糕的生活环境、同学们精致的日常和他们对我异样的眼光一直是我努力的动力，但现实是一个甜甜圈也会成为奢侈。

2015年初，家里终于偿清了造房子时欠下的债务，而我们的生活正悄悄地发生着变化。

父亲虽然不太识字，也没有受过系统的培训，但30多年的打拼为他积累了大量的装潢经验。面对各种户型各种风格父亲都能游刃有余、得心应手。“干起活来有时候觉得自己更像是一个艺术家，气枪就是画笔，墙壁就是画布。”父亲骄傲地说。父亲精湛的业务为他赢来了广阔的人脉，刚做完一处就立马有老主顾请他做事。母亲也成为本地小有名气的月嫂。有父亲的辛勤奔波加上母亲的勤俭持家，家里的存款逐渐增加，那些曾经觉得遥不可及的事物也在不断实现。

上了高中，我们搬了家，住进了整洁舒适的公寓楼。虽然还是租住，但生活环境比之前好太多太多了。

2018年，姐姐大学毕业后在律所找到了一份稳定的工作。也是在这一年，父亲大半年没有出门打工，因为我们的老家时隔12年终于要装潢了。作为设计师和施工人员，父亲每天起早贪黑，精心雕琢。当父亲接好最后一根电线，按下开关时，一束束灯光照亮了家里的每一个角落——这是这么多年来我们家最亮堂的一次。父亲当时激动地说：“给别人装潢了这么多房子，这一次终于轮到我自己了。”这是从小到大我见过父亲最开心的一次，这座房子承载了父亲太多的心血与梦想。

Quzhou
Yu Yuexiang (Class 192, Majoring in Journalism)

Remain True to Your Original Aspiration and Accomplish It

On Tomb Sweeping Day, my father took me to Cuntou Town. My father who was always taciturn and serious had tears in his eyes when he looked at the stone tablet with only a few words after burning incense to his master who had been dead for two months.

My father had told me more than once how good his master was to him. However, because of the COVID-19 pandemic, my father was unable to visit his master when he was dying.

In 1985, my father, who had failed in the entrance examination for junior high school, was taken to the town by his father to learn a trade. His master was a carpenter, and was a brother in his father's family. For my father, though it meant that he had to live under others' roof for a long time, it was merely a change in the place to eat. By contrast, my grandfather looked relaxed and did not look back.

Kaihua County, Quzhou City is located in the westernmost part of Zhejiang Province. There are many more mountains than rivers and farmlands here. Although it has a beautiful ecological environment, its economic development and living standards have been lagging behind in the whole province for a long time due to its remoteness and isolation. My father's home is in Xiaoxibian Village, a small village in the northern part of the country. On this land with continous mountains, my ancestors were born, lived, got ill, died, and worked hard on the farmland.

My father didn't do well in school. After studying in primary school in the village for five years, my father failed to get into a middle school, so he naturally discontinued his education. My father carried sand and gravel from the mine in the brigade till the day when my grandfather took him to the town to become a carpenter's apprentice.

"My master was almost your grandfather's age. He had no children and his wife died of a mental disorder early in life. He was the best carpenter in the whole town," my father said.

"In the first year of my apprenticeship, I helped my master with chores like sweeping the floor, carrying water, pulling the saw, sharpening the plane, planing and so on. During the years when he taught me, he never beat or scolded me like other masters. Even when I made a mistake he would just say, 'What a pity that you wasted this piece of wood. Be careful next time.' My master always took apprentices with him when he did his work. During the meal, my master and the employer sat on the honored seat of the eight immortals table while we apprentices could only sit on the two sides. According to the rules, apprentices must not eat until the master starts to eat, and when the master finishes eating, the apprentices must put down the bowl and not eat any more, so many apprentices were underfed. But every time my master went out to work, he would always keep an eye on me when having meals. He would eat slowly, and when he saw that I was almost done, he would speed up. When sleeping in the employer's house and there was only one bed, my master always shared the bed with me. He never docked my wages. He also recommended me to others when they needed a carpenter. He was more like a father to me, teaching me skills and how to be a human being." Looking back on the past at this place that had given him so much warmth, my father's words became even more touching.

My father learned carpentry from his master for four years. After finishing his apprenticeship, my father used what he had learned to make furniture and repair ploughs in the village. My father was a tough and skilled worker and soon became famous in the village.

"Then I heard from time to time that someone from the town had become wealthy after working in the city. Being young and restless, I also wanted to do something big." Almost without hesitation, my father took the money he had saved for several years and boarded a tractor of the brigade to the county. Then he traveled to the city and finally caught the train bound for Shanghai with the help of a policeman. It was the year of 1990, and my father was 20 years old. On April 18 of that year, the State Council officially announced the development and opening up of Pudong.

My father, who tried finding a job under the overpass and slept in the square for more than half a month, was finally hired by a construction team to decorate a large hotel in Pudong. With a much higher salary than before, my father experienced his first sweet taste of adventure.

"After work, I liked to walk around Nanjing Road in my jeans and shirts, eating pancakes and sipping set-style yogurt, walking to the Bund. Watching the buildings across the street getting higher and higher in such a short time was so amazing." As he drove the scooter, my father recalled the past days.

In 1995, after five years of working in another city alone, my father returned home and married my mother. They struggled together in Shanghai and rented a house in a town of Jinshan District. My father decorated restaurants and hotels. My mother assembled light bulbs in a bulb factory. After a few years of hard work, our family had some new articles, such as a Forever bicycle, a West Lake sewing machine, a Konka color TV, a Nintaus DVD player and so on. But my parents were faced with the dilemma of whether to stay in Shanghai or go back to their hometown after having two children. Keeping children with themselves was good, but it distracted them from work. Leaving the children with my grandparents in the hometown wasn't a good idea for my parents. After thinking it over, they decided that my mother would bring us up in the hometown while my father would work in the city alone.

In 2001, my mother took my sister who was five years older than me, and me, an infant, on a train home. Thus, the story of our family turned a new page. In 2006, after much hesitation, my parents made a difficult decision, that was to build a house. In fact, our family's savings over the years was not enough to build a new house. Although my father traveled more than half of China, due to the instability of the job, the income was not considerable. But the old house was so dilapidated that it could collapse at any moment. Therefore, my parents bought materials to build scaffolds during the day and borrowed money from acquaintances with torches at night. Soon a three-storey bungalow was built, but it was only a rough frame without any decoration. We moved the furniture into the new house and lived there. Up till now, when my father recalled that scene, he still felt very resigned and ashamed.

In 2008, with the help of my relatives who were teachers in the county, my sister and I went to primary school and middle school in the county respectively. My father continued to make money by doing decoration for others, and my mother took care of the two of us while doing odd jobs in the county. Our house in the town was an abandoned brewery with five cramped rooms inside partitioned by thin laminate, each room housing one family. The families shared toilets and kitchens, and there was no hot water. We had different neighbors. We lived here for eight years because of the cheap rent, which was only 200 yuan a month. We didn't move out until I graduated from middle school and the area was expropriated by the state.

My mother did a lot of odd jobs. She served food in restaurants, was engaged in processing trade, worked as a school handyman, nursed families and looked after children. In those days when I was ambitious and sensitive, the gaunt face of my parents, the poor living environment, the exquisite daily life of my classmates and their funny looks on me were always the motivation for me to work hard. The reality was that even a doughnut was a luxury for me.

In early 2015, our family had finally paid off the debt from building the house, and our life quietly changed.

Although my father couldn't read much, nor had he received systematic training, he had accumulated a great deal of experience in decoration through thirty years of hard work. My father could handle all kinds of decoration styles and house types with ease. "Sometimes I felt more like an artist when I was working. The air gun was the brush and the wall was the canvas," he said proudly. My father's excellent skill earned him a wide network of contacts, and he was immediately offered work by his regular clients. My mother also became a famous maternity matron in the area. Because of my father's hard work and my mother's diligence and thrift, the savings of our family gradually increased, and we were accomplishing things that used to be out of reach.

When I went to high school, we moved into a neat and comfortable apartment building. Although the apartment was rented, the living environment was much better than before.

In 2018, my sister found a stable job in a law firm after graduating from college. Also in this year, my father didn't go out to work for more than half a year, because the house in our hometown was going to be decorated after 12 years. As the designer and builder, my father worked from dawn to dusk every day. As my father connected the last wire and pressed the switch, beams of light lit up every corner of our house for the first time in years. Our house has never brighter before. My father said excitedly, "After so many decorations for others' houses, finally it's time for me to decorate my own house." I had never seen my father so happy before, as this house carried my father's efforts and dreams.

幸福都是奋斗出来的

胡鹿鸣

习近平总书记告诉我们："幸福都是奋斗出来的！"刘佳颖同学笔下的文字，没有华丽的辞藻，但却从她的视角真实地记录了一个小家庭如何通过几代人的忙碌和奋斗，奔走在通往小康生活的幸福大道上的点滴，也得出了她的答案——"幸福来自于忙碌"。"女本柔弱、为母则刚"，笔者眼中家里的两个女性，也就是外婆和母亲一生的坎坷经历，特别是一辈子忙忙碌碌的身影，使东海边小县城中朴素坚毅、吃苦耐劳的女性形象得到了充分体现。都说女性撑起半边天，刘佳颖的外婆在大半辈子用自己瘦弱的肩膀撑起了一个大家庭，就算已经把5个女儿都拉扯成人工作赚钱了，还是忙忙碌碌的"像个陀螺，不停转"，最终因积劳成疾而去世。外婆这一辈子吃了很多苦，但是她坚韧努力的品质在家族中有了很好的继承。所以到了刘佳颖的母亲这一代，不管是14岁就去做针织女工补贴家用，还是去国外的塞班岛打工，用打工积攒的钱在老家盖了楼、在县城买了房，并支持丈夫去上海闯荡等，除了一如既往的忙忙碌碌，更有一股敢闯敢为的品性。因此，这个小家正如中国大地上千千万万个小家一样，通过一家人的勤劳奋斗和吃苦耐劳，在忙碌中走向小康，在忙碌中品味幸福。新时代是奋斗者的时代，相信家人的优秀品质一定也能在笔者心中留下深深的烙印，成为其一生受用的宝贵财富。

（浙大宁波理工学院传媒与法学院党委副书记、纪委书记）

故事

宁波

刘佳颖(网络与新媒体专业 182 班)

幸福来自于忙碌

我家在象山,一个东海边的小县城。我家里的两个女人,一个是我的外婆,一个是我的母亲。她们普通又有自己伟大的地方,我在她们身上看到了“为母则刚”的力量与坚韧的精神。

1949 年,我的外婆在新中国成立的欢腾声中出生了。在老照片里,她皮肤黝黑,个子不高却很壮实,一对不大但明亮的三角眼里透着一股坚毅。外婆像那个年代普通的农村女孩一样,在同村找了个合适男孩就结婚了,那时农村还有着很强的重男轻女的观念,越穷越生,越生越穷,但外婆连着 5 胎都是女儿。我的妈妈出生于 1974 年,排行老三。“那时候老房子的外墙还是拿石头堆的,再找点土填填缝。”妈妈环顾我们居住的精致装潢的房间,略有些感慨地说:“冬天的风就从那个石头缝里钻进来,而且那时候还买不起棉花的垫被,只能用稻草垫在底下。我和你四姨睡一张,晚上睡觉时还抱在一起互相取暖。” 5 个女儿的养育压力让外婆不仅要洗衣做饭,还要帮着外公种地、养猪、养鸭,农务不忙的时候还要去针织厂里倒纱线。

但是幸运女神始终没有眷顾外婆,在妈妈 14 岁的时候,外公生病过世了,虽然前两个年长的女儿已经开始工作赚钱,但是家里一下子失去了最重要的经济来源,养家的重任还是一下子压在了外婆瘦弱的肩上。外婆就像个陀螺,不停转。“后来女儿们一个个可以上班赚钱了,你外婆也没有停下来过。反正日子就这样一天天过来了,我也不知道你外婆怎么熬过来的。”妈妈有点无奈地说。外婆操劳了大半辈子,得了罕见的恶性淋巴癌,在她即将满 66 岁的一个早晨,在女儿们陪伴下,缓缓地闭上了她的双眼。

妈妈也是继承了外婆的坚韧的品质,看到家里困难,妈妈 14 岁就辍学去做针织女工补贴家用。八九十年代,象山的针织业已经蓬勃发展起来,针织厂完成了从小作坊到村办企业到县直企业的改革,已经是象山这个小城镇主要的实体经济,所以许多女性都会选择去针织厂上班。刚开始工作时,交通还不方便,象山又为丘陵地形,很多地方也没有建隧道,所以妈妈只能每天早起,伴着微微的晨光，徒步翻过隔在家和工厂之间的山去工作。妈妈说这些时揉了揉自己的小腿："你看，我小腿这么壮，都是肌肉，就是在那时候走出来的。""我给自己买的第一双高跟鞋，我可存了大半年才狠下心去买的。"但是妈妈手脚很麻利，针线活也做得精巧，到1992年，妈妈才18岁的时候就已经成为针织厂的管理人员，工资一年有一万五。"我还得过厂里的技能比赛的第一名，赢了一台电风扇呢！"妈妈无所谓的口气中还带着点小骄傲。

后来，妈妈和爸爸经过朋友介绍，1998年结了婚，1999年生下了我。爸爸来自象山石浦镇，那时候石浦镇没有发展旅游业，只能说是一个小渔村。我们一家人一开始就住在石浦镇。爷爷也是做捕鱼和水上运输的，所以爸爸耳濡目染，找的第一份工作是做水产，收入不多。在2001年我3岁时，妈妈做了一个重大的决定——去塞班岛打工。"那时候有很多广东台湾的商人在塞班岛开针织厂，工资也要比国内高，3.01美元每小时，超出8小时每小时工资就是翻1.5倍。"妈妈说，"其实在八九十年代的时候就已经有很多人出去打工，我已经是算晚的了。那时候有政策扶持，那些国外的工厂和劳动局对接，直接和劳动局签合同，出国其实不难。"在国外，妈妈和其他工人睡上下铺，8个人一间挤在不到20平方米的房间里，洗澡也都是要去公共的地方。"我平时不怎么出去玩，都是要回国前才想到要出去拍照留个纪念。那时候唯一奢侈的活动就是和同事去吃自助餐，8美金一位，每次去前都是饿一天，专挑贵的吃，吃撑了再回来。"出国的4年里，妈妈只回来过一次，待了三天就又飞回塞班岛了，其他基本靠和爸爸互相寄照片来传达思念。

妈妈2005年回国，立马就把外婆在乡下的石头墙的老宅重建了，我们一家三口也搬离了石浦镇，在城区买了房。在一家人稳定之后，爸爸也放心地去上海寻找更好的工作机会。在妈妈回国时还有个趣事，因为在国外时妈妈有次钱被偷了，虽然数额不大，但是也让她难过了好几天。一朝被蛇咬十年怕井绳，于是回国时她用布条把美金包好，当成腰带系在腰间，坐飞机时都不敢上厕所，下了飞机与爸爸汇合时才放心去上厕所。

妈妈出国这几年，象山的针织业迅猛发展。依托在国外的工作经验，她回国后很快晋升成了车间主任，年薪10万元。但是妈妈工作依旧很拼命，经常7点上班，直到晚上7点才回家。爸爸也是在外地拼搏自己的事业，妈妈就像当初外婆帮着外公一样，她帮着爸爸，为了让对方少点压力，为了让家里的条件更好。

在2010年时，针织业已经是夕阳产业，象山的许多针织厂都纷纷倒闭，妈妈那时也想着离开针织厂寻找其他的工作，但是又觉得自己干了快半辈子的针织，真不知道还会什么，于是还是在苟延残喘的针织厂里又干了三年。2013年，妈妈听从爸爸的建议，离开了针织厂，一来爸爸在上海一家食品公司做产品开发经理，已经可以支持一家人的开销，二来也是为了妈妈的身体，长期在充满烟尘和嘈杂的工作环境里工作，妈妈的喉咙日渐沙哑，还得了慢性支气管炎。

但是妈妈和外婆一样，是一个停不下来的女人，所以筹了钱和朋友合伙开了个服装店，虽然店里生意清淡，“但就是想找件事情做，在家里闲着太无聊了。”“其实你外婆的死给我敲了很大的警钟，操劳了半辈子，没能给子女留下什么，能做到最好的就是自己身体健康。”

虽然爸爸现在是家里的支柱，给我和妈妈良好的生活环境，但我觉得这离不开妈妈在背后的努力，如果当初妈妈没有出国，积攒了一定的积蓄，爸爸也没有勇气去上海；如果没有妈妈的忙碌，也不会有我们现在幸福的小康之家。

Ningbo
Liu Jiaying (Class 182, Majoring in Network and New Media)

Happiness Comes from Busyness

My home is in Xiangshan, a small county near the East China Sea. There are two women in my family. One is my grandmother, the other is my mother. They are ordinary but extraordinary. I could see the strength and resilience of motherhood in both of them.

My grandmother was born in 1949 when people rejoiced at the founding of the People's Republic of China. In old photos, she was swarthy, short but sturdy. She had two small but bright downturned eyes, shimmering with resilience. Like other rural girls in that era, my grandmother found a suitable young man in the same village and got married. At that time, people in the countryside favoured boys over girls. The poorer they were, the more children they would have. The more children they had, the poorer they would become. My grandmother gave birth to five children, and all of them were girls. My mother, born in 1974, was the third child in the family. "In those days, the outer walls of the old house were piled up with stones and mud was used to fill up the cracks." My mother looked around the fine-decorated room we lived in, and said with a sigh, "In winter, wind blew in through the cracks between the stones. At that time, we could not afford a cotton-stuffed mattress, so we slept on straw. I shared my bed with your fourth aunt; we had to hug each other to keep both of us warm at night." The pressure of raising five daughters fell on the shoulders of my grandma who not only took care of all house chores, but also helped my grandfather do farming, raise pigs and ducks. When the farming season passed, she would also go to the knitting factory to sort out the yarn.

However, my grandmother was never a lucky person. When my mom was 14 years old, my grandpa fell ill and passed away. Even though the two elder daughters already started to earn money for the family, the sudden loss of the most important income source made it even harder for my grandmother. She worked like a spinning top that would not stop. "Even when all her daughters could go to work and earn money, your grandmother never stopped working. I didn't know how she went through all those days," said my mother helplessly. My grandma worked hard for most of her life. She got a rare disease of malignant lymphoma. On one morning shortly before her 66th birthday, she passed away with her daughters at her side.

My mother inherited my grandmother's resilience. She dropped out of school and worked as a knitting worker at the age of 14 to support her family. In the 1980s and 1990s, the knitting industry in Xiangshan flourished. The knitting factories were transformed from small workshops to village-run enterprises and county-owned enterprises, which had become the main pillar of the economy in this small town. Therefore, many women chose to work in knitting factories. When my mother first started working, the traffic was not convenient. Xiangshan is a town full of hills and mountains, and there were no tunnels in a lot of places, so my mother had to get up early every day and walk across the mountains between home and the factory on foot in the morning sunshine. "Look at my leg," my mother rubbed her shin and said, "it was muscular because I walked so much at that time." "I saved money for over 6 months before I made up my mind to buy my first pair of high heels." My mother was a fast and skillful worker and was good at sewing. In 1992 when she was only 18, my mother was promoted as the manager of the knitting factory with a salary of 15,000 RMB per year. "I also won the first place in the factory skill competition, and got an electric fan as the prize!" My mom was proud of her achievements, even though it seemed that she didn't care about them.

My mother got to know my father through a friend. They got married in 1998 and gave birth to me in 1999. My father came from Shipu, a town in Xiangshan. Back then, Shipu was just a small fishing village without the blooming tourism. Our family lived in Shipu Town at first. My paternal grandfather worked in the fishing and water transport industry. Under his influence, my father found a similar job—working in the aquaculture with a modest income. In 2001, when I was 3 years old, my mother made a significant decision—to work in Saipan. Many entrepreneurs from Canton and Taiwan opened knitting factories in Saipan, and the wage offered was higher than that in China. They were offering 3.01 US dollars per hour to work in the factory, and if I worked over 8 hours, the wage would be 1.5 times higher," my mother said, "A lot of people went abroad for work in the 1980s and 90s. I went there on later dispatches. The government was very supportive. Overseas factories established connections with our local labour administration, and workers signed contracts directly with the labour department. Traveling abroad was not difficult at all!" My mother and other workers slept in bunk beds. Eight people crammed into a room which was less than 20 square meters in area; they had to take a shower in the public bathroom. "I didn't hang out much. The photos I took in Saipan were all taken before returning home for memory. The only extravagant activity there was going to the buffet with colleagues, which cost $8 per person. I would starve myself for the whole day before I went there so I could stuff myself with expensive food and drinks." During the four years abroad, my mother came back only once for a visit; she flew back to Saipan just after three days. During that time, my parents sent photos to each other to convey their love.

When my mother returned to China in 2005, she immediately renovated my grandparents' old house with stone walls in the village. Our family of three moved out of Shipu and bought a house in the city. As soon as the family settled down, my father went to Shanghai to look for a better job. A funny thing happened after my mother returned home. Her money was stolen when she worked abroad. Though it was a small amount, it made her sad for several days. Once bitten, twice shy. When she came back to China, she wrapped the dollars with cloth and tied them around her waist as a belt. She did not even dare to use the lavatory on the airplane, and only when she got off the plane and met my father did she feel comfortable to go to the toilet.

When my mother was abroad, Xiangshan's knitting industry witnessed a rapid development. Because of her working experience abroad, she was soon promoted as the workshop director with an annual salary of 100,000 yuan. My mother still worked very hard. She usually worked from seven in the morning to seven in the evening. Likewise, my father also fought hard for his career in another city. My mother helped my father in the way that my grandmother helped my grandfather. All they did was to take stress off each other and make things better for the family.

Knitting became a sunset industry in 2010, and many knitting factories in Xiangshan collapsed one after another. My mother also wanted to leave the knitting factory and look for another job. However she felt that she had been knitting for almost half of her life, she did not know what else she could do. She worked for the dying industry for 3 extra years. In 2013, my mother followed father's advice and left the knitting factory once and for all. At that time my father was already the product development manager in a food company in Shanghai, which meant that he could afford the family's expenses. The other factor that inspired my mother's departure from the factory was health. Since she worked in a smoke-filled and noisy environment for such a long time, her throat became hoarse day by day, and she got chronic bronchitis.

Like my grandmother, my mother is a woman who would not stay idle, so she raised money and opened a clothing store with her friends. Although business was not too busy, she was just looking for something to do. "It is just too boring to be idle at home. In fact, the death of your grandmother sounded a big alarm for me. She did not leave anything precious to her kids after working for half of her life. The best gift is to be healthy."

My father is now the pillar of the family and he gives my mother and me a good living environment. But I think it can't do without the efforts of my mother from behind. If my mother had not gone abroad and saved money, my father would not have had the courage to go to Shanghai. If it wasn't for my mother's efforts, we would not have a fairly well-off family now.

阻断贫穷的代际传递

刘　玲

佳音同学的学习故事和真挚心声，仿佛是“时代楷模”张桂梅校长带领下的云南省丽江市华坪女子高中誓词的一个山谷回响。誓词有言：“我生来就是高山而非溪流，我欲于群峰之巅俯视平庸的沟壑。我生来就是人杰而非草芥，我站在伟人之肩蔑视卑微的懦夫！”这个学习的故事，是普通家庭的平凡父母鼓励孩子努力奋斗、自立自强、向上向善的故事，可谓阻断贫穷的代际传递的故事。这也是我国数以亿计实现“好好学习，天天向上”“知识改变命运”的例证。当不好好学习的故事变成“事故”，无疑是学习中没有拼搏信念、没有死磕、没有硬抗、没有压抑自我，没有奋力一跃的劲儿，无疑将无法把自己送抵祖辈和父辈无法企及的平台和轨道。背负很多压力和重托的孩子，通过好好学习获得上好大学的机会，继而获得生存之本，实现自我价值，成为对社会有贡献的人。网络上近期引发争论的两种截然不同的教育理念，即“贫穷的焦虑执念”vs“精英的随遇而安”，是对当前我国经济社会发展状况下教育问题的焦虑、反思和争论。我国已锁定于2035年建成社会主义现代化“教育强国”目标，相信在未来，孩子们能在高质量教育体系构建中好好学习，得到更多的学习获得感和幸福感，以和谐的心态、良好的精神面貌奔向更美好的生活。

（宁波城市职业技术学院思政部/基础部主任，副教授）

故事

金华

王佳音(新闻学专业 201 专升本班)

学习的故事

"好好学习"这四个字仿佛贯穿着我的学习生涯,不论是平时爱好阅读的外公,还是忙碌于挣钱抚养我长大成人的母亲,他们身体力行地劝诫家中的小辈:"知识改变命运!"

小时候,经常会看到外公坐在我的书桌前,拿起我的课外书,语重心长地对我说:"佳音一定要好好学习啊,可不能浪费来之不易的学习机会呢。"

外公出生于 1947 年,生长在浙江省义乌市的一个叫做岩界村的偏僻小山村。外公放弃家中唯一的外出学习医学的机会,决定和村子里面的其他青年一起认真做农活,成为一名地地道道的农民。他并没有停下学习的脚步,养成了热爱阅读的好习惯。自己存钱、自己买书,在忙完农活以后,认真学习文化知识,努力摆脱文盲的帽子。最终,他成功成为村子里最早的那一批识字人。

外公喜欢阅读。说来羞愧,小学时代母亲给我买来的许多课外书,如沈石溪的《狼王梦》系列作品等等,在我没有完全看完之前,外公已经看了不下三遍了。外公不是单纯地阅读某一本书籍,而是会在那本书上做自己的重点标记。他不仅自己看,还要求我一起写读后感,养成坚持每天写日记的习惯。在我不想写日记的时候,外公什么话都没说,他只是默默地,把我没有写完的笔记本拿过去,在剩余的笔记本上写他自己的阅读笔记。可以说,外公是引导我对文字有更深兴趣探索的灵魂导师,时刻监督我认真学习,不浪费能够继续学习的每一次机会。

外公不仅仅爱阅读,还爱写字。每当我练完毛笔字,外公都不舍得把墨汁洗掉。他总是默默拿起我的毛笔在纸上练习。他告诉我,他们小时候资源缺乏,他常常蹲在田地里,和着溪水,静静地勾勒着在书本上学习来的汉字。他还说,汉字是中华民族的根,千万不能忘记。

从小,母亲和我说过最多的一句话大概就是:"你一定要好好学习呀,一定要考上大学,一定不能和我一样。"

母亲小时候的生活其实是挺轻松的。那时候,外婆外公都很宠爱母亲,舅舅虽然经常会和母亲抢东西吃,但也还是很让着母亲,也会把不容易吃到的食物留给母亲。母亲不像村子里面的其他小姐妹一样,每天要做许多农活,也不用陪伴弟弟妹妹们,她放学了还能和舅舅一起玩,一起去小溪里抓小鱼小虾。

她异常后悔在那段本该学习的时光里没有努力学习。母亲的成绩很是一般,与学习成绩优异的舅舅形成对比。母亲总说,要是和舅舅一样努力,后来的人生可能就会完全不一样了吧。上初一的时候,她的视力突然变得很差,在到处寻医无果后,母亲对学习丧失了原有的兴趣。母亲选择了离开学校,和村里的小姑娘们一起去镇上的制衣厂做衣服。

舅舅比母亲大两岁,从小学习成绩优异,还擅长各种乐器,在村子里是他们那个年纪的佼佼者。出于对音乐的热爱,舅舅在初中毕业后,选择了金华师专的音乐专业学习。毕业后,舅舅回到义乌,成为一名音乐教师。经过 20 多年的努力,他成为一所小学的管理者。舅舅安稳的工作与母亲艰难的体力活形成鲜明对比,让母亲深刻地意识到了学历的重要性,改变了她对学习不重要的旧看法。

母亲是很严格的,尤其是在我的学习方面。上初中时,有一段时间内,我疯狂迷恋上阅读言情小说,导致学习成绩一落千丈,还被班主任老师请了母亲去学校。母亲在老师面前没有批评我,只是向老师保证自己的小孩不会再因为看小说而耽误学业。回到家后,母亲让我跪在搓衣板上深刻反省自己的错误行为,并让我写检讨书。那一晚,是我印象最深、具有深刻教育意义的一晚。那晚,母亲第一次和我讲述她的成长经历以及她和父亲分开后的心路历程。母亲告诉我,一个人养育小孩子的生活是非常不容易的。但是为了养育女儿,为了给女儿提供更好的生活质量,她愿意付出一切。哪怕是每天早晨只吃一个包子,中饭和晚饭只有榨菜。我觉得我的灵魂受到了巨大的冲击,母亲这么辛苦,我又有什么资格不努力呢?

母亲经历了困苦的生活,坚定了培养自己女儿的决心。母亲对我说:“我自己吃过做衣服的苦,每天起早贪黑,挣一点点钱,只能解决吃饭问题,一省再省。但是我的女儿不能再吃这种苦,我一定要培养她成为一名大学生,做体力活太辛苦了。”

我们这一代人好像总是这样,执着于自己所执着的事物,对家中长辈的谆谆教诲置若罔闻,不撞南墙不回头。高考失利后,我花费很长时间去消化那个结果,并且开始为将来发展做进一步的规划与准备。在专科期间我尝试了许多,参加了学科竞赛、社会实践等系列活动,担任了学生干部,和同学们一起举办活动,受益匪浅、感慨良多。我在不同的活动中寻找平衡点,弄清自己的渴求,发挥自己的优势与特长,找到自己前进的方向。在母亲的鼓励下,我选择了参加专升本考试。我弄清楚自己到底最想要什么,那就是提升学历,提高自我。如今,我成功考上本科院校,并且制订好下一步目标。我离我的梦想又近了一步,我还能成为自己最想成为的人。

当前,在我们家,最重要的事情莫过于表弟的学习。因为,他今年高三了,正处于人生最重要的阶段之一,即将面临人生的大考。为了让表弟拥有更好的学习资源,舅舅送他去全义乌最有名的教师那里辅导学业,哪怕一门课两小时1000 元也乐于付出,只为表弟能够在学业上取得更大的进步,能够去上一个更好的院校,能够感受不一样的大学,拥有更好的人生。可想而知,除了平时的学习课程,表弟还要上各式各样的辅导课程,形式有线上的也有线下的。随之而来,是与日俱增的压力与临近考试的紧张,这让他感到痛苦。偶尔他也会给我打电话,告诉我他的困苦与迷茫。我总是会和他说我在专科时候的经历,鼓励他坚持下去,继续努力。

拥有较好的学习资源的我们,好像缺少了上一辈人的韧劲,但是我相信,在成长的过程中,我们每个人都会发现自己最想要的是什么,并为之努力奋斗。

Jinhua
Wang Jiayin (Class 201, Majoring in Journalism)

The Story of Study

Throughout school years, I have been told to "study hard". Whether it was my maternal grandfather who loved reading, or my mother who was always working, my families always told the kids in our family-through actions or words-that "knowledge changes fate".

When I was little, often my grandfather would sit by my desk and say to me, seriously and sincerely, that I should cherish the opportunity to study.

My grandfather was born in 1947 in a remote village called Yanjie in Yiwu, Zhejiang Province. Instead of taking the opportunity to leave the village to study medicine, he decided to stay home and be a farmer like all the other young men in the village. However, he never stopped learning and got into the habit of reading. After finishing farm work, he would read the books he bought with his savings and try to be literate. He was one of the first few people in the village who were able to read and write.

My grandfather loved reading. When I was in primary school, my mother bought me a lot of extracurricular books like *Wolf King Dream* series by Shen Shixi. Before I had a chance to read them, my grandfather had already read all of them more than three times. I felt ashamed. He did not just "read" the books, but also made notes and marks while reading them. He asked me to write book reviews every day and keep diaries with him. Although he never forced me to write if I did not feel like writing, he would write his own book reviews in my notebook without saying a word. My grandfather was my mentor who helped me to develop an interest in literature. It was he who supervised me while I was studying and taught me to value every opportunity to study.

Apart from reading, he also loved calligraphy. Every time when I finished practicing calligraphy, he would take over my brush, and practice writing characters with the ink left in it instead of letting me wash the ink away. He told me that when he was young, he did not have brushes or paper for him to practice writing, so he just crouched in the fields and wrote characters he learned from books on the ground by the creeks using water. He told me that Chinese characters were the root of Chinese culture which nobody should ever forget.

One thing that my mother said to me most frequently was probably that I must "study hard to get into university, and not end up where she is now".

My mother had a happy childhood. Her parents loved her very much and though her brother and she often fought for food, he would always humor her and save for her some food not typically seen at that time. She did not have to do farm work or take care of younger siblings in the family like other girls in the village. Her after-school activities were catching fish and shrimps in creeks with her brother.

However, my mother regretted bitterly that she did not study hard enough at school. Unlike her brother who always got good grades in school, my mother never did well in her study. She always said that her life would have been so different if she had put more effort to study when she was at school. The year when she entered middle school, she had an eye disease and could not see well. She consulted a lot of doctors but it did not help, so she gradually lost interest in study and finally left school. After she dropped out of school, she went to work in a clothing factory with many other girls in the village.

My uncle was two years older than my mother. He was an extraordinary student back in school days who could also play many musical instruments. He was known as the best among all the kids at his age in the village. Because of his passion for music, chose to study music in Jinhua Junior College for Teachers after middle school. After he graduated, he became a music teacher in his hometown Yiwu. Twenty years later, he became the headmaster of a primary school. While my uncle had a nice and stable job, my mother did labor work. This sharp contrast made her realize the importance of education.

My mother has always been very strict with me, especially with my study. When I was in middle school, there was a period where I was obsessed with romantic fiction which seriously affected my study. One day, my mother was called to school for it. She did not criticize me in front of my teacher, only assured the teacher that I wouldn't be distracted from study by such fiction. When we returned home, she had me kneel on a washboard and told me to think over my mistake and write down my thoughts. That night left on me the deepest impression for I learned so much from it. It was also at that night that my mother first told me about her life when she was young, and how she felt after she and my father broke up. She told me that bringing up a child all by herself had not been easy, but she was willing to do anything to give me a better life, even if it meant that she would only have one steamed stuffed bun for breakfast and preserved mustard for lunch and dinner. I was astonished by her devotion, and therefore determined to study hard so that I would not fail her.

My mother knew how bitter life could be without education, so she tried very hard to make sure that I was well educated. I learned from her about how tough it could be to work in a clothing factory. She had to wake up very early to earn that little money which could barely cover her food expense. She said that she would not allow her daughter to have that kind of life, and that was why she wished that I could go to university.

However, it seems that our generation would only listen to the elders after we are knocked down by life ourselves. I failed the college entrance exam, and it took me a very long time to accept it. After I got back on my feet again, I started to make plans for my future. I went to a junior college, where I took part in academic competitions and social activities. I was also a student leader and held activities with some other students. I learned a lot from those experiences and gradually came to realize what I wanted and what I was good at, thus finally found my way. With the support of my mother, I took the qualification examination for university. I knew that it was what I wanted-a higher education and a chance to improve myself. I succeeded in the exam and am now a university student. Moreover, I am clear about what I am going to do next. With one step closer to my dream, I know that I am capable to become the person I have always wanted to be.

Now, my cousin's study has become the most important issue in our family. He is currently a senior high school student who is facing one of the most critical moments in his life—entrance examination for university. My uncle has sent him to study with the best teacher in Yiwu, although it takes 1,000 yuan for every two-hour lesson. It is all for my cousin to enter a good university so that he can have a better future. My cousin has been taking a lot of extra classes, online and offline, and he is under a great deal of pressure. Sometimes he called me on the phone to talk to me about his stress and confusion. I always told him about my experiences in junior college to soothe him and encourage him to keep on studying hard.

Although we have better education resources than previous generations today, it seems that we lack the perseverance they had. However, I believe that as we grow up, we will all eventually find out what we really want in our lives one day and fight for it.

日常生活绵延中孕育的浙江精神

朱小红

对于世界，你只是一个人，但对于某个人，你就是整个世界。这句话是支撑着平凡如草芥的普通人行走世界努力活下去的信念和力量。宏观社会学学者可能认为，对日常社会活动的研究是琐屑无聊的。[①] 事实上，对每日起早贪黑卖菜卖海鲜这种微观经验的研究和宏观视角的研究互相依赖、互相补充，让我们对社会的观察更为完备、更为周全。

日常生活绵延孕育出"求真务实、诚信和谐、开放图强"的浙江精神。从普通百姓到浙商群体，从鸡毛换糖到红帮裁缝，从低压电器、打火机、眼镜到纺织行业，实实在在鲜活的人群，诚实自强，艰苦创业，务实求生存，创新谋发展，敢为人先、勇为天下先是他们的特点，体现了浙江文化奋斗图强的主体意识和务实重行的重商意识。

静水流深般的日常生活绵延包含了浙江文化基因里的坚韧精神与积极社会心理。当作者回望外公外婆的一生，看到外公危中求机，腿伤之后转而改卖海鲜，从流动摊贩直到拥有固定摊位，从肩挑步行到车载货物；看到舅舅舅妈从乡村到不同的集市，从雁荡镇到湖南，从贩卖海鲜到别的行业。这种寻常而坚定、永远与生活抗争的态度和实现家庭梦想的行为影响着作者的人生态度，文化的传承和人生价值的彰显也在无言中逐渐完成。外公在起早贪黑的忙碌中总是耐心地为外孙女准备好热乎乎的一日三餐，对少不更事的外孙女发牢骚耍脾气总是默默忍受，以宽厚的胸怀把这个平常之家变成作者至今不停回望的情感意义充沛的地方。外公外婆这样的普通人坚韧、积极的品质来自浙江人普遍的积极思维，成为他们建设美好生活的主动性和创造力。

（浙大宁波理工学院传媒与法学院党委书记）

① 安东尼·吉登斯：《社会的构成：结构化理论纲要》，北京：中国人民大学出版社，2016年，第132页。

故事

温州

王亚琦(新闻学专业201专升本班)

雁荡镇上卖海鲜

“你们两个臭孩子。”外公总是这样咧嘴轻笑着说我和弟弟,常年在外劳动而被太阳晒得黝黑的脸上显露出许多条皱纹来。“不许叹气!”外婆总会假凶着脸,瞪着刚刚叹了一大口气的我。听到这两句外公外婆经常说的话,我总会哈哈笑地打马虎,然后转身逃开。

我家和外公外婆家都在温州乐清的雁荡镇上,这个小镇以景点雁荡山出名,每年都会有许多游客来,还有几部电视剧在这里取景拍摄。但这里其实还靠海,还有许多人都喜欢吃海鲜,而我的外公外婆就在卖海鲜。

我问外婆:“外婆,卖海鲜这么幸苦,你和外公为什么要卖海鲜呢?”

外婆无奈地笑,“还不是那时候没有事情可以做了。”

1991年,外公的腿在帮别人搬走打山洞时滚落的石头时意外被砸断,做不了农事并且在家休养了一年时间,这让原本就不富裕的家庭生活更加窘迫。那时候,外婆刚好听说村子里有人因为售卖海鲜挣了不少钱,于是她便去打听。

1992年,外公外婆再加上我妈妈和阿姨四个人,开始挑着装满从别人那里购进的不同海鲜的篮子走路去不同的集市售卖。那个时候没有车子,就只是自己走上一两个小时的路,挑着重重的担子一步一步地走到集市。从边上的集市开始,到白溪,到芙蓉,后来可以卖的海鲜越来越多,量也越来越大,他们决定去更大的市场售卖,1995年的时候在虹桥的菜市场购买了一个摊位,固定了售卖地点。后来妈妈阿姨都出嫁了,大舅舅也和大舅妈去了湖南打拼,只有外公外婆两个人在忙这一份海鲜事业了。但因为地点确定在这个更繁荣的镇上,而且外公外婆的海鲜既新鲜价格又便宜,有几家饭店成为固定买家,外公外婆的收入也提高了不少。

我是1997年生的,从我记事起,白天总是看到外公骑着电动三轮车去进货,以及在院子里弯着腰,低着头快速地分拣着铺在地上的花蛤、白蛤、蛏子等各类海鲜。外公从来没有固定的吃饭时间,午饭常是昨天晚上多煮的剩饭,一碗简单的面条,或者外面买来的快餐。有时吃着吃着,突然一个电话响起来,告诉外公哪里的海鲜刚打捞上来，快来抢最新鲜的，外公就匆匆吃几口后放下筷子骑车去买，就连晚上也是一样。半夜，外公还常常会设置 11 点半、1 点等各个时间段的闹钟起床给海鲜换水。以前外公都是用闹钟定点，但外公总会因为看错时间而设置错时间，为了教会从来没有上过学的外公如何使用手机设置闹钟，我也是“苦苦教导”了好几次。他有几个小本子专门记录联系人和他们的手机号码。

从小时候开始，我每天只能在晚上看到外婆，因为外婆需要每天清晨两三点钟起床，匆匆洗漱完，带着装满海鲜的塑料大篮子和水桶坐车往菜市场出发，每天晚上七八点左右回到家来做饭，吃完饭洗完碗后去洗澡然后就躺在床上看电视。往往看个 10 分钟左右，外婆就会打起呼噜睡着了。每天都是这样只睡几个小时，每天都是在菜市场和家里两个地方来回。2010 年，我开始在虹桥上初中，以前只能在晚上见到外婆的我会偶尔在周日要去学校的日子里提早去虹桥，去菜市场和外婆聊天。几乎是每一次我去虹桥的时候都会看到外婆歪着头，坐在小板凳上睡觉。我会走到边上，边摇外婆边叫外婆，外婆睁开了红红的眼睛看到我后，高兴地叫着我的名字：“琦，你来啦！”旁边的摊主看到了还会打趣：“叫你外婆少睡点，不然海鲜都要叫人偷走了呗！”

外公外婆的指甲盖总是黑乎乎的，因为总会有海鲜的泥呆在里面，身上还有海鲜的泥腥味。

外公外婆的假期一年只有一天，也就是过完年后的大年初一，外婆说这一天几乎没人来菜市场，所以她和外公两个人可以休息。但在大年三十这一天，外公外婆凌晨 12 点半就得起来，因为这一天同样会是一年生意最好的时候，然后晚上包上 6 个压岁红包分给我们。大年初一外婆会去太婆婆家看望她，再来我家和我们聊天，外婆说这一天最舒服了，连觉也不想睡。这样的生活一直过了 28 年。

我的初高中每周末只有一天半的假期时间。我不会做饭，星期五的时候总是等到外公外婆回家后 8 点多才能吃上晚饭，那个时候有一次还觉得自己好不容易回一次家还吃不上晚饭闹脾气了，我皱着眉头一脸生气样坐在饭桌旁，外公外婆都不说话，只是默默吃饭，默默地夹菜到我碗里，现在想想自己那时候真的非常不可理喻。每个星期六早上，半梦半醒的我听到“踏”“踏”“踏”的脚步声就知道外公买好早饭午饭给我送上楼来了，他总是叮嘱一句把午饭热一热再吃后就下楼继续干活去了。而我睡了一觉醒来准备去晒洗衣机里昨晚刚洗完的衣服时，都会发现外公已经将它们都晒了出去。

长大后，我开始懂得外公外婆的辛苦。于是在冬天的时候，从学校回来的时候，我都会买些东西带给外公外婆，棉袜子，热水杯，润唇膏……外公外婆也总会在周五这一天从菜市场买我喜欢吃的菜回来做给我吃。后来外婆还和我讲：“每次一到周五，我就和你外公说赶紧把剩菜剩饭倒了，不然琦回来又要说我们了。”我这才想起来，之前因为他们总是吃剩菜剩饭，我有和他们说过这样不好。但我知道外公外婆总是很忙，忙得没有时间吃饭，没有足够时间睡觉，还是会在他们手上看到冻疮。

这样的日子一天一天过去，直到去年，72 岁的外公和 68 岁的外婆才终于自告退休在家，也是因为新冠肺炎疫情，海鲜的销量大不如从前。

退休后外公外婆用挣来的钱开始建新房，他们建一整栋楼，自己睡在最底层，并且将三、四层分别给大舅小舅一家住。他们又开始了新的劳动，外公每天去帮忙建房子，做些挑材料、搅拌水泥、洒水的工作，外婆每天整理清扫楼里的垃圾，给工人们做饭，到今天已经是第二年了。外婆偷偷地和我讲，建了这座房子，这些年赚的钱也没了一大半。看着外公外婆头上的白发和时不时看着房子发呆的样子，也许 28 年的辛苦，换来了这么一栋房子，真的值吧……

Wenzhou

Wang Yaqi (Class 201, Majoring in Journalism)

Selling Seafood in Yandang Town

“Look at you two naughty boys!” My grandfather always grinned and said so to me and my younger brother. Wrinkles grew on his sunburned swarthy face after working outside all the year round. “Stop sighing!” My grandmother always pretended to be fierce and stared at me whenever I sighed. Hearing those words from my grandparents, I always laughed and pretended to be ignorant, and then ran away from them.

My family and my grandparents lived in Yandang Town in Yueqing, Wenzhou City of Zhejiang Province. It's famous for its scenic spot, Yandang Mountain, which attracts many tourists every year. Also, several TV series were shot here. Actually, it's a town at the seaside. Many people enjoy seafood, and my grandparents once sold seafood here.

One day, I asked grandmother, “Grandma, I notice it's really tiring to sell seafood, but why did you choose to sell seafood?”

She smiled with resignation, "This was the last resort for us to make a living then."

In 1991, my grandfather's leg was accidentally broken when he was moving away the stones left from the tunneling the stones, and he couldn't take on any farming and had to rest for a whole year, which made the poor family even more impoverished. At that time, grandmother happened to know that someone in the village made a fortune by selling seafood, so she made further inquiries about it.

In 1992, my grandparents, together with my mother and aunt, began to carry baskets of seafood they bought from others and sell seafood in different markets. With no car at that time, they had to walk for one or two hours step by step with heavy burdens. At first, they only sold seafood in nearby markets, such as Baixi and Furong markets. Later, the sales increased and they could sell a wider variety of seafood, Therefore, they decided to do business in larger markets. In 1995, they bought a fixed stall in Hongqiao Vegetable Market. Later, my mother and aunt both got married, and my eldest uncle and aunt-in-law went to Hunan Province to try their luck. Only my grandparents were still busy with the seafood business. Thanks to the good location in a more prosperous town and the freshness and low prices of grandparents' seafood, some restaurants gradually became regular for customers, thus my grandparents saw their income increase.

In 1997, I was born. As far as I can remember, my grandfather always rode an electric tricycle to purchase goods, and bent over in the yard during the day, quickly sorting out seafood, such as clams, white clam, razor clam, etc. He never had meals regularly. Lunch was often leftovers from last night, a bowl of noodles, or fast food bought outside. Sometimes, a phone call came informing him of the places to buy freshest seafood and then he would stop eating. Grandfather would drop his chopsticks and rush to buy the products, even if it was at night. He also set alarms at 11:30 p.m., 1:00 a.m., etc. to change water for the seafood. He used alarm clocks before but always set the wrong time because of some reading mistakes. In order to teach grandpa how to set the alarm clock on his mobile phone, I "painstakingly" taught him several times. He also kept notebooks to record his contacts and their mobile phone numbers.

Since my childhood, I could only see my grandmother in the evening every day, because she always got up at two or three o'clock in the morning, washed up in a hurry, and rushed to the market with big plastic baskets and buckets full of seafood by bus. She often returned home at around seven or eight o'clock in the evening, then prepared dinner for the family. After dinner, she was still busy with washing dishes and other housework. After a shower and 10-minute-TV time on bed, she fell asleep and even snored. Every day, she slept just for several hours and worked so hard, shuttling between home and the market. In 2010, I entered elementary school in Hongqiao. In the past, I only got to see my grandma at night. Since elementary school, I would sometimes leave for Hongqiao early on Sunday when I was supposed to return to school. On those days, I would go chat with my grandma in the market. Almost every time I got there, I would see her sleeping on a small stool with her head tilted. Then I would walk to her side, shaking and waking her up. She would open her eyes, which were always red because of fatigue, and call me by my name, "Oh, my dear Qi, it's you!" The stall owner nearby would then joke with me, "Don't let her sleep so soundly, otherwise, her seafood will all be stolen!"

The fingernails of my grandparents were always black and they always smelled fishy because of the sea mud stuck under their fingernails.

Every year, they only had one day off, the first day of the Chinese New Year. Grandma said that was because few would come to the market. But the New Year's Eve, they have to get up at 00:30 a. m. to prepare for the best time of their business. At the end of the day, they would give us six red envelopes. Also, on the New Year's Day, my grandma would visit her mother first and then came to our home to chat with us. According to her, the day was too comfortable for her to sleep. She led a life like that for 28 years.

I used to have one and a half days off every weekend in junior and senior high schools. I didn't know how to cook. On Friday, I always had dinner at eight o'clock because I had to wait until my grandparents returned from the market. Once, I even felt annoyed at the delayed dinners as I seldom had the chance to eat at home. I sat at the table frowning with an angry look on my face. They didn't speak to me, just ate in silence and put the food in my bowl. Now, whenever I think about that, I feel ashamed of my irrational behavior at that time. Every Saturday morning, half awake, I could hear the pit-a-pat of feet downstairs. I knew my grandfather was here to bring my breakfast and lunch upstairs. He always reminded me to heat the meals before eating and went downstairs to continue his work. When I got up to hang the clothes I washed in the laundry machine the day before, I would always find my clothes hung by grandpa already.

As I grew up, I began to understand my grandparents' hard life. When winter came, I would bring them something whenever I came back from school, such as cotton socks, cups, lip balm, etc. My grandparents also bought me my favorite food from the market to cook dinner for me. Later, grandmother told me, "Every Friday, I would remind your grandfather to dump the leftovers, otherwise you might scold us again." It came to me that they used to eat leftovers, and I told them it was unhealthy. But now, I know the reason is that they were too busy to eat and sleep enough. And I can still see the frostbite on their hands.

As time passes by, my grandfather and grandmother retired from work at the age of seventy-two and sixty-eight separately, which is kind of lucky. Seafood sales slumped because of the Covid-19.

After retirement, they decided to build a new building with the money they earned. They live on the first floor, and gave the third and fourth floors to my uncles. They began to work again, my grandfather helped to build the house everyday, doing things like picking materials, mixing cement and sprinkling water and my grandmother cleaned up the garbage and prepared meals for the workers. This is the second year since the construction has been started. Grandma secretly told me that the building cost them almost half of their savings. Looking at their grey hair and watching them staring at the house, I guess, maybe it's worthwhile for them to exchange with such a building their twenty-eight-year hard work.

身份触摸祖国发展的强劲脉动

崔　雨

以温州一家四代人80载光阴为主要内容，以爷爷的身份变化为主线，采用蒙太奇手法，让人穿越时光隧道，在身份变化中触摸祖国发展的强劲脉动——这是黄欣如同学的《爷爷的多重身份》给我的感受。

新民主主义革命时期，中国共产党成立，这是近代中国革命历史上划时代的里程碑。文中“三四十年代”，爷爷的身份是小镇上富家少爷。

社会主义革命和建设时期，中华人民共和国成立，开启了中国历史发展的新纪元。文中“五六十年代”和“七八十年代”中的上世纪70年代，爷爷的身份是旧知识分子——小镇上为数不多的大学生，太爷爷采用了“一哭二闹三上吊”的非常手段，于是回到小镇上小学教书。

改革开放和社会主义现代化建设新时期，党的十一届三中全会开创了中国特色社会主义的伟大事业。文中“七八十年代”中的上世纪80年代，爷爷的身份是小镇上小学老师，虽然五六十年代以及70年代也为小学老师，但由于邓小平“尊重知识，尊重人才”的提出，于是前后境况截然不同。值得一提的是，这时候，父辈汇入改革开放的大潮。文中“90年代至今”。新世纪，中国进入全面建设小康社会、加快推进社会主义现代化的发展新阶段。党的十八大以来，以习近平同志为总书记的党中央带领全党全国各族人民接力奋斗，为实现中华民族伟大复兴的中国梦奋勇前进。习近平总书记高度重视老年人养老问题，指出“让所有老年人都能老有所养、老有所依、老有所乐、老有所安”。新世纪后，作者出生；爷爷退休并开启健康养老模式——去河边钓鱼、每天看报纸。这时候，父辈在外开辟出一方天地，家庭条件慢慢好了起来……

从富家少爷到普通老人，80多载时光见证作者大家庭的时代变迁，更见证伟大祖国的快速发展。

（宁波卫生职业技术学院，副研究员）

故事

温州

黄欣如(新闻学专业201专升本班)

爷爷的多重身份

要问谁是见证中国无数家庭变化的最佳人选,我想必定是每个家庭中的老人,那些经历过不同年代的老人。我的爷爷就是其中的一位。

爷爷生活在温州的一个小镇——马屿镇上。

我不是在爷爷奶奶身边长大的,和他们接触不是很多。记得小时候,每次过年去爷爷奶奶家吃年夜饭,我都非常不情愿,哭着喊着我不要去。因为我不喜欢爷爷家破旧的房子,不喜欢奶奶当时在他们自己家楼下开的卖纸钱的小店,不喜欢他们周围的一切。

爷爷几乎很少会呆在家里。在我的印象中爷爷就是典型的农村老人。爷爷驼着背,拄着拐杖,慢慢悠悠地走在小镇的老街上,要么是去打麻将,要么就是去钓鱼。而且爷爷的老房子十分破旧,都是上个年代的装修,在翻修以前房子的墙外还写有"毛主席万岁"的大字。

是在2020年疫情期间,和爸爸偶然的交谈中,我真正地了解了爷爷。

"三四十年代"——

当时的中国是战乱的。而我的爷爷就是在这个时期出生的,还是家中独子。爷爷家好几代人都是做小糕点生意,开始生意还是不错的,曾经小镇上一整条街都是爷爷家的家产。再加上独生子的身份,爷爷从小就得到了所有人的关注和宠爱,一点重活都没有做过。在小镇上我的爷爷算得上是数一数二的富家子弟。但是,俗话说富不过三代,我的太爷爷痴迷赌博,慢慢地那条街的家产都被太爷爷赌没了,再加上当时经济萧条,爷爷家开始走向没落。

"五六十年代"——

这时的中国是全新的中国,但是小镇依旧是原来的小镇。虽然当时经济不乐观,但是太爷爷对于读书人却是非常尊敬的,一直希望家中出个读书人,于是不管家里经济条件如何,太爷爷总会省出一笔钱供爷爷上学,并且一直告诫我爷爷一定要好好读书。我的爷爷也很争气,一直努力学习,从小镇考到县城,再从县城考到杭州的一个化工学院。爷爷一直是家中的骄傲,成为小镇上为数不多的大学生。

爷爷求学的路途艰辛。当年交通非常的不发达，去往杭州的路上需要不停地转车，爷爷就和他的朋友们每人背着大麻袋，带上几天的粮食，坐几天几夜的车才来到杭州。爷爷说，那个时候所有人对于知识的渴望非常迫切，在风华正茂的年纪，都有着满腔热血。在大学里，爷爷跟着老师，非常努力地学习。毕业后，他以优秀的成绩被分配到了贵州贵阳的研究所里工作。如果不出意外，到今天我的爷爷可能成为一名德高望重的老教授了。

但是，也只是可能，那个时候发生了文化大革命，外面的世界是动荡不安的，我的太爷爷实在是不放心身为独子的爷爷独自在外，所以太爷爷“一哭二闹三上吊”，硬是把爷爷叫回了那个小镇上，让爷爷在镇上的小学里教书。

“七八十年代”——

就是在这个时期，经过我太奶奶的介绍，我的爷爷遇到了我的奶奶，我的奶奶虽然不是大学生，但在那个一穷二白、重男轻女的年代，我奶奶也读到了高中毕业，也算得上是一位响当当的知识分子。

两位知识青年的相遇却不是浪漫诗意的。奶奶嫁到爷爷家不久，就要生儿育女，学着帮着爷爷家里卖糕点，而我爷爷则继续在小镇上教书。当时爷爷教书的收入非常少，大部分都要靠家里卖糕点的收入维持生活。所以爷爷每天在学校里教完书，就要赶回家帮忙做糕点。

虽然我的爷爷是一位老师，但是他的孩子都没有从事学术工作。因为当时生活条件非常艰苦，而且需要抚养 6 个孩子，已经没有多余的钱让他们的孩子读书了。我爸爸他们趁着改革开放的热潮，纷纷外出打工。

“九十年代至今”——

这个时期，爷爷的孩子们在中国各地打拼，而爷爷依旧在小镇里教书育人，奶奶则在街上卖小糕点。开始爸爸他们创业并不是很顺利，爷爷奶奶们只能省吃俭用，省出钱来帮助他们继续创业。后来慢慢爸爸他们一个个都有了自己新的家庭，在外也开辟出了自己的一方天地，家庭条件也慢慢地好了起来。

在我出生后不久，我的爷爷就退休了，奶奶也不做糕点了，在家的楼下开了一家小店，进了些零食饮料卖，而我爷爷开始了他的退休生活。我对于爷爷奶奶的印象也是从这个时候开始的。

随着我的长大，爷爷背开始慢慢驼了，开始需要拐杖走路了，开始经常进出老年麻将馆，偶尔会蹬个自行车去河边钓鱼。爷爷虽然老花加近视，但是依旧会每天看报纸。当年一个一个出去打拼的孩子们都事业有成地回来了，把家里的老房子翻修了，让奶奶的小店停掉了，爷爷奶奶能够好好地享受老年生活了。

可是我的爷爷在家呆不住。我记得在爷爷 70 多岁的时候，骑自行车外出时出了点意外，腿摔断了，在床上躺了好久才恢复过来。刚刚可以下床没几天又开始天天往外跑，谁也拦不住。

曾经的富家少爷到如今我的爷爷，这中间经历了80多年的时光，见证了我们这个大家庭的时代变迁。我没问爷爷是否怀念曾经的满腔热血，也没问他是否后悔离开研究所的工作，回到这个柴米油盐的小镇上。只是每次我在路上遇到爷爷，他总是一个人独自拄着拐杖走着。看着爷爷一步一步地慢慢地走着，我心里就有了答案。我想爷爷每次独自一人的时候，一定是在静静地回忆自己曾经的岁月。

Wenzhou
Huang Xinru (Class 201, Majoring in Journalism)

Grandpa's Multiple Roles

Who has witnessed the most changes in a Chinese family? I think the answer must be the elderly in every family who have experienced vicissitudes of life. My paternal grandpa is just one of them.

My grandfather lives in a small town called Mayu in Wenzhou City, southeastern China's Zhejiang Province.

I haven't had much contact with my paternal grandparents because I didn't grow up by their sides. I still remember when I was young, I was always reluctant and even refused to go visit them and have the family reunion dinner with them every Spring Festival, because I didn't like their shabby house, the paper money shop that my grandmother ran downstairs at that time, or to be more specific, everything around them.

My grandpa barely stayed at home. I always remembered him as a typical rural elder, who, bent and with the help of a crutch, tottered along the old streets of the town on his way to play mahjong or go fishing. His old house was dilapidated and of a decorative style typical of the last century. There was even a reminiscent slogan of "Long Live Chairman Mao" printed on the exterior of the house before it was renovated.

It was during the COVID-19 pandemic in 2020 that I really got to know my grandfather from an unintended chat with my father.

"The 1930s to the 1940s":

My grandpa was born in a chaotic and war-torn China as the only child in his family. His ancestors ran a pastry business for generations and even owned all the shops along the street in its prime time. Born as the only child in a decent family, he consequently became the apple of the eye, having never tried anything laborious. My grandpa's family was one of the richest in the town. Yet great men's sons seldom do well—his father, indulging in gambling, gradually lost all family assets on that street. Plus, the economy was in recession back at that time, his family thus gradually declined.

"The 1950s to the 1960s":

While a New China had been established, the town remained almost the same. My great grandfather, out of respect for intellectuals despite the sluggish economy, had long hoped that his family could produce one. Therefore, he saved every penny possible to send my grandfather to school and exhorted him to study really hard. My grandpa didn't let his father down; he climbed up the academic ladder from the town to the county and was finally admitted to a chemical engineering college in Hangzhou, capital city of southeastern China's Zhejiang Province. My grandpa had always been the family pride and this time he was among a very small proportion of people in the town who could go to college at that time.

My grandpa embarked on a tough academic journey. Because of a backward transportation system, he and his friends had to take different coaches over several days while feeding on sacks of food they carried with them before they reached their universities. My grandpa recalled that every student, in their prime time, was thirsty for knowledge and full of ambition. He learned industriously from his teachers and was assigned to a research institute in Guiyang, capital city of southwestern China's Guizhou Province with excellent GPA. My grandpa could have become a prestigious professor if it was not for some unexpected events.

But it was just my imagination. Since it was chaotic and tumultuous out there because of the Cultural Revolution (1966—1976), my great grandfather, out of concern and worry for his only child, called my grandpa back using whatever means possible. My grandpa ended up being a teacher in an elementary school in the town.

"The 1970s to the 1980s":

My grandpa was introduced by my great grandmother to my future grandma, who, although not having received college education, could well be seen as a rare intellectual for she received high school education in an age of poverty when boys were preferred to girls.

The two educated young people's marriage life was by no means romantic. Shortly after they got married, my grandma gave birth to and raised up children while learning to help with the pastry business of my grandpa's family. As for my grandpa, he continued teaching in elementary school in the town. Earning a meager salary, my grandpa was unable to make ends meet simply by teaching, so he had to hurry home to help make pastries after a day's hard work—a major source of income for the family.

Although my grandpa was a teacher himself, none of his six children worked in the academic circle because there was no extra money to pay for their tuition fees under harsh living conditions. My father, with his siblings, seized the chance of reform and opening-up and became a migrant worker in the city.

"The 1990s till now":

During this period of time, my father and his siblings were working really hard in different cities across China, while my grandpa was still teaching in the town and my grandma selling pastries in the street. My father and his siblings had a difficult time starting up their own businesses, so my grandparents had to scrimp and save so as to help them. Later they formed their own families and their businesses finally took off. That was when life got better.

Shortly after I was born, my grandpa retired and my grandma, having discontinued her pastry business, ran a small store selling snacks and soft drinks downstairs. Most of my memories about my grandparents were formed at that time.

As I grew up, my grandpa, bent and with the help of a crutch, frequented the local mahjong club and occasionally went fishing by bike. Presbyopic and myopic, he still read newspapers every day. Their children, having tried their luck in cities in the past, now returned with a successful career. They had the old house renovated and persuaded my grandma out of her grocery business so that their parents could enjoy a happy and comfortable retirement life.

Yet my grandpa wouldn't be restrained at home. I still remembered that my grandpa, in his seventies, broke his legs during an accident while he was riding a bike. He, having recovered after days of rest, couldn't bear staying at home and started going out again; nobody could ever stop him.

During the past eight decades, my grandpa has turned from a carefree master of a rich family to a lovely elder. This time period has also witnessed the changes to our big family. I have never asked my grandpa whether he still held dear the past ambition, or whether he had any regret about leaving the research institute and returning to this mundane way of life, because I knew the answers to those questions whenever I saw my grandpa tottering with a crutch alone. I bet he must be reminiscing about his past.

学习作为方法：奋斗者的人生大书

文　娟

学习是人生成长的重要方法之一，借助于它，我们获得体力、智力、品性、美感以及劳动等相关理论知识和实践经验，从而在势不可挡的生活洪流中确认自我和书写命运，在塑造更为优秀的自己之时，亦为时代的美名添砖加瓦。也是在这样的意义上，从前现代的学而优则仕到当下的各种人才吸纳方略，顶层设计都在切切地倡议着努力学习的必要和可能。民间更是以实际行动诠释着努力学习与功成名就之间的密切关联，从孟母三迁到当下的教育内卷可为明证。也因得这样的上下联动，我们的中华民族才得以绵延重塑为当下的盛世中国。只是，此种关于学习的长久提倡和实践，重心都落在书面知识的习得上，以致于我们渐趋忘却了人生的大书同样是学习应该品读的对象。事实上，我们努力汲取书面知识的目的，亦是为了更好地解读生活这本大书，以便在生活中乘风破浪、奋勇前进、书写幸福和美好。

徐涵的《爷爷的奋斗》以平实笔调，述说了爷爷由普通农民成长为优秀士兵、转业厂长和成功创业者的奋斗故事，很是感人和励志。只是，行文中不断出现的“勤奋好学”“悟出了自己的特殊门道”“自己研制方案自制出来”“不断探索经验”等词句，足可见爷爷是善于向生活学习并将从中习得的经验和教训提炼内化为进阶养料的睿智之人，是认真的学习态度和严谨的学习行为成就了爷爷作为奋斗者的辉煌人生。于他而言，借助于生活，完美地实现了抽象知识和生活适实感的互动共生。

可以说，《爷爷的奋斗》激活了我们关于学习生活大书必要性的重要意义，复原了学习作为方法的双重维度，书面知识和微观生活一体两面，都需习得。在当下知识丰裕的时代，大凡成功者，多是既读一本小书又读一本大书之人。就此可言，“行走的新闻”将新闻专业主义作用于生活世相的勘察本身，已为传媒学子未来的优秀奠定了重要基础，值得他们认真学习，级级相继，播而广之。

（浙大宁波理工学院传媒与法学院讲师，博士）

故事

绍兴

徐涵(网络与新媒体专业191班)

爷爷的奋斗

爷爷是他兄弟中的老二,自我记事起,印象中的他总是严肃且不苟言笑的。许是小时候对他有些畏惧的心理,我们敞开心扉的接触与交流并没有这么多。在我记忆中,爷爷总是坐在房间的沙发上,带着他的老花眼镜,翻阅手中每日刚刚送来的报纸。他心系国家大事,关心各种新闻,常常在饭桌上与好友探讨百姓眼中的政事。而同时,他也喜欢那些老一辈艺术家的歌舞节目,从前老式的电视机里总是出现《星光大道》的影子,每次这个时候也是他笑得最多的时候。总之,爷爷是严肃却又风趣的存在,随着年龄的增长,我对他的畏惧慢慢变成了油然而生的敬意。

我的爷爷有着很多身份,他是一位农民,是一名优秀的中国共产党员,也是一名退伍军人,同时是一个披荆斩棘的创业者。

爷爷在20岁之前一直待在自家村里帮忙干农活,但他一直勤奋好学,虽然没有真正上过多久的学,但他肚子里的墨水不比别人少,尤其记得在我小学时,爷爷总是会指导我的作文,什么地方写得好,什么地方还缺点火候,这些他都能火眼金睛地看出来,那个时候我就有些佩服爷爷,他小时候的教育环境如此落后,却也能有这样一番学识。

就在那个时候,1970年,他20岁,毅然决然地选择走当兵这条路,当时已经与奶奶结婚的他纵有万般不舍,也决定去闯一闯。那一年他前往青岛北海舰队成为一名军人,这一当便是8年。1978年,改革开放的开始之年,他在4月退伍回乡。同年的6月1日,他前往当地的五一渔厂工作,并且担任厂长,从那开始,家里的条件也慢慢有了改善。凭借着优秀的工作技巧与坚持不懈的精神,他在水产养殖方面悟出了自己的特殊门道,也就是从“五一渔厂”起,爷爷在创业这条路上越走越远。

2002年6月,当时水产养殖的收益情况不错,爷爷内心的创业梦也在熊熊燃烧,他离开五一渔厂,自己成立了当时的浙江省绍兴市上虞市白马湖水产专业合作社,这也是当时的上虞市第一家专业合作社。也许是初入创业道路,爷爷的胆子很大，不断开发新的产业模式，并与朋友合作，将合作社越做越大，当时还分别被上虞市、绍兴市和浙江省评为优秀水产专业合作社。

爷爷的生意有了起色，也在水产生意人里小有名气了，在2005年他担任了农民专业合作社联合会的会长，带领着其他的合作社一起探寻合作社与农民的生存之路。爷爷从来没有被眼前这一时的名利所蒙蔽，爷爷和奶奶没有离开过农村，他们仍然住在那栋有些陈旧的自建房里，他们不舍得为自己添置好的家具，在生活起居上总是觉得这样就足够了。爷爷好像深深扎根在了农村，空闲之余也会穿着大褂背心下田去干农活，他在创业之路上同时也做着一个农民本来做的事情，因为他从农民起家，这片土地给予他的是过往挥洒的汗水以及努力的果实。

从来没有一帆风顺的道路，只有认真负责的态度。令我印象深刻的是，合作社里的品牌鱼干都是爷爷自己研制方案自制出来的，所以每到冬天最寒冷的时候，社里总是忙着晒鱼干，“鱼干就是要经过最寒的风吹，这样才会入味，才会好吃，”爷爷说道。为了制作出良心产品，爷爷总是会独自睡在社里，亲自掌控鱼干的风吹日晒，亲自监督每个环节。他每日的饮食起居也都在社里完成，直到完成鱼干的制作。一丝不苟的他会在刺骨的寒风里去查看每一条鱼干的腌制情况，也会在半夜突如其来的大雨时冲在第一个去打理。

这样的他，是工作时一丝不苟的他，是创业时昂首前进的他，他不怕困难的到来，因为他做好了充分的准备去打倒困难。功夫不负有心人，他先后两年被评为上虞市、绍兴市的劳动模范，而他的春晖牌河蟹也被评为浙江省名牌产品。他作为农业合作社的元老人物，带领着广大的农民创业者走出去、迁进来，不断探索经验，并取得成效。在合作社得到较好经济效益的同时，也带动社员致富奔小康。如今已经70岁的他仍担任着合作社的理事长一职，虽然身体早已没有了当年的干劲，但他的精神与思想仍在前进，他总会津津乐道自己关于创业的那些点点滴滴，总是在言语中表现着如同自己年轻时的那般不服输。

当爷爷说完他的这些经历时，仿佛一个年轻有为的农民创业家站在我面前，带着朴实的笑容为家人播洒汗水，不能说爷爷是多么了不起的创业者，但他的的确确是我们家的英雄，是他让原本不起色的家庭越来越茁壮成长，是他作为家中的顶梁柱使得家人凝聚在一起。作为家中的长辈，他也时常教育我们，做人要敢于闯，但这前提是要学会吃苦，不去尝试就永远没有机会。

爷爷带着些许骄傲地为我讲述着他的过去，岁月痕迹早已爬过他的脸庞，但他炯炯发亮的双眼里饱含曾经的坚定和勇敢。老一辈在那样困难的时代里走创业这一条漫长而又艰辛的道路，是勇气可嘉的，也是肩上的责任与信仰使得老一辈创业者在这条路上不断披荆斩棘，所向披靡，也为他们的后代，也就是我们的过去、现在以及未来的生活带来了美好铺垫与无限憧憬。

Shaoxing
Xu Han (Class 191, Majoring in Network and New Media)

The Struggle Story of My Grandfather

My grandfather was the second among his brothers. As far as I could remember, he was always serious and unsmiling. Probably because I was fearful of him when I was a child, we didn't open out to each other and we didn't have much communication. In my memory, my grandfather, wearing his presbyopic glasses, always sat on the sofa in his room and read the daily newspaper just delivered. He was concerned about national affairs and all kinds of news; he often discussed political affairs with friends at the table. At the same time, he also liked those song and dance programs performed by the older artists. "The Avenue of Stars" was always played on the old-fashioned TV, which made him laugh the most. In short, my grandfather was a serious yet humorous person, and as I grew older, my fear of him gradually turned into the spontaneous respect.

My grandfather had multiple roles. He was a farmer, an outstanding member of the Chinese Communist Party, a veteran, and an entrepreneur who blazed his way forward.

My grandfather stayed in the village to help with farm work until he was 20. But he was always diligent and eager to learn. Though he didn't really spend much time in school, he was no less knowledgeable than others. Especially, when I was in primary school, my grandfather always gave me advice on my composition. And he seems to have piercing eyes, which could see what was good and what should be improved in my composition. At that time, I admired him for the knowledge he had though the education in his childhood was so backward.

It was in 1970 when he was at the age of 20 that he decided to serve in the army. He had married my grandmother at that time. Though finding it hard tearing himself away from my grandmother, he still made up his mind to strike out. He went to Qingdao and became a soldier in the North Sea Fleet that year, which lasted for eight years. In 1978, the reform and opening up began. He was discharged from the army in April. On June 1 of the same year, he went to work in the local May Day Fishing Factory and worked as the factory director. Since then, the family's economic condition gradually improved. With excellent working skills and unremitting spirit, he found his unique way in aquaculture. The May Day fishing factory was also where my grandfather went further on the road of starting his own business.

In June 2002, when the profit from aquaculture was considerable, my grandfather's dream of starting his own business was burning like a fire. He left the May Day Fishing Factory and set up Baima Lake Fishery Cooperative in Shangyu County, Shaoxing City, Zhejiang Province. It was also the first professional cooperative in Shangyu City at that time. Perhaps it was because that was his first start-up that my grandfather was very bold, and he constantly developed new industrial models. He cooperated with his friends, and the cooperative grew bigger and bigger; at the same time, it was rated as an excellent and professional cooperative by Shangyu City, Shaoxing City and Zhejiang Province.

My grandfather's business gradually improved, and he was also well-known among aquatic traders. In 2005, he served as the president of the Federation of Farmers' Professional Cooperatives, leading other cooperatives to explore the development of cooperatives and farmers. He was never blinded by the fame and fortune at the moment. My grandparents never left the countryside. They lived in the old self-built house all the time. They were not willing to buy good furniture for themselves. They always felt that it was enough to keep the status quo in their daily life. My grandfather seemed to take deep root in the countryside. In his spare time, he would go to the farmland in a vest to do farm work. On his way to start a business, he was also doing what a farmer should do, because he started as a farmer, and the land gave him the sweat of his hard work in the past and the fruits of his efforts.

There was never a smooth road but only a serious and responsible attitude. What impressed me was that the dried fish in the cooperative was made by my grandfather himself. In the coldest time of winter, the cooperative was always busy drying fish. "Only when dried fish go through the coldest wind will they taste delicious," said my grandfather. In order to make quality product, my grandfather always slept alone in the cooperative. He would adjust the time that dried fish were exposed to the wind and the sun by himself; he would supervise every step of the process. He spent the whole day in the cooperative till the dried fish were done. He would check each salted fish in the freezing wind conscientiously, and he also would take care of them in the middle of the night when there was a sudden downpour.

My grandfather was meticulous in his work; he headed up boldly on his way of starting business; he was not afraid of difficulties, because he was well prepared to overcome difficulties. His efforts paid off. He had been awarded the title of a model worker in Shangyu City and Shaoxing City for two years, and his Chunhui river crabs had also been rated as a famous brand product in Zhejiang province. As a founding member of the agricultural cooperative, he led a number of farmers to go out and move in, constantly exploring experience and making achievements. The cooperative gained good profit. Meanwhile, the members of the cooperative became rich and lived a well-off life. Now he is 70 years old, and he still holds the post of the director-general in the cooperative. Although he is not full of energy any more, he is active in spirit and mind. He always enjoys talking about his own details about starting a business, and has always shown his perseverance he had when he was young.

When my grandfather finished talking about his experiences, it seemed a promising young farmer entrepreneur was standing in front of me. He sweated for his family with a modest smile on his face. I can't say what a great entrepreneur my grandfather was, but he was indeed the hero of our family, the one who made the family stronger. Being the backbone of the family, he kept the family together. As the elder of our family, he also often told us that we should be brave in life, but the premise was to learn to endure sufferings and hardships. Otherwise, we would never have the opportunity if we did not try.

My grandfather spoke of his past life to me with pride. Signs of age had crept over his face, but his eyes were bright with the firmness and courage which he used to have in the past. In such a difficult time, the older generation was courageous enough to take the road of starting their own business, which was long and difficult. It was the responsibility and belief on their shoulders that made the older generation of entrepreneurs constantly blaze a way through obstacles and be invincible on this road. They also gave their descendants, our young people, a solid foundation and infinite expectation for our past, present, and future lives.

人生骑行终向前

李　炜

历史浪潮滚滚向前，人生如骑行，又何尝不是这般！有过骑行经历的人都知道，维持动平衡比保持静平衡要简单很多，骑行者与自行车的协调至关重要，把稳车龙头、踩踏板稳健有力、合理控制速度，才能行稳致远；骑行的人，大多感受过下坡时的风驰电掣，感受过平坦路上的轻松自在，也感受过翻越陡坡时的汗流浃背，转弯、颠簸，甚至摔倒跌伤也是常见的。只是但凡骑行，总归是要向前的。正如我们的人生，往往并不一帆风顺，却也要奋力向前。人生的向前，是一种本能。我始终相信，没有人是自甘堕落、自我放弃的，有时候看似的自我堕落，本质上还是放弃了对本能的认知与坚守，就是这种放弃我想也是阶段性，是暂时的，在一个特殊的时间，本能的唤醒依然会重新开始向前的人生。人生的向前，也是一种态度。追求价值的实现、追求人生的丰满是每个人心底的渴望，相对于一个人从出生，到成长，再到凋零的向前过程，渴望成功更有助于丰富人生；当然，对于成功的定义千差万别、因人而异，但是人作为社会化的存在，成功更重要的是社会化的，而绝非仅是个体性的，并且每个人从根本上无法摆脱社会性，只有将每个人生融入社会生活与发展，才是鲜活的，也是必然的，也当是人生合适的态度。小到个人、家庭，大到国家、民族和社会，向前是主流、是趋势、是历史的决定，其中有涓涓缓流，也有惊涛骇浪；有艳阳高照，也有风雨交加；会摔倒在泥泞，也会骑行在坦途，所有的过往都在告诉我们，坚定前行的信念，总能达到心中的彼岸，《爷爷的自行车》在吱吱作响里讲述着一个普遍的人生哲理。

（浙大宁波理工学院党委宣传部常务副部长）

故事
金华
唐林源(新闻学专业202专升班)

爷爷的自行车

1978年,整个中国都处在历史的转折点。40岁的爷爷离开劳改农场,身边站着他的3个儿子。他眯着眼睛看着周围渐渐散开的人群,抓起自己的行李,拉起老三的手,不回头地走向兰溪县城。在那儿,有一份组织安排的老师岗位在等着他,在他面前展开的是崭新的未来。

1938年出生的爷爷本是家族的骄傲,毕业于兰幼师,后被分配到淳安当老师,之后又到了武汉招飞,招飞未果后于1956年被推荐至中国人民解放军天津塘沽海军勤务学院。看上去光明的前途就在眼前,可当时代的一粒尘落在一个人身上,便变成了一座山。爷爷的军人梦碎,是因为爷爷一封寄给家里的书信,被判断出有右派思想。他的军旅生涯戛然而止,被赶回家乡兰溪劳动改造。

当时的爷爷被分配到兰溪市双坝村的一个果园做看守。双坝村是爷爷的家乡,曾经村子的榜样回到家,迎接他的是村民的排挤,甚至戴高帽批斗。奶奶当时的身体也不好,又遭受到了非人的精神折磨,没过多少年就因压力太大逝世。一家人的工分全指着爷爷看护果园得来。听我父亲叙述,家里最困难时,奶奶会到池塘里捡来那些人家洗菜不要的不好的菜叶来吃。爷爷从一个前途光明的海军士官沦落为劳改农场里的果园看守,甚至要捡别人的剩菜过活,他的内心痛苦着,煎熬着。痛苦煎熬不只是为他自己,因为他的一朝失意,令整个家庭都陷入困境。但他没有办法,只有等待着,等待重新回到正轨,所有的不公平对待可以移除,一切的冤屈可以被洗清。

爷爷被安排到了兰溪市第三中学当一名总务处的老师,负责采购教学和办公所需的物资。为了方便工作,学校里给他分配了一辆自行车。在劳改农场的日子里,爷爷没有自行车,也没有资格拥有属于自己的车。经历过文革,人们对平静岁月的向往已经到了渴望的地步。爷爷住进了学校的教职工宿舍,住在一起的还有他的二儿子和三儿子。大伯当时已经参加了工作,自己住在工作单位里。当时在爷爷心中的理想就是好好生活,培养儿子长大。

爷爷踩着这辆分配的自行车为学校里购置扫帚、纸笔、老师上课写板书用的粉笔等等。机缘巧合下，一个远在杭州的亲戚向爷爷求助，希望他能帮助自己打一场官司。顺利结束这次邀约之后，和爷爷一起回到兰溪的，还有一辆临安产的28 吋自行车。在当时那个年代，自行车并不是有钱就能够买得到的，你需要有专门的自行车票，并带上现金去商场换购。那时候，能拿得出换购的现金的人家都少之又少，更甭提有车票的人家了。当时家里生活过得相对富足了，爷爷和大伯两个人的工资支持着家里，爷爷还有一笔政府发放的安置费。爷爷去买了收音机、电风扇等等，再加上这辆属于自己的自行车，我家一下子成了兰溪这座小城里最时髦的几家几户之一。

那时候兰溪城里除了人民路、延安路等几条主干道是水泥路外，大多还只是砂石路，28 大自行车的轮胎在粗糙的路面上滚过，发出吵吵的声音。那是生活向上奋进的响声，在这吵吵声中，你能听到一家人脱离苦难的欢呼，能听到社会蓬勃发展的乐章，能听到的是整个中国这辆列车重新回到前进轨道轮毂与铁轨严丝合缝时发出的令人愉悦的响声。

爷爷的第一辆永久牌自行车并没有跟随他很久，它来到我家两个月后就被爷爷卖给了他的一个同事，卖出了 170 块的价格。在当时 170 块可不是一笔小数目，足足是他 4 个月的工资。卖出了这辆车后，爷爷买了一辆兰溪本地产的凤凰牌自行车。我父亲小时候都是靠爷爷骑着这辆车带他去各处游玩。

父亲印象最深的就是那次去临仙洞的旅游了。临仙洞位于寿昌境内，这地方有全国闻名的寿昌金矿，属于典型的喀斯特地貌，多溶洞。那时候路上也没有什么路边的饭馆，家里也舍不得在外头吃一顿。一般的解决办法都是，出游的前一天家里会烙好几张饼，饼要烙得干干的，不然放不住。再带上一小袋子榨菜或是咸菜。早上从家里出发，爷爷把饼和小菜揣进袋里，把尚年幼的父亲放在自行车的前横梁上，自己潇洒地一只腿踩在踏板上，把腿从车后轮画了个圆，稳稳地踏上另一个踏板。卯足劲蹬几下，车子有了前进的基础动力，缓缓地向前走着，爷爷回头向留在家的奶奶挥挥手道别，便带着最疼爱的小儿子走上了去往临仙洞的路程。

爷爷骑完车，都会把车停进自己的办公室里，不仅办公室门要上锁，车子也要用链条连着一个水管锁住。那时候社会上的小偷很多，自行车好偷，又容易出手，自然成为他们的首选目标。车子需要不时保养，出现了毛病也得自己修理。机油、链条成为办公室抽屉里的必需品。

1982 年的时候，因为爷爷写的一手好板书，特别是空心字，街道居委会特意去请他为居委会出每周需要写的黑板报。这一写，便是 20 多年。

2010 年，兰溪的路早已全部修成了水泥或是柏油马路，可爷爷却再也不骑车了。从他的家到他出板报的地方早就通了公交车，加之他的三个儿子都不愿意再让辛劳一辈子的父亲再骑车来回。自行车就此退出了爷爷的出行工具。带上一张公交卡,他就可以免费乘坐通往兰溪各地的公共汽车。

现在的爷爷除了偶尔还会去社区里出黑板报,其余时间就会在家里看看报纸。每次和爷爷吃饭,我们都会和爷爷喝上一些酒,在我们那里有个说法,酒精能打开一个人的话门。爷爷一喝上酒,就和我们这些小辈说自己以前的故事。我们便在一旁静静地听着,时不时点头回应。

现如今,大妈给爷爷购置了一辆三轮的电瓶车。说是电瓶车,却是那种汽车似的,有单独的驾驶室,这样风就不会灌进车子里。爷爷很喜欢这辆车,常常开着这车去不远的公园散步,就连去有公交车直达的大儿子家也是骑着自己心爱的小车。

自行车伴随了爷爷的半辈子。前半辈子碍于局势,爷爷并没有感到太多生活的甜蜜,在改革开放后,是自行车载着爷爷重新回到了享受人生的正轨上。

Jinhua
Tang Linyuan (Class 202, Majoring in Journalism)

Grandpa's Bicycle

In 1978, the whole China faced a turning point in history. My 40-year-old grandpa left the reform-through-labor farm with his three sons standing by his side. He squinted his eyes at the gradually dispersing crowd around him and then grabbed his luggage. He took the hand of the third son and walked towards Lanxi County without looking back, where an arranged position of teacher was waiting for him. The new future unfolded before him.

Born in 1938, Grandpa was the pride of the family. He graduated from Lanxi Normal School of Preschool Education and was later assigned to Chun'an as a teacher. Then he went to Wuhan to participate in the pilot recruitment. He failed and then was recommended to PLA Naval Academy of Service in Tianjin City, in 1956. It seemed that a bright future was right in front of him, but a small change in era could make a big difference to an individual. Grandpa's dream to be a soldier was shattered because his letter home was said to contain rightist elements. His military career came to an abrupt end. He was expelled from the military academy and driven back to his hometown Lanxi to undergo reform through labor.

Grandpa was assigned to watch an orchard in Shuangba village, Lanxi City. Shuangba Village was his hometown where he had been a good example but now villagers marginalized him, and even criticized and denounced him by having him a dunce's cap. Grandma, already in poor health at the time, also suffered inhuman mental torture. She died of stress just a few years later. The workpoint of the whole family was earned through watching the orchard by Grandpa. According to my father, Grandma would pick up the bad leaves that others threw away at washing from the pond in the most difficult time. From a promising naval officer Grandpa was reduced to an orchard guard at the reform-through-labor farm, and even had to live on others' leftovers for a living. His heart was aching and suffering, which was not just for himself. The whole family was in hot water because of him. However, he had no choice but to wait and wait for everything to get back on track and for all the injustices to be removed and all the wrongs to be righted.

Grandpa was assigned to be a teacher in the General Affairs Office of Lanxi No. 3 Middle School. He was responsible for purchasing materials needed for teaching and office work. School assigned him a bicycle for convenience. In the days at the reform-through-labor farm, Grandpa did not have a bicycle, nor was he allowed to own one. After undergoing the Cultural Revolution, people dreamed and even longed for peace. Grandpa lived in the school's faculty and staff dormitory, together with his second and third sons. My eldest uncle had already started working then and lived in the workplace by himself. At that time, the ideal in Grandpa's heart was to live well and cultivate his sons.

On the assigned bike, Grandpa purchased brooms, paper, pens, chalks for teachers' blackboard writings, and so on for the school. By chance, a relative in Hangzhou turned to Grandpa for help in a lawsuit. After the successful setting of the case, Grandpa came back to Lanxi with a 28-inch bicycle (whose wheel diameter was 28 inches) made in Lin'an. In those days, bicycles could not be bought only with money. You needed to buy one at the shopping mall with a special bicycle coupon and cash. At that time, few people had enough cash for purchase, not to mention the coupon. Our family was relatively rich then because both Grandpa and my eldest uncle supported the family with their salaries. Besides, Grandpa also had government-issued settlement allowance. He bought a radio, an electric fan and so on. And with our own bike, my family suddenly became one of the most fashionable households in this small city of Lanxi.

At that time, except several main roads such as Renmin Road and Yan'an Road, which were cement roads, the rest were mainly paved with gravels. The tires of 28-inch bicycles rolled over the rough roads, making a rustling sound. That was the sound of striving upwards in life, from which you could hear the cheers of a family out of suffering, the movement of vigorous social development, and the pleasant sound made when the train of China returned to its forward track and its wheel hub and rail fitted together perfectly.

Grandpa's first Forever bicycle did not accompany him for a long time. It was sold to his colleague for 170 yuan two months later. At that time, 170 yuan was a considerable sum of money, which was about four months' salary for Grandpa. After that, Grandpa bought a Phoenix bicycle made in Lanxi. When my father was young, Grandpa used to take him out for a trip everywhere on this bicycle.

What impressed my father most was the trip to Linxian Cave. Linxian Cave was located in Shouchang, where the nationally famous Shouchang Gold Mine was. It features typical karst landform with many karst caves. In those days, there were few roadside restaurants and the family was unwilling to eat outside because they wanted to save money. The normal solution was to make many pancakes at home the day before the trip. The pancakes must be baked dry, otherwise they were easy to go bad. With a small bag of mustard or pickles, they would start out from home in the morning. Grandpa put the pancakes and pickles into the bag and placed his young son on the crossbar of the bicycle. Then he stepped on one pedal smartly, lifted another leg all the way from the rear wheel of the bicycle to the other pedal steadily. The wheels turned around for a few circles, and then the bicycle moved forward slowly. Grandpa turned around and waved goodbye to Grandma at home, and then started the trip to Linxian Cave with his beloved youngest son.

When Grandpa finished riding, he would park the bicycle in his office.

Not only would the office door be locked, but the bicycle would also be locked to a water pipe with a chain. At that time, there were a lot of thieves in society. Bicycles were easy to steal and easy to sell, so they naturally became the thieves' first choice. The bicycle needed constant maintenance, and you had to fix it yourself if anything went wrong. Machine oil and chains became necessities in the office drawer.

In 1982, due to Grandpa's good handwriting, especially the outline font, the neighborhood committee invited him to make the weekly blackboard newspaper. And Grandpa did this for more than 20 years.

In 2010, all the roads in Lanxi had been paved with concrete or asphalt but Grandpa no longer rode bikes. Buses had long been available from his home to the place where he made the blackboard newspaper. And his three sons were unwilling to let their father, who had has worked hard all his life, commute by bike. The bicycle then withdrew from Grandpa's life. One bus card could take you to all parts of Lanxi for free.

Grandpa now spends most of his time reading newspapers at home, except for occasional visits to the community for blackboard newspaper. We will drink every time we eat together. As the local old saying goes, alcohol can loosen one's tongue. Grandpa would tell us his old stories once he has a drink. We just listen quietly, nodding in response from time to time.

Now, my aunt-in-law has bought an electric tricycle for Grandpa. It is an electric tricycle, but looks more like a car with a separate cab so as to keep out the wind. Grandpa likes this vehicle very much and often drives it for walks in the park not far away. He even drives his beloved tricycle to his eldest son's house which can be accessed by a direct bus.

Bicycles have accompanied Grandpa for half of his life. He did not feel much sweetness of life due to the chaotic situation in the first half of his life. After the reform and opening up, it was bicycles that carried Grandpa back to the right track to enjoy life.

历史进程与家国关系的记忆叙述

陈书影

天下之本在国，国之本在家，作为最基本的社会设置之一，家庭是人以社会意义活动的最初、最基础的场所，家庭范围内的活跃是人类基本的一种群体运动形式。马克思认为，家庭是一个能动的要素，它从来不是静止不动的，而是随着社会从较低阶段向较高阶段的发展，从较低的形式进到较高的形式。促使家与国共同进步的作用是相互的，社会发展使家庭进阶到更高的形式，家庭也同样推动社会往更先进的阶段发展。国家的历史发展体现在家庭的进步上，反映在人民生活的每个细节之中；每一个家庭的进步变迁都是社会的发展记录，每个人的生命征程都是民族复兴的组成。

爷爷的一生，“像是一根轴线，撑起了一个家的进程”，换一种角度来看，他的经历同样也是我们的国家、社会前进的缩影：在爷爷一生的经历中，我们能看到义务教育的普及，家庭教育的发展，对国防与科技创新的重视，行业考核制度的逐步完善和社会的不断进步，这是时代的前进路程、国家的发展历程投射在家庭中体现在个人上的历史性体现。郭同学的记忆叙述向我们展现的不仅是一个见证了沧海巨变的老人的一生，更是一部生动的、随着时代奔腾前行的新闻与历史大合集。

“一定历史时代和一定地区内的人们生活于其下的社会制度，受着两种生产的制约：一方面受劳动的发展阶段的制约，另一方面受家庭的发展阶段的制约”，引申恩格斯的原意，国家与政府普及基础教育增加劳动者数量提升劳动力质量，与此同时，家庭坚持“立场坚定、心怀家国、严以律己、节俭重孝”的家风，为国家培养更多拥有新时代精神与优良品质的新一代接班人。中国的“伦理本位”结构使得家庭的影响深刻根植于青年人的精神图景之中，这也使得优良的、符合社会要求的家风建设与为新生代提供优秀示范的家族长辈能对社会文明进步产生极大的推进作用。爱国敬业、尽职尽责、忠厚质朴、开拓创新、勤俭节约、体恤他人，爷爷在郭同学的记忆中留下的是一个平凡但伟大的印象，这是我们的祖辈父辈的形象符号，同时也是社会、时代对我们的要求。

大国崛起与人民幸福互为因果，国家兴盛、民族复兴、社会发展离不开无数家庭的奉献，家庭的平安幸福永远要以国家的安定繁荣为前提。行走的新闻，我们需要在司空见惯中发现意义，在平凡的日常里看到“新闻”，不仅要看到历史的进程，看到身处其中的记忆叙述，更要意识到发现、记录与传承的伟大。

（浙大宁波理工学院传媒与法学院新闻学专业 2018 级学生）

故事

台州

郭心童（网络与新媒体专业 192 班）

爷爷这辈子

掰着指头一算，爷爷去世已有 8 年多时间。虽然他离开我的生活很久很久了，但每当想起，那些关于他的记忆总是清晰又亲切地浮现在我眼前。他的一生，也像是一根轴线，撑起了一个家的进程……

爷爷是在浙江温岭的一个小村子里长大的。当时才小学毕业的爷爷，就担起了一边种地一边照顾年幼弟弟的重任，把念书的机会留给了弟弟。

退学后的爷爷决定去学一门技术来养活自己，补贴家用。他在一所机械修理学校学成后，以优异的表现被推荐进了浙江杭州的一家工厂。爷爷却在刚进工厂不久，就选择了参军入伍。原来当时工厂里有参军的名额，许多人都不愿意去，怕影响了自己的收入，但爷爷凭借着一腔爱国热情和心中的责任感，选择了参军来报效祖国。曾在部队里当过兵的太爷爷十分支持，爷爷的决定也算了了他“家里总得有个孩子去参军”的心愿。

在军营中的爷爷，每个月都会有一些津贴。爷爷一再节俭，仍从牙缝里挤出不少钱寄回家里，分担家里的开销。在二弟如愿考上同济大学，三弟也考上了河海大学后，爷爷每个月只给自己留下一点点维持生活的钱，剩下的都寄给自己的弟弟们，当作他们的生活费，一直寄到他们大学毕业为止。

作为父亲角色的爷爷，可以说是一个典型的顾家男人。从部队转业后，他又回到了杭州工作。尽管杭州是他最向往也最希望留住的城市，但爷爷在姑姑出生后，为了留在家乡的妻女，选择了调回黄岩邮政局工作。

姑姑口中的爷爷，还是一个老实到吃了亏也付之一笑的人。在单位里，他永远都是不争不抢的那个人。爷爷在邮政局稳定工作了一段时间后，局里会给有一定资历的员工分配房子，按照条件来说，怎么着也应该轮到爷爷了，但最后的名单上还是没有爷爷的名字。家里的亲戚都觉得忍不下这口气，要去为爷爷讨个说法，但爷爷总是死死拦住他们，问他为什么，他也只是叹口气，说道："别人家更难啊！"

虽然房子是分不到了，但总得让几个孩子有一个安稳的家，于是爷爷东拼西凑了一些钱，在叔公的帮助下，建了一栋两层的小楼，给了爸爸、姑姑一个安定的家。就在这栋小房子里，爷爷、奶奶、姑姑、爸爸度过了平淡但幸福的童年和少年时光。姑姑曾在一篇文章里写到："我还清晰地记得，就是在这座老房子中，有一天爸爸在院子的葡萄架下对正在读初中的我说，你们逐渐长大了，我也老了……"

爷爷还有一个做手工的绝活儿，不管是什么小玩意儿，只要我能说出来，爷爷就可以用几块简单的木材和一把锯子，给我做一个像模像样的出来。姑姑说小时候家里穷，也没有闲钱买一些电器，像那些电风扇、鼓风机都是爷爷自学做出来的。她还记得爷爷曾靠着图纸自己造出了一辆自行车，这在当时可算个新式玩意儿，爷爷就骑着这辆小车子，每天黄昏载着姑姑去外边兜风，邻居的小孩看见都非常崇拜和羡慕。那辆简单却功能齐全的小车，也陪伴爸爸、姑姑度过了他们的少年时期。

爷爷曾告诉过我，他年轻的时候还"发明"过一种计算自行车骑行里程的小东西，装在轮子上就可以计算出邮局的投递员骑了多少的路程，也就能作为考核邮递员工作量的依据。那时候，全国各地的邮局都到黄岩邮政局来订购"计程表"，爷爷每天晚饭后都会带着姑姑和爸爸去局里取全国各地送来的大大小小的订单。有了制作计程表的收入，家里的物质条件也算是宽裕了不少。除了这些"正经"东西，爷爷也总会给我做一些小玩具，我一直都还珍藏着他送给我的手工乒乓球拍和木头手枪。

爷爷在我心里的还有一个印象就是十分节俭。姑婆曾经提起，有一次和生着病的爷爷一起外出，公交车等了好久都没有来，就劝爷爷坐出租车或黄包车回家，但爷爷总觉得这是浪费钱，就等了大半个小时，好不容易开来了一辆车，人家一看到是个老年人，就直接开走了，爷爷只好走了好几站路回家……

我 4 年级的时候，爷爷查出了前列腺癌。那时候的我其实还不太懂那意味着什么，只记得那时候家里的气氛总是有些凝重，但在爷爷面前，大家都装作轻松的样子。有一天爸爸把我拉到一边，说爷爷没有多少时间了，你要好好陪陪他。不久后爷爷就住进了医院，因为接受完化疗头发会渐渐脱落，爷爷索性就剃光了自己的头发，在那一夜之间，他就好像又老了10岁，曾经撑起一个家的“巨人”，突然倒下了，变成了一个干瘦枯竭的弱者。那天哥哥来医院看爷爷，也许是家人、血亲之间的那种感应和共振，哥哥在进门的一瞬间就开始掉眼泪，爷爷却只是笑着，反过来安慰他。

后来，爷爷的病情急转直下，连说句话都开始变得极其费力困难。当他想表达的时候，就会示意奶奶给他拿纸和笔出来。爷爷病倒的那段时间，我们一家子的生活都围着医院转，奶奶直接把家搬到了医院，爸爸妈妈、姑姑姑丈也是一下班就往医院跑，那时候每天下午放学，我都会直接去医院看看爷爷，有时候也会在他的病床边写写作业。医院消毒水的气味总是激得我直咳嗽。那天爷爷拿着笔，在纸上写了一句：“让童童回家安心学习吧，不要再来医院了，这里的学习环境不好。”在生命的最后阶段，他心里想的也依然都是他的家人们。但爷爷不知道，在我心目中，有他的地方就是家。

爷爷临走前留下的最后一句话，也是写在纸上的：“要照顾好妈妈，也维持好这个家，我无能为力了。”奶奶后来告诉我们，爷爷退休后一个人攒下了近30万元，自己从来舍不得花，连一些稍微贵点的药都舍不得买，说要把钱留给孩子们作为自己的一点心意。爷爷还在自己的遗嘱里一再嘱托，就算自己不在了，兄弟姐妹间也要互帮互助，千万要让这个家一直和和睦睦。他为这个家，操了太多的心。

爷爷走的那天晚上，家人们围在他的病床前，爸爸叫我到床边再喊一声爷爷，他说，这也许是你这辈子最后一次喊这个称呼了。那天晚上也是我第一次看到爸爸那样痛哭。

爷爷不需要粉饰的一生，平凡又伟大。

Taizhou
Guo Xintong (Class 192, Majoring in Network and New Media)

The Whole Life of My Grandfather

It has been 8 years since my grandfather passed away. Although I had lived without him for such a long time, whenever I recalled memories of my grandfather always appeared clearly and vividly in my mind. His life, like a time axis, took on the responsibility of the whole family.

My grandfather grew up in a small village in Wenling, Zhejiang Province. At that time, my grandfather, who had just graduated from primary school, took on the responsibility of taking care of his younger brother while farming, and he left the opportunity to study to his younger brother.

After leaving school, in order to support himself and the family, my grandfather decided to learn a skill. After graduating from a mechanical repair school, he was recommended to a factory in Hangzhou, Zhejiang Province because of his excellent performance. At that time, there were quotas for military participation in the factory, but many people were reluctant to go there for fear that their income would be affected. However, with his patriotic enthusiasm and sense of responsibility in his heart, my grandfather chose to join the army to serve the motherland soon after he entered the factory. My great-grandfather, who had been a soldier in the army, was very supportive, and grandfather's decision also fulfilled great-grandfather's wish that "there must be a child in the family to join the army".

In the barracks, my grandfather had some allowance every month. My grandpa was very thrifty, saving a lot of money and sending them home to share the expenses of his family. After his second younger brother was admitted to Tongji University and his third brother was admitted to Hehai University, my grandfather left only a little money to support himself every month, and the rest was sent to his younger brothers as their living expenses, until they graduated from university.

As a father, my grandfather was a typical family man. After he transferred from the army, he returned to work in Hangzhou. Although Hangzhou was the city he most yearned for and hoped to stay in, he chose to transfer back to Huangyan Post Office to take care of his wife and daughter in his hometown after his daughter was born.

My aunt said my grandfather was so honest that he would not be angry when he was treated unfairly. In his work, he was always the one who never fought for his own benefits. After my grandfather had worked steadily in the post office for a period of time, the office would assign houses to employees with certain qualifications. According to the conditions, it should have been the turn of my grandfather, but his name didn't appear on the final list. All the relatives in the family felt very angry and wanted to ask for an explanation for my grandfather. But my grandfather always stopped them. When they asked him why, he just said with a sigh, "It's more difficult for other people's families!"

Even though he could not get the house, the children had to have a stable home, so my grandfather borrowed some money from friends. With the help of my grandfather's brother, he built a two-story building, giving my father and aunt a stable home. In this small house, my father and aunt spent an ordinary but happy childhood with their parents' company. My aunt once wrote in an article, "I still remembered clearly that it was in this old house that my father said to me, who was studying in middle school, under the grape trellis in the courtyard, that we were growing up and he was getting old."

My grandfather was also good at making handicrafts. No matter what gadget it was, as long as I could describe it, my grandfather could make me a delicate trinket with a few simple pieces of wood and a saw. My aunt said that when she was a child, the family was poor and had no spare money to buy such electrical appliances as electric fans and blowers, which were later made by my grandfather through self-study. My aunt still remembered that my grandfather, depending on a drawing, used to make a bicycle, which was a very fashionable thing at that time. My grandfather rode this bicycle and took my aunt out for a ride every evening, which was admired and envied by the children in the neighborhood. The simple but fully functional bicycle was also a good companion for my father and my aunt when they were young.

My grandfather once told me that when he was young, he also invented a small device to calculate the mileage of bicycle riding. It could be installed on the wheel to calculate the distance traveled by the postman working in the post office, which could also be used as the basis for assessing the workload of the postman. At that time, post offices all over the country went to Huangyan Post Office to order the "meter". My grandfather would take my aunt and my father to the office after dinner every day to get orders from all over the country. With the income from making meters, the material condition of the family got better gradually. In addition to these important things, my grandfather always made some small toys for me. I still treasure the hand-made table tennis racket and wooden pistol he gave me.

Another impression of my grandfather is that he was very thrifty. My grandaunt once mentioned about her going out with my sick grandfather. After waiting for the bus for a long time, she advised my grandfather to take a taxi or a rickshaw to go home. But my grandfather always thought it was a waste of money, so he waited for more than half an hour. Finally, a rickshaw came. However, the rickshaw man went away as soon as he saw that my grandfather was an old man. At last my grandfather had to walk several stops to go home.

When I was in fourth grade, my grandfather was diagnosed with prostate cancer. At that time, I didn't really understand what it meant. I only remember that the atmosphere at home was always oppressive, but in front of my grandfather, everyone pretended to be relaxed. One day, my father pulled me aside and told me that my grandfather might not last long. He asked me to accompany him as much as possible. Soon after, my grandfather was sent to the hospital. Because his hair would gradually fade after receiving chemotherapy, he simply shaved own his hair. Over that night, he seemed to be 10 years older than before. The man, who once held up the whole family like a "giant", suddenly fell down and became a lean and exhausted weak man. That day, my brother came to the hospital to see his grandfather. Maybe it was the feeling and resonance between his family and blood relatives. My brother began to shed tears the moment he entered the door, but my grandfather just laughed and comforted him instead.

My grandfather's disease turned worse quickly later on, and it was even extremely difficult for him to say a word. When he wanted to say something, he would signal my grandmother to bring him paper and a pen. When my grandfather fell ill, our family spent a lot of time taking care of him in the hospital. My grandmother lived in the hospital directly. My parents, my aunt and my uncle-in-law ran to the hospital as soon as they got off work. At that time, after school every afternoon, I would go directly to the hospital to see my grandfather, and sometimes I would write homework by his bed. The smell of disinfectant in the hospital always made me cough. That day, my grandfather took a pen and wrote a sentence on the paper, "Let Tongtong go home and study at ease. She should not come here, because the learning environment is not good." At the end of his life, all he was thinking about was still his family. But my grandfather did not know, in my mind, home was where he was.

The last sentence left by my grandfather before he died was also written on the paper. "Take good care of your mother and maintain this family. I can do nothing anymore." My grandmother later told us that after his retirement, my grandfather saved nearly 300 thousand yuan. He was never willing to spend it. He even refused to buy some expensive medicines. He said that he would leave the money to the children as his wish and thought. My grandfather also told his family in his will that even if he was not there, brothers and sisters in this family should help each other and make this family harmonious all the time. He has paid too much for the family and worried too much.

On the night of my grandfather passing away, my family gathered in front of his bed. My father told me to call my grandfather at the bedside for the last time. He told me that this might be the last time I could call him in my life. That night was also the first time I saw my father cry so loudly.

My grandfather's whole life needs no whitewash. It is ordinary but great.

“一船五车”中的“蜂鸟效应”

周盼佳

交通工具作为一种符号展现了生活的变迁。瑞士语言学家索绪尔提出语言是一种符号系统，认为符号(sign)可分为“能指”(signifier，即符号的语音、形象)和“所指”(signified，即符号的意义、概念)。[①] 在文中，“能指”作为符号的一种物理形式，指的是“一船五车”，作为具象的交通工具。“所指”是使用者对于符号指涉对象的一种想象的概念。通过家庭中交通工具的变迁所反映出来两代人生活状态的改变，这是一种思维的变迁和时代的变迁。

在这种变迁下，交通工具的“蜂鸟效应”在文本的家庭中十分明显。侯云在《人类如何走到今天：改变世界的科技思想与发明》一书中提到，交通工具演变具有“蜂鸟效应”，是指一个领域内的一项创新或一连串创新，最终会引发表面看起来似乎完全属于另一种截然不同的领域内的变革[②]，比如在植物和蜂鸟的事例中，它们虽然是不一样的生物体，有着完全不同的需求，但植物以清楚易懂的方式明确地影响了蜂鸟的外形。这个家庭的交通工具迭代更新，不仅仅是提高了以家庭为单位的劳动生产，也导致了家庭生活品质提升和家庭结构产生根本性变化。交通工具的变化导致交通运输效率的提升，也让家里的生意蒸蒸日上。伴随着妹妹的出生，家庭多了一口人，也意味着父母的奋斗年龄要延长，笔者家庭的生活轨迹也发生了极大变化。

这些变化是从爷爷到爸爸的代际变化，从人民公社到以家庭为单位的民营小店的时代变化，从种地打工到开店经营的思维变化。这个家庭的奔向小康之路与改革开放息息相关。以小见大，这就是《浙里是我家》的意义吧！

(宁波诺丁汉大学国际传播学院在读博士)

---

① 费尔迪南·德·索绪尔：《普通语言学教程》，商务印书馆2009年版，前言页。

② 侯云：《人类如何走到今天：改变世界的科技思想与发明》，第三章：交通工具演变的蜂鸟效应。电子工业出版社2020版，第152页。

故事

绍兴

汪雅琴(新闻学专业 201 专升本班)

一船五车

爸爸 6 岁那年,爷爷带着全家落户绍兴马鞍镇的城红村,开始了新的生活。

1983 年,爷爷当上了城红村生产二队队长,他为人率真又热心,爱打抱不平。爷爷的大半生都是在务农。先是种西瓜,种了约五六年,因为行情实在是不好,改种糯稻,等到盖起了大棚,就开始种植各类蔬菜。为了养家糊口,爷爷买了挂桨机船来运输蔬菜,顺道也帮村民们把蔬菜运到城里头和粮食批发市场去。爷爷说,那艘机船可以载 6 吨左右的蔬菜,只要是村民们有要卖掉的蔬菜,他都会替人家送货。爷爷喜欢在船上喝喝黄酒,唱唱小曲儿。那时日子虽苦,但乐趣甚多。

1990 年,爷爷决定新造一栋三层楼。那会儿村子里大多是二层楼,造三层不是要娶媳妇,便是那些家底很厚的人家。爷爷说,要想日子越过越好,就得硬着头皮去干。新三楼是在下半年造好的,那会儿爸爸还在平水读高中。

1998 年,是新房造好的第 8 年,也是爸爸妈妈结婚的第 1 年。结婚后没几个月,爸爸就回上海去了。他是工地上的小队长,每年只有临近春节才会回家来过年。2001 年,城红村成了县里的第二批拆迁户,为的是"填海造房"计划。这一年,妈妈也去了上海。

我同爷爷奶奶一道搬到了永宁村的小平房里。家门口不再是来势汹汹的海了,取而代之的是一条静谧安详的小河流。河对岸是一座小石桥,石桥的角落是一家陈旧的小卖铺,但里面有好多好多新奇玩具和零食。

2003 年的 9 月,我开始上幼儿园了。幼儿园就在家不远处。

在永宁村的两年里,爷爷早已不是当初那个呼风唤雨的生产队队长了。那时候永宁村是钢铁厂的天下,爷爷力气很大,他在钢铁厂做搬运工,每天还是骑着他那辆老式自行车。爷爷说,他一个人最多一天搬过 365 斤的铁,有时候要去外地搬货,老板也就只带他一个人去。400 来斤的铜都是他自己一人背,厂里头愈发少不了爷爷,说他一人能抵上好几人……

2009 年秋,爸爸突然从上海回来,带着大半年的工资和他的行李。爸爸说,在工地里呆了10多年,和工人们吵架,老板连句公道话都不愿意讲,让他寒心。

村子拆掉后便盖了安置小区,我家分到了两套房子。爸爸在上海期间,我和妈妈一直住在外婆家,直到他回来后的两个月里,我们才搬了新家。

回家后的爸爸首先面临的问题就是找工作。爸爸说,那会儿他也是没什么办法了,要么去厂里找个机修工的工作,要么干脆自己谋出路。他想到了姑姑在轻纺城里做生意也不过两年,反正一切都是从头开始,就干脆拼一拼。

爸爸在姑姑那共呆了三个月,前一个月便是认识每块样布,包括它们的克重、米数、单价。爸爸要熟记于心的不单是挂在店里的那些,更多的是要认清楚客户手里的那些布。

爸爸估摸着学得差不多了,东拼西凑地借了10来万元,在轻纺城的北市场二楼租了间店铺,开始了真正的"单打独斗"。一间不到30平方米的小店铺,开启了爸爸的新生活,也成为家里的一个重要的转折点。开张的第一个月便接到了单子。对方客户没有因为知道了爸爸是个新手就停止了合作。爸爸在高兴的同时,也开始发了愁:没有车,他该怎么送货呢?想到回绍兴的时候,还剩着工地上发的那点工资,爸爸便狠了狠心买了第一辆车——长安面包车。

有了这辆小小的面包车后,爸爸可以送我上学,可以不用每天坐近两小时的公交车,还可以自己送点货了。店里来单子的时候,爸爸便好几天没有完整的觉可以睡,他要去厂里排队,碰到人少或者淡季的时候排到傍晚,一到9月10月的旺季排到凌晨两三点是常有的事。

面包车陪伴了我们三年。随着家里的生意逐渐步入正轨,它也到了退休的年纪。

2012年某个傍晚,一辆新的系着红带子的载货车停在外婆家的门口。它很大,颜色很新很亮,玻璃上贴了一层蓝黑色的纸,我看不见里面。我很是欣喜,跑着进去问爸爸,他说这是家里刚买的新车,那辆老面包车卖了。爸爸带我坐进了新车里,它有空调,有插U盘的口,前排还有三个座位,我可以和妈妈坐在一块儿了。新车里的一切都被透明的膜包着,我小心翼翼地触摸着它,生怕一个不小心把这张膜戳破了。爸爸在开车回家的路上,放着凤凰传奇的《荷塘月色》,"我像只鱼儿在你的荷塘,只为和你守候那皎白月光"。

载货车花了爸爸14万元,但爸爸说这个钱是值得的。有了它,去厂里拉货、送货、打包……这些日积月累的小钱都可以省下来。载货车不贵,但它代表了爸爸在那个充满激烈价格战的市场里的胜利。爸爸总说未来的路还很长,这些来之不易的点滴进步,都是这个小小的家在越过越好的标志。

2016年是我家最艰难也最幸福的一年。

我有个很励志的妈妈,她在这一年凭着自己的努力考出了驾照,还为我们家生下了一个可爱的妹妹。家里也有了第一辆轿车。这辆新轿车，带着可触屏和无线蓝牙，开门时座位下的 Logo 闪着淡淡的光，座位椅散出阵阵真皮香。

有了新车之后，爸爸负责工厂管理和运货，妈妈负责接送和店里的运营。但妈妈开车是个新手，40 分钟的路程她需要开 1 个多小时，于是店里没有订单的日子，爸爸就开车和妈妈一道去店里，有订单的日子，爸爸便先送妈妈去店里，再去厂里送货。

2018 年，家里遭遇了最为严重的经济危机——爸爸遇到了老赖，一直信誉良好的客户突然跑路，没有任何原因。他和爸爸还有几十万的款没有结清。一边是家庭的每日支出和新家的贷款，一边是定制布匹的厂商每日的催款，家里一度陷入了焦躁和绝望。爸爸去当地报警，贴寻人启事，找朋友帮忙……客户顶不住压力，和爸爸主动联系，还了一部分的欠款。但最终剩下 20 万元左右没有结清，便再也打不通电话了。爸爸选择走法律途径，这件事直到现在也还没有解决。

爸爸今年 48 岁，他时常说，有了妹妹之后他的奋斗年龄要延长到 70 岁，然后买一辆房车和妈妈去世界各地旅行。爸爸的梦想也是我的梦想，有了经济能力的我，第一个愿望便是给爸爸妈妈买梦想中的房车。

Shaoxing

Wang Yaqin (Class 201, Majoring in Journalism)

One Boat and Five Cars

When Dad was six years old, Grandpa and his family settled down in Chenghong Village in Shaoxing County and started a new life.

In 1983, Grandpa became the production team leader in Chenghong Village. He was frank and warm-hearted, and loved to fight against injustices. Grandpa spent most of his life in farming. At first, he planted watermelon for about five or six years. Because the business was really bad, he switched to grow glutinous rice instead. When the greenhouses were built, he began to plant all kinds of vegetables. In order to support his family, Grandpa bought a suspended screw boat to transport vegetables himself, and also helped the villagers to deliver vegetables to the town and the wholesale food market. Grandpa said that the boat could carry about 6 tons of vegetables. As long as the villagers needed to sell vegetables, he would deliver for them. Grandpa liked to drink yellow rice wine and sang ditties on the boat. It was a hard time, but also full of fun.

In 1990, Grandpa decided to build a third floor. At that time, most of the villages were two-story flat houses, and the three-story houses were built either for marrying, or by those rich families. Grandpa said that if you wanted a better life, you had to bite the bullet and do it. The new third floor was built in the second half of the year, when Dad was in senior high school in Pingshui Town.

The year of 1998 was the 8th year that the new house was built, and it was also the first year that Mom and Dad got married. Just a few months later, Dad went back to Shanghai. As a little team leader on the construction site, he would come home to celebrate the New Year every year only when the Spring Festival was approaching. In 2001, Chenghong Village became the second demolished households in the county for the "reclaiming sea for houses" project. This year, Mom also went to Shanghai.

Together with my grandparents, I moved to a small bungalow in Yongning Village. In front of the house was no longer a raging sea, but a quiet and peaceful river instead. Across the river was a small stone bridge, at whose corner there was an old shop. But there were many novel toys and snacks inside.

In September 2003, I started kindergarten, which was not far from home.

In the two years in Yongning Village, Grandpa was no longer the production team leader who could do anything he wanted. At that time, Yongning Village was the world of steel factories. Grandpa was very strong. He worked as a porter in the steel factory and rode his old bicycle every day. Grandpa said that he had moved 365 catties of iron at most a day by himself. Sometimes when the boss went to other places to move goods, he would only take Grandpa there. About 400 catties of copper were all carried by Grandpa alone. The factory was more likely to value him, saying that he alone could match several people...

In the autumn of 2009, Dad suddenly came back from Shanghai with more than half a year's salary and his luggage. Dad said that the boss was not even willing to say anything fair at his quarrel with workers, even though he had stayed on the construction site for more than 10 years, which made him bitterly disappointed.

After the village was demolished, the resettlement community was built, and each household was given two houses. During my father's stay in Shanghai, Mom and I lived in my grandmother's house, and it was not until two months after his return that we moved into the new house.

The first problem facing my father after his returning home was to find a job. Dad said he had no choice but to find a job as a mechanic in the factory or find his own way out. It occurred to him that my aunt had only been doing business in the textile city for two years. Since everything was starting from scratch anyway, he decided to go all out.

Dad stayed with my aunt for three months. The first month was to know each sample cloth, including its weight in grams, number of meters and unit price. Dad had to keep in mind not just what was hanging in the store, but what was in the customer's hand.

When he thought that he had learned enough, Dad borrowed and scraped together 100,000 yuan. Then he rented a shop on the second floor in the north market of the textile city and started a real "single fight". A small shop less than 30 square meters marked Dad's new life, and also became an important turning point in the family. Orders came in the first month. The client didn't stop cooperation when he knew Dad was a green hand. Dad was happy but also began to worry: How could he deliver goods without a car? Thinking of the salary paid on the construction site when he returned to Shaoxing, Dad made a great determination to buy the first car—the Chang'an van.

With this small van, Dad could send me to school and didn't need to take the bus for nearly two hours a day. He could also deliver some goods by himself. When orders came, Dad couldn't have a full sleep for several days. He had to go to the factory to line up. When there were few people or in the off-season, he would queue until the sunset. In the peak season from September to October, it was common to line up until two or three o'clock in the morning.

The van accompanied us for three years. As the family's business gradually got on track, it also reached the age of retirement.

One evening in 2012, a new truck with a red belt pulled up at the door of my grandmother's house. It was big and its color was new and bright. And there was a layer of blue-black paper on the glass so I couldn't see the inside. With great delight, I ran in and asked Dad. He replied that this was the new car we had just bought, and that the old van had been sold. Dad took me into the new car, which had air conditioning, a USB slot, and three seats in the front row so that I could sit with my mother. Everything in the new car was covered by a transparent film. I touched it carefully, for fear that I would accidentally puncture the film. When Dad was driving home, he played the song *Moonlight over the Lotus Pond* by one band called Phoenix Legend, "*I'm like a fish in your lotus pond, just waiting for the bright white moonlight with you...*"

The truck cost 140,000, but Dad said it was worthwhile. With it, you could go to the factory to pull goods, deliver goods and pack…… All those little costs that added up over time could be saved. The truck wasn't expensive, but it represented a victory for Dad in the highly competitive market. Dad always said that the road ahead was still very long, and these little progresses were hard-won, which was a sign that this little family was getting better.

The year of 2016 has been the most difficult and happiest year for my family.

Mom was very inspirational. She passed the driving license with her own efforts this year and gave birth to my lovely sister for the family. The first car came to our family, equipped with its touch screen and wireless Bluetooth. When the door was opened, the LOGO under the seat seemed to glitter with a faint light, and the real leather seats gave off a burst of fragrance.

With this new car, Dad was responsible for the factory and delivery, and Mom was responsible for the pickup and store operations. But since Mom was a green hand, it took her more than an hour to drive a 40-minute journey. Thus, in the days with no order in the store, Dad would drive to the store with Mom. When there was an order, Dad would drive her to the store first and then go to the factory for delivery.

In 2018, our family suffered the worst financial crisis ever when Dad met a deadbeat. The client who had always had a good reputation suddenly ran away for no reason. The payment of hundreds of thousands of yuan needed to be settled between him and Dad. The family fell into a state of anxiety and despair, for the daily expenses of the family and the loans for the new house on the one hand, and the daily payment reminders of the custom-made cloth manufacturers on the other hand. Dad went to the local police, posted notices for missing persons and asked friends for help... The client couldn't resist the pressure. He contacted Dad proactively and repaid part of the debt. However, the good times did not last long. Dad could not get through when there was still about 200,000 yuan left unsettled. Dad resorted to the legal proceedings, but the matter has not been resolved up to now.

Dad is 48 years old now, and he often said that he would like to struggle until 70 after my sister's birth, and then buy an RV to travel around the world with Mom. Dad's dream is also my dream. When I can make money, my first wish is to buy the dream RV for Mom and Dad.

呵护浙商精神的文化基因

郭小春

浙商足迹遍及全球，惠泽世界，声震天下。浙江正在奋力建设全国“新时代全面展示中国特色社会主义制度优越性的重要窗口”，其重要原因恐怕离不开以“顺应时势，开拓创新，敢为天下先”见长的浙商精神乃至浙江精神。提及浙商群体，关注的焦点往往是声誉卓著的上市公司、跨国企业、行业龙头企业和规模影响巨大的商业集群和商帮巨贾，这是情理所致，因为大型企业群体是地方经济的支柱，是管理者的关注点，是媒体报道的对象，易于“在场”，形成“情境空间性”。

然而，《一个家，两代人》的家庭叙事吸引读者注目万千怀揣改变命运梦想而接力奋斗的普通家庭的“小”历史。作者坦诚写出父亲认真创业终因债务链条导致失败而回归普通职员生活，这大概是创业背后不算鲜见而不引人关注的另一种图景吧？该家庭小传从非虚构、非诗意化乡村生活场景和家人历次职业变换呈现了孕育浙商精神、浙江精神的现实土壤、历史资源和人民立场。

家庭叙事当然指向对美好生活的向往。“以人民为中心”的社会治理理念寻求的是社会稳定整合，着眼于人民对美好生活的向往，强调改革开放的成果共建共享共治，消除社会成员的疏离感，增加人民群众的获得感，提升民生幸福指数。弘扬浙商精神，离不开对于人民群众日益增长的物质和精神需求的满足，需要用心呵护浙商精神的文化基因。

（宁波工程学院副教授，博士）

故事

嘉兴

顾晨琳(新闻学专业191班)

一个家,两代人

我的家乡——海宁,海宁寓有"海洪宁静"之意。

我奶奶出生在海宁一个普通的农民家庭。我奶奶特别勤劳能吃苦,十来岁的时候就能拿到和成人一样的工分。每年年末的时候,生产队会依据工分的多少给每户人家分配不同数量的钱。

在改革开放后的1983年,原来村里的生产队取消了,开始实行家庭联产承包责任制。村里按照每户人家不同的人口数分配田地,使大家的生产积极性大幅度提高,天刚刚亮就起床去田地里拔秧,为了改善生活条件,还开始养起了猪。但一年到头只有过年的时候才能吃到猪肉,奶奶回忆时说到:"当年我们平时只能吃吃土豆和番薯,如果能吃两口猪油拌饭就是天大的幸福了。"在"勤劳致富"的口号下,爷爷奶奶为了补贴家用,在兼顾农业生产的同时,还去了乡里筹建的窑厂做搬运工作,要把工厂里烧制好的砖头用扁担挑到轮船上,运往上海等地。当工厂活多的时候,甚至凌晨两三点才能回家。后来,随着农科站提高了粮食种子的品质,以及除草剂的逐渐普及,庄稼的产量也一年比一年高了。另外还开展了副业。家庭条件比刚刚结婚时好了不少。1986年,爷爷奶奶终于攒足了钱,造了一栋小楼房。

奶奶决定去开一家小店。在乡里小学的附近搭了一个铁棚,奶奶的营生就开始了。店里出售一些零食、文具和玩具,大部分的商品就是面向学校的在读学生,要是店里的商品缺货了,奶奶就会骑着自行车去街上的供货商店补货。生意少的时候,还能闲下来织织毛衣。虽然挣不了什么大钱,但基本的收入还是不错的,日子也过得安安稳稳。

我的奶奶确实是精明能干并且善于与人交流,于是她被推选为了村里妇女委员会的组长,时常要去村委会开会,负责上级文件的宣发工作,要挨家挨户地进行沟通和宣传。后来,乡里的小学搬迁了,小店也就自然而然地关闭了。

如今,我的奶奶已经年近古稀,但是她还是闲不下来,总要去地里种种小菜。傍晚时分,她会和小区里的大妈大伯打打太极拳。兴致来的时候,她会和她的姐妹们出去旅旅游。随着日子越过越滋润，奶奶再也不用像年轻时那样累死累活地干活挣钱了。国家发了养老金，她终于能好好享福了。

我父亲刚刚投入工作的时候，是拜师学做木工，给师傅打下手，师傅也会教给他基本的手艺。那时，普通的人家对于装修都只有简单基础的要求，样式也比较单一，每户人家的装修要求是差不了多少的。

后来，乡里开了一家金刚石制造厂，因为听说待遇不错，我爸就转行去厂里做技术员。厂里使用的技术在当时比较先进，不是轻易就能够上手的，于是他还专门去余杭培训了一两个月，学习装配、调试机器的方法。他有做木工的基础，没费多少时间，就把调试机器的手艺和技巧摸透了。在厂里上班的日子是很安稳的，收入也比较可观。但在工作了一段时间之后，年轻气盛的爸爸与厂里的领导发生了矛盾，原因是工资分配不均，有的人工作不上心，经常偷懒，却和勤勤恳恳工作的他拿着一样的工资，而领导视而不见，于是他一气之下就愤然离职了。

离开了工厂，他选择继续从事自己的老本行。那时候，有很多木匠都找不到活干，而我的父亲手艺精湛，大家都很信赖他，活多得忙不过来。于是他萌生了一个想法，每当他接到了活，就召集他的同伴和他一起干，他的收入也越来越多了。

1998年，父亲和母亲结婚了，和爷爷奶奶的婚姻大不相同，他俩是自由恋爱，在两三年的相处和交往之后，他们选择了相伴到老。两年后，我来到了这个世界上。当时，我爸爸已经有了一定的积蓄，他决定去盖一座新的房子。不久，一幢3层高的小楼房就拔地而起了，房子里的家具我爸都亲力亲为，他为房间的设计倾注了不少心血，住进了新的楼房，我家的生活质量无疑提升了不少。

经过了这些年的工作，我爸积攒了对生活的信心，他决定自己去创业。经过亲戚的介绍，他选择了开茶具包装厂。场址选在了海宁隔壁的小县城——海盐，每天我的父亲都要用一个多小时的路程才能到达工厂，但是他也风雨无阻。开厂，无疑需要大笔的资金，场地费、购买机器、招募工人的开支都不是小数目，我爸拿出了多年来的积蓄。在工厂的经营上，他费尽了心思，有一些生产的技术并不完善，他就自己苦心钻研。但是，厂里的生意并不景气，有客户拖欠债务，缺少资金，工厂难以运转。现实毕竟不是小说，有时候确实也挺残酷，坚持带来的未必是成功，也可能是债务持续扩大。三四年之后，我爸的工厂关闭了，原因有很多，包括机器不够先进、工人出现意外、行情不好等许许多多的因素。我印象很深刻，那几年，父亲的头发白得特别快。创业失败，我爸陷入了人生的低谷，可是生活还要继续。

如今，他是一名普普通通的在职员工，拿着稳定的工资，支撑起我们这个家，每年到头来也能有点小积蓄。

现在我们家过着安安稳稳的日子，也许平平淡淡才是真。从改革开放到今天，我们家的变化可谓翻天覆地，虽然有过挫折，但也是总体向好的。每当爷爷奶奶回忆起当年的往事，他们常常对我说："你是最幸福的一代人。"

Jiaxing
Gu Chenlin (Class 191, Majoring in Journalism)

One Home, Two Generations

My hometown is Haining, which means "seas of serenity".

My grandma was born in an ordinary peasant family in Haining. She was so diligent and hard-working that she was able to get the same workpoints as adults when she was in her teens. The production team would allocate different amounts of money to each family according to the number of points at the end of each year. After the reform and opening-up, the production team in the village was dismissed in 1983 and the household contract responsibility system was carried out. Lands were distributed to each family according to the different numbers of people in the family, so that everyone's enthusiasm for production greatly improved. People got up early to pull up seedlings at dawn. In order to improve the living conditions, we began to raise pigs but we could only eat pork during the Spring Festival. My grandma recalled, "In those days, we could only eat potatoes and sweet potatoes. It would be great happiness if we could eat two monthfuls of rice with lard." To respond to the call of "becoming rich through hard work", in addition to the agricultural production, my grandparents went to work as porters in the kiln which was established by the village so as to subsidize the family. They carried the bricks from the kiln onto the ships which would leave for Shanghai and other places. They could not go back home until two or three o'clock in the morning when there was too much work in the factory. Afterwards, agricultural science stations improved the quality of grain seeds, and herbicides had been used widely, so the production of the crops increased year by year. Meanwhile, with the help of the side business, the family conditions were much better than it used to be when they first got married. In 1986, my grandparents finally saved enough money to build a small building.

My grandma decided to open a small store. My grandma's business began by putting up an iron shed near a primary school in the village. She sold snacks, stationery and toys, and most of the customers were students. If the store was out of stock, she would ride her bicycle to the supplier store on the street to replenish the stock. When it was not busy, she would take time to knit sweaters. Although she didn't make a lot of money, she could earn enough money to live comfortably.

My grandmother was really smart and good at communicating with others so she was elected as head of women's committee in the village. She often went to the village committee for meetings. She took charge of the publicity, distributed the documents from superior department, and communicated with people from door to door. Afterwards the primary school in the village moved, and the store closed as well.

Now, my grandmother is nearly 70 years old, but she still keeps herself busy. She always goes to the fields to grow vegetables. At dusk, she will practice shadowboxing with other elderly people in the community. When she is in good mood, she will travel with her friends. As life is getting better and better, my grandma no longer works as hard as she did when she was young. Now the government is providing her with a pension and she finally lives a comfortable life.

When my father started working, he learned carpentry and worked for a master who taught him basic skills. At that time, an ordinary family didn't require much for the decoration. Therefore, the decoration style was simple and the requirements for each family's decoration was almost the same.

Later, a diamond manufactory was opened in the village. My dad changed his job to be a technician in the factory, because he heard that this job was well-paid. The technology used in the factory was advanced, so it was not easy to be mastered. My father went all the way to receive training in Yuhang on how to assemble and adjust the machine for one or two months. It didn't cost my father too much time to acquire the technique, because he had the experience in carpentry. Working in the factory was very stable and the income was relatively considerable. However, after working for a period of time, my father had conflicts with the leaders in the factory because he felt unfair about the salary. Some people didn't take their jobs seriously and were always slack in the job. However, they got the same salary as other diligent people did, including my father. The leaders turned a blind eye to that, so he quit his job indignantly.

After leaving the factory, he chose to go in for the job he had done before. In those days, there were many carpenters who were unable to find work, but my father was so skillful that everyone trusted him, so he was busy with lots of work that he could finish alone. Then it occurred to him that whenever he received a job, he would gather his friends to work with him, and he got more and more income.

In 1998, my parents got married, which was quite different from the marriage of my grandparents. Their love relationship was established at their own will. After two or three years of getting along with each other, they decided to marry so as to stay together forever. Two years later, I was born. By then, my father had some savings, and he decided to build a new house. Before long, a three-storey building rose from the ground, and the furniture in the house was all hand-made by my father. He devoted a lot of efforts to the design of the room. With the whole family living in a new building, the life quality has undoubtedly improved a lot.

After years of work, my father accumulated confidence in life, so he decided to start his own business. With the help of our relatives, he decided to set up a tea set packaging plant. The site that he chose was at Haiyan, a small county next to Haining. It took my father more than an hour to get to the factory every day, but he came and went rain or shine. Opening a factory undoubtedly required a large amount of capital. The cost of land, the purchase of machinery and the recruitment of workers all cost a lot, so my father took out his savings over the years. In order to run the factory, he racked his brain. Some of the production technique were not perfect, then he dug into it. But the business of the factory was sluggish. Some customers started to default lacking in money, so the factory was struggling to survive. The reality was not like a novel. Sometimes life was cruel, and success was not what persistence may led to; instead, the debt kept growing. After three or four years, my father's factory closed. There were many reasons, including the lack of advanced machines, the accidents occurred to workers, the soft market and so on. I remembered deeply that my father's hair went gray very fast in those years. Business failure made my father fall into the lows of life, but life had to go on.

Now, he is an ordinary employee who supports our family with a stable salary, and money can be saved at the end of every year.

Now we are living a comfortable life. Perhaps a simple life is what life should be. From the reform and opening-up to today, the changes in our home can be described as earth-shaking. Although there have been setbacks, but it tends to a good prospect overall. Whenever my grandparents recalled the past, they would say to me, "You belong to the happiest generation."

百姓家事亦国事

刘建民

“柴米油盐酱醋茶”，繁复、琐碎，甚至庸碌，早先看来，无非是引车卖浆者之流所劳心的日用家计问题，与国是无关。但是“民为邦本，本固邦宁”，关乎民生的温饱问题，若看得小了，还有什么可为国事所谋呢？《管子·牧民》里说，“政之所兴，在顺民心；政之所废，在逆民心。”民心所系，不就是各家小日子里的温饱冷暖、喜怒哀乐？一介百姓感受生活还是对居有所屋和柴米油盐来得更为切实上心。换句话说，民生之道也就在老百姓的住房、肚皮和腰包里。

平安工作、放心吃饭、安稳睡觉，这的确是一个普通百姓的最大幸福。故事的主人公作为一个石油勘探工人，常年在外工作，怎能不想要一个安稳的家？有一个地方住下来，有个自己的房子，怎能不是一个天大的梦想？这个石油工人之家从无房到单位分房，从祖宅拆迁到子女各自有房。如此琐屑，又好像一直跟这个时代关联着什么。房子就是这一家骨子里的获得感和幸福感之源。

我们应有的社会共识是有些个体问题不仅是个体行为的结果，更是由复杂的社会经济因素所决定的。从贫困走向富裕，个体、家庭和社会需要共同承担责任。“小康”这一表述中，民众家庭生活水准的概念，被延伸和扩大到整个社会，具体化为人民温饱与生活富裕的社会目标。民生民富之家事，从这个角度看就上升为国事。

一个行业工人，一个城市工人，家事如此琐屑，但求如此安稳。这个故事给我们的启示是：家事安则国亦泰。

（浙大宁波理工学院传媒与法学院，高级编辑）

故事

杭州

杨芝眉(新闻学专业192班)

一个石油工人家庭的家事

我的外公是东阳人,从小生长在东阳的卢宅里,外公家是书香门第,之前出了很多文人学子,外公的父亲也是当地小有名气的秀才,家境在当时是不错的,所以外公从小也受到了良好的教育。

我的外公是1962年毕业的。当时能读上大学是件很不容易的事,大家的受教育程度也很低,大多数人都是读到初中就回家种田了,好一点的才能读到高中。也正是因为从小受到了良好的教育,外公考上了当时的浙江省地质学校,学习的是石油相关专业。

很不幸,毕业的那年因为正好遇到了三年自然灾害,日子很苦,食物特别少,也几乎没有工作,外公告诉我:“那个时候农村里都没什么东西吃,只能吃吃野菜充饥。”所以外公就回家去做农民了。

外公很幸运,等到了1970年中国石油招工,这个工作和之前外公学习的专业知识相关,很适合外公,但是外公没有名额,只能靠走亲戚托关系才勉强获得了一个在中石油的工作,这一干就是30年。

石油勘探一般是100多人一个小支队,一个支队分为地震队和钻井队,小队里分工很明确,地震队是检查地层,看哪些地区可能有石油可以开采。外公是中石油钻井队的,主要做的是在汽车去不到的地方,把钻井机器扛过去,安装机器设备和钻井的工作。探测一个油田是否有开采价值,一般要钻井1000米,遇到地质条件好一点的地方,一般一天之内钻几米,碰上地质不好的地方,一天几厘米都有,所以是实行三班倒的机制,连续上8个小时班再休息24小时。外公说,人可以休息,但是机器不能停,要保证一直开采,所以一直都要有人看着机器。对于如何知道地层下有没有石油,那个时候主要采用的是柴油发电钻井,通过气体测量,把地层的气体抽上来,去测天然气的含量和油的含量多少,才能来判断这个地区有没有石油资源,适不适合建大型的油田。外公说不是有了油就可以开采的,要看这个地区的石油储量,达到一定量才有开采价值,比如长兴有煤矿,萧山也有油田,但是储量不大,开采价值也不大。所以真正找到一个值得开采的大油田，是很不容易的。

当一个勘探队勘探了一个油田，接下来就是开采队的事了，外公作为勘探队员又要奔赴下一个勘探地点。就这样枯燥、辛苦又一直奔波的工作，外公做了30年。由于要不停地找石油资源，所以外公带着家人一直都在外面漂，带着小孩去外面住，队伍驻扎在哪小孩就在哪上学。外公早年在长兴广德勘探，后来也去过浙江其他大大小小的地方，比如金华，衢州，宁波镇海和余姚等地。

外公说："有时候没有睡觉的床，就直接在露天打地铺休息；有些地方地势险峻，汽车无法到达，只能靠人力一点一点地把设备运进去。"

外公渐渐地年纪大了，身上也有许多大大小小的毛病。后来，钻井队的野外工作外公再也干不动了，就被调去当了队伍里的司务长，这是一个管伙食的职务，相对比较轻松。这一做大概就是10年，外公也上了年纪退了休。

1991年外公调到了大队部，有了固定的住房，外公一家在杭州安定了下来。虽然只有60平方米，但是外公其实是很开心的，常年在外奔波的人，也想要一个安稳的家。外公退休了就一直住在这个单位统一安排的小区里。但是，外公一直都是那种闲不住的人，在退休了之后还担任了小区的居委会主任，去管理小区里的生活琐事等等。

我们家的整体条件在外公做了石油勘探队的工人之后，可以说是不错的。外公的工资不低，第一个月工资就有38块。这个数字我没什么概念，所以我问了外公当时的物价，了解到当时的鸡蛋是3分1个，大米一毛三1斤，1个大饼是2毛。再加上野外津贴18块，这样的工资在那个时候已经算很多了，大概相当于一个县级干部的工资。按理来说应该可以过上好日子了，但是外公说其实不是的，因为他要养一家五口人。那个时候外公就觉得，家人才是最重要的，所以外公就下了决心把一家人带上，一起去四处勘察。所以妈妈小时候一直都是在和外公四处奔走，妈妈说，她没在一个地方连续读过两年书。

再后来，我们也没有家了。老人们常说，祖宅就是我们的根，外公家原来在东阳卢宅，因为当地政府需要征用卢宅，开发成一个旅游景点，作为东阳的一个象征。所以被征用后，外公一家虽然偶尔会被邀请回去看看，但是已经再也回不去东阳了，再后来，外公分配到了杭州的住房，所以外公一家就在杭州郊区定居了下来。而外公外婆受老一辈重男轻女的思想影响，让家中唯一的男孩舅舅得到了这份祖传的家产换来的赔偿金，舅舅和舅妈就在外面自己买了房子搬了出去。后来妈妈也搬了出去，和爸爸一起在杭州打拼，爸爸是在杭州市区工作的，所以我们家就在杭州市区安定了下来。我们一个大家庭就这样分成了几个小家，散落在杭州的各地。

妈妈学的是会计专业，毕业之后在临平找到了一份很好的工作，那个时候妈妈的工资比爸爸还要高，再后来有了我，妈妈觉得临平来回杭州路程上有点远，这样照顾我很不方便，所以就辞了原来的工作，一心一意地照顾我。我渐渐长大了，也开始上学校读书，不再需要妈妈一直照顾，妈妈就再去找了一份工作，这时候我们家的条件就慢慢开始好起来了。2008 年，等到我上了小学，我们家就从原来小小的房子里搬了出来，原来和爸爸妈妈睡一张大床的我，也终于有了属于自己的房间。

外公家和我们家都在杭州，但是一个是在郊区一个是在城里，还是有些距离的。小时候记得爸爸妈妈带我去看外公外婆的时候，总是要转两趟公交车，来去都不太方便，所以一般都是过年过节才会回去。等到后来，2010 年的时候，我们家买了第一辆车，有了自己的车子之后就可以经常回去看外公外婆了。现在的外公和小时候我记忆里的外公一样，还是闲不住，有空就在自己的小院子里种种菜，和朋友们打打牌，偶尔的，会出门远行一趟。我想着大概这是多年辗转勘探留下来的习惯吧，老人家总是想出去走走，在家就是呆不住。

现在我已经上了大学，不需要爸爸妈妈每时每刻的照顾了，我也要开始担起属于我的那份照顾外公外婆的责任。现在去看之前的日子，虽然辛苦，但是好像辛苦贫穷都是上个世纪的事，现在我们家已经过上好日子了。

Hangzhou
Yang Zhimei (Class 192, Majoring in Journalism)

The Family Affairs of an Oil Worker

My grandfather was from Dongyang. He grew up in Lu-family residence mansion in Dongyang. His grandfather's family was a scholarly family where many literati and scholars were produced. His father was also a well-known xiucai[①] in the local area. His family was wealthy at that time, so my grandpa had been well-educated since childhood.

My grandfather graduated in 1962. It was uneasy to be able to go to

① Xiucai was used to call someone who passed the imperial examination at the county level in the Ming and Qing dynasties.

university at that time. Everyone's education level was also very low. Most of them went home to do farm work after middle school. Only a few people whose family was rich could go to high school. It was because of the good education he received since childhood that my grandpa was admitted to Zhejiang Geology School as a major in petroleum at that time.

Unfortunately, there was a three-year natural disaster when he graduated. The days were extremely hard, and he had very little to eat, and almost had no work to do. My grandfather told me, "At that time, there was nothing to eat in the countryside, so wild vegetables were what people could find to satisfy their hunger." Therefore, my grandpa returned home to be a farmer.

My grandpa was very lucky, because China National Petroleum Corporation began to recruit workers in 1970. The job was related to the professional knowledge that my grandpa had learned before, which was very suitable for him. However, there was no quota for him, so he had to ask for help from his relatives. Finally he got a job in China National Petroleum Corporation which he did for the following 30 years.

The petroleum exploring team generally consisted of more than 100 people. A team was divided into a seismic team and a drilling team, both of which had very clearly—assigned duties. The seismic team was to detect the stratum to see which areas might have oil that was extractable. My grandpa belonged to the drilling team whose duty was carrying the drilling machine to the place where the car could not reach, and they should install the equipment and prepare for drilling. To detect whether an oil field was worth mining, they generally needed to drill 1, 000 meters. In places with good geological conditions, they could drill a few meters in a day. In places with poor geological conditions, they could just drill several centimeters a day, so they usually worked under the system of three shifts a day, which meant they worked eight hours consecutively and then rested for 24 hours. My grandpa said that people could rest, but the machines should not stop. It was necessary to keep mining, so someone must be there to look at the machine. Regarding how to know whether there was oil under the formation, diesel power drilling was mainly used at that time. Through gas measurement, the gas in the stratum was extracted so as to measure the level of natural gas and oil. Only in this way could they find out whether there were oil resources in this area and whether it was suitable for building large oil fields. My grandpa said that having oil didn't mean the area could be exploited. It depended on the oil reserves in this area. Only when the area had a certain amount of oil could this area be exploited. For example, there were coal mines in Changxing and oil fields in Xiaoshan, but the oil reserves in these two areas were not large and the exploitation value was not great. Therefore, it was uneasy to find a large oil field that could be exploited.

When an exploration team finished exploring an oil field, the extracting team would take over the following job. As a member of the exploration team, my grandpa had to go to the next exploration site. Such work was boring, exhausting and always kept people running around, but my grandfather stuck to this post for 30 years. Due to the constant search for oil resources, my grandfather, with his family, roved outside all the time. Their children, who lived outside with them, had schooling at the places where the team was stationed. In his early years, my grandfather explored oil in Guangde, Changxing, and later he went to other places in Zhejiang, such as Jinhua, Quzhou, Zhenhai of Nigbo City, Yuyao and so on.

My grandpa said, "Sometimes there was no bed for sleeping, so I just lay on the floor to rest in the open; in some places, the terrain was so steep that cars could not reach, so our team could only carry the equipment by our hands."

My grandfather gradually got older, and he suffered from illness, major or minor. Later, my grandfather was unable to do the drilling work anymore, so he was transferred to be the company quartermaster. This was a job in charge of food, which was relatively less demanding. He remained at this post for ten years. After that, he got older and retired.

In 1991, my grandpa was transferred to the brigade department. With a fixed house, my grandpa's family settled down in Hangzhou. Although it was only 60 square meters in area, my grandpa was really very happy. Those who had kept travelling outside all the year round also wanted a home to live comfortably. When my grandpa retired, he lived in a community as arranged for by this unit. However, my grandfather has always been the kind of person who won't stay idle. After he retired, he served as the director of the neighborhood committee of the community to handle trivial things in the community.

The living standard of our family could be said to be good after my grandpa worked as a worker in the oil exploration team. His salary as a prospector was not low, and the first month's salary was 38 yuan. I had no idea about its value, so I asked my grandfather about the price at the time. I learned that an egg sold for 3 cents. Half a kilogram of rice sold for 13 cents, and one flatbread sold for 20 cents. This salary, plus the 18-yuan allowance for working on the field, was actually a lot at that time, and it was roughly equivalent to the monthly salary of a county-level cadre. Generally speaking, he should have lived a good life, but my grandfather told me that it was not the case, because he had a family of five to raise. At that time, my grandpa thought that family should be put first, so my grandpa made up his mind to take the family to prospect with him. Therefore, when my mother was a child, she was always running around with my grandfather. My mom said that she never stayed in one school for more than two years in a row.

We didn't have a home afterwards. The elders often said that the ancestral house was our roots. The grandpa's house was originally in Lu-family residence in Dongyang, but the local government needed to expropriate Lu-family residence so as to develop it into a tourist attraction as a symbol of Dongyang. Thus, after the house was expropriated, although my grandpa's family were occasionally invited to go back to have a look, they could no longer go back to Dongyang. After that, my grandpa was assigned a house in Hangzhou, so the whole family settled down in the suburbs of Hangzhou. My grandparents were influenced by the feudal ideas of the old generation that favored boys over girls, so that my uncle, the only boy in the family, received compensation for this ancestral property. My uncle and my aunt-in-law bought their own house and moved out. Later, my mother also moved out and worked hard in Hangzhou with my father. My father worked in downtown Hangzhou, so our family settled down in downtown Hangzhou. Our large family was divided into several small families, living in different places all over Hangzhou.

My mother majored in accounting. After graduation, she found a good job in Linping. At that time, my mother's salary was higher than that of my father. After I was born, my mother thought that it was a long way back and forth from Linping to Hangzhou. It was inconvenient to take care of me, so she quit her job and took care of me wholeheartedly. I grew up gradually and started to go to school. My mother needn't take care of me all the time, so my mother went to find another job. At this time, the living standard of our family started to get better. In 2008, when I went to elementary school, our family moved out of the previous small house. I used to sleep with my parents on a big bed before, but now I finally got a room of my own.

The family of my grandpa and our family are both in Hangzhou, but one is in the suburbs and the other is in the city, so we have to travel a long way to visit each other. I remember that when my parents took me to visit my grandpa and my grandma when I was a child, we always needed to change bus twice. It was not very convenient for us to come and go, so we usually went to my grandpa's house on holidays and festivals. In 2010, our family bought the first car. After having our own car, we could often visit my grandpa and my grandma. My grandpa was the same person I remembered when I was a child. He didn't want to idle away, so he grew vegetables in her small yard, played cards with his friends, and went out for a long trip occasionally. I think this is probably a habit formed after years of exploration, so he always wants to go out, and is unwilling to stay at home.

Now that I have entered the university, I don't need the constant care of my parents. I also start taking care of my grandparents. When I looked back on the previous days, although those days were hard, it looks as if that arduousness and poverty in the past days had happened in the last century, and now our family are living a good life.

家庭变迁背后的时代发展

矫雁肇

家庭，是最具“中国特性”的本源型传统之一，它映衬着中国的过去与未来，更是当代中国社会变迁的历史起点和给定条件。《一路打拼到浙江》以“妈妈”为主线，展示了在强烈的时代历史进程中，中国个体与家庭如何在超越地域和社会限性的同时构建了新的家庭变迁特征，完成了传统与现代的历史转换。

作为个体与家庭的联结点，家庭往往透射着社会和时代的特征变化。在严文洁笔下，“妈妈”的奋斗史更像是一部浙江嘉兴历史进程的画面呈现。离开家乡四川初到浙江的憧憬；一个月不到300元工资的困窘，租住75元出租房的心酸；学习技艺改善生活的艰辛；为了生活只能春节还乡的无奈；安家浙江三次搬家建房的经历……日常生活方式和空间画面，一帧一帧地刻画了新时代变化背景下的“新浙江人”的历史侧面和发展变迁。那些细微而深刻的情感体验，生动地阐述了“励志奋进、奔竞不息”的浙江精神，构建了令人回味的家庭和历史记忆。

“家是国的基础，国是家的延伸。”在中国人的精神谱系里，国家与家庭、社会与个人，都是密不可分的整体。置身弘大历史空间的每一个家庭都是历史的载体，而以生命个体构建的历史记忆，便是中国历史的一隅。“敢想敢试、敢闯敢拼”的“妈妈”从外来妹成为浙江人；“不断尝试、勇于向前”的“我的家”走近理想生活，“海纳百川、兼容并蓄”的嘉兴从地方小县迈进经济重镇……个体的变迁与社会的发展就这样在不同的维度交叠重合，在细微的生活空间中传递着宏大的历史感，印证着新时代中国的繁荣发展，展示着浙江精神的丰富内涵，最终塑造出新型的富有时代精神和典型意义的时代。

（吉林省长春市媒体人）

故事
嘉兴
严文洁(网络与新媒体专业 191 班)

一路打拼到浙江

从四川大山里来到浙江,妈妈用她的勇敢勤劳为自己的事业创造出一片广阔的天地。在浙的 20 年打拼之路,不仅是妈妈个人的成长之路,也是独属于他们这个年代的记忆和时代缩影。

1973 年 7 月 9 日,妈妈出生在四川宜宾的一个小乡村里。因为家庭条件差,小学毕业后,妈妈就没有再继续读书了。这也成了妈妈最为遗憾的事情之一。

妈妈是在 1999 年来的浙江。妈妈不止一次地和我说过她刚来浙江的时候有多辛苦。她最初决定来到浙江务工是因为浙江的经济相比四川要好,工作机会也要更多。但是一切并不像妈妈想象的那么简单。初来乍到,首先就是语言不通的问题。这对妈妈融入浙江带来了一定的阻碍。但她没有放弃,硬是在短时间内将本地话学了个大概,到了和本地人交流没有障碍的地步。除了因为口音带来的种种麻烦,更令人沮丧的是,因为妈妈学历不高,又没有一技在身,所以她只能去做服务员。因为做不习惯刷碗的活,只做了 1 天服务员,她就辞职了。她又辗转去了袜厂。白班要做 12 个小时,晚班做 13 个小时,就这样白班夜班交替着干了 3 个月,妈妈拿到了她来到浙江的第一笔工资,3 个月 800 元。一个月不到 300 元,但是房租每个月就要付掉 75 元,还是住在一间破旧的小平房中。据妈妈说,上面盖的是瓦片,冬天的时候冷风从瓦片中直往房间里灌。床垫是最硬的棕木床,上面只有薄薄一床棉被,冬天睡到半夜会被冷醒。工资拿到手的第一时间,妈妈就去把拖欠房东的房租钱补上了。妈妈说,她永远忘不了她的第一任房东在她人生的窘境中展现的善意,直到今日她们仍然保持着联系。

这 3 个月在袜厂的工作经历,让妈妈认识到要学一门技艺在身。在袜厂从事的岗位,是最简单也最容易被取代的,所以她毅然决然再次辞掉了袜厂的工作,在熟人的介绍下,来到了一家灯泡厂工作。在灯泡厂里,她要学习如何烧制灯泡芯。自然,她需要常常与火打交道。一个不小心,就会把身上燎个泡。在刚接触这门技术时,妈妈身上总会出现涂着膏药的烫伤。即使是在干了十几年的现在，偶尔仍然会出现这种情况。冬天是很暖和，但同样夏天就会遭罪。我看着妈妈在工作时汗哒哒哒地流下来，脸上、身上都是汗水。我问妈妈，是什么让她坚持下来呢？她回答说，一方面因为这个工作坚持下来的人少，所以工资比较高，另一方面也是她性格比较倔和较真。

妈妈是通过相亲认识并嫁给了爸爸。在浙江安稳下来后，最难过的事情就是想家，妈妈说。虽然每时每刻都想回家，想念家乡的味道，独特的燃面、火锅、串串……妈妈每年最期待的事情就是回家——只有春节才有时间。回到家里呆短暂的一些日子，几乎是妈妈那时一年的回忆。

我们家的建房总共有三个阶段。第一个阶段是在 1999 年。那时就在农村挑了块地方，爸爸请了泥瓦匠、水电工就风风火火地开工了。在我出生前，房子就造好了。虽然只有两层，但是也耗尽了爸爸当时所有的积蓄，我家甚至还欠下贷款，直到我上幼儿园才逐渐还清。那座承载了我童年的欢乐和悲伤的小房子，我看着它从空空荡荡到渐渐添置起各种现代化的电器，冰箱、空调……不大，很自由，邻里之间的关系也很和睦，我小时候也经常去邻居家蹭饭，也曾有过在小伙伴家玩电脑到忘记回家吃饭，被爸妈揪回家的经历。

第二个阶段是在 2010 年左右。爸妈觉得家里太小了，没有地方放田里割下来的稻草，只能把稻草放在走廊上，下雨天草容易受潮，受潮后就不容易当柴火烧了，所以又建了个小房子。小房子总共有两间，一间用来放稻草和一些不常用的器具，一间用来给妈妈当作工作的地方。那时妈妈决定将工作地点从厂里搬到家里，上班时间可以更灵活，也更自由。我有时无聊，也回到小房子里去陪妈妈聊天。冬天很暖和，但是夏天特别热，简直就像是酷刑，不知道只有一架冷风扇的妈妈是怎样坚持下来的。那座小房子只存在了短短的两三年，我们家拆迁了。

第三个阶段是在 2013 年。我们家拆迁了。我离开了那个陪伴我 12 年的建筑，搬到了海宁我读初中附近的小区。因为新房子还没有造好，我们就暂时居住在了这里。为了让我上学方便，父母选择牺牲他们的上班时间来迁就我。妈妈因为之前就搬出了工厂，所以这次直接将工作用具搬去了姨妈家。但是姨妈家在乡下，离我们住的地方特别远。妈妈也只好像我一样一个礼拜回家一趟。也是在这一年，爸爸出了非常严重的车祸，非常幸运的没有留下什么后遗症。那一段时间，妈妈的压力非常大，她背负起了这个家。房租、治疗费、建造新房的费用，感觉随时都可以将她压垮。当时正值叛逆期的我，因为住校，和父母沟通甚少，爆发过许多十分尖锐的矛盾，妈妈自嘲，那段时间她都感觉自己到更年期了。所幸，我们一家人挺过来了。

我有时觉得，妈妈像是一棵小草，如此坚韧，什么都压不垮她；有时又觉得她像是一块石头，能承受千斤之重；有时又觉得她像是太阳，给予身边人温暖。在租的房子住了一年半后，我们成功地搬进了新家——凤翔小区。这座将会承载我们家往后喜怒哀乐的房子，装修方面也是妈妈一手操办的。大到家里的每一件家电，小到厨房的小物件，每一件、每一样都体现着妈妈对于生活的热爱、理解和用心。从选材、比价、搭配再到找装修工，她都是毫无经验，从头学起。如今，她可以滔滔不绝地讲一天关于装修的经验。

与搬到新家同时发生的好事情是我们家买车了！看着周围买车的人越来越多，妈妈从拿到了驾照的那一天起，就渴望拥有一辆自己的轿车，可以不受烈日暴雨里穿梭的辛苦。辛辛苦苦地工作了那么久，她终于拥有了一辆自己的车。

妈妈这漫漫20年在浙江生活的日子，不仅有我们这个小家变化的轨迹，更有嘉兴这个城市这20年的变迁之路。

Jiaxing
Yan Wenjie (Class 191, Majoring in Network and New Media)

Work Hard in Zhejiang

From the mountain village of Sichuan to the city of Zhejiang, my mother has created a broad world for her own cause with her courage and diligence. The 20 years of striving in Zhejiang is not only the personal growth of my mother, but also the memories of their era and the epitome of their times.

My mother was born in a small village in Yibin, Sichuan Province on July 9, 1973. Considering the poor family condition, my mother had to terminate her school life after graduating from primary school, which became one of her most regretful things.

In 1999, my mother came to Zhejiang. She told me more than once about how hard it was as a new comer here. The reason why my mother decided to head for Zhejiang to look for a job was that Zhejiang's economy was better than that in Sichuan. What's more, she was more likely to get a job in Zhejiang. However, it was not as simple as what my mother had thought. As a new comer, what my mother had to confront first was the language, which caused some obstacles to her integration into Zhejiang. Instead of giving up, my mother started to learn the dialect in a short time, and she was able to communicate with local people without any obstacles. In addition to the troubles caused by the accent, what depressed her was the only job that my mother could do was to be a waitress because she lacked education and skill. Finding herself unable to bear washing dishes, she quit this job after only one day, and left for a sock factory. The day shift was 12 hours long and the night shift was 13. After three-month changes between day shifts and night ones, my mother got her first salary since she came to Zhejiang, which was 800 yuan for three months. In other words, she earned less than 300 yuan a month, but she had to pay 75 yuan for the rent once a month. The place where she lived, according to my mother, was a shabby bungalow covered with tiles and the cold wind would blow into the room in winter. The bed was made of palm wood, which was the hardest and most uncomfortable kind to sleep on. With only a thin quilt, my mother was awakened by the cold at midnight. As soon as she got the salary, she paid off the rent which she had owed the landlord. My mother said that she could never forget her first landlord because of the kindness she had shown to her, which was the reason why they still kept in touch until now.

These three months of working in a sock factory let my mother realize that she needed to learn a skill. Working in a sock factory was the simplest job, which made it the easiest one to be replaced. Therefore, she determined to quit her job again. Introduced by her acquaintances, my mother came to work in a lamp factory. In this factory, she needed to learn how to fire a tungsten filament, which meant she was sure to deal with fire quite often. Once she was careless, her skin would blister. When my mother was a tyro to this technique, a scalded wound with plaster always appeared on her body. Even nowadays, after working on this job for more than a decade, such a case still happens occasionally. When she worked here, winter was warm and cozy but summer was insufferable. I once noticed my mother would break out in a sweat when she worked. I asked my mother about the reason that made her stick to it. She told me that one of the reasons was the salary was relatively high because few people could stay in this job, and the other reason was her stubbornness and seriousness.

My mother got acquainted with my father through blind date, and then they got married. My mother said that the saddest thing was homesick after they settled down in Zhejiang. My mother was dying to go back to her hometown all the time, missing the unique aroma of hometown, the local delicacies like Yibin Ran Noodles, hot pot, chuan chuan and so on. What my mother desired most to was to her return to her hometown, which she could do only in Spring Festival. Staying in her hometown for a few days made the memories that she had for the whole year.

There were three phases in the construction of our house. The first phase was in 1999. At that time, my father hired some masons, plumbers and electricians to start working immediately after picking a place in the countryside. The house was built before I was born. Although it only had two floors, it used up my father's savings, and my father even slipped into debt. The debt didn't pay off until I went to kindergarten. This small house witnessed the happiness and sadness of my childhood. I also witnessed its change from being empty to a house with modern electrical appliances, such as refrigerators, air conditioners and so forth. It was not big, but very comfortable. The relationship between the neighbors was quite harmonious. I usually scrounged free meals in my neighbor's house. I also had the experience of being so indulged myself in playing computer games in my friend's house that I totally forgot to go home to have a meal, and finally being dragged off to home by my parents.

The second phase happened around 2010. My parents thought that our house was too small to have a space to put the straw cut in the field, and then they had to place them on the porch. However, straw was easy to get damp on rainy days, which made it hard to serve as firewood. Therefore, they decided to build a smaller house. It was divided into two small rooms. One was for straw and some infrequently-used implements, and the other was for my mother's work. At that time, my mother decided to move her work place from the factory to home so that she could have more flexible working hours and freedom. Sometimes, I felt bored and I would go into the small room to chat with my mother. It was warm there in winter but hot in summer. The heat seemed to be cruel torture. I did not know how my mother could bear staying there only with a cooling fan. That smaller house was used only for two or three years, because our house had to be demolished.

The third phase was in 2013. As it was said before, our house was demolished. I left that house which had accompanied me for 12 years and moved to a neighborhood near my middle school in Haining. For the new house was not yet built, we stayed here as an alternative. In order to make it more convenient for me to go to school, my parents sacrificed their working time for my sake. My mother had moved out of the factory before, so this time she delivered the work equipment directly to my aunt's house. However, my aunt's house was in the village, far from where we lived. Therefore, my mother could only come back home once a week as I did. In the same year, my father had a serious car accident, yet fortunately it caused no sequelae. During that time, my mother was under a lot of pressure and she had to shoulder the burden of our family. The rent, the medical treatment fee and the cost of building a new house seemed to overwhelm her at that moment. Meanwhile, I was in the period of rebelling. Since I was living in school, there was little communication between my parents and me. Naturally, many sharp conflicts appeared. My mother once laughed at herself that she was going through menopause. Fortunately, we got through it.

Sometimes, I felt that my mother was like grass because she was so tough that nothing could overwhelm her. Sometimes, I felt that she was like a stone, because she was able to shoulder all kind of pressure. Sometimes, I felt that she was like the sun, because she brought warmth to those around her. After living in the rented house for one and a half years, we finally moved into the new one, in Fengxiang community. The house, which would carry the happiness and sadness of my family for the rest of our lives, was decorated by my mother. From big household appliances at home to small accessories in the kitchen, all this stuff reflected my mother's love, understanding and kindness to life. She was totally a green hand on decorating issues like selecting material, comparing prices, collocation, and seeking an interior decorator, so she had to learn from the beginning. Now, she can talk about her decoration experience for a whole day.

Along with the house-moving, we bought a car. Seeing more and more people around us buying cars, my mother was also eager to have a car of her own since the day she got the driving licence. Having a car would spare her from suffering the scorching sun and storm. She finally got one after working hard for such a long time.

The 20 years of living in Zhejiang shows not only the changes in my family, but also the changes in Jiaxing City.

笑迎梦想

刘连宇

读罢绍兴蒋依诺的文章《一山更比一山高》，我不禁露出了微笑。文中两个细节让我印象深刻，一个是：上海外滩，中年男子领着妻儿，指着上海国际会议中心满面自豪地夸耀，那建筑的恢弘中有我的辛劳。一个细节是：搬家的那天，爸爸把手放在背后，以视察的姿势在家踱来踱去，脸上是止不住的笑。——这两个细节画面感十足。本文看似立意很小，写一个家庭的几十年变迁，但这篇文章却展示了一个巨大的主题，那就是人该如何在梦想中起飞。

绍兴这个城市是个奇怪的城市，城市不大，但极具特点，这座城出了蔡元培、鲁迅这样的文化大师，他们代表着中华文化的精神和脊梁，这个城市有大禹陵，有兰亭、会稽山，文化积淀深厚。但绍兴吸引我的却是常人不关注的一面，这座城是一座充满矛盾的城市，绍兴是古越国故地，古越以尚武闻名于史，但尚武的绍兴却出了陆游、王羲之、徐渭这样的文人；绍兴是文人扎堆的城市，这里却保留了世界级的市井文化遗存仓桥直街。为什么绍兴会这样？去绍兴几次，我曾试图破解这个谜团。而这篇文章给了我一个解释，这个解释就是家国情怀，人要在梦想中起飞。

试想，越王勾践没有复国的梦想，怎能卧薪尝胆？没有北伐中原的梦想，陆游怎能留下万首诗歌？没有解放普天下女性的梦想，何来鉴湖女侠血洒轩亭口？没有救国救民需先救思想的梦想，何来鲁迅弃医从文？……

梦想能改变人的命运，能改变家庭的生活，也是国家富强的原动力。

谈了如此多和绍兴有关的梦想故事，再看蒋依诺的文章，小蒋所讲的故事是那么小，但没有小梦想怎么能有大梦想呢？记得我在绍兴鲁迅故居门前遇到这样一件事。那是3月时节，天气正爽，路边有茶摊，茶很香，摊主说：这茶是自家产的，过去都是自己喝，现在可以送进城，让茶卖到全国。摊主脸上带着笑，这是梦想实现的笑。

茶农把茶卖到全国，小蒋家从村里搬进了城，有了大房子，《浙里是我家》中所有同学生活的变迁，这都是小梦想得到了实现，一个又一个的小梦想汇聚起来，就是国家的腾飞。

一山更比一山高，这是一个非常好的标题。高山仰止，从足下起步，没有一步步攀爬，就没有会当凌绝顶、一览众山小的境界。想要实现梦想就得努力，如小蒋的父亲考取二级建造师证和高级施工员证，如小蒋的母亲在用破旧的缝纫机学缝纫技术。有梦想有努力，每一个梦想都像终将被我们征服的一座座高山，在高山之巅，幸福之光终将温暖每一个人。

（吉林省长春市前媒体人，现律师）

故事

绍兴

蒋依诺（网络与新媒体专业192班）

一山更比一山高

爸爸是这个时代发展的缩影，他出生于绍兴上虞金家岙村，成长于物质匮乏的年代，顺利升上高中，却没考上大学。海阔凭鱼跃，天高任鸟飞，爸爸说："如果用一个词来概括我的40年，那就是'选择'。"这样的一个新时代给爸爸带来了很多选择的机会，可以见识更广阔的天地，成就更丰富的人生，拥抱更美好的未来。

高中毕业后，爸爸兜里揣着80块钱，心里揣着梦想，启程去了上海。晚上23点，买不到坐票，他在车厢的过道上坐了9个小时。爸爸最初的职业是工业安装专业的管道工，具体是根据设计院的设计图进行施工安装，做化工厂的工业设备安装、气割和焊接的工作。初到上海，爸爸居无定所，通常是跟着项目走，就住在工地旁边的活动板房。"冬冷夏热，长年潮湿"是爸爸对板房最深刻的印象。"艰苦的条件倒是其次的，工作之外的无聊生活才是最难度过的。不像现在的活动板房，那个时候的板房里没有电视什么的，更别提空调了，有个好点的电风扇都是机遇。"

"我和寝室里的同学一起准备的，都想考个证，不做管道工了，整天跟着工地跑也不太稳定，多个证多条出路嘛。"在这样的信念之下，爸爸考出了二级建造师证和高级施工员证。

等我长大后，和家人一起逛外滩时，爸爸隔着黄浦江遥遥指着远处的圆球建筑，“上海国际会议中心的消防系统是我们承建的，看着十几年前做的工程屹立在陆家嘴嘴尖上，成就感满满啊”。爸爸的遥遥一指，是对他上海打拼生活的骄傲与满足。

1994年，也就是爸爸到上海两年之后，老家农村那矮矮的泥土瓦房翻新成了窗明几净的水泥房。那是爸爸的第一套房子，坐落于绍兴乡下老家，斜阳远近山，村外水如环，屋前有竹林，屋后有青山。爸爸对于他建的第一套房子感情很深，那好像不仅仅是一套房子，更是爸爸短期的成长史，是爸爸在上海拼搏那段岁月的见证者。

1999年，上海的发展越来越快，但是对于爸爸来说，在上海工作很难有更好的发展，“企业的技术人员大都是招聘来的，我也不想呆在上海这么长时间就只做一个小小的管道工，我就回了绍兴”。

妈妈也同样出生于绍兴上虞的凤鸣村，家庭也并不富裕。外公年轻的时候养了几头猪，妈妈除了上学之外最重要的工作就是照顾那几头猪。放学回家，她就去附近的山上砍草来喂猪。用妈妈的话来说她的童年就是“陪着猪长大的”。妈妈成绩不好，义务教育结束后也没有上高中的打算，就直接去了家附近的服装厂上班。

初到服装厂，年纪尚小的妈妈不会用缝纫机，只能做做包装产品之类简单的工作，工资低得可怜。“没有一门技术傍身是不行的”，妈妈暗下决心学踩缝纫机。包装间就有一辆快废弃的缝纫机，常年空着，给妈妈创造了学习踩缝纫机的机会。与破旧的缝纫机相映的是妈妈的技术，经过几个月的自学，妈妈也学有所成，踩缝纫机的速度已经和熟练工不相上下了。

有了一门技术傍身之后，妈妈便不再满足于包装工的待遇，跳槽去了另一家服装厂做缝纫工。在那里，加班是常态，但妈妈愿意加班，甚至主动加班。“我是住宿舍的，不加班也没地方可去，那时候附近可没有电影院这种娱乐场所，都是厂房连着厂房，加班又有加班费，何乐而不为呢?”妈妈的辛苦工作在一定程度上帮助了外婆家脱贫，短短几年后，外婆家过上了吃穿不愁的日子。

在家乡，爸爸认识了我妈妈，2000年两个人组建了幸福的家庭。2001年爸爸经朋友介绍到新昌制药厂工作，由管道工转变成了建筑施工员。工作性质的改变让爸爸有些不适应，但很快爸爸就调整好了他的状态。在新昌工作，他的收入更加可观，但依旧是居无定所。“板凳都没坐热呢，就要挪地儿了。”爸爸总是开玩笑地来说他在新昌工作的过往。这一年，妈妈也因为居住地的变更，辞去了原先在服装厂的工作，转而去了家附近的一家商场做营业员。在这一年我也出生了，那时候家里的经济条件依然不是很好，我的出生让爸爸萌生出再拼一拼的欲望。2003年，上虞杭州湾工业园区开始投入运营，爸爸便回到了上虞开始了他的再一次打拼。在这里，爸爸在上海学的知识和考的证终于有了用武之地，他在一家公司里做预算，免去了风吹日晒雨淋，不用随着工地转移居住地，生活慢慢步入了正轨。妈妈在商场做营业员也很顺利，一天只上半天班，工资也不低，工作的同时，还能照顾到家里。

2007年，家里也有了些小积蓄，在城市里买了一套小的商品房，付了首付，离开了居住多年的自建房，没有了鸡鸣犬吠，但也多了些车水马龙的声音；没有了农村夏日萤火虫的淡淡光点，却也多了些流光溢彩。从2003年到现在，爸爸一直在杭州湾工作，生活逐渐稳定，有着光明的未来。在2015年的时候，我逐渐长大，小小的商品房有些容不下了。家里的物品多到没地方放，房子又靠近环线，夜里嘈杂，影响睡眠。爸爸和妈妈又下定决心贷款买了一套更大的商品房。"房子带给我们归属感。"这是爸爸妈妈买房子的最大理由。"家庭"，虽短短两字，却是最温馨的词语了，它表达的是爱，是幸福开始的地方。第三套房子的楼层高，采光好，面积大。一切都在向更好的方向发展。搬家的那天，爸爸一直把手放在背后，以视察的姿势在家踱来踱去，脸上是止不住的笑，这是他们十几年来奋斗的结果，现在是领奖的时候，只属于他们的奖。他们用勤劳的双手、智慧的头脑、坚韧的付出，走出了原来的方寸之地，闯出了自己人生的新天地，把命运掌握在自己的手里。

"我们生在一个好时代！"爸爸总是感慨。我们的家只是这个大时代的缩影，我们家里有泪水，有汗水，有心酸，有快乐。我们都在用最大的努力，书写属于自己的故事，创造属于自己的时代。

Shaoxing
Jiang Yinuo (Class 192, Majoring in Network and New Media)

There will Always Be Higher Mountain

My father is a microcosm of the development of this era. He was born in Jinjia'ao Village, Shangyu, Shaoxing city. He grew up in an era of material scarcity. He successfully went to high school, but failed to enter university. As an old saying goes, "The sky is high and broad enough for birds to fly, the sea is wide and deep enough for fish to swim." My father said, "If I could sum up my 40 years in one word, it must be 'choice'". Such a new era had brought my father many choices, so he could see a wider world, made greater achievement and hoped for a better future.

After graduating from high school, my father went to Shanghai with 80 yuan in his pocket and a dream in his heart. It was 11 o'clock in the evening, so a seat ticket was not available. Therefore, he sat in the aisle of the train for nine hours. My father's first occupation was a plumber in the field of industrial installation; more specifically, he should install, gas cut and weld the industrial equipment of the chemical plant according to design drawings of the design institute. When he first arrived in Shanghai, he didn't have a fixed place to live. He often moved with the change of the project. He lived in a prefabricated house next to the construction site. "Cold in winter and hot in summer, wet all the year round" was his deepest impression of the prefabricated house. "As for the tough life he had experienced, the poor condition took second place, and the boring life after work was the hardest. Unlike today's prefabricated houses, the prefabricated houses at that time didn't have televisions or air conditioning. Even having a good electric fan would be a dream.

"I prepared for some certificate tests with my roommates in the dormitory. We all wanted to get a certificate instead of being a plumber anymore. It's not stable to work at the construction site all day long. More certificates meant more ways out." With this belief, my dad passed the Level Ⅱ Certificate for Associate Constructor and Senior Construction Worker Certificate.

When I grew up and went to the Bund with my family, my father pointed to the ball-shaped building in the distance across the Huangpu River, "We contracted to build the fire-control system of Shanghai International Conference Center. Seeing the project done over a decade ago standing on the tip of Lujiazui, I have a strong sense of achievement!". In fact, his pointing towards the building far away was his pride and satisfaction of his struggle in Shanghai.

Two years after my father's arrival in Shanghai, the low mud-tile-roofed house in the countryside of his hometown was renovated into a bright and clean cement house in 1994. It was my father's first house, which was located in the rural village of Shaoxing. The distant sunset looked quite near the mountain. Rivers flowed along the village. There were bamboo groves in front of the house and the green hills behind the house. My father was deeply attached to his first house. It was more than a house for him; rather, it was the brief history of his growth, and a witness to my father's struggle in Shanghai.

In 1999, Shanghai developed faster and faster. However, it was hard for my father to have a better development by working in Shanghai. "Most of the technical staff were recruited and I didn't want to just be a plumber after staying in Shanghai for such a long time, so I went back to Shaoxing."

My mother was also born in Fengming Village, Shangyu Town, Shaoxing City, and her family was not rich, too. When my grandfather was young, he raised several pigs. And my mother's most important job after school was to take care of them. When she came home from school, she went to the mountains nearby to cut grass for the pigs. In her mother's words, her childhood was "growing up with pigs". My mother was a poor performer at school, so she didn't want to continue her study at high school when finishing compulsory education. She went to work at a clothing factory near her home after graduation.

When she first arrived at the clothing factory, my mother was too young to use a sewing machine. She only could do some simple jobs like packing products, so her salary was very low. "It's bad for not having a skill!" Then my mother made up her mind to learn how to use the sewing machine. There was an abandoned sewing machine in the packing room, which was vacant all the year round. It gave my mother a good chance to learn how to use the sewing machine. After a few months of self-study, my mother had learned so well that she could finish the work as well as other skilled workers.

With this skill, my mother was no longer satisfied with the packer's treatment and wages, so she changed her job and worked as a sewing worker in another clothing factory where overtime working was common, but my mother was willing to work overtime; sometimes she would even ask for the chance to work overtime. "I lived in the dormitory and I had no places to go after work. At that time there was no place like a movie theater nearby to entertain. All we could see were just factory buildings. There was overtime pay for overtime work, so why not?" My mother's hard work helped my grandmother's family get rid of poverty to a certain extent. A few years later, there was no need to worry about food and clothing.

My father met my mother in their hometown. In 2000, they started a happy family. In 2001, my father was introduced by a friend to work in Xinchang Pharmaceutical Factory. He didn't get used to the change from being a plumber to being a construction worker, but he soon adjusted to it. Working in Xinchang, his income was considerable, but he still had no fixed residence. "The time that I stayed in a place was so short that I was unable to warm up the bench that I sat on, then I had to move again." My father always joked about his work in Xinchang pharmaceutical factory. My mother quit her previous job in the clothing factory because of the change of residence in the same year. She went to work as a saleswoman in a shopping mall near our house. I was born in this year and my family was poor at that time. It was my birth that gave my father a desire to fight again. In 2003, when the industrial park of Hangzhou Bay in Shangyu began to be put into operation, my father returned to Shangyu to start his hard work again. My father's knowledge and certificates obtained in Shanghai were useful here. He made a budget for the company, which kept him away from wind, sun and rain, and he no longer needed to change places to live because of the construction site any more. His life gradually got onto the right track. My mother did well with her work as a saleswoman in the shopping mall. She only worked half a day every day and the salary was not low. She could cope with her work while taking care of us.

In 2007, the family also had some savings, and my parents bought a small commercial house in the city. They paid the down payment and left the self-built house which they had lived in for many years. Though there were no sounds of chickens and dogs, there were the sounds of traffic. There were no flashes of light given off by fireflies in the summer days in rural areas, but there were glittering views in the city. From 2003 till now, my father has been working in Hangzhou Bay. We are living a stable life and having a bright future. In 2015, as I grew older, the small commercial house was not large enough to accommodate all of us, and household items were so many that there was not enough space to put them. Besides, the house was so close to the loop line that it was noisy at night which affected our sleep. Therefore, my parents made up their mind and bought a bigger commercial house with a bank loan.

"The house gave us a sense of belonging." That was the biggest reason why my parents bought the house. Although the word "family" is short, it was the warmest word in our heart. It expressed the love and was the beginning of happiness. Our third house was high-rise, well-lit and large. Everything was developing in a better direction. On the day when we moved house, my father kept his hands behind his back and walked around the house in a posture of inspection with a smile on his face. This was the reward they gained through decades of hard work. Now it was time to receive the prize which belonged to them only. With their diligence, intelligence and devotion, they had walked out of the small land and held their destiny in their own hands.

"We were born in good times!" My father always said that with emotion. Our family is just a microcosm of this great era. There are tears, sweat, sadness and happiness in our family. We are all trying our best to write our own stories and create our own times.

生也有涯情无限,男儿何必尽成功

刘炳辉

卫婷是一个温和的同学,文如其人。在卫婷的笔下,刻画的是爷爷奋斗的一生,操劳的一生,平凡的一生。脉脉的温情尽在岁月的长河中,这不就是我们绝大多数人的人生嘛。

世俗人眼中,看到的多半是功名利禄,看到的多半是人前显赫。有些人生动力也是需要的,但无论如何,世间的幸运儿总是少数。平凡人的平凡一生,该如何看待?心灵又该如何安顿呢?家庭和亲情无疑是最好的港湾,让每一个孤独的心灵都有长久的陪伴。

今天的时代是一个巨变的时代,是一个大争之世,家庭面临的风险、挑战和压力都不断上升,守护好自己的家庭,照顾好自己的家人,这本身就需要绝大多数普通人拼尽了全力才有可能做好。时代需要英雄,英雄的使命恰恰是照顾好绝大多数普通人。

让爱和温情在一代又一代人中慢慢传递,让家庭成为这个民族持久的基础单元,这个社会才会生生不息。我们永远怀念那些平凡的长辈,正是他们用自己操劳的一生,为子孙搭建了驶向星辰大海的码头。

(浙大宁波理工学院马克思主义学院副教授,博士)

故事

台州

徐卫婷(网络与新媒体专业 192 班)

一天一天好起来

一扇未上过漆的铁门,用红砖瓦堆砌的矮围墙,院里是一棵不太高的枣树,房屋是用深灰色水泥砌成的,高高的楼层,狭窄的阁楼,即使是夏天,屋子里也凉风阵阵。家门口是一方圆形的池塘,衢州航埠镇后坞村以此为中心分布。池水常年绿色,从小到大,我从未见过它清澈的样子,只记得小时候每逢过年,就会和弟弟们拿着用几个硬币换来的“水雷”往水里扔,看着它在水里发出滋滋的声响……然而这样的生活,突兀地断在爷爷因病去世的那一刻。之后,奶奶跟着爸爸去了外地,过年也没再回去过那个房子。

在这样一个老家,爷爷借着一辆独轮车,在生活拮据的情况下,撑起了小小的 5 口之家。

记忆中的爷爷奶奶家,墙角总是堆着一筐又一筐的橘子,它们来自离家不远的小小又紧密分布的橘田。橘子是那边的特产,家家户户以种植和贩卖橘子为生。橘田倚着只有两个篮筐的篮球场延伸开来,以前没有水泥路,只用泥泞的土路连接着。树上的橘子生得又大又圆,表皮凹凸不平、坑坑洼洼,却格外甜。我还在上小学的时候,跟着大人去橘林剪过一次橘子,刀刃短手柄长的枝剪在枝上留下平整的横截面,还会冒出一点点的汁液,也是那一次,我的食指不幸地被剪出了血液,坐着电动三轮去乡下的小诊所打了破伤风针。记忆中大约从这时起,我再也没去过橘林。渐渐地,各地更多更好的品种被生产出来,爷爷家的橘子不再有人收购,树上的橘子没有人摘,烂了一地也没有人管。爷爷那辆小推车不那么顺利地退休了。

爷爷年轻的时候很帅。虽然年轻的爷爷我也只在照片上见过——在海边,满地的石头堆,爷爷推着穿着幼稚亮片裙的我,头发浓密又乌黑,眉毛英气,鼻梁高挺。只可惜几乎没有眉毛和矮鼻梁的我没有遗传到后两样。爸爸说,爷爷的一生非常辛苦,好像在爸爸 40 岁不到的时候才算好些,不用卖橘了,也有孩子提供些生活费。以前的日子十分拮据,三个孩子的家庭只能提供两个孩子的生活费,为了节省费用,姑姑很早就辍学了。

爷爷发脾气的样子，我还真是没见过，印象里的爷爷始终都是和蔼的爷爷，说话慢慢的，过年会给我们钱去买饮料和零食的爷爷。第一次见到爷爷虚弱的样子，是在他生大病的时候。爷爷本来就瘦，我在医院见到他的那一刻，也被眼前的样子惊到了——枯黄的皮肤和凹陷的两颊，只能吃奶奶从外面买回来的馄饨，再后来，只能靠输营养液维持生命。那段时间，我感受到了爷爷对生命的渴望，以至于在医院下达病危通知书的时候，爸爸伪造了一份病历给爷爷一个人看。

小学六年级的某一天深夜，爸爸突然接我回爷爷家，我甚至不知道他白天从台州赶回了家，路上空无一人，偶尔有几辆车，夜晚的空气冷冷的，我似乎已经猜出了什么。到了目的地，门口就已经奏起了丧乐，我走进去，作为后辈上了香，一行人以家乡的习俗告别了故人。

很久之后，我才真正理解了爷爷辛劳一生的面貌。

外公外婆家的条件比爷爷奶奶家好一些，衢江区沈家村家里的院子也是两倍那么大，还有后院的田地，房子内部也要大一些。外公年轻时是村里的生产队队长，在我听起来还有些威风。外婆和外公经媒人介绍而结婚，生活条件还算好，近些年开始农活逐渐减少，老房子的拆迁也让家里不再养猪。

因为在上小学之前都和爸爸妈妈在台州生活，一年里回外婆家的次数并不多。外婆身体很好，现在依旧是一头乌黑的长发，编成麻花辫。

在一年级到三年级的时段，我一直跟着外婆生活，爸爸妈妈则留在台州工作。那时候小学里到了中午吃饭的时间，就会有同学去食堂搬运菜桶和饭桶，我和其他几个同学排着队回家吃饭，老师任命我为小队长，我就举着班牌领着大家出校门。碰上油菜花结籽榨油的季节，回家的整条路上都能闻到菜籽油的香味。

年龄再增长一点，妈妈就从台州回到了衢州，在外婆家继续住了一段时间之后，我们搬去了距离很近的舅舅家的房子。到了 2019 年，外婆家的地块被征用了，那一片的老房子全部拆迁，猪、鸭、鸡等等也在那之前全部卖完了。外公外婆也搬了过来和我们一起住。

小学之前我们一家一直生活在台州，爸爸工作的公司有员工厂房分配，我们住在顶楼的最左边一间。在此之前辗转过许多地方，我的幼儿园也从市中心转移到了其他地方。因为爸爸妈妈都要上班，所以家里留我一个人的情况比较多。我两套睡衣轮着换，头发也乱糟糟的。一到中午，爸爸会在楼底下喊我的名字，我们一起到一楼的员工食堂吃饭。

在更早的一段时间，我们家的条件非常不好，吃饭的矮桌旁边只有一张塑料板凳，让给当时还是孩子的我坐。那时候的物价也远没有现在这样高，幼儿园时期我每天有一块零花钱，似乎可以买超市里的很多东西。上了小学之后，零花钱升为两块钱，若是用这两块钱去校门口买上一份炒粉干，对于我来说也算是一种奢侈。除此之外，偶尔和外婆出门逛街，她每次都会给我买里脊肉串，在那时也算是一件人生乐事。

为了提高生活水平以及完成自己的心愿，爸爸前几年在台州成立了自己的电永磁吸盘公司，他提及政策在工业方面的扶持让他有所受惠。我们也早就摆脱连凳子都缺少的日子，生活比较安心了。

Taizhou
Xu Weiting (Class 192, Majoring in Network and New Media)

Better Day by Day

Surrounded by a low redbrick walls, the house, with an unpainted iron gate and a short jujube tree in the courtyard, was made of dark grey cement. Due to its multi-story design and narrow attic, the house was always pleasantly cool even in summer. Right in front of the gate was a round pond, the center of the village, in which the water was always green and never clear. I remembered in the Spring Festival, how I and my brothers would spend a couple of coins to buy a sort of firecrackers called "Mine" and cast them into the water to watch them fizzling for fun. However, life like this was changed abruptly when my grandfather died. I never came back to the house ever since, even in the Spring Festival, because my grandmother followed my father to relocate in another town.

Right in this hometown, my grandfather managed to feed a family of five members with a wheelbarrow.

In my memory, the corners of my grandparents' house were always piled with baskets of oranges harvested from the nearby small orchards extending along the basketball court with only two rims and connected with unpaved dirt roads. Oranges were specialties there. Growing and selling these big round oranges—rough in surface and sweet in juice—was the only living means for locals. When I was in elementary school, I tried to pick them once with adults. Unfortunately, the pruning scissors, short in edge, long in handle, was used to cut juicy branches neatly but cut my index finger instead. I was taken to a small countryside clinic by an electro-tricycle and given a tetanus shot. Since then, I did not visit orange orchards again. Local oranges, gradually replaced by other better varieties, were left unwanted and rotten all over the trees and ground. My grandpa's wheelbarrow was thus forced to retire prematurely.

My grandfather was very handsome when he was young, though I only saw his young face from pictures. Along the seaside which was covered by pebbles, my grandfather with thick black hair, handsome eyebrows and a prominent nose, carried me, a little girl in a childish sequined dress with a baby carriage. Unfortunately, I did not inherit his pretty eyebrows and nose. My father said that my grandfather's life was bitter. With three kids to feed, he could only afford to pay for the education for two of them. In order to save money, my aunt had to drop out early. Life did not turn better until my father reached his late thirties, when my grandfather no longer needed to sell oranges thanks to the financial support from his children.

I have never seen my grandfather lose his temper. It seems to me that he is always a kind old man talking slowly and offering us pocket money for soda and snacks. The first time for me to witness his weakness was when he fell sick. Even though I already knew he was slim, I was still shock by the way he looked—what a pale complexion and hollow cheeks! He was too weak to eat anything except for the wonton bought by my grandma. Later, he became so sick that he had to live on life-support nutrient solution. At that time, I knew how much he wanted to live and my father even fabricated a less harsh medical chart only for my grandpa to read when the hospital issued the notice of critical illness.

One night when I was in the sixth grade, my father took me to my grandfather's home. Until then I did not even know he came all the way from Taizhou during the day back home. In that late night marked by cold air and empty streets with few cars, I was struck by a sense of foreboding. Sure enough, we were greeted by the funeral music at the doorway. I offered incense to my grandfather and said goodbye to my grandfather in a customary way with my relatives.

It took me a long time to fully understand my grandpa's life of hardship.

My maternal grandparents were better-off than their counterparts. The house they lived in is with a courtyard twice the size, backyard fields and bigger rooms. My maternal grandfather, who was the leader of the production team when he was young (a quite decent title to me) married my grandmother after being brought together by a matchmaker. Thanks to the relocation of the old house, recently they could be saved from the toil of farm labor and pig breeding.

Seldom did I visit my maternal grandparents before I entered my elementary school since I lived away from them with my parents in Taizhou. Until now, my maternal grandmother, with long black braided hair, is still in good health.

I was living with my maternal grandmother for the first three years of my elementary school, while my parents were working in Taizhou. When it was time for lunch, some of my classmates would carry barrels of food from the canteen to the classroom while I, as the team leader holding up the sign indicating our class number, would lead other classmates back home for lunch. I would never forget the fragrance of rape seeds on the way home in the season for rape flowers to seed.

When I was a little bit older, my mom came back from Taizhou and moved into my grandma's place. Living there for some time, we moved to my uncle's house which was in the vicinity. In 2019, my grandparents' properties, along with the nearby land, were expropriated, and they sold all the pigs, ducks and chickens and came to live with us again.

Before the elementary school, we moved frequently and ended up living in the left-most room on the top floor of a staff dormitory provided by my father's company in Taizhou. I had to transfer from a downtown kindergarten to another one. Since both of my parents had to work, I was often left home alone, unkempt and alternating between two sets of pajamas which were all that I had. At noon, my father would call me by my name downstairs, taking me to the staff canteen on the first floor for lunch.

When I was even younger, my family was poor. The only plastic stool in my house, placed right beside our dining table, was the privilege for me to sit on as a little kid. In my kindergarten days, everything seemed so affordable that I could buy so many items from supermarkets with my daily pocket money of 1 yuan, which doubled when I entered the elementary school. Thanks to this "upgrade", I could enjoy the treat of a portion of fried rice noodles cooked by the vendors at the school gate. Besides, I also enjoyed the grilled pork my grandmother bought me during our occasional shopping.

To seek for a better life and realize his personal ambitions, my father incorporated his own company dedicated to electro permanent magnet chucks several years ago under the favorable government policies. We have long since got rid of a life even in want of stools and led a better-off one.

路很长，唯梦想不能停歇

陈雪军

无论在哪个时代，知识都是改变命运的力量。郑玺同学的爷爷扮演着大家眼中伟大的人民教师、亲戚眼中的家族领袖和“我”眼中普普通通的和蔼老人，一生中经历过诸多坎坷，有幸读书的童年、遭遇饥荒的少年、经历文革的青年和教书育人、乘上改革开放东风的后半生。不断变化的是年龄和复杂的外部环境，但一直不变的是爷爷对知识的渴求和心中一直念念不忘的“大学梦”。

近年来我们一直提倡的是不忘初心，牢记使命，不断强调初心二字。那么，到底怎样才算是不忘初心呢？我认为不忘初心的背后是不计代价，不问收获，默默耕耘，不求回报。正如郑玺同学的爷爷那样，对心中的大学梦念念不忘，郑玺爷爷用自己的一生去践行了“路很长，但梦不能停”的信仰，为青年一代树立了不懈奋斗的榜样。

郑玺爷爷的求学之路上遭遇了很多意外，有过吃不上饭饿着肚子但仍然坚持坐在教室的经历，也有中途被迫停止学业的遭遇，但尊重知识、培养人才的信念和心中燃起的大学梦成为经久不熄的灯塔，指引着郑玺爷爷不断向前。倘若心中对知识的梦想早早停歇，或许郑玺爷爷就无法变成如今受人景仰的老教师，或许郑玺同学就不再会有“疫情过去之后，陪爷爷逛大学校园”的机会，或许这个家庭的生活，会是另一番模样。

如今我们的社会已经发生了天翻地覆的变化，但不变的是知识的力量，不变的是我们对知识的尊重和敬仰，不变的是我们学习科学知识的时代任务。这让我们明白：即使路再长，心中的梦都不可辜负。

（浙大宁波理工学院传媒与法学院，教授）

追寻着更高的人生价值

刘　玲

著名教育家鲁洁先生曾说:远离了意义的教育,也就从根本上远离了生活。一方面,教育中迷人的意义世界来源于生活世界。人的生活是需要有意义的。在生活论的视域上,生活的意义来自生活本身,存在于生活之中。陶行知先生说"生活即教育"。"爷爷"以其一生的奋斗,在时代的沉浮变迁中,找到了真实生活的事实与意义的联结,创造了有意义的生活,从而领略了迷人的意义世界。意义世界不断生成的过程,是由一连串的生活事件、生活联系、生活故事组合而成的过程。"爷爷"丰富的阅历成为他理解、体验、创造生活意义不可或缺、最直接、最切近、最真实的基础。另一方面,"爷爷"是一位懂得教育真谛的好教师。他善于讲好时代故事,引导"学生"感受祖国的尊荣、时代的成就,在他们的心灵中逐步构筑起热爱生活的基本态度,打好健全人格、德性发展的根本基础,让"学生"在生活中认识到"我对于生活是有意义和价值的"。在追求生活意义中,"爷爷"自身期盼圆梦大学,追寻着更高的人生价值。如今,国家有了社招生的政策,"爷爷"如仍有志向、有决心、有毅力、有精力,可以通过考试入校,圆自己一个大学梦,欢迎求知若渴的"爷爷"来到大学,从想逛校园的客人成为真正的校园主人。

(宁波城市职业技术学院思政部/基础部主任,副教授)

故事

温州

郑玺(网络与新媒体专业 191 班)

一位老教师的大学梦

自我有记忆以来,爷爷便一直陪伴着我长大。在年幼的我眼中,我的爷爷只是一位和蔼的普通老人,当然,这仅仅只是对于我来说而已;在别人的眼中,爷爷是一位值得尊敬的人民教师;在亲戚的眼中,爷爷更是家族中最有影响力和号召力的长辈族领。出生于 20 世纪 50 年代的他如今依旧身体健康,而我也通过眼前这位和蔼的老人,了解了那一个个尘封的故事,那一段段存在于他们脑海中的回忆,以及我现在生活的这个家的故事。

1951 年,我的爷爷出生在温州苍南县的一个农家。爷爷说,他自己也没有想到,将来会选择成为一名教师,并且一干就是几十年。

曾祖父虽说没有受过多少教育,但他还是将我的爷爷送入了学校。那时候,农村住户的家庭经济条件都十分的不好,让孩子去上学是一件奢侈的事情。年龄虽小,6 岁的爷爷却也或多或少懂得这些道理,在对待读书这件事上,爷爷是付出了十分的精力去对待的。在班上,爷爷的成绩一直名列前茅,这也让曾祖父与曾祖母十分高兴,认为这笔钱花对地方了。后来,遇上了三年大饥荒,我的老家,爷爷那时的家,一片萧条的景象,没有一户人家是吃得饱的,即使是平时最为勤快的几户人家,也经常会碰上吃不饱的情况。

“何止是吃不饱啊,有时候一天只吃一餐呢。”爷爷在听了我的话后,如此对我说,“还好我们村比较能干活,农民们也都身强体壮,不然早就饿死一大片了!”因为大饥荒,学校里也是一片惨淡的景象,很多家庭都让孩子呆在家中,在校学生人数变少,但爷爷即使空着肚子依旧坚持去学校。在大饥荒逐渐结束后,爷爷的学业又再一次回归了正轨,顺利地上了一所好初中。

爷爷说:“原本我的计划是要一路读到大学的,但后来发生了文化大革命,我的学习生涯就在初中毕业后停止了。”

十年文革过后,全国终于迎来了光明。理性又一次洒在了中国的大地上。这消息,对于爷爷他们来说,无异于最大的喜讯。在文革期间,我的爷爷结识了我的奶奶,二人得以结为夫妻,并生出了我的姑姑以及我的父亲,这样的一个小家庭，逐渐变得热闹了起来。家庭的人数变多了，家庭经济的负担也就变多了，需要有人为这个家庭站出来去支撑。

那时候，村里的学校正处在百废待兴的时期，一些师资力量重新回到了学校中，但仍有诸多的空位需要被填补，因此学校便开始招聘师资。当爷爷得知了这个消息后，便立刻行动了起来，先通过了教师考试，后来顺利地成为村中学校的一位老师。

在说到教师考试时，我爷爷还微笑着和我述说了一个故事以教育我们这一辈人，他说："在那场考试前的10分钟休息时间，我看了一道题目的解析，结果考试时就考到了，这就说明了考前临时抱佛脚的重要性，所以在考试前做的一切努力都是有用的。"

在顺利通过教师考试并成为一名人民教师后，我们一家的收入来源总算是有了稳定的保障。爷爷将教师认作自己这一辈子要一直奋斗的职业，将学校认作这辈子要一直奋斗的岗位，他认为教书育人，传授知识给这些生在农村的儿童，让他们得以上大学，得以改变命运，是顺应了国家改革开放的潮流，同时也算圆了自己曾经的大学梦吧。

而奶奶，在外曾祖父的资助下，拥有了那时候的老三件之一——缝纫机，并在家做起了缝纫的生意。听说那个时候村里少有缝纫机，因此许多人都来找奶奶做手工活，家庭的经济在二人的日积月累下，逐渐从重创中恢复了过来。

"后来，随着改革开放慢慢地兴起，我们村的经济也逐渐复苏了，许多家庭都不再是以前那样连温饱都无法解决。"爷爷如此说，"我们家的钱也越来越多，这是一个由少到多的过程，是没有那么快的，没记错的话，应该是过了三四年，我们的家庭条件算是达到了一个过得去的水准"。

慢慢地，随着家庭条件的转好，爷爷建了一个属于自己的家，并在家中添置了电视、电冰箱、收音机等贵重物品；同样地，他也为曾祖父与曾祖母买了这些物品。

爷爷止不住地赞叹："改革开放好啊，邓小平说过'不改革开放，只有死路一条'，看看现在，改革开放给我们带来了多大的福祉。以前我父母把我养大，不知道多辛苦咧，而我把你父亲与姑姑养大时，却完全不会有经济问题来困扰我们。"

2011年，爷爷光荣地从岗位上退休，离开了工作几十年的学校。直到现在，爷爷偶尔还会回到学校，与曾经的同事聚一聚，唠唠嗑。那学校啊，可是爷爷曾经奋斗过的地方啊，不管是读书时，还是工作时。

作为族中最有威望的人，爷爷仍经常回到老家，去帮人处理各式各样的事情，真的是就算是退休了也依旧在奋斗呢。说到老家啊，老家也不再是从前那番模样，早已拉上电线，开了道路，通了网。田地里，年轻的农夫卖力地耕地、播种；

树荫下，老人躺在椅子上，手执大蒲扇，惬意地乘凉，好一派平静的农村生活。

2020 年，暑假回到家。饭桌上，爷爷问："下一次，让我送你去学校，顺便看看你的校园怎么样，你说行不？"我知道，爷爷心中的那个大学梦还在。不管到什么时候，爷爷总是怀揣这个梦，我能十分确定，在这一点上，我觉得称爷爷为老顽童也不为过了。

"啊，可以啊。"我说，"等疫情彻彻底底地过去，我就陪您去逛一逛大学！"

Wenzhou
Zheng Xi (Class 191, Majoring in Network and New Media)

The University Dream of an Old Teacher

For as long as I could remeber, my grandpa has been accompanying me as I grew up. When I was a child, he was just a kind and ordinary old man in my eyes. Of course, this was only for me. In the eyes of others, my grandfather was a respectable teacher. In the eyes of our relatives, he was the most influential and appealing leader in the family. Born in the 1950s, he is still in good condition. Through this kind old man in front of me, I learned all those past stories, the memories in their minds, and the story of the home I live in now.

In 1951, my grandfather was born into a peasant family in Cangnan County, Wenzhou. My grandpa said that he did not expect that he would have a career as a teacher for decades.

My great-grandfather, who himself did not receive much education though, sent my grandfather to school. At that time, the financial status of rural households were dreadful, and it was a luxury for children to go to school. Despite the young age, my 6-year-old grandfather understood the situation more or less, so he put 100 percent energy into studying. My grandfather always ranked top of the class, which also made my great-grandparents pleased, believing that the money was worth it. Later, there was China' s Great Famine from 1959 to 1961. My hometown where my grandfather's home was located was a desolate scene. No one could be replete with food. Even the most diligent ones often couldn't have enough food to eat.

"It was not just about being underfed. Worse still was that we could only have one meal a day sometimes." My grandfather said to me after hearing what I said, "Fortunately, our villagers were better at farm work, and the farmers were also strong. Otherwise many people would have starved to death!" The school was a bleak scene owing to the Great Famine. With children of many families staying at home, the number of students at school decreased. But my grandfather still insisted on going to school even with an empty stomach. After the Great Famine ended, my grandfather's schoolwork was back on track again and he was successfully admitted to a good middle school.

My grandpa said, "I had planned to go to university, but then the Cultural Revolution happened, so my education ended after graduating from middle school."

After ten years of Cultural Revolution, the whole country finally ushered in a bright future. The reason was once again all over the land of China. This was definitely the most rejoicing news for my grandpa and all the others. During the Cultural Revolution, my grandfather met my grandmother. They finally got married and gave birth to my aunt and my father a year later. Such a small family gradually became lively. However, more family members also meant more financial burden. Someone needed to step up to support the family.

At that time, everything in the village school was waiting to be rebuilt. Some teachers returned to schools, but there were still more vacancies to be filled, so schools began to recruit teachers. When my grandpa learned the news, he immediately took action. He passed the teacher qualification examinations first, and then became a teacher in a village school.

When talking about the exams, my grandfather smiled and told me a story to educate people of our generation. He said, "During the 10-minute break before the exam, I read the analysis of and answer to a question which was tested later in the exam. That truly shows the importance of last-minute effort, so all the efforts you make before the exam are useful."

After successfully passing the teacher certification exam and becoming a teacher, our family income was finally secured. My grandpa regarded teaching as a career and school as a position that he would struggle for all his life. He believed that educating people and imparting knowledge to rural children to help them go to university and change their destiny can be regarded as a response to the trend of the nation's reform and opening-up and a fulfillment of his own university dream.

With the funding of her father, my grandmother owned a sewing machine, one of three new prerequisites for marriage. Thus she started a sewing business at home. It was said that there were few sewing machines in the village at that time, so lots of villagers came to grandma to do needlework. The family's financial situation gradually got better from the severe damage. Due to the accumulation of the couple's income.

"Later, with the gradual rise of reform and opening-up, the economy of our village recovered little by little. Many families no longer lacked food and clothing as they used to." My grandfather said, "Our family had more and more money. But this process of accumulation took time, as far as I can recollect, it should be three or four years. Our family conditions were considered to be at a decent level."

With the improvement of family conditions, my grandfather built his own home equipped with valuables such as TV, refrigerator, and radio. He also bought these items for his parents.

"Reform and opening-up was great. Deng Xiaoping once said that if there was no reform and opening-up, we had no way to go but only a dead end. Look at us now, how much blessing has been brought to us by reform and opening-up! You had no idea how hard it was for my parents to bring me up, and when I raised your father and aunt, there were no financial problems to bother us at all." My grandpa couldn't help saying with admiration.

In 2011, my grandpa retired from his post honorably and left the school where he had worked for decades. Until now, my grandpa would occasionally go back to that school, gathering with former colleagues to have a chat. That school was a place where my grandpa used to struggle for study and work.

As the most prestigious person in the clan, my grandpa still returns to his hometown frequently to help people deal with all kinds of things. Even if he has retired, he is still working. Speaking of my hometown, it is no longer what it used to be. Wires have pulled up; roads have been paved, and the

Internet has been connected. In the fields, young farmers work hard to plow and sow; under the shade of the trees, the old man is lying on a chair with a fan in hand, enjoying the cool comfortably. What a peaceful rural life!

In 2020, I returned home during summer vacation. During the dinner, my grandfather asked: "Let me take you to school next time and see how your campus is, yeah?" I know that his university dream is still there underneath. It has always been there. I can be quite sure that it's definitely not too much to call my grandfather a kidult at this point.

"Ah, yes," I said, "When COVID-19 epidemic is completely over, I will accompany you to visit my university!"

小家庭，大社会

曾晓燕

家是最小国，国是千万家。家作为最小的社会组织，是社会的基石，也是宏观社会的缩影。中国社会学和人类学奠基人费孝通先生在《江村经济》(*Peasant Life in China*)中通过深入细致观察，刻画了中国东部一个村庄整体生活的方方面面，开创了以小型社区窥视中国社会的实验性范例。尽管存在争议，微观观察仍然在社会学研究方法中具有无可取代的地位。

《在溪口打拼》这个一家三代人奋斗史的平实描述，看似琐碎平凡，却也在不经意间印刻出时代的剪影。“耕地”“粮站”“办厂”，这些字眼恰好映射出中国从上世纪 50 年代至今经历的计划经济、以家庭为单位的联产承包责任制和市场经济的巨大变迁。故事中的人与家庭，走出村庄，走向城市，也是轰轰烈烈城镇化进程中的沧海一粟。

时代塑造人，社会变迁、社会转型必然导致人行为方式、价值观念等各个方面的变化。农耕、分配工作、小作坊、经商，过去的每一天，樊佳瑜一家跟随时代的脉搏努力奋斗。从一家三代人身上，我们不难看到自己同时代的祖辈父辈、亲朋好友相同或相似的人生选择。人创造时代，成功的变迁与成功的转型必然是人与社会的充分协调。每一个小家的努力，都在 960 多万平方公里中国土地上积累，在近 14 亿中国人民手中凝聚，千千万万吃苦耐劳的中国百姓家，是创造今日“中国奇迹”的主体。

通过了解一个小家的生活，“我们犹如在显微镜下看到了整个中国的缩影”，这便是微观观察超越个体的价值所在。

（浙大宁波理工学院党委宣传部）

故事

宁波

樊佳瑜(新闻学专业192班)

在溪口打拼

在上世纪50年代末,我的爷爷去参军了,当炮兵。当了兵,入了党,在军队服役7年后爷爷回到了村子里,经由父母的牵线搭桥和奶奶结了婚,那一年,爷爷27岁。

父亲是家中的第三个儿子,出生的时候爷爷因为曾经是军人就已经有了在粮站的稳定的工作,但是家里的条件还是不好。随着时间的推移,大伯二伯逐渐到了成家的年纪,爷爷就把家里的房子和田都分给了他们。父亲那个时候只有20岁,不想在大伯二伯的田里当农民,就去入伍,成了我们家里的第二个军人,去广东当了一名侦察兵。

本来父亲也应该像爷爷一样在部队里呆的时间久一些,可惜好景不长,两年后父亲在一次对打训练中被战友踢伤腹部导致脾脏破裂,以伤残军人的身份提前退役了。但是国家也没有忘记我的父亲在部队中的贡献,每个月都会发放抚恤金直到今日。

退役后父亲回到了家中,发现整个奉化都兴起了办厂的热潮。父亲说,那个时候的人都是"从小工开始做起,技术学会了就借钱开厂,教更多的人在自己的手下学技术,把厂变大,最后成了大老板",我的大伯也是其中之一。

大伯在我父亲去部队服役期间在县外办了厂,极大程度改善了爷爷奶奶家的家庭条件。家里住的房子从以前那间窄小潮湿的老屋换成了有大院子和房间数目多的独栋房子,其中一楼开成了零售店,主要卖烟酒。奶奶主管收银,爷爷就提前退休和二伯一起在大伯的工厂打下手,也会在空闲的时候去打理已经给了大伯的田,自己种东西吃。

父亲退役后,爷爷就把父亲推荐到了自己原先上班的粮站。父亲在粮站里工作到了1999年,觉得这么多年在粮站里的工资都没有大的改善,然而物价却已经涨上去了。父亲就决定辞掉粮站的工作,去溪口打拼。

从小村庄到县城,这就是父亲个人的奋斗方式。

母亲的家在武岭西路,隔了一堵墙的邻居是在历史上留下浓墨重彩的蒋介石。母亲家里的收入来源有两个，一是在景区中心开饭店，二是等奉化水蜜桃成熟的季节卖桃子。农商结合，就是对母亲家庭的最好概括。母亲家的饭店类似于夫妻饭店，厨师是我的外公，服务员是我的外婆和放假在家的母亲和舅舅，舅舅有时也会和外公一起学着烧菜，在忙的时候当厨师。

每年的节假日，溪口的客流量大幅度增加，这个时候母亲就会充当店里的临时服务员，给客人点菜、送菜、结账，全家人一起忙，直到中午用餐高峰期过了一家人才能吃上中饭，那往往已是下午 2 点半左右。

在景区开饭店的人家也不只母亲一家，竞争比较激烈，在中午和晚上母亲就站在步行街口招揽客人，向客人推荐自家饭店，在酷热的夏天这样的招揽更加费力，往往一站就是一小时，5 分钟就汗流浃背，极为辛苦。

夏天还有另一项工作，那就是卖桃子。外公家里有一整片的桃林，不舍得花钱找人打理，都是自己进行除虫除草，在桃子快成熟的时候还要用报纸把桃子一个个包起来防止鸟儿啄食。等桃子成熟了，还得由我的母亲去步行街摆桃子摊。外公外婆太忙，舅舅不会用秤，这项活儿一直都是属于我母亲的。母亲说，卖桃子的摊子很多，需要她不停地吆喝，有时候还会遇上城管驱赶，她跑得不快，每次都会被抓住，有一次还让城管夺去了装桃子的筐，给丢进了剡溪，她一气之下把洗桃子剩下的水泼了过去，被叫到派出所写了 1000 字的检讨。

母亲的日子充实又忙碌，而这些付出的努力也为家庭增加了收入。溪口如今日新月异，旅游业的发展蒸蒸日上，对于桃农贩卖桃子的管理也更为科学规范，很少出现小农商和城管之间的冲突了。母亲在一家工厂里做了车间主任，不再卖桃子，但依旧会去现在属于舅舅的饭店帮忙，毕竟这是财富一点点累积起来的地方。

在我的印象中，父亲和母亲在工作这条路上做了不少尝试。在最开始，因为母亲以前是开家庭饭店的，因此让父亲也开了一家家庭饭店。父亲作为厨师掌勺，在冬天的时候往往做菜做得满手都是冻疮，母亲也一直在不停地端盘子洗盘子。

房子的一楼二楼都作为饭店和它的包厢，我们一家三口生活的地方只有第三层楼。房子隔音效果并不是很好，小时候印象深刻的就是在三楼做作业时听到从一楼二楼传来的划拳声。

饭店收益不高，工作又太辛苦。4 年后，父亲终于支撑不住，决定改行做别的生意。那一天，父亲去离家不远的商业街转了一圈回来后，就决定要开足浴店，家里的房间也足够容纳员工。于是饭店的招牌被换下，我们家的足浴店就开始正式经营了。

足浴店由我父亲负责看管，母亲就去外面的工厂找工作，进了一个厂一呆就是 12 年，从基层的流水线员工逐渐做到了车间主任。家里的收入逐渐高了，家庭条件也好起来了，于是父亲就在我的小学附近买了新房子。父亲的足浴店主要是从下午开始经营，一直到晚上 2 点，母亲的加班次数也很多，所以晚上几乎都是我一个人在家，我也早早适应了这样的生活。

父亲的足浴店一直从我小学开到了我高二，高二时家里的收入已经十分可观，但是父亲的健康情况却有所下降。他本就因为缺少了一个脾，免疫系统不是很强大，再加上足浴店需要天天熬夜，父亲逐渐觉得心有余而力不足，而我又面临高考，于是父亲就决定关掉足浴店，把原来开店的房子全部租出去，自己来我上学的地方陪读。父亲不仅仅是家庭收入的顶梁柱，同时也在我学习压力最大的时候做我的坚实后盾。

我时常会问父亲，为什么好多次动心要卖掉原来四层楼的房子，但是到最后也没有卖掉。父亲说，对于我们这一家三口，那不仅仅是一栋房子，也是一个生活过的真正的家，我们的财富都是从那里创造的，我们的亲情也在那栋房子里变得更为紧密。

Ningbo
Fan Jiayu (Class 192, Majoring in Journalism)

Work Hard in Xikou

At the end of the 1950s, my grandpa joined the army. He served as an artillerymen in the army. After that, my grandfather returned to the village where he met my grandma through the introduction of his parents and got married. He was 27 years old that year.

My father was the third son in the family. When my father was born, my grandfather got a steady job at the grain station because he was a soldier before. However, the family was still poor. As time went by, two elder uncles had grown up and reached the age to get married, so my grandfather distributed to them all the houses and the farmlands. My father was only 20 years old then. He didn't want to work for the uncles as a farmer on the farmland, so he also joined the army and became the second soldier in our family. He went to Guangdong to be a scout.

My father should have stayed in the army as long as my grandfather did. Unfortunately, my father was kicked by his comrade in a sparring training two years later, causing his spleen to rupture. Finally, he had to retire early from the army as a disabled soldier. Fortunately, the country had not forgotten my father's contribution to the army, and he received the pension every month till today.

After his retirement from the army, my father returned home and found that there was an upsurge of setting up factories throughout Fenghua. My father said that at that time, people all started as workers. After they learned the technology in the factories, they would borrow money to open their own factories and taught more people to learn technology from them. Finally the factory became bigger and those people became big bosses. My uncle was also one of them.

My uncle opened a factory outside the county when my father served in the army, which greatly improved the living conditions of my grandparents. The small and damp house that we used to live in had been replaced by a detached house with a large yard and many rooms. A retail store was opened on the first floor, and it mainly sold cigarettes and alcohol. My grandma was in charge of the cashier in this store, while my grandpa retired early and worked as a helper with my uncle in my eldest uncle's factory. When my grandpa was free, he also took care of the farmlands that he had given to my uncle and planted something to eat.

After my father retired from the army, my grandfather recommended my father to the grain station where he used to work. My father kept working in the grain station until 1999. Then he thought that the salary he earned in the grain station hadn't been increased for so many years, but the prices had already risen. So he decided to quit his job at the grain station and went to Xikou to make a living.

The way of my father's personal struggle is leaving the small village for the county.

My mother's home was on Wuling West Road, and the neighbor living next door was Chiang Kai-shek, who was one of the most influential figures in history. There were two sources of income in my mother's family. One was running a restaurant in the center of the scenic spot, and the other was selling peaches when fenghua peaches were ripe. Combining agriculture and commerce was the best description of my mother's family. My mother's restaurant was similar to a mom-and-pop restaurant. The chef was my grandfather. When my mother and my uncle spent their holiday at home, they would help with my grandmother as waiter and waitress. My uncle sometimes learned how to cook from my grandpa. When it was busy, he would work as a cook.

The number of visitors in Xikou would increase greatly during holidays each year. At this time, my mother would take a job as a temporary waitress in the restaurant doing things like ordering, delivering food and checking out. The whole family were so busy that. they weren't able to have lunch after the lunchtime rush, so they often had lunch around 2 : 30 in the afternoon.

It's not just my mother's family who opened restaurants in the scenic spot. The competition between restaurants was fierce. My mother would stand at the pedestrian street to win customers at noon and night. She also recommend the restaurant to the customers. In the hot summer days, it was more laborious to win customers in this way, because she would have to stand under the scorching sun for at least an hour. She would be drenched with sweat in 5 minutes, which was extremely tough.

Another job in summer was selling peaches. My grandfather had a peach grove, and he was reluctant to spend money on asking someone to tend it. He always weeded and disinsected the grove by himself. When the peaches were about to ripe, he would wrap the peaches one by one with newspaper to prevent birds from pecking them.

When the peaches were ripe, my mother would set up a stall to sell peaches at the pedestrian street. My grandparents were too busy to help, and my uncle didn't know how to use a steelyard, so it had always been my mother's job to sell peaches. My mother told me that there were a lot of people selling peaches, so she had to keep peddling to attract more customers. Sometimes she would be chased by chengguan, the urban management officer. As she could not run fast, she was caught each time. Once the urban management took the basket with the peaches, and threw it into the Shengxi River. In a fit of anger my mother splashed the water that she used to wash the peaches over him, and then she was called to write a 1000 words self-criticism at the police station.

My mother lived a fulfilling and busy life, and all the efforts she had made increased the family income. Now Xikou is changing rapidly. The development of tourism is still thriving, and the management of peach selling is more scientific and standardized. Hence, there are few conflicts between street hawkers and chengguan. My mother works as a workshop director in a factory nowadays, so she no longer sells peaches. But she will still go to my uncle's restaurant to help. After all, this is a place where wealth is accumulated little by little.

In my memory, my parents have tried many kinds of jobs. At the beginning, my father decided to open a mom-and-pop restaurant, because my mother opened one before. As a cook, my father's hands tended to have frostbite because of cooking in winter. My mother also never stopped carrying plates and washing dishes.

The first and the second floors of the house were used as the restaurant and its private rooms. The third floor was where my family lived, and the house reduced sound badly. The deep impression in my childhood was the sound of finger-guessing game from the first and the second floors when I was doing homework on the third floor.

The profit of the restaurant was low and the work was too hard. Four years later, my father could not bear it anymore, so he decided to change to another business. That day, after my father came back from the commercial street less than 20 meters away from home, he decided to open a foot massage shop. Our house was also large enough to accommodate employees. Therefore, the restaurant's signboard was replaced, and our foot massage shop officially opened.

My father took care of the foot massage shop while my mother went to the factory to find a job. She stayed in a factory for 12 years, and gradually became the workshop director from a grass-root employee at the assembly line. As my family's income gradually increased and the family conditions had been improved, my father bought a new house near my primary school. My father's foot massage shop was mainly opened from the afternoon until 2 o'clock at night, and my mother always worked overtime. Thus, I was almost always at home alone at night everyday, but I adapted to this life early.

My father's foot massage shop, which opened when I was in primary school, was kept opened till my second year of high school. In my second year of high school, the family's income was already considerable. However, my father's health got worse gradually. Because of his lacking in a spleen, his immune system was not very good. In addition, he had to stay up all night to tend to the foot massage shop. My father gradually felt that he was unable to do what he hope to do. As I was facing the college entrance examination, my father decided to close the foot masage shop, and rented out all the houses that were used to open shops before and accompanied me at school. My father was not only the main support for family income, but also a solid backup for me when I was under the greatest pressure of studying.

I often asked my father about why he had thought about selling our original houses so many times, but never decided to sell that four-floor house. My father said that it was more than a house for the three of us. It is a real home we live together, where our wealth is created and our kinship has become closer.

浙江富民之路的典型呈现

刘建民

温岭市大溪镇前溪村工业区，是当地推出10个工业地产产业园之一，故事的主人公和其他温岭老板们一样，相中了这个地方。温岭作为中国民营经济先发地区和台州市工业经济第一强县(市)，始终坚持“工业立市、工业强市、工业兴市”不动摇。近年来，当地通过高强度建园区，全力“筑巢引凤”，主攻泵与电机、新能源汽车、数控机床和时尚童鞋，打造四大现代产业集群，构建新型制造体系，打造台州“制造之都”最强板块，最终跻身全省工业强市第一阵营，建设成为浙江打造世界级产业集群的先行区。

这个故事的主人公、作者的父亲就在这里开了一家水泵厂。《扎根前溪村工业区》，我们读到的是一个普通的创业故事：“2006年底，到了我快上小学的年纪，父亲终是决定带着我们一家回到浙江温岭老家生活。一回来，第一件事就是联系在当地开水泵厂的朋友，决定和自己的亲兄弟一起办个水泵厂。”

我们看到了一个创业者的乐观精神、责任感、学习能力，更看见了地方“筑巢引凤”所做所为及政策支持。作者的父亲总是告诉孩子：自己有准备，有魄力，敢做、敢冲的同时，国家颁布的政策支持是一个重要的前提：“我们真的是借助于国家政府的支持，才有今天的发展。”

这些话，这个故事，不免一再令人感慨：浙江富民之路，也是浙江各级党委政府锐意改革和无数基层干部“拎着乌纱帽”顶住压力保护老百姓首创精神的一个见证：最早允许农民务工经商，最早允许农民长途贩运，最早允许对农民开放城乡市场，最早推进农村工业化，最早推进城乡区域统筹……

浙江的“老百姓经济”特色鲜明：全省企业大都是中小民营企业，劳动力充分就业，遍地都是“小老板”，大批普通民众成为股东、老板、法人。中小企业多、“小老板”多，使大批普通百姓拥有企业、房产、土地收益等股本和资产，跻身“有产阶层”。“打工只能解决温饱问题，要想致富还是要靠创业。”浙江各地普遍推崇这一理念，拓出的道路也会越走越宽。

（浙大宁波理工学院传媒与法学院，高级编辑）

故事

台州

郑婧怡(法学专业 193 班)

扎根前溪村工业区

父亲 1971 年出生于浙江温岭一个普通的农村家庭。父亲高考失利,为了能尽到家中长子的责任,分担家里的经济负担,18 岁的他选择离开浙江,跟着村里的长辈去到上海打拼。

初次来到上海,父亲说自己完全是傻了眼。“大城市啊,八九十年代上海已经是大城市的样子了,毕竟我是农村来的,没见过。”对于初次来到上海的农村小伙子,一切都是新鲜的。可这份新鲜劲没过多久就被挫败感替代,在上海找一份稳定的工作成为他的大难题。父亲起初在徐汇区的某一购物中心的服装店做工,可没过几个月便因服装店倒闭而失去工作。于是父亲另寻出路,在电脑维修店打工,也因此学会了很多维修电脑的技术。通过三个月的刻苦学习,父亲虽然掌握了维修技术,却因店面将搬离上海而再失去工作。“其实也有收获,”父亲笑着说,“家里的电脑不都是我修的?现在朋友还找我修呢”。

再次成为无业游民的父亲始终没放弃在上海打拼的希望,向同在上海的朋友四处打听,终于找到了一份新的工作——买卖废旧电器。他来到徐汇区一家专门买卖废旧电器的公司,主要工作就是去指定地点收购废旧的电器,再运送至公司卖给前来购买的散户,按收入的百分比结算工资。好在这份工作稳定,工资不错,父亲工作刻苦努力,后来当上了管理人员,上海话也越来越溜。在努力工作 4 年后,终于有了些积蓄。

在某一次回温岭的假期中,父亲偶然经人介绍认识了母亲,两人互生好感,父亲回温岭的次数也逐渐频繁起来。在 1995 年,两人结为夫妇。父亲将母亲接到上海的出租屋一起生活。在 2001 年,我的诞生让我的父母多了一个新的身份,同时多了一份责任。他们想拿着这几年的积蓄回到浙江办一个水泵厂,但不能下定决心。于是我们一家继续在上海生活了几年,上海也成为我幼年记忆中的一部分。还能想起小时候,在拥挤的出租屋里,父亲时不时会问我:“想不想爷爷奶奶,想不想回家?”

直到 2006 年底,我到了快上小学的年纪,父亲决定带着我们一家回到浙江温岭老家生活。回来第一件事就是联系在当地开水泵厂的朋友，决定和自己的亲兄弟一起办个水泵厂，准备用这些年在上海的积蓄租场地、租设备。几经周旋，以合适的价格在隔壁村租下了 200 平方米的厂子，设备由父亲的朋友提供，这件事给了父亲一些希望。

但当时的父亲对于水泵行业还是个门外汉，到处打广告，才招揽了一批工人与技术人员。在技术方面遇到困难时，父亲便亲自去镇上和开水泵厂的朋友们讨教，自己慢慢了解和摸索。到 2007 年中，父亲和叔叔的水泵厂才开始出现好的苗头。

2007 年，浙江温岭的水泵行业得到了政府的重视，多家小型工厂也得到了技术与补贴上的支持。在长达一年的时间里，父亲每隔一个月就要去镇上开会，听取在该行业上的前辈给予的建议与技术上的讲解，政府每月也会给予一定的资金补贴，这些都让父亲在这条路上走得更有了些底气。讲到这，父亲还感叹道："这对于我们初进入这个行业的人来说，帮助真的很大。有时候我有不懂的，还会在会议结束后去讨教，前辈们还真的会告诉你怎么去应对，所以说大老板的格局是不一样的。"

接下来的几年里，附近的工厂越来越多，村里的流动人口也越来越多，外地的务工人也越来越密集。于是父亲又发现了一个新的商机，可以将家里的一处房子装修成出租屋给附近的工人居住。父亲既要完成工厂的日常工作，下了班还要兼顾出租屋的情况。2013 年 7 月，出租屋建设完成，迎来了第一批租户，不出意外，都是附近的务工人员。

随着水泵厂的发展，父亲与叔叔希望能继续扩大工厂的范围，寻找一个更大的厂房，同时拓展新的业务范围。可是寻访了附近很多的工业区，厂房的价格对于父亲与叔叔来说过于昂贵，费尽口舌也谈不拢价格。正当他俩准备放弃时，突然听到了市政府要在隔壁前溪村建设工业区的消息，而且听说政府在厂房的出租价格上也会有一定的控制，预计在 2019 年完工。这个消息可把父亲和叔叔高兴坏了，当晚买了几瓶酒在我家的一楼喝了起来。我依稀还记得那是个夏日的晚上，父亲一个人坐在家门口竹椅上口吹风醒酒冲我笑的样子。"谁都没想到这个时候市政府会出这个政策，再说当时确实是我和你叔叔资金不稳太着急了。确实是可以说帮了我们一个大忙，省了一大笔钱。"

前溪村工业区的建立历时两年，直至 2019 年，即在新中国成立 70 周年之际正式完工。在完成相关手续之后，父亲和叔叔的水泵厂终于在前溪村工业区正式"落户"。同年，父亲和叔叔决定开辟第二条生产线，拓展新的产品，继续投入到产业发展的路上。

前溪村工业区的建立对当地的影响是巨大的，吸引了不少工厂搬迁至此。

附近的几个村一下子变得热闹起来，餐饮业、房屋租赁行业在附近很是吃香。在2019年底，我家出租屋的一楼开设了便利店，取名为“群兴便利店”，也来凑一波工业区带来的福利。对于自家的出租屋的福利更不用说，每当迎来开工之际，父亲的手机总是响个不停。“租房啊，没有了，对对对，再见。”这句话快成了父亲那段时间的口头禅。

“我们真的是借助于国家政府的支持，才有今天的发展。”父亲总是告诉我，国家颁布的政策支持，前提是自己有准备，有魄力，敢做，敢冲。机会是给有准备的人的，这是父亲教给我的道理。

我们一家子从离开浙里到回到浙里，一直在进步和发展，同时也不乏艰辛与磨练。我敬佩父亲的“敢”，也感谢国家的政策支持，我们一家终是在浙扎根。

Taizhou
Zheng Jingyi (Class 193, Majoring in Law)

Settle Down in Qianxi Village Industrial Zone

My father was born in an ordinary rural family in Wenling, Zhejiang in 1971. He failed the college entrance examination. In order to fulfill his responsibilities as the eldest son and share the financial burden of the family, he chose to leave Zhejiang and follow the village elders to Shanghai to work hard.

My father said that he was completely dumbfounded when he first came to Shanghai. "Big city! Shanghai was already a big city in the 1980s and 1990s. After all, I came from the countryside and I hadn't seen it before." For the rural young man who came to Shanghai for the first time, everything was new. But it didn't take long for this freshness being defeated by frustration, and finding a stable job in Shanghai became his big challenge. My father first worked in a clothing store in a shopping mall in Xuhui District. He lost his job after a few months because the clothing store closed down. So my father tried another way out to work in a computer repair shop, and he learned a lot of computer repair skills. After three months of hard study, my father finally mastered the repair skills, but he lost his job again because the store would move out of Shanghai. "Actually, there were gains," my father said with a smile, "It was me who repaired all the computers at home. Now my friends still ask me to repair their computers."

My father who was unemployed again never gave up the hope of working hard in Shanghai. He sought information from his friends in Shanghai and finally found a new job, which was to buy and sell used electrical appliances. He came to a company specializing in buying and selling used electrical appliances in Xuhui District. His main job was to go to a designated place to purchase used electrical appliances, and then deliver them to the company so as to sell them to the individual customer. The salary was calculated according to the percentage of income. Fortunately, the job was stable and the salary was good. My father worked hard and became a manager later. His Shanghai dialect became more and more fluent. After four years of hard work, he finally saved some money.

During a vacation in Wenling, my father was accidentally introduced to my mother. They felt well-disposed toward each other, and the number of times my father returned to Wenling gradually increased. In 1995, they finally married. My father took my mother to the rental house in Shanghai and lived together. In 2001, my birth gave my parents a new identity and an extra responsibility. My father wanted to return to Zhejiang with his savings of the past few years and set up a pump factory. However, he dared not make up his mind. So my family continued to live in Shanghai for a few years, and Shanghai became a part of my childhood memory. I could still remember when I was a child, in a crowded rental house, my father would ask me from time to time, "Do you miss your grandparents? Do you want to go home?"

By the end of 2006, it was time for me to go to elementary school. My father finally decided to take our family back to my hometown in Wenling, Zhejiang. When we came back, the first thing my father did was to contact a friend who opened a pump factory in the local area. He decided to set up a pump factory with his own brothers and planned to use the savings gained in Shanghai over the years to rent a factory site and equipment. After several attempts, he finally rented a 200-square-meter factory in the village nearby at a reasonable price. The equipment was provided by his friends, which gave him some hope.

But at that time, my father was a layman in the water pump industry. He advertised everywhere so as to recruit a group of workers and technicians. When he encountered technical difficulties, he went to the town in person and asked for advice from friends who ran water pump factories. He learned and explored little by little. Then in mid-2007, my father and my uncle's pump factory began to show good signs.

In 2007, the water pump industry in Wenling of Zhejiang received much attention from the government. The government also provided technical and subsidy support to many small factories. In this year, my father would go to town meetings every other month to seek the advice and technical explanations given by his predecessors in the industry. The government would also provide certain financial subsidies every month. All of these made my father feel more confident about his factory. Speaking of this, my father said with a sigh, "This is really helpful for those who just entered this industry. Sometimes when there was something I didn't understand, I would ask for advice after the meeting. They would tell me how to deal with it, so the perspective of big boss was different."

In the next few years, there were more and more factories nearby. The number of migrant population in the village became bigger and bigger, that is, more and more migrant workers came to the village. Hence, a new business opportunity that my father found was to renovate a house in the family into a rental house for nearby workers. My father had to complete the daily work of the factory, and he had to take care of the rental houses after work. In July 2013, the construction of the rental houses was completed and the first group of tenants came. Not surprisingly, they were all migrant workers nearby.

With the development of the water pump factory, my father and my uncle wanted to expand the scale of the factory, so they were looking for a larger plant and stretching out into new business scopes at the same time. They visited many industrial areas nearby, but the price of the factory was too expensive. They spent a lot of time on negotiating, but still could not agree on a reasonable price. Just as they were about to give up, they suddenly heard the news that the municipal government was going to build an industrial zone which was expected to be completed in 2019 in Qianxi village, and the government would also have a certain control on the rental price of the factory building. The news made my father and uncle excited at the time. They bought a few bottles of wine that night and drank them on the first floor of our house. I vaguely remember that it was a summer evening when my father, sitting on a bamboo chair alone, sobered up at the door of the house with a smile. He said, "No one had thought that the municipal government would adopt this policy at this time. Besides, at that time, your uncle and I were too anxious and we don't have enough money. Indeed, this policy helped us a lot and saved us a lot of money."

The establishment of the Qianxi Village Industrial Zone lasted for two years. It wasn't officially completed until 2019, which was the 70th anniversary of the founding of New China. After completing the relevant procedures, the pump factory finally officially settled in the Qianxi Village Industrial Zone. In the same year, my father and uncle decided to open a second production line to develop new products, and continued to invest in industrial development.

The establishment of Qianxi Village Industrial Zone had a huge impact on the local area, attracting many factories to move here. Several nearby villages suddenly became lively, and the catering and housing leasing industries thrived in the surrounding area. At the end of 2019, a convenience store was opened on the first floor of our rental house to make use of the benefits brought by the industrial zone as well as the benefits of our rental house. The store was called Qunxing Convenience Store. Whenever people were back to work, my father's cellphone never stopped ringing. "Rent a house? No vacancy, goodbye." This sentence almost became a pet phrase of my father during that time.

My father always told me that it was because of the support of the national government that we could make today's achievement. The policy support issued by the government requires preparation, courage and ambition. Opportunities are for those who are well-prepared. This is what my father taught me.

From leaving Zhejiang to returning to Zhejiang, our family has made progress. We also have gone through a lot of hardship. I admire my father's courage, Meanwhile, I am grateful to the policy support by the government. Our family settled down in Zhejiang at last.

小人物的大能量

聂迎娉

作为一切社会关系的总和，人的本质属性表现在各种社会关系中。文中的"奶奶"不仅是一位奶奶，还是一个女儿，一个妹妹，一个妻子，一名知青，一名中共党员，一名国家公职人员……在各种社会关系中人物角色的切换，构成了一个完整的人。

这种现实的人，会基于自身和社会需要去从事一定的实践活动。基于女儿和妹妹的身份，年仅8岁的"奶奶"将家庭需要优先于个体学习需求，承担了家庭中照顾生病哥哥的重任，奔波于医院和家庭。基于知青的身份，"奶奶"去到了公社，去到了乡镇卫生院，在从事着力所能及工作的同时，作为一位母亲努力照料着自己的儿女。作为一名中共党员，一名国家公职人员，"奶奶"在妇联工作岗位上做得尽善尽美，发光发热，哪怕退休也仍然阻挡不了她"爱管闲事"的热情。一张张照片，记录下了这些不同社会关系中的"奶奶"，生动、真实，却活灵活现地再现了奶奶的故事。

"奶奶"是一个典型的人，是广大人民群众的鲜活个体，然而每一个个体的作用是不容忽视的。因为就每一个个体而言，他或她在一定意义上谱写自己个体"历史"的同时，也"通过每一个人追求他自己的、自觉预期的目的来创造他们的历史"，他们是整个人类社会历史的创造者。因为整个社会历史就其整体性而言，是一定群体的认识活动和实践活动及其产物的演进过程。正是一个个像"奶奶"一样鲜活的人，在不同的社会角色中创造了人类赖以生存的社会物质财富、精神财富，推动着社会的变革和国家的发展。

（浙大宁波理工学院马克思主义学院副教授，博士）

故事

湖州

张辰怡(网络与新媒体专业 192 班)

照片会说话

我的奶奶 1949 年出生于浙江嘉兴。新中国成立之初,政府鼓励妇女生育,并对多生育的妇女实行奖励政策。我的曾外祖母一共生了 4 个孩子,我的奶奶还有两个哥哥和一个妹妹。随着思想的进步,女性的地位也渐渐得到了提高,我奶奶也得到了上学的机会。奶奶到了 8 周岁,曾外祖母就为她报了名上学。但是奶奶的哥哥在奶奶要去上学的时候意外生了病,作为家中比较年长的女儿,年仅 8 岁的她就担起了照顾哥哥的重任,在医院和家两头奔波着,送饭、打水、每日为哥哥擦身,在哥哥痊愈后才去了学校报到。

"所以我拼音学得不好",在讲起这段略有遗憾的经历时奶奶露出了无奈的笑容,"但是也没有办法,父母都在务农,照顾哥哥的重任就落在了我的头上"。虽然奶奶的拼音不是特别好,但是她还是认真地跟着老师学习了一口标准流利的普通话,这为她以后的人生也打下了良好的基础。

奶奶读完初中之后,因为并没有取得理想的成绩,便响应国家号召,上山下乡,成为一名知青。原本住在嘉兴市的她被派到了位于含山乡的公社插队,并在那边认识了我的爷爷——比她大 11 岁的湖笔制造商。两人结婚后,便在含山乡定居了。1970 年奶奶 21 岁时,诞下了他们的第一个孩子,也是我的父亲。奶奶开始在别人的介绍下到含山乡社区卫生院做着挂号、收费的工作。在她的描述中,我了解到,一边喂养孩子一边上班并不是件容易事。

"那个时候人手比较少,我一个人要做好多事,挂号、收费,还有给病人打针以及开药。"奶奶一边端详着手里的老照片一边对我说,"那个时候我就把你爸爸放在我旁边的小凳子上,等到了时间就给他喂奶。"说到这里,她看向爷爷,"你爷爷那个时候很忙,经常到外地去卖湖笔,我就一个人住在医院的宿舍里面,到要生你姑妈的时候你爷爷害怕,都不敢进产房。"听到这时我也明白了爷爷和奶奶没有一张合照的原因,虽然爷爷经常在外地出差,但是也参与了父亲和姑妈的成长过程。

父亲说,爷爷那个时候对自己是"散养",经常任由自己到村口去和别的孩子

“瞎混”，父亲带了一身伤之后回家便受到奶奶的数落。

奶奶长期在卫生院积攒的良好口碑和对乡亲们无微不至的照顾使她在上世纪 80 年代初获得了含山乡副乡长的职位。作为一名中共党员，她关心着邻里的生活，把脱贫攻坚工作放在首位，得到了许多人的尊敬。

90 年代末，奶奶被选为了善琏镇妇联主席。善琏为镇历史悠久，据清《湖州府志》记载：善琏镇在府城东南七十里，一名善练（善琏），以市有四桥，曰福善、庆善、宜善、宝善，联络市廛、形如束练，故名善练。又据嘉、湖方志记载，在清初时期，善琏的住户已达千户至数千户之多，商贾云集，店铺林立，十分繁荣。由此可见，其已属江南水乡重镇之一。在善琏镇的街头有很多居民自己开的湖笔小作坊，湖笔看似结构简单实则工序繁琐，一支好的湖笔无疑是一副完美书法作品的“基石”。湖笔选料讲究，工艺精细，品种繁多，粗的有碗口大，细的如绣花针，具有尖、齐、圆、健四大特点。制作一支能为书法家所用的湖笔是一件需要花费巨大精力和智慧的事情。

在双学双比活动 10 周年之际，奶奶代表了善琏镇去北京人民大会堂出席了全国妇联双学双比 10 周年大会。为了弘扬善琏镇的优良湖笔文化，她带了一位湖笔择笔技术突出的妇女与她一同前往，向来自全国各地的妇女展示了善琏镇的风采。

现在的奶奶已经退休了，和爷爷住在湖州吴兴区一个老小区里面，过着清闲的生活。爷爷虽然已经 80 岁高龄了，但每隔一个礼拜还是会去善琏的老家看看他的“老宝贝”。善琏的老房子已经被父亲卖掉了，所以爷爷就挤在一个小车库里继续他的事业。小小的车库里面只有一张一米二的小床，在酷暑 7 月，爷爷就坐在小床上，一台快要报废的电风扇吱呀吱呀地响着，微热的风吹在他被汗浸湿的背心上。我们全家除了奶奶没有人支持他这样的做法。父亲经常一听说爷爷回到了那个车库里，便火急火燎地开车去了善琏把他接回来，在车上还少不了一顿数落：“都多大了年纪了还去摆弄这些东西”，“这么热的天气，连空调都没有，晕在里面都没人知道”。爷爷也一般是左耳进右耳出，手里攥着的老式邮差包还有刚才来不及归到原位的笔杆。

奶奶依然还是改不了“爱管闲事”的习惯，街坊邻居发生了什么大事总要背着手过去瞧一眼，能帮上忙就帮一帮，帮不上就扇着扇子在一旁默默地记下，等回家之后原模原样地复述给爷爷听，爷爷则是一边看着刚从图书馆借来的书一边敷衍地点头。奶奶的爱好和所有这个年龄段的老年人一样，打打麻将、买买彩票，每天晚上守着双色球的直播。“没中也没事的，也是上交给国家了，”奶奶一边对着号码一边对我念叨着。

Huzhou
Zhang Chenyi (Class 192, Majoring in Network and New Media)

Pictures Can Tell

My grandma was born in 1949 in Jiaxing, Zhejiang Province. At the beginning of the founding of the People's Republic of China, the government encouraged women to have children and implemented incentive policies for women who had more than one child. My great grandma had four children, and they were my grandma, her two elder brothers and a younger sister. With the enlightenment of people's minds, the status of women gradually improved, so my grandma also got the opportunity to go to school. When my grandma was 8 years old, her mother enrolled her in school to study. However, my grandma's brother accidentally fell ill when she was about to enter the school. As the elder daughter of the family, the 8-year-old girl shouldered the responsibility of taking care of her brother. She shuttled back and forth between the hospital and home, delivering meals, fetching water, and scrubbing her brother's body every day. After his brother's recovery, she went the school to register.

"That was why I was not good at Pinyin," she said with resignation when she told about her regretful experience. "But there was nothing I could do about it. My parents were engaged in farming, so I had to shoulder the responsibility to take care of my brother," said my grandma. Although her Chinese Pinyin was not so good, she still earnestly followed the teacher to learn standard and fluent mandarin, which laid a good foundation for her later life.

After my grandma finished middle school, because she did not achieve ideal results, she answered the national call to go to the countryside and mountain areas, becoming an educated youth. Originally living in Jiaxing, she was assigned to live and work in the commune in Hanshan village where she met my grandpa—a manufacturer of Huzhou-style writing brushes who was 11 years older than her. After they got married, they settled down in Hanshan. In 1970, when my grandma was 21, she gave birth to their first child who was my father. Introduced by others, my grandma began to work in Hanshan Community Health Center, handling stuff like registration and charging. In her description, I learned that it was not easy to raise a kid and work at the same time.

"At that time, the health center was understaffed, so I had to do lots of things by myself, including registration, charging, and giving patients injections and prescriptions." My grandma looked at the old photo in her hand and said to me, "At that time, I would put your father on the stool next to me. When he was hungry, I could feed him." Speaking of this, she looked at my grandpa. "Your grandpa was extremely busy at that time. He often went out to sell Huzhou-style writing brushes, so I lived alone in the dormitory of the hospital. When I was about to give birth to your aunt, your grandpa was afraid to enter the delivery room." When I heard this, I actually understood the reason why my grandparents didn't have any group photos with each other. Although my grandpa often went on business in other places, he also participated in the growth of my father and my aunt.

My father said that at that time, my grandpa was a free-range parent to him, so my father was often allowed to go to the village to muddle along with other children. Then he was always scolded by my grandma when coming home with wounds everywhere.

My grandma's good reputation in the health center and meticulous care for the villagers earned her the post of deputy head of Hanshan Village in the early 1980s. As a member of the Communist Party of China, she cared about the surrounding environment of the neighborhood and put the anti-poverty work in the first place, which was respected by numerous people.

In the late 1990s, she was elected chairman of the Women's Federation of Shanlian Town. Shanlian is a town with a long history. According to the records of *Huzhou Prefecture Chronicles* of the Qing Dynasty, Shanlian was 35 kilometers southeast of Huzhou. There were four bridges in Shanlian called: Fushan, Qingshan, Yishan, Baoshan. These four bridges connected the town together in a shape like white silk, so it was named Shanlian. According to the records of Jiaxing and Huzhou local chronicles, in the early

Qing Dynasty, there were thousands of households in Shanlian. With many merchants gathering here, shops could be found everywhere, which made it a prosperous place. Thus it can be seen that it was one of the most important water-bound towns in the south of the Yangtze River. In the streets of Shanlian Town, many small workshops of Huzhou-style writing brushes were opened by residents themselves. The structure of the Huzhou-style writing brush seems simple, but the process was complicated. A good brush was undoubtedly the cornerstone for a perfect calligraphy work. The Huzhou-style writing brush was exquisite in material selection, fine in craftsmanship and various in variety. The size of the big brush was like the size of a bowl, and the small brush was like an embroidery needle. It had four characteristics: sharp, even, round and durable. It took a lot of energy and wisdom to make a Huzhou-style writing brush that could be used by calligraphers.

On the occasion of the 10th anniversary of the "Dual Learning and Competing Campaign", my grandma, on behalf of Shanlian Town, went to the Great Hall of the People in Beijing to attend the 10th Anniversary Conference of all China Women's Federation. In order to promote the culture of Huzhou-style writing brushes in Shanlian Town, she took a woman who was skillful in choosing the Huzhou-style writing brush with her, showing the elegance of Shanlian town to women from all over the country.

Now my grandma has retired. She now lives a leisure life in an old community in Wuxing District of Huzhou with my grandpa. Although my grandfather is 80 years old, he still goes to Shanlian to watch his "precious brushes" every other week. My grandpa's old house in Shanlian has been sold by my father, so he huddled in a tiny garage to continue his "career". There is only a double-size bed in the garage. In July when it was scorching hot, my grandpa just sat on the bed. An electric fan that was about to be scrapped creaked, and the slight hot wind blew on his sweat soaked vest. No one in my family but my grandma supported him. As soon as my father heard that my grandpa was back to the garage, he would drive to Shanlian in a hurry to pick my grandpa up. My father couldn't help scolding him in the car, "You are too old to play with these things. In such hot weather and without the air conditioner, you will even faint there with nobody knowing that." My grandfather usually let these words go in one ear and out the other. In his hands were the old-style postman bag and the pen holder that he didn't have time to put back to where it used to be.

My grandma still can't change the habit of being nosy. She always took a look at what happened to her neighbors. If she could help, she would help. If she couldn't, she would fan herself and keep the whole thing in mind quietly. When she got home, she would retell the whole story to my grandfather. My grandfather nodded perfunctorily while reading the book that he just borrowed from the library. My grandma's hobbies are the same as other elders at her age, that is, playing mahjong, buying lottery tickets, watching the live broadcast of the two-color ball a kind of lottery every night, "It's fine if you don't win, because the money will be handed over to the country." My grandma talked to me while looking at the number.

建构和谐互惠的人地关系

胡晓梅

靠山吃山，靠水吃水。人类从生存之日起就不断向自然索取，两千多年的农耕文明更是形成了中国人对于土地的深深眷恋。人们依山而居，溯流而上，在自然资源丰沛的地方聚集成群，再慢慢形成乡村和城镇。人与自然的关系在千百年的发展变化中已然成为一个命运共同体。自然成为人类“赖以生活的无机界”，而人则和自己所处的环境一起生存发展。

人类依靠自然赋予的资源不断进化，但只有真正尊重自然、敬畏自然的人，才能获得自然的丰厚馈赠，就像张恬同学的外公外婆那样。张恬同学的祖辈世世代代靠着翁家山的茶山茶地生存、繁衍。那一亩亩的茶园既是小孩子们自小玩耍的乐园，更是全家人维持生计的希望，一大家子人伴着这三亩五分茶地迎来新中国的成立，也迎来一代又一代新成员。绿油油的茶园见证了家族的代际延续，更见证了从土地集中制到包产到户制的改革开放步伐，见证了从计划经济到市场经济的巨大变化。唯一不变的，是这片茶园里人和自然的关系。张恬的外公年轻时在茶园里辛勤劳作谋生活，采取传统的方式制作茶叶，年纪大了也时时记挂着茶园，没事就要去茶山上晃一圈看看茶树长势，关心茶树会不会缺水或受冻。于他而言，这片茶园就像一个多年的老朋友一直陪伴在他身旁，也像自己的孩子，带给他力量，也带给他幸福。

在我写这篇小文时，张恬同学的外公刚刚去世。但我们可以预见的是，这三亩五分地的故事还会继续，外公的子女孙辈会像他一样，继续细心地呵护这片茶园。因为“绿水青山，就是金山银山”，只有用心对待自然，人与自然才能建立更长久更和谐的人地关系，我们才能从自然中得到更丰厚的回馈。

（浙大宁波理工学院传媒与法学院讲师，博士）

故事

杭州

张恬(网络与新媒体专业 183 班)

这三亩五分茶地

我的外公家在翁家山村,那里主要产的就是西湖龙井茶。翁家山村的村民们,也世世代代靠着这茶山茶地生存、繁衍、生活,一步步踏上小康之路。

小时候放暑假,爸爸妈妈工作繁忙没空管我时,就会把我“丢”在外公家。而我那时候也很喜欢外公家,印象中的外公家的独栋小房子里永远弥漫着茶香,还可以在放眼望去全是绿色的茶园里肆意玩耍,当个“野孩子”,记忆里每每都是和表妹玩得一身泥回来还嘻嘻哈哈地傻笑受“骂”。那时候还小,也不懂守着这几亩茶地的辛苦,就是觉得茶园到处充满着清新的茶香。看着外婆带着雇来的采茶工们一钻进茶树堆里就是几个小时,双手一起又快又准地采下一大把一大把茶叶,再丢进背后的茶篓里。那时,小小的我看着这一系列眼花缭乱、行云流水的操作,只觉得很酷。采下来以后的茶叶要先经过半天左右的晾晒,接着便是炒茶,这一步骤必须是手工完成。长大后看到外公宽大的手掌上满满的厚厚的茧,才觉守着这三亩五分茶地的不易。

这次趁着端午时节全家在外公家团聚的机会,也和外公聊了起来。“以前我们是农民嘛……”这三亩五分茶地的故事由此开始。外公说最早以前,茶地就是他们家自己的,每家都是固定的。和现在的承包到户不一样,以前就是一家一户的。“我们家那时候一共就一亩土地。以前的生活,一大家子人就依靠着一亩茶地的产出维持生计。”听到这里,我忍不住发出了感叹:“一家就一亩地啊! 那哪里够生活的啊!”外公听到我的发问,边点头边流露出点怀念的神情,他的眼睛好像在看着我,又好像在透过我看着那些不会再回来的岁月,“是啊,一大家子就只有一亩地。那也没有办法,我们就只能去山上砍柴,砍下来第二天一大早到城里去卖,到那个清波门、现在的吴山广场,城里各个地方,我们都去卖,才有这个钱来维持基本的生活。”虽然每天都很辛苦,有时候也会吃不饱饭,但那时候一大家子人一起努力生活的充实感却让外公有些怀念。

1949 年,这个时间节点对整个中国来说都难以忘记,而对于外公来说,也同样重要。虽然外公当时也还小,就十几岁的年纪,但也能清楚记得日本人在中国做的种种恶行，也能清楚记得 1949 年新中国成立时的欢庆氛围。而对于外公家当时身处的农村环境来说，随之而来的土地改革，对他们的影响更为深刻。“1949 年的时候，我是 12 岁，那时候刚经历了解放，然后就是土地改革。土地改革，就像刚才我说的，原来属于个体的茶地，后来都变成集体的大家的，所有人一起干活。把茶地都集中起来，他家的我家的都集中起来，组织成生产队，就大家一起干活。生产队嘛，就自然有生产队的队长。”我来了兴趣，笑着问外公有没有当过生产队的队长。“当过！我还记得我是 60 年左右当上的生产队队长，大概 20 岁的时候。”当我问到队长的主要职责是什么的时候，“队长嘛，就是要带领整个生产队干活。那时候，主要就是靠村里的大喇叭喊。”外公还兴致勃勃地给我模仿了下当时的场景，“诶——！今天早晨——！我们要到茶山上去干活了！×××你今天要去哪里哪里干活！××你……”一听到这个大喇叭，村民们就知道了自己今天的任务。大家就听着队长的安排，回家去拿干活的工具。“要用刀的就去拿刀，要用铁耙的就回去拿铁耙。工具都拿齐了，就一起去山上干活，这个样子。”

回忆起从前的岁月，令外公难以忘却的，还有人民公社化运动的那段时间。“然后国家就搞了集体公社，人民公社化。就是吃饭不要钱，大锅饭嘛。那段时间，大家都不珍惜粮食了，盛一大碗饭有时候就吃一点点，剩下的就这样浪费了，慢慢地粮食就没有了。”外公回忆道。再往后，就碰上了艰难的三年自然灾害。粮食不够大家吃，大米在当时十分稀缺，就只能用瓜、菜这些东西代替饭来勉强填饱肚子。“一样的，全国都是一样的，都没有饭吃。这么几十年中国发展过来，碰到的事情很多很多，到你们现在这个时代社会已经发展得很好很好了，现在的生活已经是很稳定的了。”外公想着这几十年的生活变迁，感叹道。

“那后来茶地又是怎么从集中再分到现在各户人家的?”

“后来啊，后来就是 1982 年的时候，想想到现在也已经快 40 年了。那个时候搞了个农村土地承包到户的制度，把之前属于集体的土地按每户人家的人头数分，五分茶地一个人。还记得那时候我们家一共 7 个人，我们夫妻两个再加上我妹妹和 3 个子女，一共是三亩五分茶地。”

1982 年实行土地承包责任制之后，外公就和外婆带着一家子人勤勤恳恳搞生产，慢慢地一年比一年更好了。当我问起外公是怎么和外婆认识并最终组成家庭的时候，外公回忆起和外婆的初识往事，还有点小羞涩呢。“我是 30 岁那年认识的你外婆。是经过人介绍的，说是‘那个山里有个姑娘，挺好的，你去看看’，然后我就去了，两个人就这么相处下来了，过了大概一年就结婚了。”之后外婆就嫁到杭州这个小山村里来，和外公一起，守着这三亩五分茶地，直到现在。

以前外公总是早早地四五点就起床了，没事就去茶山上晃一圈，不干活，也会看看茶地的长势，就像对待自己的孩子一样爱护着这片茶地。即使现在腿脚不利索了，上山的频率少了很多，外公还是时时牵挂着。连续多日大晴天时，他会想着茶地会不会太干旱了会不会缺水了；冬天连续低温时，也会想着防寒措施有没有到位。现在外公外婆的年纪大了，有些比较辛苦的活儿就不能亲力亲为了，像给茶树打农药除虫、定时修剪茶树这些要耗时比较久的体力活，就会雇其他人去做。虽然现在每年的茶叶采摘量不如以前那么多了，赚的钱也少了，但外公外婆的几个子女有空时也会去茶山上帮忙，帮着他们一起守着这养了他们几十年的三亩五分茶地。

守着这三亩五分茶地，是外公坚持了一辈子的事情，他的出生、成长、结婚生子、摆脱贫困、走向小康，他人生道路上的每一步都离不开这三亩五分茶地。

Hangzhou
Zhang Tian (Class183, Majoring in Network and New Media)

A Tea Plantation of Three and a Half Mu

My grandfather's house is in Wengjiashan Village, where the main product is the West Lake Longjing tea. The villagers there, from generation to generation, rely on the tea mountains and tea plantations to survive, to breed and to live. That is how they step on the road to prosperity.

In my youth, when it was time for summer vacations, if my parents were too busy to take care of me, I would be sent to my grandfather's house, which I was very fond of at that time. In my impression, grandfather's small house was always filled with the fragrance of tea, and I could play freely as a wild child in the tea garden which was all green as far as the eye could see. Everything in my memory was that my cousin and I went home with mud all over and got scolded with a cheeky giggle. I was young at that time, and did not understand the laboriousness of guarding the acres of tea, but just felt that the tea garden was full of fresh tea fragrance everywhere. My grandmother, together with the hired tea pickers, entered into the pile of tea trees and worked for a few hours. They picked a large handful of tea-leaves quickly and accurately, and then threw them into the tea basket behind. At that time, I was little and just felt cool while watching the series of dazzling and skillful operations. After the tea leaves were picked, they had to be dried for about half a day, and then they were to be fried, which was a step that had to be done by hand. It was not until I grew up and saw the thick calluses on my grandfather's big palms that I realized that it was not easy to keep this tea plantation of three mus and a half.

Taking the advantage of the family reunion at my grandfather's house at the Dragon Boat Festival, I chatted up with my grandfather. "In the past, we were all farmers..." The story of this three-mu-and-a-half tea plantation began. My grandfather said that the tea plantation was of their own long time ago and was fixed for each family. Different from the work contracted to households nowadays, every household had their own land at that time. "At that time, our family had only one mu of land. In the old days, we, as a large family, depended on its output to make ends meet." Hearing it, I couldn't help sighing with surprise, "One mu of land for a family! How could it be enough to live on!" Hearing my question, my grandfather nodded, showing a bit of nostalgia. His eyes seemed to be looking at me, and as if looking through me at those days that would not return, "Yes, a family only had one mu of land. We had no choice but to go to the mountains to cut firewood and to the city early the next morning to sell them. We sold at the Qingbo Gate, the current Wushan Square and other places all over the city so as to have the money to maintain a basic living." Although it was hard every day and sometimes they were unable to get enough to eat, a sense of fulfillment when a family worked hard together to live made my grandfather feel a little nostalgic.

The year 1949 was an unforgettable time for China, which was also an important year for my grandfather. Although he was still young at that time, just being a teenager, he could clearly remember all the evil things the Japanese had done in China and the celebratory atmosphere of the founding of New China in 1949. For the rural places in which grandfather's family lived at that time, the ensuing Land Reform had an even more profound impact on them. "In 1949 when I was 12 years old, just after the liberation of China came the Land Reform. Land reform, as I said earlier, meant that the original tea plantation belonging to the individual later became a collective property, and all of the people worked together. The tea plantations were pooled together, all families were organized into production teams so as to work together. It was natural for a production team to have a captain." Being interested, I smiled and asked my grandfather if he had ever been the captain of a production team. "Yes, I had been the captain! I remembered that I became the production team captain in the 1960s, when I was about 20 years old." When I asked what the main duties of the captain were, my grandparents said, "The captain was to lead the whole production team to work. At that time, I mainly used the loudspeaker in the village." My grandfather excitedly imitated the scene for me. "Hey! This morning we are going to work on the tea plantation! today you have to go to work at someplace!" As soon as they heard voices coming out of this loudspeaker, the villagers would know about their tasks today. Everyone would just follow the captain's arrangement and went home to get the tools for work. "Those who needed a knife went to get the knife, and those who needed an iron rake went to get the iron rake. After getting all the tools, we went to work together from the mountains. More or less like this."

As he looked back on the old days, what was unforgettable to my grandfather was the period of the Movement of People's Commune. My grandfather recalled, "Then the government established the collective commune as the People's Commune. It meant free meals, in other words, eating from the same big pot. During that time, people did not cherish food. Sometimes they ate just a little bit of a big bowl of rice, and the rest was wasted, and slowly there was no food left." Later, they encountered a difficult three-year natural disaster. There was not enough food for everyone, and rice was very scarce at the time, so they had to eat melons and vegetables instead of rice to barely appease their hunger. "The whole country was the same. There was no rice to eat. China has developed over so many decades, and has encountered many things. In the present era, the society has developed very well, and life now is quite stable." My grandfather sighed as he thought about the changes in life over the decades.

"And then how come the previously collectively-owned tea plantations were distributed to different households as it is now?"

"Speaking of it, it has been almost 40 years till now. It was in 1982 when a system of rural land contracting was put into use, and the lands previously belonging to the collective were distributed according to the number of family members. One person could be distributed half of a mu of tea plantation. I still remembered that at that time our family had seven people in total. They were my wife and I as well as my younger sister and three children, so we could get a tea plantation of three and a half mu in total."

After the implementation of the system of rural land contracting in 1982, my grandparents led their family to work hard on production, and the family got better and better gradually. When I asked my grandfather how he met my grandmother and eventually formed a family, my grandfather was a little shy when he recalled his first acquaintance with my grandmother. "I was acquainted with your grandmother when I was 30 years old. Someone introduced her to me. I was told that there was a nice girl in the mountain and was asked to meet her. Then I went, and we two got along with each other and got married after about a year." After that, my grandmother married the small mountain village of Hangzhou. She guarded the tea plantation of three and a half mu with grandfather till now.

My grandfather always got up early at four or five o'clock before, and wandered around the tea mountains. Even if he might not have to work, he would check the growth of the tea. He cared for the tea plantation in the same way he treated his own children. Even though he is not agile in walking now, and does not go to the mountains as frequently as before, he is still always concerned about the tea plantation. When it was sunny for many days, he would worry the tea plantation might be too dry and lack water. When the temperature was low for many days in winter, he would also worry if the winter protection was done well. Now, my grandparents are getting older and cannot do some of the laborious work personally, so as for such time-consuming physical work as spraying pesticides to the tea tree for pest control and pruning tea trees regularly, they will hire others to do. Although the annual amount of tea picking is not as much as before, and the money earned is less, but the children of my grandparents will go to the tea mountain to help when they are available in time, helping them to guard the three-mu-and-a-half tea plantation that has been raising them for decades.

Guarding the three-mu-and-a-half tea plantation is what my grandfather has insisted on for a lifetime. He was born, grew up, got married, and had children here. It was also in this place that he got rid of poverty and went towards a well-off life. Every step in his life couldn't be possible without the three-and-a-half mu tea plantation.

回归初心:守住幸福最本真的模样

胡晓梅

对于幸福的理解千人千面。物质财富上的优渥与从容、身份地位上的优越与俯视是一种幸福;拥有自己擅长的事,能够从事自己喜欢的工作,是一种幸福;拥有和谐温馨的家庭,有相爱相守的家人,也是一种幸福。对于张纯熠同学而言,家人健康、家庭和睦,就是幸福。

张纯熠同学的家庭是数亿中国家庭中的一员。爸爸是电信局的职工,妈妈开着一家小五金店,两个人凭借努力和省吃俭用让孩子接受好的教育,又买了大房子,换了好一点的车。这是一个再普通不过的家庭,与其他很多家庭相比,这个家庭并没有特别突出的地方。这又是一个不普通的家庭,爸爸小时候被寄养在别人家,父母二人都只有初中学历,但却一点一点努力,慢慢与环境抗争,为张纯熠建立起一个温馨美满的家庭。

当下的中国在各方面都正处于急剧变动之中,从物质到精神,从社会结构到财富分配,人们的生活在不断发生着变化。德国著名社会学家乌尔里希·贝克曾直言:"当代中国社会因巨大的变迁正步入风险社会,甚至将可能进入高风险社会。"离婚率反超结婚率、对财富的极端追求、价值观沦丧……当前社会出现的种种现象似乎正印证着他的断言。在这时来看张纯熠同学这篇文章,会感觉到格外的安心和宁静。不忘初心、牢记使命,对于每一个平凡的人来说,初心就是做好我们份内的、擅长的、能够完成的事,守护好我们身边的人,让老有所养,幼有所学,让每个家庭都朝向它建立时所设立的幸福目标一步步前进。

(浙大宁波理工学院传媒与法学院讲师,博士)

故事

温州

张纯熠(网络与新媒体专业 183 班)

知足而常乐

我的妈妈出生在浙江省温州市平阳县鳌江镇,我的爸爸则在隔壁的龙港镇(现龙港市)。说来也凑巧,爸妈都是各自那边辈分最小的,命运的红绳将这两名“年轻人”拴到了一起。妈妈小时候的生活处境比爸爸要优越得多,每次外婆都是让大阿姨和二阿姨分担家务,最小的妈妈就承担了吃、玩的“工作”。爸爸儿时的生活就不是那么如意了。爷爷奶奶生的孩子比较多,又无力养这么多的孩子,就把孩子分别寄养在他人家里。爸爸被安置在了山里的一户人家。爸爸 18 岁时,被奶奶强制要求去参军,为的是爸爸以后能够有一份稳定的工作。

爸爸退伍后进入了龙港电信局工作,妈妈则留在家里开办的五金店里帮忙。经他们之间朋友的一系列机缘巧合的操作后,爸妈王八看绿豆——对眼儿了。

“你不可以跟他谈恋爱的,我不同意的。”外婆在电话里对妈妈说,“不是他呐,我跟另一个人好的,有正式工作的。”妈妈解释着这一出小闹剧,“哦,那没事了,听上去这个小伙子不错啊。”这段对话还残留在爸妈的第一个房子里。

这间房子是外公和外婆年轻时就买下的,高度有三四层左右,后来又将第一层改成了五金店。空间十分的狭小,在墙与墙之间还特别设计了一个夹层用来存放零部件,这个夹层直到我年幼时都还在那儿。第二层是一家人做饭用餐的地方,以前没有空调,一到了夏天,大家都是在这儿匆匆吃完饭后就逃命般的跑到楼下去避暑了。第三层,就是卧室了。外公年轻时主要的工作是木匠,铁制的工具随处可见,还有几张时代的见证——粮票。我的目光落到了几本书上,妈妈说那是关于养生的书,外公以前是一个酗酒成性的人,白酒都论斤喝,经常是半夜喝醉倒在门外,为此没少招外婆的唠叨。后来完全戒除了酒精,2008 年外婆因糖尿病去世后,外公就开始注重养生,现在 80 多岁了身体完全没有大碍。顶楼原本就是一个空旷的平台,后来外公外婆开始在上面养些花花草草,几株类似爬山虎的植物都挂到了三楼窗外的大街上。

爸爸的老家也就是爷爷家,从观感上看来更加的“宜居”,房子要穿过一个小巷才到,屋前屋后都是院子式的结构,进去时能够感受到一种明显的生活气息。

第一层前面是厨房,后面是餐厅,有时也会作为亲朋好友聚会的场所,后面的门板打开是一片开阔地,作为大型聚会的场所。往上数二三层则都是卧室了,一般都是闲置着,或者作为提供给远亲的临时住所。

爸爸妈妈都是只有初中水平的学历,爸爸还多上了一段时间的夜校,此后便没有接受过任何的教育了。爸爸自退伍之后便进入电信局工作,过着朝九晚五标准的普普通通上班族的生活。由于电信局是国企,工作岗位比较稳定,稳定的工作收入能够满足生活的需要,除了每周三都要在单位开会不回家吃饭、偶尔要赶去灵溪开会以外,爸爸业余时间都基本上会回家陪伴家人。那时爸爸上班用的还是单位的车,学车也是单位组织的,据说当时大夏天的,倒车一练就是几个小时,爸爸和几个同事只能像微波炉里的面包一样闷在里面。在刚入职以及后来相当长的一段时间里,爸爸都是负责联络、外出修电线、宽带网络的工作。想必现在头发稀少都是那时候熬没的。妈妈的五金店虽说只需要坐在店内,但毕竟是老建筑,地势低洼,空间狭小。夏天只能靠风扇勉强散热,遇到台风天气店内就会被雨水淹没。而金属零部件一旦泡水就相当于废了,为此妈妈都必须把一楼的零件连夜搬运至高处才能使这些小家伙们免遭天灾。

1998年,爸爸妈妈买下了属于他们自己的第一套房子,位于之前的老鳌江小学,现如今的鳌江镇政府附近,大约有80多平方米。当时的房子周边可以说没有什么基础设施,大门的入口没有栅栏门的设计,完全与主道路接壤,附近也没有专门的小卖部,地下停车场的顶棚也是塑料材质的,单元楼没有大门和电梯,只能走楼梯。这也没有办法,毕竟爷爷奶奶外公外婆没有钱赞助给爸爸妈妈。

2008年之后,我们家的经济状况开始稳中向好,连续地完成了几个大手笔。先是把原来只有手摇窗的轿车换成了东风日产,前两年又换成了大众途观。我们全家也从原来的80多平方米老房子搬进了现在的新小区,128平方米的大房子。

要说为什么变化这么大,一是全家人的省吃俭用,二是爸爸的事业也有了起色。爸爸从原来外出工作的普通员工成为一班之长,也就是说爸爸不用再那么辛苦地重复无论寒冬酷暑都要外出的日子了,现在他只需要负责接收问题再派人出去就行了,而且曾经是外出人员的爸爸还能享受到提前退休的福利。原本领导还想要把爸爸提升为副主任,但被爸爸婉言谢绝了。爸爸说自己的文化水平并不高,现在这个职位已经足够了,再向上攀的话,第一自己的能力可能不够,第二应酬势必增多。他已经不想再为了工作而舍弃陪伴家人的时间。

我的家庭不跟住洋房的大户人家比吧,就跟同阶段的人们比较我认为已经是一个温馨美满的家了,知足者常乐嘛。只要每个人都能够健康,自己不给父母添麻烦，爸妈的感情能够和睦如初，就已经很好了。小康，其实也并不一定要钱越多才幸福，家跟人一样，精神上的幸福远比物质上的富足来得更重要，更加弥足珍贵。小孩子们珍惜童年好好玩耍，年轻人好好学习好好工作，老年人保持健康颐养天年，每个人都做好自己，这样每个人都能过上自己的小康生活。

Wenzhou
Zhang Chunyi (Class 183, Majoring in Network and New Media)

Happiness Lies in Contentment

My mom was born in Aojiang Town, Pingyang County, Wenzhou City, southeastern China's Zhejiang Province, while my father in the nearby Longgang Town, today's Longgang City. It was a coincidence that both my parents were the youngest child in their families and fate brought two young people together. My mother led a much better life than my father when they were still kids. As the youngest child in the family, my mom was assigned the "task" of eating and playing while her two elder sisters were asked by my grandma to do chores. By contrast, my father didn't live a smooth and stable life. His parents had several children but couldn't afford to raise them up. Therefore, they found foster parents for their children, with my father sent to a family in a mountainous region. When my father turned 18, he was forced by my grandma to join the army for the sake of a stable job in the future.

He landed a job in Longgang Telecommunications Administration after being discharged from the army while my Mom became a helper in the family-run hardware store. They fell in love with each other after being paired off by their friends.

"I won't allow you to be in a relationship with him," my grandma told my mom over the phone, mistaking my father for another jobless man. My mom explained, "Not him, Mom. I am dating another man who has a formal job." "Well, then it's all right. Sounds like that chap is a nice guy," said my grandma. To this day, this conversation still lingered in my parents' first ever house.

The house, with a height of three or four stories, was bought by my maternal grandparents when they were young and the first floor was later altered into a hardware store. Considering its confined space, an interlayer was installed between walls to store parts, which remained there even when I grew up to a little kid. Upstairs was the place where we cooked and had meals. In the past, no air-conditioner was available, and we would rush downstairs to escape the heat after a quick meal in summer. The third floor was designed as bedrooms. My grandpa worked mainly as a carpenter when young, so iron tools could be seen everywhere in his bedroom. There were also several food stamps, which witnessed the changing times. My eyes fixated upon some books which, according to my mom, were about regimen. My grandpa used to be an alcoholic, taking swigs even of baijiu (a kind of Chinese liquor). He would even crumple on the doorstep in a dead faint at midnight, incurring my grandma's constant chatter. He later finally hauled himself out of alcoholism and started to follow regimen after my grandma passed away due to diabetes in 2008. As a result, he is in good health now in his eighties. The top floor, used to be an empty platform, was later used for gardening. Some creeper-like plants even wound around the windows of the third floor, stretching their leaves far into the streets.

The house of my paternal grandparents, which was also my father's home, seemed more livable judging from the exterior. Walking through an alley, you would find this house of a rectangular structure and feel a strong vibe of life when entering. There was a kitchen in the fornt and a dining room in the back of the first floor, which would sometimes serve as a place for parties for relatives and friends. A large empty open space would unfold before your eyes once you opened the door, an ideal place for big gatherings. Upstairs on the second and third floors were bedrooms, which were mostly idle and sometimes would be used to accommodate remote relatives.

My parents discontinued their studies after graduating from the junior high school—my father went to the night school for some time afterward. He then had a nine-to-five job at the Telecommunications Administration after leaving the army. Working in a state-owned company meant a stable monthly salary which could well meet our life needs. My father would accompany us once he was off duty except for every Wednesday when he was supposed to have meetings in the company and days when he attended meetings in Lingxi County. At that time, my father was still using the company's car to commute, and his company also organized staff to learn how to drive. I was told that he, together with some colleagues, had to stay in the car like bread in the microwave oven when they learned how to back the car in the scorching hot summer season. Shortly after he entered the administration, he was in charge of liaisons, wire maintenance and broadband internet connection, which he continued for a fairly long period of time. Presumably his current sparce and wispy hair was attributed to the harsh work back at that time. As for my mom, though the work in the hardware store was not heavy and all she needed to do was to sit there, the store itself caused much trouble. An old and low-lying building with confined space, the store would only be cooled off by fans and would be flooded once a typhoon struck. Metal spare parts would be at risk of being totally ruined once soaked in water. As a result, my mom had to move those spare parts from the first floor to high terrains overnight so as to spare them of the natural havoc.

In 1998, my parents bought the first house of their own, located near the former old Aojiang Primary School (now Aojiang Town Hall). The house covered an area of about 80 square meters. There were no facilities around the house without a fence gate, the entrance was directly connected with the main road. There were no small shops nearby and the roof of the underground parking lot was also made of plastic. With no gate or elevator for the apartment building, residents had to take the stairs. However, there was no way to get a better house. After all, my grandparents did not have money to support my parents.

Life gradually improved after 2008 and we made several big purchases. Our first old-style car with hand-operated windows was replaced by a Nissan, which was once again upgraded into a Volkswagen Tiguan a few years ago. We also moved from the old and cramped house to the 128 square meters one where we currently live.

Those changes were partly due to our frugal way of life and partly due to my father's career success. After promotion, my father became the head of his department and was no longer an ordinary worker, meaning he now only needs to dispatch personnel instead of personally going out in freezing cold winter days or scorching hot summer days. And my father once a field worker, was entitled to an early retirement. His boss once wanted to promote him to be the deputy director, but the offer was turned down by my father who believed he, not well educated, was not competent for such a high position. Besides, he wanted to spend more time with families while a job promotion would definitely mean that he had to devote more time to work.

Although not a match to those families living in villas, my family is already a happy and warm one compared with other average households. Happiness lies in contentment. It is a blessing already that every family member is in good health, my parents are affectionate towards each other as before and I haven't given them any trouble. To have a moderately prosperous life doesn't necessarily require a large amount of money, since spiritual happiness is much more important and valuable for a family as well as a person than material affluence. As long as kids cherish their childhood and play hard, the young study and work hard, and the elderly keep healthy, everyone can lead a well-off life.

中国传统文化的积极传播

郭小春

张微的舅公是传统的知识分子。喧嚣的社会秩序和社会关系剧烈变革中成为社会风尚压舱石和文化传播指向标的，恰恰是这样众多微小社会个体身上卓然的“穷则独善其身，达则兼济天下”的儒家风骨。杜维明先生认为，儒家的终极关怀是自我转化，即一种社群行为，具有人文主义特质。[①] 儒家文化浸润的中华民族以改革开放建设小康社会的征程也是传统文化积极传播的历程。多面迷人的中国传统文化又是通过每一个中华儿女所言、所行、所思而保留传承。

儒家心怀天下，主张个人“重视主观精神的修养”[②]，以“富贵不能淫，贫贱不能移，威武不能屈”的境界存身立世。传主从私塾到学堂直到大学，从江南到大兴安岭，从努力工作到“被别人嫉妒”，于时世变幻中靠着自身实力为政一方，赢得认可；无论年富力强，还是年迈老衰，既身体力行，还不忘谆谆教诲后辈“要做一个对社会有贡献、有回报的人”。中国文化的滋养在不经意间流露出来，“天下兴亡，匹夫有责”的儒家入世精神如此亮眼，也映照出强烈的现代公民意识。世界经历着百年未有大变局，虽多难而奋斗不屈的中国行稳致远，背后是无数沐浴儒家传统文化的普通人不屈不挠、勉力务进的韧性和付出；传统文化积极向上呵护世界的价值观的传承和传播，与经济繁荣、技术进步共生互荣，中华民族命运共同体才会健康地持续发展。

（宁波工程学院副教授，博士）

① 杜维明：《〈中庸〉洞见》（中英文对照本）。北京：人民出版社，2008年版，第117-157页。

② 程裕祯：《中国文化要略》。北京：外语教学与研究出版社，1998年版，第73页。

故事

宁波

张徵(网络与新媒体专业182班)

只要肯登攀

我的外曾祖母共生育了8个孩子,舅公是最大的那一个。孩童时代,家境殷实的舅公不用像其他小孩那样需要学做草帽、草扇等来维持家中生计。受外曾祖父的影响,舅公从小便对书法产生了浓厚的兴趣,每天做的事情便是练习书法。后来家中突遭变故,舅公一家财产散尽,日子开始变得穷苦起来。

尽管生活艰难困苦,外曾祖母还是为舅公请了教书先生。后来家附近设立了学堂,舅公便去学堂念书。舅公聪慧过人,凭借自己的勤奋努力,顺利念完了大学。从学校出来之后,国家正处于严重的经济困难时期,舅公便留在宁波跟着一起进行社会主义教育运动。

慢慢地,舅公的能力被上级领导发现,文革还没结束,舅公就被分派到黑龙江的大兴安岭工作。那会儿大兴安岭正在进行林区开发,舅公被任命为革委会的秘书。之后舅公不停锻炼自己的工作能力,一步一步升职,最终靠着自身实力成为一个地方官。

1997年舅公退休,回到了慈溪定居。退休后的舅公全身心投入到对书法的钻研中,尤其是对草书的研究颇有造诣,其作品也获奖无数。直到现在,他仍然对书法如痴如醉。

舅公刚到黑龙江的时候,常常因为工作能力强的缘故被别人嫉妒,无论是工作上还是生活方面,被下绊子是常有的事。但舅公并不在意,正如他之前说的那样,他看重的只有自己的工作能力。

不过后来遇到的一个领导令舅公印象深刻,他不喜欢别人的溜须拍马,会虚心接受他人提出来的意见和建议。所以他很喜欢舅公,两人在一起有说不完的话。舅公提到他时,也是满脸笑意。“这样的领导是有水准的。”舅公这样夸奖。

那个时候每年冬天,舅公都要去林场劳动,在那里一待就是两个月,中间也不能回来。几个人需要一起把五六米长的大木头从冰冷的水底抬起来,舅公刚来,不懂抬的技巧,受伤是常有的事,腰的毛病也就是在那个时候落下了。“那个时候,生活真的挺艰苦的。”舅公说道,“我们刚去的时候,那里冬天喝水的井只有一口。每天都得去打水，如果打不着啊，就只能去凿冰。把河里结得厚厚的冰凿回去，用来烧水做饭。”

舅公在那儿担任最高决策机关的常委秘书的时候，会在第一时间得知一些内部消息。某次开会后组织决定要对一个人进行处分，没想到这个消息竟然马上就被泄露了出去。组织进行调查后，认为是舅公泄露出去的，结果舅公被下放，还有专门人员进行监督。最后组织调查清楚了，那与舅公没有关系，又将舅公调了回来。

“无论是在学校读书，还是进入社会工作，总是会遇到很多不愉快的事。尤其是工作之后，社会是很复杂的，会碰到形形色色的人。你要学会的就是一个字——‘忍’。”舅公指了指心，认真说道。

舅公脾气耿直，心里藏不住话，有时候会直接说出来，这在小帮派中特别不受欢迎。那个时候舅公的人缘特别不好，经常受到排挤，甚至被告状到组织部去，也一直接受调查。直到发生了那件事。

舅公当副书记的时候，一次会议上，有一个干部因为犯了错误而要被公开处分。会议结束后，舅公思索了很久，觉得那人虽然犯了错，却不至于要公开处分，只需面对面批评教育即可。于是他在第二次会议上向那干部道歉，表明此次的惩罚过重，是他的失误。那个时候向下级低头道歉的领导很少，舅公受到了很多好评，之前排挤他的那些人也对舅公的印象有了很大的改观。“大家慢慢习惯了我这个耿直的性子，之后我的朋友也多起来了。没有想到这个举动，竟然让我开始受欢迎了。”舅公笑着说道。

退休之后的舅公闲在家中，又重新拿起毛笔开始钻研书法。退休二十几年，他把精力都投入到了书法中。舅公常说：“要做一个对社会有贡献、有回报的人。”现在他能做的便是顺应时代潮流，根据国家需要，把满腔的爱国热血投注到书法之中。舅公写得最多的便是毛泽东的诗词，尤其是那首《水调歌头·重上井冈山》他最为喜欢。词中最后两句“世上无难事，只要肯登攀”是他经常挂在嘴边的话。“世上无难事，只要肯登攀。最主要的是登攀，这是最重要的，你不要怕。”舅公反复对我说。

在舅公那里学书法的小朋友也不少，舅公从不收费，只是一门心思地教小朋友。舅公一直认为学书法应该从基本笔法开始，然后到偏旁部首，再到字的上下左右结构。他不会叫小朋友练字帖，他认为打好基本功是最重要的。小的时候我也去舅公那里学习过书法，每周日上午的那两个小时应该是我最放松的时候，舅公严格但不严厉。我自己练习的时候，舅公就会去他的写字台那里专心写字；休息的时候就会带我参观他院子里的花花草草，还会为我准备点心。

舅公有很多作品，平时也一直练字，家人朋友有喜欢的他都会大方送人，包括奖杯和奖章也是。去他家做客，回来的时候手里都会拿着舅公的书法作品和奖杯。他也不在意那些荣誉，对于他来说，写的过程才是最享受的。记得舅公有一个朋友，身体一直不好，但他每天都会看一会儿挂在房间里的舅公的作品，他对舅公说："你的字是活的，看到你的字，我也会感觉我自己是活着的。"

五年前，舅公不幸脑梗，左手无法动弹，这给他的生活带来了很多麻烦，但却丝毫不影响舅公对书法的痴迷。直到今天，他还是会在空余时间提笔写字，日日如此。

经历了这么多事的舅公，在问及他对自己这一生的总结时，他只说了三个字：挺好的。

舅公这一辈子，也算是走南闯北，受过苦，挨过冻，也遇到不少明枪暗箭，但他自始至终认为，提高自己的能力，干好自己的事才是最重要的。就像他一直挂在嘴边的那一句：世上无难事，只要肯登攀。舅公这一辈子，就是在不停地向上登攀。踏踏实实做事，爱国家，也爱小家，做个对社会有贡献的人，这就是舅公一辈子的信仰。

Ningbo
Zhang Wei (Class 182, Majoring in Network and New Media)

Nothing Is Difficult if You Put Your Heart into It

My great-grandmother had eight children, of whom my granduncle was the eldest. In his childhood, my granduncle, enjoying a well-off life, did not need to learn to make straw hats and straw fans to support his family as other children did. Under the influence of my great-grandfather, my granduncle developed a strong interest in calligraphy from childhood. What he did every day was to practice calligraphy. His world was later shattered as his family lost every penny, and life suddenly became hard.

Despite the tough life, my great-grandmother hired a teacher for my granduncle. A school was set up later near their home and my granduncle went there for education. With his hard work and intelligence, my granduncle successfully finished university. When he graduated, the country was in serious economic difficulties, so he stayed in Ningbo to join the socialist education movement.

My granduncle's ability was discovered by leaders gradually. Before the Cultural Revolution ended, he was assigned to Heilongjiang's Greater Khingan Ridge, where forest development was underway, to work as a secretary for the revolution committee. After that, he kept improving his working ability, and was promoted step by step. Finally, thanks to his own ability, he became a local government official.

In 1997, my granduncle retired and settled down in Cixi. After retirement, he devoted himself to the study of calligraphy and became a man of great attainments in the study of cursive script, and he won numerous awards for his works. Until now, he is still infatuated with calligraphy.

When my granduncle first arrived in Heilongjiang, he was often envied by others because of his excellent working ability. It was not uncommon for him to be tripped up in both work and life. But he did not care, as he had said before, what he cared about was only his ability to do his work.

However, my granduncle met a leader who impressed him a lot, because this leader did not like others' flattery and would humbly accept the opinions and suggestions of others. He liked my granduncle very much and they had a lot to talk about together. My granduncle smiled when he mentioned him and praised him, "Such a leader was very professional."

Every winter at that time, my granduncle would go to the farm to work for two months and could not come back during these two months. Several people needed to lift five-or-six-meter-long wood from the cold water. It was common to be injured for my granduncle, a newcomer who did not know the skills of lifting wood, so he had a backache finally. "Life was really tough at that time," said my granduncle. "There was only one well to drink in winter when we first came. Every day we must fetch water, and if we could not get water, we had to go to chisel ice in an icy river to be boiled for cooking."

When my granduncle served as the secretary of the standing committee of the highest decision-making body, he would be informed of some inside information in the first place. During a meeting, the organization decided to punish a person. Unexpectedly, the news was leaked immediately. After the investigation, my granduncle was considered to be the one who leaked the news. As a result, my granduncle was sent down to the lower level and supervised by specialized personnel. Finally the organization found out that it had nothing to do with my granduncle, and they brought him back.

"No matter you are going to school or going to work, there are always a lot of unpleasant things. Especially after work, the society is very complex and you will meet all kinds of people. All you have to learn is one word——forbearance." My granduncle pointed to the heart and said seriously.

My granduncle was frank and candid. He could not keep the truth to himself and would sometimes speak out, and this frankness was unwelcome among groups. At that time, my granduncle was not popular in his organization, and he was often sidelined. Some people even filed a complaint to the organization department, so he was always under investigation until something happened.

When my granduncle was a deputy secretary, a cadre was to be publicly punished for his mistake in a meeting. After the meeting, my granduncle thought for a long time and felt that although the man had made a mistake, he would not punish him publicly but only criticize and educate him face to face. He then apologized to the cadre at the second meeting, saying that the punishment had been excessive and that it was his fault. At that time, few leaders would apologize to their inferiors. Because of this, my granduncle received a lot of praise, and the people who had rejected him before also had a great change in the attitude. "People gradually got used to my straight temper, and then I had more friends. I didn't expect that it would make me popular," said my granduncle with a smile.

After retirement, my granduncle idled at home and picked up the brushes again and began to study calligraphy. In his two decades of retirement, he devoted himself to calligraphy. My granduncle often said, "Be a contributor and a giver to the society." What he can do now is to follow the trend of the times and devote his patriotic passion into calligraphy according to the needs of the country. What my granduncle wrote most was Mao Zedong's poems, especially the one called "Head of Water-Melody Song: Re-Climbing Mount Jinggang", which he liked the most. The last sentence of the poem—"Nothing is difficult if you put your heart into it"—was his constant refrain. "Nothing is difficult to the man who is willing to try, and trying is the most important. Though it is hard, don't be afraid."

A lot of children learned calligraphy from him, but my granduncle never charged them any money. He just got immersed in teaching children. He has always believed that learning calligraphy should start from the basic brushwork, then to the radicals, and then to the structure of characters. He would not ask children to practice calligraphy on a copybook because he thought that a good basic knowledge was the most important thing. When I was younger, I also followed my granduncle to learn calligraphy. The two hours every Sunday morning should be the most relaxing time for me. He was serious but not strict. While I practiced by myself, my uncle went to his desk and concentrated on his writing; during breaks, he would show me the flowers and plants in his yard and prepared snacks for me.

My granduncle has the habit of practicing calligraphy, and naturally, he has many pieces of work which he would generously give to family members and friends upon request, including trophies and medals. Every time I paid a visit to him, I came back home with his calligraphy works and a trophy in my hand. He didn't care about the awards. For him, the process of writing itself was the most enjoyable. I remembered that my granduncle had a friend who had been in bad health, but he would still take time to appreciate my granduncle's work hanging in the room. He said to my granduncle, "You make these characters alive. Every time I see the characters you wrote, it encourages me to live on."

Five years ago, my granduncle had a cerebral infarction, which left him unable to move his left hand. It caused a lot of trouble in his life, but it did not affect his obsession with calligraphy. Until today, he still picks up a brush and writes in his spare time, day in and day out.

I asked my granduncle how he would sum up his life after experiencing so much. He replied with three words: It was good.

For his whole life, he had traveled far and wide. He had suffered distress and cold; he had taken shots from the back, but he had always believed that it was most important to improve one's competence and do things well. As he always said, "Nothing is difficult to a man who is willing to try." My granduncle has been positive and hardworking all his life. He has been doing things in a down-to-earth way; he loves his country and loves his home. He aspires to be a person who can contribute to the society, which is the belief in his life.